The Bogota Connection

by

Peter W. Rainier

1663 Liberty Drive, Suite 200
Bloomington, Indiana 47403
(800) 839-8640
www.AuthorHouse.com

First published by AuthorHouse 11/14/2005

ISBN: 1-4208-8278-3 (e)
SBN: 1-4208-6943-4 (sc)

Library of Congress Control Number: 2005906176

Printed in the United States of America
Bloomington, Indiana

This book is printed on acid-free paper.

- 1 -

Florentino Chavez had enjoyed his assignment. It pleased him that he had been able to earn the girl's trust so easily. He had met her, seemingly by accident, as she was returning to the Ambassador's house with a load of groceries. He chatted pleasantly while he helped her with the groceries. She agreed to meet him on her day off; she had never been to see the Tequendama Falls and he was offering dinner as well. The rest was easy. He seduced her in the afternoon, then talked her into having her picture taken on the edge of the cliff overlooking the falls. A quick push off the cliff and it was all over. They would never find the body nor connect him to her disappearance. He had been careful not to be seen by the staff at the Embassy.

* * *

Craig Fox waited for the opportunity to slip out of the dining room. He would have stayed if the teacher being honored deserved the fine words showered on him. The whole school knew Mr. Llewelyn was about to be fired, but forewarned, he had elected to resign and return to England to join the army. Quietly Craig eased his chair back, and waiting until the Headmaster was talking to a teacher, tiptoed out a side door and along the corridor to the lobby of the Bolivar Hotel. The doorman smiled and opened the door leading to the side entrance.

"Buenas Noches, Señor."

"Gracias, Buenas Noches."

At an elevation of eight thousand feet, nights are cool in Bogota. Craig paused at the top of the steps. He turned up the collar of his blazer and was about to step down to the poorly lit street. Two young men, startled in mid conversation, turned their heads towards him. Quickly they jerked their faces away from the light streaming out the side door of the hotel and hurried down the street into deeper shadows. Stunned at what he had overheard Craig stood immobile, one foot below the other, gaping at the receding figures. He recognized one of the young men. It was Richard Bannerman, the Senior Prefect at Craig's Boarding School. There was no mistaking the tall athletic figure in the navy blue blazer, the blond wavy hair and the prominent chin. The other man was shorter, slim, in tight black pants and short dark jacket that made him appear to fade into the gloom behind him. But it was not the clothes that Craig noticed, It was the face that embedded itself in Craig's mind. Features almost asiatic with high cheek bones and black oily hair. But the dark complexion had to be that of an Indian. The dark eyes flashed briefly in the light before swinging away. The young Indian had been holding a small photograph in front of Richard as he spoke.

"The girl is dead! I pushed her over the Tequendama Falls yesterday. She will never be found. I took this picture of her floating at the base of the falls. See! Here is the proof. Now you can pay me the rest of...."

Those words were to haunt Craig for many days. Recovering from his shock, Craig walked back to the school wrestling with what he had heard, unaware he was followed. That night in bed he lay awake staring at the ceiling. Was it possible he had misunderstood? No! There was no misunderstanding the Indian's words. But was Richard Bannerman truly capable of murder. "Yes... yes! Richard is capable of murder." Craig decided.

As a young 'New Boy' at the boarding school, Craig hero-worshipped Richard Bannerman. Soon after arriving at the school, Craig was invited by the senior boy to share his room. Immensely flattered, Craig accepted. Tall, handsome, and an outstanding athlete, Richard excelled at track-and-field, swimming, and rugby. His athletic abilities, combined with exceptional intelligence, and a witty and pleasant personality, charmed both the staff and schoolboys. Wherever he went he was usually surrounded by admirers. But Craig was no longer an admirer. Craig had moved out of the room they shared two years ago after an incident that shocked him. Richard proceeded to discredit Craig with subtle innuendoes to the staff. Craig was nearly expelled through Richard's shrewd manipulations, but was saved by the Headmaster who had his suspicions about Richard.

The morning after the incident outside the hotel, Craig was summoned to the Headmaster's office. Noting the boy's worried features the Headmaster reassured him with a smile.

"Craig, I have a telegram from your father. He won't be able to pick you up on Friday. Some problem at the mine. You will have to take the bus I'm afraid. Those bus drivers are rather reckless sometimes, so take care."

He was fond of the young man. Always polite, cheerful, and popular with the other boys. But Craig was no angel. In the three years the boy had boarded at the school he had been summoned before the Headmaster four times. The most serious offense was for raiding the tuck shop late one night with two other boys. The other misdemeanors were minor. One in particular amused the Headmaster although he had to discipline the boy.

Craig had managed to capture a snake and sneak it into Mr. Llewelyn's bed. The snake was harmless but Mr. Llewelyn didn't know that. An average student, Craig needed to study more and be less interested in sports.

On his way back upstairs Craig read the telegram:-

"Sorry. Cannot meet you. Serious accident at the mine.
Take bus. Manuel will meet you at Ubala with Dick.
Be careful! Bandits active in our area. Love Dad."

His father, Robert Fox, manager of Chivor Emerald mine, had been feuding with a local bandit, Joaquin Chavez, for several years.

"Damn!"

His father had promised Craig could drive the next time he came to pick him up. It was a four hour drive from Bogota to the village of Ubala on a gravel road over two mountain passes with sharp dangerous curves. Craig had been secretly practicing on one of the teacher's MG sports car and was anxious to impress his father. From Ubala, it was a two day horseback ride to the emerald mine again over several mountain passes, a rare opportunity to have his father to himself.

* * *

Joaquin Chavez, the oldest of ten illegitimate children, was born in a dirt floor shack. At the age of twelve he stole a calf from his employer, the local landowner. Other thefts followed from his former employer and other landowners in the Chivor district. He induced other boys to join the gang. Eventually the local landowners banded together forcing the gang off their land. Joaquin set up camp in an isolated valley. Over the years his reputation grew. Landowners, and subsistent Indian farmers, to avoid trouble, supplied his gang with meat and fresh vegetables. But this did not stop the occasional raid to kidnap their daughters. One thirteen year old gave birth to a boy. She died giving birth; the boy lived. Joaquin named him Florentino. Two years later a fourteen year old girl produced a baby girl. The mother, Conchita, lived. She named her daughter Teresa, after her grandmother.

When digging for emeralds began at Chivor Mine, Joaquin arranged for some of his men to be hired by the mine. He showed them how to hide emeralds between their bare toes. Soon little green rocks were filtering into his hands. Mine managers came and went. Their efforts to stem the flow were abandoned when none-too-subtle threats were received. Prudently, they departed. The shack in the hidden valley gave way to a two story house, then expanded to include a stable for the horses that Joaquin bought or stole, and bunkhouses for the men that did his dirty work. Emeralds became common tender in the area.

Then a new manager arrived on the mine.

Joaquin's reputation for cunning, ruthlessness, and ability to inflict brutal revenge on any that opposed him terrorized the district. The local landowners, the tenant farmers, the police, and town people feared him. The only man who did not was the new mine manager, Señor Fox.

* * *

Robert Fox graduated from the University of Toronto just in time to be sucked into the slaughter of the First World War. Any romantic ideas that he may have had about the glory of war quickly shriveled in the daily horror of the trenches. Young men and close friends were sacrificed in useless attacks. His courage and leadership qualities were recognized and he was placed in command of more and more troops.

After the War, Robert was assigned to the occupation forces, and it was in Germany that he met his future wife, Margaritte, the daughter of a minor aristocrat, the owner of a country estate in Westphalia where he was billeted. Margaritte was popular and much sought after by young aristocrats streaming out of Dusseldorf at the slightest excuse. She had turned down several marriage proposals in a tactful and considerate manner. She was pretty, but not exceptionally so. Her appeal was her warm caring personality that made all who met her feel they were special friends. Traces of Celtic ancestry remained, the reddish brown hair that she kept trimmed short just below her earlobes, and the freckles sprinkled lightly over smooth glowing cheeks and nose. Her lips hovered on a smile ready to pucker her cheeks with laughter. In spite of the stern shell wrapped around Robert, Margaritte was immediately attracted to this tall handsome man. She realized that behind the piercing blue eyes and stern features was a highly intelligent man with a dry sense of humor. Margaritte was a few years younger than Robert but exuded a mature confidence and intellectual curiosity that he found stimulating. An accomplished horsewoman and tennis player in spite of her small trim frame, she was also an excellent pianist. Robert was in love with Margaritte within days, but hesitated revealing his feelings for many months, knowing the estate had been ruined by the War and the father was anxious for Margaritte to marry a more eligible and wealthy aristocrat. It was Margaritte that forced the issue and made it clear she was going to marry Robert. Six months later they were married.

On Robert Fox's release from the army he worked as an engineer in the diamond mines of South Africa for fifteen years before moving back to Canada during the Depression. The two children, Valerie and Craig, were born in South Africa, two years apart. Valerie, the older child, was fourteen when she entered high school in Toronto. An intelligent young lady, she developed an interest in literature at an early age and was gradually developing her writing skills. At school she usually took honors in arts. Craig, on the other hand, was an average student more interested in sports.

Advertisements for professional engineers were rare during the Depression, but browsing through a mining Journal one Sunday afternoon, about a year after returning to Canada, Robert spotted an interesting advertisement,

> EMERALD MINE
>
> ---
>
> Requires experienced manager. Must have at least ten years experience with emerald or diamond mining and a mining degree from a reputable university in North America. Location Colombia, South America. Knowledge of Spanish desirable but not essential.
> Apply Box 3020, Chrysler Bldg. N.Y.

Robert Fox was hired the day he walked into the office in the Chrysler building. The man on the other side of the desk mentally doubled what he was willing to offer as soon as Robert entered the room. The tall broad shouldered man striding through the door projected an aura of strength and power. The chiseled jaw, iron gray hair cut short, the clipped mustache, and the icy cold blue eyes marked him as a man used to being obeyed.

Two months later the family was on Chivor Mine, numb from the shock. They were perched on the remote summit of the Eastern Cordillera of the Andes in Colombia, two days from the nearest motor road and civilization, among primitive Indians with whom they could not communicate, and living in a bungalow that was filthy, rat infested, and in need of extensive repairs. Water for washing and drinking came out of buckets carried in by the maid. The lavatory was a smelly shed behind the house.

Nevertheless within six months all was changed; water was piped in through a long rubber hose, and a flush toilet of sorts now performed its duty in a small room at the back. Margaritte's musical ear allowed her to pick up Spanish easily and quickly, whereas Robert was forced to spend long evenings struggling with the language so critical for his work. The children soon became fluent in Spanish, besides English and German.

The mine had made little or no profit for several years. Robert Fox's predecessors had failed to stop the theft of emeralds, and departed after being threatened by Joaquin that their life might be in danger. It did not take Robert long to figure out that his major problem was Joaquin. The mine could be very profitable if he could only get rid of the bandit and his gang. For several years Robert Fox was to spend half his time thwarting Joaquin's schemes.

The steady flow of illicit emeralds decreased after the new mine manager weeded out the more suspicious characters and hired two young Colombian adventurers for protection. Now only small and poor quality gems were dropping into Joaquin's hands. Joaquin responded by raiding the workings at night. Robert retaliated by covering the emerald bearing rock with a ton of dirt each evening. This pile of dirt had to be cleared each morning. That reduced the rate of recovery but stopped the raids. A thorough inspection late one night convinced Joaquin he did not have enough men to remove the dirt in the hours available before daylight.

The emeralds were kept in a wall safe in Señor Fox's office. A servant informed Joaquin that the safe was cemented to a large concrete block too heavy to carry off some night when the manager was away; nor did he have the means to open it. Joaquin gave up on the mine for awhile, concentrating on more traditional activities. Murdering Señor Fox would not produce more emeralds, just another manager, and the murder of such a prominent foreigner would force the police in Bogota to descend on his territory.

* * *

Florentino Chavez, a sickly child, would not have survived without the efforts of Conchita, his aunt and his father's new mistress. Initially Joaquin took an interest in the child - his only son - but was soon ashamed of this puny thing he had spawned. Conchita's daughter, Teresa, was born two years after Tino. Unable to produce any more sons, his father took out his frustration on Florentino, and to a lesser extent on Teresa, usually after returning from one of his drinking bouts in Gachala. Tino became Teresa's protector and learned to make himself scarce, hiding Teresa with him whenever his father came home from these trips. Teresa developed an intense devotion to Tino. She was devastated when his father took him away to Gachala to school. Joaquin could not read nor write. This was a handicap. Perhaps his son might be useful to him, if he could be taught to read.

At the age of twelve Tino rode to Gachala on the rump of his father's horse. Their first stop was the local store where he was fitted for his first pair of shoes, new pair of shorts and a shirt. The next stop was the Chief of Police's house. Joaquin dismounted and banged a large knocker on the door leading to the inner courtyard. He banged again impatiently before the door opened. The Chief was informed that Tino would be boarding with him and was now his responsibility to see that he went to school.

Tino didn't see his father again for eight years and was delighted to escape his cruel beatings. His first few weeks at school were difficult. His slight build and baby face encouraged the more sophisticated town boys to tease and bully him. He acquired a knife to protect himself from his tormentors. He struggled to learn the alphabet, arithmetic, and writing skills. With his quick mind he soon caught up to his peers. Within a year he had left them and the teacher behind. Soon the younger boys were looking to him for leadership and protection. Tino's growing and maturing body demanded more food than was being provided by the Police Chief. To satisfy this constant hunger he organized the boys to raid food stalls in the local market, and when they became bolder, some of the stores for food, clothes, and knives. Initially curious as to why The Police Chief had agreed to board him, he discovered that the large house belonged to his father and was loaned, rent free, to the policeman in return for his loyalty. The policeman feared his father. Tino used this fear to his advantage. Although aware that Tino and his gang of boys were shoplifting, the policeman did nothing about it until the merchants' complaints began filtering up to his superiors. Tino was informed he was being sent home. Instead he fled to Bogota.

* * *

There was a steady improvement in emerald recovery for several years, then abruptly, Robert Fox was recovering far poorer emeralds from dikes that he knew should have been producing high quality gems. From his South African experience he suspected what might be happening. Taking his powerful binoculars Robert climbed a hill half a mile away from the pit where the miners were working. For two days he spied on them. His suspicions were soon confirmed. The afternoon of the second day he walked back down the hill followed by the two bodyguards. Usually the two brothers, Alberto and Jorge, indulged in cheerful banter between themselves, but sensing that there might be some action to relieve the boredom they followed in silence watching Robert as he wrestled with the problem.

Jorge and Alberto were not twins but it was still difficult to tell them apart. Both dressed much the same, riding boots up to the knee, faded khaki colored britches and tattered black fedoras over brown curly hair. Their emerald green eyes were the only inheritance from the wild Irishman that had loved and promptly deserted their mother. Both were trying in vain to grow a mustache to make their smooth faces more masculine. Fortunately they favored different colored shirts, one brown the other gray, otherwise Robert didn't know whether he was talking to Alberto or Jorge.

Robert slowed. He stopped and pointed behind him. "Go back and empty the dynamite shed. Pick up your rifles and meet me in front of my office. Make sure your revolvers are loaded. I am going to stop this stealing and arrest the men involved. Be prepared for trouble."

Robert seldom carried a firearm. His presence alone was usually enough to intimidate most Indians, if not, his steel blue eyes overawed the more aggressive ones. Nevertheless his old service revolver hung on an easily accessible nail by the office door. He took it down, strapped the belt around his waist, opened the flap and loaded the chambers. Glancing up Robert saw Margaritte walking across the yard. Quickly he hooked the belt back on the nail. He went out to greet her. Sensitive to his moods she knew immediately something was bothering him. His smile greeted her warmly but his eyes, troubled and cold, betrayed him.

"Is there is a problem at the mine again?"

He squeezed her hand gently, "Yes, but I will be careful. Please go back into the house. I shall be back shortly."

Half an hour later Robert and the two brothers, rifles in hand, descended into the pit where the men were finishing up for the day. The miners stopped work when they saw the guns. Robert called the foreman over and pointed out ten men.

"Tell those men to come over here."

They straggled over and stopped some ten feet in front of Robert looking apprehensively at the rifles. One man seemed to be the leader. He scowled at the three men before him. Robert remembered his name. He called himself "Jose."

"You have been swallowing emeralds. I am going to arrest you and shut you up in the dynamite shed until you produce the emeralds you swallowed. Each man that delivers a stone to me will be released." Knowing that indians were never separated from their knives, Robert ordered, "Jorge take their knives and search them then lock them up."

Jorge handed his rifle to Robert, cautioning him to be alert. He knew the brothers were not popular with the local young men. Too many girls had succumbed to these smooth 'Romeos' with plenty of money to buy them trinkets. Jorge beckoned one of the men towards him, ordered him to drop his knife, searched his clothes then checked the inside of his mouth. He repeated the routine with several others until he reached Jose. This man was not going to submit peacefully. He hunched down in a crouch, feet planted wide apart daring Jorge to approach. Knowing his reputation was at stake Jorge did not hesitate. He walked quickly towards the Indian. Jose's right hand grasped his knife pulling it out of the sheath in one continuous motion. Jorge's brother, Alberto, dropped to one knee, cocked his rifle, and fired once. Jose screamed. The knife spun to the ground some distance away. Blood gushed from a hole in his palm. He held it with the left hand, jumping up and down, cursing, threatening revenge. The remaining men quickly threw down their knives and submitted to being searched. Alberto and Jorge escorted the men to the shed while Robert walked over to the remaining miners to warn them.

"From now on we will be watching you carefully from that hill. Any miner that steals emeralds will be fired and the rest of you will lose a day's pay."

The men glared at him. They picked up their shovels and started digging again muttering angrily to each other.

"One thing more." They eyed Robert warily, "each week that no emeralds are stolen you will receive a bonus of one day's pay." Mollified, but still resentful of this strange foreigner, they went back to work.

Within two days the prisoners presented the required emeralds, were released and fired. Each day one of the brothers sat on the hill with the binoculars watching the digging. A few emeralds were still disappearing under the toes of the men - an acceptable loss.

* * *

Florentino Chavez arrived in Bogota with only a few centavos wrapped in a dirty handkerchief, a shirt, shorts, and a pair of scruffy shoes too tight for his maturing body. Just another street urchin that drifted into the city to scratch out a living in the trash cans or whatever could be stolen. Some sold the only asset they had - their bodies. Tino joined a group of shoeshine boys. They donated an old shoe box which he repaired and painted, showed him how to steal shoe polish, and assigned a spot for him in the "Parque de Independencia" where he set up his stand. It didn't take Tino long to realize that where they had located him was not going to take much business away from the other boys. Friendship went only so far - business was business. His stand was well out of the main traffic flow opposite a bench that was seldom used.

Also his new friends neglected to instruct Tino in the art of polishing shoes. He made a mess of the few shoes that were coaxed onto his stand, much to the annoyance of the owners. He pondered the problem for a few days then took initiatives that were to raise him above his peers and set him on his first fumbling steps to power and money. He contacted Rafael, the bootblack at the Bolivar Hotel, and offered to help him polish the guest's shoes each night in return for lessons. Late one night he dragged another park bench close to his stand. The next day he reduced his prices. Gradually his clientele increased as his skill improved. Every few months he raised prices but still they came. Both benches were usually full by 10 o'clock in the morning, while business men waited for a shine, and didn't empty until late in the afternoon.

One evening, Tino was confronted by four older boys. He knew who they were - a gang of bullies that extorted money from the shoeshine boys and controlled the young prostitutes on the street. They watched him clean up. The moment Tino began to move away they grabbed him by his shirt. The leader, known as "Chico" - a misnomer for he was a tall heavyset young man - picked up the box from where it had fallen and smashed it with his boot. Among the brushes and tins scattered on the ground was a roll of paper money and a bag of coins, Tino's earnings for the day. Chico stuffed the paper money in his pants and handed the coin bag to one of the boys. Leaning over Tino, he sneered.

"Pretty Boy. We will come every evening and you will give us half of what you earn each day."

"Never!" Tino hissed, aiming a vicious kick at Chico's groin. Chico screamed and collapsed on the ground holding his bruised genitals. The sudden attack confused the other boys momentarily. Tino slipped out of their grasp, but Chico clutched his leg tripping him. They dragged Tino behind some bushes, ripped his pants off, and took turns raping him while holding him face down on the grass. After taking turns pummeling him with their boots, the boys left him lying on the grass. For the last time in his life Tino cried.

Soon they were to wish they had killed him for he was to wreak a terrible revenge on each boy in turn.

Picking up his broken shoe box, Tino gathered the brushes and tins and hid them behind a bush. He had no friends. He needed help. After some thought, Tino wandered over to the Bolivar Hotel and knocked on the door of the hotel's bootblack. Rafael took him in, washed his bleeding body and put Tino to bed on a mattress on the floor. Tino stayed a week while his body mended.

Through Rafael's discreet inquiries, Tino located where each of his attackers slept. Late one night Tino positioned himself under a stairway across the alley from the shed where one of the boys lived - the one that had kicked Tino in the groin. He waited in the dark. The only light was from the street at the end of the alley. Tino saw the boy enter the alley. Quietly he took off his shoes and tiptoed behind the boy. Reaching up he wrapped his hand around the boy's face, jerked it back, and slashed his razor-sharp knife across his throat. The scream choked in blood before it left the boy's mouth. Emotionless, Tino watched the dying boy thrashing in the dirt. After a few minutes he rolled the body on its back, emptied the pockets of money, and took off the pants. He made a deep cut across the abdomen to expose the boy's entrails, cut off his penis, then stuffed the organ in the boy's mouth. He wiped the bloody knife on the boy's clothes, pinned a note to the shirt, put on his shoes and strolled out to the street.

The next morning an urchin delivered the note to Chico. He described in detail the fate of one of his gang. The note read:-

"Chico. You will die like this after I kill the other two. Florentino Chavez."

Chico gathered the rest of the gang and went looking for Tino. He was nowhere to be found. Not even beating up the bootblacks elicited Tino's hideout, nor did ransacking his lodgings give them a clue. The following morning the badly mutilated body of another boy was discovered on the roof of a factory. He was the one that had kicked Tino in the head. A second note was delivered to Chico:-

"Chico. One more then you. Florentino Chavez."

The last of Chico's boys went into hiding. Chico did not. He did not dare show his fear to the street urchins he controlled, but he did not sleep at night. Four days later a third body was found by a garbage bin. The final note read:-

"Chico. You will die like the others. Florentino Chavez."

Chico announced that he was going to visit his family in Medellin. He did not return to Bogota, nor did he cross paths with Tino again for twenty years, but Florentino Chavez did not forget the evil inflicted on him by Chico.

Tino retrieved his shoe box, patched it as best he could with the help of Rafael and returned to his usual stand. His former clients came back but it was not the same as before. This boy no longer smiled nor offered a cheerful greeting to each customer. He was not surly but he had enveloped himself in a shield. Any attempt to penetrate was rebuffed by the lowering of the eyebrows and a cold stare that discouraged any further overtures. His clients gradually drifted over to friendlier bootblacks. The bootblacks no longer chatted with him. They had heard about the killings and were afraid of his anger. With the departure of Chico some of the street boys and girls came to seek his protection from other pimps and bullies. Tino did not coerce them into giving him money but offered protection only to those that paid him a fixed weekly fee.

One morning a well dressed foreigner approached and sat at Tino's stand. He watched Tino carefully while the boy polished his expensive shoes. When the boy finished the man handed him a large bill, saying, "keep the change." The man hesitated for a moment as if trying to come to a decision. He shook his head, arguing with himself, then walked off briskly. Five minutes later he was back, cleared his throat and spoke to Tino in a slightly husky voice.

"I have several pair of shoes in my room at the Hotel Bolivar that I want you to clean. I will pay you well. It is room 612. Be there at two o'clock."

Tino eyed the man suspiciously but said nothing. The man turned and walked back across the park. Watching the receding figure with a cold calculating look Tino digested the solicitation. It was not the first time he had been approached by men but before he had always been able to deflect their attentions with light hearted banter. Now he was no longer capable of light hearted banter. He was bored shining shoes and business was declining. He knew that his slim body and exotic looks appealed to a certain kind of man. By the time the short fat man disappeared behind a statue at the far end of the park, Tino had come to a decision.

He had been well paid, nevertheless, Tino was tempted to steal the man's wallet. It was lying partly open on the fat man's dresser, stuffed with American money. Reluctantly, he walked past the wallet and opened the door to the suite. Behind him the fat man sat up in the bed and spoke in a low voice, almost pleading.

"Tino, will you come back tomorrow?"

His lips and nose bunched in a sneer, Florentino nodded briefly before closing the door behind him. He took his payment and opened an account at a bank. He gave his shoe box to another boy. Florentino Chavez embarked on a new career.

* * *

Joaquin Chavez's finances were suffering at the hands of Señor Fox. His income from stolen emeralds had been reduced drastically leaving little money to bribe landowners and local officials. Nevertheless Joaquin, an enterprising man, eventually conceived what he considered to be the perfect plan. The young son of Señor Fox would be kidnapped and ransomed for emeralds. Enough emeralds to allow him to disappear and live very comfortably for the rest of his life. Joaquin's spies kept him up to date on all activity on the mine, and he knew young Craig was in school in Bogota, but he needed to know when the boy was coming home for the summer holidays. The boy had to be captured before he reached the mine. After neglecting Tino for eight years Joaquin decided to enlisted the help of his son. Florentino's notoriety had filtered down to Gachala. He was reputed to have a large stable of girl and boy prostitutes and a reputation as an assassin for hire. A courier was sent to Bogota with orders to find Tino and deliver a sealed envelope containing secret instructions.

The courier had no difficulty finding Tino. The young man was now well known in the city's underworld. A few discreet inquiries and within twenty hours a young street urchin was leading the courier through a labyrinth of back alleys to a dingy apartment block, along a dark grimy hall on the ground floor to a door near the rear of the building. The inside of the small apartment however was bright, clean, and garishly decorated in red and black colors. Tino didn't bother to rise when the courier walked in behind the boy. The little guide disappeared into a back room. The two men stared at each other. They had been friends as boys, but the young man facing the courier no longer acknowledged the past. Tino uncoiled from the couch.

"What brings you here?"

The courier had been warned during his search that Tino was dangerous. Tino's eyes bore into the man. The courier lowered his eyes. He handed Tino the envelope.

"This is from your father. I am to return immediately with your answer." No sooner had the words left his mouth than he regretted the tone of his voice.

Tino leaned into him menacingly, "you will have my answer when I am ready. Come back tomorrow. The boy that brought you will take you back."

* * *

Richard Bannerman was finishing his final year of school. In four weeks he would be nineteen and returning to Canada to join the Royal Canadian Air Force. The Battle of Britain was now being fought over England and the glamor of this struggle exhilarated him. He envisioned himself dueling in his Spitfire with some German ace. But there was one problem that might wreck this glorious future. It was the maid at the Canadian Embassy where his parents lived. The maid was pregnant and threatening to go to his father and the authorities. His father was not a cause for worry. In fact he would probably be amused at Richard's philandering. It was the publicity that could hurt Richard's image if it became public knowledge that the son of the Canadian Ambassador was consorting with Indian girls.

Richard was an only child. After several miscarriages and a difficult birth that precluded any more children, his mother enveloped the boy in a protective cocoon. She idolized him, catering to his every whim. He was spoiled. He soon learned, even at the age of three, that screaming tantrums would very quickly bring his mother running. She provided him with toys as a child, a labrador retriever when he was eight, and a horse on his thirteenth birthday.

The dog was the only creature that Richard ever truly loved. He carried the pup around in his arms the moment he came home from school; slept with it every night, initially on top of the blanket while his parents were up and under the blanket as soon as they were in bed. Each summer he roamed the half section family farm west of Toronto with a shotgun on his shoulder and Rex trotting by his side. With his quick reflexes and sharp eyes it didn't take long for Richard to master the art of deflection shooting. A skill that was to make him an ace fighter pilot a few years later.

Rex was run over by a truck while trying to retrieve a bird that had fluttered into the bushes on the other side of the highway. Dry-eyed, Richard buried the dog in a remote corner of the property. His mother suggested a cross over the grave. Richard shook his head. Instead, he painted the dog's name on a board and buried the board, and his compassion for living creatures, with the dog. He sat by the grave for two days and nights, then rose and returned to the farmhouse. His mother met him at the door. She tried to put her arms around him. He shook her off, glaring at her.

"Leave me alone."

"Richard, I'll get you another dog."

"Don't you dare. No dogs. Ever again!"

On Richard's birthday, a young groom brought a horse out of the barn. It was huge. At least it appeared huge to the thirteen year old boy. Too short to reach the stirrups, the groom moved the horse next to the gate leading to the pasture. Richard climbed the gate and into the saddle. Sitting on the back of the beast was initially intimidating. Determined to master the creature, Richard dug his heels into the animal's ribs. The horse broke into a trot almost toppling Richard backwards. He grabbed the front of the saddle with his left hand and yanked back on the reins with his right hand. The horse stopped. Keeping his left hand on the front of the saddle, Richard pressed his heels into the horse once more, this time gently. The horse began walking forward.

Within the hour Richard had firmly established his dominance over the horse. Pulling the right rein moved it to the right; pulling the left rein moved it to the left. A sharp dig in the ribs and the horse trotted. Smacking the whip across the rump produced a fast gallop. Finally, hauling back on the reins would slow the horse to a full stop. Returning the horse to the barn, the groom noticed the heaving chest and froth drooling from the horse's mouth.

"You're not supposed to whip the horse so hard."

Sitting up straight Richard towered over groom standing below him. He was tempted to strike the pimply face with his whip. He leaned over hissing, "Don't you dare tell me what I can do."

Seeing the look on Richard's face the young man stepped back several paces. He waited until Richard slid off the horse's back before moving forward to take the reins.

The next day the groom didn't move the horse to the gate, instead he crouched low and beckoned Richard to place his left boot on his upper thigh. With his left hand under the boot and his right hand between Richard's thighs, the groom hoisted him into the saddle. He didn't remove his right hand immediately. For almost a minute Richard didn't move, allowing the man's fingers to stroke his growing hardness. Abruptly Richard grabbed the groom's wrist and yanked his hand out from under his buttocks. Leaning over he snarled.

"Don't ever do that again." And much to his own surprise at his next words, he continued, "unless I say you can."

The groom smiled slyly, "Yes sir, any time you say."

The groom stepped back and smacked the horse's rump. The horse jumped forward breaking into a gallop almost tumbling Richard off its back. He grabbed the front of the saddle with his left hand while pulling back on the reins with the other hand. The horse slowed to a walk. The groom watched Richard guide the horse out of the paddock and through the gate into the field. Richard dug his heels into the horse's ribs. The horse began to trot. Richard's britches rubbed back and forth against his penis. He could feel himself becoming hard again. Leaning forward increased the pressure sending sensations into his belly and down his thighs. Richard jabbed his heels hard into the horse's flank. It broke into a gallop. Richard opened his legs wider, leaning forward and pressing himself into the saddle.

When Richard returned to the barn, the groom was standing at the entrance, shirtless; revealing a thin hairless almost concave chest with the ribs plainly visible. The youth's jeans were low over his buttocks. The pubic hair and bulge in his jeans plainly visible. The crafty grin on his face infuriated Richard. He raised his whip to strike the groom. Immediately the youth turned his back bending over instead of moving away. Richard had only intended to threaten the groom but the pale flesh offered was too tempting. He slashed across the back leaving a red welt extending from the shoulder to the waist.

"Christ! Not so hard. That hurt."

Richard struck again, leaving a red 'X' on the pale skin. The groom ran into the barn. Richard slid off the horse and followed him in. He was hard again.

Richard's mother bought him a sports car on his sixteenth birthday, and recently in response to his desire to join the R.C.A.F., she arranged flying lessons. She was not happy about his decision to go to war but perhaps the lessons would increase his chances of surviving. James G. Bannerman was more encouraging. He had plans for his son's future. A few years in uniform would give Richard the right sort of credentials for a career in politics. He was aware of Richard's ruthless nature and had no doubt that with his exceptional intelligence Richard could fight his way to the top to become Prime Minister of Canada. Through his connections he would make sure that Richard stayed clear of any fighting. Richard however had no intention of avoiding combat. He was convinced his destiny was to be a fighter ace. But right now he had a matter to resolve. He knew where to look for help.

At their regular Friday dinner at the Anglo-American Club, Richard informed his father of the maid's threats. As expected, his father merely warned him to take care of the problem quietly and make sure his mother didn't hear about the girl. She would be shocked that her darling son could consort with such women.

Richard tripped and nearly fell going down the stairs. Realizing he had sipped too many glasses of his favorite red wine on top of a couple of drinks of scotch before dinner, he paused before opening the door to the street. It was drinking that had created the breach between Craig Fox and himself. Through one stupid drunken action he had nearly exposed his true nature. Ever since the incident with Craig, Richard avoided possible exposure at school and bought his pleasures in the park across the street. Richard stepped out, looked up and down the street to make sure he was alone, before crossing to the heavily treed park. Little did he know that tonight he was to meet the person who would influence his actions and career for the rest of his life.

Florentino Chavez saw him enter the park. Another foreigner, tall, broad shouldered, with blond hair reflecting the street lights behind him. The face was not visible, all he could distinguish was the outline of the man approaching. A boy stepped out of the shadows in front of Tino and walked towards the foreigner. Tino growled at him. The boy turned angrily. Recognizing Tino, he slunk back into the shadows.

Richard walked further into the gloom of the park until he heard a voice on his left.

"Are you looking for company?"

A young man was leaning against the concrete rim of a fountain that had been shut off for the night. The slim athletic youth was dressed in black. Richard studied the boy for a few moments, then nodded. Tino in turn studied Richard. He could see his face now. He was young, which was unusual.

"My fee is a hundred pesos. I have a room in a hotel across the street. Please follow me. The manager will not talk as I pay him well." Tino turned and walked off rapidly, not looking back. Richard followed.

* * *

Florentino Chavez dressed slowly, aware that Richard was watching him from the bed. Combing his hair, Tino was vigilant. He made sure he could follow Richard's movements in the mirror. Tino had learned that Richard was sadistic when aroused. He had to be careful with this young man. Richard got up from the bed to dress. Tino decided it was time to demand his fee. Sometimes this was the dangerous part of his business. Now that they had had their fun they haggled at the price.

"Ricardo. Last night I said my fee was one hundred pesos, but you have hurt me so it is now one hundred and fifty pesos."

Expecting Richard to object, he was surprised when Richard smiled instead. Tino allowed a brief smile to flit across his lips, 'I must have flattered his male pride.'

Richard opened his wallet and checked the contents.

"You did not touch my money."

"No Ricardo. I never steal money from my clients. The price has been agreed beforehand and it is not good for business. They do not come back if I steal from them."

Richard handed over the one hundred and fifty, then held up a one thousand peso note. He sat on the bed and waved Tino to the only chair in the room.

"I think you are the man I have been looking for. I want you to find me a man that will kill somebody for me. I will pay you this money now, and another three thousand pesos when you prove to me that the person is dead."

It was twice the amount Tino had in his bank account. Nevertheless, his culture impelled him to negotiate.

"Ricardo, I have killed many enemies. I will kill this person for you." A slight smile softened his face briefly. "My fee is always five thousand pesos, and I guarantee my work."

Richard's lips pursed momentarily then he nodded. "Bueno. The person is a maid who is pregnant by me. I want her dead."

"A girl! That's different, I..."

Richard's hand shot up, palm open towards Tino, "five thousand no more!"

Tino saw the clenched jaw and flashing eyes. The negotiations were over. "Bueno, Amigo. Five thousand pesos. One thousand now. The rest when I give you proof she is dead."

"Remember, I need proof."

"Okay, as you Americans say."

"Remember! Proof!"

"I will remember. Ricardo, I need some information from you. You said you go to school at the English School. When do you finish school?"

"In five days, why?"

"There is a boy in your boarding school that I am interested in. I want to know when he leaves the school to go home for the holidays. His name is Craig Fox."

Startled, Richard glanced quickly at Tino. "What is he to you? What do you want from him?"

"I will tell you, my friend, when I know you better. After I take care of your girl. Come, it is time for us to leave."

"You should know that his father comes to Bogota to take him home."

"I know. But not this time."

"Why?"

Tino smiled but didn't answer the question, "Vamonos, Amigo."

* * *

Standing in the street near the side door of the Bolivar Hotel, Florentino waited impatiently for Richard to come out from the dinner party he was attending. Ten minutes later Richard crept up behind him.

"Why did you come that way?"

"I wanted to make sure we are alone."

"The girl is dead. I pushed her over the Tequendama Falls yesterday. She will never be found. I took this picture of her floating in the water at the base of the falls." Tino held up a small picture. "See! Here is the proof. Now you can pay me the rest of..."

They both looked up at a shadow that had appeared above them. A boy was standing at the top of the steps leading down from the hotel door. Quickly they walked down the dark alley. In a low voice Richard said.

"That is the boy you were asking about. That is Craig Fox. Why are you interested in him?"

"His father is the manager of a very rich emerald mine, Chivor Mine. My father is planning to kidnap his son on his way home and ransom him for emeralds. I am to follow him when he goes home and help capture the boy."

Tino followed Richard to his sports car. Richard unlocked the glove box and took out an envelope. He handed it to Tino.

"Here is the rest of your payment. There is four thousand pesos in this envelope which is the balance of the amount I agreed to pay you. You did very well. Everybody is wondering where she is. I suggested to my mother that the girl has probably gone home to her village. There is no suspicion that she was murdered."

"Ricardo, my friend, anytime you need me you know where to find me."

"I think I need you now."

"Who do you want to kill now?"

"Craig Fox."

"Why him? He is just a boy. Tino's eyes searched Richard's face, "Unless?"

"Not that. But I'm sure he overheard you telling me about the girl."

"But I was speaking Spanish."

"He speaks excellent Spanish. I want you to kill him."

"Do you want me to kill him tonight?"

"No! No! Are you mad? Not in Bogota. The police might connect me to him. You said your father wants to ransom him?"

"Si."

"Well then kill him after he is ransomed but before the boy returns to Bogota. Nobody will suspect me if he is killed out in the jungle."

"If you want him killed I can arrange that after the ransom is paid. The fee, Ricardo, will be the same as before. Five thousand pesos."

"Don't forget, I am leaving for Canada in thirty days and I want you to kill him before I leave. Here is a thousand pesos. The rest with proof he is dead."

Watching Richard drive off in his little red sports car Tino muttered to himself.

"Ricardo, today I follow your orders, my friend. But now I have something over you, and one day you will obey my orders."

Tino walked back out to the street to follow Craig Fox, to make sure he would recognize him again.

* * *

The three-days before Robert Fox was to leave for Bogota to pick up Craig a dynamite blast buried nine men. This happened soon after the miners descended to the floor of the open cut mine and were removing the overburden protecting the emerald-bearing dike. By the time Robert arrived the survivors were digging frantically, hoping to save their friends. The pit foreman walked over to Robert shaking his head.

"Señor, I think there are nine workmen under there. One is my brother, Jesus. There can be no survivors with all that rock on top of them.

Somebody planted some dynamite up there on the wall and set it off while we were working. There was no warning." Leaning closer to Robert, he continued in a low voice, "I think some of the men knew what was going to happen because several walked away just before the explosion."

"Point them out to me."

The foreman mumbled, head bowed, eyes averted, "Señor, I am sorry, I-I don't know what they look like." Robert understood. To reveal the identity of Joaquin's men would be his death sentence. The foreman was his most trusted employee. He could not ask him to risk his life.

"I understand. I am very sorry about your brother. Come let us see what we can do." Robert patted the man on the shoulder and walked back to where one of the bodies was being recovered. Assessing the damage he estimated that it would take several days to remove the slide. He would have to shut the mine down for a day while the miners attended the funerals. He could not leave the mine for at least a week. Craig would have to come home by himself. Margaritte would not be happy at the thought of Craig traveling through bandit territory unescorted. He would send Manuel for the boy. Manuel had worked for them for several years and could be trusted. He was older, honest, and fond of Craig. Having no family of his own, he had become attached to the boy and treated him like a son.

A messenger left at noon for Gachala with a telegram for Craig.

That afternoon Robert worked his way up the slope through the rubble of the slide until he reached the top of the pit. The evidence was there. Pieces of primer cord were strewn about, burnt matches used to light the primer cord lay scattered along the edge of the cliff, and a stick of dynamite was still wedged in a crack in the rock with the fizzled primer in it. Fifty yards away under a tree a pile of cigarette butts showed where the perpetrator had waited for the appropriate moment. Robert sat on the edge of the cliff watching the men below moving the heavy rocks with their bare hands, shovels, and picks. Filling his old battered pipe from a well worn tobacco pouch, he settled down for some thinking.

There was no question that Joaquin was behind this atrocity. But what was the purpose? The dike that Joaquin had so thoroughly covered was nearly mined out and was to be abandoned in a few days and the miners moved to a new location. This dike had yielded some of the finest high grade gems that Robert had ever seen; flawless, dark green, hexagonals. He now had a fortune in emeralds sitting in his safe, ready for shipment to Bogota at the end of the month. Through his spies Joaquin was certainly aware that the dike was nearly mined out and knew about the emeralds in the safe. So what was he after? Killing the miners would attract the attention of the authorities, which Robert doubted Joaquin would welcome. Nor would it make it easier for him to steal the emeralds.

The sun was setting behind the far range of Andean peaks when he got up, beckoned to his two bodyguards, and walked down the path towards the house. He still had not figured out what Joaquin was up to.

* * *

The Headmaster was right, it was a hair-raising ride, but it wasn't so much the driver's nonchalant maneuvers around the sharp curves that was worrying Craig, it was the presence of the young Indian that he had seen outside the Bolivar Hotel, seated on the other side of the bus several rows behind him.

Soon after boarding the bus in Bogota Craig noticed the young man. He looked familiar. Whenever Craig looked back, the young Indian was watching him, but quickly turned away whenever their eyes locked. His striking facial features, the high cheek bones, smooth almost translucent hairless skin, and black shiny hair slicked back gave him a slightly asiatic look. His dark eyes, deep in their sockets under thin eyebrows, seemed to smolder when they refocused on Craig. The realization of who was sitting behind him flooded in. It was the young man that reported the murder to Richard.

Craig was inured to Colombian drivers. Even so, every time the bus slid out towards the edge of the road Craig's hands clenched. Plunging towards each sharp curve in the road, the driver leaned on the horn with one hand while steering with the other. At the same time he was trying to convince the passenger on the front seat across from him that his favorite bullfighter was the best in the business. Between each curve in the road, he half turned, lifted his hand from the horn, and waved it in the face of the elderly man. The old man nodded his head in agreement while keeping a frantic eye on the road ahead. Each time the bus lurched towards the next curve the terrified passenger pointed desperately ahead. Without pausing in his praise, the driver turned, punched the horn, and attacked the curve. The rattling of the old bus and the horn gave ample warning to the Indians on the road. They could be seen plastered up against the rocky face as the bus bounced by in a cloud of dust. Craig stole a glance at the old Indian lady sitting next to him. She was sleeping peacefully even though her head was rolling from side to side. Some of the other passengers were sleeping in spite of the jolting and noise. Others were talking quietly oblivious to their peril, or if aware of it, had already given God the burden of looking after their souls. It was no problem while the bus labored slowly up to the passes, but when they began the final descent to the town of Ubala, Craig tensed once again. The driver was pumping the brakes with little effect and relying on the gears to control the speed. Curious as to whether the Indian was nervous like himself Craig looked back when the bus skidded around yet another curve. The Indian was watching Craig with a slight smile on his lips. Embarrassed at being caught staring Craig turned back to the void beneath him. Far below in the valley he could see the village of Ubala, a large cobble-stoned plaza, surrounded by red tiled roofs paying homage to a church dominating the far end. The huge bell in the church tower tolled the noon hour, but he could hear nothing above the rattling of the old bus as it bounced over the ruts, sending gravel machine-gunning up into the metal underside. The road zigzagged down the mountain for several thousand feet then stretched across the valley and entered the village of Ubala. Horn blaring, the bus came to a stop in the plaza with a final protest from the smoking brakes. Ubala was the end of the motor road. Craig eased himself through the mass of Indians crowding the exit of the bus and made a dash for the urinal behind the bus stop.

Working his way back through the crowd Craig picked up his saddlebags and looked for Manuel, his bodyguard, and Dick, his horse. According to his father's telegram, they were here to pick him up. Manuel was nowhere in sight but he spotted Dick. A strange Indian was holding his horse, certainly not Manuel. The man was younger, taller, armed with a rifle slung over his shoulder and a revolver strapped to his waist. He was talking to the young Indian Craig had seen on the bus. The young Indian spotted Craig approaching. He nodded towards Craig, said something, and walked away rapidly. The man picked up the horse's bridle and gave it a jerk, forcing the horse to follow. Dick's neck arched up, ears laid back, and nostrils flaring, nervously resisting the rough treatment. The horse was afraid of the man. The Indian smiled, greeting Craig.

"Buenos dias, Señor."

There was no warmth in the smile nor in the greeting. The cold black eyes locked with his own briefly then turned away. His smile vanished as quickly as it had flashed. He had not even bothered to lift his hat, the usual courtesy. Craig had lived for several years among the Indians and considered them gentle and courteous, but this man's greeting was cold and certainly not courteous. The Indians he knew were not well armed either. The only guns they possessed were the muzzle loading blunderbusses that were relics of the eighteenth century. This Indian was carrying a high powered rifle and a heavy caliber revolver, besides the usual two knives most Indians carried. A two foot 'penilla' for cutting through the jungle, and a small knife for cutting meat or enemies, hung from his belt. His cheeks were heavily pockmarked, the nose bent slightly to one side as if it might have been broken in a fight, and a long purple scar was clearly visible slashing diagonally across his throat. Craig was instantly wary remembering his father's warning about bandits.

"Buenos dias. Where is Manuel?"

"Manuel is sick." A faint smile appeared as if remembering some joke, "Your father sent me instead."

The horse recognized Craig when he picked up his scent, gave a gentle snort, and nibbled at the side pocket of Craig's riding breeches, where he knew Craig kept cubes of sugar for him. Craig took out a lump and held it in the palm of his hand. Dick gently wrapped his thick lips around the tidbit, then bumped the pocket asking for more.

"Later, my friend, if you behave."

Patting the long gray neck, he took the reins from the Indian, checked the cinch under the horse's belly, strapped the bags behind the saddle, took out and put on his spurs, then eased himself into the saddle.

"What is your name?"

The man hesitated before replying, "Jose, Señor."

Craig wondered why he was reluctant to give his name. Gently he dug his spurs into Dick's belly, followed the Indian out of the plaza and down a narrow side street flanked by high walls. Craig watched Jose carefully. His clothes were clean and his rope sandals were not muddy. The man ignored the greetings of the Indians they passed, walking brusquely through the throng. Whenever Craig returned a greeting, Jose turned his head with a disdainful look. The walls on each side of the street had long ago lost their plastered brilliance and were now weathered to a dull yellow color. The large wooden doors shielding the private inner courtyards from passersby showed their age, weathered and pitted like the iron railings on the tiny balconies above the doors. The clatter of the horse's hooves on the cobblestones attracted the attention of a young lady. She came out onto a balcony above him. Seeing Craig she waved. He smiled, took off his hat, and waved back. Silently she watched him ride down the street until he turned a corner. With a quiet sigh she walked back into the dark gloomy bedroom.

At the edge of the village they came to a junction, one branch snaking back up the mountain that the bus had just descended, and the other meandering down the valley towards the town of Gachala, a four hour ride over a mountain pass. They took the road to Gachala, the horse leading with Jose a few yards behind. Gradually the cultivated fields gave way to scrub, and the road, now more a mule trail than a road, entered the jungle. An hour later rain burst over them. The raindrops drumming on the leaves long before they reached them gave them warning of the approaching deluge. Craig had time to unpack his raincoat, and Jose to unroll the "ruana" he carried over his shoulder. The Indian put his head through the slit in the middle of the heavy woolen blanket and draped the ruana around him before the rain struck. Looking back Craig could barely see Jose some twenty feet behind him through the sheets of water sluicing down. The storm was gone as quickly as it had come.

Late that afternoon they were still some distance from Gachala. Near the equator there would be no long twilight to guide them into town. When the sun set it would be pitch black. Jose had been following some distance back, but moved closer behind the horse when the sun set. When it got dark Jose came forward and walked beside Craig with one hand on the back of the saddle. Craig chuckled to himself. Indians are terrified of the dark, and he was amused to see that in spite of his 'macho' demeanor Jose was no different.

An hour later they entered the village of Gachala along a wide cobble stoned street. A shallow stream babbled along one side and the high walls of private homes lined the other. The occasional street lamp cast shadows on the walls beside them. From time to time the shadows were blurred by soft filmy mist drifting up from the stream, or by the occasional spark from the horse's iron shoes. They clattered across a plaza and entered the courtyard of the only hotel in town. Craig dismounted, handed the reins to Jose, and walked inside with his saddle bags. Jose walked off with the horse towards the stables behind the hotel. Señor Trujillo owned the hotel that Craig's family had frequented for several years, but it was Doña Isabela that controlled the establishment, including her husband. She was a short, slightly plump lady with a round smooth olive tinted face, and shiny black hair that she kept pulled back in a bun. The tiny lobby was empty. Craig dropped the saddle bags next to the little reception desk, took off his spurs, and was about to walk towards the kitchen noises, when Doña Isabela emerged drying her hands on a towel. As soon as she saw him she flung the towel away, and rushed forward embracing Craig, crushing him to her bosom. He was pleased but embarrassed. He could feel her breasts against his chest.

"Querido! We have been worried. Es muy tarde. Your father sent us a letter saying you were coming. Mirate. Estas muy mojado. Your room is ready. Please go up and change your clothes or you will catch cold. When you finish come and eat before your dinner gets cold."

Later when Craig entered the dining room he noticed several families dining. He bowed slightly to the ladies, as was the custom, and seated himself at a small table. He was ravenous. Doña Isabela hovered near him making sure that he had all he could eat. She liked the young man. He was pleasant and courteous, not too tall like most North Americans, but a little thin for his age. The brown hair and the faint sprinkling of freckles over his fair skin gave him a slightly softer look than his father, but the strong chin was the same as the father's. The blue eyes were even more brilliant than Señor Fox's.

The boy appealed to Doña Isabela. He had such an infectious smile. His cheeks crinkled up, almost closing off those luminous pools of blue whenever the smile took over his face. There was a trace of a mustache on his lips. He must be sixteen or seventeen by now. She had known the family since Craig was a boy. They stayed at her hotel several times a year when they traveled to and from Bogota. A much nicer young man than his father, Señor Fox. Doña Isabela sat across from Craig, her ample bosom resting on the table. Craig concentrated on his dinner, a large soup bowl containing several large chunks of boiled meat and "yucca". Craig was not fond of "yucca", a very starchy root, but was too hungry to be fussy.

"Is your sister still in school?"

"Si Señora. Valerie is in her last year in school in Toronto. Do you know where Toronto is?" Doña Isabela shook her head. "It is in Ontario in Eastern Canada. She is talking about going to university. She wants to be a writer. She is very good at it. She is the clever one in the family."

"Querido." Reaching over to pat his shoulder, "I do not believe that."

Craig finished the large dish of his favorite thick sweet dessert, thanked his hostess, and walked out of the now empty room. Outside in the courtyard Jose was again talking to the young Indian Craig had seen on the bus. The moment they saw Craig both walked away rapidly. 'I wonder why he is following us.' He mused, 'something is going on.' Craig climbed the stairs to his room, locking the door before getting into bed.

In the morning the dining room was empty when Craig entered. He wasn't looking forward to the long ride ahead of him. It would be a long day. Other than a few clearings laboriously hand cut by homesteading Indians, his whole day would be taken up riding under the canopy of the jungle. It was boring and tiring. The mule trail was narrow, muddy, and subject to frequent heavy rainstorms, particularly on the high passes on the way to the mine on the slopes of Chivor Peak. The occasional waterfall would do little to break the tedium.

Three fried eggs, ham, sweet rolls, jam, and thick black coffee improved his spirits. Out in the courtyard Jose was waiting for him with Dick. When the man handed him the reins Craig noticed a scar on Jose's right hand. The roundness of the scar on the back of the man's hand could only have been caused by a bullet. Jose saw Craig looking at it and scowled. Craig was about to ask him about the scar, but the scowl warned him not to inquire. The man's pockmarked face was flushed and puffy, his eyes bloodshot, his clothes rumpled. He returned Craig's cheerful greeting with a brief surly nod. Craig's good spirits evaporated. Angrily he leapt on the horse, jabbed the spurs into the horse's flank, and galloped out of the courtyard. The man was drunk on that deadly alcohol the locals called "Aguardiente." Realizing that he was taking his anger out on the horse Craig slowed to a walk and patted Dick's neck.

It was Saturday morning - market day, and Indians were bringing their produce to sell at stalls set up in the town square. Men and women passed him on the trail leading into town; heavy string packs on their backs filled with the root of the "yucca" plant, their staple diet, or a heavy load of sugar cane; or occasionally some chickens hung upside down from a rope over their shoulders. In spite of the heavy loads the men were dressed in their best clothes; rope sandals; black trousers rolled up above bulging calf muscles; white embroidered shirts; and the usual two knives in fancy sheaths. The women wore black skirts; red or black embroidered shirts under black shawls, or short black jackets. They stepped to the side of the road as he passed and lifted their straw hats politely with a brief smile. They eyed him curiously. They did not live near the mine and had not seen this young foreigner before.

Craig, worried the young Indian from Bogota might be following them, glanced to the rear whenever Jose was not watching. That afternoon he was certain they were being followed. They had crossed the first high pass and were following the steep trail zigzagging down the flank on the far side when Craig heard a rock clattering down the trail high above him. Jose, some yards below him, looked up quickly then back at Craig before continuing down the trail. Later in the day Craig picked up the sound of iron shod hooves some distance behind them.

"Somebody is following us."

"No, I heard nothing." Jose muttered without stopping or turning around, but he did take the rifle off his shoulder and insert an ammunition clip. They were now in bandit territory. Craig hoped the gun was for his protection.

The few Indians that were now passing were local men who knew Craig. They greeted him warmly until they spotted Jose behind the horse. Quickly they pressed to the side of the track. A few miles from the mine Craig saw in the distance his young friend, Eduardo, approaching to greet him. The boy stopped while still some distance away, stood still watching them approach, then suddenly turned and ran off into the trees. Jose cursed and ran past Craig to the spot where Eduardo had disappeared but the boy was gone. Craig was now convinced he was in danger.

At a junction in the trail Jose stopped and pointed to the right fork. "This way, Señor."

Craig shook his head, "That is not the road to the mine. I know the way."

"Si Señor. This is the way. There has been a landslide and that road is closed. This road will take us to Chivor Mine."

Craig knew it would not. Jose grabbed Dick's bridle to prevent Craig from taking the left fork. Suddenly the clatter of hooves behind them startled Craig. Turning in the saddle he saw the young Indian from Bogota galloping towards them, hands flailing from side to side whipping his horse and digging his spurs cruelly into the horse's flank. The Indian shouted to Jose.

"Stop his horse! Hold the bridle!"

Craig realized, too late, that he must escape. Thoroughly frightened he leaned low in the saddle digging in his spurs. His horse smashed into Jose spinning him off to the side of the trail before he could unsling the rifle. A brief feeling of exultation flowed over Craig as he galloped away. He had escaped.

The Indian shouted at Jose. "Stop him ! But don't kill him!"

Craig heard the sharp crack of the rifle. The horse bucked and rolled over throwing Craig forward into oblivion when his head hit a rock.

* * *

Florentino Chavez stood on his stirrups and hauled back on the bridle, bringing his horse to a stop. He leapt off and ran over to where the white boy lay crumpled on the side of the road, spread-eagled in the mud, with his head half buried in a shallow pool of muddy water. Blood was flowing from a cut over his left ear. The horse had rolled over the edge of the road and crashed upside down against a tree preventing him from rolling out of sight over a cliff. The horse was thrashing feebly as he died, blood flowing from the hole in his flank.

"You have killed the boy."

"No. Patron. He is only injured. See! He moves his hand. You came just in time. He was very suspicious."

"Pick him up and take him to the house. I will go and report to my father. My father will not be pleased with you if he dies. I will send a horse for you. Where did you throw Manuel's body?"

"Down there, Patron." Grinning, Jose pointed over the cliff below the dead horse. "Manuel would not beg for his life, so I shot him in the legs: then in the knees; but he didn't beg. Stupid old man. I threw him over the cliff. Alive!"

Florentino shrugged and rode off towards his father's compound. The manner of Manuel's death was of no interest to him. His immediate concern was how and when to kill Craig. Five thousand pesos was a lot of money... Maybe he could also steal some of the emeralds from his father?

Looking off to the left Tino caught a glimpse of the tin roofs of the mine buildings glinting in the late afternoon sun. Thrusting his middle finger towards the buildings he jeered. "You are in for a big surprise, Señor Fox."

- 2 -

Teresa paced up and down the length of her room. Every few minutes she paused before the full length mirror, ran her hands nervously through her hair, tucked her blouse more firmly under her skirt and smoothed the folds around her knees. 'Will he remember me? I was so young when Tino left... what's he like now?... He was such a wonderful brother. My protector... Father sneered when he told me Tino was coming, said he was a pimp and a prostitute... I don't believe that. The Tino I knew would never do that.'

Teresa heard noises and voices in the courtyard. Racing out of her room she peered over the iron railing. Two men were carrying a white boy up the stairs from the courtyard. One was that horrible man, Jose. The other had to be Tino. Although he was much taller than when he left eight years before she knew it was him. They came up the stairs. Tino glanced at her, briefly nodded but didn't greet her. She followed, watching them carry the young boy into the bedroom next to hers. He was unconscious his mud spattered head lolling backwards, his mouth open. Gurgling sounds, more like moans, bubbled out of his mouth with every step they took. They dumped him on the bed. The boy's head thumped against the headboard and began bleeding from a deep cut on his temple. Jose laughed, leaned over and squeezed the cut. Tino barked.

"Leave him alone! Go and tell father the boy is here then bring some rope to tie him down."

Jose left the room slamming the door behind him. Teresa waited for her brother to acknowledge her presence. She was close to tears, heart thumping chest tight with emotion, terrified of what his response might be. He had changed so much and not only physically. He was now a man but with a personality so different from the sensitive boy she had adored. He was still beautiful, but no warmth emanated from him. She waited, fingers fiddling nervously with the top button on her blouse.

Tino, satisfied the boy was not about to move, raised his head. Silently he ran his eyes up the length of her body appraising the little girl that had matured into a young woman. 'She is beautiful, like myself'. Slim, fairly tall, not short and stocky like most Indian women. But it was her facial features that set her apart. 'We could have been twins'. Her skin, tanned to a very light brown, was stretched over high cheek bones giving her the same asiatic look as himself. Her hair, black and lightly oiled, was pulled back into a bun and held in place with a comb. Her nose was fairly large, straight, with slightly flared nostrils. The lips though, were thin and brown. He noticed her chin trembling. Tino walked forward and embraced Teresa. She burst into tears.

"Teresa you are all grown up. You are a beautiful young lady."

She felt a deep shudder in his chest and a slight warmth in his embrace. Abruptly he pulled back. Jose came back with several ropes. She turned her back to hide her tears from Jose. When they finished tying the boy's legs and arms to the bed Jose left. Tino pointed at the boy's head.

"Teresa, the wound must be washed otherwise it will become infected. I have to go and see father now but I will return later to talk to you. I must see what father is planning to do with the boy. I have heard Señor Fox is a very ruthless man. Father must be very careful." Nodding towards the boy, Tino warned her, "He is very dangerous. Make sure the ropes are tight all the time."

Tino went out closing the door behind him. Teresa approached the bed. The wound had stopped bleeding but the pillow was soaked with blood and the boy's hair was matted with dried blood and mud. His face and clothes were muddy also. His boots were on the floor. She picked them up and placed them neatly at the foot of the bed. She stared at the boy for several minutes. He certainly did not look like an evil foreigner. His father might be a monster, but this boy certainly was not. His pale face was gentle, no harshness there. She took her handkerchief and wiped some of the mud from his face. His warm breath tingled the hairs on the back of her hand. A strange ache spread up from her chest forcing a sigh to relieve the tightness. She leaned over and lightly brushed her lips on his. Shocked at her boldness she moved her head back quickly. Blushing she hurried out of the room. A few minutes later Teresa returned with with a basin of hot water a clean towel and a bottle of permanganate. The boy's eyes were now open staring straight ahead, unfocussed. She gazed at them fascinated. Such blue eyes! She had been told these foreign devils had evil blue eyes that could cast spells. His eyes were not evil. They were beautiful like precious stones.

Vaguely aware there was somebody in the room, Craig turned his head and immediately winced letting out a groan. Every heart beat exploded in his head.

"Ooh! My head!"

Teresa had never heard English spoken before but understood what he said. Gently she washed his wound and face. Then warning him it was going to hurt she poured a few drops of disinfectant on the open wound. He jerked his head up in agony gasping in Spanish,

"Caramba! That hurt!"

Carefully she put a few more drops in the wound while he clutched the side of the bed clenching his teeth. She wrapped a clean towel around his head and removed the basin from the room. By the time she came back it was dark. Teresa brought a kerosene lamp with her and placed it on a chest across the room. She sat on a wooden chair by the chest. The light from the lamp cast soft shadows under her cheeks and nose, giving her face a more sculptured look. Craig watched her, fascinated. His head was still throbbing but the pounding had receded. He could now think rationally.

"Where am I? What am I doing here?"

"You are in the house of Joaquin Chavez, my father. The young man that brought you here is my brother. His name is Florentino. He is an important business man in Bogota." Craig stared at her, incredulously. 'She can't really believe that.'

"Your father is a very evil man and he is to be punished for the things he has done to our people. My father has taken you prisoner and he is going to send your father a message that you will be returned to him unharmed, but he must pay for the suffering he has inflicted on the Indians for making them work for nothing in his mine. Señor Fox will have to donate all his emeralds for you to be released. My father will collect the emeralds and distribute them to everybody."

Craig knew all about Joaquin, the bandit. In spite of this naive girl's sincerity, he was certain the local Indians would never see any emeralds. Also, knowing his father, Craig doubted any ransom would be paid. Some daring rescue would be more likely. But he was not about to warn anybody not even this beautiful girl.

* * *

Robert Fox was working late. Usually by six in the evening, he and Margaritte would be sitting in front of a warm fire enjoying a drink of Scotch and a smoke. Tonight though, he was worried and trying to relieve his anxiety by finishing up the slow process of grading the pile of emeralds on his desk. It was hard to concentrate with Margaritte bursting in every fifteen minutes to announce, once again, that Craig should have been home hours ago and still had not arrived.

Robert picked up another stone from the pile and with his knife scraped off the iron oxide from one side of the hexagon. Rotating the stone, he made a similar window on the opposite side. Holding the the stone in front of the light he was immediately bathed in a dark green light.

It was flawless. It had no cracks nor impurities. It was dark green yet he could see through it easily. He was holding a fortune between his fingers. With a satisfied grunt he put the emerald in a tray on his right, next to a dozen similar gems. Hearing Margaritte approach, Robert got up and put the emeralds in the tray and back in the safe. He opened the door for her as she rushed in, very agitated,

"Craig's young friend, Eduardo, is in the kitchen. He says Craig has been captured by the bandits. He wants to see you urgently. Come quickly."

In the kitchen, the maids were milling around, some moaning, hands cupped around their heads, others flailing their arms up and down, talking in loud voices.

"They have captured the boy." "The boy will be killed!" "He is dead by now." "He was such a nice boy."

Robert could see Margaritte was losing control. Craig was popular with the staff but he had to stop this uproar. He picked up a plate and shattered it against the kitchen stove.

"Parate!" There was instant silence.

He beckoned Eduardo to follow, leading the way into the living room. He eased Eduardo into a chair but the boy was too upset to sit. He popped up as soon as Robert took his hand away,

"Eduardo, please calm down. Try to tell me what you know about Craig."

"Señor Fox, Craig has been hurt." A tear plowed its way slowly down the brown face. Eduardo wiped it away with the back of his hand. "Señor, I had not seen Craig for months and wanted to meet him on the road so we could come home together. I waited for him at the junction a few kilometers down the road. When I saw him I went to meet him but then I realized that it was not Manuel with him. It was that man, Jose. Joaquin's man. When Jose saw me he chased me. I ran into the trees and hid but I could still see them. There was an argument at the junction about which road to take. Craig was trying to take the road to the mine but Jose wouldn't let him. Just then another man galloped up. Craig tried to flee. Jose fired his gun. The horse rolled over and Craig fell to the ground. Señor, he didn't move. I thought they had killed him but it was the horse Jose killed. I think Craig is badly hurt, Señor. They took him away to Joaquin's place."

"Did you see Manuel?"

"No Señor, but I heard Jose tell the other man he shot Manuel and threw him over the cliff alive."

"Thank you Eduardo. You can go now"

Eduardo hesitated. His anxiety overrode his awe of the man standing before him. Nervously rubbing a bare foot up and down the back of his leg, he persisted, "Señor, What can you do to save my friend?"

Robert's jaw clenched. He patted Eduardo on the shoulder, "We will save your friend."

Margaritte watched the Indian boy walk back towards the kitchen door. She was fond of the boy, the illegitimate son of Consuela, the cook. Eduardo was the same age as Craig but not as tall. Although slimmer than Craig he was fast filling out; the muscles on his calves were more pronounced and his face was losing its boyish chubbiness. A trace of fuzz on his upper lip was barely visible on the brown face. He was wearing some of Craig's old clothes. Seeing them, she controlled herself with difficulty. She had sorted Craig's wardrobe in preparation for his return and given those that were too small to Eduardo. The pants, cut off at the knees, looked baggy on his smaller frame. At the door he turned around as if to say something, but instead gave Margaritte an anxious smile before walking back into the kitchen. Seeing her worried look he had decided not to mention the wound and blood on Craig's head. She had enough to worry about.

Margaritte approached Robert. He was standing in front of the fireplace, staring into the fire, methodically filling his pipe.

"What are you going to do?" She nearly added, 'You should have gone to bring him home', but realized it would not be fair. It was impossible for him to leave after the mine disaster. Robert didn't reply. He continued to stare into the fire, one hand on the mantelpiece, the other holding his unlit pipe. Margaritte was about to repeat the question when he looked up.

"Sorry, did you say something?"

"Yes! What can we do? Why have they taken Craig?"

"All of a sudden it hit me like a ton of bricks. its so obvious now. For days I have been trying to figure out Joaquin's motive for dynamiting the mine and killing all those men. It just didn't make sense. Now it does. The only way the bastard can get emeralds is by ransoming Craig. He didn't dare attack me while I was with Craig. Dynamiting the workings prevented me from going for Craig. We get our son back in exchange for the emeralds. You can be sure that the wretch knows I have a safe full of high grade emeralds. He'll probably want the lot." Repeatedly stabbing a finger in the direction he assumed was the location of Joaquin's lair, Robert growled, "You can be sure, Joaquin, you bastard, that I will get Craig back. Alive!"

"How?"

"I have a plan."

Robert walked over to the kitchen door and summoned Eduardo, "Go find Alberto and Jorge. I want to see them Immediately."

Ten minutes later Jorge appeared.

"Where is Jorge?"

"I am Jorge!"

Slightly exasperated, Robert asked again, "Where is Alberto?"

Jorge knew, but wasn't about to disclose the whereabouts of his lecherous brother.

"He will be here shortly."

"I want you both to ride as fast as possible to Bogota. Gather at least five of your wild friends and return immediately. Ride day and night. They must be good with guns. You have heard Craig has been kidnapped. I plan to get rid of Joaquin and I need some help. It is no good going to the police in Gachala, I know they are on his payroll. We will rescue Craig and break that gang for good. I shall expect you back in four days. By then I am sure we will have heard from Joaquin. Go quickly, find your brother and leave tonight."

* * *

Walking along the upper level of the inner courtyard, Florentino had to admit that his father had done rather well in the eight years since he had left. The house was built in the traditional spanish style with living and servant quarters on the ground floor, accessed from the inner courtyard, and bedrooms on the second floor opening onto an inner balcony. Heavy wrought iron railings lined the stairway and balcony. There were no doors nor windows on the outside walls; all rooms faced inward. Entrance to the courtyard was through massive wooden double doors with planks three inches thick. A fortress on the outside. A comfortable home inside. His father probably determined what should be on the outside, but it was obvious a feminine touch had guided the interior layout. The rooms were large, but without outside windows, the interiors were dark. Though sparsely furnished the colorful prints and brightly colored tapestries softened the gloom. Teresa had lined the courtyard and the balcony with huge earthen pots, some over four feet tall. In each pot Teresa had planted a number of tropical bushes noted for their scented flowers.

Joaquin was in the kitchen, his favorite retreat, sitting in an armchair at the end of a large heavy wooden table. He looked much like Tino remembered him; a short, massive and powerful body, now spreading in the middle. A round face that had once been smooth, was now blueprinted with the record of his dissolute life. The face was puffy and blotched; the eyes red and dull. Watching his father take a large swallow from a bottle half full of clear colorless liquid Tino wondered whether his father was afraid of Señor Fox and was bolstering his courage with alcohol.

Joaquin waved Tino to a bench by the table, examining him carefully while he approached and sat down. Tino had certainly changed. There was a certain magnetism to him. When his eyes locked with Tino's it was the father who dropped his eyes. He offered Tino the bottle.

"Have a drink of Aguardiente, my boy."

"I do not drink, and I am not your boy! But I will have some coffee." Waving a hand towards the upstairs bedrooms, "The boy is tied up in a bedroom upstairs. I have done my part so tell me what is your plan?"

Joaquin eyed him suspiciously, then swiveled around and growled at the Indian woman standing with her back to them. She was stirring a pot on the stove.

"Bring him some coffee."

The woman turned. Tino had difficulty recognizing his aunt, Conchita. She smiled shyly at him, put down the large wooden spoon, picked up a cup from the counter and the coffee pot from the stove. She brought them to the table. Her movements were slow and weary. Though still slim she had aged prematurely. The once shiny clear skin was now dull, wrinkled, the hair streaked with gray, the hands thin and knobby. Tino thanked her, faced his father and waited for an answer to his question. Joaquin shifted his eyes down to the bottle and took another gulp. Usually secretive about his plans he was reluctant to divulge them to anybody, even his son. Tino forced the issue.

"Father! You must tell me. I know about Señor Fox. I heard many things about him in Bogota. He is a very dangerous man. You have taken his only son and he will do everything to get him back. You are a fool if you think he will let you escape him after he has paid the ransom to you. He will track you down and kill you. You must have a good escape plan and a good place to hide. I can look after Teresa. She can come with me to Bogota. She will be safe with me."

Joaquin pounded his fist on the table, rattling the coffee cups, "Nobody calls me a fool! I could kill you for that." Sneering, "Go back to Bogota to your boys and girls but Teresa stays with me. I need her."

Tino shrugged. He stalked out of the room muttering a curse under his breath. He went back upstairs, looking for Teresa. She was still in Craig's room, talking to him. He didn't like the atmosphere in there. It was obvious there was too much mutual attraction developing between the two. He beckoned her out and requested a room. Teresa showed him one on the opposite side of the balcony. About to return to Craig's room, he took her hand to restrain her.

"Teresa, I must talk to you. Come here and sit on the bed. I want you to come to Bogota with me. I need somebody to keep house for me and you could help me with my business. I know father will not want you to leave him but you are a grown woman now and should be able to leave if you want to go with me."

"Oh Tino! Please take me away from here. Please. Father is so cruel, and he wants me to marry one of his stupid men so he can keep me here forever to write his letters for him." Teresa paused, dreading the answer to her question, "Tino, what is your business?"

Tino had never explained his business before. He searched around for the right words; words that would give her an idea without shocking her.

"Father says you are a prostitute and have young boys and girls working for you. I find it hard to believe that. But Tino, even if its true... I want to go with you."

Startled, Tino looked at her with more respect. Deciding at that moment he would no longer offer his body for sale, he said, "I am not a prostitute, but I do have young people that I protect from bullies that beat them up and steal their money. In return they pay me a regular fee each week. I have a nice apartment you could live in and keep house for me. In Bogota you might meet somebody you could marry."

"Father will never let me go."

"We won't ask him. We will just leave. But before we do I have some business to take care of with that white boy. You must not get too friendly with him. Listen carefully. It is very important for our future. It means a lot of money we can use to start a good business and make money. Your father thinks I came to make sure Jose delivered the boy to him, but that is not the real reason." Tino placed his arm around her shoulder, "Teresa, Listen carefully. Sometimes I help people get rid of bad men that are threatening or blackmailing them. It's a service I perform for a large fee. This boy has been threatening one of the boys in his school. I will be paid a large sum to kill him. I have to kill him, Teresa. But before I do anything I must know father's plan, but he won't tell me."

She stared at him, stunned, appalled that her brother could commit murder, and from the lack of expression on his face, probably enjoyed it.

"Oh Tino! You mustn't do that! He is just a boy. He cannot be evil like you describe. He is a nice boy." Her chin fluttered, close to tears, "Tino, please don't kill him." Hesitating, "If you do I'll never forgive you. I won't go to Bogota with you."

Tempted to lash out, he controlled his anger. His sister was the only person that cared for him. He would have to be careful not to turn her against him. Handled carefully, he could use her affection for his benefit.

"For me to be paid I have to prove the boy has died." Pacing around the room, Tino delayed replying until he could think of something to pacify her. "Maybe we can take a picture of his wound, say he died, and collect the reward."

"Oh yes, yes. I will help you. Thank you, thank you Tino."

Teresa leapt up and hugged him. Chastened by his lack of response she left the room. He barely noticed her leave, thinking, 'I will have to work out a way to kill him without her finding out.'

* * *

Robert Fox was increasingly worried. He had heard nothing from Joaquin for two days. 'Did they accidentally kill Craig during their clumsy capture of the boy? Are they torturing him? Is he seriously hurt while I'm sitting here doing nothing?' Robert did not dare reveal his concerns to Margaritte. She was already too distressed. Initially he had hoped that whoever delivered the ransom note would reveal Joaquin's hideout but quickly decided that was not realistic. 'He knows I would attack it immediately. So I had better take steps to locate the rat's nest.' There was no point asking the miners, or the kitchen staff. If they knew they were too afraid to tell him. In any case they probably had only a vague idea where it might be located. He knew that much himself. Eduardo was Craig's friend, he might be more helpful. Robert went looking for him. Eduardo was not in the kitchen. He found him sitting on a bench in the yard sharpening a long machete. Robert sat besides him and watched, silently, for a few minutes. The boy became increasingly nervous.

"Why are you sharpening your Penilla?"

"I know you plan to rescue Craig. I am coming with you, Señor, to save Craig."

Robert observed him closely, "Do you know where Joaquin lives?"

"Si Señor! Craig never told you but last year he and I discovered where he lives."

"Oh!"

"Si, Señor. We followed one of Joaquin's men. We kept far back. When he reached a clearing around a big house another man came out from a small shack hidden in the trees. They talked for a few minutes then walked down to the house. We crept through the jungle and had a good look at it."

"Christ!" Robert shook his head in disbelief. "That boy... Describe the house to me."

"The house is in a cleared valley about a hundred meters from the edge of the forest. The road leads down through a cornfield to an entrance into a courtyard. The entrance is through a double door. It looks very heavy. I think the house has two floors but there are no windows on the outside so we couldn't be sure of the two floors. To the left is another low house. I think it is where the men sleep. To the right of the big house is the stable."

"Did you see any other guards?"

"Si Señor, there was a guard on a platform above the entrance to the courtyard. Señor, please let me come with you when you rescue Craig. You will need me to show you the way."

Robert stood up, lifted the boy and hugged him. "Eduardo, you will certainly be coming with me. This afternoon you and I will be taking a little trip to scout Joaquin's hideout Then we will draw up a map of the location."

Robert ruffled the boys hair and walked off. Eduardo watched his friend's father enter his office. 'I wish everybody wouldn't treat me like a little boy. I am sixteen. I have a girlfriend and she doesn't treat me like a little boy.' Chuckling, Eduardo picked up the file and resumed sharpening the machete.

* * *

Eduardo burst into Robert's office, for once too excited to be intimidated by him. He gasped,

"Joaquin's man Jose is coming up the road!"

Robert rolled up the rough plans of Joaquin's compound; put a rubber band around the drafting paper and inserted it in the rack with the other mine plans. Looking out the window while he strapped on his revolver, he saw a rider approaching warily. Still too far away to identify the rider, he was near enough to see him glancing around as he approached. He was holding a rifle across his lap. Quickly Robert lifted his battered Lee Enfield rifle from the rack and inserted a clip of .303 bullets before walking out the door and across the yard. He walked through the gate and closed it carefully behind him, never taking his eyes off the rider. The man stopped the horse when he saw Robert's rifle. It was Jose. He kept his eye on Robert's rifle while gripping his own on his lap. Glowering at Robert, he leaned over the side of the horse and spat a wad of chewing tobacco on the ground between them. Robert didn't move. Gaining courage, Jose snarled:

"Señor, we have your son. If you want him to live you will do as I say."

With difficulty Robert ignored the insulting manner. Thinking he had the upper hand Jose began to raise his rifle. Robert's rifle was on his shoulder aimed at Jose's head before Jose's gun was off his lap.

"Stop! If you move that gun you are dead! Get off your horse slowly. Very slowly."

Jose hesitated for a few moments, measuring his chances. Robert's face convinced him. With his courage draining out of him he dismounted slowly. Robert recognized the saddle immediately; it was Craig's saddle. In a fury he cocked the rifle in one quick movement, aiming it at the man's heart.

"Robert! Don't!"

It was Margaritte. She was standing behind him on the other side of the gate. "You must not kill him otherwise we'll never save Craig."

Robert lowered his aim and fired between Jose's legs. The bullet kicked up a spurt of dust by Jose's heels before whining off into the distance. The horse reared up and galloped down the road. Jose frantically threw his rifle down.

"Señor! Please understand I am just following orders. I had nothing to do with the capture of your son. I was sent to give you a letter." Motioning towards his shirt pocket, "it is here, Señor." The gesture exposed a gun belt under his jacket.

"You lie! It was you who killed Manuel and kidnapped my son. You will be sorry before I finish with you. Drop your gun belt. Very slowly... Good! Now drop the envelope, lie down on the ground and put your hands behind your back." Motioning to Eduardo. "Bring me some rope from the storeroom."

While Robert kneeled on Jose's back searching for other weapons, Jose, face down in the dirt, tried to salvage the plan Joaquin had explained to him.

"Señor, Joaquin will kill your son if I don't return by tonight. I have to give him your answer to his letter."

Robert ignored him. When Eduardo returned with the rope, he tied the Indian to the fence post in full view of the kitchen staff and any miner that might come by. His message was clear: 'Nobody challenges Señor Fox, not even Joaquin!' But he would have to move fast if Jose was telling the truth. Even if he was not, he couldn't risk Craig's life. Craig would have to be rescued that night even if Jorge and Alberto had not returned. Robert picked up the envelope and tore it open. He was not surprised at the contents. He handed the letter to Margaritte.

"Joaquin will deliver Craig tomorrow morning in return for all our emeralds."

Margaritte read the letter, becoming visibly agitated. She handed it back, "What are you going to do?"

Robert took her arm and led her back into the house. He needed time to sort things out and besides, the gossipy servants watching the drama didn't need to know his plans. Inside he sat her down and began methodically filling his pipe. Margaritte watched him impatiently. Finally, when he began wandering around the room looking for matches, she burst out.

"They are in the top drawer of the buffet! Robert what are you going to do?"

Robert moved to a chair opposite Margaritte, extracted a box of matches from his pocket, lit a match and held the flame to his pipe. Satisfied with the cloud of smoke he was puffing out, he answered her.

"Margaritte, I need your help in working things out. We have to rescue Craig tonight. It is only three days since the brothers went to round up their friends, and assuming they rode day and night and were lucky to find six in one day, that were available and interested, they won't be here until tomorrow. That is too late."

"So what can we do?"

"I have a little secret to confess to you. Last year Craig and Eduardo sneaked up to Joaquin's hideout. Eduardo told me this. Yesterday afternoon Eduardo led me through the jungle to the compound. I have made a sketch of the outside of the buildings but I still don't know the inside layout nor where they are keeping Craig."

"Surely Jose knows the interior of the house and where Craig is located."

Robert stared at her, "Of course!"

There was a sudden commotion in the kitchen. Eduardo ran in. "Many horsemen coming up the road!"

Robert walked rapidly to the window. There were seven approaching at full gallup. Assuming they were bandits coming to rescue Jose he picked up his rifle and pointed it out the window. Jose evidently thought so too. Jumping up and down laughing. He turned and spat in Robert's direction. Robert recognized Alberto and Jorge leading the pack. So did Jose. He slumped back against the fence post.

Robert turned back from the window. "Margaritte, help has arrived!"

She began to cry. He hugged her quietly.

* * *

"Why does somebody want to kill you?"

Craig lifted his face up towards Teresa, who was hovering over him while she cleaned the wound on his temple. "I thought I was to be ransomed?"

"Si, Father is going to ransom you but Tino says he is supposed to kill you after the ransom is paid. A boy at your school wants you killed because you have been threatening him... Is that true? Where you threatening him?"

"No! That's a lie. Teresa, believe me, I never threatened this boy. I overheard Tino telling the boy that he had killed a girl the boy paid him to kill. The boy is the son of a very important man and must be afraid that I will expose him."

"Tino is to be paid a lot of money, but don't worry! I have pleaded with Tino and he has promised not to kill you. Somehow we will make it look like you have been killed so he can collect the money from this boy. Tino says the money will help him start a business in Bogota and I'm to help him."

Craig was not convinced. In fact he was very skeptical. Tino's manner with him over the last few days didn't suggest any thawing in his hostility. Although Tino was shorter and slimmer he was surprisingly strong, as Craig had found out that morning when he tried to overpower Tino. On his regular trip to the outhouse in the corner of the courtyard Craig was usually escorted by Jose, but this morning it was Tino that untied the ropes around his arms and legs. Coming out of the outhouse Craig saw a chance to escape. Tino was standing with his back to Craig combing his hair. It was a spur of the moment decision. Craig ran forward, wrapped his left arm around Tino's neck and with the other hand tried to twist Tino's right arm behind his back. He had attacked a coiled steel spring. Tino snaked around and in an instant was holding a knife to Craig's throat, with his right hand holding Craig's in a crushing grip. Pulling Craig's face close to his own, he hissed,

"Carajo! You foolish boy! Do not. I repeat, do not ever try that again or I will kill you."

Teresa finished cleaning the wound. She was pleased with how quickly it was healing. Seeing how troubled he was she couldn't resist gently touching his face with her fingers. She cupped his head lifting him towards her.

"Querido, I am so sorry I have upset you. Please forgive me, but Tino has promised no harm will come to you."

Seeing her lips so close to his own Craig pushed up with his elbows and kissed her. Her lips were cold against his. He had intended a quick furtive kiss only, but when he slumped back on the bed her hands, now trembling, held him firmly. She kissed him on the lips, cheeks, forehead, and eyelids. Gently she eased his head back on the bed and rubbed her cheek against his. She kissed his ear and ran her hands down each side of his neck. Breathing heavily she tried to unbutton his shirt but her hands were trembling too much. Low moans from deep in her throat alarmed Craig.

"Teresa, I didn't mean to make you cry. You are so beautiful I had to kiss you."

She searched his face; there was no guile there. 'He has no experience with women. He must be a virgin.' Overjoyed she showered kisses on his face. "Oh Querido! I am not crying, it is my love for you."

"Teresa, please untie me. Please?"

"Tino said I was not to untie you after what you tried to do this morning. You would hurt me and try to escape."

"Teresa, please. I just want to hold you. I will never hurt you. I won't try to escape. Please?"

Reassured Teresa fumbled with the ropes around his wrist. Once free Craig pulled her down kissing her firmly on the lips. They were warm now. Tentatively he ran his fingers over her cheeks along the back of the ears and around her neck to the front of her blouse. She shuddered. Low moans fluttered up though her lips. She smiled, encouraging him. Slowly he unhooked the round pearl shaped buttons on her blouse and eased the blouse off her shoulders. He stared at her breasts. He had never seen breasts in the flesh before. They were beautiful! Large soft brown globes with a dark brown circle around each erect nipple. Unsure what he was supposed to do with them he cupped his hands around them. The more experienced lover leaned forward until her nipples brushed his lips. Gently he licked each nipple. Gaining confidence he sucked one then the other. Unable to unbutton his shirt with her trembling hands he did it for her. Teresa slid her lips from his mouth to his chest. She could feel his heart pounding. She kissed his nipples, sat up and began unbuckling his belt. In a sudden panic Craig tried to stop her realizing his manhood was about to embarrass him, but she was not about to be thwarted. Firmly she put his hands to one side.

"Querido, Amor mio! Do not worry. It is what I want."

Unbuttoning his trousers, Teresa could feel his hardness underneath. Craig noticed her hands no longer trembled. Although her breathing was still heavy her moans were lighter, more like a whisper. Teresa tried to ease his pants down but he resisted, pressing his buttocks against the bed. 'Oh Lord! She's about to pull down my pants and I have no idea what I'm supposed to do.' He gave in when she persisted, closing his eyes to hide his embarrassment. When she started on his underwear he was more cooperative but kept his eyes firmly closed trying to think of something that would prevent him losing control. He heard the rustle of clothes. He opened his eyes in time to see her drop her clothes on the floor. Quickly he closed his eyes again. She climbed on the bed and straddled his torso. Suddenly her warm hands wrapped around him guiding him into her warmth. Craig lost control immediately. Arching his back he groaned. "Ooh God!" He erupted. Dizzy and faint he could feel his lips tingle as the blood drained from his face. His whole body twitched uncontrollably. After a few moments he calmed down enough to open his eyes and look up at her. Teresa smiled down at him leaning over to kiss him. She continued to move her hips gently. He was surprised he was still hard. Teresa leaned back, placed her hands on his thighs, arched her back and began to thrust harder; her breasts rising and falling with each thrust. Eyes closed, face contorted, she gasped every time she thrust forward. Craig wrapped his hands around her breasts to slow their movement. He rubbed the nipples gently. Her cries became louder and louder, until with a wail she collapsed on his chest. He grabbed her buttocks and forced himself into her. This triggered his own climax, less intense than before, but enough to make his legs twitch.

Teresa lay heavily on him until her breathing subsided, then eased up enough to kiss him gently on the lips. She lifted herself off his torso and climbed off the bed. She dressed slowly, allowing him to admire her. Picking up a towel Teresa wiped his body, chuckling at his quick reaction to her touch. He smiled, no longer embarrassed. She helped him dress. She retied the ropes around his wrists, this time so loose he could easily slip out of them.

"Amor mio! We will make love again. Tonight I will come when everybody has gone to bed... I'll be back in a few minutes with your dinner."

In the kitchen, Conchita was ladling boiled chicken and potatoes onto a platter. She looked around when Teresa entered, handed her the platter, silently motioning towards the table. Tino was talking to his father. He looked up at Teresa while she filled a bowl with a chicken thigh and some boiled potatoes. He noticed the tight look around her lips and chin was gone. She nodded, a faint smile on her lips, before leaving the room. Tino confronted his father once again.

"Padre! You must tell me. Que va hacer? It is now dark and Jose has not returned."

"I will wait until morning."

"Why?"

Joaquin gave Tino a sly look. Unable to resist showing off his craftiness he chortled. "Señor Fox has sent his gunmen to Bogota to get help, but according to my spies they won't be back for two more days, by then it will be much too late."

"But what if Jose does not return tonight?"

"If Jose has not returned by morning, I will tie that boy to a horse and ride with all my men to the mine." Joaquin pounded his fist on the table, "I will show Señor Fox the boy with a gun to his head, and I will demand he give me all the emeralds in exchange for the boy's life. He will not let his only son die."

His father was right. Señor Fox would not let his son die, but he would be relentless in his vengeance after the ransom was paid. Joaquin would not survive if he did not flee. Tino was certain the crafty old man must have plans to escape and disappear with the loot. No doubt leaving the rest of them to suffer the wrath of Señor Fox.

Silently Tino ate his dinner. He used a knife and fork, his father his hands. Tino ignored his father's smirk while concentrating on trying to figure out a way to kill Craig after the ransom was paid, and yet be able to escape before Señor Fox attacked. He would have to escape with Teresa before Joaquin rode out to confront Señor Fox, then hope he could kill Craig later. Tino wiped the inside of his bowl with a piece of corn bread, thanked Conchita and left the room. Suspicious eyes followed his exit. Upstairs Teresa was sitting on Craig's bed feeding him with a spoon. Her left hand was holding his head up gently.

"Teresa, I must talk to you. Come to my room."

"I will come in a minute, when I finish feeding Craig."

Tino glared at Craig; Craig glared back. He could see Tino's anger flaring and was concerned he might strike Teresa. With his hands tied there was little he could do about it. Abruptly Tino turned and stalked out of the room. A few minutes later she entered his room. He had regained his composure.

"Teresa, listen to me. We must leave this place tonight otherwise we will die here. Father is no longer thinking straight and he drinks too much. I know Jose won't return tonight. Señor Fox will kill him for what he did to his son, and he will torture him to find out all about this compound and Joaquin's plans. We have to figure out a way to leave without anybody seeing us."

"Tino, we must save Craig. Please? If you help me save him I will do anything you want. I will come and help with your business and look after you but you must save him Tino. Please?"

"But it will be hard enough for us to escape."

"I know where there are two rifles, and..." Teresa hesitated. She was beginning to realize Tino was not to be trusted, "I know how to leave the compound without being seen."

"How do we get out?"

"I will show you later." A trapdoor in the back of the kitchen was used to bring in the firewood for the stove. Only Conchita and the maids knew it existed. Tino might leave without her and Craig if he knew about it.

Tino eyed her coldly then shifted them to a poster advertising the beauty of the Tequendama Falls. Teresa watched him anxiously. 'He's so cold. Whatever happened to the brother I loved. Something terrible must have happened.'

Finally Tino nodded. "We will take him with us but we must leave tonight while everybody is asleep. Do not untie Craig until the last minute in case they check on him. Do not tell him we are leaving. To avoid suspicion do not pack any clothes. Go to bed. I will wake you when I think it is safe. Now go to bed."

Tino closed the door behind her, took off his boots, and lay back on the bed 'Maybe if we are chased by father's men a stray bullet might take care of the Craig problem. Or, perhaps I can provide the stray bullet.'

His gaze went back to the poster. It showed the Tequendama hotel with the waterfall in the background. He allowed his thoughts to drift back to the hotel and the girl he had seduced there. A slight smile crossed his lips. 'Maybe I was too eager to throw her over the cliff.'

* * *

Robert opened the office door and beckoned the men to enter. He studied each man in turn as they filed past. Alberto and Jorge he knew and trusted; hot headed but dependable. The other five were an unknown quantity; could they be trusted to carry out his orders? He had no choice; he would have to rely on them but he would make sure they were aware of the consequences if they didn't perform. Three were about the same age as the two brothers, and according to Jorge, long time friends. He said he would vouch for them and as Robert respected Jorge's opinion he was not too worried. The fourth man was older, probably in his late forties, so thin and pale Robert wondered if he was ill. Jorge assured him he was not. The skin was drawn tight against the teeth; cheekbones prominent; jaw thin and pointed; his clothes a dull dirty gray. Only the eyes and boots were black. Jorge knew him by reputation only and warned Robert he was a killer wanted by the police. When introduced, he had not offered his name. When pressed, he had muttered, "Pedro." The man's eyes, deep in their sockets, watched Robert unwaveringly, while Robert unfolded the map he had made of Joaquin's compound. They arranged themselves around the wooden table; Margaritte sitting at one end, himself standing on the far side and the others on each side. Robert unhooked a high pressure gas light from a bent wire above the table and placed the lamp in front of Margaritte. The fifth man, a pimply faced boy, squeezed between Alberto and Jorge. Robert was not impressed when the boy was introduced. Round faced with a juvenile mustache struggling on his upper lip. Jorge had shrugged his shoulders sheepishly when Robert questioned him about the boy. Jorge explained that Juan had been instrumental in helping him contact the others and he had to bring him along as a reward. Jorge had promised to look after the boy. Robert had relented but was to regret his decision to include the boy in his attack plan.

On the top half of the map was a rough sketch of the main building, bunkhouse, and stables. That portion of the map was based on Robert's observation of the Compound. The bottom half of the map showed the layout of the main and second floor of the house. The location of the room where Craig was being held was clearly marked. This information had been extracted from Jose.

Robert was about to speak when a slight noise at the door made him turn around. Eduardo's face hovered, uncertainly, behind the partly open door. Robert beckoned him before turning back to the group. Beaming the Indian boy moved in behind Margaritte's chair.

It was time to present his plan of attack. "Caballeros! Tonight we will rescue my son from Joaquin. Then we will put an end to Joaquin's gang. First, we must save my son. Listen carefully." Robert paused, leaning forward eyes boring into each face around the table. "I am warning you. If my son is killed because one of you has not followed orders, I will kill you myself. Jorge, here, will tell you I mean what I say." Jorge nodded. Juan, the teenage boy, giggled nervously. Pedro glared at Robert. Without shifting his eyes he made a defiant gesture by lighting a cigarette. Robert flared at his insolence.

"Put out that cigarette!"

The man's face flushed. After a long pause his eyes dropped and he ground the cigarette under his boot. Immediately Robert regretted his outburst. He had humiliated the man and made an enemy when he needed all the help he could get. Margaritte tried to repair the damage.

"Señor, my husband should have told you cigarette smoke makes me very ill. I am sorry he didn't tell you. Please accept our apologies, Señor."

The man bowed coldly. Robert gave Margaritte a grateful smile before proceeding.

"Jorge has told you what you will be paid, but..." Robert held up a sheet of paper, "but I am confirming in writing what you will receive. For helping me destroy Joaquin the mine will pay each of you five thousand pesos. For helping me save my son... alive. I repeat, alive, each of you will receive another five thousand pesos from me."

Juan clasped his hands over his head and did a little jig; the young men clasped hands; the old outlaw slid his hand down his side, clasping his hand around the yellowed ivory handle of his pistol.

Robert motioned to Alberto. "Show them the dynamite."

Alberto extracted a dynamite stick from a box on the floor and brought it to Robert. It was studded with two inch nails. A black primer cord, eight inches long, protruded from one end. Holding up the homemade grenade, Robert continued.

"Once this is lit you have approximately eight seconds before it explodes. We have checked the time on several sticks, but be sure to throw it as soon as you light it because the time can vary depending on the condition of the primer cord. Five of you will be supplied with two bombs each... Here is the plan. Pay close attention."

Robert turned on a small flashlight, using the focus as a pointer. "This is a road leading to Joaquin's compound. It is about ten kilometers to the houses from this junction." Pointing to the intersection of the mine road and a trail leading off into the jungle he continued, "we will leave the mine at exactly eleven o'clock tonight and ride up this trail until we reach this clearing I have marked here. The horses will stay there and we will walk the rest of the way. It is one kilometer from the clearing to the compound." Pointing at the teenager. "You, Juan, will stay and watch the horses."

"No! No! Señor! You cannot do this to me. My honor will not permit it." Pointing at Eduardo, he pleaded, "the Indian boy here can look after the horses."

Curbing his anger Robert tried to appease the boy's honor. "Everybody's job is equally important. The horses must be kept quiet otherwise they could give us away. We will be less than a kilometer from the guard located here at the entrance to the clearing surrounding the compound. Any little noise will alert him. Besides I need Eduardo as you will see in a minute. He has a very difficult and dangerous job to do which only he can do because of his size and agility. Juan, you will look after the horses, otherwise you stay here."

Robert ignored the young man's sulky expression. He pointed to the entrance to the clearing where he had sketched the outline of a small hut.

"There is a guard here that has to be eliminated. We think he is there all night but by two in the morning he may not be too alert."

Pedro spoke up. "Señor, I will look after him."

"Be very careful. He might be asleep, but don't depend on it."

Irritated at being cautioned, Pedro snapped back. "Señor! I know my business. I am an expert."

Although annoyed at the man's tone Robert was gratified he had volunteered. He had already chosen him for the job. He was the kind of killer that preferred to operate on his own.

"We will wait for you by the horses. When you return signal us with a flashlight that I will give you. Two quick flashes. We will walk to the edge of the clearing. Once there, if all is clear we will break into two groups. Pedro, you will come with me and Eduardo. The rest of you are to go with Jorge. I insist you follow his orders." Pointing to the bunkhouse next to the big house. "You are to surround this bunkhouse where Joaquin's men sleep. You are to do nothing, I repeat, nothing until you hear shots from inside the big house. Then light these sticks of dynamite and hurl them through the doors and windows as fast as you can. The success of this attack depends on your following these orders." Robert moved the penlight to the front of the house. "Eduardo, Pedro, and I will go to the front gate of the big house. There is a guard that sits on a platform above the gate. He may or may not be asleep. Pedro, you will watch out for him while I hoist Eduardo over the gate into the courtyard. The moment Eduardo opens the gate from the inside, Pedro and I will rush into the courtyard, up these stairs shown here, and into this room where Craig has been tied to a bed. We shoot anybody that gets in the way. Hopefully the servants will have enough sense to stay in their room when the shooting starts."

Robert looked at each man in turn ignoring the teenager's sulks. "Do you understand? Any questions? Good! Now, empty your pockets of everything that might jingle, coins, watches, also your spurs. I see you are all wearing fairly dark clothes. Good. In this tin is a mixture of charcoal and mud. When we get to the clearing smear some of this on your faces. I have flashlights here for each man. We have to be careful we do not shoot each other in the dark. Flash twice if anybody challenges you." Robert checked his watch. "We leave in one hour. There is food for you in the kitchen."

The men filed out. Robert beckoned for Jorge to remain. He filled and lit his pipe, waiting for Margaritte to leave the room. "Jorge, I have not had time to thank you for returning so quickly from Bogota. I wasn't expecting you for at least another day. How did you do it?"

"I sent a telegram to Juan from Gachala asking him to contact my friends. It saved a day and a half. Juan did a good job that's why I had to bring him along."

"The description of the inside of the big house is excellent. Did you have difficulty persuading Jose to tell you about it?"

"No, Señor, he was very cooperative."

"Where is he?"

Jorge hesitated for a moment. "I regret, Señor, the man tried to escape and would not stop when we warned him. We were afraid he would warn Joaquin if he got away so we shot him. He is dead, Señor."

Robert had expected that some force might be used on the man but had not anticipated the man being executed. However Jose's execution was not something to be concerned about; before this night's work was finished many more might die. He just hoped Craig would not be one of the casualties.

* * *

The long wait was affecting the men. It was pitch black with only the occasional bluish green glow from fireflies fluttering through the trees, and the red flare from nervous smokers puncturing the black wall around them. Fortunately, the rain had stopped, but Robert could hear the heavy drip every time a slight breeze sent a shudder through the trees. Looking up he could see nothing above, no moon, no stars. The heavy clouds gave warning it might rain again. The cool air seeping out of the damp jungle penetrated their clothes already wet from the last downpour. Robert could feel the goose pimples on his back from the moist clammy air enveloping him. Eduardo, standing beside him, was shivering, his teeth chattering. The horses too were becoming restless, anxious to return to their stables. Robert, standing some distance up the road from the others could hear the stamping of hooves, snorting, and jingling of bridles whenever the horses shook their heads. The men were muttering among themselves with young Juan's voice clearly audible. He could hear Jorge trying to calm them. Robert, once again, pointed his flashlight up the road. He flashed twice. There was no response.

"Where the hell is that man?"

Pedro should have returned at least half an hour ago. Something must have gone wrong. He could wait no longer. Robert walked up the road for several hundred yards and flashed twice again. A faint pinpoint of light flashed twice.

"Thank Christ!"

Quickly he strode back to the men. "Pedro has returned. Vamonos! We've got to hurry. It's very late." Robert grabbed Juan's upper arm.

"Juan, it is most important the horses are tied down so they won't to follow us. You will stay here to watch them. You understand?"

Robert couldn't see the boy's face but could feel his hostility as the boy stomped off towards the horses. There was no time to deal with the boy's bruised ego nor was he inclined to try. There were more pressing things to attend to. Robert marched down the road to meet Pedro. The rest followed. Pedro was sitting on a log, smoking. Sensitive to the man's prickly conceit he didn't ask him why he was so late. Pedro volunteered the explanation.

"The guard was awake, not asleep like you said he would be." Robert ignored the rebuke. "It took me a long time to reach him without making a noise. He has been eliminated." Pedro ran a finger across his throat to illustrate the method of "elimination."

Robert noticed Pedro had replaced his boots with a pair of soft rope sandals. Annoyed he had not thought of it himself he was about to ask the man why he had not suggested they wear sandals but decided he didn't need another confrontation. Regardless of how careful they might be, boots would make more noise than sandals.

"Muy bien. Gracias. Caballeros! Vamonos. We must hurry."

Half an hour later they came to an open clearing. The house and men's quarters was barely visible in the pitch dark, except for a faint glow from inside the house, probably from a lamp left on all night. Robert motioned to Jorge pointing to the bunkhouse. Jorge signaled for the others to follow and led them towards the building. Robert crouched down and picked his way down the road towards the big house taking care not to step on rocks in the path. Eduardo padded silently behind him in his bare feet with Pedro bringing up the rear. Robert stopped some ten feet in front of the massive gate. He pointed up at a platform above the gate. Pedro nodded. The guard was not visible, but Robert could hear heavy breathing coming from there. Pedro moved away and leaned against a tree. He gently cocked his rifle and aimed it at the platform. Robert waited until he could see the others were in position around the bunkhouse. Taking Eduardo by the hand he moved towards the gate. The boy's hand was trembling but he did not hesitate to follow. Robert leaned over and whispered in his ear.

"You are a very brave young man. I am very proud to have you with me."

Eduardo gripped Robert's hand tighter but said nothing. Robert turned his back to the gate. He leaned carefully against it. The heavy gate did not move. He clasped his hands together and crouched down. Eduardo placed a bare foot on the clasped hands, grabbed the lapels of Robert's jacket, and was about to step up to reach for the top of the gate. They both froze.

A thunder of hooves shattered the silence. A horse at full gallop burst into the clearing. A frantic Juan trailed the horse cursing and shouting. He stopped at the edge of the clearing but the horse did not. Iron shoes clattering on the stones it raced towards them. For one stunned moment nobody moved. A light came on in the bunkhouse. The scraping of boots on the platform above him warned Robert the guard was awake. Quick action was needed or all was lost.

"Pedro, shoot him! Jorge, quick, the dynamite!"

At the same time he stood and flung Eduardo over the gate. Eduardo clutched the top of the gate and eased himself down the far side. Pedro fired. The guard pitched over the platform landing with a dull thud beside Robert, a neat bullet hole in the middle of his temple. Robert could hear muffled shouts from inside the house and Eduardo's grunts on the other side of the gate, trying to wrestle the heavy crossbars holding the gate closed. Impatiently, Robert muttered under his breath.

"For Christ sake! Eduardo, get a bloody move on! This is going to be a disaster in a minute."

Eduardo flung the gate open and Pedro rushed into the courtyard. Before Robert followed, he glanced towards the bunkhouse just in time to see four sparkling bombs arcing into the windows. Racing through the gate Robert grabbed Eduardo and flung him behind the gate yelling, "Stay there! Do not move!" He raced to catch up with Pedro at the bottom of the stairs. A kerosene lamp on a table by the stairs cast a dim light, but it was enough to illuminate the courtyard and reveal two men standing by the kitchen door, aiming their pistols at Pedro. Robert raised his rifle, firing as he warned Pedro.

"Lookout! By the kitchen."

Robert's target slammed back against the wall and slid to the floor. The second man's bullet hit the iron railing close to Pedro's head. Pedro crouched and fired back but the man had slid behind a large clay tree planter.

"Keep him pinned down. I am going up the stairs to find my son."

Robert took the stairs at a run. Four explosions from the direction of the bunkhouse made him pause momentarily. It nearly cost him his life. The loud bang of a rifle somewhere behind him, preceded by the zing of a bullet close to his ear, galvanized his leap to the top of the stairs and through the bedroom door. The room was empty! Craig was not there. His hat was on the floor together with the ropes that had tied him to the bed. A candle flickered feebly on a small chest. He put his hand on the rumpled bed. The sheets were still warm. Craig was alive! He must have been moved not many minutes before.

More dynamite explosions and shooting from the bunkhouse echoed through the house. Also sporadic shots in the courtyard below. Pedro needed help, but before he did Robert had a problem of his own to resolve. Who was shooting at him? And from where? According to the house plans Joaquin's room was on the second floor on the far side of the building, diagonally across from himself. Robert blew out the candle. Hoping the light from the lamp downstairs was too weak to illuminate the second level corridor, Robert crouched down and peered out the door. Ten feet to his left a large clay pot might provide some shelter. He made a run for it. There was no shot. Pedro was still exchanging fire with the gunman hidden behind the clay pot in the courtyard. Robert leaned over the balcony and put a bullet in the man's leg. Screaming the man dropped his pistol and clutched his upper leg. Pedro ran over to the man and shot him through the head. Robert, angered at the unnecessary murder, didn't have time to protest. A bullet had just smashed into the wall behind him. The flash from Robert's gun had given his position away. Quickly Robert dropped to the floor and crawled back behind the clay pot.

Robert remained hidden debating his next move. Outside the shooting had stopped. Robert could hear his men shouting to each other as they rounded up Joaquin's men. Soon they would be rushing into the courtyard and would be able to secure the building. All he would have to do is stay hidden behind the clay pot until they arrived. But where was Craig? He could not sit here on his butt while Craig was in danger; maybe a hostage of Joaquin's. He would have to go on the offensive to force Joaquin to expose himself. Robert leaned around the clay pot trying to locate Joaquin, but it was too dark at the far end of the corridor. Suddenly he noticed a small figure climbing up a vine covered trellis on the far side of the courtyard in full view of the bandit.

"Oh my God!" He cried, "it's Eduardo. What is that boy doing? He'll get killed."

A shot echoed through the yard, muffling Eduardo's cry. The boy let go with his hands. His body rotated outward and dropped to the cobblestones. In a white hot rage Robert jumped out from behind the clay pot and fired two quick shots towards the flash of Joaquin's rifle. Instantly a flash, five feet to the left of the previous flash, sent a bullet ricocheting off the metal railing in front of Robert. He leapt back behind the pot.

Robert reviewed his options again. He would have to outsmart the old fox. Joaquin would have to make a move soon otherwise he would be captured. What could the bandit do? To make his escape Joaquin would have to eliminate Robert first and do it quickly before the others arrived. To eliminate Robert he would have to move along the corridor towards Robert until he was close enough to flush Robert from behind the clay pot. But would he approach using the left or the right corridor? Upright Joaquin would be a faintly visible target. To approach unseen he would have to crawl. If he was crawling he couldn't shoot quickly. This should give Robert three to five seconds to move to a new location. Robert checked his surroundings. On his right was the stairway and Craig's old room. Too far. On his left was the entrance to another bedroom. The door was closed but there was no light under the door. Hopefully it was empty. Robert inserted a fresh clip in the rifle. Knowing there was only enough bullets in the clip for one quick burst he would have to decide which corridor Joaquin was using to approach him. He chose the left corridor. Slowly Robert moved around the clay pot, then made a dash for the bedroom emptying the clip along the left corridor as he ran. He was rewarded with a roar of rage. He smashed through the door into the bedroom. Quickly he put a fresh clip in the rifle. A shuffling of boots along the corridor warned him that the bandit was wounded but still dangerous. Robert swung around the door just as Joaquin lunged. Joaquin wrapped his hands around the rifle barrel trying to wrest the rifle from Robert. Robert fired twice before the gun was wrenched out of his hands. Joaquin staggered back against the railing, flung the gun out into the courtyard, and toppled backwards over the railing, hitting his head on the cobblestones with a soft squelching sound. Robert looked over the railing. Pedro was leaning against a clay pot. He took a puff on his cigarette, flicked it away and strolled over to check the body. He gave it a kick to make sure the man was dead.

"Quickly Pedro. My son is missing. He is not in the room. We must look for him. Go tell the others to search the whole area. I am sure he is alive."

Pedro gave Robert an insolent stare and spat on the floor before nonchalantly strolling towards the gate. Furious Robert reached for his revolver, tempted to put a bullet between the man's legs. Instead he rushed down the stairs and leaned over Eduardo's body. Pedro, misinterpreting Robert's movements, swung around revolver ready in his hand, and aimed at Robert. Robert ignored him. He was not about to add another notch to Pedro's gun. He put his head against Eduardo's blood soaked shirt. There was slight movement. Robert picked up the boy's limp wrist and checked his pulse. It was there but weak. He ran into the kitchen. Three women huddled against the stove, terrified.

"Señoras, have nothing to fear. You will not be harmed. There is a boy out here that has been hurt and you must come and look after him."

An older woman stepped forward. “Please, Señor, is my daughter Teresa safe?”

“I have not seen your daughter, Señora, but Joaquin is dead.”

The lady crossed herself. “Gracias a Dios!”

“Where is my son? He is not in his room upstairs.”

Frightened at the mention of Craig, the women protested their innocence. Conchita, the oldest and self appointed spokesman, pleaded. “Señor, we had nothing to do with the kidnapping of your son. Señor, please believe us. He will tell you we looked after him well. I don’t know where he is. He was in his room tonight when I gave him a drink of water.”

“Señoras, you have nothing to fear. Please hurry! The boy will die unless you come quickly.”

Beckoning them to follow Robert returned to the courtyard. Somebody had turned up the light at the foot of the stairs. The women brought in a basin of warm water and some towels.

A few minutes later Robert whipped out his revolver towards a sudden commotion at the front entrance. Craig rushed in. Behind him Jorge was wrestling with a young Indian. The Indian was trying to extract a knife from a sheath on his belt but Jorge had a firm grip on the man’s wrist. He removed the knife and pushed the Indian forward. An Indian girl followed them into the room. Robert rushed over to Craig and hugged him.

“Craig! Thank God! You are safe!”

Overwhelmed by his father’s uncharacteristic outburst of emotion, Craig buried his face in his father’s chest, while wrapping his arms around the powerful torso. After a few moments they separated, a little embarrassed by their display of emotion.

“Craig where were you? Your room was empty. I couldn’t go looking for you until the place was secure.”

“Teresa, Florentino, and I slipped out through the trapdoor in the kitchen before you attacked. We were saddling some horses when you attacked. It was safer to hide in the stable until it was all over. Jorge found us.”

The girl, frightened by the men entering the courtyard with the remnants of Joaquin’s gang, moved closer to Craig putting her arm across his shoulder. The young Indian moved to one side eyeing the men warily. The three women huddled over Eduardo. He regained consciousness, groaning softly when they removed his blood soaked shirt. He glanced around. Suddenly he became very agitated and began speaking in a very low voice. Conchita leaned close to his face, nodded and turned to Robert.

"Señor, the boy must speak to you."

Robert knelt beside the boy and put his ear close to Eduardo's mouth. "That man standing over there," glancing in the Indian's direction, "is the man that kidnapped Craig. He helped Jose."

Robert stood up slowly. Turning towards the young Indian he slid his hand down towards his revolver. He walked towards Tino. "What is your name?"

Tino had been evaluating each of the gunmen and had determined that Pedro was the most dangerous one. Watching the older man approach Tino realized, by the look on the man's face, that he had been wrong. Señor Fox was more dangerous. The man's steel blue eyes glittered in a face chiseled in stone. For the first time in many years Tino dropped his eyes.

"My name is Florentino Chavez. Joaquin is my father."

Pointing to a body sprawled on the floor in the far corner of the courtyard. "Joaquin is dead," Robert paused at the slight gasp from the girl, "We have destroyed his gang and will not allow you to start another one to terrorize the district. You kidnapped my son and nearly killed him. For that I will kill you!"

Robert raised his revolver. Craig leapt in front of Tino. "No! Father! You must not shoot him."

"Craig, stand aside!"

"No Father. I cannot let you murder him in cold blood. You are not like that. Father, please don't!"

The girl moved over and put an arm around Craig's waist. He did the same. Watching his son standing resolutely before him Robert's anger slowly dissipated. His boy had become a man. He cocked his head slightly, thinking. 'The girl beside him probably had a lot to do with it.'

"Very well, Craig, but remember this well. Some day you will regret the day you saved his life."

Turning to the men Robert ordered, "We will burn this place down." Pointing to the prisoners, "they will bury the dead then you can release them, but they take no guns. Make a stretcher to carry Eduardo back to the mine." Facing the women, "Señoras, you have half an hour to collect your belongings before we burn everything here."

After the men left Robert walked over to the girl. "You must be Joaquin's daughter. I am sorry, but it was necessary to kill your father. He tried to kill me. I had no choice."

"My father was a bad man, still, I am sorry you killed him. He said you were an evil man but you cannot be bad if you are Craig's father."

"You have looked after Craig very well and I thank you for that. I notice his wound is healing nicely and I'm sure you are responsible for that."

Silently Robert observed Craig and Teresa attending Eduardo. Looking up he saw young Juan hovering by the front gate. Smiling he waved the boy in. Craig was safe. He could afford to forgive the boy. Juan approached tentatively still unsure of his reception.

"Señor, I am so sorry about the horse but a noise frightened him before I could tie him down and he took off down the road. I couldn't catch him in time."

Robert patted him on the shoulder before walking into the kitchen. He found a clean mug on a shelf, helped himself to coffee on the stove and sat on a bench by the table. Craig came in as Robert was lighting his pipe.

"Father, I'm sorry about what happened outside but I had to stop you because of Teresa. She has nobody now except for Tino. He is going to take her with him to Bogota."

"What do you know about him, this young man, Florentino Chavez?"

"He is an assassin. He kills people for money. He has a contract to kill me."

"Good Lord! And you saved his life! Who could possibly want to kill you? Whatever for?"

"A boy at our school, Richard Bannerman, the son of the Canadian ambassador. We had a confrontation at school some years ago and he has hated me ever since. I overheard him and Tino discussing a murder that Tino committed for Richard. A pregnant girl Richard wanted killed."

"So when is Tino supposed to kill you?"

"He said he is not going to kill me now. He and Teresa will make it look like I have been killed so they can collect the five thousand pesos Richard has promised Tino. You have probably guessed, I am very fond of Teresa and want to see her safely in Bogota."

"My dear boy. Your Teresa and her brother are free to go to Bogota but it is up to him to figure out how to collect the money. I have no respect for the Bannerman clan but will not be a party to stealing their money." Robert paused while he re-lit his pipe. "Your mother will be anxious to know you are alive and well. Also if we are to save Eduardo's life we must get him home quickly. I want you to organize a stretcher party to carry him back. Mobilize some of Joaquin's men to carry the stretcher. Make them do a good deed for a change. Tell your mother that all is well and I shall be home after I finish burning this place down."

* * *

"Robert, what is the matter with Craig? He has been moody all week, ever since he returned. Other than helping with Eduardo he sits outside staring off into space. I can't get him to talk to me."

They were both in the living room sitting in front of a crackling fire and enjoying a quiet drink before dinner. Robert smiled. "I suppose this is as good time as any to talk about Craig."

Margaritte waited patiently while Robert filled his pipe and lit it. She had learned long ago her husband went through this routine while organizing his thoughts.

"Craig is in love. Joaquin's daughter Teresa looked after Craig's head wound while he was their prisoner and now he is in love with her." He did not mention his suspicion that more was involved. "She is a beautiful Indian girl. Teresa and her brother have gone to Bogota. For that reason I do not think it would be wise for Craig to return to the boarding school in Bogota. I think he should go to Toronto to live with Valerie. He can live in her flat until he finishes high school. Knowing Craig I expect he will want to join up when he graduates."

"Oh Robert! He's just a boy. I don't know if I can let him go so far away."

"Margaritte! He is almost seventeen and I know he has matured in the last few weeks."

"I know you are right. But it's hard for a mother to cut the umbilical cord. Particularly the youngest child."

She looked so dejected Robert rose and sat next to her, putting his arms around her slumped shoulders. "I know, dear." They sat quietly for a few minutes before Robert ventured to raise another subject. "There is something else I would like to discuss with you... Young Eduardo."

Margaritte's face perked up. "I'm glad you mentioned Eduardo. He helped rescue Craig. He is a fine boy and we should do something for him. I have been thinking that I could teach him to read and write. It would give him a better start in life."

"I was going to propose sending him to school in Gachala but if you would like to teach him I think that is an excellent idea. If he does well we could then send him to school."

He didn't mention that teaching the boy might compensate for the loss of Craig. Nor did he mention that he would like to adopt the boy. Perhaps if her affection for Eduardo blossomed, Margaritte would propose that step herself. He had no doubt that Craig would approve. His sister Valerie might not be so enthusiastic.

* * *

- 3 -

Squadron Leader Allan Sharp, D.F.C. and Bar, was aware before he even met the man that Richard Bannerman wielded considerable influence in Canada. The day before Bannerman arrived on his Squadron, Allan was informed by Group Headquarters of Desert Air Force that the young man was the son of a very important government official in Ottawa and was not to be exposed to too much danger. His response to the request did not endear Allan to H.Q. "How the hell could I keep a pilot out of danger on a fighter squadron unless he doesn't fly?"

His animosity towards the new pilot was reinforced the moment he entered the Commanding Officer's tent. Squadron Leader Sharp had little respect for the upper class dandies that gravitated to the R.A.F., and he fully expected Pilot Officer Bannerman to arrive nonchalantly flaunting his superiority and sneering at his scrawny C.O. with his working class accent, skinny legs, and crooked teeth. Sure enough, the young man sauntered into Allan's hot steamy tent impeccably dressed in a safari jacket, shorts, knee socks, desert boots, a silk scarf around his neck, and a silver handled fly swish in his left hand - just like those H.Q. types sipping their gin-and-tonics at the Gezira Club on the banks of the Nile.

The cool Canadian accent was polite, "Where can I find the C.O.?"

"I am Squadron Leader Sharp."

Allan stood up from behind his work table and put on a mottled salt stained khaki shirt over his thin sweaty body. He had no doubt who the man was, but asked anyway. Richard raised a casual salute but snapped to attention when saw the decorations on the other man's shirt. Allan noticed the reaction - the dirty little bits of ribbon made him the equal of any man.

"Pilot Officer Bannerman reporting, sir!"

"Sit down."

Allan watched Richard lower himself into a canvas chair, folding one long elegant leg over the other. The peak cap was carefully removed without disturbing the blond wavy hair. The face turned slightly away from Allan, emphasizing the cleft chin and dimpled cheeks. The pose irritated Allan even more.

"Are you the only replacement?"

"Yes sir."

"Christ! I lost two pilots this morning. I'm down to half strength and they send me you."

Again the cool controlled voice, "Sir, my father has been pulling strings to keep me back at H.Q. but I managed to get a posting to your squadron, which according to the reports I've read, is the best in Desert Air Force. Here are my papers." Extracting a brown envelope from a side pocket of his jacket, Richard placed the envelope on the table. Richard leaned back. Suddenly his right hand flicked up and clutched something in the air in front of him. Nonchalantly Richard opened his hand, and with a small puff, wafted the dead fly away. Slowly he turned back to Allan a trace of a smile on his lips. In spite of his dislike of the man, Allan was impressed.

"You'll see," pointing to the envelope, "I was top of my class all the way through training. I am an above average pilot. Sir, I'm sure you will not regret my posting to your famous squadron."

He was right. During the next two years Richard Bannerman developed into a superb leader and a ruthless killing machine. Sometimes too ruthless Allan suspected. On two occasions Allan received reports from army headquarters of parachuting enemy airmen gunned down by a Spitfire. He suspected Richard was the perpetrator, but Richard was his best pilot, and the squadron was desperately short of good pilots. Allan merely informed H.Q. none of his pilots could possibly do such a thing.

On Richard's second day on the squadron, Allan was surprised to see him sitting in the cockpit of his Spitfire with the tail propped up with ammunition boxes as if in level flight. Richard was squinting through his gun sight, shouting orders to his mechanic while the young man raced across the front of the plane carrying a board on which was painted the rough outline of an ME109. This scene was to be repeated many times as Richard practiced his deflection marksmanship. Even though the new German ME109G's and FW.190 were faster planes than the Mark V Spitfire, Richard handled his Spit with the skill of an artist, outmaneuvering his opponents, and frequently coming back with another kill added to his score.

Richard soon realized that his connections and good looks did not carry much weight on a squadron trying to survive constant attacks by a superior and better trained enemy. Quickly he shed the mannerisms that offended Allan and the other pilots. He was attentive to the more experienced pilots, never hesitating to ask their advice, and pleasant with the ground crew, thanking them for keeping his Spit in tiptop order. When he became more experienced, he initiated lectures in aerial tactics for the new young pilots. Showing them how to survive when up against the more experienced German pilots with their faster planes. Richard was an enigma to Squadron Leader Sharp; a complex personality with two sides to his character; generous with his friends and admirers, but ruthless with competitors or enemies. Allan Sharp's initial dislike did not last. Slowly and reluctantly he was forced to accept that Richard was an exceptional leader with talents far superior to his own. Gradually their relationship changed with Richard becoming more assertive with his Commanding Officer.

Allan Sharp was no fool. Raised in the grimy industrial heartland of Britain he nevertheless obtained a London Matriculation Certificate. For several years the Air Force refused to consider Allan's application to join but eventually relented when they were desperate for new recruits. He was short, thin, sallow faced with hair growing every which way, and without the right sort of accent. He graduated as a Sergeant Pilot a week after the war began and was posted to a fighter squadron in France. By the time of the Dunkirk evacuation, Allan Sharp had shot down five German planes, been promoted to Pilot Officer, and awarded the Distinguished Flying Cross. During the Battle of Britain, two Hurricanes were shot out from under him, but by the time it was over he was a Flight Lieutenant with a singed left leg, a Bar to his D.F.C., and a score of twelve planes to his credit. In 1941 he was promoted to Squadron Leader and posted to the Western Desert in Egypt to Command a fighter squadron, 241 Squadron. There he met Richard Bannerman.

Allan Sharp didn't have the education nor the right accent expected of Commanding Officers, but he was a superb organizer and a good administrator. When he arrived, what was left of the squadron, after Rommel's spectacular advance across the Libyan desert, was licking its wounds on the outskirts of Tobruk harbor. Four hurricanes were all that was left of the normal complement of sixteen aircraft, and they looked barely operational with torn ailerons and elevator fabric. Three quarters of the transport with most of the spares, ammunition, and bombs, was scattered across four hundred miles of desert. Half the ground crew were now marching across the desert into prisoner-of-war camps. Those that were left were lying in their tents, dirty and unshaven. Nor were they very impressed when their new C.O. showed up. The pale faced, skinny little man didn't inspire confidence, even with the decorations on his shirt.

It took Allan six months to turn the squadron around. He drove four of the remaining trucks to the Air Force store depot in Alexandria, five hundred miles away, and refused to leave until the officer in charge agreed to give him the spares, ammunition and bombs he demanded, plus new tents cots and blankets. When daily phone calls to R.A.F. headquarters in

Cairo did not produce more planes and pilots, he flew to Cairo in one of the hurricanes and persuaded the Air Officer Commanding to come out to the airport at Heliopolis to look at his battered hurricane. A month later the squadron was re-equipped with Mark V Spitfires. He took the remaining pilots up, one by one, and taught them the skills they must have against the Germans. By pointing out that half the credit for the Battle of Britain victory belonged to the ground crew, he convinced both pilots and ground crew that they had to work as a team. He drilled them relentlessly until the airmen could refuel and rearm the planes and have them back in the air within twenty minutes of landing. Over the objections of his superior officer, a Wing Commander of the old school, Allan moved the sergeant pilots into the Officer's Mess. He wanted an elite cadre of pilots that would allow inexperienced Officers to fly as number two to more experienced noncommissioned pilots. 241 squadron was a happy squadron with the best record of any squadron in the Western Desert.

By the time the Squadron moved onto a small air base a few miles south of Naples, Richard was in command of 'A' Flight and was being written up in the Canadian press as "Canada's Ace". Squadron Leader Sharp did nothing to discourage the publicity. In fact, he encouraged it. He planned to emigrate to Canada after the war and his association with this rising star could be beneficial. He made sure the best pilots went to 'A' Flight. This not only enhanced Richard's image, but the better pilots could protect Richard. When the Squadron was supplied with the much more powerful Mark IX Spitfires, 'A' Flight was equipped first.

* * *

Squadron Leader Sharp entered the trailer. Startled Richard looked up at the intruder. Quickly he closed his diary and put it in a small drawer on his right. He locked the drawer, sliding the key into his pocket. Flight Lieutenant Richard Bannerman D.F.C. had no intention of letting anybody on the Squadron read his diary.

Allan placed four brown envelopes on the small desk in front of Richard. "Dick, here's the gen on the new pilots that arrived this afternoon. There's two good ones that might interest you. The others are fairly average. Let me know who you want by this evening, I'll give the rest to 'B' Flight."

Richard's ritual with his personal diary amused and intrigued Allan. Why should this supremely self confident young man be so flustered over being discovered doing a simple human activity? 'I wonder what he writes in those diaries that he ships home regularly. He must be leaking something to the press. They seem to get hold of so many details about his activities'.

Allan pulled up a canvas chair and faced Richard across the battered wooden desk. He was about to speak but was forced to wait until four Spitfires from 'B' Flight started up and rattled down the metal runway for their evening patrol. When the peculiar whine of the Rolls Royce engines faded he spoke up.

"Richard, I know you have flown twice today but I want you to lead another patrol tomorrow morning. It's important. The Beachhead at Anzio is in trouble. The German bombers and fighters are creating havoc. The whole Beachhead is stalled and may have to be pulled out. We're fairly certain the Germans are launching an offensive tomorrow. The Americans are sending over fifty bombers in the morning to try to break up the offensive but need some additional fighter cover. I'm sending you up. Take a flight of six of your best pilots including yourself. The bombers are due to arrive at Anzio by ten A.M. You should be there fifteen minutes earlier to chase off the German fighters."

"Allan, you know I look forward to this kind of sortie. I'll lay on a flight to take off at nine thirty. I'll give you the names of the pilots this evening."

Dreading what he might be about to hear, Allan hesitated before proceeding. "You lost Rene Gauthier today."

Richard spread his hands out, shrugging. "It happens. I'm sorry too. He was a good friend."

Rene Gauthier was a French Canadian from a little town in northern Quebec. When he announced he was going to join the Royal Canadian Air Force to fight for the 'English' his parents were shocked; forbade him to go; and finally pleaded. But Rene felt it was time to forget the defeat on the Plains of Abraham and leave Val Barrette to fight for a greater cause. The R.C.A.F. was not impressed with the short stocky slightly bowlegged young man with a rugged peasant face who spoke little English. Anxious to encourage French Canadians to join, they accepted him, even though they doubted he would survive the course. He surprised them. He developed into an above average pilot. His aerobatics were smooth and precise, and his gunnery reflected the skills acquired goose hunting each Fall. When he joined the Squadron, Richard Bannerman took him into his flight. He tutored him in aerial tactics between daylight patrols and in English in the evenings. Rene learned quickly. In his first month on Operations he shot down a FW190 after a spectacular dogfight fought over the air base. The Canadian Minister of Defense and reporters happened to be visiting the Squadron at the time. Sergeant Gauthier was an instant celebrity. Rene shot down three more German fighters in the next six months and was promoted to Pilot Officer. Richard Bannerman no longer gave him lessons in aerial tactics. This morning Richard and Rene went on patrol. Richard returned alone.

For several weeks Squadron Leader Sharp had been monitoring Richard's growing resentment of Rene's popularity and had been considering moving him to 'B' Flight. There he would not only improve the quality of the Flight's pilots, but keep him away from Richard's vindictiveness. Now angry with himself for not following his instincts, Allan tried to restrain his temper.

"What happened to Gauthier?"

"We took off before dawn and headed up past Rome to the Po Valley looking for trains and transports. It was daylight by the time we came down into the Po Valley and started our patrol at about two hundred feet. We followed the railway line between Bologna and Parma. Rene was about two hundred yards behind me. He must have become careless and didn't see the ME109 come up behind him. The German shot him down before I could come to the rescue. Rene crashed in flames. The ME109 zoomed up into the clouds before I could catch it." Richard shrugged again. "There was nothing I could do."

"Did you check to see if he was alive?"

"Of course! The plane was enveloped in flames. He couldn't possibly survive. Even though there was nothing I could do I feel responsible."

Allan looked at Richard accusingly. "One more Jerry and he would have been eligible for the D.F.C."

Richard didn't like Allan's tone. He glared at Allan but said nothing.

Allan had known Richard long enough to understand that he had to be the star, the only star, but the Canadian Press had discovered a new star, Rene Gauthier. Richard resented the attention Rene was getting, but surely not enough to kill him! Angry at losing one of his best pilots, Allan stormed out of the trailer slamming the door behind him. Sergeant McFadden spotted his C.O. emerging from Flight Lieutenant Bannerman's trailer. The sergeant was about to request some additional help for his overworked mechanics but hesitated as his C.O. approached. The sergeant had rarely seen Squadron Leader Sharp so angry. The face flushed and scowling, the fingers jabbing at some phantom figure before him, a stream of curses spewing out of compressed lips. The sergeant had no doubt who was being cursed. The C.O. should get rid of Flight Lieutenant Bannerman before he killed off all their good pilots. The sergeant stepped to one side. His request would have to wait until his C.O. was in a better mood.

In his trailer Allan sat in a canvas chair staring at the field telephone on the table in front of him. Twice he picked up the phone to ring headquarters. Twice he put it back and lit another cigarette. If he picked up that phone and called headquarters about his suspicions, they were more likely to reject his concerns and assume he was jealous of Richard's success and popularity. Allan had been passed over for promotion several times even though his squadron was the best in Desert Air Force. He knew he had no future in the postwar R.A.F. He suspected his working class background and poor language skills had something to do with it. But he had to acknowledge that he could be too outspoken at times, particularly when the welfare of the squadron was involved. It was almost dark before Squadron Leader Sharp put out his fifth cigarette and turned on the small light over his desk. There would be no phone call to headquarters. He did not want to return to an impoverished Britain, condemned to work in some menial job because of his poor education. Richard Bannerman had considerable influence in Canada. Allan had no doubt that Richard's future path in that country was already sprinkled by the stars. Richard must be his ticket to Canada. But Allan had no illusions. He was hitching his future to a dangerous man.

For over two years Allan had been creating a shield to protect himself. It was a diary recording Bannerman's offenses. Initially he had started the diary to refresh his memory should Bannerman ever be exposed and court-martialed. Allan continued the diary when it became evident that Bannerman was becoming impatient with his Commanding Officer and too famous to be court-martialed. Allan unlocked a drawer in a filing cabinet and took out the diary. There were several entries.

Now convinced that Richard had either led Rene over some heavily defended German fighter base or shot him down himself, Allan made another entry in the diary.

Feb.15,44.Pi Off. Gauthier shot down Po valley.

6-7 AM. By ME109? No. By Bannerman?

He replaced the diary in the file and locked the drawer. The dusk patrol from 'B' Flight was returning. Allan stood on the steps of the trailer watching them land, one behind the other. Three landed. He waited for a few minutes hoping the fourth would show up. It didn't. He muttered, 'Damn! We've lost another one.' He walked over to the Operations trailer to debrief the pilots.

Richard finished writing the letter to Rene's parents. He was quite pleased with his account of Rene's heroic battle with the German fighters. A less heroic account would be written in the diary that would be leaked to the press. He signed his name to the letter, adding his rank and decorations below the signature. Placing the letter in a tray for the clerk to forward in the morning Richard picked up the four envelopes his C.O. had left on the desk. He sat up abruptly.

The name on the top envelope was Pilot Officer Craig Fox!

Richard unclipped the flap and pulled out the Pilot's Training Record. Among the papers was the Entrance Application Form outlining the young man's academic record. The pilot had gone to school in Bogota, Colombia. In a low voice he mumbled to himself.

"It is Craig Fox. I paid that little bugger, Tino, five thousand pesos to kill him and now he's here?"

Richard opened the filing cabinet and pulled out an old envelope addressed to him care of the Canadian Embassy in Bogota. It contained a brief note from Florentino Chavez, and a newspaper clipping from some rural Colombian paper describing Craig Fox's death at the hands of bandits. Richard reread the clipping before putting it back in the envelope. Muttering to himself he put the tattered envelope back in the filing cabinet. Speaking in a louder voice.

"Tino, you fucking bastard! I'll get you for this."

For a long time Richard stared out the window drumming his fingers on the desk. At this moment Craig must be sitting in the Officer's Mess waiting for Richard to appear. Chuckling to himself Richard spoke to the empty chair on the other side of his desk.

"Well, well, well. This is going to be interesting"

Richard checked the Pilots' records in the other envelopes and wrote two names on a sheet of paper. He went looking for the C.O. He found him talking to the pilots in 'B' Flight. He beckoned to Allan handing him the sheet,

"I'll take these two in 'A' Flight."

Allan held up the paper in the fading light. "Philip Euston is a good choice but I'm surprised you are taking Pilot Officer Fox. He's not an exceptional pilot."

"I know, but he is an old school chum and I'd like to take care of him. I'll make him my wing man until he learns the ropes."

"Fine, but not tomorrow. That's an order. It's going to be a hard day and you must take your best pilots."

Richard walked away frowning. 'There will be another day.'

* * *

Craig dreaded meeting Richard. What should he say? What could he say? Should he accuse Richard of murder or pretend he didn't know Richard tried to kill him? A hand on his shoulder and a familiar voice behind him left Craig no choice.

"Craig! How wonderful to see you. Welcome to the Squadron."

Reluctantly Craig turned to face his enemy, forcing himself to hide his distaste for the handsome man standing before him. He was surprised how little Richard had changed, the same blond wavy hair, cut shorter than when they last met, the prominent chin and nose and wide sensuous lips. But there was a difference, the aura of supreme self confidence, and an arrogance that he barely concealed. Craig was quick to notice the young pilots gathered around Richard, waiting for him to acknowledge them.

"You're a lucky fellow to end up on this Squadron. This is the best Squadron in Desert Air Force. We have a small contingent of Canadians here, five pilots and about twenty airmen. We try to take care of each other. I asked the C.O. to put you in my Flight.... "A' Flight."

Craig shook the outstretched hand a tight smile on his lips "Richard. I am honored. I've followed your career with great interest. As you no doubt know, you're written up every day in the Canadian papers." The slight sarcasm in Craig's voice alerted Richard.

Craig knew!

"I appreciate your taking me into your Flight. I'll do my best to live up to your expectations."

Richard patted Craig on the shoulder before walking over to the other end of the bar. Craig was too familiar with Richard's personality to take comfort from his friendly approach. Sipping Scotch at the bar, and later during dinner, Craig sensed he was being watched, but whenever he glanced at the far end of the table, Richard was looking elsewhere, either talking to the C.O., or writing on a sheet of paper.

Near the end of the meal Richard showed the paper to the C.O. The Squadron Leader nodded, stood up, and leaned forward to bang a spoon on his wine glass. "May I have your attention, please. We believe the Germans will launch a big offensive tomorrow against the Anzio Beachhead. The Americans are sending over about fifty bombers to try to break up the offensive and have asked us to help out with additional fighter support." Waving the sheet of paper above him, he continued. "Flight Lieutenant Bannerman is leading a flight of six Spits. On this sheet we have listed the names of the pilots selected for this very important sortie. I will post this notice on the bulletin Board. Take off is at nine thirty tomorrow morning."

Craig was disappointed he wouldn't be flying on "Ops" the next day, but much to his surprise, relieved at the same time. He got up and walked out to the large garden at the back of the estate. A lady was leaning over a rose bush inhaling the delicate scent. She lifted her head as Craig approached. It was dark but there was enough light filtering out through the dining room door for him to make out her blond hair and handsome features. He guessed she must be the Countess, the owner of the property.

Craig greeted her politely. "Bona sera, Signora."

"Ah! Parla Italiano!"

"I'm sorry, Countess, that's the only Italian I know. But I speak Spanish and hope to learn your beautiful language soon."

"Si, It is a beautiful language. You have just arrived?" Her soft Italian accent made her English sound so.... he could only describe it as.... sensuous!

"It is so sad" she continued, "all you beautiful young men come to my house and in a few days you disappear.... for ever.... such a waste."

"I assure you, Countess, I have no intention of disappearing."

"Then you must come to visit me soon. I live in the little cottage on the far side of the garden. What is your name?"

Craig. Craig Fox, Signora."

"English names are so hard." She began walking away from him along a path between the roses. Over her shoulder she reminded him, "Don't forget to visit me before you disappear. Bona Sera, Signor."

Craig watched her fade into the darkness. Squadron Leader Sharp strolled out smoking a cigarette. "You have met our Countess. Her husband was killed in the Western Desert in 1940. I should warn you, she consumes young men then spits them out when she has devoured them. The only exception is Richard Bannerman." The C.O. smiled slyly, "he seems to be able to keep her amused."

"Sir, may I speak to you confidentially?"

"Of course."

"Could you please assign me to some Flight other than 'A' Flight?"

"Good Lord! I thought you would have been pleased to be in Richard's flight. According to him you were great friends at school."

"Sir, that is not correct. We have never been friends. Anything but friends. Sir, I am anxious to do well on your Squadron but my relationship with Richard might make that difficult."

Squadron Leader Sharp took a long puff on his cigarette then flicked it into the garden. Pointing off to the left he said, "See over there. You see that glow against the clouds. That's Mount Vesuvius. It's been acting up lately. Good night."

"Sir?"

"Good night, Mr. Fox."

The C.O. walked into the garden in the direction the Countess had taken. He paused a few yards away, stepped on his cigarette butt and faced Craig briefly. "I will take your request under consideration. In the meantime keep this conversation to yourself."

"Yes sir."

Craig went up to his room. Philip Euston was unpacking a small haversack. The rest of Philip's things were scattered on a bed by the window. The only other bed was across the room in a dark corner. Cursing himself for being so slow, Craig dumped his kit bag on the other bed and sat on a small chest to establish ownership before Philip claimed it too.

"We're very lucky to be in 'A' Flight. They tell me that Flight Lieutenant Bannerman is a super person and a great leader. I heard you were in school together. What was he like?"

Craig hesitated before answering. "Richard was several years ahead of me at school so we were not friends. He was very popular and a great athlete."

* * *

Philip Euston came from a small town in central Rhodesia with the unlikely name of Gwelo. He explained to Craig that it was a Bantu word, and shrugged his shoulders when Craig asked what it meant. Philip and Craig had met while doing their final Spitfire training at the Operational Training Unit in Ismailiya on the Suez Canal. Philip did his initial flying training in Rhodesia under the Empire Training Scheme. Craig earned his wings in Southern Alberta under the same scheme. They became unlikely friends. Both were much alike physically, but their personalities were on opposite ends of the spectrum. Craig was slightly taller at six feet. Both were nineteen, although Philip's long exposure to the African sun made him look older. Philip was aggressive, self confident, and considered himself irresistible to women. Craig envied the ease with which Philip acquired beautiful admirers. His own approach to women was more circumspect, unaware that his piercing blue eyes and quiet shy manner was very appealing to most women. Philip considered Craig naive and definitely a virgin. However Philip had learned that behind Craig's quiet demeanor there was strength, character, and a temper. If he became too aggressive Craig's eyes would suddenly lash Philip like a lance.

* * *

The next morning the new pilots piled into a jeep to drive to the airstrip. They parked beside the Operations Trailer and jumped out to watch some Spitfires taxiing out to the end of the metal runway. Six planes took off, one behind the other. Squadron Leader Sharp was standing at the door of the trailer watching the planes leap off the runway, form up into Battle Formation and head north towards Anzio. Craig thought the C.O. looked grim, as if he didn't expect any of them to come back. The C.O. was about to reenter the trailer but a slight cough from Philip made him aware of their presence. He reached behind him and picked up a sheet of paper. Holding it in front of him the C.O. spoke to the new pilots.

"Gentlemen, each of you is assigned an aircraft. I'll read out your name and the number of your aircraft. You are responsible for looking after your aircraft. Go to your Spitfire and meet your ground crew. Your life depends on these men so treat them with respect. Take off in half an hour and become familiar with the area. But keep well south of Naples to avoid German aircraft. I want you to become thoroughly familiar with these more powerful Mark IX Spitfires, so take them up and throw them around the sky. If you handle them well you will survive. If you don't you won't. Keep a sharp lookout for Jerries."

Craig selected a parachute from the trailer, slung it over his shoulder and walked along the metal runway looking for his Spitfire. It, like the other planes, was parked in a revetment, protected on three sides by sandbag walls. It was not a new plane. Here and there paint had chipped off and he could see where bullet holes in the fuselage had been repaired. Nevertheless it was the most beautiful machine he had ever seen - and it was his.

A sergeant was checking the 20mm. cannon jutting out from the port wing. He looked up and was momentarily taken aback thinking it was his son approaching, although he knew Jamie was still in Burma. The young man's pleasant features and ready smile when he came near reminded the sergeant of his son. The prominent nose, clear slightly freckled upper cheeks, and the wide friendly mouth was the same, but the brown curly hair and blue eyes were not Jamie's. The sergeant murmured to himself. 'Christ! They get younger every day. Jamie is older than that boy.' He smiled at the young pilot and introduced himself.

"My name is Sergeant McFadden. My friends call me John for reasons unknown to me as my name is not John Thomas." Craig chuckled. 'John Thomas' is R.A.F. slang for the male appendage. "I make sure those chappies over there," pointing at two grinning mechanics behind him, "keep your plane in fighting trim. She may look a little worn but that engine is the best in the squadron."

Craig was pleased the sergeant did not salute. It made him uncomfortable when men old enough to be his father saluted him. He liked the good humored sergeant immediately. He had the rugged handsome features of the Scottish Highlander. Long sideburns streaked with gray adorned the side of his face. A luxurious mustache covered his jowls extending almost to his ears. A powerful torso with thick neck supported the large head.

One of the airmen helped Craig into the cockpit, clipped on his safety harness and plugged in his earphones, then moved along the wing and sat with his legs dangling over the leading edge. He gave Craig the 'all clear' sign. Craig pressed the starter button. The 2000 horsepower Rolls Royce engine spun into life with a roar. Craig throttled back and released the brakes. Following the airman's directions Craig taxied out to the end of the runway. He applied the brakes and waved the airman away with a brief salute, then ran through his cockpit check. The moment the control tower gave him a green light, Craig pushed the throttle forward, applied full right rudder and control stick to the right to counteract the tremendous torque from the powerful motor. He was slammed back in his seat as the four bladed propeller gouged out huge chunks of air, propelling the sleek machine down the runway and into the sky in seconds. At fourteen thousand feet the supercharger kicked in giving Craig another jolt. Craig leveled out at 20,000 feet and headed south. It was a clear day except for smoke streaming up from Mount Vesuvius on his left. Below was Naples; in front he could see Pompeii, and beyond, the island of Capri.

"Rat-a-tat-tat! Rat-a-tat-tat! You're dead!" Burst into his earphones and jerked him out of his reverie. He recognized the voice, it was Philip Euston. Furious, Craig spun his plane into a tight turn as a Spitfire flashed by. 'Damn him! He'll boast he caught me dreaming when I should have been watching my tail.' Craig flipped his Spit on its back and dived down on Philip, but the other Spit went into a tight turn. Craig followed, but Philip was slowly gaining in the turn and would soon be back on Craig's tail. The 'G' force was beginning to drain the blood from Craig's head. Black spots were beginning to appear in front of his eyes. 'In a few seconds I will lose consciousness unless I do something'. In desperation Craig put the flaps down, hoping his speed wouldn't wreck them. In five seconds he was on Philip's tail.

"Rat-a-tat-tat to you too! You're dead."

Craig followed Philip back to the airstrip, landed, and taxied back to his parking space. By the time he climbed down, the sergeant was peering under the wing examining the flaps. They were not flush to the wing. Each flap was slightly bent. The sergeant straightened up and faced Craig. He wasn't pleased.

"Sir!" The sergeant said grimly, "you must not use flaps at high speed. Only when your speed is below a hundred miles per hour." He stared at the embarrassed young man before him thinking, 'Except for the blue eyes and brown hair he could be Jamie.' The sergeant peered under the wing again. "I think I can fix it without making a report. Sir! Please be more careful."

"I'm sorry, Sergeant, it was a stupid thing to do." Craig walked back to the Operations Trailer feeling more like a schoolboy than an officer.

That evening in the Officer's Mess Philip made no mention of him catching Craig dreaming, nor the dogfight Philip lost.

Richard Bannerman came into the bar. He hesitated at the door, looking over the heads of the pilots until he spotted Craig. He joined Craig and Philip at the bar and bought them a round of drinks. A bandage covered Richard's left thumb. It was prominently displayed for their benefit. Craig ignored the thumb. 'I am damned if I'm going to ask him about it.' Philip did.

"Sir, were you hit today?"

"Oh. It's nothing, just a scratch. I got jumped when my number two wasn't watching my tail. He, unfortunately, got shot down.... So, Craig, you are now my number two. Tonight, after dinner, I want both of you in my room for lessons on tactics and combat. I want to make sure my number two knows how to protect my tail."

Craig had difficulty getting to sleep. He was still awake when Philip walked in. Craig had seen him wander off across the garden towards the Countess's cottage. Craig was sure Philip would want to talk, but Craig was in no mood to listen to Philip's exploits. He faced the wall pretending to sleep.

They took off before sunrise and climbed up into the morning sun. Craig was alert, tense, but no longer nervous. The four planes in the flight leveled off at 10,000 feet and headed north in Battle Formation towards the Anzio Beachhead. Craig searched the skies on his right, at the same time keeping an eye on Richard, one hundred feet in front of him. To his right, a hundred yards out, were the other two Spitfires, hopefully keeping an eye on the sky behind Craig. Philip was number two to a senior experienced pilot, Anton Havel, a Czechoslovakian. Richard began weaving. They were over enemy territory. Craig did the same. Below him he could see no sign of a front line. Craig had expected to see trenches and barbed wire. There was nothing that suggested war, just villages and farmland.

Richard led them in a wide sweep around the Anzio Beachhead. Here there was a war going on. Black puffs followed them. Some puffs were so close Craig could hear the 'thunk' of the exploding Ack-ack shells over the roar of the engine. Remembering the lessons learned from the instructor at O.T.U., Craig weaved more energetically. "Never fly in a straight line." He had said, over and over again, "if you do, you're a dead duck." The instructor had demonstrated on a blackboard the result if you did. The gunner on the other end of an Ack-ack gun would track your course, calculate your speed, and fire at the spot in the sky where you and the shell would intersect, and "it's up your arse, matey."

On the ground black oily smoke was gushing from several vehicles, probably tanks, but they were too high to be sure. Yellow flashes along a two mile front marked the battle line. They completed a second swing over the battle. Suddenly a voice broke the radio silence.

"Crystal Red Leader, two bandits, eight o'clock below." It was Philip. "I'm sure they're Stukas dive bombing."

Richard's voice came on. "I see them. Good work. Red three and four peel off and attack the Stukas. Red two and I will stay up here and cover you in case they have fighter escort."

Craig rolled over on his back and followed Philip in a steep dive. Without taking his eyes off the quarry Craig turned on the switch activating the machine guns, cannon, and cine camera. The two Stukas dropped their bombs, finished their dive, and were scrambling to regain height. They spotted the two Spitfires zooming down and in desperation rolled over and dived for the ground. Craig pressed the button on his joystick, giving the nearest Stuka a long burst. He missed. He was too far away. Cursing his stupidity for being so hasty he took a quick look around before closing in for another shot.

It saved his life.

Two ME109s shot past him as he whipped his Spitfire into a tight turn. They were going too fast to follow him around and continued their dive after Philip. He was firing at a Stuka unaware of the danger behind him.

Frantically Craig screamed into the radio. "Philip! Look out behind you!"

He was too late.

Cannon shells smashed into the Spitfire. Craig watched in horror as his friend's plane rolled over on its back and spiraled down towards a hill, slowly turning round and round, smoke trailing behind like a corkscrew. He could not bear to watch the end and turned away to look for the German fighters. Two Spitfires dived past him chasing the ME109s.

Craig yelled into his radio, "You fucking bastards! Where have you been. You're too late!"

Nobody replied. The Spitfires disappeared behind a hill. The Stukas and ME109s were gone. He was alone over the battlefield. Craig headed home, climbing as he flew south. He landed, parked his plane, brushed by the sergeant without returning his greeting, and marched into the Operations Trailer. He didn't knock. Squadron Leader Sharp looked up from his desk when Craig slammed the door behind him.

"Philip is dead! And it's all Richard's fault!"

"Sit down! Young man. I said sit, and keep your voice down. Now tell me what happened."

"We were over Anzio when Philip spotted some Stukas dive bombing. Richard ordered Philip and I to go after them while he and Havel stayed above to cover us. They didn't cover us. Two ME109s jumped us while they sat up at 10,000 feet with their fingers up their arse. The ME109s shot Philip down but I was supposed to be the one to get it."

"Pilot Officer Fox, you are suggesting that Flight Lieutenant Bannerman, D.F.C., a commander whose first concern has always been for his pilots, would sacrifice two of his pilots. This is ridiculous and I will not tolerate it. They were probably busy chasing other planes and couldn't go to your rescue immediately."

"Sir! There were no other planes in the area, other than the Stukas and the two ME109s."

"Young man you are being hysterical. Your charges are completely unfounded. You are to say nothing about this to anybody. I repeat, to anybody. If you do I shall throw you off the Squadron and strip you of your commission. You will be finished in the R.A.F."

The two glared at each other. Finally Craig said. "Sir, will you move me over to 'B' Flight?"

"No!"

Craig was about to plead his case further, but the C.O.'s face convinced him he was close to jeopardizing his future in the R.A.F. He stood up, saluted, and marched out of the trailer. Craig walked back to his plane looking for the sergeant. He found him leaning against the sandbags in the revetment smoking his pipe.

"Sergeant, I'm sorry I was rude but I was upset at losing my friend."

"I am sorry to hear that." Attempting to distract the young man he changed the subject. "Sir, I noticed you fired the guns. Did you hit anything?"

"No, I opened fire too far away. I know better but I was too anxious."

"Everybody makes the same mistake on their first mission. We're supposed to aim the guns for a point three hundred yards out, which is best for the two twenty millimeter cannons, but most pilots find that the four point five millimeter machine guns are more effective at a hundred and fifty yards. They like to shoot when they are closer to the enemy. I'll adjust your guns this afternoon."

"Thank you, Sergeant."

Both watched two Spitfires land. It was Bannerman and Havel. A few minutes later they walked by carrying their parachutes. Richard ignored

Craig. Anton smiled at Craig, said something to Richard, and turned back to Craig.

"I'm sorry, I didn't see the ME109s in time. They came from behind me. Richard should have seen them but he must have been looking somewhere else. They were attacking you before I saw them and could dive down to help... I'm sorry about Philip."

Craig turned away abruptly to hide the tears welling up.

* * *

Squadron Leader Sharp appeared not to hear Richard Bannerman enter and sit opposite him. He was staring out the side window, eyes unfocused. Richard waited impatiently for a few seconds.

"Was Craig Fox in here?"

His eyes now focused on Richard, Allan said, "He accuses you of causing Euston's death. Claims he was the intended victim."

"That is nonsense! You'll have to do something to shut him up. I can't have him spewing lies about me and tarnish my reputation."

Allan forced himself not to react to Richard's insolent manner, unaware that by doing so, he was walking through a door through which he could never return. "I have told the young man that he was being ridiculous and hysterical over the loss of his friend. He was never to mention his suspicions to anybody, otherwise I will strip him of his commission and hound him out of the R.A.F."

"He has been an albatross around my neck too long."

Intrigued, Allan leaned forward, "what's between you two?"

"None of your business."

Furious, Allan leaned forward. He glared at Richard. But he hesitated too long. After a long pause he continued,"He wants me to move him to 'B' Flight."

Richard snapped, "Not necessary." He stood up and leaned over, "Don't worry. I'll look after him." Richard walked out not bothering to salute.

Allan resumed his musing, digesting the implication of Richard's last words, while his unseeing eyes looked out the window. 'I have to do something about Richard Bannerman. The man is becoming a liability to the Squadron. If it ever comes out that Bannerman is carrying out a personal vendetta by killing off rivals and enemies, it will destroy the reputation of the Squadron. It will destroy me also.

Several hours later, Allan picked up the phone and rang Group Headquarters. He asked for and spoke to the Air Officer Commanding.

"Sir, I will be forwarding to you my recommendation for a decoration and promotion for Flight Lieutenant Richard Bannerman, D.F.C. He is a brilliant pilot and a superb leader. He is presently in command of 'A' Flight. He works very well with the ground crew; trains the young pilots in aerial tactics before they go on 'Ops', and does not send them on dangerous missions until they have gained some experience. I recommend a promotion to Squadron Leader, and strongly recommend he be given command of a squadron. I will be sorry to lose him but it would be unfair of me to hold back such a talented pilot and leader."

"Very well, send in your recommendation and I will look at it. I happen to have a squadron that needs a good commander."

* * *

Craig stayed in his room before dinner sorting Philip's things, but he was not making much progress. He sat on his bed with his friend's clothes strewn around him, holding a picture of Philip and himself standing next to a camel. The pyramids of Gizeh were in the background. The camel had drooled on Philip's brand new officer's cap and Philip had been furious. Craig had collapsed on the sand laughing. Remembering, Craig's eyes blurred.

Just then Richard marched in. Craig greeted Richard with a cold stare. He put the picture back in Philip's wallet. Richard pulled out a chair from under the table holding Philip's toilet kit, personal letters, and Officer's cap, and sat with his elbows propped across the back.

"Craig, I'm terribly sorry about Philip." He continued, a tight smile on his lips, "the C.O. tells me you blame Havel and I for his death."

"I do."

"I can understand you being upset at losing your friend but you've no right to blame us. Havel didn't see the two ME109s and they slipped under us, attacking you before we could stop them." Richard spread his hands out, tilting his head sympathetically, "These things happen. I am sorry, Craig."

Craig's anger rose at the blatant lie. He believed Havel's version of the tragedy rather than Richard's. He got up quickly and walked to the window, fists clenched. Breathing deeply he brought his anger under control. In a low voice, he spoke, "He didn't have to die like that. He was a super pilot and my friend."

"I'm sorry." Richard unfolded his long legs and stood up. He put the chair back under the table. He was about to pat Craig on the shoulder, but Craig, anticipating the gesture, moved away. Pausing briefly at the door Richard glared at Craig's back.

"Don't forget you are still my number two and I expect you to cover my arse when we're up there."

"I'll do my best, sir."

Richard gave Craig's back a suspicious look before closing the door quietly behind him.

Craig listened to Richard's steps fading down the hall. He paused by Philip's bed. The thought that some other pilot would be occupying Philip's bed wrenched a sob from his chest. He sat on the bed but leapt up immediately as if he had, inadvertently, sat on somebody. He almost said, 'Sorry!'

He whispered. "Oh God! I wish I'd let you talk to me last night."

* * *

Craig continued to fly as Richard's wingman. He dutifully protected his leader's tail, while making sure his own was safe. In spite of his intense dislike of the man, Craig had to admit that Richard was a superb combat pilot. His quick maneuvers invariably shook off the German fighters, and often placed him in position to attack them. But it didn't take Craig long to figure out that Richard was going out of his way to expose Craig to enemy fire. On several occasions Richard dived down into a gaggle of German fighters, then chased off after a plane, leaving Craig desperately trying to extricate himself from the other planes swarming around him. Relying on the Spitfire's ability to turn inside most German planes, Craig's solution was to hug the joystick to his belly and keep the plane in a tight circle, while firing on any German fighter that crossed his gun sight. To his, and Richard's surprise, in three months of operations he shot down an ME109 and damaged two others. Also he learned combat tactics, which was not what Richard had intended.

* * *

A brief knock was followed by the squeak of the bedroom door and the rattle of tea mugs. The single light bulb hanging from the ceiling flicked on. Craig scrunched down into the bed pulling the thin blanket tighter around his neck. A hand shook his shoulder gently. Above him a soft Irish voice whispered.

"Sir, It's after five." The huddled body didn't move. In a louder voice Paddy persisted, shaking the shoulder more vigorously. "Sir! Sir! You take off in an hour. You must get up. I brought you some tea."

Craig surrendered. Stretching his legs he rolled on his back exhaling a cloud of vapor. "Christ it's cold. Paddy, I've been cold all night. Do you think you can steal another blanket from somewhere?" Craig sat up and put his feet on the cold floor. The batman's freckled face crinkled in amusement. Craig was fully dressed, sweater under a blue battle dress top, and heavy woolen socks pulled up over his trousers. Craig reached over and picked up the mug of tea from the chair beside him. He took a small sip of the muddy liquid and nearly spat it out.

"Jesus Christ! When are you Brits going to learn to make a decent cup of tea."

Paddy took no offense. From somebody else he would have resented being called a "Brit". He liked his young Officer. 'Treats me like a human, not like some of the others. He's a real gentleman.'

"I'll get a couple of blankets for you today, Sir. Mr. Havel didn't come back last night so I don't think he will be needing his for awhile." Craig stopped rubbing his eyes to look up at the batman. "He's all right, Sir. He bailed out but was nabbed by the Jerries."

A blond head jerked up from the other bed. "Did you say Flying Officer Havel was shot down?"

"Yes Sir."

"Blast! I was supposed to fly with him this afternoon. He was great to fly with. He didn't take stupid risks." A sudden thought hit him. "Christ! I hope the Jerries don't execute him for being Czechoslovakian." The young man sat up in bed and ran his fingers through his long stringy hair. Watching Craig tie his shoes he asked, "Where are you going?"

"Bannerman is leading four of us north of Rome on an early morning 'Recce'. There's supposed to be a long column of Jerry tanks and lorries moving south to reinforce their Anzio defenses."

"You lucky bugger flying with him. But you can't fly in this weather. It's pissing down."

Craig cocked his head. Charles was right. He could hear the rain pounding on the slate roof above him and drumming on the window glass. "Paddy, did nobody tell you flying was canceled?"

The batman shook his head, "No sir."

"Well! Go and find out."

Craig watched the young airman stumble out the door, an apology on the tip of Craig's tongue. He shouldn't have been so sharp with him. The Irish boy was still trying to adjust to a world very different from his remote village in some corner of County Cork.

Paddy was back in less than a minute. "You're to come down immediately and eat breakfast. Mr. Bannerman says the weather will clear soon."

"Thanks, Paddy. Thanks for the tea."

On the way to the dining room Craig stepped out into the courtyard. The wind was sloshing the rain against the walls of the building and gusting along the trees in the driveway. Above it was pitch black. "He's crazy! There's no way we can fly in this." In the dining room Richard and two other pilots were drinking tea and waiting for food. Richard's was the only cheerful face. The other senior pilot, Flying Officer John Hancock, must have just finished arguing with Richard when Craig walked in. He was scowling into his tea mug.

Craig could see that Richard was losing patience. "But John, I spoke to H.Q. a few minutes ago and they assured me it would clear in one hour." Seeing Craig, Richard asked. "Craig, did you go outside?"

Craig nodded. "Yes, it's pouring down and very windy." Looking for support Craig glanced over at the young pilot sitting at the end of the table, but Desmond Cooper, a new pilot on the Squadron, was not about to offer an opinion, although he knew enough to know this was not flying weather.

The batman walked in balancing four plates. Craig noticed he placed one in front of Richard, the second in front of Hancock, the third in front of himself, and handed the fourth to Cooper, the new pilot. 'I guess Paddy considers me higher in the pecking order than Cooper.' Craig pulled the plate towards him. A greasy glob of powdered egg mush slid to the far end of the plate, followed by a slab of slimy ham. Quickly he pushed the plate away. His stomach was too knotted to accept that kind of food.

"Don't you want that?" Without waiting for an answer Richard reached over and put Craig's plate over his empty one. Two minutes later it too was empty.

"According to the forecast the weather will clear in about one hour. I intend to be north of Rome in one hour. Jerry won't be expecting us in this weather and we should be able to catch him with his pants down. We'll fly out to sea and up the coast then cut in north of Rome until we hit the main highway between Rome and Florence. Stay close to the water to keep under their radar screen. There should be enough light by then to see the waves under you." Richard stood up. "The jeep is leaving for the airstrip in ten minutes. I shall expect you gentlemen to be on it when I drive off." Richard glared at Craig as if to say, 'in particular that means you.'

Back in his room Craig pulled out an airgram and wrote a quick note to his sister, Valerie, in Toronto. It was his first letter to her since arriving on the Squadron. She was his only contact at home since his parents had died. Thinking of them, he stopped writing. There was something suspicious about the way they had died. His father was an excellent driver. There was no reason for their car to plunge over a cliff.

"Mr. Bannerman is waiting, Sir."

Quickly Craig sealed the airgram, wrote the address on the front, and handed it to his batman. "Paddy, if I don't come back please mail this."

"Oh sir! You'll be back for sure." Paddy held up a package wrapped in an old greasy newspaper. "Sir, the cook made you a ham sandwich."

Craig put the sandwich in the breast pocket of his battle dress. "Thank you, Paddy. Thank the cook for me."

It was still raining when Craig climbed into the back seat of the jeep. The wind was strong enough to splash them as they sloshed through mud puddles on the way to the airstrip. By the time Craig was hoisting himself up towards the cockpit of his Spitfire his trousers were soaked. Sergeant McFadden checked to see that the longrange tanks were firmly in place under the Spitfire then helped Craig strap in. Before he closed the canopy he placed his hand on Craig's shoulder.

"You be careful, my boy."

Craig lifted his pale face. "I will, thank you, Sarge."

The sergeant stepped back off the wing. He watched Craig start up and follow the other planes towards the runway. He shook his head, muttering to the two mechanics standing beside him.

"I don't like the look of this. That crazy Bannerman is going to get them all killed in this weather."

One by one the Spitfires taxied out and roared down the metal runway, rapidly disappearing behind a curtain of spray sucked up by the huge propellers. A jeep bounced through the mud and slewed to a stop in front of the sergeant. The C.O. jumped out and confronted the sergeant.

"Who the hell authorized taking off in this weather?"

"Mr. Bannerman, Sir."

"I specifically told him not to take off unless the weather had cleared."

Sergeant McFadden motioned the two mechanics away. He waited until they had disappeared behind the sandbag revetment before speaking, "With all respect, sir. The impression around here is that Mr. Bannerman does whatever pleases him and you do nothing about it. You may not have noticed, but some young pilots are being sacrificed so that bastard can look like a hero. For some reason, young Mr. Fox is sick to his stomach most times he flies with Mr. Bannerman. When I was strapping him in just now I overheard him whisper. 'Dad! Please help me!', and he wasn't speaking to me."

"Damn you, Sergeant! You and I have worked together for years but you are going too far. I will not allow it!"

"I'm sorry, sir. But I must speak for the sake of our Squadron. This Squadron is my life, and I think, yours too. We have made it the envy of Desert Air Force, and that man up there," pointing in the direction the planes had taken, "is going to destroy what you and I have worked so hard for."

Allan looked up at the sky. Some light was beginning to filter down outlining the lumpy gray clouds. He exhaled slowly, allowing his anger to deflate before speaking to his friend. "John, I am very proud of this Squadron. I have no intention of letting anybody destroy much less tarnish what we have made of it." He took out a crumpled cigarette pack, extracted a cigarette and offered the pack to the other man. The sergeant shook his head pulling out his pipe. "For your information, John, and keep this to yourself. I have arranged for Mr. Bannerman to be posted to another Squadron. His posting came through yesterday evening. I'll tell him as soon as he returns."

* * *

Craig couldn't see. The plane taking off in front of him covered his windshield with streaks of mud. he pulled back the canopy and stuck his head out the side. The muddy rain blurred his goggles. He shoved them up and pushed the throttle forward, blinking rapidly. The slipstream smashed the rain drops into his face blinding him. The drumming sound of the wheels on the metal airstrip stopped suddenly. Realizing immediately that he had veered off the airstrip, Craig hauled back on the joystick, praying he had enough air speed. The propellers clawed at the air pulling the Spitfire off the ground and over the apple orchard on the side of the airstrip. He felt a slight bump when the wheels brushed the top of a tree. By the time he could close the canopy his upper body was soaking wet.

"Crystal Red Flight, form up in Battle Formation. Craig, I'll waggle my wings so you can get in position behind me."

Craig accelerated until he was in position one hundred feet behind Richard. He could barely see the other two planes on his right. They leveled out at two hundred feet just below the charcoal gray lumps of cloud above them. Some light filtered down as they headed out over the sea. Craig could now see the outline of Richard's plane clearly, and the white caps on the sea below. They descended to fifty feet.

Craig's grip tightened on the control stick. The white caps were now coming towards him so fast they were a blur beneath him, and it was difficult to judge his height above them. A mile offshore they turned north, following the coast. Approaching the Anzio Beachhead they made a wide swing to the west to keep well clear of the British and American warships bombarding the Beachhead. Naval gunners had orders to shoot any aircraft approaching.

Beyond the Beachhead they swung back east and continued north a half mile offshore. Passing Ostia they approached a large fleet of fishing boats clearly visible in the early morning light. They flew higher to avoid the masts. Within seconds tracer shells streaked towards them from a jetty jutting out from the town, forcing them back down among the boats. The tracers followed searching for them among the boats. Several boats were hit. Many collided in their panic to avoid the white hot streaks. In a minute they were through, leaving behind the chaos they had created. South of Elba Island Richard waggled his wings and the three planes formed line astern behind him. Turning east they roared over a fishing village heading into the hills at treetop level. The clouds above them were breaking up, confirming Richard's prediction. It was now light enough to see the trees and power lines. In less than five minutes they crossed the main Florence - Rome highway. It was empty - no tanks, no lorries.

"Crystal Red Two and Four break off and follow the road south towards Rome. Hit whatever you see then head for home. I'm going north towards Florence with Red Three. See you back at base... Good hunting, chaps."

"Roger, Red Leader."

Hancock and Cooper wheeled over and headed south along the highway. Richard turned north. Craig followed with mounting apprehension. Evidently Richard's scheme was to eliminate him hundreds of miles behind enemy lines where the only witness would be the enemy.

A few minutes later Hancock's eager voice rattled their earphones. "Richard! They're down here. Lorries and tanks." A few seconds later. "Cooper, watch out! Flak! It's very heavy. Don't forget to weave."

Richard ignored the message. He continued north. 'The bastard knew all along where Jerries were. Now he's got me where he wants me.' Craig was tempted to break off and flee south to join the other two Spitfires. At least there he might survive the flak and do some damage to the enemy. 'But if I do turn back Richard will brand me a coward. So! It's just him and me now. OK, Richard, you murdering bastard, I'm ready for you.'

Richard flew along the highway straight and level at a height of two hundred feet. He was not weaving. 'I'll be damned! I think he wants me to shoot him so he has the excuse to attack me.' Craig soon realized he was wrong. Richard was flushing out the flak. He was obviously counting on the few seconds that it would take for the flak gunners to swing around and track him. This would allow him to flash by, quickly out of range, and bring the following plane, Craig, into their sights. Craig dropped down to treetop level keeping a sharp lookout for power lines. The road led into a narrow valley with steep sides. Craig spotted 88 millimeter Ack-ack gun emplacements halfway up each side of the valley. Richard dived towards them. Craig yelled into his radio.

"Fuck you! Richard, I'm not that stupid!. I'm going back."

He hauled back on the stick and zoomed up in a steep turn away from the valley, but he was too late. White puffs exploded all around him peppering shrapnel into the belly of the Spitfire and through the ailerons. Craig headed west towards the sea, keeping low and weaving his way through the hills. The damaged ailerons made it difficult for him to control the plane. Very much aware that Richard was not through with him yet he kept a sharp lookout behind him. There was no sign of Richard's Spitfire. Suddenly black oily smoke began pouring out from the exhaust ports and the motor shuddered, shaking the whole plane. 'Oh God! I'm too low to bail out and there's nothing but bloody trees in these hills, and the smoke will attract Richard.'

Richard was furious. Craig had disappeared. Unable to come out of the valley because of the flak above him, Richard was forced to fly low beneath the guns until he was through the valley. By the time he circled back there was no sign of Craig. 'Blast, I've lost the bugger. If he gets away I'm in trouble. I've got to find him.' Craig could be heading south, or more likely west for the coast. That would be the safest route for him. Richard climbed until he was clear of the hills and headed southwest to cover both possibilities. Five minutes later he saw a trail of black smoke streaming through a valley off to his right. That had to be Craig. He pushed the throttle wide open and cocked his guns. He did not turn on the cine camera. Ahead Craig's Spitfire was belching heavier smoke. Richard rolled over and dived, gaining speed rapidly.

Craig caught the glint of the sun bouncing off Richard's canopy. He watched his attacker approach until he dared wait no longer. Craig yanked his Spitfire into a tight turn at the same time he flicked on the flaps with a brief apology to the sergeant. The flaps tightened the turn and saved him. A stream of cannon shells and machine gun bullets passed behind him. His maneuver put him on Richard's tail, but by the time Craig turned on his firing button Richard's superior speed had carried him out of range. A grinding noise warned Craig his motor was overheating. A glance at his instruments showed the temperature gauge on red. The motor screamed, red hot metal scraping across red hot metal. The propeller ground to a stop. Desperately Craig looked around him. He had to land before Richard could swing around and finish him off. He spotted a break in the trees ahead - small field. He ejected the canopy and the longrange tank. He pushed the stick forward hoping he had enough speed to reach the clearing. Remembering the flaps he tried to raise them but they were jammed down, slowing the plane. He mouthed a silent prayer.

"Oh! Please, Dad! Help me!"

Craig eased the stick back trying to retain altitude, but eased it forward again when the plane's shuddering warned him it was close to stalling. The plane was sinking too fast to reach the clearing. Just short of the field his left wing sheared off against a tree spinning the Spitfire counterclockwise. It hit the ground and spun into the trees beyond the clearing. The plane burst into flames.

Richard was surprised he had missed hitting Craig. He seldom missed his target. He was even more surprised when he discovered Craig on his tail. 'He's a better pilot than I gave him credit for.' Swinging round to attack again he saw Craig drifting down to a grassy field, smoke and coolant pouring from his dead motor. Richard watched the plane hit a tree and gouge a path across the field before smashing into the forest. Immediately flames belched up around the engine and cockpit. Richard waited for Craig to appear. He did not. 'Good! He's probably dead but I'll make sure.' Richard swung around and dived on the flaming wreck emptying his cannon and machine guns into the Spitfire. The plane exploded shooting flames up towards him as if Craig were making a final effort to reach up to destroy his nemesis. Richard gloated.

"Finally, gotcha you bugger."

Richard loitered near the burning wreck for a few minutes, just to make sure, then climbed over the hills and out to sea. Turning south he flew home.

* * *

Valerie got up to answer the doorbell. She had rented the small bungalow two days ago and had yet to inform her friends of the change of address. Wondering who might be at the door she was startled by a young boy thrusting a brown envelope towards her. his bicycle was propped up against a clay pot at the foot of the steps.

"I had a hard time finding you, Miss. Your old place wasn't too sure where you lived."

"Thanks."

He picked up his bicycle. He thought he should say something sympathetic but was too young to know the right words. With a quick glance at the young lady tearing open the brown official envelope he jumped on his bicycle and raced away hoping to be out of sight before she read the telegram inside.

Dreading what it might contain Valerie didn't read the message, instead she clutched it in her hand while stumbling back into the kitchen. Supporting herself with one hand on the kitchen table Valerie lowered herself into the seat she had vacated only moments before. She unfolded the wrinkled paper.

"The Royal Canadian Air Force regrets to advise you that your brother, Pilot Officer Craig Fox, was killed in action on May 15, 1944. His personal effects will be returned to you in due course.
His Majesty offers his deepest sympathy."

She had waved Craig goodbye only six months before when he boarded the train to Halifax and overseas. He had looked so handsome in his brand new blue-gray officer's uniform, with the shiny R.C.A.F. wings proudly displayed over his left pocket. Now he was gone.... forever. The ready smile, the chuckle always hovering on his lips, the boyish pranks that had so annoyed her - now remembered with regret - all gone. Surprised that she wasn't crying, couldn't cry, Valerie stared at the crumpled paper on her lap. She felt only anger at the waste.

Ten days later an airgram arrived from Craig. This time she burst into tears.

- 4 -

Antonio was not in a good mood. Things were not going well. Two nights ago one of his men had blown off his fingers and part of his face trying to demolish the railway line between Leghorn and Florence. The owner of the farm was becoming difficult, insisting he move his Partisans to some other location. Yesterday one of his couriers didn't return from Florence. This had never happened before. He hoped she had not been intercepted by the Gestapo. But what really bothered him was that he was getting nowhere with Maria. He considered himself an expert when it came to women, but Maria seemed to be immune to him and the other men.

Antonio watched her cut off a thick slice of bread from the loaf on the table, pick it up in her long slender fingers and hand it to him. Instead of taking the bread he wrapped his hand softly around her wrist pulling her gently towards him. With his other hand he put the bread on a plate then folded his hands around hers. She tried to retrieve her hand without hurting his feelings.

"Tonio, please. There's no time for this. The British are going to make a drop tonight and you have to be there before dark to set up the flares."

"But Maria. I love you so much. You are so beautiful, so lovely, so kind, so gentle. When I am near you I can hardly breath, my passion for you is so great. When you are not here I am desolate, inconsolable, unable to think or plan. Please, Maria, put me out of my misery."

Maria wrenched her hand away, slapping his wrist with the other. "Antonio! You're just like all those other men. You say that to all the girls. It hurts your Italian pride that you have not been able to seduce me in the year we have been together. You are a good friend, even though you are a communist, but that is all. Now eat your bread and I'll give you some coffee."

In spite of her heavy mountaineering boots, Maria moved with athletic grace, effortlessly placing one foot carefully in front of the other, as if picking her way through a forest. Watching her glide over to the small stove at the far end of the kitchen, he mentally peeled off Maria's heavy woolen shirt and skirt. Unaware of his thoughts, Maria cupped her hands around her breasts then down to her slim hips to straighten the shirt. The gesture inflamed Antonio. Maria picked up a piece of wood, opened the grate, lowered herself to her ankles in one smooth movement and inserted the firewood over the coals. She peered into the stove's entrails. Satisfied, she stood up lightly, pulling a loose strand of auburn hair back behind her left ear.

Her cheeks were flushed from the hot stove. Maria wrapped a rag around the handle of the coffee pot and brought it over to the table. Antonio looked up at her oval face while she poured the coffee into his chipped mug. There was a hint of a smile on her lips. He suppressed the temptation to reach up and pull her face down to kiss those moist lips. He knew from experience any attempt at familiarity would reward him with a hard slap to the face. Maria might be slight but Antonio respected her strength and stamina. In spite of her middle class background she could carry heavy loads up and down the hills as well as any man. Antonio had referred to Maria's lips as "sensuous" in front of Giovanni. Shocked, Giovanni insisted her lips were "generous", not "sensuous". Giovanni worshipped Maria.

With an exaggerated sigh he stood up "I am desolate, but I must go and wake Giovanni. The rain has stopped and it's getting light outside. We must leave soon."

He walked through the door and clumped down the hall. She heard him yell. "Benito! Wake up we have to go." She smiled. Giovanni hated being called by that name. It had been given to him by his mother. She had worshipped Benito Mussolini when the boy was born. But the boy had grown up to be a communist; the little strutting dictator had been overthrown and was now a German puppet. Benito changed his name to 'Giovanni'.

A door slammed. A rasping voice croaked, "You woke my wife with your yelling and noise." It was the old man who owned the farm. "I let you use my house so you can play your stupid war games but that does not give you the right to frighten her. She is very sick. If you do not respect us you must leave."

"Be quiet, old man. When the war is over we will take over and everything will belong to the State, including this farm. You will no longer be able to exploit the peasants."

The owner shuffled into the kitchen. He slouched into a chair, slumping over the table. Maria poured him a cup of coffee. She noticed he had been sleeping in his clothes. The heavy woolen jacket and baggy pants were heavily creased. A woolen cap covered his bald head. Seeing his worried expression Maria tried to reassure him. "Don't pay attention to what Antonio says. The Italian people will never become communists, and anyway the British and Americans will never allow that to happen. So don't worry."

He shook his head grunting. "I'm not so sure. I'm not so sure. A country foolish enough to allow Mussolini to become dictator could become communist."

Antonio walked in followed by a thin young man in his early twenties. Giovanni was Maria's favorite; kind; helpful; good humored, but vain like most Italian men. His face was too thin, with a sharp pointed nose, a slightly receding chin, and a prominent Adam's Apple, to be handsome. He kept a comb in his back pocket which he used frequently to comb his shiny black hair straight back. Maria handed him a chunk of bread and a mug of coffee.

The old man shook his finger at Antonio, "This is still my farm."

Antonio ignored him. "Giovanni, eat quickly. We must go."

Giovanni ran his fingers through his long hair before covering it with a gray peaked woolen cap. He followed Antonio out the door.

* * *

Two hours later Ack-ack guns thumping off to the east made them pause and listen. Antonio and Giovanni were following an overgrown logging road that meandered along the top of a ridge. The sound echoed through the hills. A few minutes later an engine in trouble could be heard approaching from the east. It sputtered and coughed towards them. Giovanni ran up the trail to a gap in the forest where he could look into the valley below. Pointing he called to Antonio.

"Quick! Come and see. It's an English plane. It's on fire."

Antonio joined him. The plane wasn't on fire, but the motor was spewing black smoke from the engine.

"Look there is another one." Giovanni pointed to the sky above and behind the crippled plane. "It's attacking the other one. It must be a German plane." It was accelerating rapidly, diving on the other plane. The markings on the fuselage were soon visible. "No! Look! It's an English plane. I can see the English markings."

The crippled plane seemed to be unaware it was being attacked but suddenly it whipped around in a steep turn just as its pursuer opened fire. The roar of the cannons startled the two men. They dived to the ground. Sheepishly avoiding each other's eyes they stood up and brushed the wet leaves from their clothes while searching for the planes. Giovanni pointed down the valley. The smoke gushing from the crippled plane was much thicker now, it's propeller no longer turning. It was drifting down towards a small clearing, the other plane circling above it. The English plane hit a tree, breaking off a wing, skidded across the field and smashed into the forest on the far side. Immediately flames and smoke flared up around the plane. The other plane swung around in a wide slow turn and dived on the flaming wreck. A long burst of cannon and machine gun fire bracketed the plane. The fuel and ammunition exploded sending a sheet of orange billowing up licking the bottom of the fuselage of the attacker as it zoomed up over the trees. The plane circled twice then flew away. Silently Giovanni and Antonio looked at each other, too surprised to speak. Antonio recovered first.

"Come. We must go there quickly to see what we can salvage before the Germans get there. All that smoke and gunfire will attract them." Giovanni looked nauseated, his thin lips curled in disgust. "Giovanni, you are going to have to get used to seeing dead and burnt bodies if you want to be a Partisan. Come, hurry."

They couldn't find a trail leading to the field and were forced to zigzag around the heavy brush as they worked their way through the forest. The sun had burnt off the low clouds but the trees were still heavy with moisture. It was noon before they broke through into the clearing; wet; hot; scratched, and irritable. At the far end of the clearing the remains of the plane was surrounded by black charred trees with their stripped branches crisscrossed over it as if offering a final benediction. A thin wisp of oily smoke drifted up through the bare branches. Part of a wing lay on the near edge of the clearing. It had ripped off when the plane hit the tree and was badly crumpled. The containers holding the ammunition had been smashed and 20mm cannon shells and machine gun bullets were scattered around. The barrel of the cannon was bent. It was useless. The blow against the tree had wrapped the leading edge of the wing around the barrels of the machine guns. Antonio peered into the broken wing and tried moving the guns. They were undamaged but there was no way of extracting them from the wrecked wing.

"These guns are exactly what we need and I don't have the tools to cut them out." He kicked the wing in frustration. "By the time we come back with a saw and crowbar the Germans will be here." Antonio removed his knapsack and began picking up the cannon shells and bullets. "Giovanni. While I am doing this you go to the plane and see what you can find that might be useful." After a few minutes he looked up. Giovanni hadn't moved. "Jesu Christo! What are you? A girl? Hurry! The Germans will be here any minute. Go! Go! Go!"

Antonio watched the young man walk slowly towards the burnt plane. He shook his head. 'How do they expect me to fight a guerrilla war with boys like him.' He filled the knapsack and took the heavy load some distance into the forest, emptied the contents behind a tree and covered the ammunition with leaves. Retracing his steps he made sure he left no trail for the Germans. Looking across the clearing he saw Giovanni still had not reached the wreck. Reluctantly Antonio followed him hoping Giovanni would have finished his grizzly inspection before he was forced to do the same. But Giovanni avoided looking into the cockpit, instead he pretended to inspect the charred fuselage while waiting for the older man to approach. The fuselage looked like a sieve. Bullets, cannon, and shrapnel from the ammunition had ripped holes everywhere. Exploding fuel from the punctured tanks had torn the plane apart and seared the paint from the aluminum frame leaving a black residue. Antonio forced himself to peer into the cockpit. He expected to find the gruesome remains of what was once a man. It was empty.

The few pieces of burnt canvas on the seat were all that remained of what had been a parachute; the rubber pads on the controls were gone; the instrument panel was smashed; but no burnt skeleton.

"Giovanni! There is nobody here. Come and look." Suspicious that Antonio might be trying to lure him to look in the cockpit, Giovanni hesitated. "Giovanni! There is no corpse." Antonio waved his hand in the empty cockpit. "See. Look around the bush. Maybe he was thrown out by the explosions."

Giovanni found nothing. Antonio joined him and together they searched a wider area. In a small depression some fifty meters from the wreck they discovered a paper bag. Antonio peered into the wet bag crumpled it and threw it aside. He studied the depression. The grass had been flattened; it was now slowly recovering.

"Look, Giovanni. The pilot must have survived and hid here. Quick. We must find him before he stumbles into the Germans. They will be searching for this plane. But we must take care we don't get caught ourselves. Giovanni. Come, let's go."

* * *

The moment the plane had come to a shuddering stop the flames had belched up over the engine cowling, quickly enveloping the cockpit. Craig had wasted no time. He unclipped the harness and parachute, yanked out the oxygen tube and radio jack, crouched on the seat and hurled himself out of the cockpit through the flames. He landed on his back, winded, but knowing what was coming Craig ignored the pain. He scrambled to his feet, looked around briefly, searching for an easy escape route. His heart pounded furiously pumping adrenaline through his system. His mind racing. 'The smoke and flames are behind me. Good. Richard can't see me. He's going to make sure I'm dead and will attack any second. I must get far enough away before all hell breaks loose.' Quickly Craig ripped off his helmet, oxygen mask, and goggles and flung them through the flames into the cockpit, then plunged off to the right between two thorn bushes. Ignoring the thorns slashing at his face he plowed through the forest until he heard the roar of an accelerating motor. Richard was attacking. Craig hurled himself into a shallow hollow behind a tree and covered his ears. Just in time. For the next sixty seconds there was a frenzy of exploding shells and bullets combined with the high pitched wail of shrapnel flying over his head, followed by the fuel blowing up sending a wave of searing heat over him. The heat set the ammunition in the plane popping off in all directions. He dared not move. Finally it was over except for the snap and crackle of burning leaves. He could hear Richard circling overhead. Cautiously Craig rolled over on his back. The trees shielded him from Richard. He waited until he could no longer hear the whine of the Rolls-Royce engine before sitting up.

Carefully Craig checked himself over. Running his fingers over his face he was surprised it was not burnt except for a small streak along his upper cheeks where there had been a gap between his goggles and oxygen mask. He ran his fingers along his arms and legs. There was no pain there but his clothes were wet and badly singed. The wet clothes had protected him from the flames when he made his desperate leap from the cockpit. But there was something cold and squishy on his belly.

"I'm bleeding!"

Cautiously Craig unbuttoned his battle dress, eased his hand under his sweater and pulled out a soggy paper bag. Inside were the crushed remains of a sandwich. It was the sandwich Paddy had given him before he took off so long ago that morning. He collapsed laughing hysterically, then sobbed with relief. He held up his hands. They were trembling. Staring up at the sky through the branches above him he whispered.

"Thank you, Dad, for saving me."

Craig tried to decide what he should do now that he was hundreds of miles behind enemy lines, but the horror of what he had been through dulled his mind. He was too tired. Other than the occasional crack and pop from some burning logs there was now no sound. Craig stretched out closing his eyes. The sun filtering through the trees permeated his damp battle dress relaxing his jangled nerves. 'God, I'm hungry'. Remembering the sandwich he ate it slowly. He lay back and drifted off to sleep exhausted from the morning's ordeal.

Craig awoke with a start. He sat up listening intently. His keen ears had picked up something. What was it? All he could hear was the birds. They had returned after fleeing the gunfire and explosions. Then he heard the murmur of voices in the distance. Slowly he stood up and worked his way quietly to the edge of the clearing. Peering out from behind a bush he spotted two men pulling on a jagged piece of metal from the broken wing of his plane. They were talking, arms waving. Italians. Unsure of what their attitude to him might be, Craig remained hidden. They could be Fascists who would turn him over to the Germans, or Partisans who might help him escape. The two men approached his wrecked plane. A tall man and a younger thin man. The tall man was clearly the leader. He walked with a confident stride, right hand resting on the butt of a pistol tucked into his belt, head swiveling as he checked the forest around him. Craig retreated into the forest but stayed within earshot. He listened carefully trying to determine who they were. When the older man picked up the paper bag Craig swore silently.

Craig did not want to startle the armed man. He spoke in Italian from behind a tree. "Signor. I am here. Do not shoot. I am unarmed." He walked out slowly with his hands out to the side, palms open. The tall man jerked the pistol from his belt and pointed it at Craig's head. For the first time in his life Craig was staring into the black hole of a gun barrel. Under his woolen peaked cap the man's swarthy features were grim; black eyebrows curled into a scowl; lips clamped. He was intimidating in spite of the thin mustache. Craig could not be certain of the man's intentions. 'Are they Fascists or Partisans?'

Antonio was puzzled, not quite sure what he expected to see emerge from behind the tree, certainly not this innocent looking young man. What terrible thing had he committed for them to want to kill him? He would have to watch him carefully.

"Giovanni. Check him over. Make sure he has no weapons - guns or knives." The young man stood in front of Craig and began going through his pockets. "You fool! Don't stand in front of him. You are blocking me. Stand behind him."

The boy moved behind Craig. He ran his hands along Craig's arms and up his legs. "He is unarmed."

The young pilot put his hands down. He was wary, unsure of his reception but unafraid. His uniform was dirty and badly charred in places. Thin angry streaks under his blue eyes were the only evidence he had been burned by the flames. Antonio uncocked the pistol and slipped it back under his belt. The young pilot smiled.

Gruffly Antonio asked, "Who are you?"

"I'm Pilot Officer Craig Fox, Royal Air Force."

Antonio was anxious to find out why one of the pilot's comrades would want to kill him. The answer to that question would help him decide whether the young man should be helped, but now was not the time.

"The Germans will be here soon. Come, we must leave immediately. Follow me but don't make any noise."

* * *

Maria rolled the heavy quilt to one side and sat up. Leaning over the side of the bed she felt around in the dark for her boots. Sliding her feet into the damp boots she shivered slightly even though she was fully dressed in heavy woolen clothes. Maria, like the others, slept in her clothes in case of a surprise attack by the Fascists or Gestapo. In the kitchen Maria lit a kerosene lamp, poked the stove into life, prepared the coffee, and sat nearby to warm herself. She was tired. Up very late helping the men store the explosives, guns, and ammunition carried back from the drop zone, she had not slept long. But also thoughts of the young Englishman sleeping in the barn behind the farm kept intruding all night. Waiting for the men to drift in for their early morning coffee Maria allowed her thoughts to return to the young pilot.

She had been startled when the Englishman followed Antonio and Giovanni into the kitchen carrying Antonio's heavy pack sack on his back. He dropped the pack in the corner of the room, then leaned against the wall. She watched him from across the room. His expression was wary. He studied the group milling about, his blue eyes flicking from face to face, reflecting the light from the lamp as they moved. Two red welts under his eyes made him look slightly owlish. Seeing her his expression dissolved into a warm smile. He bowed slightly in her direction. Maria smiled in return. She poured coffee into a mug and carried it over to Craig. Offering the cup to him, she apologized.

"I am sorry but we don't have any sugar."

He had learned enough Italian to understand. He placed his hands around the cup and took a sip. "Grazia, Signorina."

"I am Maria. All these men you see here are good patriotic Italians fighting to liberate us from the Fascists. Do not worry you are among friends. Antonio you know. He is our leader. Some of the men are communists, others like me are not. What is your name?"

"Craig Fox."

She smiled retrieved the empty mug and walked back to the stove. Craig forced himself to pay attention to the men. There were only eight men in the kitchen but it sounded like twenty. If it weren't his fate they were discussing he might have been amused. So different to Colombians, so passionate, so emotional. His Italian was now fluent enough to understand the gist of the disagreement. Should he be allowed to join the Partisan group until the British could pick him up with one of their small aircraft, or was his presence among them too much of a risk? Why did the British try to kill him? Was he a spy? Glancing over at Maria Craig noticed she was not participating. She was slowly stirring the coffee pot on the stove with her back to the men, occasionally shaking her head. Antonio stood up and banged his empty coffee cup on the table. He banged several times before the arguments subsided. Pushing the men aside he faced Craig.

"Englishman, who are you? Why did your friends want to kill you? Giovanni, give him a chair. Sit and tell us who you are so we can decide what to do with you."

Craig thanked Giovanni with a brief smile and sat down slowly while he organized his thoughts. His response to Antonio's brusque question could determine whether he was accepted or thrown out to fend for himself. He hoped they would not be put off by his Italian.

"Signore. I am a pilot in the Royal Air force. I am a Canadian but I grew up in Colombia, South America. I hope you will forgive me if sometimes by mistake I use Spanish words instead of Italian. I am still learning your beautiful language." The group smiled nodding appreciatively; except Antonio, he scowled. His reaction cautioned Craig to be careful with his rhetoric. "I was in school in Colombia with the man that tried to kill me. He made a servant girl pregnant and arranged for a young assassin to have the girl killed. I found out and he has been trying to kill me ever since. He is also Canadian, a skillful pilot with many decorations and very popular. He is a hero in Canada. I am the only one who knows his secret and could ruin his career. Unfortunately, I ended up on his squadron and this last attack was one of many he has made trying to eliminate me. He nearly succeeded as Antonio and Giovanni saw. I hope you will help me go back to my squadron but while I am with you I would be honored if you will allow me to help you fight the Fascists."

Craig was about to ask Antonio and Giovanni to provide him with written testimony of what they had witnessed, but glancing at the faces before him he decided to leave that for another day. He had evidently won them over. They smiled at Craig. One man patted him on the shoulder. Craig's eyes locked with Antonio's. He was observing Craig with a pensive look. The fingers of his left hand gently stroked one side of his mustache while he digested Craig's story. Silently they stared at each other. Then abruptly Antonio banged the cup on the table to silence the murmur around him.

"Englishman. You have told us a story that I find hard to believe, but you may stay with us until we can send you back to the British. I warn you, Englishman, if you betray us or endanger my men I will kill you. Do you understand?"

"Si, Signor."

Maria picked up a lamp and beckoned to Craig, "Come, I will show you where you can sleep." He nodded to the group before following her out the door. A light drizzle washed his face when they emerged from the house. Maria led the way to a barn a few meters from the house. In a corner of the barn she pointed out a wide manger. It was stuffed with hay. An old saddle at one end served as a pillow. Maria pulled a dirty brown saddle blanket off a rack and placed it over the hay.

"I'm very sorry but this is the only place you can sleep. The house is full. Wait here and I will bring you a blanket." Craig leaned against the manger until she returned. "These two old blankets were all I could find. I hope you will be warm enough. It is wet but not too cold tonight. I know you must be very tired. Have a good rest and do not worry about getting up too early." Maria picked up the lamp and walked towards the entrance to the barn. Over her shoulder she said, "Good night Craig."

"Signorina, you are very kind. Thank you. Good night."

* * *

Antonio came into the kitchen and peered through the window. It had stopped raining but a gentle breeze was shaking the trees, sprinkling the ground. The sky was clear. It would be a warm day when the sun cleared the hills. He straightened up ran his fingers through his long greasy hair and sat next to Maria.

"Antonio. How do you do it?"

"What are you talking about?"

"Your clothes. They are not even wrinkled. Don't you sleep in them?"

"Maria, that is my little secret. I take them off hoping you will come to me in the night."

Maria slapped his knee. "Antonio, stop that nonsense. I think you are too vain to sleep in them."

Watching her carefully Antonio changed the subject, "What do you think of the Englishman?"

Maria shrugged, "He seems to be sincere. It is too early to tell but I think he is telling us the truth."

"I'm not convinced. His story is too incredible. I think he is lying but why I don't know yet." Although satisfied with her response he continued, "We must be very careful." He hoped she understood he was addressing those words to her. He didn't want her to become interested in the young man.

"Antonio. What is more important right now is where is Lucia?"

"I know. I'm very worried. She should have been back day before yesterday after delivering our report to the Commandante. At her age she should attract little attention. Something has happened to her. If she has been captured they will force her to reveal our location."

"We should move immediately."

"Yes. We should move today. This evening we'll move to our safe house at San Casciano. If everybody including the Englishman carries a load we can move in one trip and reach the safe house before tomorrow morning. The British have instructed us to blow up the railway bridge across the Arno to stop the Germans resupplying the front at Anzio. We will reconnoiter the bridge the following day and attack it the next night. I will go and wake the others."

Antonio squeezed Maria's thigh and moved away quickly before she could elbow him in the ribs. He took one stride and stopped his head cocked to one side. Maria was about to speak. He silenced her with a quick motion.

"Listen!"

For a moment there was nothing then faintly in the distance - Phut phut phut.! She had heard that sound before. There was no mistaking it. German automatic pistols.

"Gestapo!"

"Maria, who is on guard duty this morning?"

"Carlo."

"They must have surprised him. Quick! Call the men upstairs. I'll wake the others. We must flee into the forest. Tell them to meet at San Casciano tonight."

"What about the old man and his wife?"

Antonio shook his head, "We'll have to leave them. They are old and cannot keep up."

"And the Englishman?"

"Good riddance! Let them capture him then we don't have to worry about him. Hurry! Call the people upstairs."

"Antonio, he'll give them information about us."

"He doesn't know where we're going. Come on, hurry."

The men stumbled bleary eyed into the kitchen. Antonio and Maria hoisted packs on their backs and pushed them out the kitchen door making sure they did not follow each other into the forest. Stepping out the door the gunfire helped speed them on their way.

"What's all the noise? You woke my wife again." The old farmer shuffled into the room as Antonio was about to leave.

"Go back to bed old man. We're leaving you and won't be coming back. It's all yours now." Antonio ran out the door.

"Antonio. You are so cruel." Maria leaned over and spoke in the old man's ear. "Signor. Please take your wife and hide in the forest. Quickly! The Gestapo will be here any minute. You must hide or they will kill you. Please hurry."

Maria followed Antonio, but instead of racing after him she ran into the barn. In the gloomy interior she didn't see Craig walking towards her and collided with him before she could stop.

"Signorina, I can hear shooting and men running. What's happening?"

"The Gestapo are attacking! Quick! You must flee into the forest. Please hurry or you'll be killed. I must go." She adjusted the pack on her back and rushed towards the door. "Do not follow me. Goodbye."

"Signorina, I would not put you at risk by following you." Addressing her back he continued, "I hope we'll meet again, Signorina."

His words made her pause at the door. She look back. His uniform was rumpled charred and dirty, his hair spiked in all directions, and his face was streaked with dirt below the angry red welt on his cheeks. To her own surprise she broke the rules.

"Craig. Head north but keep away from roads and towns. We'll be meeting in a safe place near the village of San Casciano. I can't tell you where in case you are captured. Go to the church in the village and wait for me there. Somehow get rid of your uniform. Go into the church at night otherwise you might be recognized. Goodbye and good luck."

Wondering what Antonio's reaction would be to her breach of security Maria ran into the forest.

Cautiously Craig approached the front of the barn. He was about to make a run for the forest but he was too late. Half a dozen soldiers were trotting up the road towards the farm. They had not seen Maria but would spot him if he tried to leave the barn. Quickly he looked around the inside of the barn. There were no windows nor rear exits visible. He was trapped! He would have to hide... But where? Craig stood behind the heavy barn door weighing the pros and cons of potential hiding places. Outside a German voice ordered the soldiers to attack. Immediately there was the sound of glass breaking, and a few seconds later muffled explosions from inside the farm house. A woman screamed in agony. Craig noticed bales of hay stacked in the loft. He ran over to a ladder leaning against the front of the loft. A broken ax handle lay beside the ladder. He picked it up by the jagged end and waved it up and down. Satisfied with his weapon, he climbed up the ladder quietly pulling it up after him. About to burrow into the stored hay he noticed a thin streak of light behind the hay. He worked his way around the hay to the back wall. It was a trapdoor used to put hay in the loft. Craig unlatched a bolt and eased the door open slowly, stopping every time the rusty hinges screeched, but the German soldiers were making too much noise to hear him.

He heard the voice of the old man begging. "Signore, please, please help my wife. She is terribly wounded and..." The dull thud of a pistol butt hitting bone ended the old man's plea. Craig winced.

Craig poked his head out the loft door, checked around, jumped to the ground and walked slowly into the forest making sure the barn was between him and the farmhouse. Looking back he saw smoke. Craig worked his way through the trees until he could see the house. It was on fire, probably from the grenades. Well hidden behind a tree he watched the Gestapo.

A short fat man in an officer's uniform came out the kitchen door. "Bring that old man out here. He must know where they've gone."

Two soldiers followed, dragging the old farmer between them. The left side of his head was bleeding from a cut on the temple. He tried to push them away but they forced him to kneel. He raised his blood soaked head challenging the officer, "You monsters. You have killed my wife, now kill me. I am old and have no need to live now that my wife is dead... kill me."

The officer lifted his riding crop and slashed the old man across the face. "The traitors were here this morning. Where have they gone? You let them stay on your farm. You are a traitor too. For that you should be executed, but if you tell me where they have gone I will spare your life." The officer stood back, straightened the uniform over his belly, and waited, the riding crop flicking impatiently against his boots. "Come old man. Speak."

"Sir. Look what I found." A soldier ran out of the barn holding a silk scarf. Craig felt the front of his shirt. 'Damn! It's my scarf.' The officer took the scarf and held it up. "You have been hiding a British pilot. Where is he? You must tell me now." Leaning over the kneeling man he slashed each side of his face with the crop. "Where is he?"

Unable to watch anymore Craig turned away, seething with frustration at his inability to rescue a brave old man. He walked deeper into the forest, the sound of blows haunting him. A few minutes later he stumbled onto a narrow trail leading away from the farm. Craig was about to step out and follow the track. Instead he jumped back and hid behind a large bush. A soldier was coming towards him, evidently intent on finding a comfortable place to relieve himself. His belt was unbuckled and he was looking down, unbuttoning his uniform as he approached. The man stopped on the other side of the bush. Craig's heart was pumping so furiously he thought the soldier must be able to hear it. Movement on the other side warned Craig the man was coming towards him. Craig raised the ax handle over his shoulder. The soldier came round the bush facing away from Craig, his trousers part way down his thighs. He was about to squat but instinct warned him of danger. He jumped up and swung around to face Craig. Yesterday Craig would have hesitated, but not today. He swung the ax handle in a wide arc smashing it into the man's temple as the soldier opened his mouth to call for help. The soldier collapsed in a heap, blood spurting from the wound. One of his legs twitched for a few seconds. He gave a long sigh. His muscles relaxed releasing his bowels and bladder. Craig sat down abruptly, trembling violently.

"Oh God! I've killed him."

He had killed before but they were in airplanes, not face to face. He had never thought of those pilots as being other young men like himself or the soldier lying before him.

Realizing he still clutched the bloody ax handle, Craig flung it into the bushes. He forced himself to look at the body. It was a young boy probably younger than himself. His trousers had fallen below his knees when he tried to protect his head from the blow. The boy lay on his side, one hand clutching the blond head the other across his groin as if to cover his nudity. Craig leaned over and turned the boyish face towards him. It was covered with blood. Craig took out his handkerchief and tried to wipe the blood off but stopped when he noticed the dead green eyes staring at him as if asking 'why?'. Gently, Craig closed the eyelids. In a low voice he apologized in German.

"I am so sorry."

Craig rolled the body over, pulled up the trousers and buttoned the tunic, as if by the act of restoring the boy's dignity he might be forgiven for taking his life. He pulled the body deeper into the forest away from the trail, straightened the tunic and put the soldier's felt cap back on his head. Retracing his steps the glint of metal on the ground made him pause to investigate. It was a small harmonica. The boy must have been a musician. Heavy with guilt Craig picked up the harmonica and returned to the boy. He bent over to replace it in his tunic. Looking at the young face beneath him Craig changed his mind. Speaking once more to the boy who would never hear again,

"No. I will keep this to remind me of what I have done."

Slowly Craig walked back to the trail. He checked to see that it was clear. The soldier's rifle was propped against a tree some fifty feet closer to the house. Craig ran back, threw the rifle into the trees then loped away from the farm. Taking his bearings from the sun, Craig determined that the trail was guiding him more or less in a northerly direction. After some twenty minutes Craig slowed his pace. At each curve in the trail he approached slowly, listening before proceeding. Late in the afternoon he heard the faint sound of voices ahead. He stopped to listen. The words were too faint and muffled to decipher but they did not appear to be getting louder. Craig eased around the curve in the trail. It led out into an open field. In the distance two farmers were plowing. An older man guiding the span of oxen while a young man steered the plow. Craig retreated into the forest and picked a spot warmed by the sun. He would have to wait until it was dark before he could move on.

* * *

The two kilometer hike to the village of San Casciano from the 'safe' farmhouse did not deter Maria from making the pilgrimage for the second night in the hope that Craig would turn up. Antonio was not only furious that she had put the whole group at risk by revealing to Craig their new location but now he was unable to attack the bridge across the Arno. The Gestapo and Fascists, suspecting that the British pilot who had murdered the German soldier was in the area, were searching villages and farm houses. Antonio didn't dare go out to reconnoiter. Maria was certain that there was more to Antonio's anger than he let on. At times, much to her annoyance, he could be very possessive, almost treating her as his personal property. She suspected that he thought she might be attracted to the English pilot. Maria liked Craig but doubted whether she could become romantically involved. After all, he was several years younger, scarcely more than a boy. Nevertheless Maria was determined to look for Craig. She had told him she would meet him at the church and she had an obligation to fulfill. Antonio warned her she was endangering the group again by wandering into the village at night where Fascist patrols might detain her. She had promised him this would be her last trip.

Maria approached the village piazza through a narrow alley between two stores. She stepped carefully around the puddles, her thin raincoat clutched over her head in a vain attempt to keep out the rain. She was cold and wet. It was May, yet a cold wind was gusting through the alley. At the entrance to the piazza Maria stopped. The street lights had been switched off at the beginning of the war and the piazza was dark, so dark she could barely see the church on far side even though it was a not more than two hundred meters away. Maria stepped into a dark doorway and forced herself to wait for five minutes. There was no sound except for the faint murmur of voices behind her on the other side of the door. Satisfied it was empty, Maria walked carefully around the piazza keeping close to the buildings. She paused by the stone steps of the church and again made sure there was nobody around. Quickly she ran up the steps and over to a narrow side door. She lifted the latch and very slowly opened the door, but the rusty hinges betrayed her. Their squeal echoed through the rafters inside the cavernous interior. Once more Maria waited, peering out the door. Nothing moved in the piazza. She felt her way into the church, hands outstretched feeling for a pew. Two small candles on each side of the altar cast a faint flickering light on the lonely crucified body of Jesus stretched on the cross behind the altar. The church was empty. Maria genuflected and crossed herself before walking along the aisle checking each pew hoping to find Craig asleep on one of them. Disappointed she returned to the front of the church.

"Signorina, I am here."

Startled Maria jumped back, banging her heels against the back of a pew. She froze. The echo bounced off the rafters then quickly died away. There was no other sound.

"Where have you been," she whispered, "What happened?"

"I'll tell you later but I think we should leave quickly. I've been here for over two hours and people keep coming in to pray. I thought one of them was you. I nearly spoke to her. I was about to leave when you came in. Come, let's go." Craig led the way out of the church. They left the side door ajar.

Craig refused to let Maria share her raincoat and by the time they reached the safehouse he could feel little trickles of cold water running down his back over his buttocks and along the insides of his legs. Maria fumbled around looking for the handle of the door. She opened it releasing a flood of light into the yard. She motioned Craig to enter the kitchen. She followed closing the door behind her. Antonio was standing in front of the stove warming his back with his arms folded in front of him, a grim expression on his face. Giovanni and four other men were seated around the kitchen table. Giovanni smiled but the rest ignored his greeting, contemplating him suspiciously. Maria motioned Craig to follow her.

"Come, I'll try to find you some dry clothes."

Craig did not move. He knew he had to face this hostile group first. He unbuttoned the stolen wet greasy overalls covering his uniform, stripped them off and stepped away from a pool of water forming under him. He straightened his uniform before facing Antonio. Maria picked up a tin cup from the table and was about to pour coffee but Antonio gestured angrily at her.

"Maria! Sit down. Englishman, I warned you that if you endangered the lives of my group I would kill you. You killed a German soldier and now the Fascists and Gestapo are looking for you. We don't dare go out.

We can't operate until they catch you. I'm supposed to blow up a bridge to help the British but I can't while their patrols are everywhere." Antonio pointed a finger at Craig. Raising his voice he growled, "Because you killed the soldier the Gestapo executed the old man and his wife and burnt their farm down."

Craig retorted angrily. "No! That's not true. The Gestapo threw grenades into the house thinking you were still in there. The grenades killed his wife and set the house on fire. I was in the barn and saw it all. Then they dragged the old man outside and began beating him. The old man refused to tell them where you had gone. I escaped and hid in the forest but was discovered by a soldier." Craig paused and looked down at his hands. "I just wanted to knock him out but... I was angry... I hit him too hard. I killed him."

"I don't believe you, Englishman."

"It's the truth." Motioning to the men seated around the table Craig accused them, "You all knew the Gestapo had discovered your hiding place and would execute anybody they found there, yet you all ran off and left the old man and his wife knowing they would be tortured and killed. Now you are trying to blame me for their death. I will not accept that. I am responsible for the death of the soldier. I accept that burden... You must accept responsibility for the death of the farmer and his wife."

Before Antonio could explode Maria spoke up, "He's telling the truth. When I ran away I heard the officer give the order to attack and the wife scream when she was killed by the grenades. We should have tried to save them. I'll always feel guilty that I didn't."

Antonio glared angrily at Maria. Turning to the men around the table he was about to explain his reasons for deserting the farmer and his wife but seeing their faces he said nothing. The men got up from the table and shuffled out the door avoiding Antonio's eyes. Maria beckoned to Craig and led him out of the room closing the door behind her.

Antonio watched them leave. For a few moments he stared at Maria's raincoat hanging behind the door then leaned over the stove and pulled a burning twig from the grate. He put a cigarette between his lips and carefully lit the end before replacing the twig. 'I will have to be more careful. The Englishman is popular with my men and Maria likes him too much. I'll arrange for the British to pick him up in the next few days. I can't allow him to take Maria away from me.'

* * *

"Englishman!"

Startled, the Partisans swung around to face Antonio. They were on benches, leaning over the table drinking coffee before collecting the dirty dishes. Antonio was sitting in a kitchen chair on the far side of the stove. He was waving a sheet of paper in his hand. Craig was, as usual, sitting next to Maria. This annoyed Antonio, particularly because she didn't appear to mind.

"Englishman, I contacted the British to arrange for them to send a small plane to pick you up. I heard nothing for several days and was going to send another message but this was just delivered to me. I will read it to you." Antonio paused giving Craig a rare smile relishing his next words. 'Commandante Antonio Vesco.' Antonio smiled slyly. "I like the new title they have given me. I hope my Commandante will not be too annoyed with me because of the British mistake." Antonio glanced at Maria. Impatiently she shook her head.

"Antonio! Please, What does it say?"

'Commandante Antonio Vesco. Our records show that Pilot Officer Craig Fox was killed in action on May 15th, 1944. The man traveling under that name is an impostor. Signed: Group HQ. Desert Air Force.'

Antonio waved the paper at Craig. "Englishman, you do not exist."

Craig stood up slowly. Without taking his eyes off Antonio he eased himself around the kitchen table and walked over towards him. Seeing the expression on Craig's face Antonio got up from his chair, curling his right hand around the pistol in his belt. Craig was taller than Antonio. Craig leaned forward with his nose a few inches in front of the other man's face.

"I exist, Signor Vesco. I am alive and I am here. Because they think I am dead does not mean I don't exist. Now, would you please send another message saying I am alive. That I escaped alive even though my leader was trying to kill me - No, don't say that. That can wait. Say I survived the plane crash with minor injuries."

Antonio backed away from Craig. He glanced at the men sitting beside Maria. Their sympathies were with Craig. He shrugged.

"Bene, I will send another message but they will say the same thing as before... That you are dead."

Craig returned to the bench beside Maria.

"Craig, why don't you want to tell them about your attacker?"

Craig shook his head, "No, Maria. That will not help me at the moment. I have to prove to them I am who I say I am." Craig's face brightened. Looking up at Antonio he spoke in a more conciliatory tone. "Antonio, an impostor would not know where I went to school. Please include in the message that I went to school in Bogota, Colombia."

Antonio shrugged, "Very well. We shall see, Englishman."

* * *

Antonio led the group up through the woods to the edge of a clearing on the crest of a ridge. He motioned them back while he went forward on his hands and knees. Crawling between two bushes he was able to look down on the Arno River and the railway bridge less than a kilometer away. He pulled out a powerful Zeiss binocular from his pack and panned along the river to the bridge and beyond. A pillbox guarded each end of the bridge. He couldn't see the sentries but was sure they were there, probably in the sentry boxes. There were no other German soldiers patrolling the area. A hundred meters upstream on the far side of the bridge the muzzle of an 88 millimeter Ack-ack gun thrust skyward from a sand bag emplacement. Another was located a similar distance downstream. The spring runoff from the Apennines had raised the level of the river to the top of the banks. The churning dirty brown water was slopping over the iron girders supporting the railway track. Without looking behind him Antonio beckoned the Partisans forward. Maria crawled up on Antonio's right, Giovanni next to her. Antonio made sure Craig moved up on his left beside the fifth member of the group, Vittorio.

Pointing angrily at the river Antonio muttered. "Look! Englishman, it is all your fault. We were supposed blow up that bridge a week ago and the only way to do it would have been by floating down at night to set the dynamite on the girders. Now the water is too high and it is too dangerous. If you hadn't killed the soldier we wouldn't have been forced to hide from the Gestapo. Now it too late. The British are angry because they supply us and we do nothing. Look at all those bomb craters on both banks. They've been bombing the bridge for two days and still have not been able to hit it. What's the matter with you Englishmen, don't you know how to bomb a bridge? Any Italian pilot would have destroyed it on his first try."

Craig was about to point out the difficulty of hitting a two meter wide bridge while diving down from three thousand meters at over seven hundred kilometers an hour. He was going to illustrate the difficulty by asking Antonio if he could hit a string with a stone from a height of fifty meters but the words were never uttered. The ear numbing blasts of a hidden Ack-ack gun, less than fifty meters behind them pumping shells up into the sky, forced them to clamp their hands over their ears to protect them from the rapid concussions. The other guns added to the roar. Looking up Craig spotted six planes high in the sky weaving to avoid the white puffs bursting around them. They were in line astern preparing to dive bomb the bridge. Craig recognized the planes.

"Spitfires!"

The leader peeled over into a dive leaving the others circling above. At a height of five hundred meters the Spitfire released three bombs and pulled up into a steep climb, weaving to avoid the flak. Trying to make himself heard above the crashing thunder of the guns, Vittorio yelled in Craig's ear.

"Why don't the others dive?"

"They are protecting him while he's diving in case German fighters attack. They will dive one by one."

The bombs exploded just upstream of the bridge sending huge sheets of muddy water over the bridge. The sentries abandoned their boxes, racing away from the bridge in opposite directions along the railway track. Both had taken off their helmets, looking up as they ran. One tripped, fell, rolled back up on his feet like an acrobat and continued along the track without loss of momentum, still clutching his helmet. When they saw the second plane begin to dive the soldiers flung themselves off the track into ditches beside the rails. Half way into its dive the Spitfire exploded into a huge ball of red fire, quickly elongating downwards as the carcass of what had been a plane tumbled down. Two seconds later the blast from the explosion struck the stunned witnesses. Craig prayed the plane was not from his squadron nor somebody he knew. He heard the cheering from the gun emplacement nearby. Vittorio leaned towards Craig.

"What happened?"

"A shell must have hit his bomb just after it was released."

The leader was still climbing when the other plane blew up. Craig saw the leader's plane flip over into a dive straight down towards them. Vittorio began scrambling back down the slope. Craig grabbed his shirt and held him.

"But he's attacking us! let me go!"

"No! No! He is attacking the gun."

The Ack-ack gun stopped firing abruptly. The gun crew had fled. The Spitfire sprayed the gun emplacement with cannon and machine gun fire and zoomed over the Partisans not fifty meters above their heads. The squadron lettering on the side of the fuselage was clearly visible. It was not Craig's squadron.

Even Antonio was impressed. "That is a very brave man to fly straight into the muzzle of one of those guns. Look at him now! He is flying around trying to make the other guns shoot at him so the others can bomb safely. That takes courage."

Craig watched in rapt fascination. The plane tossed around the sky dodging the shells bursting around it. The Ack-ack gunners were determined to revenge the strafing of one of their guns and concentrated their fire on the one Spitfire ignoring the others. The next plane to dive was way off target. Craig could appreciate why; a friend's plane exploding would unnerve anybody. The bombs from that plane exploded on the far bank at least a hundred meters beyond the bridge. The fourth plane followed close behind the other. It's three bombs straddled the bridge, one on each side and one between the tracks, lifting one section of girders and dropping it into the rushing river. Craig stood up waving his arms over his head cheering silently.

Nobody noticed four FW190's streaking towards the Spitfires. But the two pilots circling above had. They jettisoned their bombs and turned to meet the German fighters. Two German fighters leveled out to confront the Spitfires. Two continued diving to attack the three below. Immediately the Ack-ack guns ceased firing. The two Spitfires that had finished their bombing runs made the fatal error of continuing to climb instead of diving to gain speed to elude their attackers.

Craig jumped up waving his hands frantically. "Dive! Dive, you bloody fools, dive!" Vittorio leaped up and dragged him down.

Two long bursts from the FW190's caught the Spitfires struggling to gain altitude. One Spitfire rolled over and dived straight down hitting the far ridge at high speed. The second Spitfire burst into flames and began gliding down the river valley. The pilot ejected his canopy and jumped over the side but his parachute didn't open, instead Craig saw him tumbling down until he disappeared behind a ridge. A few minutes later they heard the crash of the plane behind the same ridge.

"Why didn't his parachute open?"

"I don't know, Vittorio. Maybe he was going too fast and hit his head on the tail of the plane when he jumped. Look! They're now attacking the leader."

The Spitfire pilot, the one that had been taunting the gunners, made no attempt to climb up to meet his attackers. Instead he appeared to be cruising along oblivious to the two FW190's streaming down behind him. But Craig could see from the increased exhaust issuing from the plane that he was accelerating. Just a split second before the leading German plane opened fire the Spitfire zoomed up into a vertical climb, rotated 180 degrees, and dived down behind the FW190 that only seconds before had been behind him. A quick burst at close range and the FW190's right wing broke off tumbling the plane into the ground near one of the guns. The Spitfire zoomed up again to attack the second FW190, but the German pilot decided he was not in the same league as the British pilot and used the only maneuver effective against a Spitfire, he flipped his machine onto its back and dived towards the ground knowing the heavier machine could dive faster than the Spitfire. The English pilot made no attempt to follow. Instead he flew behind the ridge to look for the fallen pilot. The Ack-ack gun on the far side of the bridge fired three shells at the disappearing Spitfire but it had already gone behind the ridge. The shells plowed into the hill and erupted, one by one. The sound echoed up the valley toward the group on the hill before fading away. Now the only sound was the thrashing of the flood water through the broken girders. Nobody spoke.

Maria had grown up in Milan in comfortable middle class surroundings. She had been to parties and air shows where handsome Italian pilots in their gorgeous uniforms strutted in front of admiring females. They led glamorous lives doing incredible aerobatics and setting speed records around the world. The thought that they also had to do other things, not nearly so glamorous, had seldom occurred to her. Maria was stunned by the vicious air battle she had witnessed. She looked over to where Craig was sitting. He was staring down the valley a forlorn expression on his face. He looked so vulnerable. She moved over towards him on her hands and knees, glancing at Antonio as she passed. He was glaring at her. Concerned with Antonio's growing hostility toward Craig which she knew was sparked by jealousy, Maria had tried to discourage Craig's infatuation with her, but not any more. Maria clenched her jaw. Ignoring Antonio she stood up and walked over to Craig.

Craig didn't notice her approach until she spoke. "Craig, until today I thought you led such a glamorous life. It must be terrifying. How can you do that every day?"

Craig forced himself to pay attention to what she was saying, "Oh... ah... When one is up there one is too busy to be afraid. Its only before and afterwards that one worries."

"The pilot of that plane, Is he good?"

"Yes. Very good."

"Do you know him?"

Craig nodded. As far as he knew there was only one man who used that maneuver... Richard Bannerman - but what was he doing in a different squadron?

Craig followed the others through the forest. Maria was in front of him. Antonio made certain that he and Vittorio were between Maria and Craig. She kept looking back a worried look on her face, hoping he would lift his head and return her look but he didn't look up. Craig had seemed so happy until today, happy to be with her and not too worried about getting back to his squadron, but now he was moving away from her his thoughts back on the other side.

Craig lifted his eyes. Seeing Maria's troubled face he gave her a brief smile before disappearing back into his thoughts. 'I have only now finally realized that I cannot win against Richard. He is too formidable. A man with the ruthless courage he displayed today will not hesitate to use any means he can command to eliminate me. I will have to be cunning if I am to stay alive.'

* * *

For once Craig and Maria were alone. Sipping coffee at one end of the kitchen table Craig followed Maria's movements while she filled her cup, replaced the coffee pot on the stove and seated herself across from him. He reached out for her hands. Gently he caressed her palms. He lifted his head searching her face.

"You know I'm in love with you."

Maria nodded smiling. "I know." She disengaged her hands from his. "Craig, I'm very fond of you too but we must not allow our emotions to interfere with our work. I am a Partisan and I have a responsibility to my companions."

Craig persisted. "I think of you night and day. When you are away I count the minutes until you return, terrified that you may have been captured. When you smile at other men I am jealous and have to force myself to accept that you are kind and considerate with everybody." Emboldened by her smile he went on, "When can we be together? Just you and I without the others. All day, every day, there's somebody with us. I have been here for several weeks and have not been able to talk to you. There are so many things I want to tell you and time is running out for us. Any day now we'll get a message that a plane is coming for me and I haven't had a chance to tell you how much you mean to me."

"It's all Antonio's doing. He is determined to keep us apart. I'm sure you must know he is in love with me and is very jealous of you. That's why we're never alone."

"Well, I'm going to change that. It's a beautiful day. Come let's go for a walk to the village. I'll tell Antonio we're going."

"He won't let us to go."

"We'll see. Where is he?"

"In his room."

Maria watched Craig stride down the hall, hands clenched at his side. He knocked on the door, entering without waiting for a response. Antonio swiveled around. He was holding a photograph of a building in one hand and a magnifying glass in the other. He glared at Craig.

"Englishman. I didn't say you could come in. What do you want?"

Craig was tired of being called an 'Englishman'. He was proud to be English but Antonio sneered whenever he spat out the word. However he had never given Antonio the satisfaction of reacting to his sneers and did not intend to do so now.

"Antonio, I am sorry to interrupt you but I would like to talk to you about Maria." Antonio scowled. Craig held up his palm. "Antonio, listen, please. I know that Maria means a great deal to you, and you will not allow anybody to harm her. I too love her very much and will protect her with my life. I think she loves me too but I don't know for sure. Soon I will be going back and I must know before I go how she feels about me." Craig took a deep breath before continuing. "I have invited her to go with me to the village."

"I forbid you to go. It is too dangerous. The police are still looking for you and will recognize you."

"Antonio, you know that's no longer a problem. My Italian is now very good and I am dressed the same as any other Italian." Trying a little diplomacy, but hoping his offer would be rejected, Craig suggested, "Why don't you come with us? You've been working too hard these last few days. We will be sitting by the taverna on the piazza."

Antonio eyed him suspiciously then shook his head. "No. I am too busy. Englishman, if you endanger Maria I will kill you." Antonio turned his back to Craig and resumed peering through the magnifying glass. Craig waited quietly for a few moments his eyes on the hunched shoulders of the other man. Reluctant to defy Antonio but determined to visit the village with Maria, he walked out the door, closing it gently behind him before returning to the kitchen.

"What did he say?"

"I invited him to come with us but he said he was too busy."

"Did he say we could go?"

"We-e-ll. At the end he didn't say we couldn't go... So let's go. Get your coat and I'll meet you outside."

Through the window Antonio watched them walk out of the yard. Antonio stared gloomily after them as they wandered off along the tree lined lane. He had to do something soon otherwise Maria would be lost to him forever. Her growing attachment to Craig had to be curbed somehow. His jealousy had impelled him to include Craig on several dangerous assignments hoping a bullet might solve his problem, but the young pilot seemed to have a charmed life. Briefly he had considered sending Craig out on some errand then betraying him to the police, but that was too risky. They would force him to reveal their hideout. Disturbed that he should even contemplate risking his Partisans and his mission just to eliminate his rival, Antonio paced up and down the room muttering to himself, alternatively shaking his head or poking his finger at his invisible rival in the recently vacated chair. Staring out the window he stroked his mustache. Finally, nodding to himself he sat down and pulled out a sheet of paper and a pen.

"To. Headquarters, Desert Air Force.

Now you have confirmed the pilot is not an impostor most urgent you pick up Craig Fox. Gestapo looking for him for killing a German soldier. His presence here very dangerous for Partisans in area. Repeat. This most urgent.

Signed: Commandante A. Vesco."

Antonio reread the message and folded it into an envelope. He yelled down the corridor. "Giovanni! Come here. I want you to take this message to the Commandante for transmittal to the British."

Giovanni came out of his room. He had been sleeping and hadn't taken time to comb his hair. He leaned over the railing, "What! Right now?"

"Yes. Now. It is important and urgent."

Giovanni shrugged, put on his heavy jacket, pulled out a comb from his back pocket and peered in a small mirror while he combed his hair. Antonio waited impatiently. Seeing Antonio's scowl Giovanni put the comb away. He shuffled down the stairs, took the envelope from Antonio's outstretched hand and ambled out the door.

* * *

The lane had not been repaired for many years and it was becoming too awkward to negotiate the mud puddles while holding Maria's hand. She had allowed him to retrieve her hand when she was sure Antonio couldn't see them. Reluctantly Craig surrendered the hand. Instead he walked behind her as she glided smoothly around the puddles. Her hair was pulled back into a loose bun allowing the sun to shimmer in the reddish brown of each strand. Sensing his gaze Maria stopped and turned towards Craig. She lifted her face to him. He had intended to wait until they were out of sight of the farmhouse before kissing her but could wait no longer. He cupped her head in his hands, kissing her on the lips. Her response surprised him. She gasped, pressing herself to him, one hand around his neck the other around his waist. She kissed him again, then abruptly put her hands against his chest. Pushing him away she pleaded.

"Please, no. We mustn't."

"But, I love you, Maria. I must know how you feel about me before I go back to my squadron. In so many ways I wish I could stay here with you but I must go back."

Maria looked up at him. "Is it because of the man that tried to kill you?"

"No. That's not the reason. That will have to wait until after the war. No, I have been trained as a pilot and it's my duty to help win this war."

"I understand, but if you go back I'll never see you again. You'll be killed in some battle like the one we saw the other day."

Craig shook his head. Clenching his jaw he continued, "Somehow I have a feeling that I am not going to die in this war. I'm not a religious person but intuitively I know I am going to live for many years." Craig whispered to himself, "Unless I get careless against Richard."

Craig paused at the corner of the street before entering the piazza. It was busy. Sturdy peasant women and children mostly. A few older men sitting on benches reading or arguing at small tables in front of the taverna. He could see no Germans nor police. The women lugged their heavy baskets from store to store, bargaining for each item on their shopping list. Young boys ignored their screaming mothers, chasing and splashing each other from the fountain in the middle of the piazza. The girls clung to the mother's skirts while casting envious glances at their unruly siblings. Craig found a small table in the shade outside the taverna. Discretely hidden beside a large bush they could talk quietly without being overheard by the other tables. Three tables were occupied. Two elderly couples at two tables and two old men at the third table. The old men were in the midst of a heated argument, their voices bouncing back off the far buildings. A young girl came out to take their order.

Craig smiled at her. "Duo vermouth, Por favore, Signorina."

The girl placed a small dish of black olives on the table and went back inside.

Maria leaned towards him, "Your Italian is good but sometimes you slip in a Spanish word. You have a slight accent. It is not as soft as most Italians, but if somebody asks you could say you were born near the Austrian border. There is a strong German influence in that part of the country. That would also explain your blue eyes."

The waitress placed two small half filled tumblers on the table. Craig waited until the girl left before picking up his glass. "To our future." Maria lifted her glass and clicked it against his. Craig took a small sip of the sweet liquid. He replaced the glass on the table next to hers. She was tense, her eyes roving around the piazza, but Craig was too busy trying to organize his thoughts to notice. He reached over for her right hand. For a few moments he caressed the palm. Clearing his throat Craig spoke slowly.

"Maria, I love you very much but being English I am not very good at telling you how much. I'm sure some handsome Italian would be so much more romantic with words and gestures, but that does not mean I don't love you more than he possibly could."

Maria smiled remembering Antonio's passionate expressions of devotion. She squeezed his hand. "Craig, I know you love me." She hesitated then suddenly blurted. "I love you too." Immediately she wished she could take back her words, but it was too late.

Thrilled with her declaration Craig wrapped both hands around hers. "When the war is over I'm coming back and I'm going to ask you to marry me. Please don't answer me today. I will ask you again and you can think about it until then. Please don't answer today."

Shocked she leaned back in her chair spluttering, "But... but I am a Catholic."

"I know you are a good Catholic. I'm not Catholic. I'm a Protestant but not a very good one. If you'll marry me I'll become a Catholic."

"But my parents would want me to marry a catholic Catholic."

"Don't you think your parents will approve if I become a Catholic?"

Maria smiled, wearily shaking her head, "They're so old fashioned and traditional. I know they would disown me if I married a Protestant. They don't approve of what I am doing now. They don't say anything but from the way they look at me when I visit them I know they think I am sleeping with all the Partisans. That is not true, Craig, I am a virgin."

"Maria I know you are. But even if you were not I would still love you. I'll take you back to Canada. I want to go to university to be a mining engineer like my father. I'm not rich. My father left me some money but only enough to help me through university. You would have to work while I go to school."

"Will I not see you again until the war is over?"

Craig sighed, "After I go back I don't know when I will see you again. This war goes on and on. Even the Germans must realize they have lost the war, yet they won't surrender."

"It'll come to an end someday."

They sat quietly holding hands, both silent, both sad in their own thoughts. Craig was the first to surface. He noticed it had suddenly become very quiet. The old men had stopped arguing and were looking across the piazza at a black sedan approaching. The car slowed and parked by the taverna. The doors opened. Three German officers stepped out. They straightened their uniforms while they surveyed the silent onlookers. Satisfied, they walked slowly between the tables nodding to the old men and bowing slightly to the ladies. The officers sat down three tables away.

Maria hissed. "Gestapo."

Craig was facing the officers but had avoided looking at them. He snapped a quick look. Maria felt his hand tighten in hers. She whispered.

"What is it, Craig?"

"The short fat officer is the one who murdered the old farmer and his wife, and he is staring at me. I'm the only young man here. He is probably wondering why a young man is drinking and not working at this time of the morning."

"We should leave."

"No. If we do he will know something is wrong. We must sit here for awhile. Maria, talk to me about something, anything. Tell me about your family, brothers, sisters, cousins, but start talking."

Maria forced herself to chatter. Fluttering her hands she described her relatives, occasionally grabbing Craig's hands between giggles. Craig hoped she wasn't overdoing it. Leaning forward he looked over her shoulder. The fat officer was giving his order to the young girl, but as soon as he finished, he again stared in their direction. One of the other officers spoke to him and the fat one finally turned away but not for long. He continued to glance in Craig's direction while chatting with the other officers. Craig decided they should leave. He beckoned the young girl over in a loud voice.

"Signorina, por favore, il bilete."

She nodded and brought the bill over. She leaned over and spoke in a low voice to Maria. "Signorina, be careful. The fat one has been asking me whether you two are from this village. I told him you were. I am not sure he believes me. You should leave but go slowly."

Craig thanked her loud enough for the Germans to hear. "Grazie, Signorina."

He left a large tip on the table and limped after Maria, making sure the peak of his cap was low enough to hide his eyes. He could feel his scalp tingling under the cap knowing the fat Gestapo officer's eyes were boring into his back. When they were out of earshot Maria whispered.

"Why are you limping?"

"I am hoping he will think I am a wounded Italian soldier."

Maria was anxious to leave the piazza but Craig deliberately dawdled, stopping to buy bread in one shop and cheese in another. He waited until the Germans drove away.

"Maria, we can't go back to the farm for awhile. They may be watching us or may have a spy following us. Let's sit in the church until it is safe."

Craig stopped outside a dusty curio shop near the church.

"Wait here, please."

A few minutes later Craig emerged with something hidden in the palm of his hand. He guided Maria to a pew in the church. He presented her with a thin silver ring.

"I'm sorry they didn't have any gold rings... With this ring I promise to love you and protect you." He kissed her firmly on the lips. "I love you, my sweet Maria."

Craig, not sure where an engagement ring was supposed to go, lifted her right hand and slipped the ring over her little finger. He looked up. Tears were flowing down her cheeks. She leaned forward. She pressed her lips against his.

"Craig, I do love you. Caro Mio, I will marry you."

Maria transferred the ring to the proper finger on her left hand.

* * *

Craig was surprised Antonio said nothing when they returned. He was sitting behind the kitchen table facing the door when they came in. Craig was unaware he had seen them approaching the farmhouse, not along the lane from the village but across the fields. Antonio had been pacing in front of the window for several hours. He moved to a bench before they entered. Antonio didn't need to say anything. His face warned Craig he had turned a rival into a bitter enemy. Without taking his eyes off Craig, Antonio ground his cigarette into a plate in front of him that was already overflowing with crumpled butts. His eyes bored into Craig, icy cold black under the sharp vee of thin eyebrows; his lips compressed under the thin mustache, jaw clamped. Craig motioned Maria to leave the kitchen. He watched her close the door behind her before sitting on the bench opposite Antonio. He waited for Antonio to speak. Antonio didn't. Instead he plucked another cigarette from the pack on the table and lit it. Craig noticed Antonio's hands shook while lighting the cigarette.

"Antonio, I have spoken with Maria. I have asked her to marry me. She accepted."

Antonio lifted his chin. He sneered down his nose at Craig, "You are just a boy. She will come to her senses long before the war is over."

Waving Craig away with his hand he continued, "Anyway that's not important right now." Leaning forward across the table towards Craig, "What is important is where have you been for the last six hours? It is almost dark and you left the house this morning. If you had not arrived in the next two hours I would have had to assume you and Maria had been captured and I was going to evacuate this house. Obviously you do not understand that I am responsible for the lives of my men and Maria... and unfortunately you too. Do you think we are playing games here? Where have you been?"

"We had a drink at the taverna while we talked. We bought bread and cheese which we ate on a bench in the piazza, then we sat in the church until we came home. I am sorry, Antonio, I was not thinking. We should not have stayed away so long."

"Why were you walking across the fields instead of using the lane?"

"It was just a precaution in case we were followed."

Pointing a finger at Craig, Antonio threatened, "If you leave the house before the plane comes to pick you up I will have you shot. Do you understand me?"

Craig nodded. Antonio was right. He had been reckless. It had been a near thing with the Gestapo officers. They could have easily walked over to their table and demanded identification. "You are right. I have been thoughtless and have not paid enough attention to your concerns. I am sorry. I will stay in the house until the plane comes. Antonio, the fault is mine, not Maria's."

Antonio sneered, "Very noble."

"Have you heard from the British?"

"No, but I expect to hear they will be picking you up in one or two nights from now. You are very reckless and thoughtless and a danger to us. I have requested an urgent pickup for you."

Antonio took one more puff. He squeezed the cigarette between his thumb and finger before dropping it in the plate. Again Antonio waved his finger at Craig.

"Englishman. I will not warn you again. Do not leave the house."

Craig watched Antonio leave the room. He felt chastened and chagrined for allowing his immaturity to be exposed by Antonio, and angry with himself for having put Maria's life at risk.

* * *

The following evening Antonio called everybody into the kitchen. "The British and Americans have started their offensive and the Germans are retreating everywhere. The Americans have broken out of Anzio and will be in Rome in a day or two. The Germans have declared Rome an 'Open City' and are retreating north. We have been instructed to keep behind the German line. So we go north also. You," pointing at Craig, "will be picked up tomorrow night."

"Where?"

"You will not be told until you get there in case we are intercepted. Giovanni, you will go with him to set up the flares. We move out the following night, but before we leave I will have to find out where our new location is. The Commandante will decide." Antonio paused. He looked at Craig before addressing Maria. "Maria, tomorrow morning you are to go to the Commandante in Florence and bring back our instructions." He noticed the quick visual exchange. Turning back to the others. "I understand we will have a two night march. Take only what you can carry comfortably. The British will resupply us at the new location. Start packing. We will leave as soon as it is dark two nights from this evening."

Antonio shuffled some papers on the table, picked up a crumpled slip and read it aloud, "To Commandante A. Vesco, Pilot Officer Craig Fox pick up at 23:00 Hrs. Friday night. Location Delta. Code:- Charley, Freddie. Signed. HQ. Desert Air Force"

"Giovanni, that means you are to flash the letters 'C' and 'F' with your flashlight when you see the plane otherwise it will not land. I will tell you the designated landing place before you leave. Englishman, you are to put on your uniform before you leave. Do not, I repeat, do not take anything other than your identification."

Maria waited until the group dispersed to pack then sat across from Antonio. "Please, Antonio, let me go with Craig to the plane. I won't be seeing him for a long time maybe never. Please allow us a little time together."

"I cannot allow that. I do not trust him. He is liable to force you into the plane. You must not go with him."

Maria left him determined to find a way. In her room she laid out fresh clothes for her bus trip to Florence while searching her brain for solutions. 'I must say goodbye to Craig when he flies away. I don't care what Antonio says. But I don't know where the plane will be landing and I'm sure Antonio won't tell me.' Standing in front of a small mirror Maria combed her hair back into a bun. Carefully she tied a black ribbon around it. 'The bus from Florence won't be back until ten o'clock tomorrow night but that will be too late. Craig and Giovanni will have left before that.' Sitting on the bed she was about to take off her boots. She stopped, an idea germinating in her brain. She hurried over to Giovanni's room and spoke to him for a few minutes before going to Craig's room. He was in his uniform. She had forgotten how well the uniform suited him even though it was spotted with black streaks where the flames had singed the material. The light from the candle on the stool by his bed highlighted his face, the strong chin, straight nose, brilliant blue eyes, and the barely visible burn scars on his cheeks.

"I feel strange wearing this again."

"Oh Craig! You look so handsome."

Craig moved forward and lifted her into his arms. "Maria, it is you who are beautiful. Oh God! I love you so much."

Catching her breath between kisses Maria whispered in his ear, kissed him again and left the room. Before she closed the door behind her she gave him a long backward glance trying to imprint a picture of Craig on her mind for future reference.

* * *

Maria awoke with a start. 'Somebody is in the room!' A hand touched her gently on the shoulder. She gasped, sitting up abruptly.

"Ssh. Maria it is me."

"Craig! What are you doing here? Antonio will kill you if he finds you in my room. Please go. Please."

"I can't sleep. I've been tossing in my bed for hours thinking about you. You'll be gone in the morning and I will be gone when you get back from Florence. I won't be seeing you again for a long time, maybe never. I had to come."

"But I told you I made arrangements with Giovanni to leave me a note when he finds out where the plane is landing."

"I know, but things may go wrong. I had to see you before I leave."

She couldn't see Craig in the blacked out room. From the sound of his voice she deduced he was kneeling beside the bed. She reached out to touch his face. The soft day old stubble on his chin made her shudder and propelled her into his arms. Craig held her tightly, then gently eased her back on the bed. Slowly he unbuttoned her blouse and pushed it aside. He cupped her head in his hands kissing her gently on the lips. They were warm and moist. Softly he kissed her ears, her neck, and the vee between her breasts. Craig cupped the sides of her breasts, squeezing them against his face. Maria's chest heaved with short sharp gasps.

"No! No! Please, Craig. Please stop. Antonio will kill you."

Craig wrapped his hands around her breasts. The nipples were erect. Gently rubbing one he sucked the other into his mouth, caressing it with his tongue. The pain in his groin was becoming unbearable. He released the nipple and pushed his hand slowly down her belly. Maria's sobbing filtered through his lust forcing him to stop. She was pleading with him.

"Please, please stop! Caro Mio! Antonio will find us and kill you. Please stop."

"Oh Maria! I am so sorry... I... I lost control. Please forgive me. It's just that I want you so much."

"I know. I know. Now please my love. Go before he finds you."

Craig kissed each breast before buttoning the blouse. He wiped the tears from her cheeks with his lips then silently disappeared into the blackness of the room.

* * *

Antonio knocked on Craig's door. "It's time to leave, Englishman."

Craig put his identification papers in one breast pocket, the harmonica and a small Italian dictionary in the other. He gathered a pile of papers from the bed and took them down to the kitchen. He stuffed them into the stove. Antonio moved towards him.

"I have to search you. It is necessary. You must understand you might be captured."

Craig nodded. While Antonio was checking his pockets Craig glanced over Antonio's shoulder at Giovanni waiting by the door. Giovanni gave Craig a thumbs up signal. When Antonio finished Craig offered his hand.

"Antonio, thank you for your help in returning me to my squadron. I will make sure that every body knows what an excellent commander you are. Thank you."

Antonio ignored the hand. "You must leave now. Giovanni, be very careful that you are not seen. Don't forget he is in uniform."

Craig turned towards the door. Giovanni was holding two buckets filled with oily rags. he handed one to Craig. "Here, you carry this one."

"What are the buckets for?"

Behind him Antonio snorted, "They are flares to show the plane where to land."

Walking down the lane away from the house Craig made the request that was crucial if he was ever to defeat Richard Bannerman. "Giovanni, I need to ask you for a favor. You saw the British plane attacking me when I crashed." Giovanni nodded. "When the war is over I want you to give me a letter describing what you saw. I will need it when I charge that man with attempted murder. Will you do that, please?"

"Craig, I will be pleased to help you. You are a good man."

"Where will I find you? Where will you go after the war?"

"I don't want to be a communist any more. We shouldn't have deserted that farmer. The Communists are no better than the Capitalists. I'm going home. I'm from Udine. My mother has a bakery. Papa is dead, killed in Albania. I'm going back to help her."

"Where is Udine?"

"North of Venice. My mother's bakery is called 'La Venetzia.' It's the best one in Udine. Everybody knows where it is. Ask anybody and they will tell you where it is."

* * *

Craig tried to stay calm but it was becoming more and more difficult for him to sit quietly waiting for Maria to come. Fortunately the plane was late. For that he was grateful. The longer the plane was delayed the more likely Maria would be able to come to him. But it was now past eleven thirty. 'She should have been here a long time ago. She had plenty of time even if she was delayed in Florence.' For the third time he quizzed Giovanni.

"Are you sure the note was well hidden under her pillow?"

Patiently Giovanni responded for the third time, "Si, si, Craig."

"Are you sure that is where she told you to put the note?"

"Si, that is where she asked me to put it."

Craig could sit no longer. He got up and walked back and forth, fifty paces over to where Giovanni had placed one of the buckets and fifty paces back to where Giovanni was sitting smoking. After a few minutes he stopped and listened. Faintly he heard the hum of an engine. It faded for a few seconds then he heard it again louder this time.

"Giovanni the plane is coming."

"I hear nothing." Giovanni cocked his ear. "Si, I hear it now. Craig, quick take the other bucket to the far end of the field. Here's some matches. Light the bucket when you see me light mine then run back here."

A small black speck was moving rapidly towards them from the west. The moon had risen behind them. Craig could see the moon's reflection flickering on and off the plane's windshield as the pilot swung from side to side searching the ground. Craig picked up a bucket and raced for the far end of the field. It was not very long, not even a thousand feet. Craig hoped it was long enough. Giovanni's flashlight flashed the code letters. The plane's navigation lights flicked on briefly. The pilot turned towards the field, throttling back. The moment Craig saw Giovanni light his flare, he lit his then ran back to Giovanni hoping to see Maria beside Giovanni. She was not there. Craig heard the thrash of the wheat stalks against the plane's wheels, then the gentle rumble when the wheels made contact with the ground. It was a high wing monoplane, a 'Lysander', designed for short take off and landings. The pilot opened the throttle and taxied rapidly towards the flare. He swung the plane around facing the flare at the far end of the field before applying the brakes. He kept the throttle partly open with the brakes on. Craig forced himself against the slipstream and opened the side door. The pilot was young and very nervous. From the way he was looking around he clearly expected to see a squad of German soldiers attacking at any moment. He was wearing a leather jacket over his uniform, the kind favored by the Americans. Craig made a stab at his rank.

"Sergeant, switch off your motor. We can't leave just yet."

"Not bloody likely! We have to leave right now. We've got to be back before dawn. Why the fuck they decide to pick you up in the middle of a bloody offensive I'll never know. By daylight there'll be fucking planes all over the sky shooting at anything that moves. Hop in, sir. We are leaving now. Right now!"

"Sergeant, wait! Please, it's most important."

"Get the fuck in here! God damn it!"

The pilot released the brakes and pushed the throttle forward. Craig grabbed the wing strut and heaved himself into the passenger seat beside the pilot. He looked back despairingly. Giovanni and the flares disappeared from view behind the plane. Too despondent to argue with the pilot Craig slumped back in his seat. The pilot headed west towards the sea.

* * *

The first familiar face Craig saw was Sergeant McFadden. He was standing in front of a Spitfire peering at the plane taxing across the tarmac towards him. It was early morning. Too early to be able to see who was in the plane. The pilot maneuvered the Lysander around until it was facing the runway before putting on the brakes and idling the motor. As soon as Craig stepped down the pilot eased the throttle forward and taxied away. Craig faced Sergeant McFadden. The sergeant smiled. It was as if granite had shattered. A huge wide smile creased his cheeks and forehead into deep folds, the handlebar mustache was forced up towards his ears, his eyes buried in the folds of his cheeks. The sergeant marched forward but instead of shaking Craig's outstretched hand he wrapped his arms around the young man, crushing him in a bear hug.

"My Boy! You are alive!"

Gasping for air as the sergeant released him Craig nodded. "Yes Sergeant, I am alive and I intend to stay that way in spite of Bannerman."

"Well. You don't have to worry about that bastard anymore. He was posted to another squadron the day you were shot down. He reported you made a forced landing and blew up on landing." For the first time he noticed the singed uniform. "How did you escape?"

Craig shook his head wearily. "I'll tell you some other time. Just now I'm too tired. Please, could you drive me to the Officers Mess. I need some breakfast and should report to the C.O. Is Squadron Leader Sharp still here?"

"Yes. He is still here but be very careful what you say about that Bannerman bastard. He is still very popular here especially with the young pilots." Frowning the sergeant went on as if speaking to himself. "I don't know about the C.O. I've known him for a long time but lately he seems so... so angry. As if he doesn't like himself anymore. He gets annoyed whenever Bannerman is mentioned. Be careful."

"Thanks. I intend to be. I will say nothing until after the war." Climbing into the sergeant's jeep Craig put his hand on the sergeant's arm to stop him from turning the ignition key. He faced the older man muttering, "but after the war I am going to try to stop that bastard. He is evil. He tried to kill me after I crash landed, but I have witnesses. Two Partisans saw the whole thing."

"Sir, I repeat, be careful. Do not tell anybody what you just told me. Come, I'll take you to the Mess."

Wending his way around the potholes the sergeant snapped occasional glances at Craig beside him. The young man sat slumped in his seat, shoulders hunched forward, hands in his lap, staring vacantly out the side window. His face was thinner, more mature, eyes sunken over a trace of burn scars. He noticed an old scar on the young man's temple. The sergeant had never noticed it before. Only the eyes retained their blue brilliance. In front of the Mess Craig shook the sergeant's hand.

"Thank you, Sergeant."

"Good luck, sir."

Craig waited until the jeep drove off before turning to enter the house. Paddy was holding the door open for him a huge grin crinkling his freckled face.

"Welcome back, sir. It's good to see you."

"Thank you, Paddy. Where's the C.O.?"

"He's upstairs. He's expecting you. He asked me to send you up as soon as you arrived."

Craig stopped part way up the stairs. "Oh Paddy, I want to thank you for saving my life."

"Me?"

Craig chuckled, "Yes, you. The morning I left you gave me a sandwich to take with me. When I got shot down it kept me going all day. It was the best sandwich I have ever eaten. Thank you."

Paddy beamed. "Thank you sir! As soon as you finish with the C.O. I'll give you some breakfast."

The bedroom door was ajar. Craig knocked before entering. Squadron Leader Sharp was seated at a small desk facing French doors leading to a balcony. He got up and shook Craig's hand. Craig was surprised to see him fully dressed so early in the morning; battle dress jacket and trousers; black tie; officer's hat, and a row of decorations under his pilot's wings. This was to be a formal meeting even if it was in the C.O.'s bedroom.

"Welcome back, Craig. It is always a great relief to me when one of my pilots turns up alive. I mean that very sincerely young man."

"Thank you, sir."

"Now, sit over here and tell me how you survived your crash landing and what you have been doing for the past two months. Later today I want you to write a full report. For now just give me the highlights."

"Yes sir." Craig sat. He clenched his hands on his lap determined not to allow his emotions to reveal his anger at the man who had shot him down. He took a deep breath before looking up at his C.O. "As you know, Sir, on that morning there were reports of heavy German traffic coming south towards Rome. Richard led us up the coast north of Rome then inland until we crossed the main road to Florence. He ordered Hancock and his wingman south while we went north. I was hit by flak and my motor began belching smoke so I was forced to crash land. I tried to land in a field but ended up smashing into trees on the far side. The plane burst into flames. I managed to leap out just before the fuel and ammo exploded. I was not hurt."

Allan had noted Craig's singed uniform and the two burn scars on his face as soon as Craig entered the room. Craig made no mention of them. "You confirm what Richard reported but he didn't see you get out and assumed you perished when the plane exploded."

"I ran into the forest to escape the flames and all that ammo flying about. He probably couldn't see me in the trees."

"Why didn't you come out of the forest to let him know you were alive?"

"Aah... I was a bit stunned by the crash and the explosions. It was awhile before I pulled myself together and went back to the clearing. Richard had left by then."

"Richard is no longer with us."

Craig decided not to let on the sergeant had told him. He tried to sound surprised. "Oh!"

"Yes. Squadron Leader Bannerman left the day after you were shot down."

"Oh!" Now Craig was surprised. "Squadron Leader?"

"Yes. Squadron Leader. He was promoted to C.O. of 93 Squadron. The squadron was in bad shape and needed somebody with Richard's drive. Unfortunately the Canadian Government has demanded he return to Canada. They want him to go on a cross country speaking tour. Something to do with War Bonds. However, please go on, Craig. I understand you teamed up with the Partisans?"

"Yes, the Partisans took me to their camp and I lived and worked with them for the two months I was away. Antonio Vesco, the leader of the group I was with, allowed me to participate in some attacks against bridges, an ammunition factory, and two German columns."

"Very good. Write this all down this afternoon. I can't make any promises, young man, but you might be in line for a medal."

Craig nodded. He understood. A medal would depend on what he wrote. "Thank you, sir."

"I want you to take the day off. I'll assign a new plane for you tomorrow and you can take it up for a practice flight. Move back into your old room. There is a spare bed in there. Unfortunately your personal effects were shipped back to your family. Your sister isn't it?" Craig nodded. "You should write to her today. I'm sure she will be very pleased to hear from you. Now go and have some breakfast."

Paddy was waiting for him in the dining room. Two bleary eyed young pilots were at one end of the table. They glanced at him briefly, grunted in response to Craig's greeting and went on eating. They were new. Paddy poured him coffee before going back to the kitchen. He returned almost immediately putting a large plate in front of Craig. Four fried eggs and several slices of ham floated in grease. This time Craig attacked the meal with relish.

- 5 -

Valerie opened the front door. Clutching her dressing gown tighter across her chest she peered up and down the street hoping that nosy Polish lady next door hadn't started her morning vigil. Satisfied the coast was clear Valerie made a dash for the paper, muttering curses at the paper boy for leaving it on the bottom of the steps. Safely back in her little kitchen she put the kettle on the hot plate and flicked on the switch. She settled down at the kitchen table to enjoy her only cigarette of the day. While waiting for the water to boil she removed the elastic band around the paper and spread it on the table. The editor of the *Toronto Star* expected his reporters to know what was in the paper before they came to work.

The bold two inch type splashed across the front page left no doubt Toronto was about to welcome home a native son.

-TORONTO'S ACE COMES HOME TODAY-

> Squadron Leader Bannerman. D.F.C. & Bar, 19 confirmed kills, seven unconfirmed German planes to his credit, landing this morning at Toronto Airport. He will be greeted by Toronto's Mayor, His Worship Jeremy Thomson, who will be presenting Squadron Leader Bannerman with the keys to the city. The presentation will be followed by a signing ceremony at City Hall. The hero of "Desert Air Force", the legendary Air Force that swept the German and Italian air forces from the skies over the Western Desert and Italy, will be giving a lecture tomorrow night in the Crystal Ballroom of the Royal York Hotel in support of Canada's War Bond Drive. The lecture will commence at 8:00 P.M. and is open to the public...

The rest of the front page covered the hero's early life, his skill as a fighter pilot and pictures of the 'Gallant Ace' in the cockpit of his Spitfire. The Swastikas painted on the side of the fuselage, recording his victories, were prominently displayed.

'Bannerman, Bannerman... why is that name familiar?' It wasn't until she had finished her coffee and the one piece of unbuttered toast she was restricting herself to, that the name meant something. Valerie leaned over and extracted three letters from a drawer in the kitchen cabinet. Two were from Craig; the third was a tearstained official one marked 'O.H.M.S.' Valerie opened it one more time.

The Royal Canadian Air Force regrets to advise you that your brother, Pilot Officer Craig Fox, was killed in action on May 15, 1944. His personal effects will be returned to you in due course.

His Majesty offers his deepest sympathy.

To her surprise she nearly cried once more. Valerie opened the letter she had received just yesterday. She reread the airgram from Craig.

My Dear Valerie, July 17, 1944.

I hope you are sitting down when you read this. I am very much alive!!

I was shot down by 'Jerry' but got out of the plane without a scratch. I have just come back from two months behind enemy lines, living and working with the Italian Partisans. It was pretty exciting but can't tell you much about it. Met a wonderful person and would like to bring her back after the war if she will marry me. I won't give you her name in case this letter falls into the wrong hands. She is a lovely person and very brave. I love her very much and am sure you will too.

Love,

Craig.

There was no mention of Bannerman in that letter. Valerie opened the third letter. It had been mailed the day Craig was shot down. It contained only a brief reference to Bannerman. "My leader is Richard Bannerman. We were in school together in Bogota."

* * *

Several times during the morning Valerie tried to speak to the editor, Brian Shirley-Dale, but he kept putting her off while he dealt with the afternoon edition.

"Later, Valerie. I'm busy."

"But I must speak to you."

"Later! Please."

Late that afternoon he waved her into his office. Although Valerie was his junior reporter Brian was sure she would soon be one of his best. If anybody had suggested his opinion of her might be influenced by a growing attraction he would have been shocked. Brian was content with a bachelor life devoted to the *Toronto Star* and his rare collection of antique books. Women were a distraction and a responsibility he had successfully avoided. Or that was what he told himself. Looking at himself in the mirror each morning he assumed no woman could possibly find him attractive with his large hooked nose, pale lifeless skin, receding hairline, and weak watery gray eyes, magnified by large horn rimmed glasses. Better not to be involved and risk rejection. But Brian had to admit he enjoyed having Valerie around. She was intelligent, and possessed a dry sense of humor that matched his own. She was not exceptionally pretty; with her strong chin and regular features she could be mistaken for a man except for the wavy auburn hair and the prominent bulges under her blouse. She was tall for a woman, carried herself with an aura of self confidence, and had a habit of thrusting her chin forward if she didn't get her way. Brian noticed her chin led the way into his office.

"Okay Valerie. What are you so hot and bothered about? Aren't you supposed to be covering some fashion show?"

"Yes but I got Isabel to cover for me."

"Who? Isabel?"

"Really, Brian. Isabel Lafleure. She has been here six months and you still don't know her name." Realizing this wasn't helping her get what she wanted Valerie retreated. "I'm sorry, I know how overworked you are. I'm not being fair... who is covering Squadron Leader Bannerman's talk tomorrow night?"

"I am, why?"

"My brother, Craig, flew with him in Italy and I'm sure the Squadron Leader would be pleased to know Craig is alive and well."

"He's alive?"

"Yes! Isn't that wonderful! His letter arrived in the mail yesterday. He survived the crash and lived with the Partisans behind the German lines for two months. I would like to meet the Squadron Leader to tell him. Please let me go with you?"

"Mmmm... it might make a good story." Drumming his fingers on the desk the editor's eyes drifted off into space. Valerie sat quietly, a slight smile on her face. It was a familiar scene whenever Brian began composing suitable headlines in his head. Valerie watched his lips forming words only to discard them with a shake of the head. She liked Brian. He had hired her and was always encouraging with constructive criticism and an explanation for any change he made to her submittals.

"Well, I'll work on that some more... yes, you can come with me."

* * *

The ballroom was packed. Fortunately seats had been reserved for the Press in the front row. Valerie followed Brian and the photographer through the crush of guests. It was slow going. Seats near the front were in demand, mainly by young ladies with a sprinkling of eager matrons. Relieved that the aisle seat in the front row was still unoccupied Valerie quickly claimed it by laying her raincoat across the back. A lectern had been set up on the platform some twenty feet in front of her. She should be able to catch his eye from where she sat. A large map of the Mediterranean area was pinned to the wall behind the lectern. Libya, Tunisia, and Italy, had been highlighted.

The hum of voices continued until the skirl of bagpipes entering the room from the rear brought everybody to their feet. Valerie watched the procession approach up the aisle through a sea of bobbing female heads eager to get a glimpse of the guest of honor. He was third in line behind the piper and the Mayor. Tall, broad shouldered with wavy blond hair, and looking very handsome in his blue air force uniform. He smiled modestly to acquaintances as he passed them in the aisle. She recognized the elegant man behind him as the recently appointed Justice Minister, the Right honorable James G. Bannerman, M.P. Valerie assumed the lady following the Minister was Richard Bannerman's mother. The guests of honor filed past Valerie and seated themselves in the front row on the other side of the aisle. The Squadron Leader was nearest Valerie. He gave Valerie a warm smile when he sat down. His mother appropriated the seat next to him and took possession of his right hand while gazing adoringly at her son. He seemed slightly embarrassed. Valerie felt a surge of sympathy for him. The piper disappeared through the rear door taking with him the fading wail of bagpipes. The Mayor heaved his ample torso up onto the bandstand. Firmly grasping the lectern in both hands he launched forth into a long speech which at times sounded more like a campaign speech than a tribute to the guest of honor. Restless murmurs from the hall forced him to wind down and introduce the speaker. A drum roll of applause followed. Richard Bannerman bounded effortlessly onto the platform and bowed slightly to the audience. He smiled at Valerie, or so she thought.

Thanking the Mayor for his introduction Richard apologized for some of the exaggerations in the Mayor's eulogy before describing the seesaw battles in the Western desert, Montgomery's triumphant march across North Africa and the fighting in Italy. He wove his narrative with numerous anecdotes, some humorous some sad; alternatively the audience responded with laughter or wept over the death of some gallant young pilot, like the French Canadian, Rene Gauthier. There was no mention of any of his own exploits except when required to explain a particular incident.

It was a masterly performance.

Richard was amused. He toyed with their heart strings. First raising his voice then lowering it for the sad stories, he led them through an emotional roller coaster. From time to time he focused on individual ladies in the audience leaving them drained the moment he moved on to the next. He kept coming back to the girl in the front row. She was particularly affected; mouth slightly open; eyes glazed, and a wet handkerchief clutched in fingers that appeared to be pulling it apart.

Richard concluded by thanking the Mayor for giving him the keys to the city. A standing ovation went on for several minutes. Valerie didn't clap. She was too drained besides being disturbed by her own reaction to such a charismatic man. She believed herself to be a practical sensible person and yet she was being swept up by strong feelings she was afraid she might not be able to control.

Brian put a hand on her shoulder. "Valerie. We'll wait until the crowd around him moves away then we'll try to take a picture of you telling him about your brother... hey! Are you Okay?"

"Yes! Yes! I'm Okay."

The crush around the guest of honor began to thin. Soon she would have to go over and introduce herself. Valerie forced herself to look at the King's picture hanging on the wall behind the lectern while she counted to ten slowly. Gradually the thumping in her chest eased. Taking a firm grip on her purse she walked over to where he was standing, head cocked to one side, smiling at her while he listened to a portly matron gushing in his ear. He retrieved his ear and leaned towards Valerie.

"Miss. I do hope you enjoyed my talk. It is so important that Canadians understand the sacrifices their sons are making."

"Yes, thank you, I did... I believe you know my brother, Craig Fox."

"Yes, I knew him. A brave young pilot. It was an honor to fly with him. If he had survived I am sure..."

"But he is alive! I just got a letter from him yesterday! Craig survived the crash and was behind the lines for..."

The transformation was so dramatic it left her speechless. The eyebrows clamped down into a deep furrow; the eyes, so warm and gentle a moment before, froze over. Glittering cold gray daggers glared down on her. The smile vanished replaced by a grim chin and a thin line where the lips had been. The cold voice was almost menacing.

"I'm pleased to hear he is..." Just then the flash made him jerk his head around. "Stop that! Don't you dare take a picture without my permission. I want that negative now!"

The photographer looked to Brian for guidance. He nodded. The photographer scowled, tore out the negative and handed it to the angry man in front of him. Squadron Leader Bannerman stuffed it in his pocket, and once more in control of his temper, smiled coldly at Valerie.

"Madam, I'm very pleased to hear about your brother... now, if you will excuse me we must leave."

With a curt nod to the Mayor the Squadron Leader led the way out of the room.

The next morning two letters were mailed both addressed to the same Squadron in Italy; one was for Pilot Officer Craig Fox describing Valerie's strange encounter with Squadron Leader Bannerman and would he please explain what was going on between him and Bannerman; the other letter was for Squadron Leader Sharp requesting details of Craig Fox's resurrection.

* * *

A month later Richard received a copy of Craig's report covering his experiences behind enemy lines. It was attached to a letter from Squadron Leader Sharp. Richard skimmed through the report. Craig made no mention of Richard's repeated attempts to get him killed by the German Ack-ack, nor the final attack after Craig crashed. Allan Sharp's covering letter was more disturbing.

Dear Richard, August 30, 1944.

Pleased to hear your lectures are going so well. Never doubted you would do a great job. Congrats! Sorry you heard about Craig Fox at such an inopportune moment. I had planned to write to you but didn't have your address in Canada.

"That's bullshit! H.Q. Desert Air Force has my address"

In any case no harm done. I'm sending you a copy of his report. As you can see it is not critical of you, rather it is mildly positive. However I must warn you, although the young man is much more mature and self confident he has not mastered the art of lying.

The morning he returned he gave me a verbal report which is the same as the written report I am sending you but I could tell he was less than truthful about your involvement. Also we had received reports he had killed a German soldier which he didn't mention in his report. The Partisans complained that he was jeopardizing their ability to operate because he was being targeted by the Gestapo.

I don't know what happened between him and you that day and I do not wish to know, but Richard, by his manner I suspect Craig feels he has something on you. He is much more assertive around the Squadron even with me.

Finally, we've got 'Jerry' on the run. I'm sure you've heard

Rome fell to the Americans and 'Jerry' is fleeing north to his Gothic Line in the Apennines. Now that we have finally landed in Normandy, hopefully the war will be over this year and I can start thinking of the future. You and I have talked from time to time of my coming to Canada. I know that is where my future lies and I look forward to seeing you there and working with you.

Yours faithfully,

Allan

P.S. I have recommended young Fox for a medal for his work with the Partisans. I hinted it depended on what went into his report.

Richard grunted. "I'll fix that!"

Richard picked up the phone and booked a call to his father in Ottawa for three o'clock that afternoon. It didn't come through until seven, an hour before he was due to commence his lecture.

"Richard, sorry I could not come to the phone earlier but have been in the House answering stupid questions from idiots. I shouldn't say this on the phone but sometimes I think Hitler has a better system of government than we do... ha,ha... I'm just joking of course... my boy, how are you?"

"Fine, Thanks... Dad I..."

"Where are you? You sound so far away."

"I'm in Regina at the Saskatchewan Hotel. I'm lecturing downstairs in an hour."

"From the newspaper reports you are wowing them in the prairies."

"With all these flying training schools out here they want to hear all about their fly boys. But that's not why I called."

"I thought not. What can I do for you, my boy?"

"Dad, I've got a problem. It's not urgent right now but it might get sticky when the war is over."

"Richard, what have you done now? Knocked up another girl?"

"Shit no. I could take care of that by myself. I don't want to go into details on the phone. I can do that when I'm in Ottawa next month. But I'm going to need a good lawyer. You're the new Justice Minister. You must know some good ones. I want this kept quiet. No publicity hounds."

"It sounds pretty serious. Isn't there something I can do to head this off? Richard, your future looks so bright we can't risk a cloud over you."

"Maybe there's a couple of things you could do from your position that might discredit and weaken my opponent. I'll drop you a note tonight. Thanks Dad. Give my love to Mom. Bye."

"Richard, if this is serious maybe you need some protection. I'll get in touch with the R.C.M.P. and arrange for some security."

"No! No! Dad. The last thing I need is a guardian."

"Mmmm... the more I think about it the more I like the idea. A leak that there have been rumors of an attempt on your life requiring the Mounties to provide a guard will enhance your profile."

Thinking about it Richard had to admit his father was probably right. "Very well, Go ahead. Bye."

"Bye son. Come and see us soon. Your mother keeps asking when are you coming home."

"I will soon, bye."

* * *

Flying Officer Fox led his flight south. It had been a good "recce". All four planes dropped their bombs on the engine factory outside Milan and on the way home destroyed a train loaded with petrol. Diving down south of Leghorn Craig zoomed over the town of Cecina and rattled onto the new metal airstrip north of the town. The Intelligence Officer was waiting to debrief him. When he finished the Intelligence Officer motioned towards the C.O.'s trailer.

"He wants to see you."

Craig zipped up his heavy sheepskin jacket while easing himself down the slippery steps of the "I.O.'s" trailer. The weak December sun filtering through the broken clouds was not strong enough to melt last night's freezing rain. Craig skated across the tarmac finishing his glide with a clumsy pirouette in front of the C.O.'s trailer. He bowed to the airmen applauding nearby and knocked on the trailer door.

"Come in."

Craig was surprised to see the C.O. smiling at him. "That was quite a performance. You must have had a good flight."

"Yes sir. Even though the flak was heavy over the target all the bombs landed on the factory. Great sheets of flames and heavy black smoke. To top it off we caught a train before it could hide in a tunnel. It was loaded with petrol and some ammo. It was quite a sight... you wanted to see me, sir?"

"Yes... I..." Squadron Leader Sharp turned away. He fumbled in his breast pocket for a cigarette. He lit it and inhaled deeply, exhaling before continuing. "I'm sorry, I have some bad news for you. Your medal has not been approved. Headquarters approved it but the Canadian Government turned it down." The C.O. shrugged uncomfortably, "Why I don't know."

Craig glared at his Commanding Officer but clamped his mouth shut determined not to blurt out what he was thinking. Slowly he turned around and walked out without saluting. The moment the door closed behind Craig, Allan began another letter to Richard.

* * *

"Brian, what's going on?"

"Valerie, what are you talking about?"

"Look at all these clippings I've cut out of our paper." Valerie threw a wad of crumpled paper on her editor's desk. "What are you trying to do to Craig? All these innuendoes, hints, rumors... look at this... 'have been unable to confirm reason for turning down his medal, but unofficially have been told Flying Officer Fox may have exaggerated his role with the Partisans, and may even have jeopardized their activities to the point they made an urgent request that he be picked up and returned to his squadron'... Brian! For Heaven's sake! Those are absolute lies."

"Valerie, we get these reports from Ottawa and we have no reason to question what comes down the wire. Unless I know it is not true I just make sure it is in good English. I'm sorry, Valerie, I'm sure your brother is a fine young man but unless you can prove to me it is all lies I will continue to print this stuff. Although I'm inclined to agree with you that somebody is probably orchestrating a smear campaign against him. Somebody with influence in Ottawa."

"That somebody has to be Richard Bannerman. When I wrote Craig about these smears he warned me it could be him."

"Oh come on, Valerie... Richard Bannerman! That is not possible."

"Craig is out there risking his life every day for his country and what does he get, nothing but dirt thrown at him. It's disgusting."

"Valerie, I'm sorry, there is nothing I can do. I wish I could... Valerie, please, I must get on with the business of putting out a paper."

Valerie picked up the clippings one by one and flattened them into her notebook. Resting her clenched fists on the desk she leaned over, snapping. "I am not going to allow my brother to be ruined by you and your newspaper. I thought you were different. I guess you're just like the rest."

Brian watched her pick up the notebook and march out the door giving him a last contemptuous look before she closed the door behind her. It was not the first time he wished he had chosen a different career.

* * *

Constable Keith Calder was late. An accident at the intersection of Ninth Avenue and Fourth Street delayed him for fifteen minutes and he wasn't familiar enough with Calgary to risk taking a detour. Approaching the front of the Palliser Hotel he was relieved to see Squadron Leader

Bannerman was not waiting at the entrance. Keith parked the car in the taxi rank, ignoring the muttered glares of the drivers, and sprinted up the front steps into the lobby. The Squadron Leader was sitting near the dining room reading a paper. Constable Calder took off his hat and approached with some reluctance, unsure of his reception with the unpredictable and short tempered hero. Richard spotted the young Mountie crossing the lobby towards him. He flashed him a smile before folding the paper.

"Good morning, Keith. It looks like a beautiful morning out there. Is it cold?"

Relieved, Keith responded enthusiastically, "Yes sir, It's a crisp sunny morning. No wind. We had some snow last night and the streets are a bit icy, but..." Realizing he was babbling to cover his nervousness he stopped abruptly.

Richard dug into his breast pocket. "I'd better take my overcoat. Here's the slip. Go and fetch it from the cloakroom. I'll meet you at the front entrance. We're going to City Hall to meet the honorable gentlemen that run this hick town."

Richard watched the tall athletic figure stride down to the far end of the lobby. The Mountie was doing his best to ignore the admiring glances from the young ladies at the reception desk. His red uniform and red hair was the only splash of color in the gloomy mahogany paneled lobby. Richard had made it clear to the R.C.M.P. that if he was to be escorted the Mountie was to wear dress uniform

* * *

Constable Calder had been assigned to Richard in Regina. He had knocked on Squadron Leader Bannerman's hotel door at eight one morning. After a few minutes the door was wrenched open and he was confronted by a tall bare chested angry young man.

"What the hell do you want at this hour?"

Startled Keith stepped back and saluted. "Constable Calder reporting for duty. I was told to report to you, sir."

"You should have phoned before you came up. Now wait for me downstairs. The next time phone before you come up."

Before the door was slammed in his face the young Mountie caught a glimpse of long blond hair flowing out from under rumpled bedclothes on the bed behind the Squadron Leader. From then on he was careful to follow his instructions.

* * *

Keith Calder was born and raised in Regina. His father had taken his young Irish bride to Canada after he was released from the British

Army at the end of the First World War. Why Canada? In France Allan Calder was attached to the Princess Patricia Regiment as signalman and was seduced by stories of wide open spaces and unlimited opportunity in that huge country. For a young man with no skills, limited education, and a pregnant wife, Canada would enable him to provide a good home for his family. The reality turned out to be far different. From the moment they landed in Halifax until they reached Regina six years later it was a desperate search for any kind of menial employment, while his wife, Nancy, and the baby girl shivered in cold damp basement rooms. The little girl sniveled and coughed until she died of pneumonia at the age of three. A year later Keith was born; a carbon copy of his mother, red curly hair, clear almost translucent skin, green sparkling eyes, and a cheerful gurgling personality.

In Regina Allan Calder's luck turned for the first time in his life. He was hired by the telephone company that was busy stringing lines all over town. With his first paycheck he took Nancy to a dress shop on Main Street and insisted she buy a dress. With his second paycheck they went looking for a house to rent. With his third paycheck he bought himself a bicycle. Seven years later Allan Calder was killed falling off a telephone pole. A poorly maintained safety harness snapped and he landed on the sidewalk head first. The company denied any blame but paid for the funeral and gave Nancy six month's pay. To survive Nancy took in boarders. Keith delivered papers in the early morning and groceries after school. They were poor but more fortunate than the thousands of men riding the rails looking for work.

When he was twelve Keith decided he wanted to be a Mountie. On the Sundays he was able to slip away from weeding the vegetables in the back yard Keith rode across town on his father's bicycle to watch the young cadets training at the R.C.M.P. Academy. The day after Keith finished high school he pedaled to the Academy and joined the R.C.M.P. A month after his graduation parade he was told to report to Squadron Leader Richard Bannerman at the Saskatchewan Hotel. It was not an assignment he viewed with enthusiasm. He was hoping to get into intelligence work, instead he was told to coddle some puffed up war hero. Little did he know that the man he was to meet would dominate his life and propel him into positions of power he could not have accomplished on his own.

* * *

Squadron Leader Bannerman picked up his peaked cap from the table beside the chair and dropped the paper on the chair making sure his picture on the front page was prominently displayed, then strolled over to the reception desk. He chatted briefly with the two flustered girls leaning over the counter. With barely a moments hesitation they accepted his invitation for drinks in his suite that evening. Walking to the entrance he was about to push open the heavy door but the doorman spotted him through the frosted glass and held it open for him. Richard thanked him with a brief nod.

"It's very cold, sir. You'll need your coat."

"It's coming, thank you."

It was cold. It quickly penetrated his uniform, sending chills along his spine and up his legs. He stamped his legs for a few minutes, then with a muttered curse retreated inside. Constable Calder was hurrying towards him with Richard's heavy Air Force greatcoat draped over one arm.

"Where the hell have you been? I've been freezing my balls out there."

Taken aback by the unexpected attack Keith nearly dropped the coat he was handing to Richard. In a low embarrassed voice he tried to explain. "I'm sorry, sir, I had to take a leak."

"Well. Take a piss on your own time. Not when I'm freezing to death outside."

"Yes sir."

"Now, go and get the car."

Richard climbed into the back seat of the Oldsmobile before Keith could jump out to open the door. He ignored Keith during the drive to the gray stone City Hall. The Mayor dashed down the steps to the kerb before the car pulled up. This time the Squadron Leader waited for Constable Calder to open his door. Richard squeezed himself out of the back seat and shook hands with the Mayor before speaking to the Mountie.

"Officer Calder, come back in an hour. Make sure you have enough gas to take us to and from High River." Turning to the Mayor, "Your Worship, how far is High River? I'm supposed to have lunch there and give a talk to the cadets at the Flying Training School. Do you know where the school is?"

"Yes. I sure do. I was born in High River. The school is a couple of miles south west of the town. You can't miss it. High River is about forty miles south of here."

"Thank you. Did you get that, Calder?"

"Yes sir."

The Constable saluted smartly. The Squadron Leader returned the salute with a vague wave of his hand towards the visor of his cap. The Mayor waited until the crunch of tires on ice faded away before speaking.

"That is a fine young Mountie. It is young men like him and yourself, sir, that makes me so proud to be Canadian. You do great honor to our city. I can assure you that nobody in this lovely city would ever think of causing you any harm. You are perfectly safe here."

Irritated at the hint that he might be afraid Richard replied brusquely, "Your Worship, there is no threat to my life. It is the newspapers that are trying to spice up my tour now that it is becoming fairly routine."

"I'm glad to hear that. I can't imagine why anybody would wish to harm you. You have brought so much honor to this country. Come, the others are waiting for us upstairs."

Keith hovered over the boy filling the gas tank, making sure the metered amount of gas was going into the tank and not into some other container. He knew all the tricks attendants used to get around the rationing, having used some of them himself in his teens. He handed over the gas coupons and within the hour was back at City Hall standing beside the shiny black Oldsmobile. On the hour, Bannerman and the Mayor appeared at the front door of City Hall. The Squadron Leader extricated himself from the Mayor and walked rapidly down the steps. Constable Calder opened the rear door. He saluted smartly. Bannerman didn't bother to respond. Bending over to climb in the back seat he muttered, "let's get the hell out of here."

* * *

Driving south on the McLeod Trail, Keith checked the face in the rear view mirror whenever the traffic allowed. Richard's head was tipped back, eyes closed as if asleep. But the lips were moving silently mouthing the words of wisdom he would unveil to the cadets at the Flying School. Occasionally the head would nod appreciatively at a well turned phrase or smile at some joke. Keith was fascinated and had difficulty keeping his eyes on the road. He had witnessed these rehearsals on several occasions and looked forward to the subsequent performance. Each speech, delivered without notes, was carefully crafted for the audience; the ebb and flow of battles for business lunches; personal anecdotes for women's clubs; and stories of comradeship and bravery for the younger audience. Keith had heard the same stories a number of times, yet Richard could still tug at his emotions. The carefully orchestrated buildup of suspense, the pause just before the climax of some air battle while the audience, and Keith, held their breath, followed by the audible release of tension at the climax. Richard never flaunted his own heroism and rarely mentioned his exploits, and then only briefly. This disturbed Keith more and more, concerned that Richard was being too humble about himself. This tall handsome fighter pilot Ace should tell the audience what they came to hear. It wasn't as if his exploits were a secret. The papers across the country were serializing his victories one by one.

One evening, distracted and irritated by some women chattering next to him in the back of the lecture hall, Keith stood to ask a question.

"Sir!" Richard looked to the back of the hall. Recognizing the speaker he frowned. "Could you please tell us how you shot down your first German plane?"

Richard dismissed the question. "I'm sorry, sir, but I don't have time to go into that today, besides..." smiling at the audience. "I'm sure you are all tired of reading those stories in the papers."

A ripple of laughter flowed across the room. Mortified that he had once again incurred Richard's wrath Keith slumped in his chair, dejected and discouraged. He never seemed to be able to do or say the right thing to earn Richard's approval. Richard said nothing to Keith until they were back in his room in the hotel. Expecting a tongue lashing Keith was surprised and relieved when Richard calmly waved him to a chair.

"Keith. What you did this evening is totally wrong for several reasons. Each lecture I give has a beginning, middle, and end. You interrupted that sequence and I lost control of the audience. But, most important, everybody knows you are with me and would immediately assume I had arranged for you to ask the question. That would leave a very negative impression and I cannot have that... do you understand? Besides who do you think is writing the stories that are in the paper every day?"

"Ooh. I see, sir."

* * *

The pavement ended at the city limits. The gravel road south was icy with the occasional pothole. Keith drove cautiously weaving the car around the potholes to avoid disturbing Richard. Suddenly.

"For Christ sake Calder! I'm supposed to be there for lunch today not tomorrow. Pull over, I'll drive."

"Sorry, sir." Keith trod on the accelerator spinning the wheels. The car slewed sideways. Keith spun the steering wheel back and forth until he regained control. "You were working on your speech and I didn't want to distract you."

"I said, pull over! I'm driving."

"But, sir. The road is very icy and you have no experience driving on icy roads." The moment he spoke Keith wished he hadn't.

"Stop the fucking car! Right now!"

Keith slowed, moving over to the shoulder. Before he could stop the back door was flung open and Richard leapt out. Keith put the car in neutral and slid over to the passenger side. Richard jumped in slamming the door shut. He ground the gears into first then stomped on the accelerator. The car lurched sideways towards the ditch before the spinning wheels found some traction on a patch of gravel, sending the car lurching down the road. Keith braced his feet against the front fire wall, clutching the door handle in anticipation of the inevitable disaster. He saw it coming. A sharp curve to the left a half mile ahead.

"Sir, you're going too fast. You'll never make that curve."

"Shut up!"

They didn't. Half way around the curve the car began to slid sideways. Richard tried to steer into the curve; the car began to spin; he compounded the error by jamming on the brakes; the car spun around three times, heading towards the ditch on the outside of the curve. Richard gave a gleeful 'whoop', shouting.

"Hang on there, Keith. Just watch me ride this bugger."

Startled, Keith took his eyes off the looming ditch for a quick glance at Richard. The man's behavior kept pulling his eyes back. Richard sat forward on the seat with his left hand gripping the steering wheel, the right hand shifting gears, his feet smoothly working the pedals. But it was the face that fascinated Keith. It was alive! The cold inscrutable unemotional face was gone. It glowed. The eyes were electric, sparkling blue flashes, darting left and right mapping the surrounding hazards, or it suddenly dawned on Keith, watching for enemy aircraft. This is what he must be like when he is flying into combat, all his senses raised to their highest level, every muscle ready to respond instantly, the brain absorbing what the eyes revealed and analyzing the situation before issuing commands. Even though the car was diving into the ditch Keith's grip on the door handle relaxed, confident that Richard would lead them out of danger.

Richard steered the car into the ditch at the same time he geared down to second gear, then used the opposite bank to force the car along the bottom of the ditch. Slowly he applied pressure to the gas pedal, accelerating gradually without losing traction on the mixture of broken ice and gravel. Keith was about to warn him of the culvert ahead when Richard barked.

"Hang on! Here we go."

Richard forced the gas pedal to the floor turning the wheel at the same time. The back wheels churned through the ice into the gravel, ejecting the car back onto the road. It was now sliding towards the other ditch. Richard took his foot off the pedal and steered towards the slide using the engine to slow the car. The slide eased off and Richard headed down the road accelerating. He ignored the potholes but eased off on the curves. A mile from the entrance to the Flying School, which they identified from the Harvards taking off and landing, Richard stopped at the side of the road grinning at Keith.

"Well, Keith. That's restored my sizzle. Now let's go and wow them."

Richard patted Keith on the knee before moving to the back seat. Keith glanced in the rear view mirror, the face reflected there had reverted to its enigmatic expression.

Returning to Calgary late that afternoon Richard sat in the front seat, and for the first time shared some of his private thoughts and plans with Keith.

"On my twelfth birthday my father took me into his study and told me I would grow up to be the Prime Minister of Canada. From that moment I have dedicated my life to reaching that goal. Everything I do, my flying, my medals, these lectures, the newspaper articles, are steps towards that objective. I do not allow anything to deflect or obstruct my path. I demand a great deal from others, as you may have noticed, but I reward those who are loyal to me." Patting the constable's knee Richard continued, "Now I want to talk about you... I was told your father died when you were very young and your mother ran a boarding house."

"Yes sir. I delivered papers and groceries and worked at a service station."

Keith, from now on I'd like you to call me Richard when we're alone like this."

"Thank you, sir... Richard."

Offering his hand Richard continued. "I have been studying you over the last few weeks and am most impressed with your character and willingness to work hard. After the war men like yourself will be the builders of this great country."

Keith grabbed Richard's outstretched hand. "I would be honored to work for you, sir... Richard."

"Do you have a girlfriend?"

"Yes. In Regina. We went to high school together. We'd planned to get married whenever the force would allow... but I'm not so sure now."

Richard didn't bother to comment. Abruptly he ordered, "Tomorrow at eight. Don't be late again."

* * *

Craig was tired. So exhausted he rarely thought about Maria. During the winter thoughts of her had churned through his mind all day long, but now the daily struggle to keep flying and survive left little room to worry as to why she had not come to say goodbye. Over the winter months flying was canceled for days at a time. This allowed him to brood in his room, staring gloomily out at the streams of water drumming against the window. But now that the "Spring Offensive" was driving the Germans out of the "Gothic Line", their winter bastion in the northern Apennines, Craig would be roused by Paddy before dawn with foul tasting brown tea and greasy ham and eggs. Bleary eyed he would climb into his Spitfire, lead his patrol up and over the Apennines and down into the Po valley looking for trucks or trains. A few hours later he would be back in the air on a dive bombing mission with three bombs strapped to his wings and five planes following him down to strike at bridges or factories. Late in the afternoon he would be back in the Po valley for the third time. The constant flying and the stress from heavy flak had reduced him to a robot, numb to the mounting losses of young pilots, his sluggish brain capable only of concentrating on the mission, achieving the objective, avoiding flak, and bringing his pilots back alive. The pilot training schools had been shut down and the squadron was no longer receiving replacements for the pilots killed in action. Fewer and fewer pilots did more and more. In the evenings he was drinking too much, collapsing on his cot sometimes fully clothed too tired to make the effort to undress, unaware of Paddy taking off his flying boots before covering him with a blanket. Any stray thoughts of Maria quickly bogged down in the torpid recesses of his brain.

He had made one attempt to locate Maria. That was back in February. Flying had been canceled, and according to the weather forecast, flying was not likely to resume for several days. Some of the younger pilots were ordered to stand by, ready to scramble if the Germans took advantage of the weather for a sneak attack. The rest were given three days leave. Craig used the opportunity to look for Maria. He borrowed a jeep from the Officer's Mess and set off in the rain. According to the map he carried with him the distance from his airstrip at Cecina, a few miles south of Leghorn, to the village of San Casciano was only forty miles, but it took Craig most of the day, steering around muddy potholes, grinding through heavy mud, or waiting at the side of the road for long lines of military convoys to slosh by. Late in the afternoon he drove into the village square in San Casciano and pulled up in front of the taverna. Craig sat in the jeep shocked by the devastation around him. He knew there had been some heavy fighting in the area the previous August, but locked in his mind was the idyllic scene of Maria and himself sitting in a lovely piazza sipping wine and holding hands in the warm spring sunshine; children playing around the sparkling fountain; and the locals arguing amiably at the little tables outside the taverna. The tables were gone; the bush they had sat beside was now a stump barely visible above ground; the fountain was in pieces the victim of a grenade; several buildings on the other side of the piazza had been demolished; and tank tracks had chewed long gouges out of the ornate brick designs in the piazza. Except for a few bullet holes in the plaster walls of the taverna it was undamaged, testament to the importance soldiers on both sides attached to the liquor stocks inside. Light filtered through the partly open wooden door.

Craig pulled his raincoat tight around his neck and stepped out into the rain. Hunching over he made a dash for the door. A young girl looked up from the counter at the sound of the door squeaking open. It was the same girl that had served Maria and himself seven months before. She was washing the counter with slow listless movements. The rag was dirty. Two old men were sitting at a small table in one corner, staring down at the chipped glasses in their angular wrinkled hands. Craig took off his raincoat and cap, hung them on a peg near the door and approached the girl. She eyed him curiously but didn't recognize him.

"Bona sera, Signorina."

The girl nodded while her eyes checked the blue uniform. She was acquainted with the uniform of the British and American soldiers that occasionally stopped at the taverna. But this one was unfamiliar. She saw the wings on his jacket. He must be a British flyer. But what was he doing here? The blue eyes; where had she seen those before. The face looked vaguely familiar.

"Could I order a vermouth, please?"

She smiled, "Si Signor."

Craig greeted the old men who were now staring dully at this intrusion into their melancholy thoughts. He sat at a table next to them. Craig wasn't too hopeful they could provide him with much information but he had to start somewhere. The girl kept glancing at him while she half filled a small tumbler from the solitary bottle on the shelf behind her. She placed the tumbler on the table.

"I am sorry, but as you can see we are very short of vermouth just now. We were supposed to get some supplies this week but it has not come. We are not sure when it will come. We are not sure of anything anymore."

"Signorina, Do you remember me?"

"No, but you look familiar."

"Seven months ago, I sat out there with a young lady and you served us some of this excellent vermouth."

"But that is not possible, the Germans were still here."

"Yes, it was last July and the Germans were still here. I am a pilot and was shot down. I was living and working with the Partisans. I was sitting out there in civilian clothes with my girlfriend and some German Gestapo officers were sitting out there too. You came to warn us they were asking questions about us... do you remember?"

"Aah Si! Si! I remember."

Oh yes. How could she have forgotten the young man sitting out there with the beautiful girl. They were such a handsome couple. He with those warm blue eyes and that deep baritone voice that thanked her every time she served them. She had spied on them through the window wishing it was her that was sitting at the table holding hands with him. For days after they left she had to be reminded by her mother to stop her daydreaming and get on with her work. But he wasn't smiling now. He looked sad with little sparkle in the blue eyes that had so fascinated her before; there were dark circles under them; the pale face was almost colorless, thinner than she remembered. The skin was tight over the cheek bones and chin making him look older than she remembered.

"Signorina, I'm trying to find that young lady and I'm hoping you can help me."

"But, Signor. I had never seen her before you came... and she has not been back."

"Her name was Maria Castellone. When I was with the Partisans we lived in a house out in the country about two kilometers west of the village. Our leader was Antonio Vesco. There were ten in the group including the young lady."

One of the old men slowly straightened, raising his head to look at Craig. He became agitated pointing a gnarled finger at Craig.

"Signor! Signor! I remember. That house belongs to my cousin Leone. He was one of them. Stupid man. He could have been killed or lost everything if they had caught him." The old man began to laugh, a dull croaking rasp. "The house was destroyed in the fighting last winter so he lost everything anyway."

"What happened to the Partisans that were living there?"

"They left and went north when Rome was captured by the Americans. I saw them go. My cousin Leone went with them. He told me to look after the house but there is nothing to look after."

"Was there a girl with them when they left?"

"No, there was no girl."

"Are you sure there was no girl with them?"

The old man barely acknowledged the question with a feeble shake of his head. His interest had shifted back to the contents of the tumbler in front of him. The young girl hovered near Craig. After some minutes he looked up.

"Signorina, is there somewhere I can spend the night?"

"Oh yes, there is a room in the back that used to be for our waiter but we don't have one now. You can sleep in there."

"Grazie, Signorina. I will pay for it and a meal."

"Come, Signor, I will show you the room and prepare some food for you. I hope you like soup. That is all I can give you."

"I am sure it will be much better than the food I have been eating."

The next morning Craig drove along the familiar lane to what had been the 'safehouse.' There was not much left of the house that contained so many happy memories. The doors and windows were gone; the front and one side wall had collapsed exposing the bedroom on the main floor that Antonio had occupied and Maria's bedroom above. Strips of corrugated iron covered gaping holes in the roof. Homeless urchins had set up residence inside. Three boys were outside chopping up what was left of the furniture. They stopped chopping when he drove up, watching him warily as he got out of the jeep. An older boy approached Craig.

"Cigarettes?"

"No. No cigarettes."

The boy shrugged stuffing a thick wad of paper money back into the pocket of his shorts. The boys followed Craig around the house while he searched for anything that might reveal where the Partisans had gone. There was nothing. Driving back through the village he had a thought. He stopped in front of the taverna once more and went inside. The two old men were inside.

"Signor, did your cousin Leone tell you where they were going?"

The old man eyed Craig, suspiciously for a moment then shook his head. Craig pulled out a 1000 lira note. The old man reached for the note but Craig held it back.

"Your cousin told you. Didn't he?"

"He said I was not to tell anybody."

"I am a friend of the Partisans. I only want to find the girl. We are going to be married after the war."

Craig put the note on the table and added another one.

"My cousin Leone said they were going to some village north of Bologna." The old man snatched the money from the table, "but he would not give me the name of the village... that's all I know, Signor."

Craig studied the man's face for a few moments before resigning himself to the fact that he had reached a dead end. Bologna was behind the German lines and there was nothing more he could do until the Germans were driven out of that area. He said good bye to the young girl and took the melancholy road back to the base at Cecina.

* * *

On May 8, 1945, Germany surrendered. A month later Craig set out once again to find Maria. This time he made rapid progress thanks to the

German prisoners working on the roads and bridges. After a brief stop for lunch in Florence he was climbing the western slopes of the Apennines by early afternoon and would have reached Bologna by late afternoon except for a two hour delay at a bridge crossing over a deep ravine. When Craig approached the bridge a young German Officer standing in front of a barricade flung his right hand up in what to Craig looked very much like a Nazi salute.

"Halt!"

Craig stopped the jeep a few feet in front of the Officer. He leaned out and asked in German, "Can I drive across?"

The Officer marched up, clicked his heels and saluted. He didn't smile. He spoke rapidly before clamping his mouth shut, "This bridge is closed until it is fixed."

"How long before it is fixed?"

"Three hours."

"Is there a detour?"

"Nein!"

The Officer saluted, turned on his heel and marched back to where a squad of soldiers were repairing a large hole in the middle of the bridge. A bomb crater probably. Craig got out of the jeep. He watched the men working for a few minutes while sorting back through his memory trying to recall if he had bombed this bridge. The German uniforms began to trouble him. The soldiers eyed him curiously from time to time but were not menacing. One or two even smiled at him, yet he was becoming increasingly disturbed watching them. Suddenly he realized why. Abruptly he walked back up the road past the jeep. He sat on a rock looking out over the ravine away from the soldiers, a small harmonica clutched in his right hand.

"You may now cross the bridge."

Startled, Craig looked up at the Officer clicking his heels beside him, "That was quick."

"We are Germans. Not Italians. My men wanted to make sure you could pass before it got dark."

"Dunker Shun."

Craig started up the jeep and drove onto the bridge. The soldiers lined up on both sides saluting as he passed. Craig stopped the jeep at the far end of the bridge and climbed out to return their salute.

"Thank you very much. I hope we can all go home very soon."

A dozen hands clasped overhead to a chorus of "Ya Ya Ya" before a bark from the Officer brought them to attention. Craig drove down the road, his faith in human nature restored. Tomorrow he would see Maria again. He began to whistle the few bars of "Lilli Marlene" he knew. He couldn't remember the last time he felt happy enough to whistle.

A large sign on the main street in Bologna directed Allied personnel arriving in the city to report to the Allied Occupation Headquarters. A grizzled old Major was just leaving the headquarters as Craig drove up.

"Sir, where can I find a room for the night?"

"My boy, you won't find a bed anywhere. The place is flooded with refugees from all the bombed out villages that you chaps destroyed, which we in the Royal Engineers are now trying to repair. Come. Maybe my batman can find a room for you in our Mess."

"Sir, Have you come across any Partisans in the area?"

"Hummph! Bunch of bloody Communists. They started all kinds of trouble here. Rallies and parades. Trying to take over the city. I soon put a stop to that. Chased them out of the city and warned them I would arrest any communist who dared to show his face. On the surface things are peaceful but I know they're here stirring up the young ex-soldiers."

"Are they active in the towns nearby?"

"Oh yes! Are they ever. Particularly in San Giovanni north of here."

That night Craig checked the map he had brought with him. It was the same one he had used on operations; now wrinkled, torn, and splattered with oil, but still legible. San Giovanni lay twenty five kilometers to the northwest. Maria was only twenty five kilometers away from him. That night there were no nightmares. Maria came to him in the night, took his hand and led him back to their piazza, now miraculously restored. Craig was about to embrace Maria...

"Sir. Wake up! You asked me to wake you at seven. Here's your tea."

Craig eyed the gray sludge with disgust but forced himself to drink it. After breakfast he drove the Major back to his headquarters, requested a chit for petrol for the jeep, thanked the Major, and headed north after refueling.

San Giovanni was untouched by the war. The British Eighth Army had broken through and overrun San Giovanni before the Germans could organize any defenses. Approaching the center of town Craig could hear the hum and roar of a crowd. The entrance to the piazza was blocked off and beyond the barrier Craig could see a mass of arm waving men and women. A grim young man with a red bandanna around his neck waved him back. Craig parked the jeep and approached to get a better look. On the far side of the piazza a speaker was hurling invective at the capitalists from a truck festooned with red hammer and sickle flags. Craig tried to get closer but the young man pushed him back.

"You cannot go through, Englishman. You are not welcome here. Leave now."

Several faces turned to see what the altercation was about. A young man left the crowd and came forward peering at Craig from under a peaked cap. As soon as he lifted his cap revealing his long stringy hair Craig recognized the pale face, the long thin nose, and the prominent chin. It was Giovanni. Enveloping Craig in a hug he exclaimed.

"Craig! My friend. It is good to see you have survived the war." Turning to the puzzled young Italian beside him Giovanni motioned him away saying, "It's all right, he is an old friend."

"Giovanni. I didn't expect to see you here. You said you were sick of the communists and were going home to help your mother?"

Giovanni shrugged, smiling sheepishly. "I know," leaning forward he whispered, "but I am going soon."

Craig tilted his head towards the speaker ranting at the crowd. "That man up there, is that Antonio?"

"Si, that's him. He's now a very important man in the Communist Party."

"I thought it would be him."

"But don't let him see you. He has vowed to kill you."

"Why?"

"Because of Maria."

"Where is Maria?"

"Oh my friend. You do not know... Craig, Maria is dead."

Craig blanched slumping back against a wall. "No! No! Maria is not dead... please, Giovanni, do not say that."

"I'm so sorry, my friend, but it is true."

Head clutched between his palms Craig asked in a low choked voice, "What happened to my lovely Maria."

Giovanni put his arm around Craig's shoulder. He helped ease him into the jeep. "Craig, we must leave here before Antonio hears you are here. I will tell you about Maria but we must leave. Antonio is now very powerful and no longer afraid of the British. He would not hesitate to kill you. Come, let's go."

Trying to back down the narrow street Craig scraped the jeep against the buildings on each side. He found a place to turn around but dented the rear fender. "Giovanni, please. You drive."

Craig eased himself over and slumped in the passenger seat oblivious to the grinding of gears as Giovanni searched through the gearbox. Giovanni drove to his lodgings in an old house on the outskirts of the town. He hid the jeep behind the house and guided Craig down some wooden steps to a small room in the basement. Craig sagged into a chair by the door, took off his cap and looked around vaguely for a place to put it. Giovanni took it from him placing it on a chest by the bed. Craig leaned his head on clenched fists, eyes closed.

"Giovanni, please tell me what happened to Maria."

Giovanni fiddled around the room for a few moments trying to decide how he should deliver the sad news to the distraught young man. He sat on the bed facing Craig.

"Remember the night you flew away, Antonio sent Maria to Florence... Craig, she never returned. She didn't come back to say goodbye to you. She didn't come back the next night... Craig, Maria never came back. A week later we heard she had been captured by the Gestapo in San Casciano before she could board the bus for Florence. The Gestapo Chief had recognized her."

"The fat one?"

"Yes, the fat one."

"Oh God! Oh my God, I killed her!" Shaking his head from side to side, chest heaving Craig gasped for air. "I killed her, I killed her. I shouldn't have taken her to the Piazza. Oh Maria! What have I done to you... oh my love."

Craig leaned forward, sobs wrenching his chest. Giovanni, embarrassed and unsure how he should respond to the young man's grief, got up and went over to the window. Minutes passed before Craig was able to lean back. Wearily he murmured.

"Go on."

Giovanni returned. He didn't sit, instead he stood beside Craig with one hand on his shoulder. Reluctantly he continued, "A few days later the priest found her huddled in the church. We had left to go north but Father Guiseppe got in touch with us and I came back for her... but she was too sick to travel. She died from pneumonia the next day. She is buried in the cemetery."

"Was she tortured?"

Giovanni nodded.

"What did they do to her?"

"I will not tell you any more... before she died she whispered to me, 'I know Craig will come looking for me. Do not tell him I was tortured. Just say I got sick. Tell him I love him. Give him this from me.' She took a silver ring from her finger and handed it to me. I have it here in a drawer."

Giovanni got up and rummaged in the top drawer of a chest. He handed the ring to Craig then turned his back unable to watch his friend's grief. Craig placed the ring against his wet cheeks murmuring to himself. "Maria, Maria." He leaned forward and cupped his face in his hands with the ring against his cheek. He closed his eyes to imprint the image of Maria so he would always remember her. After a few minutes Craig lifted his head.

"Giovanni, may I stay with you tonight? Tomorrow I would like to speak to Antonio."

"No! No! No! You must not do that. He will kill you. I know he will. He has killed others. He has become very ruthless since Maria's death. He loved her and blames you for her death. Please Craig, go back. You cannot stay. You must not stay. He will kill me if he finds out I helped you..." Abruptly Giovanni sat down. "Oh Mama Mia! That young man will tell him you came and I took you away. He will know I helped you." Giovanni leapt up and paced around the room running his hands through his long stringy hair. Speaking rapidly with hands pointing at himself Giovanni sputtered.

"He will kill me. I must leave now. Soon he will be looking for us and he knows where I live."

"Giovanni, I can give you a ride to Bologna. Come with me. There is nothing here for you. You're not a communist. Go home to your mother. In Bologna you can catch a train for Venice. Come let's go."

Giovanni nodded. He pulled an old cardboard suitcase from under the bed. Laying it on the bed he threw in the contents of the dresser, a suit hanging in the closet, and a pair of shoes. He pulled out his wallet and showed it to Craig. It was empty.

"Craig, Will you lend me some money? See, I have no money. The Party pays once a month and that won't be until next week. I have to leave some money for the rent and I will need some to get home."

Craig took out his wallet and pulled out all the bills. Folding them he offered them to Giovanni. "Please accept this as a gift to repay you for all your kindnesses."

"No, No, I'll repay you when I get home. Give me your home address and I'll send the money."

"Please take it. I can get more in Bologna."

Giovanni counted the money. "I owe you 12500 Lira."

He picked up his suitcase and followed Craig out the door. At the top of the wooden steps he motioned Craig to wait while he went out into the street. Satisfied it was empty Giovanni signaled Craig to bring out the jeep. They followed the back streets avoiding the center of town until they reached the road leading to Bologna. An hour later Craig pulled up in front of the railway station in Bologna, parked the jeep and walked around to help Giovanni retrieve his suitcase from the back of the jeep.

"Giovanni, do you remember the pilot that tried to kill me?"

"Si, si, I remember."

"I will be going home soon. When I do I will try to send that man to prison. He is an evil man. You and Antonio are my only witnesses. From what you say I know Antonio will not help me, but will you?"

"Craig, I will help you, but I do not have the money to go to Canada."

"I will look after that. I will be in touch with you when I need you."

"Don't forget. My mother's bakery is in Udine. It's called 'La Venetzia'. I will be there."

They hugged, patting each other on the shoulder. Craig climbed back into the jeep and waited until Giovanni disappeared through the ornate entrance to the station before going to the Allied Commission Headquarters. The sentry at the door directed him to the Major's office. The Major looked up from a cluttered desk when Craig entered the room. Smiling he waved Craig to a chair in front of him, pushing aside two heaps of files to get a better view of the young pilot.

"Well, my boy. Did you find your lady love?"

Craig leaned forward, putting his head down to hide the sudden gush of tears. Shaking his head he murmured, "She is dead."

The Major eyed him silently, unaccustomed to giving words of sympathy. When Craig recovered he asked.

"Do you want to talk about it?"

"She was captured and tortured by the Gestapo. She was so badly tortured she got pneumonia and died. She is buried in San Casciano. I must find her grave."

"San Casciano... Um... Ummh... Major Schiller again."

"Is he fat?"

"That's him! We've been looking for him, but he disappeared before we could catch him. We have been compiling a list of his crimes. It is now a very long list and growing daily. He terrorized most of northern Italy."

"I saw him torture and kill an old couple. I hope to God you find him."

"Good! Now, I want you to go into the next room and put down all you know about him. Is there anything else I can do for you, my boy."

"Yes please, I need some money."

The Major nodded and pressed a bell. A sergeant opened a side door.

"Flying Officer Fox has information on Major Schiller which he will write down for us. Give him pen and paper and 10,000 Lira." The Major stood up and shook Craig's hand. "Good bye and good luck."

Two hours later Craig was on the road to Florence. He drove all night, reaching San Casciano just as the farmers were leaving the village to work their plots of land. Craig stopped an old man pulling a cart to ask directions to the cemetery. It was a small cemetery, nevertheless it took him half an hour to find Maria's grave. Searching through the long grass in the far corner of the cemetery he stepped on a small wooden cross. Picking it up Craig was barely able to decipher the name, Maria Castellone. Craig pressed the weathered cross to his chest, tears streaming down his cheeks. Carefully he sat in the long grass to one side of the slight mound.

"Maria... Maria... I have thought of you day and night ever since we parted. I love you so much. I had a beautiful speech memorized to tell you how much I love you and to ask you to marry me. Now I find I am responsible for your death. I shall carry that terrible burden until I die. I cannot ask you to forgive me but I promise you, Maria, I shall always love you."

Returning from his morning rounds Father Guiseppe stopped before the rusty iron gate of the cemetery. Every day he struggled up the hill to offer a brief prayer for the souls of his villagers now resting in peace. Every year it was becoming more and more difficult to get up the hill but he knew he would come even if he had to crawl up on his hands and knees. It was his way of serving God. He took off his broad brimmed hat and wiped his bald head and wrinkled jowls with a dirty rag. Preparing to kneel a distant blur of blue caught his eye. He wiped his watery eyes with the rag and peered through the iron gate. Shaking his head he reached into his black robe and brought out a pair of chipped glasses held together by wire. The blur became a young man in a blue uniform kneeling at the far end of the cemetery. Father Guiseppe approached quietly. It was a British Officer. He was pulling weeds from a grave. Father Guiseppe knew the name of every soul in his cemetery.

"Sir, that is the grave of a beautiful Signorina. She was tortured by the Gestapo."

Startled out of his deep grief Craig stood to face the elderly priest. "Yes, Father. I came to ask her to marry me and I find her here."

"My son, you must be the British pilot she said she loved. It was a terrible thing they did to her. I am so sorry for both of you."

"Father, I have to go back to my squadron but I want her to have a marble headstone not this wooden cross... I will pay for it... could you please buy one for me with her name on it and the dates. She was born on July nineteenth, 1924... when did she die?"

"I remember it very well. It was on July thirtieth, the day before my birthday."

"Also put my initials at the bottom. It is CPF." Craig held up the silver ring. "Father, this is her ring, could you put it under the headstone?"

"It will be done, my son."

"Thank you, Father... I will make a donation to the church to make sure her grave is looked after and I will send money every July for flowers to be put on her grave."

Craig opened his wallet and placed all his money in the outstretched hands. The priest folded the money and put it in his robe. The priest's eyes followed the young man walking down the gravel path to the road, head down, shoulders slumped, with one hand clutching a wet handkerchief. He waited until he heard the jeep drive off. Kneeling beside the grave Father Guiseppe prayed for the souls of the two lovers.

- 6 -

Late one afternoon Webster Madison's secretary alerted him that Brian Shirley-Dale was on the line. He hadn't heard from the editor of the Toronto Star in over a year. Usually when he called Brian was looking for free legal advice, which Webster provided with some friendly ribbing about those lunches that were promised but rarely materialized.

"Webster, I know you are a busy man but can you spare a few minutes of your time to listen to a young man who needs help? You're well known for your practice of defending the underdog. This young man claims that a very famous and important person has been trying to kill him for many years but no lawyer will listen to him. I find his story hard to believe, however there seems to be a very well organized campaign emanating out of Ottawa to discredit and dishonor the young man. If what he's saying are lies why would somebody in Ottawa be so determined to destroy his credibility? Webster, would you speak to him then make up your own mind?"

"Brian, I'm sorry. I'm really much too busy just now to take on anything else."

"Webster, I know you're very busy. His sister is one of my better reporters and I would like to do this for her... please. Just listen to him for a few minutes. You're so good at separating the wheat from the chaff, if I may use that worn cliché on you, and would know immediately if he is lying."

"I suspect the young lady is more than just a reporter to you."

"Oh No! No! It's just that she's a very good reporter, besides she's young enough to be my daughter."

"Okay I'll see him, but you won't hold it against me, old friend, if I decide not to represent him. However you've sent me some interesting cases in the past, maybe this will turn out to be another one."

"If what he says is true I have no doubt you'll take it... thanks Webster. I'll have Valerie send you all the clippings she has collected to give you the negative side of his story. His name is Craig Fox. I'll have him call your secretary to set up an appointment."

"Aah... I seem to recall reading about him."

"All very disparaging. Thanks, Webster. We must have lunch soon. I'll give you a call next week."

"I think I've heard you say that before. Bye, bye."

When Craig entered the lawyer's office he was surprised to see Webster Madison sitting in a wheelchair behind his desk. Noticing Craig's hesitation, Webster said, "didn't Brian tell you I'm paralyzed from the waist down?"

"No sir."

"The sly old bugger." Pointing to a heavy leather couch at the far end of the room he invited Craig to sit. "Would you like some coffee?"

"Yes please."

The lawyer backed his thick torso away from his desk and propelled the wheel chair effortlessly across the room. The powerful shoulders and arms guided the chair smoothly around the furniture to a small table in the corner of the room. He lifted a metal coffee pot from a hot plate and sniffed the spout. "Hope you like strong coffee?"

"Yes sir, I do."

Craig retrieved the two mugs the lawyer waved in front of him, placing them on the low table in front of the couch. The lawyer wheeled over to a bookcase returning with a file which he placed on the low table.

"Craig, these clippings are all I have in your file. Before the day is over I hope the file will include some of my own notes. However before we start I want to take a few minutes for us to get to know each other. If these clippings are to be believed you're a pretty nasty fellow." Craig leaned forward to protest but Webster waved him back. "I'll let you tell your side of your story in a minute. I don't know what my friend Brian may have told you about me, but as he didn't tell you I have a disability, I suspect he preferred that you make your own judgment."

"He said you are a very busy man and that I have only a half hour of your time."

"We-e-ll. I start my day at six in the morning and by three I'm generally finished. I have set aside the rest of the afternoon for you. So relax young man."

"Mr. Madison, I appreciate your taking the time to listen to my story. I have contacted other lawyers. They either put down the phone as soon as I give my name or throw me out of their office the moment I mention Richard Bannerman."

"Craig, when I was a young man like yourself I was looking forward to a career as a professional hockey player," smiling, "I would have been a good one too but I was slammed into the boards and received a spinal cord injury. I was devastated. For a long time I was bitter and sorry for myself. Eventually my father read the riot act, talked me into going to law school and here I am twenty years later. I don't know whether Brian told you that because of my disability I have more sympathy for the losers, the underdogs, in this world. This is why Brian sent you to me. He said you were fighting a losing battle against the powerful. So, drink your coffee and tell me about yourself. I understand you were a fighter pilot during the war?"

"Yes, I was, and a fairly good one too. Not the idiot Bannerman makes me out to be."

"What are you doing now?"

"I'm in my second year working towards a degree in geology. My father was a mining engineer and I would like to follow in his footsteps. I admired him very much."

"You said he was a mining engineer. I gather he is no longer alive?"

Craig was impressed. He nodded, "My father and mother were killed in Colombia several years ago. The car my father was driving went over a cliff under very suspicious circumstances. I know who did it."

"Was Richard Bannerman involved?"

"No, for once he wasn't the perpetrator."

"You have proof it was no accident?"

"No, but my father was an excellent driver and he had been over that road many times. Witnesses said the car swerved suddenly and went over a cliff."

"A reasonable conclusion but in our profession we require proof. Craig, please keep that in mind as you try to justify your charge of attempted murder against Richard Bannerman... now, tell me your story."

For the next two hours, Craig did, in detail. Beginning with the seduction of a servant girl in Colombia by Richard Bannerman; the murder of the pregnant girl by Richard's hired assassin, Florentino Chavez; Richard's contract with Florentino for Craig's assassination; Craig's capture by the father of the assassin, a notorious bandit; the killing of the bandit by Craig's father; and Craig's rescue from the bandits. While he spoke Craig studied the lawyer, trying to assess the lawyer's reaction to his story. The moment Craig mentioned the murder of the servant girl the lawyer picked up a clip board from the table and laid it over the gray pinstripe trousers covering the remains of his legs. He began making notes on the foolscap pad clipped to the board. His thick callused hands were wrapped around the pencil so firmly Craig expected the pencil to snap each time he scratched a note on the pad. Whenever Craig's extraordinary experiences bordered on the unbelievable, the lawyer sat back fixing him with a stare as if trying to penetrate Craig's head to determine the truth of what he was saying. From time to time he would raise his hand signaling Craig to stop. At these pauses he would lean back, push his black horn rimmed glasses up to the bridge of his nose with the index finger of his left hand, and fix his eyes on the ceiling, while running his left hand backwards through his hair. In spite of the absent minded stroking the black hair remained undisturbed, flowing straight back off the prominent forehead. He wore a gold ring on his left hand. Noticing Craig's glance shifting from his hand towards a family picture behind his desk Webster smiled.

"Yes, I do have a family. It's only my legs that are crippled." Noting Craig's embarrassment he changed the subject. "Craig, it's not clear to me why Bannerman wanted you killed by this young assassin."

"Primarily because I overheard them talking about the murder of the girl. You really have to know Richard to understand why he is capable of murder. He is a very clever manipulator of people and very ruthless. He is talented and very ambitious. I think Richard probably would like to be Prime Minister of Canada. He will try to destroy anything that jeopardizes that possibility. I was, and am a threat to his reputation. Also, he is a sexual predator and not very discriminating."

"What do you mean?"

"The assassin, Tino, told me he used to be a male prostitute and Richard was one of his clients. When I first went to the boarding school in Bogota Richard got drunk one night and tried to get into my bed. I repulsed him and ever since he has been trying to discredit me."

"This Indian girl, the sister of the assassin. You said her name was Teresa. Would she be prepared to testify that her brother had been contracted by Bannerman to kill you?"

"No, she adored him."

"So why would she have told you about her brother's contract?"

"We were good friends."

"You mean you were lovers." Craig nodded. "Craig, you must be frank with me, otherwise you might as well leave."

"I'm sorry. It won't happen again."

"The young assassin, Tino, is he the one you believe responsible for your parent's death?"

"Yes. There is a very strong tradition in Colombia with respect to family honor. My father killed his father the bandit. He had to avenge that."

"I see. Continue."

During another pause, while Webster stared at the ceiling, Craig allowed his eyes to stray around the room. It was tidy, very tidy. The large oak desk was neatly arranged; two wooden trays, each containing one file, were located precisely at each corner, a pen stand was exactly half way between the trays, with six pencils neatly arranged in front of the pen stand. Large books were in the middle row of the bookcase, the small ones in the top row. The bottom row contained files separated by name tags, which Craig had no doubt, would be in alphabetical order. Before the pause, Craig had been describing Richard's many attempts to have him killed by the Germans while on fighter patrol In Italy.

"Are you trying to tell me your Commanding Officer, Squadron Leader...?"

"Squadron Leader Sharp."

"Squadron Leader Sharp was aware of all these attempts to kill you and he did nothing?"

"He would get furious and threaten to have me court martialled every time I complained. He was very proud of his squadron and didn't want anything to mar its reputation. It was the best squadron in Desert Air Force. But it was more than that, he seemed to be intimidated by Bannerman. The best pilots went to Bannerman's flight. The newest and best planes were in Bannerman's flight, and the best mechanics were there too."

"According to these clippings you were not a good pilot. So why were you in his flight, if that assertion is correct?"

"He wanted me in his flight as his wingman so he could maneuver me into dangerous situations. Richard is a brave man. He believed he was the best pilot in the world with a charmed life. He was prepared to take enormous risks, supremely confident he would survive. I may have been a mediocre pilot to begin with but as I became more experienced I developed into an above average pilot. Not exceptional like Bannerman, but better than most. I did shoot down four planes in combat, and by the end of the war the C.O. had promoted me to Flight Lieutenant."

"Did you get any medals?"

"No. The C.O. recommended me for one but it was turned down by Ottawa. I don't have to guess who was responsible."

"What was the medal for?"

"For my work with the Partisans."

Picking up and waving the newspaper clippings in front of Craig the lawyer said, "but these tell me you were a disaster behind the lines."

"Lies! Everybody, including the C.O., thought I deserved a medal for my work with the Partisans until the negative campaign began in Ottawa."

"Where is Squadron Leader Sharp now?"

"I don't know. He talked about coming to Canada. He may be here by now."

"Do you think he would confirm what you are saying?"

"I doubt it. He would probably support Richard. In any case his recommendation must be on file somewhere."

"Good. Continue."

A few minutes later the hand came up again. "Stop! Stop! Go over that again. Slowly, while I make notes."

"There were four of us on this early morning patrol looking for a German armored column. It was reported to be heading south to attack the Anzio beachhead and drive the British and Americans back into the sea. Richard broke up the flight, sending the other two south towards Rome while he and I went north. Richard kept leading me, at low level, across Ack-ack nests. He would be safely beyond them by the time they were ready to shoot and I would be the one to get their full attention. Finally, when he tried to drag me through a very heavy concentration of guns, I broke away but was too late. I got hit and the motor caught fire. Richard tried to shoot me down but I eluded him. My motor died. I crashed into some trees behind the lines. Richard attacked the burning plane with cannon and machine guns, but anticipating his attack, I scrambled out of the plane and hid in the forest. He was convinced he had killed me and reported I had been killed. He didn't know I had survived until my sister, Valerie, told him. She was shocked at his reaction."

"If what you say is true and can be proved he will go to prison."

"I have proof. There were two witnesses to the attack."

"Good. Tell me about them."

Craig leaned forward. Staring down at his tightly clenched hands he hesitated before he replied. "It is very painful for me to talk about this. The two witnesses were Partisans. They took me back to their camp, an isolated farm house. It was attacked the next day by the Gestapo. The Partisans fled leaving an old farmer and his wife behind. I hid in the forest. I saw the Gestapo torturing the old man. Unfortunately I was discovered by a young soldier... I... I hit him with a big ax handle. I was so overwrought by the torture I had witnessed that I hit the boy too hard... I killed him... I regret what I did. He must have been a musician. A little harmonica fell out of his pocket... I kept it." Craig reached into his breast pocket and pulled out a small harmonica about three inches long. The cheap tin cover was scratched in several places. Craig put it back in his pocket. "Every once in a while I pull it out to remind myself I should control my emotions better." Looking up at Webster, Craig continued, "lately I am having more and more difficulty doing that."

It was at that moment that Webster made up his mind. He would take the case. He had been moving in that direction reluctantly, very much aware there was little hard evidence to support Craig's allegations.

But there was no artifice to this young man. He was transparent. It was impossible for him to be devious. His face and mannerisms would betray him immediately.

"Go on."

Craig stood and walked over to the window, facing away from Webster. The lawyer waited for Craig to regain control of his emotions. Looking out the window Craig cleared his throat before continuing.

"I'm sorry, this is difficult... one of the Partisans was a girl... she and I fell in love. We were to marry after the war... after I returned to the Squadron she was captured and tortured by the Gestapo... she died of her injuries."

Webster waited until Craig returned to the couch. "What about the two witnesses, will they be prepared to testify?"

"One has agreed to testify. I have not asked the other one because I know he wouldn't. In fact he has vowed to kill me."

"Oh! Why?"

"He was the leader of the Partisans, and he too was in love with Maria. He was very jealous. He concocted all those negative reports about me and arranged to have the R.A.F. send a plane to pick me up from behind the German lines."

"But why has he vowed to kill you?"

"He blames me for Maria's death... I blame myself also. I thought it was safe for us to spend an afternoon together in the village. He warned me not to go but by then my Italian was very fluent and I could pass for an Italian, so we went... the Gestapo drove into the village and sat at few tables across from us. They became suspicious. Two days later they saw her getting on a bus and captured her... she refused to betray me. She contracted pneumonia because of the torture and died... I didn't find out until after the war that she had been captured and tortured."

"What are the names of these two witnesses, and where are they now?"

Craig ran his hands slowly down the length of his thighs straightening the creases in his trousers. He raised his eyes and focused on the face in front of him. Even though he was reassured by the smile and warmth in the eyes, Craig hesitated.

"Mr. Madison, the only hard evidence I have against Bannerman are these two witnesses. If he finds out who they are he will have them killed. You can be sure of that. I have not revealed their names to anybody, not even to my sister Valerie."

"Craig, the testimony of these two men is crucial. Without their testimony you have no case. You are very wise to be cautious, but if I am to take your case I must know who they are, and arrange for a lawyer in Italy to write down their evidence."

Craig's face lit up. "Did you say you will represent me?"

"Yes, I will. Provided you can give me a satisfactory explanation of your motive for pursuing this case. Is it a personal vendetta? Are you concerned that he will kill you unless you can put him away? Or is there some other reason you haven't told me about?"

"There are several good reasons but the two most important grounds for sending this man to prison are justice, and I hesitate to say this, patriotism. I know that sounds corny but I love this country. In addition to trying to kill me, there were stories among the airmen on the Squadron about talented pilots disappearing while on patrol with Richard. Knowing what he tried to do to me I have no doubt Richard was responsible for some of the deaths. He did not tolerate competition. He should pay for those murders. Richard is ambitious and ruthless. I hate to think what he might do if he becomes too powerful."

"We will see what we can do, but you must realize it is going to be a long hard battle and very expensive. My fees will be nominal, however there will be many other costs involved. We will be up against powerful and wealthy opponents who will spend whatever is necessary to defeat us."

"My father left me some money. It is not a great deal but I'm willing to spend it if we can stop this dangerous man."

"We'll try to keep our costs down. At least at the beginning... first," Webster wrote the word on his pad and underlined it. "I have to get in touch with the R.C.M.P. to prepare a charge against Richard Bannerman... second," The word was also underlined. "I'll contact a lawyer in Italy, Rome probably, and have him get a statement from your witnesses."

"Antonio Vesco was the Partisan leader. He is now the Communist Mayor of a town north of Bologna called San Giovanni. He's the one that has vowed to kill me. You won't get any help from him."

"We'll have to try. We need all the evidence we can get."

"The other man is Giovanni Bellini. He lives in Udine, a town near Venice. I looked it up on a map. It's sixty miles northeast of Venice near the Yugoslav border. He and his mother own a bakery in the town. It's called "La Venetzia". I don't have the exact address but according to Giovanni the bakery is well known in the town."

Craig studied the lawyer's face while Webster wrote down the names. The thin eyebrows curved downwards in concentration; the pale, almost translucent cheeks, were pushed forward, puckering his lips as he scrawled the names on the page. If anybody could win against Richard surely this man could. He was methodical, and as was evident in the room, well organized; astute and intelligent. But did he fully understand what he was getting into?

"Mr. Madison, I hope you don't consider me too impertinent, but I must warn you that by taking this case you will be exposing yourself to all the negative mud that Bannerman will throw at you."

"Craig, I crossed that bridge before you entered this room."

Nevertheless Webster Madison didn't have to wait very long before he was forced to realize the mud would be much slimier than he had anticipated. Webster Madison was incensed at the newspapers for painting him as a sleazy lawyer grubbing after publicity. For over twenty years he had been careful to base his practice on the merits of a case rather than its publicity value. Among his peers he was respected for his honesty, his sensitivity, and his willingness to handle cases shunned by his more mercenary colleagues. Craig Fox became his client because Webster believed Craig was right to charge Richard Bannerman with murder. Not because Bannerman was a famous war hero and convicting him would enhance Webster's legal practice.

A week later he received a call from the Toronto Star editor. "Webster, I see you have taken on young Craig Fox's case."

"How did you find that out? Brian, that is supposed to be confidential."

"I've just received a little gem about you from Ottawa. There wouldn't be any reason for them to put you on their shit list unless you were representing him. I'll send you over a copy but don't name me as the source... Okay?"

"Sure, but tell me, Brian, why is this stuff coming from Ottawa? Richard Bannerman lives here in Toronto."

"Yes, but his father is in Ottawa. He's probably the one responsible. He's a Senator now. You may remember James Bannerman was Justice Minister in the last Parliament but lost his seat in the election. He really messed up in that Department."

"I know, I was involved in getting him moved out of that Portfolio."

"We-e-ll, you can bet your bottom dollar he hasn't forgotten the names of those responsible. By having this stuff come out of Ottawa, it makes it look official and keeps Richard out of it."

"Thanks, Brian. When are we going to have that lunch?"

"I'll give you a call next week. Bye."

* * *

The phone rang. Richard cursed. A most inopportune time. He rolled out of bed and staggered to his feet. 'Damn! I've had too much to drink again.' He picked up the dressing gown he had thrown on the floor only minutes before. He had trouble putting his arms through the sleeves. Richard leaned over to pat the smooth round buttocks before pulling the sheet over them.

"Sorry, I'll only be a minute."

The boy rolled over. "Can't you ignore the bloody thing?"

"I'm afraid not. It just keeps on ringing. Too distracting. Won't be long."

Richard opened a drawer in the chest beside the bed and pulled out a tattered magazine. He threw it on the bed, "Here, read this. It'll keep you in the right mood while I'm gone."

Richard extracted a cigarette from a silver cigarette case on the dresser, lit it with a silver lighter, filling his lungs with smoke before leaving the room. He made sure the door was closed behind him. At this time of night it was usually his father calling. Knowing Richard's habits his father didn't call unless it was important.

"Yes?"

"Richard, it is me. I gather from the tone of your voice I'm interrupting something."

"Yes."

A leering chuckle rasped in Richard's ear, "Knowing you I bet she's a luscious little bitch."

"Dad! You have something you want to tell me?"

"Richard, my sources tell me that young bastard, Craig Fox, has finally found a lawyer willing to fight for him. I've crossed swords with Webster Madison before, and I must warn you he's good. He doesn't lose many cases. Charges have been filed against you for attempted murder and the police will be contacting you tomorrow. There are rumors floating around he has witnesses to your attempt to kill him. We cannot let this sort of thing jeopardize your career... Richard, it's time to take the gloves off, but if we're going to get nastier you're going to have to tell me exactly what went on between you and Craig Fox. I can't help you if I don't know the truth."

"Okay... " Richard took another puff before crushing the cigarette in the ashtray by the phone. He exhaled before continuing, "Craig Fox and I go back a long way... all the way back to Bogota and boarding school. He was three years behind me at school. Unfortunately I got drunk one night and did something foolish. He's been trying to blackmail me ever since. Also do you remember me telling you about our servant girl in Bogota?"

"No-o."

"I told you I knocked her up and you said to get rid of her. So, I got rid of her."

"Ooh. How?"

"I hired a young man to do it. Craig found out. He overheard me talking to the young man."

"Shit! That bloody thing between your legs is going to destroy you some day. Go on."

"So I hired the young man to kill Craig, but the little bugger lied to me. He told me he'd killed Craig and I paid him 5000 pesos. Next thing I know, Craig turns up on my squadron. He had so much dirt on me I had to get rid of him. I exposed him to all kinds of danger hoping the Jerries would finish him off for me, but that bastard seems to have a charmed life. Instead of crashing in flames he became a skilled pilot. On that final day he did get hit and his plane caught fire. It crashed into some trees. I didn't think he could have survived the crash, but to make sure I blasted the wreck with my guns. It was a very remote valley. I certainly didn't expect my attack to be witnessed."

"Richard, we have to find out who the witnesses are and buy them off."

"We-e-ll, I'm not too sure buying them off is good enough. I think a more permanent solution would be better. Dad, do you still keep in touch with some of your old associates?"

"No. I set them up with good retirement incomes to keep them quiet. Most are probably dead by now. Oh, wait a minute, there is one. He's pretty old but his son might be available. The son has been in and out of prison many times. I saw his name when I was Justice Minister. What do you have in mind?"

"We have to get the names of the witnesses. I'm sure Craig Fox will have told his lawyer their names. Somebody has to go into the lawyer's office and get those names without him knowing he's been broken into."

"Richard, we have to be very careful this can't be traced back to you. I'll get in touch with my old friend and have him arrange for his son to do it. I know the old man would not betray me. I won't even tell you his name."

"Thanks Dad. As soon as I have the names I will make other arrangements . I know who can help."

"Who?"

"The same young man that got rid of the girl for me."

"But he cheated you about Craig Fox, and he's way down in Colombia."

"I know, but I needed a little problem in the boarding school cleared up so I got in touch with him. He's done very well for himself and has moved to Cali. I'm sure he would jump at the chance to travel with his way paid."

"Fine, but do be careful. I'll be in touch when I have some information. Good night my boy. Give her a pat on the bum for me."

Walking back to the bedroom, Richard was too preoccupied to notice the bedroom door was now slightly ajar.

* * *

Mrs. Bannerman was anxious that Richard settle down and marry. After considerable discussion between Mr. and Mrs. Bannerman, Barbara Bourne-Smith was selected. Barbara was the only daughter of the richest and most respected family in Toronto. There was no question such a union would benefit Richard's political career. Mrs. Bannerman contacted Mrs. Bourne-Smith, and was pleased to learn Mrs. Bourne-Smith already had Richard Bannerman on her short list of eligible bachelors. A scheme was concocted between the two for a surprise meeting.

Richard was cool to the idea of marriage. He had just breezed through Queens University graduating with honors. While there he had been pursued by countless eager young bodies only too anxious to be bedded by such a famous hero. Marriage would put a stop to that. Next month he would be entering Osgoode Hall to complete his law degree, and he had no intention of curbing his social activities, at least until he finished law school.

Barbara had been warned many times by her mother to beware of handsome men. 'They are vain self centered philanderers, always seeking reassurance of their attractiveness.' Barbara had met many handsome young men and had had ample opportunity to confirm her mother's sage advice. So when she was introduced to Richard Bannerman, she was immediately wary.

On the appointed day, Barbara's mother lured her to the gazebo beside the pool, ostensibly to discuss the plays they would see in London during their visit in the fall, but it didn't take Barbara long to figure out her mother had something else in mind. Mrs. Bourne-Smith appeared to be more interested in looking at her watch than in discussing plays and the tea table was set for four rather than for two. Well aware that her mother was in the middle of a campaign to get her married off by parading eligible bachelors through the house, Barbara knew that another thoroughly vetted offering was about to appear. When the offering did appear, Barbara was surprised her mother had allowed such a handsome man through the front door. Tall and broad shouldered, he walked with an athletic spring. The maid guided Mrs. Bannerman and son through the garden to the gazebo. As they approached the late afternoon sun sparkled through his thick blond hair and accentuated the slightly flared nose and strong chin whenever he nodded in response to his mother's whispered instructions. Mrs. Bourne-Smith rose to greet them. Both mothers made an elaborate pretense of affection with a peck on the cheeks. Richard shook hands politely with Mrs. Bourne-Smith then glanced at Barbara with a hint of a smile on his face. Noticing her amused expression he gave a slight shrug of his shoulders, acknowledging that both were victims of parental intrigue.

"Richard, this is my daughter, Barbara... Barbara,this is Canada's greatest war hero, Richard Bannerman."

Barbara noticed the brief compression of lips and brow as he controlled his irritation. She gave her mother a withering look. 'Mother! how could you make such a stupid introduction.' Although Barbara had never met him before, she had read about Richard's exploits in the papers and didn't need to have his heroics shoved down her throat.

Quietly he took her hand, and in a low modulated voice said, "Barbara, I'm so pleased to meet you. My mother has been telling me a great deal about you."

Muttering to herself 'I bet she has,' Barbara stood up. "Come, we are now required to get to know each other." Glowering at the two matrons' startled expressions, she went on, "so let us go for a stroll through the garden."

Following Barbara across the lawn towards the tennis courts Richard had to admit she was unusually attractive. Spirited, athletic, with a mischievous sense of humor. Her stride was springy, legs long, tanned and smoothly muscled beneath her tennis shorts. Waist slim, flowing outward to rounded hips and upwards to firm breasts and squared shoulders. Barbara was the Granite Club tennis champion. 'She probably has a wicked serve.' Richard had not had much time to check out Barbara's face but had noticed she wore no makeup nor lipstick. She turned to face him.

"Would you like to play some tennis?" Looking him over, "You have much the same build as my brother John. You could wear his clothes."

"Aah. Thank you. No, not today." Tennis was not his best sport. "I sprained my ankle last week and I think I should not strain it so soon. Some other time... Barbara, could we talk for a minute without me chasing you all over the garden."

Chuckling, Barbara pointed to a nearby bench. "Why don't we sit there?"

"Barbara, I want you to understand that I had nothing to do with this conspiracy. Mother insisted I accompany her on a shopping trip and suddenly we were here."

"I understand what you are saying. My mother thinks that because I am twenty-two years old I'm practically an old maid. She's determined to get me married off but I have no desire to marry for a few years. I plan to go to Oxford this fall for a Fine Arts Degree and read History of Art, then travel around Greece and Italy."

"I certainly have no plans to marry either... now that we understand each other, maybe we should rejoin the ladies for tea?"

"Before we do I wonder if you could tell me a little about Italy. Rome is a place that has always fascinated me. I know you spent quite a long time in Italy during the war."

"I'm sorry, Barbara, but I left Italy before we captured Rome. I was dragged back here and sent on a lecture tour."

"Oh yes, I remember. Wasn't there some threat and you had to be given protection by the Mounties?"

"We-ell yes. That was mostly newspaper talk."

"Who threatened you? Is it the man that is saying you tried to murder him?"

Abruptly Richard leaned over to retie his shoes. Barbara didn't notice the back of his neck was suddenly flushed. In a few moments he sat up. Gently shaking his head he continued, a benign expression on his face.

"it's a sad case. We were good friends in school in Colombia and ended up on the same squadron in Italy. He wasn't a very good pilot and became jealous of my success. He got shot down while on patrol with me and now claims I shot him down... Barbara," raising his hands, palms open, "Why in the world would I want to do that? I thought he had been killed but he survived and joined the Partisans. He made such a mess of it with them they pleaded for the British to fly him out. I'm told he tortured and murdered a German soldier and betrayed a Partisan girl to the Gestapo."

"How terrible! He should be in a mental institution."

Richard smiled, "He's not that bad, just confused. But he does claim he has witnesses to my attack so we will probably end up in court. It shouldn't go that far, but unfortunately he has a lawyer that is trying to make a name for himself. Enough of that. Come, if we don't go back soon, they..." nodding towards the gazebo, "will conclude we're already engaged."

Over his teacup Richard was able to study Barbara without seeming to. He decided she was attractive without being exceptionally pretty. Her brown hair was pulled back into a loose bun, straight eyebrows and nose bracketed her pale blue eyes; full lips and a hint of peach fuzz over the lips hinted at a passionate nature. Her face was long and sprinkled with a few barely visible freckles under her tan. She caught him looking at her and crinkled her nose at him.

Barbara was beginning to like him. He seemed modest in spite of his fame, showed considerable sympathy for the wretched man attacking him, and was not vindictive. He appeared to have a sense of humor, an attribute important to her. Obviously not interested in her money or in marrying her. But like all men, unwilling to expose his male ego to humiliation by a female tennis player. She shook her head. One of these days she was going to lure him onto the tennis court.

* * *

The intercom interrupted his concentration. "Webster, there's a young man on the phone claiming he has very important information on Richard Bannerman he is willing to sell. I think you should talk to him. He won't tell me what it's about."

"Thanks, Fran. I'll talk to him. Yes? who is this?"

A young male voice asked, tentatively, "Mr. Madison?"

"This is Webster Madison. Who am I speaking to?"

"I would rather not say, Sir, but I have information on Richard Bannerman. He is planning to kill somebody and I can tell you who it is if you give me ten thousand dollars."

"I'm sorry young man. I cannot give you that kind of money. If you have information that somebody is planning a murder you should go to the police. After you have given your information to the police I would be happy to talk to you, but no money... do you understand?"

The tone was now petulant. "I can't go to the police. They don't like us. They beat us up all the time. I need the money," becoming agitated, "if Richard finds out I've been talking to you he'll kill me. He's a real brute. I need the money so I can leave town and go home... please, I need money to go home."

"Where's your home?"

"I can't... I guess it's okay to tell you. I'm from Moose Jaw. Sir, please give me some money so I can go home."

"Okay, okay. You come and talk to me and I will contact the police. When we finish, I will give you money for a train ticket to Saskatchewan." Webster paused, quickly flipping through his appointment book, "I can't see you this week. Come to my office next Tuesday at four in the afternoon.

My address is in the phone book. Do not, I repeat, do not tell anybody you are coming. Is that understood?"

"Yes sir, I have your address."

Webster replaced the receiver and wheeled over to the bookcase to make a brief notation in Craig's file.

* * *

She would have to do something about Craig. Two years was much too long a period for a young man to be mourning. Quietly Valerie puffed on her one morning cigarette while she studied her young brother, who was absently stirring his coffee, unfocused eyes staring blankly at the remains of the porridge congealing in his bowl. At least he no longer wept silent tears drifting down his cheeks. She had watched his agony, yearning to fold him into her comforting arms. She loved her brother but couldn't break the bonds suppressing her emotions. It was almost a year after his return before he was able to talk about Maria. His wrenching sobs during his confession of guilt over Maria's death had been too much for her reserved nature. She had risen to go over to him but the scraping of her chair had caused him to raise his head. He had smiled weakly through his tears, shaking his head.

"It's okay, Sis. It's okay. I'm all right. I'm sorry, but I loved her so much. I feel so guilty."

Now he was allowing this wretched business with Richard Bannerman to dominate his life. He was on a crusade to stop the man before he became too powerful. Granted, Valerie would like to see Bannerman brought down and Craig's reputation restored, but even if it wasn't she was sure that over time the notoriety would fade and Craig could get on with his life. But she knew Craig wasn't as concerned with his reputation as with stopping Bannerman.

Feeling the pressure of her gaze on him Craig looked up. "Yes?"

"Is it Maria or Bannerman?"

His face flushing he smiled sheepishly. "Actually I was thinking about a girl I saw in the cafeteria yesterday."

"Well, I'll be damned. Halleluya! Our boy is alive again. Who is she?"

"Her name is Audrey Brown. She reminds me of a girl I knew in Colombia. The same clear almost translucent skin. High cheek bones. Dark brown hair that curls around her head just below her ears... like this," cupping his hands below his ears, Craig lifted his chin towards Valerie. "Her eyes have that brown smoky mysterious, look... intriguing and seductive. No! No! That gives the wrong impression. She's not a flirt, just warm and friendly."

"Is she Oriental?"

"Oh no. Well, there might be some of that in her background, but she is definitely not Oriental. She was sitting with three guys but she saw me. She looked away quickly when I looked at her. She has a great sense of humor."

"Did you meet her?"

"No."

"So how do you know that?"

"Her whole face would light up every time one of those silly asses opened his mouth. She would laugh hilariously."

"Where is she from?"

"She lives in Toronto. She's captain of the basketball team and is taking a degree in nursing."

"You have been busy."

"I spent all afternoon asking questions around the campus. She's very popular. Usually has a football or hockey star mooning around her... I doubt if somebody like me would interest her."

But Craig was wrong.

Audrey Brown was interested. She had been quietly observing Craig for many days but he had been too preoccupied to notice her. She knew all about him and had been trying to reconcile what she had read with the solitary young man eating by himself every day. The odd time that friends came by to jostle him out of his pensive posture he was invariably courteous and friendly, listening attentively to their idle chatter. There was one girl in particular that was a frequent interrupter of his thoughts. She would sidle up behind him, tap Craig on the shoulder and giggle as she whispered in his ear. He would stand, greeting her politely, smiling in response to her inane jokes, but it was plain to see that in spite of his cordial manner she was not his favorite person. Audrey found herself becoming irritated at the silly girl's persistence and was tempted to warn her to leave him alone. Rather surprised at her own emotions, Audrey continued studying Craig with increasing interest. He appeared to have no girlfriend... maybe he didn't like girls. That might explain why he betrayed that Italian girl to the Germans... but it was hard to imagine the quiet young man sitting across from her doing that. The sudden flash of blue as he lifted his head and looked at her trapped her eyes for a second before she could unlock them and lower her head, chagrined at being caught staring. The knowledge that he was now aware of her presence heightened his appeal. She sneaked glances at him hoping he might be looking elsewhere, but more often than not he was studying her. This was unsettling and she found herself giggling and laughing absurdly at her companions' banter. Irritated with herself Audrey made excuses to the three boys and walked out of the cafeteria. When she passed Craig's table she could feel the back of her neck tingling but did not trust herself to look at him.

On her next visit to the cafeteria Audrey took her lunch tray to a table away from the crowd hoping Craig might come and sit with her. But he didn't show up, which was just as well. She was quickly surrounded by boys and knew he wouldn't approach her through all the young men around her table.

The next afternoon Audrey was leading her team to victory against a squad from the Phys. Ed. Department when Craig showed up. She was lining up for a penalty shot when she spotted Craig sitting up in the balcony behind the hoop. She missed. From that point on she had difficulty keeping her concentration. Fortunately he left at half time and she was able to recover and refocus on the game. Leaving the sports complex after the game Audrey saw Craig sitting on the grass outside. Slightly irritated at having her game spoiled she approached him. Craig got up to greet her.

He blurted, "My sister has asked me to invite you to dinner."

Audrey collapsed on the grass, sputtering through her laughter, "That is the most original overture I have ever heard."

Embarrassed at his clumsiness Craig tried to recover the initiative. "What I meant to say was, would you come to dinner at our house. My sister is anxious to meet you." Realizing he wasn't doing any better Craig tried again. "I'm Craig Fox ..." He waited for a negative response. Hearing none he continued, "would you come to dinner at our house?"

"I would like to very much. To meet your sister, of course."

They both laughed.

* * *

A large black delivery van eased up to the stop sign on Avenue road. It waited for the traffic to clear before turning left on to Avenue Road. The van turned left again on Lawrence Avenue then right on Yonge street. Before reaching Eglinton Avenue it pulled into a lane between two buildings, stopping beside a small grocery store. The window rolled down and Webster's face leaned out. He addressed the rear end of a short stocky man who was dragging a bag of potatoes out through the door of the grocery store.

"Paolo. How are you on this beautiful Monday morning?"

With one hand on the small of his back to ease the pain, the man straightened and faced Webster, his face beaming. "Ah, Signor Madison, so good to see you. How is your beautiful lady and bambini?"

"Very well, Thank you."

"Wait. Please, I have a little gift for you."

Paolo walked slowly into the store. A few minutes later he returned with a brown paper bag, handing it to the lawyer. Webster placed the bag on the seat beside him without opening it. He knew what was inside. In the summer it would be three oranges, in the winter three apples. It was a Monday morning ritual Paolo initiated two years ago after Webster saved Paolo's son from being convicted of stealing from his employer. Webster had accepted no payment for proving it was the head accountant, not his assistant, that had his hand in the till.

"Thank you, Paolo."

Webster rolled up the window and drove to a reserved parking space behind a four story building. Carefully he reversed the van, easing it backwards until the back wheels bumped a small concrete barrier. When he felt the bump he reached down to pull a small lever on the floor beside the gear shift . Small hydraulic pistons pushed open the rear doors of the van and another piston lowered a ramp. Webster switched off the motor, unlatched the clamps holding his wheel chair to the floor, swung around and rolled the wheel chair down the ramp. Webster pressed a switch to lift the ramp and shut the doors. Satisfied the van was secure he rolled up to the back door. Opening the door he noticed some scratches near the lock but thought nothing of it at the time. The building was old and overdue for renovation, but the owner kept putting off his promises to paint. The creaky elevator deposited Webster on the second floor in front of the door to his office. Two other offices shared the floor. Both at the front. Webster's office was at the back facing east away from the street noise on Yonge street and the hot afternoon sun.

The moment he entered the room and closed the door behind him Webster was enveloped by a growing sense of unease. He wheeled over to the coffee stand, put the brown paper bag beside the hot plate, lifted the metal coffee pot to be sure the cleaning people had filled it with water, and added several tablespoons of dark coffee from a tin placed conveniently where he could reach it. He put the coffee pot on the hot plate and turned on the burner before swiveling around to examine the room. Something was disturbing him and he couldn't figure out what. Everything appeared to be in it's correct place. The cleaning staff had strict instructions that other than vacuuming the floor they were not to touch anything except the coffee pot and mugs. Carefully his eyes roamed the room. Nothing was out of place. He moved towards the bookcase glancing at the desk as he passed.

"There! That's it!"

One of the trays on his desk was not properly aligned. It had been moved, only slightly but enough to disturb the lawyer's serenity. Relieved he had found the source of his unease, Webster made a mental note to again remind the cleaners not to touch his desk. Proceeding to the bookcase he extracted Craig Fox's file from behind the 'F' tab and moved to his desk. The moment he opened the file he knew it had been tampered with. The notes he had made during Craig's interview were no longer precisely aligned with the top of the cover. Webster folded the file slowly. Leaning back in his chair he tried to work out the implication of this discovery. The coffee pot burbled frantically for several minutes before it could attract his attention. Webster wheeled over and turned down the burner, poured coffee into a mug and carried it back to the desk. It sat there. By the time Webster remembered to drink the coffee it was cold.

There could be no question that this was Richard Bannerman's doing. He would check the other files to be absolutely sure but Webster had no doubt they would be untouched. Bannerman must have wanted to find out what Craig had revealed to his lawyer. But the notes had not been removed. They were still in the file. They must have been laboriously copied over the weekend or photographed... probably photographed. Bannerman now knew the names of the witnesses and where they lived.

Shaking his head Webster muttered to himself, "I'm beginning to feel like some character in a grade 'B' movie. How did I let myself get into this. I'm a lawyer not a detective."

Craig would be devastated... should he tell him? Of course he had to know, it would be unethical not to tell him... what now... what would he, Webster, do if he were in Bannerman's shoes? Bribery! 'We must get the witness statements before Bannerman's agents reach them'. Webster took a sip of cold coffee, and without waiting for his secretary to arrive put in a call to Rome, followed by a call to Craig.

* * *

Even though Webster Madison's voice was unruffled, Craig could detect the lawyer was not his usual self by the tone of his voice, and by his reluctance to discuss the reason for his summons over the phone. Craig decided it was important enough to skip his nine o'clock summer school class. Mineralogy wasn't his favorite subject, and anyway it was too hot to be sitting in a stuffy classroom. He caught a streetcar going up Yonge street, hoping to use the ride to figure out what the problem might be, but the car hadn't gone three blocks before it was blocked by a leisurely road crew tearing up the asphalt. Too impatient to wait Craig decided to walk. The humid morning air wrapped itself around him sucking sweat from his pores.

Hot and irritated Craig entered through the empty secretary's office and opened the door into the inner office. Mr. Madison was speaking into the phone but waved him in pointing towards the coffee stand. Craig poured himself coffee, then carried the pot over to the desk to refill the mug the lawyer was holding in front of him. Craig sat on the couch leafing through a magazine trying not to listen to the discussion between the lawyer and his client. A few minutes later Mr. Madison put down the phone, picked up his coffee mug in his left hand and with the other rolled his chair to the low table in front of the couch. Webster sipped his coffee quietly for a few moments, studying Craig while he decided how he would break the bad news.

"Craig, I asked you to come over because we have a serious problem. A very serious problem. Somebody broke into this office over the weekend and went through your file. It wasn't a common burglary, it was a very professional job and the only thing they touched was your file."

"Bannerman?"

"Yes, I have no doubt he's responsible."

"So they took all your notes and he now knows the names of my witnesses."

"The notes and the rest of your file are still in the folder." Seeing relief spreading across Craig's face, Webster raised his hand to push back the optimism, "But I have no doubt they photographed all the relevant material. You are correct, he knows every thing. I'm sorry, Craig. This has never happened to me before. I don't keep any of my files locked up but that will change as of today."

"Now that the horse is out of the barn you close the barn door. For heaven's sake! Why don't you lock your files?"

Webster allowed the rebuke to pass without comment. "I can understand your concern, and believe me, Craig, I too am very worried about this development. As soon as I realized what had happened, I phoned our lawyer in Rome and demanded he send somebody out immediately to get statements from Bellini and Vesco. I wanted to make sure he did that before Bannerman's agents bribed them. He was most upset that I could think Italians could be bribed but I insisted he go immediately."

Craig leaned back against the couch. The cold from the leather permeated his damp clothes chilling his back. The chill spread up and down his body. Craig reached into his pocket and pulled out a small harmonica, caressing the warm metal in his cold hands while he tried to keep his emotions under control and figure out how to salvage his crusade from this disaster.

"Mr. Madison, I have a question. If your lawyer is able to obtain these statements and we eventually go to trial, is that enough to convict Bannerman or will it be necessary for Bellini to come here to testify?"

"I very much doubt that any judge would accept a written statement even though it is certified by a lawyer and signed by witnesses. If we want to be sure of winning, Bellini must come here in person."

"And Bannerman's lawyers will have the right to see these statements before the trial?"

"Of course, that's the law."

"In that case we've already lost."

"Why?"

"Bannerman will never allow him to reach this country alive. He will have him murdered before he leaves Italy..." Craig was about to continue but stopped when he saw the expression on the lawyer's face, "Sir, what is it?"

"Oh my God! Is that who he meant." The lawyer spun his chair around and gave the wheels a vicious spin, propelling him at high speed towards the bookcase. He grabbed Craig's file and returned to the table. He lifted his notes from the folder and held them up before Craig's astonished face.

"Last Thursday I had a call from a young man offering to sell me, for ten thousand dollars, information about a murder Bannerman is planning."

"And what did he tell you?"

"I haven't seen him yet. I couldn't fit him in to my schedule. He's coming tomorrow afternoon."

"Tomorrow afternoon!"

"I wanted him to report to the police first but he seemed frightened of them. I made it clear he was not getting ten thousand dollars. He's terrified Bannerman will find out he's been talking to me so I offered to pay his train fare home."

"Where can I get hold of him? Do you have his phone number? I will gladly pay him ten thousand dollars for his information. Mr. Madison! For God's sake. That's the only chance we have to thwart Richard."

"No! No! Craig, calm down. If you pay him for his information it is unacceptable in court. It would be as if you had bribed him to say what you wanted. Totally unacceptable. In any case I have no way of contacting him. I don't even know his name. I jotted down some notes at the bottom of this page to make sure I have a record of..." The lawyer's voice sank to whisper, "... of what the boy said."

Shouting angrily Craig shook his fist in Webster's face. "God damn it, Mr. Madison. You should have kept that file in a secure place. You should have seen him right away. You have doomed the boy and our only chance to beat Richard."

Realizing he was crushing the harmonica in the tightly clenched fist Craig slouched back relaxing his hand. Running his thumb over the dent in the metal he tried to control his anger.

Shocked at Craig's rebuke Webster forced himself not to respond. Craig was not being fair. Webster was a lawyer not an espionage expert, but he realized this was not the time to try to justify his actions. The young man had spent years trying to build a case against Bannerman and the whole case he had so carefully constructed was collapsing before his eyes. Webster waited until he judged Craig was in a mood to listen.

"Craig, after this boy comes tomorrow we will have a better idea what Bannerman is planning. If he is after your witnesses we can warn them."

"I don't wish to appear rude again so soon but I don't think you have fully grasped how efficient and ruthless Richard can be. Mr. Madison, that boy will not be here tomorrow."

"Fine!" The lawyer snapped. In a calmer tone he continued, "Let's assume he won't be here. Do you agree there is no way we can contact the boy before tomorrow. Nothing we can do to warn him?" Reluctantly Craig nodded. "The next question is how do we keep Bellini and Vesco alive until the trial which at the earliest won't be for another year?" Craig shrugged, throwing out his hands in a hopeless gesture. "Okay, Craig, why don't you go home and think about it, and I will too. Come back tomorrow around six. By then I will have finished with the boy if he has turned up. If he hasn't we will have to come up with some new ideas."

"Sure. Sorry I lost my temper."

"Don't worry about it. See you tomorrow. Lock the door as you go out. Bye."

Craig stood by the elevator for several minutes, impatiently punching the down button before giving up and going down the stairs two at a time. Out on the street he looked around for a cafe. Some place where he could wash away the bitter taste of the lawyer's coffee and deal with the trauma of the last hour. Seeing none Craig walked quickly down Yonge street, unaware he was jostling people on the sidewalk and interrupting traffic in the intersections as he wrestled with a nagging sense of guilt in one part of his brain and bitter frustration in another part. Guilt for not being able to do more to save a boy's life; frustration at being defeated at every turn by Richard's cunning and everybody's assumption that Richard would conduct himself according to the rules of civilized behavior. In spite of all Craig had revealed to him, Mr. Madison was still unable to accept that the boy would be murdered unless he was warned and taken to a safe place. Craig knew that even though the lawyer had been almost flippant in his dismissal of the boy's life, 'do you agree there is no way we can contact the boy before tomorrow. Nothing we can do to warn him', the lawyer was not callous by nature. He was trying to divert Craig's attention from the boy who he didn't consider to be in danger, on to things more important such as the two witnesses in Italy.

Unaware he had walked nearly ten blocks along Yonge Street Craig noticed a cafe across the street and weaved through the traffic to reach it. It was just opening. An Italian waiter was noisily removing metal tables and chairs from inside the cafe and setting them up on the sidewalk. Suspecting that if he asked for coffee in English he would be told the cafe was not yet open, Craig spoke in Italian. He was rewarded with an appreciative smile.

"Si Signor, por favore, sit here," rushing over to wipe off a table. "I'll have some coffee for you in a few minutes. We are just opening and I still have to make the coffee, but please sit here and enjoy the beautiful morning and all the lovely Signorinas going by."

The waiter arranged a cup and saucer on the table. A few minutes later he brought hot coffee in a small metal pot. He hovered nearby hoping Craig might relieve his boredom with idle chatter but soon realized his guest was trying to resolve some personal problem and was in no mood to talk. The young man was hunched forward with elbows on the table and hands clenched under his chin. His eyebrows were pulled down in a frown; eyes staring at some spot in the pavement beyond the table. The waiter quietly walked back inside.

Craig knew the lawyer was not convinced Richard would murder Craig's witnesses. Bribery he was familiar with, not murder. Craig had no doubt about Richard's intentions, so he would have to figure out a way to keep the two Italians alive. Knowing Richard, Craig was sure Richard would not wait until the trial began next year before eliminating them. If he only knew how Richard intended to kill them he could plan accordingly. The boy knew. He would have revealed everything. He must locate the boy, not only to obtain this information but more important to save the boy's life. Familiar with Richard's habit when drunk, the boy was obviously a male prostitute... but who was he? Where did he live? Where did all these street kids live? Where did they hang out, selling their bodies in order to survive? Who among his friends might know where these outcasts lived? Reviewing his few faithful friends Craig quickly eliminated them. It would be impossible to explain his reasons for wanting to contact these young prostitutes. He considered asking the waiter but dismissed the idea for the same reason... 'my sister, Valerie? Of course! She's a reporter working for the city's largest newspaper. She should know.'

* * *

"How the heck would I know where prostitutes live!"

Valerie had sat back in her chair with an indignant expression when Craig asked the question. He had fretted through a dull lecture on crystallography in the early afternoon before he could catch a bus to the Star building. Then was forced to wait a half hour while Valerie was in some meeting. She had been surprised to see him sitting across from her desk when she finally emerged.

"Well, you're a reporter. Surely it's not all flower shows and garden parties you write about. You must also write about some of the seamier side of life?"

"That happens to be a sore point right now but we won't go into that. Why do you want to contact prostitutes? I thought you had just met a nice girl? I didn't know you went in for that kind of thing."

"For heaven's sake Valerie! I have to try and find one of these kids before our friend, Bannerman, has him killed... is there somebody in this office we can ask?"

"I don't dare ask the other reporters. They would want to know why I want to talk to prostitutes."

"What about the editor, Brian Shirley-Dale? He's familiar with what I'm trying to do."

Valerie picked up the phone. She held the phone to her ear with her left hand while doodling with her right. The rough outline of a face was materializing on her pad by the time the call was answered. The slight frown on her brow disappeared. Her face softened. The pencil was dropped on the pad, allowing her right hand to smooth the curls over her ears while she spoke.

"Brian, Craig is sitting here in my office and would like some information on prostitutes. No! No! Funny man. He wants to know where they live so he can warn some kid his life is in danger... yes, it's Bannerman again... what's that? Jarvis Street? Is that a pretty seedy area? Okay, I'll tell him to take care. Thanks Brian ... tonight?... for dinner? Love to. See you at eight then." Reluctantly Valerie put down the receiver, "They do their business on Jarvis street and probably live in the same area. Brian says to watch your step. It's a very dangerous neighborhood."

"Thanks, you've been a big help." Craig leaned over the desk and kissed Valerie on the forehead. "Good luck, enjoy your dinner." Her writing pad hit the wall beside him before Craig could duck out through the door.

* * *

Turning on to Jarvis Street Craig stopped to glance up and down the street. He hesitated at the corner trying to decide which way to go. It looked equally depressing in either direction. Three and four story brownstone buildings lined each side of the street. The paint on the woodwork was beginning to peel from balconies and stairways. The brown light from the setting sun magnified the bleak brownness of the street. The area did not appear to be dangerous; crumbling perhaps but not dangerous. What once had been elegant homes lining Jarvis Street were now offering shelter to the humble, the poor, the unskilled, the servant girls, the immigrants, and no doubt, the prostitutes. Many residents were sitting on stairs or balconies, enjoying the last rays of the sun before surrendering the street to those who earned their living at night.

Craig was a bit at a loss where to start asking questions. He turned to the left. Walking slowly along the sidewalk, he stepped carefully around dog droppings, slippery garbage and broken pavement. He was aware he was being scrutinized even though he had put on clothes he usually reserved for chores around the house. The sun was now a thin sliver between the buildings. As he passed each group sitting on the stairways leading down from the front of buildings the idle chatter ceased and heads turned. Craig nodded to each group, hoping that a friendly response would give him an opportunity to ask questions. Some returned the nod others eyed him suspiciously. Realizing it was the older residents that were friendlier he decided to approach an old couple sitting by themselves on the stairs of a smaller two story house. He stopped beside them and delivered his carefully rehearsed speech.

"Excuse me, Sir. I'm looking for my young brother. He ran away from home yesterday and I'm wondering if he might have come down into this area. My mother wants me to tell him all is forgiven and please come home. He's probably with the street kids. Sir, would you know where these kids live?"

The old man removed a grubby old pipe from his mouth with a gnarled callused hand and turned his head to one side to delivered a stream of brown spittle to a gap in the pavement close to Craig's boots. Looking up at Craig he snarled.

"He's probably one of them taking my tomatoes." The old lady tugged at his sleeve but he ignored her, "The buggers steal everything. Then come around here at night peddling their asses."

"Ssh. John, stop it. The young man only wants to find his brother." Looking up at Craig she said, "It's so sad. They should do something about these poor kids so they wouldn't have to do what they do. Nobody cares. They live in an old warehouse. I know cause I've seen them go in and out of there... go to that corner," pointing back the way Craig had come, "turn left and go down about five blocks. If your brother is with them that's where you'll find him."

"Thank you so much. You are very kind." The old man grunted. He aimed another stream at the growing puddle near Craig's boots.

Craig had no difficulty finding the warehouse. There was only one on the street. Large gray concrete blocks rose up on each side of a huge wooden double door covering most of the front of the building. The door was securely locked with a thick rusty chain and padlock. A few chips of gray paint clung to the bleached wood. The tin roof had rusted through in many places, leaving gaps and jagged edges fluttering in the evening breeze. Streaks of brown rust slashed down the gray side of the building. Grass a foot high outlined the broken slabs of what had been the driveway. Craig walked around to the side and followed a narrow well-used path through tall weeds to a low window covered with a long dirty strip of canvas. The strong odor of cigarette smoke filtered through the canvas. He could hear a murmur of voices from inside. He hesitated briefly before pulling aside the canvas and stepping through the window. The murmur ceased immediately. Craig allowed the canvas to slide back cutting off the daylight. He stood still for a few moments while his eyes adjusted to the smoke and gloom inside. The inside of the warehouse was divided into stalls, each marked with a white crudely splashed number on a wooden crossbar over each stall. In number eight, across from him, a small candle on a wooden crate outlined the figures of two girls sitting on rumpled bed clothes on each side of the crate. They had been chatting and smoking until they heard the rustle of the canvas. Now they faced Craig, cigarettes suspended in slender hands. He could not distinguish their features, just the shape of their ears and a faint glow on the side of their faces from the light of the candle.

"Please excuse me for intruding, but I'm looking for a young man that's..."

One of the girls jammed her cigarette into the dirt beside her in an angry gesture before jumping to her feet. She jabbed her hand towards him screaming, "Fuck off you queer! Why don't you get the fuck out of here and leave us alone! Go and look for your boys some where else. Fuck off! You..."

"No! No! Please listen. This boy is in danger. His life is in danger. I must find him to warn him. He has been with a man that is now looking for him to kill him. Please you must help me find him. I don't know anything about him except he comes from some town in Saskatchewan. I don't know what he looks like, whether he is tall or short, or the color of his hair. All I know is that he comes from a town called Moose Jaw in Saskatchewan. Do you know this boy?"

Although he couldn't see her eyes, Craig could sense her gaze probing him from head to foot. The girl leaned over and whispered in the other girl's ear. The one sitting shook her head vehemently. The girl straightened and jabbed her fingers at Craig once more.

"Why do you want to help him? What makes you different to all those other men who use us?"

"Miss, I just want to find this boy and give him the train fare so he can go home before this man finds and kills him. Miss, please believe me, this is very serious."

"Well, Mister, he don't need your money." The girl sitting tugged at the other girl's skirt but her hand was brushed aside, "He's probably on his way home right now with a big wad of money. He took all his things away two days ago saying he was going home after he got paid."

"Did he say how much?"

"Yes. Thousands of dollars."

"When was he going home?"

"Jesus man! I just told you, he's probably on his way."

"What is his name?"

The girl on the bed reached up and yanked at the other's skirt. "Jean! Don't tell him!" Turning to Craig she hissed. "Mister, why don't you get the fuck out of here and leave us alone."

Craig had noticed other figures gathering in the gloom beyond the stall. They were silent though he could feel the menace in the increasing rustle beyond the glow of the candle. But he had to make one more attempt.

"Okay, okay, I'll leave now, but if he comes back please have him call this number." Craig took a pencil and a small pad from his breast pocket and wrote his name and home number on a sheet before tearing it out and offering it to the girl sitting on the bed. She refused to accept it. The other girl did.

"Thank you, miss, for your help. Please make sure he gets this."

Craig eased himself out through the window, rearranged the canvas cover, and took several gulps of the fresh evening air before walking back through the weeds to the street.

* * *

Webster Madison was sitting behind his desk with an open bottle of Glenlivet in front of him when Craig entered the room. His right hand was resting loosely on the desk with a small tumbler half full of amber liquid nestled in his fingers. A file lay open on the desk beside the half full bottle. The lawyer was holding a piece of paper in his left hand. He lifted his head and smiled at Craig before putting the paper back in the file.

"Please come in, Craig. As you can see I have finished for the day and am unwinding before I go home. Would you like a drink? It's scotch, the best, straight malt."

"No thank you." Craig moved a chair up to the desk and sat across from Webster. He glanced at the file. His name was written across the top.

"Did the young man turn up?"

Webster shook his head. "No. I'll stay for awhile in case he calls."

"In that case I think he's dead."

Webster eyed Craig skeptically, "How do you know he's dead?"

Craig unrolled a newspaper. He laid it on the desk. It was the afternoon edition of the Toronto Star. He pointed to a small paragraph on the back page of the front section "I'm sure this is him. The police found a body in a lane behind Jarvis street. The boy had been hit on the head and stabbed several times. He was supposed to be carrying a lot of money so the police suspect robbery was the motive. They identified that he was from Moose Jaw."

Webster emptied the tumbler, slowly refilled it and emptied it again. He leaned back in his wheelchair. He raised his eyes to the ceiling. Next he stroked his hair back with his left hand in what was now a familiar gesture to Craig. After some moments he straightened to face Craig. His face was pale, strained.

"Craig, I'm not quite sure I can phrase correctly what I want to say to you, but if you will bear with me I will try... although I believed every thing you told me about Bannerman, I did so only on an intellectual level... that might not be the right word... it's as if I was reading a story. A report of some distant happening that didn't touch me ... what you have just told me has ripped apart the shield all good lawyers build around themselves. A shield they must hide behind in order to be objective. I now have this terrible guilt. Oh God! I should have told the boy to come and see me immediately."

Craig bit off a quick angry retort. Instead he clenched his hands and said nothing for several minutes waiting for the lawyer to regain his composure. Webster corked the whiskey bottle and replaced it in a drawer in the credenza behind him. He settled back in the wheelchair looking at

Craig expectantly. Craig's hands now rested calmly on his lap. Craig took a deep breath.

"We must warn your lawyer in Rome that he must alert Giovanni Bellini his life is in danger. I don't know how Bannerman plans to murder him." Craig avoided looking at Webster in case the lawyer interpreted his look as a reprimand, "But knowing how Richard operates I'm sure he will not risk his reputation by killing Giovanni himself, as I'm sure he did not kill the boy himself. He must have contacts that are prepared to murder or break into your office. He will send somebody to Udine to look for Giovanni. Mr. Madison, we must move quickly."

"Yes, you are right. I will phone the lawyer again the first thing in the morning."

"Why not tonight?"

Webster looked at his wrist watch. "It is now six thirty and because of the time difference the lawyer's office in Rome will be closed. I will phone him as soon as I come in tomorrow. Why don't you plan to be here. Say, six tomorrow morning?"

"I'll be here." Craig got up to leave. "Good night, Sir, I'll see you at six."

"Craig, one moment, please," Craig paused at the door with one hand on the doorknob, "I have a question for you that has been nagging me for some time. Bannerman made many attempts to kill you while you were in the R.A.F., why has he made no attempts to kill you since then?"

Craig closed the door behind him and walked back to the desk, a tight smile creasing his face. "Knowing Richard, I made sure as soon as I was back here that the world knew. By that I mean that the newspapers knew that Richard had made many attempts to kill me and that I had witnesses. I gambled on Richard not daring to attack me physically because if he did kill me he could not avoid being linked to my death. As you know, he was reduced to using smear tactics against me."

"That took a great deal of courage. I'm impressed."

"Oh, I don't know. I've studied Richard for so long I didn't think it was too risky. He wants to be Prime Minister and he's far too smart to risk killing me."

"Thank you for telling me. Good night. See you in the morning."

"Good night, Mr. Madison."

* * *

One week later, Webster Madison received a telegram from Rome:-

Regret unable interview Giovanni Bellini.
He disappeared three days ago. His mother told me a foreign

man came to see Giovanni. Said he was a friend of Craig Fox. They went away together and have not returned. Will continue to try to contact him. Have statement from Antonio Vesco. It is very critical of your client. It is in mail to you. I await your instructions.

Webster read the telegram again. He removed the bottle of whiskey from the drawer behind him. Half an hour later he dialed Craig Fox's number to inform him Richard Bannerman had won again.

- 7 -

"Audrey, please sit down. I have to talk to you."

Craig had waited until they had put the two boys to bed and washed and dried the dinner dishes before broaching the subject he dreaded. Audrey moved to one side of the small dining room table across from him. From the strained look on his face, Audrey sensed that what she was about to hear was not good news. Craig reached over, folding her hands in his.

"I was fired this afternoon."

Audrey snatched her hands up to her face. "Oh God No! Why?"

"Gerald took me out to lunch. I could tell something was wrong while we were eating. He kept avoiding my eyes and just playing with his food. As you know he usually has a big appetite. He gave me the bad news in his office."

"But why did he fire you? What reason did he give? Craig, he can't fire you after all the things you have done for the company. That reef discovery near Stettler. All that land you leased for them in Southeastern Saskatchewan that is now part of the Weyburn field. Your geological ideas made that little company... Gerald can't fire you."

"Of course he can. He's the President. Paradoxically, it's the very success of the company that cost me my job."

"What do you mean?"

"Because the company has been so successful the value of the stock has increased at least ten fold, and as a result the big eastern speculators became interested and bought control of the company. Gerald was instructed to close down the geological department, fire the geologists, hire petroleum engineers, and buy producing properties instead of conducting 'high risk' oil exploration. Presto! I'm out of a job. I give you one guess who is behind that move."

"Richard Bannerman."

"Although he is not listed as a share holder he probably controls our company through nominees. While checking over the company he must have spotted my name."

Audrey squeezed his hands. "Oh Craig, I'm so sorry. After all your hard work to reestablish your good name."

Her eyes caressed the gloomy features of her husband. Seeing the distress in his eyes was painful for her. It had been such a struggle for him... for her too. Craig's abortive attempt to have Bannerman sent to prison for murder had caused them years of strife. The legal costs had consumed all the money Craig had inherited from his father, plus left him several thousand dollars in debt. When Craig's case was thrown out, Richard Bannerman held a press conference to announce he would not sue Craig. The negative publicity orchestrated by Richard was compounded by Richard's refusal to sue Craig for libel. Richard's generosity enhanced his reputation and ruined Craig's.

When Craig approached Audrey's family for permission to marry their daughter, permission was refused and Craig was asked to leave the house. It was not until Audrey threatened to elope that permission was given.

Labeled a psychopathic liar, a man consumed by envy with a disreputable wartime record, Craig was rejected by one mining company after another. He turned in desperation to the oil industry in Alberta, only to have the major oil companies turn down his application after checking his background and credentials. Finally after scratching a living at menial jobs for two years a "Junior" oil company offered Craig employment at a minimum salary.

In the last three years life had improved; they had paid off their legal costs; made a down payment on a small bungalow, and bought a second hand station wagon. Audrey had hoped their years of struggling to wash away the dirt that Richard Bannerman had dumped on Craig were over. It was not to be; Richard had struck again.

She couldn't understand why Bannerman would bother after all these years; surely Craig was no longer a threat to him. There must be more to it than just revenge. Something must have happened between the two long ago that Bannerman is terrified Craig might reveal. 'I must ask Craig about it when he is in a better mood.'

Audrey tugged at Craig's hands to draw his eyes up. "Craig, what are we going to do? There's only a few hundred dollars in our account; we're paying one hundred and ten dollars each month on our mortgage and we still owe money on the wagon?"

"We'll sit down in the morning to work things out." Craig released Audrey's hand and stood slowly, a hand on one hip to ease a creak in his back. "Tonight I'm too tired. Sweetheart let's go to bed, please?"

Later that evening Audrey managed to revive Craig's interest in things other than the loss of his job. Later still she murmured in his ear, "At least Bannerman can't take that away from us." Then she started giggling.

"You monkey, what are you giggling about?"

"I was just thinking of our canoe ride on the Bow River the first summer we were out here. You insisted on making love to me while we bumped our way down that rough stretch of water. Wow! That was really something. No wonder Donald is so lively."

They both giggled then made love again.

Craig was awakened by persistent shaking of his shoulder. Rolling over he was confronted by a worried five year old. It was Robert.

"Daddy, you'll be late for work."

Craig reached over and pulled the slender little body to his chest before covering the boy with the blankets. He kissed the furrowed little brow and whispered in his ear.

"Daddy is staying home today to be with you and Donald."

"Daddy, why you naked? You have no clothes on. Won't you catch cold? Mummy has no jamas on. When's it going to snow?"

"I think it's going to snow today."

Reassured, the imp in Robert took over. He lifted his cold feet and planted them in the middle of his mother's back. Audrey awoke with a shriek. She spun around threatening him in a mock growl. "Just you wait." Running her fingers under his undershirt she tickled him. "Just you wait, I'm going to tickle you forever."

Leaving them to romp on the bed, Craig got up to go to the bathroom. On the way he peeked into the boys' bedroom. Donald was fast asleep. He had managed to throw off his covers and jam his head into one corner of the crib. Craig decided to leave the child alone rather than risk waking him. Audrey would be upset he didn't move him but he wasn't in the mood for crying babies at the moment. Moving on from the bathroom Craig turned on the coffee pot before returning to the bathroom. He showered, shaved, put on clean under clothes, and dressed in his good casual clothes. It was important to be properly dressed when things were at their bleakest.

Donald was now awake and demanding attention. Craig drank his coffee while Audrey attempted to spoon mush into Donald. The one year old wasn't too fond of Pablum. He was dribbling it out of his little round face faster than his mother could spoon it in. Deciding that, as usual, Donald was winning the contest, Craig poured himself a fresh cup and wandered into the living room. For a few minutes he stared glumly out the window. It was late September and the forecast was for snow. He could see a few flakes streaking past the window, blown along by gusts of arctic air. The flakes swirled through bare stalks of dead flowers, rose bushes, and a small pine tree, before sinking into the brown grass of the lawn. Audrey had lovingly planted these same bushes only three months before.

Shaking his head Craig turned his back on the window and headed for an easy chair by the fireplace. 'I'll never get used to these long Canadian winters. Nine months. Ugh!'

They couldn't go on living forever with Richard's sword hanging over them, poised to strike every time Craig managed to put their lives together after another of Richard's attacks. With his growing reputation as a developer of carefully researched geological prospects, Craig was confident he would be able to obtain employment with another oil company, but it would not take Richard long to track him down, particularly now he knew Craig was a career petroleum geologist. Maybe he could get a job in foreign exploration?... but only the major oil companies were involved in international exploration and they had turned him down before... if he did get a job overseas, he would be throwing away his years of hard work learning the geology of Alberta and Saskatchewan... he should be able to use that expertise for his own benefit... but how?

Audrey came in with Donald and started setting up his playpen with one hand while she held the squirming baby with the other. She had nearly finished setting it up before Craig noticed. He leapt up to finish the job, apologizing, "Sorry, Sweetheart, I should have noticed."

"You were so far away I think it would have taken a cannon blast to bring you back. What were you thinking about?"

"Our future."

"I hope it is going to be better than what your face was telling me."

Audrey peered into Craig's coffee cup. It was full. She dipped her finger into the liquid. It was cold. She took the cup into the kitchen, returning with two fresh cups. She handed Craig his cup and placed the other on the floor next to her near the playpen. Donald was throwing out the toys in his pen, one by one. While she waited until Craig was ready to talk, Audrey busied herself putting Donald's toys back into the pen. Donald glared at her then proceeded to hurl the toys beyond her reach on the other side of the pen. Audrey made a face at him. She sipped her coffee, her eyes on Craig. She could hear Robert playing with his train set in the basement. Finally she could wait no longer.

"Craig, what are we going to do?"

"Okay! Okay! I haven't worked out all the details but I've figured out a way to get around Richard so he can never hurt us again. I'm going to work for myself. I'm going to become a consulting geologist. This way nobody, and I mean nobody, not even Richard can get me fired. I have several geological ideas that I was going to develop for the company. I'll do some research on them to see if I can mature them into good geological prospects, then sell them to one of the small oil companies, hopefully retaining a small override on each one. But there are problems to overcome."

"Money?"

"Money for one. I'll need an office and I can't afford to rent one. I need well files, seismic and geological maps, and those are very expensive to buy."

"Could you set up an office in the basement?"

"Of course! You clever girl. I don't need to be downtown. I can work just as easily here. But I'll need money to buy all that data, and most important, we need money to live on until I can work up these prospects. That's going to take me three to four months."

"I'm sure Dad could lend us the money. He did for the down payment on the house and we paid that back on time. So I'm sure he would be pleased to help out again."

"If he could do that it would be marvelous. I know he was opposed to our marriage because of the bad publicity but I think he likes me now. I'll work out how much we need for the next four months and we'll phone him tonight. It's going to mean a loan of several thousand dollars."

"I'm sure Dad can help." Audrey got up, threaded her way through the toys and sat on the arm of Craig's chair. She hugged him. "Oh Craig! I know you can do it. I feel as if a twenty pound weight has been lifted off my shoulders." She hugged him again.

Within a week the office in the basement was operational. Three months later Craig sold his first prospect. It was unsuccessful. Three more prospects came up with dry wells. The fourth well was a successful oil well but not in the reservoir Craig had projected to be full of oil. That reef was full of salt water. A shallower sand reservoir, one that Craig hadn't anticipated to be there, was the one full of oil! Smiling sheepishly Craig tried to explain to Audrey, "Geology is not an exact science. There's a lot of luck involved." On this prospect he had been able to negotiate a one percent gross overriding royalty. Within a year fifteen oil wells were producing on the property. Three months before the loan was due to be repaid Craig and Audrey flew to Toronto to return the borrowed money and personally thank her father.

On the flight east Craig was unaware his old squadron commander, Squadron Leader Allan Sharp, was seated ten rows in front of him in the First Class section.

* * *

Squadron Leader Sharp was not offered a 'Permanent Commission' in the Royal Air Force after the War. This setback was not unexpected. In spite of his outstanding war record his working class background and lack of higher education was against him. The R.A.F. sent him to the Far East for two years before he was demobilized and shipped back to England. He wrote several letters to Richard but received no replies. Swallowing his pride, Allan applied for a clerical job with a small manufacturing company making bicycles for export. Bored and restless he handed in his notice after one year. He was about to book passage to Canada when a letter arrived from Richard Bannerman. It included tickets for passage from Southampton to New York on the "Queen Elizabeth" and train fare from New York to Toronto. Shaking his fist in the direction of the setting sun, Allan muttered, "it's about time! You bastard, you owe me this."

Richard needed help. Together with his father, Richard had formed the "Three Star Corporation," an investment vehicle through which they could acquire control of successful resource companies. The small 'start up' company was to be controlled by himself and his father through a blind trust. To run Three Star, Richard had hired an economist away from a senior position in a bank hoping to benefit from the man's financial background. He was to be responsible for an efficient organization, but no more. Otherwise he was to do as he was told. But the man did not follow orders. In fact he became impossible to control. Not only was he President in name but insisted on behaving like one. The "President" took over a whole floor in a new building and staffed his organization with banking bureaucrats, more adept at writing memos than evaluating acquisitions. Moreover the man was not an administrator. Three Star was unraveling. Richard fired the president and contacted Allan Sharp.

Over his father's objections Richard hired Allan Sharp. He explained to his father that the Squadron Leader had run a fighter squadron efficiently during the War, making it the best in 'Desert Air Force.' He was intelligent, hard working, and most important he would have no choice but to do as he was told or be thrown back to some menial job. Allan Sharp was appointed President of Three Star. His mandate was to sort out the mess in three months or be fired. Allan interviewed the staff, fired half of them, hired a mining engineer, a petroleum engineer, and an economist, to be the nucleus of a research and evaluation department. He sublet half the office space to an accounting firm contracted to do the company's book work in return for a reduced rent. Allan Sharp was confirmed as President of Three Star well before the three months were over.

Allan knew that the Bannerman family was wealthy, but the amount of money passing through the blind trust into Three Star Corporation was much more than what the Bannermans' could possibly provide. Allan once made the mistake of asking Richard, during one of their meetings, about the source of the money. He was warned it was none of his business, and not to try to find out because the investors wished to remain anonymous. Richard's wife, Barbara, was also from a very wealthy family, but her money was not in Three Star. It was in a trust set up by her father. Richard had tried to break into the trust without success. This much Allan knew and was secretly pleased. He liked Barbara Bannerman.

Allan Sharp traveled first class. He was paid an extravagant salary, provided with luxurious executive offices and a company car, but had no authority. He did what he was told to do. Richard controlled Three Star through a blind trust. Richard never came to the Three Star office, nor did he attend any of the company meetings. Allan was never to contact Richard at his law firm. Meetings between the two were held in Richard's house in the late evenings. Richard issued instructions to Allan by phone. There were never any written orders. In addition to his duties as President some of the assignments Allan was instructed to carry out had nothing to do with his position as President of the company.

* * *

Richard had heard through his contacts that Craig Fox was reestablishing himself as a geological consultant. Allan was summoned to a noon meeting in Richard's house and instructed to go to Calgary immediately to see what could be done about it. One feature of his instructions intrigued and puzzled Allan.

"I've arranged a driver for you. He is an R.C.M.P. Sergeant. He does work for me on occasion, mostly undercover work. He's familiar with our problems with Craig Fox and keeps an eye on him for me."

Retrieving his bag from the baggage rack at the Calgary airport Allan looked around for a uniform. There were no uniforms in sight. Walking towards the exit a voice beside him called out his name.

"Mr. Sharp?"

Allan turned to face a tall young man in civilian clothes. "Yes, that's me."

"I'm Keith Calder."

"Oh! I expected you to be in uniform."

"No sir, I can only drive you around while I'm off duty. Sir, I'll lead the way to the car. Please follow me."

The Mountie offered to carry Allan's briefcase but Allan waved his outstretched hand away. He never allowed anybody to carry his briefcase in case a very secret diary fell into Richard's hands. Allan followed Calder as the tall man marched out the door of the terminal. Even out of uniform there was no doubt he was a Mountie; red hair cut very short; squared shoulders; neatly pressed trousers; and shiny brown regulation off duty shoes. Allan resisted joining the march to the exit. He slowed his pace. By the time he reached the car the back door was open for him. The car was parked in a 'No Parking' zone. Allan ignored the invitation to sit in the back and opened the front passenger door.

"If you don't mind, Calder, I would prefer sitting in the front seat with you so we can talk."

"Thank you Sir. My pleasure."

Calder walked around to the driver's side to open the door, but before he could get in a Commissioner came up waving a piece of paper. Expecting a rude confrontation between the two, Allan heard only a soft murmur of voices before the Commissioner walked off smiling. The sergeant eased himself into the driver's seat, grinning at Allan.

"I hope you don't mind, Sir, I told him you were the head of the R.C.M.P. I was late picking you up and there was nowhere else to park."

Threading his way through the traffic Calder explained he would be on duty that evening and the following afternoon, otherwise he was free to drive Allan to his meetings around town. Sitting in the front seat Allan made an attempt to probe the relationship between the Mountie and Richard Bannerman, but all he was able to elicit from Calder was that he had been Richard's bodyguard during the War while Richard was on his lecture tour, and from the tone of Calder's remarks, that he was one of Richard's admirers.

Over the next three days Allan held perfunctory meetings with a number of small oil companies. He had already expected what their response would be from the information in his files, but went through the motions anyway to satisfy Richard. Craig's reputation among the oil fraternity was too well established. None of the 'Junior' companies were prepared to trade Craig's work for vague hints of future financial assistance.

Allan was more interested in Sergeant Calder. What was his connection to Richard? What had Richard told this upstanding young Mountie to convince him that he should spy on Craig Fox? Was Calder stupid, or had Richard so completely dominated the young man into believing Craig was a criminal. Allan had an extensive file on Craig and nowhere in that file was there any hint that Craig was involved in any illegal activity.

"Sergeant Calder, I understand from Mr. Bannerman that you keep an eye on a man by the name of Craig Fox?"

"Yes sir."

"Do the R.C.M.P. have any reason to suspect this man?"

"I'm sorry, sir, but I'm not at liberty to discuss what the R.C.M.P. may or may not have on Mr. Fox."

The next day Allan tried another tact. “Sergeant Calder, as you know one of the reasons I came out from Toronto is because we want to know what Craig Fox might be up to. I take it you know where he lives?”

“Yes sir.”

“Could we drive by his house?”

“Of course. I’ll take you there now.”

They drove slowly by the house. Craig didn’t look up from his mowing the first time they passed. The second time he did. The driver with the red hair was vaguely familiar but the passenger was just a dark shadow.

On the way back to the hotel Allan sprung a trap for the Mountie, hoping for an honest answer. “Does the R.C.M.P. know you have Craig Fox under surveillance?”

“Ah... hu-m-m. No sir.”

“As you know I’m out here because of him. Mr. Bannerman and I need your help. Has Mr. Bannerman told you why he wants you to watch Mr. Fox?”

“Yes sir. It’s a long story going all the way back to when they were in school together in Colombia. Mr. Bannerman believes that Craig Fox has connections with criminal elements in that country, but he needs proof before he can expose him. Mr. Bannerman has helped me so much with my career that I’m delighted to be able to help him unmask this man. Craig Fox has said some terrible things about Mr. Bannerman over the years. Perhaps you don’t know about the lies? It happened while you were still overseas.”

“Yes, I know all about those stories.”

“Mr. Bannerman is such a credit to this country... it angers me that a man like Craig Fox is walking around free to spread malicious lies. He should be put away and I will do my best to make this so.”

Allan turned his face away as he spoke, “Yes, I agree he should be put away if he is guilty.”

Later Allan made another entry in his secret diary.

* * *

Allan was comfortably seated in the fifth row of the first class section when the second class passengers began filing in. He had no difficulty recognizing Craig. Allan spotted Craig entering the front door but Craig was too busy restraining a three year old trying to extricate himself from his father’s clutches to notice the other passengers. To avoid being recognized Allan opened the Calgary Herald and lifted it up to hide behind it. If discovered, Craig might wonder what Allan was doing in Calgary.

Allan ordered two double scotch which he hoped was enough to last him until the plane was well beyond the Saskatchewan border. He had long ago given up trying to understand how drinking in the air over that province would corrupt the morals of those below. During the long dry stretch across Saskatchewan Allan planned to catch up on company paper work and write a secret report on Craig Fox for Richard. Richard would not be too pleased with his report. There was nothing Richard could do against Craig. He couldn't get him fired; he couldn't stop him consulting; he couldn't prevent companies buying his geological prospects; nor could Richard cut off Craig's royalty income from producing oil wells. Craig Fox was free of Richard. Allan was relieved. Although he had long ago crossed the barrier of morality it still bothered his sense of British fair play to be forced to continue harassing Craig.

On the Squadron, Craig's unwelcome complaints against Richard had angered Allan. He had categorized Craig to be a habitual complainer and whiner. However after Bannerman left the squadron, Allan soon realized that Craig was not a grumbler and was doing his best to carry out his duties. Craig developed into a good pilot able to assume responsibility. By the time the war was over Allan had promoted Craig to Flight Lieutenant over the objections of Ottawa. Though President of Three Star, Allan was forced, reluctantly, to pursue Richard's vendetta against Craig and in the process began to realize that much of what Craig had asserted against Richard might be true, but it was too late to do anything about it. Allan was now too compromised.

Allan shook his head, irritated at his own naiveté. It had been a subtle process. Little by little Richard had guided Allan deeper and deeper into his web. He should have known better than to trust Richard's assurances that the stock manipulations and accounting maneuvers he was encouraged to make were accepted practices; or that buying stock in companies Three Star was about to acquire was perfectly legal. Allan Sharp, the President of Three Star, was guilty of fraud and insider trading. Richard frequently reminded Allan of the consequences whenever Allan balked at some order. Although Allan objected vigorously on occasion, life was too good to risk throwing everything away on some principle. He was paid well; received generous stock options; belonged to several prestigious clubs; traveled first class; and not least, he would regret leaving Three Star, an efficient organization that he had created. Allan resumed his gloomy musing while staring down at Calgary receding below his bleak stare.

* * *

Barbara punched in the code numbers to open the tall iron gates, waited impatiently for the slow opening, then raced through not bothering to close them behind her. She trod on the accelerator. The Jaguar growled up the driveway spraying gravel from the rear wheels. Barbara skidded around the circular drive narrowly missing the car parked in her usual parking slot. Muttering a brief curse, she backed up and slid in next to the offending car. She would have to remind Mr. Sharp, once again, not to park his Buick in her parking spot. Richard's Cadillac was parked next to the Buick. Richard was home. Barbara ran her fingers through her tangled hair, stared briefly into the rear view mirror and stuck her tongue out at herself... she felt great! It had been an exhilarating and challenging afternoon of tennis. She had been having problems with her backstroke recently, but a few hints from the new tennis pro had helped. This afternoon her backstroke had devastated her opponent. She would have to take some more lessons from the pro.

Barbara grabbed the tennis bag and racquet from the seat beside her and raced up the steps to the front door. She was careful not to slam the front door before running lightly upstairs. She didn't want Richard to know she was home. She looked forward to savoring her victory in the privacy of her room. Richard was not interested in her tennis prowess, and she had long ago stopped talking to him about it. On the way up the stairs Barbara glanced towards Richard's study. The door was closed. He must be having another one of his meetings with Allan Sharp. These meetings usually took place late at night. It must have been something important for Allan to come so early. Barbara sometimes wondered what went on in there but had never been invited to attend; nor did Richard like to discuss his business with her.

Barbara had been surprised and disappointed when she first met Allan Sharp. Expecting to meet another war hero in the mold of Richard, tall and handsome, she was taken aback at meeting Richard's former commanding officer. The man was short, slim, some might call him skinny, with dark brown hair that could only be kept in place with generous application of Brylcream, sallow skin, and a prominent nose. She had never seen his teeth even when he smiled. His redeeming feature was his north country accent. She loved it. He gradually lost the R.A.F. slang but the accent remained. Just to hear his voice Barbara often invited Allan to stay and have a drink after his meetings with Richard. Through these informal meetings Barbara began to understand why Richard had chosen this man to run his company. Beneath the unprepossessing exterior, intelligence and humor sparkled through his brown eyes. Through subtle hints and suggestions Barbara was able to influence Allan's choice of clothes, but she stopped short of commenting on the Brylcream. His teeth and hair appeared to be sensitive issues. Allan was not married, and as far as Barbara knew, had no regular lady friend. Barbara's one attempt to change the situation was quietly rebuffed. Barbara was unaware that he was having an affair with a widow who hoped to marry him. The widow satisfied his biological needs, but in his current position he did not think she would make a suitable wife. He would have been shocked if he had been told he was taking advantage of her. Allan believed he was doing her a favor by providing the lonely widow with companionship and intimacy.

On occasion Barbara could hear the sound of fierce arguments pounding through the walls of the study, but whenever Richard joined them for a drink, Richard was always courteous and treated his former commanding officer with respect. Nevertheless Barbara could detect tension in their relationship. The odd flash of anger from Allan when he responded to some remark by Richard and his reluctance to linger over a drink whenever Richard was present, usually departing with some vague excuse as soon as courtesy would permit. It was as if he resented taking orders from his former subordinate. In Barbara's eyes Allan had no right to feel that way considering all the things Richard had done for him; hired him as President of a company even though he had no previous business experience; paid him a generous salary with all kinds of perks; and allowed Allan to run Three Star Corporation much as he pleased. Richard seemed unaware of Allan's resentment or, at least he never showed it in her presence.

In her room Barbara undressed and showered. Coming out of the shower she wiped the steam from the full length mirror in the bathroom and pirouetted in front of it. She patted her buttocks... no fat there. She lifted her breasts... still firm. Drying herself, Barbara wondered if she could seduce Richard into making love to her tonight. It had been rather a long time since he had. He was away so much these days, giving talks all over the country on the current political situation, the economy, and on international affairs. When he was home, the dinner parties for prominent business men and politicians kept him up late at night. Richard was preparing to run for Parliament, but was delaying his final decision until he could decide which party was likely to win the next election. He had made it clear to Barbara that he had no intention of wasting his time on the opposition benches. Barbara agreed he shouldn't waste his talents like that. She looked forward to the excitement of an election campaign. She had attended a few of his lectures and had seen how he could sway his audience. She had no doubt Richard could win an election.

But right now she was feeling in need of some sex.

Rolling back the mirrored closet doors in the bedroom, Barbara selected a red cocktail dress. Red was Richard's favorite color. Also it complimented her rosy cheeks, now flushed in anticipation and glowing from the hot shower. She tried several brassieres, selecting the one that flattered her bust. Agonizing on whether to wear stockings she deciding not to. She checked her legs to see if they needed shaving. Satisfied they didn't Barbara wedged her feet into a pair of red sandals. She seldom wore high heels but tonight she would put up with the discomfort. Sitting at her dressing table she started to put on lipstick but decided she looked better without it. Barbara removed the red spot with a paper towel. She combed her hair and rolled it into a loose bun at the back, adding a pair of pearl earrings and a single strand pearl necklace. The final touch was a dab of Richard's favorite perfume behind each ear and on her right wrist. She was ready for Richard. She hoped he was ready for her.

Going down the stairs Barbara glanced towards the study. The door was still closed and she could hear the murmur of voices. In the living room she poured herself a weak scotch before carrying it over to the record player. Sifting through the stack of records she spotted Harry Belafonte's Calypso record. "Ah, Yes!" Memories of their honeymoon in Jamaica flooded in. She danced across the room keeping time to the music. It had been the most wonderful two weeks. Richard had been fantastic in and out of bed. Particularly in bed. Barbara's decision to lose her virginity in high school had been a disappointing disaster. The boy had she selected was clueless. He was finished before she even got started, besides making a mess of her party dress. Not Richard. His hands explored all her erogenous zones one by one, some that she didn't even know she had, lifting her ever upward to one climax after another. When he finally entered her it was almost unbearable. His gentle thrusting made her gasp for air. When she climaxed she fainted. She never fainted again. It was never the same again. It took a while but eventually it dawned on her that Richard was programmed to make love in a certain way. It was as if he had a check list he ticked off as he progressed, so many seconds here, another minute there. It exasperated her, wishing he would get on with it. On a couple of occasions Barbara tried to sidetrack the methodical sequence with a few initiatives on her part but soon realized this irritated and shocked Richard. She resigned herself to going along with the preliminaries for the sake of the prize at the end. Richard was good at delivering that.

The door to the study opened and Richard came out followed by Allan. Richard's face was grim, eyebrows pushed down in a frown, eyes cold, mouth clamped shut. He crossed the hall and entered the living room. His eyes strayed over her briefly while he accepted the scotch Barbara had prepared for him. Behind him Allan lifted his hand, palm out, shaking his head, silently refusing the proffered drink. Richard walked over to the record player to turn down the volume. As Harry Belafonte's voice sank to a whisper so did her desire. Richard turned. He gave her a smile which did nothing to lift her spirits.

"I'm sorry, Barb, but Allan and I have to go to his office to work on some papers. It can't be helped. The deadline for closing on a deal is midnight tomorrow and we still need to sort some things out." Richard put down his empty glass and lifted Barbara's chin to gave her a kiss on the lips. "Tell the cook I won't be home for dinner. Come, Allan, let's go."

Barbara waited until the sound of their cars died away before she walked over to the record player to turn up the volume. She poured herself another scotch, stronger this time. She sat in a chair by the fireplace toying with her drink, trying to decide whether to go back to the Club or stay home with a book. It was Friday and there was always a dance on Fridays at the Granite Club. Maybe the tennis pro would be there. Surprised at herself Barbara rang the bell for the maid. When she appeared Barbara stood up, handing her the empty glass.

"Anna, Mr. Bannerman won't be home for dinner and I'm not very hungry. Could you please tell Greta I'll just have some of her delicious soup up in my bedroom. A fire in my bedroom would be nice. Could you see to that, please."

"That would be nice, Mrs. Bannerman. I'll do it right away."

"Thank you, Anna."

Barbara walked upstairs into her bedroom. She hung up her red dress and put away her sandals. In her dressing gown Barbara settled into an easy chair by the fireplace. Vaguely watching Anna put a match to the papers stuffed under the logs, Barbara's thoughts struggled with disturbing notions.

* * *

Richard made his excuses to Barbara and followed Allan's Buick downtown. Richard was furious and had been taking out his irritation on Allan during their meeting. The evaluation prepared by Allan's research department was very clear. The assets and income would not support the amount of money Richard wanted to offer for the Berry Creek gold property in British Columbia. Richard questioned the estimate of reserves, daily production figures, costs, and cash flow. He refused to accept the conclusions and insisted on Allan returning to the office to revise the figures. But that wasn't what was annoying him. He didn't really care whether they bought the property or not. It was the phone call that had provoked his irritation. He was furious at Florentino Chavez for calling during the day.

The phone had rung in the middle of his discussion with Allan, and unfortunately Allan picked up the receiver before it rang five times.

"Richard, it's a long distance call for you. The operator says it is from Colombia. Here." Allan offered the receiver to Richard.

"No! No! Tell the operator I am in a meeting and cannot be disturbed. I will call back later."

"Shall I take the number?"

"No! No! I know the number! Just put the bloody thing down! Let's get on with it."

Richard was angry at himself for allowing the call to fluster him. He should never have blurted out he knew the number. Florentino Chavez had strict instructions to call Richard in his study, and only late at night. He was to hang up after five rings. Richard would return the call at a suitable time from a public phone. What the hell was Tino up to calling him so early in the evening. Lately the little bastard was becoming more insistent. Their relationship was shifting and Richard was not quite sure what he could do about it. He certainly had no intention of letting the little bugger think he could start treating Richard as an equal even though Tino was now a rich man and the major investor in Richard's trust fund.

Richard allowed Allan's Buick to disappear into the traffic ahead of him before turning off to look for a pay phone. He would not go to Allen's office. The call to Colombia was more important. He made his call at a pay phone outside the post office.

* * *

Allan parked the car in the basement. He waited briefly for Richard's car to appear, and satisfied Richard was not coming took the elevator to the ninth floor. The receptionist and clerical staff were gone, their desks clean and tidy according to his instructions. His research staff was assembled in the conference room, summoned by phone an hour earlier from Richard's house. Allan delivered the revised parameters for their evaluation. He agreed with their objections but insisted they proceed regardless. Ignoring their grumbling Allan retreated to his office and locked the door behind him. He opened a small fridge in his credenza, dumped some ice in a tumbler and half filled the glass with scotch. He swiveled his chair around, plunked his feet on the credenza in front of the plate glass window and stared out into the night. Below him the evening traffic pulsed from traffic light to traffic light but the flashing tail lights didn't register in his brain. Allan slowly sipped his drink.

Why was Richard demanding a revised evaluation based on unrealistic numbers which even Richard knew were false? Allan respected Richard's ability to sort through pages of numbers and in a matter of minutes extract those numbers that determined the soundness of an evaluation, but tonight he had been way off base... 'strange'... The review of the report on the gold property had been proceeding normally and Richard appeared to agree with the assumptions Allan's staff had used to arrive at their conclusions, but then Richard suddenly became irrational demanding changes to the assumptions... 'What triggered this sudden shift in his thinking?' There were no interruptions except for one phone call... 'That's it! the phone call!... Could that phone call have been so upsetting it derailed his usual good judgment? If so, why?... why was Richard fuming over a phone call?... Was it because I picked up the receiver and now know Richard was communicating with somebody in Colombia?... Was it true Craig Fox had criminal connections in Colombia and Richard was trying to get confirmation?... If this is so, surely Richard should not be so upset that I picked up the phone... in fact, if he was checking up on Craig Fox he could have explained the call to me, seeing that Richard knows I am aware of his hatred of Craig'... Allan dropped his feet off the credenza with a crash... 'Maybe the reverse is true!'

"I'll be damned, you bugger! Is that where your money comes from?"

Allan picked up the briefcase he had dropped on the floor next to the desk, spun the combination and took out a black diary. He jotted the date and hour at the top of a fresh page and filled the page with notes. Allan walked over to a book shelf, removed some books hiding a safe, opened the safe and placed the black diary on top of two other similar diaries. He closed the safe, carefully replacing the books on the shelf. He poured himself another drink and reclaimed his seat to resume speculating on the dangers to his future which now looked riskier. He would have to be doubly careful from now on. Careful that Richard didn't compromise him further by getting him involved in his illegal activity, and most important that Richard didn't become suspicious Allan had grasped the significance of that phone call. Allan had no doubt Richard would arrange something if he thought Allan might be a threat. If Richard was capable of shooting at Craig's plane he was capable of eliminating his former commanding officer.

* * *

"Ricardo, thank you for returning my call so soon. Amigo, how is your Señora, in good health?"

Richard controlled his anger with difficulty. He couldn't let Tino's crude interest in Barbara's barrenness irritate him. Tino's frequent references to Richard's inability to produce offspring was becoming increasingly irksome. Richard had tried to explain he didn't want children, but for a Latino the lack of children implied lack of manhood.

Richard's Spanish was no longer as fluent as it had been in his youth. The only time it was exercised was on the phone to Colombia. "Tino, why did you call so early, and why didn't you hang up when the phone was answered?"

"I'm so sorry, Amigo. It's my sister's fault. I told Teresa not to call so early but she forgot. She was worried about her son. She's nervous about him going to Canada."

"Who is coming to Canada?"

"My nephew, Enrique. I want him to go to school in Canada to learn to be a like a Canadian. He speaks good English. He's been going to the American School in Bogota for two years but now he can't go there any more."

"Oh, why?"

"Ah... the school found out I am his uncle and don't want Rico back. I am sending him to you. He can stay with you and go to a good school in Toronto."

"What! You cannot do that. He cannot stay with me. Tino, listen. I would be unable to explain to Barbara, or for that matter to anybody else, who he is. He cannot stay with me. That is final."

"Very well, Amigo. Please find him a nice apartment in a good area. I will send you money for him through our usual channels to pay the rent, the private school, and his living expenses. He's not to have a car. It would make him too conspicuous and I want him to be like the other boys."

"How old is he?"

"Sixteen."

"When is he arriving?"

"He is flying up to Miami next week and is going to take care of some business for me," a chuckle in the background at the other end of the line gave Richard a clue to the nature of the business the boy would take care of, "I will let you know when he is arriving. He'll be flying up to Toronto. Ricardo, my friend, my sister and I will be very grateful if you take care of him. I have great plans for him when he grows up. He helps me even now. Adios, Amigo."

Richard didn't bother to respond before slamming down the receiver.

* * *

Richard recognized him immediately. The sight of this young Indian walking towards him spun him back eighteen years to when he began his walk on the edge, discovering the thrill of the illicit and the forbidden. This boy was a carbon copy of Tino as he remembered him. Taller, but with the same sinewy lithe self confident stride, high cheek bones and taut skin that had given Tino a slightly oriental appearance. Enrique entered the lobby and lit a cigarette as soon as he was through the arrival door. He took off his sun glasses with his cigarette hand to look around at the waiting crowd. He spotted Richard, replaced the glasses and approached smiling, hand extended.

"Señor Bannerman, it is an honor to meet you."

His English was better than Richard had expected. The words were soft, melodious. Richard accepted the handshake, surprised at its firmness. "Enrique, welcome to Canada. I'm sure you will like it here." The boy gave Richard's hand another squeeze before releasing it. "Enrique, how did you recognize me?"

"My uncle gave me a good description of you. You are a very distinguished man, Señor."

Richard, aware he was being flattered nevertheless found his resentment dissipating. His indignation at Tino's impudence had been building for a week, ever since Tino had had the temerity to suggest the boy live with Richard, then to top it off, making the boy his responsibility. Reluctantly Richard had decided he better meet Enrique otherwise the boy was sure to turn up at the house. The day before he arrived Richard reserved a room in a modest hotel and made preliminary inquiries at a private school.

Waiting for Enrique to recover his bags Richard was able to study him more carefully. The boy's clothes were casual, expensive and cut in the form fitting European rather than North American style. Even though jostled by the other passengers, Enrique smiled courteously waiting his turn to pick up his bags. Walking back towards Richard with a bag in each hand, Richard noticed Enrique's hair was not black as he had first thought but dark brown. 'Must be all that grease on it that makes it look black.' In the parking lot Richard lifted the trunk of an older model Chevrolet, motioning Enrique to throw in his bags. Enrique put in the bags and stood back to examine the car.

Richard explained, "It is not my car. It's rented. I will explain while we drive into town."

Richard got in the car, picked up a hat from the passenger seat and put it on, tilting it forward low over his face. It didn't fit him very well but it hid his blond hair and most of his features. Richard paid at the toll gate and headed towards the city. It was raining heavily. Richard noticed the boy didn't remove his sunglasses.

"Your uncle wanted you to live with me but that is not possible. It is nothing personal. Do you understand what I am saying, Rico? May I call you Rico?"

"Si, Si, Señor, I understand more English than I speak."

"It is most important that nothing connects me to your uncle. If you stayed with me, as much as I would like that, my wife and servants would want to know who you are and why you are there. These things have a way of becoming public and I cannot allow anything to interfere with my future plans. I have reserved a room for you at a hotel. The reservation is in your name. Do not mention my name, ever. Tomorrow I will pick you up at noon and take you to see a small apartment near the school you will attend. On Friday afternoon, at three, you are to present yourself to the Headmaster of a private school I have selected. Don't forget your school records from the American School. Tomorrow I will show you the location of the school so you can find your way there by yourself. I did not give them my name. So, remember, do not give my name."

Rico nodded his head impatiently. "Si, Si, Señor, my uncle told me never to reveal your name."

"Good. Here is a thousand dollars to cover your hotel and meals for the next few days."

Richard parked the car a half block from the hotel. He handed his keys to the boy, waiting in the car until Rico retrieved his bags and handed the keys back through the window. Rico thanked Richard for the lift, picked up the bags and walked towards the entrance of the hotel while Richard watched. Richard didn't notice the smile on Rico's face. Rico's uncle had been disappointed his nephew couldn't live with Richard, but nevertheless Tino would be pleased at the progress Rico was making with Mister Bannerman.

* * *

Enrique Chavez was illegitimate. This didn't bother him. Most of his friends were fatherless also. Rico had no need to find out who his father was. His uncle provided for everything; a luxurious home, clothes, money, and a car with driver to use as he pleased. The few times he asked his mother about his father he had done so more out of curiosity than any concern with what his parentage might be. His mother burst into tears each time he asked. As a boy, this disturbed him; as a teenager this irritated him. He made the mistake of asking his uncle and immediately wished he hadn't. Tino had leaned forward, his hands tightly clenched on the arms of his chair. The face was flushed, menacing.

"Your father raped my sister. I know where he is and one day I will kill him. I will kill him with my own hands. I will revenge my sister's honor."

Rico didn't dare ask the name or location of his father.

At age thirteen Rico went to night school, graduating with honors at the end of one week. Tino took him to his best brothel, selecting the senior most experienced girl to be his tutor. The lady was instructed to choose a young virgin and supervise the two children's education. The room chosen for Rico's rite of passage was small, barely large enough to contain a narrow bed; the walls were covered by heavy red brocaded curtains, and the room was lit by four spotlights; two on the floor and two on the ceiling; all focused on the bed. A white sheet covered the bed. The lessons started promptly at nine each evening. Rico and his partner were to enter the room fully dressed, slowly undress each other, then follow the instructions from the tutor hiding in the curtains behind the head board. The moment the two children entered the room the curtains on three sides of the room rolled back to reveal floor to ceiling mirrors. In the beginning the tutor found it necessary to plead with them to slow down and prolong their coupling for a full hour. It wasn't until the third day that Rico discovered the reason for the late hour and extended play. The room was a stage! The mirrors surrounding the bed were not mirrors but one way glass! On the other side of the glass, small cubicles with narrow beds faced the stage, all for the benefit of rich clients in need of extra titillation while they were entertained by young girls. The newly discovered knowledge that he was being watched, inspired Rico to repeat performances. The tutor no longer pleaded. On the fourth day another Indian boy was added to the show. Reluctantly and at his mother's insistence, Rico went home at the end of the week.

It wasn't until he went to the American School in Bogota that Rico found it convenient to deflect questions about his parentage, and concoct a story of a mother widowed and father killed in a car accident. The story was modified after he made the mistake of taking off his sun glasses to kiss a girl from his class. Startled she leaned away from him to get a better look.

"Rico! Where did you get those beautiful eyes? They're so blue!"

"U-u-u-mm... from my father... he was an American, but he's dead. Killed in a car accident crossing the street in New York."

"I'm so sorry. Do you miss him?"

"Yes, very much. He was killed when I was fairly young, but I still remember what he looked like. Very tall, very handsome." Rico dropped his eyes and managed a sigh, "I miss him very much."

The girl hugged him, lifting her face for him to kiss. Rico slipped his hand up her back under her blouse, and in one quick expert move unhooked her brassiere.

In his second year at the American School, Rico made the mistake of tantalizing three boys into going with him to a brothel, by painting vivid pictures of the luscious nubile young girls available and willing to satisfy their slightest wish. Unfortunately the boys, bursting with pride at their newly discovered manhood, bragged to their friends. Within hours the escapade was the talk of the school and by that evening the parents had heard the shocking news. The next day a large delegation of American fathers and mothers besieged the Headmaster's office demanding the expulsion of Rico. The Headmaster angrily ushered Rico out the front door between a long line of students, some cheering and wishing him good luck.

Tino was not amused. He had planned on Rico graduating from the school. Returning to the house late in the evening, Teresa with some hesitation informed him that Rico had returned to Cali from Bogota. With considerable apprehension she added that he had been expelled from the American School. Reluctantly she gave him the reason for the expulsion. Rico was in his room, sitting at his desk pretending to study an English text book when Tino entered, quietly closing the door behind him. This silent deliberate motion warned Rico his pretense at studying would not placate his uncle. He swiveled around to face Tino. His uncle dragged a chair across the room and sat three feet in front of Rico. In a low menacing voice, Tino spoke.

"You stupid boy! Don't you know those crazy stupid Americans don't let their boys do what young men should be doing. They don't tell them anything about the aching thing growing between their legs... so you take them to a brothel. Suddenly they think they are supermen and have to boast to their friends." Tino whipped out a long thin dagger from a sheath strapped to his leg. He held it under Rico's chin; the tip touching Rico's Adams apple each time he swallowed nervously. "You have wrecked my plans for you." The tip was now beginning to dig into flesh. "I have killed for less provocation, Rico, I will kill you if you ever disobey my orders again. Even though you are my sister's son, I will kill you. Don't forget, you are also the son of the man I have sworn to kill." Slowly Tino removed and sheathed the dagger. He stood up. "Now I have to think. Somehow you must learn English. We will speak again." At the door Tino paused before he turned the door handle. Pointing a finger at Rico he repeated his warning, "Remember what I told you, I mean it."

Rico had no doubt he did.

* * *

Tino beckoned. "Rico, come in here."

Rico followed the older man into his office. "Close and lock the door behind you." Even though his uncle's voice had no menace in it Rico was apprehensive. He had never been invited into the study before. Looking around he was surprised at its sparseness. A huge map of North and Central America was pinned to one wall. The room was small but the map made it look large. It dominated the room. In front of the adjacent wall five black telephones sat ominously on top of a red credenza. They appeared to stare at Rico. The white disk in the middle of each phone were like eyes glaring at him. Numbers were printed in large letters on each white disk. All the phones were connected to a small speaker and to a recorder. Tino lowered himself into a swivel chair in front of a large desk. It was painted a mustardy yellow color. He motioned Rico to the only other chair in the room. This chair was brown but countless nervous hands had worn through the paint on each arm revealing the cheap wood underneath.

"Enrique, it is time for you to learn some business. My business." Pointing to the wall map over his left shoulder, "see this map... up there is Canada and the United States and down here is Central America and all these Caribbean Islands. The islands and these countries down here are only stepping stones to reach those rich countries up there. That is where my future is. In the United States and Canada... but I don't speak English. I need somebody I can trust who not only speaks good English but understands these people. You are going to learn English. Is the door locked?"

"Si, Si, I locked it."

"Enrique, I'm going to tell you about my secret business. What I'm going to say now you must not repeat to anybody. If you do I will kill you. Do not whisper it into the ear of a girl you may be trying to impress as you make love to her. Do not even tell your mother. Do you understand?"

"Si, Si, but everybody knows what your business is. It is prostitution. You own brothels. You control those kids on the streets. Why do you want me to keep quiet about that when it's well known what you do?"

"Because that is not all my business. That part of my business has been good to me, but it is not growing. I can control Bogota and Cali, but to open brothels in other cities I have to bring in others and I cannot make any profit because they steal most of it. It's terrible," shaking his head in disgust, "you can't trust anybody these days." Tino didn't notice Rico's brief smirk. "For some years I have been supplying drugs locally, cocaine and heroin, mostly cocaine, but only the rich can afford to buy them and there are not many rich people in Colombia." Waving his hand towards the top of the map, "That's where the rich people are. I will supply them and make money, much money, and more money, and when you grow up you will run my North American organization. But first you have to become a North American. A Canadian."

"Why Canadian? Why not American?"

"Two reasons," holding up two fingers, "I will explain... Reason number one," holding up his index finger, "is competition. There are six or seven, ummh... 'families' in the drug business here in Colombia. All except one will not survive. I or the 'family' in Medellin will eliminate them. The 'family' in Medellin is run by an old enemy. He knows I have been trying to kill him for years and makes sure he is well protected. He too has been trying to kill me. That's why we have the guards, the electric fence, and your bodyguard. My spies tell me he is trying to set up a distribution organization through Florida. There are many Latinos there, but the Americans will stop most of it with their huge navy. I have a better idea. See this long border between Canada and the States. I hear it is undefended. It is over seven thousand kilometers long! It is much too long to patrol... imagine! Seven thousand kilometers of undefended border. It should be very easy to move drugs into the States through that border and the Canadians don't have a big navy. That is reason number one. Do you understand what I am saying?"

"Si, muy claro."

"Reason number two is a man in Canada. He is a very famous man in Canada. He is a war hero. He shot down many German planes. His name is Ricardo Bannerman. I met him when he was going to school in Bogota. We became friends... well, maybe not friends." Tino allowed a cynical smile to flick across his face. "Associates might be a better word for our relationship. I provided him with certain services, including assassinating some people that were creating problems for him. He is planning to go into the government there and I have been sending him money to invest in his company. He will use some of that money when he decides to campaign. He is a brilliant man and when he is in government will very quickly rise to the top, maybe become the "Jefe" of the country. He will make it easier for me to bring in drugs through Canada. But I have a problem with him. He thinks I am a stupid Indian that is here for his benefit to call on whenever he needs me. He is becoming unhappy with me because I am starting to tell him what I want him to do for me. I have things I can blackmail him with but that is old stuff. I need something better to make him understand that things are changing and he will have to do what I want. I have tapes of phone calls and receipts of payments he has made to me, plus transcripts of money transfers to his company. It is a beginning, but I need something better, something that will completely destroy him if it becomes public. Enrique, this is where you become involved and the reason I want you to go to Canada. I..." A low buzz interrupted Tino. He swiveled away from Rico and picked up the receiver of the middle phone, leaving Rico wondering how his uncle knew which phone to select.

"Si?... un momemto," Tino covered the mouthpiece with his free hand and motioned with his head for Rico to leave the room. "We'll talk some more tomorrow."

Tomorrow didn't come for a week. When he was finally summoned into the study, Tino was in a good mood smiling at some joke. "I just finished calling Mister Bannerman and somebody else answered the phone. He refused to take the call but I made sure the other man knew the call was from Colombia. Now we will wait for a call from Mister Bannerman and I know he will be angry. I will put him on the speaker so you can hear him but don't let him know you are listening. Rico sit down and I will tell you about Mister Bannerman... here," Tino held out a packet of cigarettes, "I know you smoke." They were an American brand.

Surprised at his uncle's amiability, Rico slowly extracted a cigarette from the pack while he probed the face in front of him to gauge the other's purpose in offering the cigarette. Rico examined the cigarette before placing it between his lips. It was a Camel. His uncle was now holding a lighter before him. Rico leaned forward. His uncle was in an unusually good mood.

"Rico, you have to help me blackmail Mister Bannerman." Tino held up his hand to silence the question Rico was about to ask. "I will tell you how. Just listen. Mister Bannerman," Rico was amused at his uncle's derisive pronunciation of 'Mister.' It sounded like the hungry meow of a cat. "Me-e-e-ester Bannerman is a pervert. He likes boys. He..."

"Tio! You don't expect me to..."

Tino waved his hand in front of the boy. "No! No! Listen. You don't have to go that far," he shrugged his shoulders, "Unless you like that sort of thing." He waved his hand again as Rico was about to explode, "No, all I want you to do is to seduce him by encouraging him to make advances. You will be staying in his house while you go to school and this will give you many opportunities. At the right moment you will agree to meet him at the apartment I own in Toronto that I will fix up with cameras and microphones. But you have to be very careful. He is a clever man and not easily fooled. So, go very slowly. It may take you a year to lure him. Also, he only chases boys when he is drunk."

"Is he strong?"

"Yes, tall and strong." Tino didn't add that Bannerman was also cruel.

Rico didn't ask how his uncle knew Bannerman only liked boys when he was drunk. He suspected there was more to his uncle's relationship to Mister Bannerman than he was being told. He had heard some rumors in Bogota about his uncle's early history but decided it would be wise not to probe too deeply.

"Enrique, next week I am going to fly to Miami. You are to come with me to be my translator as I don't speak English. After we finish some business you will go on to Toronto to meet Mister Bannerman."

"Do you have business in Miami?"

"Oh yes! The manager of one of my brothels ran off to Miami with my money. When we have recovered the money you can go to Toronto."

Rico was intrigued by the challenge of discrediting the clever Mister Bannerman. Rico was not entirely unfamiliar with such men.

The angry buzzing of one of the phones warned them Mister Bannerman was on the line.

-8-

Craig was worried. Robert had not made his regular first of the month call. It was an arrangement they had insisted on when Robert informed them he was going to be involved in a top secret mission, and that there would be no way they could keep in touch with him. Robert refused to explain what type of R.C.M.P. operation was underway, but in a private conversation with his father had hinted it involved drug counterintelligence. Robert was not supposed to communicate with them, but to reassure them he was still alive and well, he would on the first day of each month call from some anonymous call box and mutter a brief "Sorry, wrong number" if somebody picked up the phone, or leave the same message on their answering machine if nobody was home. This cloak-and-dagger arrangement amused Craig, but it was typical of Robert. The boy had always loved intrigue and the Mounties had broadened this appeal.

Robert decided he wanted to become a Mountie the moment he saw them ride by in the Calgary Stampede Parade. The 'Musical Ride' was to be a feature of the Stampede the year Robert was seven. Robert had been sitting on the ground in the front row when the Mounties rode past on their sleek jet black horses, spurs and reins jingling, eyes straight ahead, arrogant chins thrust forward. The red tunics and lances captivated Robert. He jumped to his feet and saluted. A snappy salute from one of the troopers clinched it. Robert tugged at his father's hand, and eyes glowing, announced, "I'm going to be a Mountie when I grow up." Robert's interest in the 'Force' continued in spite of Craig's efforts to discourage him. In his teen years Robert struggled through school, more interested in sports, hiking, mountain climbing, and girls, than academic achievement. It was only when he realized that he would not be accepted into the Mounties unless he graduated with good grades that he applied himself. Craig, concerned that Robert should receive a good education, insisted he go to the University of Calgary. When Robert failed his first year, Craig relented and Robert flew off to the R.C.M.P. Academy in Regina, barely able to hide his joy, even while kissing his tearful mother goodbye.

Craig hesitated to bring it up as he had no doubt Audrey had forgotten the date, otherwise she would have been fretting that Robert had not called. At the moment she was so absorbed, as usual, in her latest water color landscape and totally oblivious to her surroundings. Although Craig was never allowed to see a painting in progress, he could judge when the evolution of the painting had reached a critical stage; either to be trashed or finished in triumph. Today Audrey was barely acknowledging his existence, disappearing behind the closed doors of her studio for most of the day. Even at the dinner table she was somewhere else, either staring through him, or answering in monosyllables when he attempted to draw her back to his world.

"Is it going well?"

"Terrible!"

"But yesterday I got the impression you were pleased with your progress."

"No! I'm not!"

"Can I see it? Maybe I can make some suggestions."

Audrey gave Craig one of her disdainful looks. "Of course not!"

Audrey considered her husband's artistic development to have stopped somewhere between the Neanderthal and Cro-Magnon age; or to put it in terms he understood, between the Pliocene and Pleistocene. Unless he could see recognizable human figures he didn't think it was art. "I can paint better than that" was his usual comment when presented with an abstract painting.

Craig suppressed the retort on the tip of his tongue, and got up to put the dishes in the sink while he debated whether to remind her Robert hadn't called. Hoping Robert might have called and Audrey neglected to tell him, Craig spoke up.

"Audrey, did you get a call from Robert yesterday?"

"No. Was yesterday March first?"

"Yes it was. I didn't get a call from him either. You have been so involved in your new painting I hesitated asking you."

"Oh how awful! I didn't even notice yesterday was the first of the month. Here I have been stewing about my stupid painting and I didn't realize he didn't call. I wonder why. Something must be wrong. Who can we phone to find out? Can you phone the R.C.M.P.? Craig, phone them in Montreal. That's where he was based the last time we talked to him... why are you shaking your head?"

"Audrey please. Robert told me he is in a top secret unit. So secret that even the names of the men in the unit are confidential and known only to the Commissioner in charge. There is no way I can make inquiries because Robert doesn't exist as far as the Mounties are concerned. Robert told me his computer files have been moved to a top secret location. Audrey, I'm sorry. There is nothing I can do. We will just have to wait. He will probably phone in a couple of days to explain."

"Craig! Don't you think something must be wrong? He has always called on the first day of every month for the last year, and if he didn't call yesterday something must be wrong. I just feel it."

"Okay, okay. Let me think about it for awhile. I'll have to figure out how to make some discreet inquiries. Maybe I can talk to Steve Martin. I saw him in the Petroleum Club the other day. He mentioned he is on some Parliamentary Committee that monitors the R.C.M.P. Maybe he can help. I'll call him in the morning."

Craig never made the call to his M.P. Four o'clock the next morning the phone rang. Craig had been up all night. He was in his office when it rang. Audrey was supposed to be asleep in the bedroom. She answered the phone before he could.

"Hello?"

"Please, could I speak to Mr. Craig Fox?" The English was excellent but the French Canadian accent was unmistakable.

"Yes, this is Craig Fox speaking. Who is this?"

"Mr. Fox, what is the name of your oldest son?"

"Robert. Who is this?"

"This is Deputy Commissioner Boulanger. Mr. Fox, I am sorry for the question, but as you know there are several Fox's in the Calgary phone book and I had to make sure you are Robert's father. Sorry to..."

Audrey's voice, pitched higher than usual, interrupted, "Is he all right? Where is Robert?"

"I am sorry, Madame, this is why I am calling. Your son, Robert, has been hurt. Very badly hurt. He is in a coma in a hospital here in Montreal. Mr. Fox, I think you and Madame should come to see him immediately."

"My wife and I will come as soon as I can get a plane... could you please reserve us a suite at the Hotel Bonaventure for tonight... for an indefinite stay. They know me there so you should have no problem getting us rooms."

"I am sorry, Sir, I cannot do that. Robert was doing very sensitive work so there must be no connection from him, or his family, to the Force. That is why I am calling from a public phone. Please make your own arrangements. Also, most important, do not tell anybody why you are coming to Montreal. Please, this is most important. I will explain when you get here. I will phone your room at six this evening. Until this evening, au..."

"What is the name of his hospital?"

"I am sorry, Madame, I cannot tell you that over the phone. It is a very good private hospital. He is getting the best treatment I assure you.

I am very fond of the young man. I have no children so he is like a son to me."

"Thank you, Commissioner. We look forward to your call tonight."

"Au revoir, Monsieur, Madame."

* * *

Audrey had seldom seen Craig so upset. He was pacing up and down the suite; over to the window to glance briefly at the traffic stopping and starting in jerky spasms below him as it moved from light to light on the Rue De La Gauchetiere; then back behind her chair to the bathroom door. There, he stared vacantly at nothing as he fiddled with the change in his pocket for a few moments, before raising his arm to check his watch for the umpteenth time. Crossing the back of her chair he gave Audrey's shoulder a gentle reassuring squeeze each time he went by. Audrey watched each traverse with growing concern, 'He is worried. I've never seen him so worried in the twenty five years we've been married. It's not six o'clock yet, too early for the Commissioner to call, and he's pacing up and down. Usually he's so calm. Ever since we bypassed Bannerman's harassment, Craig has been able to control his life and career, but this is a situation beyond his control and I know that must bother him. However, it shouldn't upset him that much... Craig must know something that he hasn't told me'

The phone rang next to her elbow causing her to jump. The Commissioner was early. "Mrs. Fox, this is Marcel Boulanger." Craig picked up the phone by the bed. "Is Mr. Fox with you?"

"Yes, Commissioner, we are both here."

"I am speaking to you from a public phone across the street from your hotel. I am going to take you to see your son. Please exit your hotel on the Rue Mansfield side and turn right. Half way down the block you will see a parked black sedan. I will be waiting for you in the car. Get in the back seat. I shall expect you in about fifteen minutes. It is snowing outside so wear a raincoat, Madame."

Mr. and Mrs. Fox slid into the back seat. Marcel leaned over the back of the front seat to greet them. He was surprised at how young the couple appeared to be. She in particular. He knew she must be nearly fifty, but would have guessed her age to be closer to thirty. The moist evening light accentuated her almost translucent, unwrinkled olive complexion. Her hair, dark brown with no trace of gray, was pulled back from her forehead before curling down over her ears. Her smile, as she shook hands, was warm and friendly. He liked her instantly. He was about to tell her he owned two of her paintings but decided to leave that to a more suitable occasion. Him, Marcel had expected to dislike. This was the notorious Craig Fox that had tried to ruin Richard Bannerman, but this man did not fit Marcel's mental image of a psychopathic liar and coward. Commissioner Boulanger had given Robert and his family a thorough background check before admitting Robert into his counterintelligence unit. He was familiar with Mr. Fox's history. The man before Marcel was tall, well built, with regular features now lined with experience, a strong jaw, a straight nose, hair still brown with a white streak covering an old scar on one temple. The eyes were not evasive. Instead, brilliant blue eyes were appraising Marcel steadily and carefully as they shook hands. There was no craftiness there. The smile was friendly, self confident. He was dressed in expensive clothes and must be wealthy to be able to afford a suite at the Bonaventure. They both looked at him expectantly. Marcel eased the car into the evening traffic, and began his explanation, glancing at them in the rear view mirror from time to time as he weaved slowly around the slower vehicles.

"I know you must think that I'm being overly dramatic. Maybe playing silly games with you for effect. Please let me explain. Your son is in great danger even if he recovers. Somebody within our organization has betrayed him. I do not know who it is, but if that person finds out that your son is alive, he, or they, will make sure that he does not survive a second time. You see, Robert knows who is the head of the Drug Cartel in Canada. He knows his name, where he lives, how he operates, and who he controls. Robert is my best operator. He infiltrated the Hell's Angels and..."

"The Hell's Angels!" Craig and Audrey exclaimed simultaneously.

"Yes, the Hell's Angels. I know it is hard to imagine your upright son with long greasy hair and beard in a black leather nail studded jacket. He was very good. So good he was soon noticed by the Angels' hierarchy and through them met the Colombian 'Jefe'. Robert told me over the phone this Colombian's nickname is 'Rico'. Robert was supposed to meet me last Monday evening and was going to give me all the details... he never showed up."

"Rico is short for Enrique. It also means rich in Spanish."

"Interesting. That is useful information, I had forgotten that you speak Spanish. Thank you. On Wednesday two young boys stumbled across Robert's body in the middle of a corn field. Robert had been shot six times through the chest..."

A shocked cry from Audrey; a deep grunt from Craig.

"He was barely alive. Fortunately the boys reported their discovery to the local police instead of to the R.C.M.P. I am always tuned into the police radio reports on this radio here," pointing to the unit in the dashboard, “and heard them reporting another attempted murder by the Hell’s Angels. I guessed it might be Robert and managed to get the police to let me handle the investigation. I was able to divert the ambulance to a private hospital. Robert has been under intensive care for the last twenty four hours and his condition has stabilized. I had his hair and beard cut off this afternoon to make him presentable for you.”

“Thank you, Commissioner. My son, Robert, was very secretive with us about his work, but he did tell me that each operator in your counterintelligence unit was never informed what the other operators were doing; nor did he know their names. They all reported to you, and only to you, so how could one of them betray Robert?”

“Mr. Fox, that question has been keeping me awake all night. I don’t know how anybody could have found out about Robert. I’m the only person who knew what he was doing. There are no written reports that anybody could have seen. No recorded telephone messages... nothing.”

Craig, unsure whether his questioning might be resented, nevertheless knew he had to proceed if he was to save Robert’s life. He took a deep breath before he went on, “Do you report to anybody?”

“Of course! I report to the Solicitor General.”

Craig exhaled slowly. He muttered in a low voice to Audrey, “I thought as much.” He continued, “Do you report to him directly, or do you communicate through one of his assistants?”

“I report to him directly, no one else. As Solicitor General, Mr. Bannerman became very concerned at the extent of the drug traffic coming into Canada, and through Canada into the States. He asked me to set up a top secret counterintelligence unit reporting to him. I report to him on a secure private line to his apartment in Ottawa that only he answers. So there is no leak there. He has been most helpful. He is a very competent and decisive Minister and it has been a pleasure working for him.”

Realizing he would have to proceed even more cautiously, Craig decided to wait a few moments to allow the Commissioner time to digest the implication of where Craig’s questions were leading. His next question was more personal and designed to give the Commissioner more time.

“Is Mr. Bannerman aware Robert is my son?”

“No. He does not know the names of any of my men. He knows only their code names. I am aware of your dispute with Mr. Bannerman and thought it best not to tell him your son works for me. In spite of his reputation for fairness he might have been tempted to interfere. I select my men on their suitability and competence... your son, Mr. Fox, was near the top of my list.” The Commissioner pulled into a parking space across the street from an 'Emergency' sign. "Now shall we go and see your son?"

As the Commissioner was about to open the car door, Craig leaned forward and put his hand on the Commissioner's shoulder. "Commissioner, Please, could you wait a few minutes? I have a few more questions."

The Commissioner closed the door and swiveled around to confront Craig. The light from the hospital 'Emergency' sign shone on the Commissioner. It was the first time Craig had got a good look at him. The Commissioner was not in uniform. Instead he wore a gray tweed jacket and a conservative striped tie over a white shirt. His expression was grim. Craig was struck by the Commissioner's resemblance to his own father; he was, perhaps, a little shorter. It was difficult to judge his height in a sitting position. He had the same chiseled face, salt and pepper hair, cut short; the same steel blue eyes flashing angrily as he waited for Craig to lead him to a conclusion he was not prepared to accept. Audrey squeezed Craig's hand trying to warn him to stop, but Craig was determined to force Commissioner Boulanger to confront the source of the leaks.

"Commissioner..."

"Mr. Fox! That is enough! I am very familiar with your history. Do not continue with this questioning. It only confirms the reports about you. Now, do you want to see your son?"

Defeated, Craig leaned back and reached for the door handle. "Of course, Commissioner. We will follow you. What floor is Robert on?"

"The fourth floor. Come."

The Commissioner led the way past the reception desk. Audrey and Craig followed in single file. The middle aged nurse looked up as they passed. Recognizing the Commissioner, she smiled and greeted him in French.

"Bon soir, Monsieur Boulanger, it is not good for your patient to be having so many visitors."

"It is just his parents and we won't stay long."

"Two gentlemen went up to see him a few minutes ago."

"Mon Dieu! Who are they?"

Craig didn't wait to find out, he brushed past the Commissioner and raced for the elevator. His French was rudimentary but he had understood enough to be alarmed. He punched the 'up' button repeatedly muttering curses. "God damn you, Bannerman! Damn you! Damn you!" Although the Commissioner's thoughts were in turmoil as he stood waiting beside Craig, he decided to say nothing in case the man fuming next to him vented his frustration on him. As soon as the doors opened they both jumped in. Audrey was about to follow but Craig pushed her back as the doors were closing.

"Audrey, stay here!"

There was no arguing with his tone of voice. She turned back to face the startled receptionist, and began pacing the floor in front of the desk. The lady shrugged apologetically.

"I am so sorry, Madame, they said they had been sent by Commissioner Boulanger. I should have asked for identification. I am so sorry."

The moment the doors opened on the fourth floor, the Commissioner pushed Craig behind him and leaned out into the corridor. He was holding a small Berretta pistol in his right hand. He glanced to the left and right. Satisfied the corridor was empty, he put a finger to his lips and motioned Craig to follow him, but the noise of the elevator doors opening alerted the intruders. A face appeared on the left side of the corridor three doors down, immediately followed by a hand holding a revolver equipped with a silencer. Craig dived for the floor. Two quick shots above him boomed and echoed down the hall. He looked up just in time to see the man's head snap back before he collapsed into the hall. The index finger of his hand twitched twice, sending two silent bullets into the wall somewhere above Craig's head, then the gun slid off his fingers and clattered on the linoleum floor. The Commissioner ran forward to pick up the revolver, but was bowled over by a black blur as the second intruder spurted out the door. The Berretta flew out of the Commissioner's hand as he fell. The man quickly kicked it away. Craig lunged for it. Before Craig could grab the gun, the intruder, dressed in black like a panther, took two quick steps towards Craig and aimed a vicious kick at Craig's head. Craig saw it coming, ducked his head, grabbed the foot as it arced over him, and heaved the man backwards. Instead of crashing onto his back, the man coiled his slim body and spun around in the air like a cat, landing lightly on his hands and feet. His dark glasses rattled onto the floor. With a quick backward glance at Craig, the intruder snatched his glasses off the floor, sprang upright and raced down the corridor weaving from side to side. The Commissioner scooped up the revolver with the silencer and fired twice. The glass exit door at the end of the corridor shattered. Moments later the man leaped through the cascading shards and disappeared down the stairs. Craig, confused by the face he had seen, squatted on his haunches for a few moments before picking up the Berretta and rushing into Robert's room, leaving the Commissioner to pursue the intruder.

Craig approached the bed with some reluctance, afraid of what he might find there. Only Robert's face and the left arm were exposed. His torso lay under a sheet. There was no movement under the sheet to indicate he was breathing. The face was deathly white. Where the beard and long hair had been was even whiter. With mounting apprehension, Craig leaned over the bed and put his right ear close to Robert's face. He was rewarded with a gentle breath on his cheek.

"Oh thank God! He's alive!"

He heard footsteps racing down the corridor towards him. Quickly, Craig wiped the tears from his eyes and faced the door, pointing the Berretta at whoever might appear. It was Audrey, followed by the Commissioner. Audrey hesitated briefly, then stepped over the body on the floor and ran into the room.

"Is he all right?"

"Yes, thank God."

Audrey hadn't waited for an answer. Her fingers were clasped around Robert's left wrist feeling for his pulse. Her lips moved silently for close to a minute before she looked up at Craig.

"His pulse is there but weak."

She checked the intravenous to make sure the fluid was still flowing into the vein in Robert's wrist, then leaned over and kissed him lightly on the forehead. Craig turned to the Commissioner with a puzzled look on his face.

"Why did nobody come into the corridor while all the commotion was going on? Are there no other patients on this floor?"

"I had the floor cleared." The Commissioner nodded his head, slightly abashed, "to increase security."

"What about the body out there?"

"I will arrange for it to be taken to the morgue and fingerprinted. Somebody should be here soon."

Audrey suddenly exclaimed, "Look at that!" Pointing to an object on the floor next to the bed. A syringe lay on its side with the needle embedded in the stopper of a small bottle half full of a clear liquid. Craig leaned over to pick it up. The Commissioner snapped.

"Don't touch it!"

Commissioner Boulanger took out his handkerchief and wrapped it around the syringe and bottle. Carefully he extracted the needle from the stopper and placed the two objects side by side on the table by the bed.

"The liquid in the bottle is probably the poison the assassin was about to inject into the intravenous tube. Very clever. Nobody would have suspected Robert had been poisoned. There will be finger prints that will help us identify the assassin."

"I already know who the assassin is, Commissioner."

Startled, the Commissioner turned to Craig. "Monsieur! You do?"

"You have just met 'Rico' the Canadian 'Jefe' of the drug cartel. The man you have been trying to arrest for years has just disappeared down the stairs."

"Mr. Fox, How can you be so sure it is him?"

"I had a good look at his face when he dropped his glasses, and for a moment I thought I was looking at an old enemy, Florentino Chavez... the man that tried to kill me many years ago... the man who is now, if the newspaper reports are correct, one of the kingpins of the Cali drug cartel... but that man must now be close to fifty. This fellow is much younger yet the resemblance is uncanny. The same slim body, olive skin and high cheekbones. He looks more Asiatic than Indian. I have no doubt he is related to Florentino Chavez, most likely his son." Craig hesitated. "One thing more. His eyes are blue."

"Blue!"

"Yes, blue. Most unusual for an Indian."

Audrey interjected. "The receptionist downstairs told me the two men asked for your man. They used your name. How did they know Robert is your man?"

The Commissioner didn't answer. He shook his head then slumped into a chair with a frown on his face. Craig seized the opportunity while the Commissioner appeared to be confused.

"Commissioner, you must listen to me, otherwise you will fail and the drug cartel will take over this country. Audrey will look after Robert while we have the discussion you do not want to hear. Please listen to my story, then make your own assessment as to its validity. I have respect for your courage and integrity, Commissioner. I know you are very loyal and it will be very difficult for you to sit and listen to a person saying villainous things about a man you admire. But please listen to me before you make a judgment."

"Bien. You may proceed with your story, Mr. Fox. But I warn you that everything you say I may end up using against you."

"Fair enough. I shall begin at the beginning... I first met Richard Bannerman in boarding school in Bogota, Colombia. He was three years ahead of me. We were not friends for reasons that are not relevant at the moment..."

"Mr. Fox, If you wish to convince me you must give me reasons for the enmity between you."

"Very well. Soon after I arrived at the school he tried to get in my bed. He was drunk at the time. That's why I omitted the incident. From then on he tried to get me expelled with trumped up assertions."

"Such as?"

"That I was having affairs with boys, stealing, cheating at exams. Things like that."

"Were you?"

Craig chuckled. "I probably tried to cheat at an exam but that was all. Richard can be very charming and considerate with those he considers useful to him, but he is ruthless with anybody that opposes him. Unfortunately one night I overheard a conversation between him and a young indian. Hearing that conversation was my death sentence. He has been trying to destroy me ever since."

"What were they talking about?"

"The Indian was reporting that he had thrown a girl over a waterfall and had taken a photo to prove it. He was asking for his money."

"Who was the girl?"

"I learned later that the girl worked in the Embassy. Richard's father was the Canadian Ambassador to Colombia at the time. The girl was pregnant by Richard. He had contracted the young Indian assassin to kill her and agreed to pay him five thousand pesos, which in those days was quite a lot of money. I also learned later, that suspecting I had overheard the conversation, Richard contracted the young assassin, Florentino Chavez, or 'Tino' as he is generally known, to eliminate me also. He was to be paid another five thousand pesos."

"What proof do you have that any of this took place. I find these stories hard to believe."

"Tino's sister told me, and when I confronted him, Tino admitted it. But unfortunately, Commissioner, I have no proof. Although I heard that Richard's mother tried to find out what had become of the girl and contacted the police. Maybe the Bogota police have some record of their search for the girl."

"Knowing something about the police in South America, I doubt they would bother to look for some poor Indian girl, much less make a record. Since you are standing before me, I assume this assassin, 'Tino', failed to kill you and did not earn his five thousand pesos?"

"He nearly succeeded. This scar you see on my forehead is the result. Tino and his father, a bandit, captured me by killing my horse. I was thrown and hit my head. My father..."

Craig heard a noise in the hall and reached for the Berretta on the side table. Two orderlies in white coveralls appeared pushing a wheeled trolley. They stopped in front of the doorway and bent over to pick up the body. It was beginning to stiffen. The dead man's trigger arm was at an angle to the body. Before they lifted him, one of the orderlies knelt down and pushed the arm towards the torso. The three spectators in the room watched fascinated, holding their breaths, expecting to hear the sound of flesh tearing as the arm moved slowly towards the body, but there was no sound except for the grunt of the orderly as he pushed. The two orderlies had no sooner disappeared when another orderly appeared with a mop and bucket and began mopping up the blood that had lain under the dead man's head. It was now a sticky red goo clumping on the mop as he swirled it around. The orderly, a small thin ancient man, with a wrinkled bald head, dirty yellow tobacco stained mustache, and wire rimmed glasses held together with tape, could be heard muttering curses as he swished the mop around in the bucket trying to dissolve the blood.

A young nurse came in carrying a small tray with bandages and medication. She greeted them in a soft voice before she glided over to the bed. She put the tray on the bedside table and hovered over Robert, straightening his pillow and smoothing the sheet. Her gaze lingered on him for a few moments before she picked up Robert's hand in her left hand, folding her fingers in his. She felt his pulse with her right hand. The intimate gesture was hidden from the others, but Craig noted her fingers gently caressing Robert's hand. He glanced up at her face. Her cheeks glowed pink; her eyes were half closed; her lips moved, silently counting his heart beats. Craig smiled. 'Even at death's door, Robert can make a conquest.'

Audrey spoke to the girl haltingly, slowly extracting each word from her limited French vocabulary. "Mademoiselle, we will be staying here for a few days to look after our son... we need a room... for my husband and I."

"Oui, Madame. There are several rooms on this floor you could use. I will speak to the matron."

"Merci. Craig, Robert must be moved to a safe and secret location, but he is too sick to move for a day or two. I am going back to the hotel to pick up some of our things. Why don't you go with the nurse and talk to the matron about a room up here. I'll order a taxi and be back as soon as I can. Commissioner, could you please stay here while Craig is downstairs?"

"Of course, Madame."

When Craig reentered the room the Commissioner was holding the small bottle of poison in his handkerchief. He had removed the stopper and was holding the open bottle to his nose. "It smells of almonds. I suspect it is cyanide in some liquid. A deadly substance." He replaced the stopper and put the bottle back next to the syringe. He returned to the chair.

"Your wife, Monsieur, is a very remarkable lady."

"Yes, she is. Audrey is a trained nurse and whenever anybody gets sick she knows exactly what to do. She has not forgotten her training. She is a very efficient nurse... also a very talented artist."

"Yes, I know. I am a great admirer of her work. I have two of her paintings in my living room. But we must move on. You were about to tell me how you avoided being killed."

"Yes. I will try to be brief. It is late and you are probably anxious to go home."

"I live alone. My wife died ten years ago. Please continue."

"I was captured by Tino and his father and taken to their hiding place. My father raided their camp with some other men and rescued me. Joaquin, Tino's father, was killed by my father during a gun battle. Tino, at my insistence, was not killed and was allowed to leave taking his sister with him."

"Why did you save his life?"

Craig glanced towards the door before replying. "This is something I have never told my wife. A beautiful Indian girl looked after my head wound while I was a captive of Joaquin. At least to me, a romantic sixteen year old boy, she was beautiful. We became lovers. She is Tino's sister. After my father killed her father there was nobody to look after her other than Tino, so I begged my father to spare him; which he did reluctantly; warning me I would regret my decision. He was right. Tino murdered my mother and father some months later.

"How did he kill them?"

"By sawing partly through a rod in the steering mechanism of my father's car. Going around a sharp curve the car swerved off the road and plunged over a cliff killing my parents. It was only recently that I was able to confirm my suspicions that Tino was the perpetrator. For years I tried to get hold of the police accident report but could never get the police to respond. Finally, through a Colombian friend of a business associate I received a copy of the report. It proved what I had known all along. My parents didn't die in an accident. Tino killed them."

"Did the report name Tino?"

Angrily, Craig retorted. "No! They didn't have to! It was obvious. He was the only person that could have done it... to revenge the death of his father."

The Commissioner wisely said nothing. Craig turned around and gazed at his son for a few moments. Looking at the body of his son lying on the bed, one faint breath away from eternity, Craig seized up, his chest suddenly tight, heaving, 'Robert, you were prepared to risk your life for an ideal. I must not fail you. The Commissioner is a good man. I must convince him I'm telling the truth.'

Facing the Commissioner again Craig apologized. "I'm sorry, Commissioner. I tend to become emotional over my parents' death... if only... always, if only. If only I had allowed my father to execute Tino they might be alive today. I'm certain that Richard Bannerman was not involved in this crime because by then he had graduated as a pilot and was overseas."

"Mr. Fox, according to the information in the your file that I was given, you also became a pilot and were on the same squadron in Italy. You became jealous of Mr. Bannerman's success as a fighter pilot and accused him of trying to kill you when you were shot down behind the front line. Please, please don't get annoyed, I'm merely quoting from your file. After the war you tried to have Mr. Bannerman charged with murder but the case was dismissed for lack of evidence."

"That part is correct. The case was dismissed for lack of evidence. What is not in your file is the reason I lost."

"And that was?"

"Two witnesses saw Richard's Spitfire shooting at me, before and after I made a forced landing. Knowing that my whole case depended on their evidence I told nobody who they were. My lawyer was the only person who knew their names and where they lived. Somebody broke into my lawyer's office and extracted their names from my file. Please note, Commissioner, only my file was touched... none other. I leave you to make the only possible conclusion as to who organized the break-in."

"I agree a reasonable conclusion points to Mr. Bannerman, but no proof."

"Then a few weeks later my one good witness, Giovanni, disappeared. A young man with a foreign accent came to Giovanni's bakery in Udine, Italy, asking for him. They left the bakery together. Giovanni never returned. His body was found weeks later with multiple stab wounds in the back. When I heard he had been murdered I wrote to his mother to tell her how much I had liked and admired her son. She wrote back and described the young man that had come looking for Giovanni. The young man fitted the description of Tino, the young Indian assassin! Some years later I was able to obtain a copy of the police report covering the murder. I have kept his mother's letter and the police report in a safety deposit box. I can show them to you. I ask you, Commissioner, why would some little 'two-bit' hood from Colombia travel all the way to Italy to murder a young man that worked in a bakery? The only possible link between Giovanni and the assassin is Richard Bannerman!"

The Commissioner appeared not to have heard Craig's last remark. He was staring at the floor, brows furrowed, lips pressed together, and fingers absently stroking his chin. In the silence that now lay between them, Craig could hear the faint scratching of the fingernails against the stubble on the Commissioner's chin. Craig waited, trying to decipher the Commissioner's reaction to his accusations. Finally, the Commissioner looked up at Craig and spread his hands out, palms open, in a gesture of resignation. Before speaking he stood up.

"Mr. Fox, you have given me much to think about. I pray that there is a simple logical explanation for what you have told me. I cannot believe Mr. Bannerman is capable of what you accuse him of doing. In all my dealings with him, he has been most insistent that I conduct our drug investigation in an ethical manner and within the law. I'm aware that he can be ruthless at times, is ambitious, and would like to be Prime Minister. But that is not illegal. A strong Prime Minister is what this country needs right now. Wouldn't you agree?"

"Absolutely! But not a Prime Minister controlled by a powerful drug cartel."

"Mon Dieu! Non! Look... I am very tired, I have not slept for two days. I must go home, Monsieur, and sort out what you have told me. I will return in the morning and we can talk some more. I will leave the two guns with you. I would send you somebody to help you guard Robert, but I don't know who to trust."

"Is this why earlier this evening, you told me it was fortunate the two boys who found Robert reported their discovery to the local police, rather than the R.C.M.P.?"

The Commissioner nodded. "For some time I have been concerned that some of our officers may have been corrupted. In confidential memos that are circulated within the Force, there have been a number of reports on operations that have been compromised by leaks within the organization. It is very disturbing. One last question. What happened to the second witness?"

Craig snorted, a smile spreading across his face. "He was killed by an irate husband. Antonio fancied himself as a ladies' man. After the war he became the communist mayor of the city of Bologna and must have thought that as a mayor he could demand favors from the ladies. One of the husbands objected and gunned him down in the main piazza. This happened long after my case was thrown out. We had tried to get him to agree to testify for me but he refused. He was the one that had concocted those stories about what happened while I was with the Partisans. I'm sure you have seen those lies in my file?"

"Yes, I have."

"Commissioner, what I have been telling you this evening occurred many years ago... it is history. Tomorrow when you return I will bring you up to date. I will outline for you how the drug cartel has succeeded in extending its power into resource companies, transportation, newspapers, radio, and television. You keep insisting on proof. I can not give you that. My evidence is circumstantial, but my story is credible and logical. With your resources you should be able to check my conclusions."

"You are a good story teller, Mr. Fox, I'm sure it will be interesting. If you know so much, why have you not done something about it?"

"Commissioner, knowing how ruthless Bannerman can be, my first priority has been to protect my family. But over the years I have done some investigating. Very carefully while trying to ensure that suspicions are not aroused. What I have managed to find out is frightening. The Cartel has been spreading its tentacles for years and I have watched this spreading corruption with growing apprehension. Because of my family I have done nothing." Pointing to the inert body of his son, Craig continued, "But now that my son has been attacked I can no longer remain passive. I know that within days, maybe hours, Mr. Bannerman will know that Robert is my son. Not only is Robert in great danger, so is my family, my wife and my son, Donald... and, I suppose, myself. As soon as Robert can be moved I'm taking him to some secret location."

"Where?"

"I'm sorry, Sir. As much as I respect your integrity, Commissioner, I cannot tell you that. You will be making a report to the Solicitor General, and as a loyal Officer you will be answering questions truthfully. If you don't know, you cannot tell him where we have taken Robert."

"Perhaps you are right. I must leave now. I'll take the bottle and syringe with me and have it analyzed. Good night, Mr. Fox."

"Commissioner, would you please call me Craig? I'm not used to so much formality. We're very casual in the west."

The Commissioner hesitated briefly in the doorway, head tilted slightly sideways, while he considered Craig's offer. Turning, he said, "I think not, Mr.Fox. For the time being I prefer to keep our relationship on a formal level. I hope you will understand. Good night."

Ten minutes later Audrey rushed in, followed by an orderly carrying two small suitcases. She thanked him hurriedly and hustled him out the door. She peered out to make sure he was out of earshot before speaking to Craig in a low voice,

"Craig! There's some of those men outside watching the building."

"What men?"

"Agh! The Hell's Angels of course! Three of them were standing across the street when I drove up in a taxi."

"Are you sure?"

"Yes! Yes! I'm sure. They had long hair and were dressed in dark clothes... looked like leather. One had a beard. I was paying off the taxi when the Commissioner came out. He didn't notice me, or them. He seemed preoccupied about something."

"I know. He's having trouble accepting what I told him about Richard Bannerman."

"When the Commissioner drove off in his car, the bearded one jumped into a car and followed him. The other two are still there. They watched me enter the building but I don't think they were suspicious."

Craig walked across the hall into the room opposite. He switched off the overhead light, closed the door behind him and felt his way over to the window in the dark. After a few moments of adjusting his eyes to the street lights below, he spotted them. One was leaning against a car parked in the shadow between two street lights, and appeared to be talking to somebody sitting in the driver's seat. Every few moments he would lean over and say something to the man inside, nod his head, then resume his careless posture against the car, arms folded across his chest. Craig recrossed the hall and eased himself behind Robert's bed to check his window. He peered out into the dimly lit parking area behind the hospital. The window was sealed and as the building was fairly modern there were no exterior emergency ladders.

"Good! Nobody can get at us through the windows, so they will have to come up in the elevator or up the back stairs. If they use the elevator, they'll have to come in through the front door and pass the receptionist. Which means that they are more likely to use the back stairs. They are probably accessed from the parking lot in the back of the building."

"Do you think they will try again?"

"I have no doubt they will. From what the Commissioner told us they have to kill Robert before he recovers from his coma. Right now they are organizing their next move. While those two keep an eye on the front, somebody is probably watching the back to make sure we don't slip Robert away. The bearded one that followed the Commissioner probably went to report the Commissioner's departure. With the Commissioner gone they will be more confident of success and will try again very soon before the Commissioner returns with more men."

"But the Commissioner is not coming back!"

"I know, but they don't know that."

"Craig you must get some help. If the R.C.M.P. won't help, phone the Montreal police."

"We-e-ll." Craig hesitated, then nodded his head. "Yes! You're right. We need help. You can speak better French than I do. Dial an outside line and phone 9-1-1."

Audrey picked up the receiver and pressed some keys. She held the receiver to her ear. A frown furrowed her brow. She replaced the receiver momentarily then dialed again. She held the receiver towards Craig. "The line is dead!"

Craig took the receiver and put it to his ear. He dialed again, listened for a moment then put it back on the cradle. "They've cut the line. They must be nearly ready to attack." He punched two more keys. "The internal line is OK."

"We're trapped! What can we do?"

"I'm going to take the gun with the silencer and I'll guard the top of the stairs. From there I can hear anybody coming up. But in case they come up the elevator we'll need the receptionist to give us a warning. Audrey, I know this is risky, but could you go down and talk to the lady downstairs. If the men outside didn't suspect you when you came in, you should have no problem even if they do see you. Ask her to phone us here if any suspicious looking characters walk in. She's probably feeling guilty about letting the two intruders come up and is anxious to help."

"Hope you are right."

"When you get back, take this Berretta and sit in a chair over there. Let me know if you get a warning from downstairs. If you hear a commotion from the stairs lock the door and don't open it unless I knock three times."

"Craig, you're going to get yourself killed. We can't fight off that mob forever."

"I know. I have to figure a way out of this mess. Why don't you go downstairs and talk to the receptionist?"

Ten minutes later Audrey returned, very annoyed. "The receptionist was pleased she could help. She said it is almost after visiting hours, so it should be easy for her to keep track of any suspicious looking men."

"So why are you looking like that?"

"She suggested we talk to the Matron about moving Robert to another floor."

"Good idea."

"I went to the Matron's office. She refused to allow us to move him to another floor. Said she was not prepared to risk the lives of her other patients, and more or less told me we should move Robert out of her hospital. I guess I lost my temper with her and told her that for a person who should be in intensive care, Robert was not getting much care. That we had seen his nurse only once when he should have a nurse with him constantly. She mumbled something about the nurses being too frightened to come to the fourth floor because of all the shooting. She finally agreed we could move him to another room on this floor."

"Could we move Robert to another hospital if we had to?"

Audrey shook her head. "No. Moving him to another room is no problem, but I think he is too feeble to move any distance at present. He's barely hanging on."

"It's a risk we might have to take. For the time being we'll move him to another room down the hall. The one closest to the elevator might be the best."

"Why that one?"

"It's furthest from the back stairs."

Audrey started to make an objection, but realized this was not the time to discuss options. She clenched her jaw and followed Craig, who was already striding down the hall. Craig entered the room next to the elevator and closed the heavy curtains before switching on the overhead light. The room was the same size as the other one, with a single bed on rollers, a side table, and a chair. He pushed the bed to one side.

"We can use this bed to sleep on, if that ever becomes possible. There's enough room for Robert's bed over here. I'll roll his bed across while you carry the I.V. stand and bottle."

Back in Robert's room, Craig positioned himself at the foot of the bed. Audrey picked up the I.V. stand. They nodded to each other and Craig began pulling the bed slowly towards the door. Audrey followed making sure the I.V. tube didn't become disconnected. Gently they pushed the bed into the other room. Audrey adjusted the stand, raised the bottle slightly, and checked the tube to make sure the liquid was dripping. Craig folded Robert's left hand in both his and bent over to kiss his son's forehead. For a moment he thought he felt a slight twitch in one of the fingers but decided it was his imagination. He walked back to the other room and returned with the suitcases and a tray holding Robert's personal effects. He took the Berretta out of his coat pocket and put it on the empty bed. Audrey saw the butt of the other revolver weighing down the top of his trousers. Suddenly frightened she reached up and pulled him towards her in a tight hug. He hugged her back just as tight.

"Oh Craig! Please take care."

"You too! You too! Remember if you hear a commotion in the stairs, lock the door. Don't forget to phone the receptionist to give her the new room number. I'll go and guard the stairs, and try to think of some way of getting out of here... alive!"

Craig stepped carefully over the broken shards of the stairwell door and looked over the cement banister. He could see all the way to the ground floor in the gap between each flight of stairs, and part of the stairs as well. He should be able to detect anybody climbing the stairs provided they didn't hug the wall. He leaned out and looked up. One flight of stairs above him led to a heavy metal door. A sudden thought galvanized him. He raced up the stairs and opened the heavy door to the roof. Satisfied the hospital had a helicopter pad, he closed the door and slowly returned to the fourth floor, whispering to himself, "Maybe... maybe."

The glass shards by the door gave Craig an idea. Picking up a large piece of glass by one corner, he leaned into the stairwell and spun the glass towards the stairs three levels down. The shard shattered against the wall on the third level scattering broken glass on the third floor landing. "Darn!" On the next piece, Craig put less spin on it. The shard arced downwards between the stairs and exploded into tiny slivers on the stairs leading up from the ground floor. "Bingo! I dare anybody to come up without making a noise." Craig dropped two more pieces without spinning them, covering the ground floor with crunchy slivers. He positioned himself on the fourth floor landing where he could guard the corridor behind him as well as the stairwell below him.

Craig didn't have long to wait.

The crisp sound of grinding glass followed by muffled curses alerted him. Craig checked the corridor to make sure it was still empty, and cautiously eased his head over the banister. Two dark figures were tiptoeing up the first flight of stairs. A third man was hunched over peering at the ground and stepping carefully as he tried to avoid the glass on the ground floor. One of them, Craig assumed it was the one hunched over, growled in a low voice, "Who the fuck did this?"

Another voice hissed, "Shut up!"

A noise behind him spun Craig around. Audrey was running down the corridor towards him waving her hands frantically. Craig slumped against the banister.

"Oh God! They're coming up the elevator too!"

But Audrey was beaming, a smile splitting her face. She couldn't wait until she reached him. She yelled,

"He's come back! The Commissioner has come back with the police. The receptionist phoned me. He's on his way up in the elevator."

"Thank God!"

Audrey slowed when Craig put his finger to his lips. She put her arm around his waist. He did the same with his left arm. His right arm held the revolver pointed down the stairs. They listened. There was no sound from below. Then,

"Did you hear that?"

"Yea! Whatchu gonna do?"

"Let's get the fuck out of here! This ain't worth the money. Come on, move it!"

The exit was noisy. Hobnailed boots slithering on glass, the thump of somebody landing on his butt, a yelp, followed by curses and promises of vengeance on whoever put the glass there. Craig gave Audrey's waist a squeeze, chuckling,

"I hope they won't be able to sit for a week."

"What did you do?"

"I littered the stairs with broken glass."

Audrey pulled his head down and kissed him on his nose. "If you weren't so conceited I'd have said that was clever."

Craig heard the elevator doors opening at the far end of the corridor. A moment later the head of the Commissioner appeared. He saw Craig and Audrey, arms around each other, smiling at him from the door at the end of the hall. He turned and spoke to somebody behind him. The Commissioner and two policemen entered the hall, each with a gun in his right hand. Walking past the door of the first room, the Commissioner saw Robert lying in bed. He halted, waiting for Craig and Audrey to join him. He put his gun back in a shoulder holster. The two policemen did the same. As soon as he could reach it, Craig grabbed the Commissioner's right hand in both his.

"Commissioner Boulanger! I don't know how to thank you enough. They were coming up the back stairs. There were three of them. I don't know how long I could have held them off."

"Not very long with the gun you were holding, there's only two shots left in the chamber."

"Oh-oh! You're right, I had forgotten four had been fired. I tried to phone the police but the outside line has been cut."

"I know. I phoned you from the police station to tell you I was coming with help but the line was dead. I realized then you needed help quickly."

"Thank you! Thank you! We thought you had gone home. What made you decide to come back?"

"The three men standing across the street. I saw them as soon as I went out the front door. I also saw..." nodding towards Audrey, "Madame, but I thought it best not to say good night to her as it would alert them she was connected to Robert. One of them took off in his car as soon as I left."

"Yes, I saw him follow you down the street and around the corner."

"He wasn't really following me, Madame, he stopped at a phone booth a few blocks away. I presume to report I had left the hospital."

Craig gestured towards the two policemen. "I didn't hear any police sirens."

"No, I'm trying to avoid publicity. If the T.V. and papers hear about this they'll want to know everything and we must keep Robert's identity a secret. I know that somebody, probably one of the staff here, is going to reveal there has been an attempt to kill a patient. I hope by then you will have transferred Robert to your secret location. Have you made any arrangements?"

"No, Commissioner. Audrey and I have been busy," Craig gave him a wry smile to emphasize the understatement, "but as soon as the telephone is repaired I'm going to start making some phone calls."

"There are some public phones downstairs in the lobby, you can use those. They're on a different line to the hospital and wouldn't have been disconnected. I suspect it was somebody inside the hospital that cut the outside line. Probably one of the orderlies. Mr. Fox, through a friend in the Montreal Police Department I have arranged for these two men to stay here until six o'clock tomorrow night. That is all the time he could give me without reporting the assignment. I'm sorry, but that is all the time you have. One man will be in the room and the other will guard the corridor. Now, if you will excuse me, I must get some sleep... and make a report to the Minister." Seeing Craig was about to object, the Commissioner raised his hand, palm open towards Craig. "Please, Mr. Fox! Don't try to lecture me, I'm too tired. I have told you before and will say it one more time. The Minister does not know the names of any of my men... So! He does not know you are involved. Good night, Sir! Madame."

Craig followed the Commissioner downstairs and was about to continue out the front door with him but the Commissioner shook his head and motioned Craig back with his hand.

"You must not be seen with me."

"Are they still out there?"

"Oui, Monsieur. Somewhere close by. They must watch the building in case Robert is moved."

"But can't you arrest them?"

"On what charge? It is not illegal to park on a street after hours. At least not in Montreal. Good night."

"Good night, Commissioner, and again thank you."

"Robert is also my responsibility. Good night, Monsieur."

Craig closed the door of the phone booth behind him. He phoned the Calgary operator for information. Cradling the phone against his shoulder he took out his wallet looking for something to write on. He scribbled the number the operator gave him on the back of one of his business cards and dialed the number using his phone card. Fifteen minutes later he emerged from the booth and smiled cheerfully at the receptionist. Remembering her help, he stopped at the desk to thank her. Coming out of the elevator on the fourth floor, Craig was confronted by a policeman standing five feet in front of him, feet planted firmly apart, both hands clasped around a black revolver aimed at the middle of his head. It had been many years since he had looked into the black hole of a gun barrel. The policeman recognized him and lowered the gun, but did not smile. He spoke slowly in stilted English.

"Monsieur, it is dangerous. Before you come, you telephone."

Scratching around in his head for a suitable French words of apology, Craig uncovered "Pardone Moi" from some long forgotten corner of his brain.

Unimpressed, the policeman gave Craig a curt nod and returned to the seat he had vacated. The other policeman was friendlier. He and Audrey were chatting amicably when he entered the room. Craig waited a few minutes until Audrey had exhausted her French vocabulary before tipping his head towards the other room. She followed him into the room across the hall and closed the door behind her. Craig motioned her to a chair while he leaned against the wall.

"I got hold of Ken Watson in Calgary..."

"Ken who?"

"Ken Watson. He owns Allcan Aviation." Audrey still looked puzzled. Craig explained, "You've probably forgotten but ten years ago Ken needed some help getting the company started so I put up some seed money. I'm still a director and a large shareholder. I explained our problem and asked him to send one of his Gulfstreams or Learjets to Montreal to pick up Robert to take us back to Calgary."

"You told him about Robert!"

"Yeah, he's okay. I play squash with him at the Glencoe Club whenever we are both in town. Squash brings out the best and worst in people; I think I know him pretty well. He is arranging a flight. I'm to call him at ten o'clock Calgary time tomorrow morning to confirm arrival time at Dorval Airport. Audrey, you're a trained nurse, do you think you can look after Robert on the plane?"

"Um-m-mh, I don't know. It's been so many years. The hospital should be able to provide a nurse, besides, we'll need one while he's in the ambulance on the way to the airport."

"There won't be any ambulance to the airport nor can we use any of the staff."

"Why not?"

"They are still watching this building. They are there in case we move Robert. The moment we leave in an ambulance they will attack and I don't think the drug cartel takes prisoners. Also, the Commissioner thinks one of the orderlies might be involved. There may be others. A nurse might slip Robert the wrong medicine."

"So how do... Craig! Is there a helicopter pad on the roof? Most modern hospitals have them. Go and check."

"I already have. It's the only way out of here. Ken is going to organize that also. The hoods downstairs will not be able to follow us in their cars and by the time they track us to the airport we'll be gone. I'll go back downstairs and phone Ken again and see if he can arrange for some medical help on the plane. Also, we'll need somebody on the helicopter."

Audrey got up and walked over to her husband. Sliding her arms around his chest and up his back, she squeezed him to her. She reached up to kiss him on the lips. "Craig, you wonderful man. I'm so glad I married you."

Craig kissed her back. "Sweetheart, don't count your chickens yet. Ken may not be able to get a plane here before tomorrow night. Well past the six o'clock deadline when the two policemen must leave. I suspect that by now the cartel knows the exact time the two policemen go off duty, and may try again as soon as they leave. But right now we can relax and get some sleep. We'll takes turns watching Robert. You try to get some sleep in here and I'll stay with Robert."

- 9 -

The Right honorable Richard Bannerman M.P. Solicitor General, Deputy Prime Minister, D.F.C. LLB. was not in a good mood. The limousine driver's "Good Evening, Sir" was acknowledged with a curt nod of the head as Richard skipped down the steps in front of the mansion and plunged into the back seat, slamming the door behind him. The driver, after two years of trying to decipher the Solicitor General's temperament at any particular moment, eased himself behind the steering wheel and waited for instructions. Thirty seconds later the man behind him exploded.

"What are you waiting for! Take me home."

"Yes sir."

Approaching the gate, the driver briefly flicked his lights on high to warn security the Minister was approaching. A Mountie opened the gate and saluted Richard as the limousine glided by. The driver turned right on Sussex Drive and right again onto Wellington Street. Passing the Parliament buildings, Richard gazed glumly at the brooding Gothic structure. It was late and only a few windows were lit. The thought that somebody besides himself was working late, lifted Richard's spirits for a moment, but his thoughts quickly returned to the Prime Minister.

He muttered, "Bloody fool! He can't get it through his head that he is the problem."

The driver smiled. He knew who was the target of the Minister's displeasure. It was not the first time the Minister had come out of number :24 Sussex Drive in a temper. It was no secret that the Minister wanted to become Prime Minister and was actively campaigning across the country to gain support. According to the polls, if Richard Bannerman was Prime Minister the Party would be a clear winner in next year's election. Without him the Party could go down to a resounding defeat from which it might take years to recover. The Party was in the fourth year of its mandate and an election would have to be held within fifteen months. And yet, the Prime Minister, Trevor Goodrich, dithered, unable to make up his mind whether to retire or run again. Editors and pundits were becoming increasingly strident in their criticism of the government's inability to control inflation, create jobs, and cut back on government spending; and Richard Bannerman's name was mentioned more and more frequently by the same experts as the man to lead the country out of the quagmire into which it was sinking; a man that was decisive and honest; the man that had done so much to combat the criminal elements by building more prisons, and increased funding for local police forces and the R.C.M.P.; the man that was making the streets safe again.

In front of the apartment, the driver opened the rear door and stood beside it. He waited patiently for the Minister to finish stuffing some papers into his briefcase and emerge. When he did the Minister smiled as he closed the door behind him.

"I'm sorry to have kept you up so late, Jim, but he does love to talk. Go on home, I won't need you in the morning. Good night."

Surprised, the driver responded, "Good night, sir!"

Richard punched the combination to open the lobby door before entering the empty lobby. On his right a triple row of brass mail boxes glistened dully in the dim lobby light. His box was on the top row, far right. A flood of letters spilled on the floor when he opened the box. Richard gathered them up, shuffled through them and picked two. One was from Barbara, 'I wonder what she wants?' The other was also from Toronto. The sender's name was not on the envelope but the writing was familiar. The rest of the letters were from constituents. He stuffed them in his briefcase for his private secretary to handle.

Inside his apartment, Richard dropped the keys and letters in a tray, closed the curtains in the living room and poured a jigger of brandy into a goblet. He emptied the glass, swished it around in his mouth and swallowed. He poured another one. This one he sipped while busying himself changing into pajamas. Occasionally he glanced at the two telephones on the chest by the bed. He didn't have long to wait. The shrill ring and flashing red light on one phone could only mean that Enrique Chavez was calling. Both Rico and the Commissioner had access to his secure line, but the Commissioner never called at night. Neither was aware the other used the same line. Richard sat on the bed. He took a sip of brandy before lifting the receiver.

"Hello?"

"Ricardo, this is Rico. Can you talk?"

"Si, Amigo, I'm alone. Did you get him?"

"No! I did not! Your Commissioner Boulanger turned up and killed Jaime. I had to make a run for it before I could inject the stuff into the tube."

"What kind of shape was he in? Was he alive?"

"I don't know. He didn't seem to be breathing but I didn't have time to check. The instant the Commissioner shot Jaime I ran... I had bribed the hospital orderly to tell us when the the coast was clear so I didn't expect the Commissioner. You told me he was going home."

"That's what he told me... who is Jaime? Will they be able to trace him to you?"

"No, I brought him in a month ago. They won't have any finger prints of him... Ricardo, the Commissioner was not alone. There was another man with him."

"One of his men?"

"Are you sitting down?"

"Go on."

"Craig Fox."

"Craig Fox! Are you sure?"

"I'm sure."

"I didn't know you knew him. What the hell was he doing there?"

"Not personally, but I've been keeping an eye on him for a couple of months."

"Whatever for?"

"Craig Fox has been making too many inquiries in Colombia. The police alerted Tino. My uncle thinks it is time something was done about him, and asked me to find out where he lives and what he is up to... the question right now is, what has he got to do with Commissioner Boulanger?"

"Hu-m-m. Good question. Why would he go to the hospital with the Commissioner? Is he a close friend of the Commissioner and just happened to be with him... not likely... or because Craig Fox is related to the young man in that bed. He has two sons and one happens to be in the R.C.M.P.... that must be him! His son Robert! But what is the connection between Craig and Commissioner Boulanger? You said you thought Robert might be dead?"

"No, I didn't say that, but if he isn't he's very close to being dead."

"The Commissioner must have brought Craig over because his son is dying. I wouldn't be too concerned about Craig Fox, he's a light weight anyway. I wrote him off years ago."

"Ricardo, the way he flipped me over this evening does not put him in the light weight category for me. Don't underestimate him. I have been wondering for some time who has been making discreet inquiries about some of our companies. Now I suspect it is Craig. This ties in with what my uncle told me about him asking questions down there. I think he is dangerous. He probably recruited the Commissioner some time ago and talked him into making his son an undercover agent to infiltrate us."

"How come you let him get so close to you?"

"We won't go into that now. The man who brought Robert to me won't do it again... ever."

"What are you going to do about Robert?"

"If Robert is alive he is too sick to move. The Commissioner has two policemen guarding Robert, but the orderly tells me they are only there until six o'clock tomorrow night. After they leave we'll make another attempt and hopefully eliminate Craig Fox at the same time."

"Why wait?"

"We have fairly good relations with some of the Montreal police and I don't want to upset them by killing off their men."

"So how are you going to handle it this time?"

"The orderly tells us there is a helicopter pad on the roof. We'll come in that way, grab Craig and inject his son. We'll do it soon after dark when there's still enough traffic on the streets to muffle the noise of the helicopter."

"Good luck. Ciao!"

The line emitted a low buzzing sound. Rico had hung up. Richard put the receiver back and gulped the rest of the brandy. He padded back to the living room in his bare feet and poured two inches of brandy into the goblet. He picked up the two letters he had left in the hall and carried them into the kitchen. He put water in the kettle, plugged it in, and dumped a large teaspoon of instant coffee into a mug. Richard sliced open both envelopes. Barbara's he put aside to be read sometime. He unfolded second the letter. It was from Miss Roberta Masse, Allan Sharp's secretary. Her report was routine; Mr. Sharp had cut back on his drinking; was spending two hours a week at a fitness center; his teenage son was in some kind of trouble; she hadn't been able to find out what the problem might be, but Mr. Sharp was on the phone a lot so it must be serious. Richard crumpled the letter and dropped it in the garbage can. He was more concerned about the connection between the Commissioner and Craig Fox than about Allan Sharp's teenager. Taking the coffee and brandy into the bedroom he placed the mug and goblet on the small chest by the bed, threw back the covers and propped more pillows against the head board before climbing into bed. He reached over for the brandy. Sipping occasionally he began analyzing the Craig Fox enigma.

'What is the connection between those two? Rico suggested that Craig Fox recruited the Commissioner... from what I know of Commissioner Boulanger, I don't think the Commissioner is the type of man that can be "recruited" much less so by a man like Craig Fox... nevertheless the two men must know each other if they appeared together at the hospital...

my earlier conclusion has to be correct that it is Craig Fox's son, Robert, in the hospital, and the Commissioner brought the father in because the boy is dying... but why did the Commissioner select Robert for his team? The Commissioner claimed he recruited the best from a long list of young Mounties... was Robert one of the best? The son of Craig Fox being one of the best? Doubtful... there had to be some other reason for recruiting Craig's son... maybe I will have to take a closer look at the Commissioner... maybe put somebody I can trust into the organization who could keep an eye on the Commissioner... I'll have to think about that. it'll be interesting to hear what the Commissioner has to say when he calls tomorrow morning.'

Richard swallowed the rest of the brandy and turned off the light. Three minutes later he was asleep. He had forgotten to drink his coffee.

* * *

The phone rang. Richard rolled over and propped himself on his elbow. He glanced at his watch before picking up the receiver. It was precisely seven. That would be Commissioner Boulanger on the phone.

"Hello?"

"Good morning, Minister. This is Commissioner Boulanger."

"Good morning, Commissioner. I hope you have some good news for me. How is your young man doing? Is he going to live?"

"He is very weak but his condition has stabilized. I think he will live. He is still in a coma so cannot give us any information on the cartel."

"Do the doctors think he will come out of the coma soon?"

"They don't know, but in their opinion they think it's only a matter of a few days. He's young and was in good physical condition."

"Is he being guarded?"

"He is now."

"What do you mean 'now'?"

"We-e-ll Sir, I assumed that nobody knew I had put John in that hospital so guards didn't seem necessary, but two men tried to poison him last night. Luckily I arrived just in time. I killed one but the other one got away... now I have two policemen guarding John."

"I thought you told me his name was Robert?"

There was a silence on the other end.

"Commissioner, are you there?"

"Yes, Minister. I think you must be confusing him with one of our other under cover men whose code name is Robert."

"Oh! I see. Commissioner have you notified his family?"

"Yes, they are with him now."

"Had you met them before?"

"No sir." After a long pause, "why do you ask?"

Richard ignored the question. "The man you killed, have you identified him?"

"No, but from his appearance and clothes I have no doubt he is Colombian. We checked his fingerprints and nothing came up."

"The man that got away, was he Colombian?"

"Yes, I have reason to believe he's the one running the cartel in Canada."

"How do you know that? You've never met him."

"No sir, I haven't met him. Maybe I am premature in assuming he is the man we are looking for, but knowing the importance they would attach to making sure John does not talk, I think the 'Jefe' would want to handle the assassination attempt himself. If he had succeeded in injecting the poison I doubt that anybody would have suspected John had been poisoned... Minister... but the problem I am trying to sort out right now is who told them John is in that hospital?"

"That is a very good question, Commissioner, and it brings up a subject I have been considering for some time, particularly since this latest incident."

"Oh! You already knew about last night?"

"Oh no! Of course not! You have a security leak in your organization. You are now one man short. You need some help and I think I have just the man for you. I'm sure you will be pleased. He's a very competent senior officer. I can arrange to have him transferred in a couple of days."

There was no response from the other end.

"Commissioner?"

"Minister. I don't think that is necessary. I have enough men, and I am certain the leaks are not from within my organization... Minister, I think somebody may be tapping into this line and listening to our conversation. I'm going to have the line checked today."

"Commissioner! That will not be necessary... Ah-h... I've had the line checked already to make sure that was not the problem. You do not need to check the line. It is secure."

"Yes, Minister. But I insist, sir, I do not need any more personnel. If I may remind you, sir, you have given me authority to recruit my own staff, and their identities are carefully guarded even from you."

"Yes! Yes! I know, but circumstances have changed. I am assigning another officer to work with you. That is an order, Commissioner."

Richard waited for the Commissioner to continue his objections; his left hand holding the receiver to his ear; his right hand reaching for the cigarette pack on the side table. There was silence at the other end. Richard jerked the pack, ejecting a cigarette part way out. He put it between his lips, dropped the pack on the bed, and felt around the side table for his lighter. He lit the cigarette, inhaled, and exhaled.

"Good! Now that we have got that settled, what else do you have to report to me?"

"I'm at home at present. I will give you a full report later in the day after I have talked to my staff. Will you be home around noon, sir?"

"Yes, I'm here all day. I was up very late last night with the Prime Minister. Oh! One more question."

"Yes, sir?"

"What are you going to do about... Aah... John, when the two policemen go off duty?"

There was a long silence. When the Commissioner finally answered, his voice, for the first time, was dull, defeated, "I don't know. I'll have to make some other arrangement. I'll let you know when I come up with a plan. Good day, sir."

"Goodbye, Commissioner."

Richard put down the receiver. He took a long puff on his cigarette. Slowly he allowed the smoke to drift through his nostrils. Suddenly Richard slapped his thigh. "Damn!" Scowling at his bare feet at the bottom of the bed. 'How could I be so stupid! The Commissioner said nothing to me about the two police officers going off duty. It was Rico who told me that. Now the Commissioner must be wondering who told me the policemen were going off duty at six. However, the Commissioner probably suspects me already, now that that bugger, Craig Fox, has been talking to him about me... my stupid slip has probably confirmed his suspicions... now for sure I will have to get somebody to keep an eye on the Commissioner.'

Richard unlocked a small drawer in the side table and pulled out an address book. He opened it at the letter 'C', and ran his index finger down the page until he came to the name of Inspector Calder. Richard dialed the Ottawa number.

* * *

Long after the Minister had hung up, the Commissioner was still holding the phone to his ear. A persistent loud buzz from the receiver nudged Marcel Boulanger out of his gloomy apathy. Wearily he put the receiver back on the cradle and pushed himself back from his desk. Hands on the desk, he rose slowly, picked up the notes he had scribbled and carried them down the hall to the kitchen. The Commissioner sank slowly into a kitchen chair and stretched his long legs under the table. He surveyed the food before him with distaste, wishing, as he had so often, for his wife's cooking. The housekeeper had laid out his breakfast the night before; English marmalade and butter on the table, next to two croissants on a plate neatly covered with a small napkin, a sugar bowl, an empty cup and saucer. There would be, as usual, a small glass of juice in the fridge. The coffee pot waited, patiently, on the stove. All he had to do was to switch on the element. This he neglected to do for some minutes.

"Mon Dieu! Can it be possible?" Marcel shook his head as if that gesture of denial could obliterate the terrible thoughts that were streaming round and round inside his head. "Non! It cannot be true."

Lifting the cup to his lips, Marcel realized it was empty. He put it back on the saucer and reached around behind him to turn on the element under the coffee pot. As soon as it boiled, he poured the coffee and slowly ate the croissant, using generous helpings of marmalade to improve the taste. He had never liked croissants, even when his wife made them. When he finished, Marcel dropped the dishes into the sink, chipping the cup as it clattered against the saucer. He shrugged indifferently, picked up his notes and returned to his desk. Taking out a fresh sheet of foolscap paper, Marcel rearranged his notes into the proper sequence leaving room below each heading for additional comments and conclusions.

<u>Craig Fox:-</u> Not what I expected -- Strong character -- Good marriage.

<u>Break in at Lawyer's:-</u> Bannerman's doing? -- Reasonable assumption -- No proof.
<u>Murder of Witness:-</u> If description of Colombian assassin is correct, then no doubt Bannerman is involved--Proof relies on Craig Fox's description-- Can Craig Fox be believed?--I think so!
<u>Location of Hospital:-</u> Bannerman is the only person informed.
orderly in hospital recognized Robert --Not likely.
leak in my organization --I don't see how.
Telephone to Bannerman tapped --Not likely.
Conclusion:- Bannerman probable culprit!
<u>Robert's name:-</u> How did Bannerman know his name?
I never told him Robert's name
The cartel didn't know his name
The hospital does not know Robert's name
Did the assassin recognize Craig Fox when they wrestled on the floor? --Craig didn't say he knew the assassin.
Conclusion:- Maybe an honest mistake by Bannerman.

<u>*Policemen on duty:-*</u> *I didn't tell Bannerman they would be on duty only for a short time --Somebody else informed him. Bannerman has no contact with Montreal police. But I know the cartel does*
Conclusion:- THE CARTEL TOLD BANNERMAN!

Marcel put his pencil on the pad and leaned back on his chair, hands clasped together across his waist. After a few moments he leaned forward again and reread his notes. He made no changes. Across the bottom of the page, Marcel added one short sentence... in large letters... in ink.

BANNERMAN IS GUILTY!

'What to do now?... I have supported and admired this man for many years... by next year he will be Prime Minister of Canada... and the cartel will control Canada ... Mon Dieu! That would be a disaster! He must be stopped... but how?'

Marcel began writing again on a fresh sheet of foolscap.

OPTIONS
============

1- Inform the Prime Minister.
Weak man -- Would avoid doing anything unless I had film of Bannerman talking to the head of the cartel... which I do not have

2 - Contact the news media.
According to Craig Fox much of it is already controlled by the cartel, and those organizations that are not would want more than just circumstantial evidence that relies on Craig Fox's word --a notoriously unreliable person in their eyes.

3 - Report to the Chief Superintendent of the R.C.M.P.
No friend of mine --He resents my direct contact with the Solicitor General. Would need hard proof for him to do anything. He may even be one of Bannerman's men and could report me to him

4 - Do my own investigation - Only option.
A - Talk to Craig Fox --He seems to know more about the cartel than I do after years of undercover work.
B - Find out who owns the company that controls so many T.V. stations and newspapers.
C - Contact Italian Police re murder of Craig's witness.
D - Contact Colombian police.
No! According to Craig they report every thing to the cartel at some point may have to take a chance.
E - BE VERY CAREFUL!

Marcel read his notes again. He made no changes. He underlined the last sentence with a red pen, and pushed his chair back firmly, rising quickly. Ten minutes later he was heading towards the hospital, one ear tuned to the radio in the dash board

* * *

Craig called Calgary twice. Each time Ken Watson was out of the office. Frustrated he left the number of the telephone he was using with Ken's secretary and moved a chair in front of the booth to prevent anybody else using the phone. The receptionist took pity on him after fifteen minutes and brought him the morning paper. It was in French. To show his appreciation he tried to read it. The phone rang long after he got tired of pretending.

"Ken, is that you?"

"Yep! Who else would it be?"

"Have you got the jet organized?"

"Yep! A Lear jet will be taking off this afternoon and should be landing at Dorval around nineteen hundred hours and the heli..."

"Ken! that is not good enough! Seven o'clock is too late. We'll all be dead by then."

"Oh for Christ sake, Craig! This is Canada. Not some two bit country like Panama."

"Ken, listen carefully. This is the Colombian cartel we are dealing with and they mean to get Robert come hell or high water. They pumped Robert full of bullets and dumped him in a field thinking he was dead. When they found out he was still alive... someday I'll tell you who told them but at the moment you wouldn't believe me... they tried to kill him with cyanide and would have succeeded if we hadn't arrived in time. We killed one of them but the other one got away. Ken, listen, please... we have two policemen guarding Robert but they must leave at six this evening. The moment they leave I know that gang will make a third attempt."

"You mean they've made two attempts already?"

"They gave up the second attempt when the police arrived. Ken, you must try to be here before... hold on... there's somebody hanging around outside the booth. It's a damn orderly. Probably the one working for that gang. Hold on... it's okay, he moved off when I opened the door. Ken can you get here before six?"

"I'll try. The jet is being serviced right now. I'll speak to the crew. Craig, I have a helicopter flying over from Ottawa. I had a hell of a time getting one and it won't be available until it finishes another job."

"When will that be?"

"They promised it would be finished by five o'clock."

"How long will it take to fly to Montreal from Ottawa?"

"As the crow flies it's a shade over one hundred miles, depending on which way the wind is blowing, I'd say one hour."

"Is there no way you can get it here sooner?"

"Craig, I'll do my best."

"What about medical help?"

"My son Roger is an intern at the Foothills Hospital here in Calgary. He has agreed to come."

"I hope you warned him it could be dangerous."

"I will make sure he knows."

"Thanks, Ken. I'll take care of any expenses. What's a good time to call you to confirm your time of arrival?"

"Call me around four your time... good luck."

"Ken, one thing more. Is there any way you can avoid revealing that you are carrying a sick man on the return from Montreal?"

"No problem, my friend. Already taken care of. We are delivering some engine parts for one of my planes sitting at Dorval and the Lear jet is returning empty."

"Fantastic! You are a marvel. Thanks, Ken. I'll call you at four."

Coming out of the booth, Craig spotted Commissioner Boulanger striding past the reception desk. He returned the paper to the receptionist, gave her a smile, and followed the Commissioner. Together they entered the elevator.

"Bon jour, Commissioner."

"Bon jour, Monsieur. You are learning our beautiful language. Bien."

On the fourth floor the Commissioner paused to speak to the policeman standing at attention by the elevator, then followed Craig into Robert's room. The second policeman was helping Audrey wash Robert's back and didn't notice the Commissioner until he spoke. Unable to salute his superior officer he bobbed his head instead.

"Monsieur Fox, may I call you Craig?" Without waiting for Craig's reply he continued, "Please come with me, I must speak to you."

Craig, surprised and pleased at the Commissioner's friendlier tone, followed, taking long strides to keep up with the older man's march down the hall.

"Craig. We'll use this empty room... here sit over there, I'll take this chair... I want you to tell me what you know about the cartel. Their organization and what they control. I know you said you have no proof, regardless, I want all the details... I have a lot of catching up to do. Please proceed."

"I am sure you have noticed that Richard Bannerman's name is frequently in the news... on T.V., radio, and newspapers... Bannerman at some conference; Bannerman addressing such and such convention; Bannerman making public announcements of one sort or another; Bannerman the man on the white horse who could save this country if he was Prime Minister. It has been building up for some time. There was so much coming out about him, I began wondering if this was being orchestrated, and if so, by whom... Commissioner, in your file on me it says I was jealous of Richard. Believe me, Commissioner I am not jealous of Richard. I am afraid of him, and of what will become of this country if he is Prime Minister."

"I regret that I have come to the same conclusion. He is a man I have admired for many years... and now, I suppose, I must try to destroy him. Please continue."

Craig's face brightened. He continued, "I made a list of the T.V. stations newspapers and magazines that reported on Bannerman more frequently than other stations or publications. Then I traced their ownership through their annual reports and the stock exchanges. All! I repeat, all are owned or controlled by one corporation... a privately owned conglomerate... the Star Corporation."

"I'm not familiar with that company."

"I am! Very! Years ago the Star Corporation bought up a small oil company just to force the President to fire me. Later, when I became a consulting geologist, the Star Corporation tried to induce some of the smaller oil companies not to accept my work. Fortunately for me, they liked what I was doing and continued to work with me... Commissioner, who do you think would..."

Quickly, Marcel held out his hand to deflect Craig's rhetorical question, "I know! I know!"

"And guess who runs the company?... none other than Allan Sharp!"

"Who is he?"

"Squadron Leader Sharp was the Commanding Officer of our Spitfire Squadron in Italy. Both Bannerman and I were attached to that squadron. Bannerman had something on the Squadron Leader. I never was able to figure out why Sharp let him get away with so much, but Bannerman got the best pilots, aircraft, and ground crew. Sharp was born and raised in Britain. He knew nobody over here except Bannerman. He had no university nor business background... so, how did he get to be President of a huge conglomerate? It had to be Bannerman... conclusion, Bannerman controls Star Corporation."

Boulanger's brow furrowed, "I find that hard to believe."

"There can be no other explanation."

"Is Star Corporation huge?"

"Very! I don't know the full extent of what it controls. Your staff is probably better equipped to do the research, but what I was able to dig out is frightening. Besides the T.V. stations newspapers and magazines I mentioned earlier, it controls several oil companies, including two very large ones with production in a number of foreign countries including Colombia. It controls several gold and silver mining companies; one large base metal company in northern Manitoba; one of the largest undeveloped nickel deposits in eastern Canada; and a large bauxite deposit in South America... but where did it get the money to buy into these companies? Adding up the money required to buy control of the companies that I know about, would have required several billion dollars... Commissioner, I said billions! I know Bannerman is wealthy, and so is his wife, but they do not have the resources to spend billions. I could find no evidence that the Star Corporation did any public financing or borrowed money from the banks... it had to be cartel money. The cartel has been laundering it's profits by investing in the Star Corporation, a company controlled by Bannerman! And now they are financing a media campaign to propel Bannerman into this country's highest office."

"But you have no evidence the cartel financed Star's acquisitions."

"I know. However, let me give you another thread to help you tie the knot around Bannerman... who is Florentino Chavez?"

"He is, from the information we have been able dig out, the head, or one of the heads of the Cali Cartel."

"Right! He is also the man Bannerman contracted to kill the pregnant girl; the man he contracted to kill me, and the man that killed the only witness to Bannerman's attempt to kill me. Florentino Chavez is reputed to be a billionaire several times over. He would have no problem funneling billions into Star."

Boulanger gave his head a slight shake. "It is a very thin thread you are using to conclude he is financing Star Corporation."

"I agree, but I think the last twenty four hours has..." Craig hesitated, a little apprehensive he might be touching a sensitive area, "has demonstrated there is a rope, if I may continue with my analogy... a rope tying Bannerman to the cartel... only he could have told the cartel where Robert is recuperating."

Marcel nodded. Abruptly his head jerked up, "I'm sorry, I should have asked before. How is Robert?"

"His breathing is stronger, and he actually let out a moan when Audrey moved his arm. I think he'll be OK. Thank you."

"Craig, the young man that escaped after you bowled him over... what's his name?"

"Rico."

"Had you ever met him before?"

"No! Never."

"Are you sure?"

"Absolutely. Why?"

"Bannerman may know that it is Robert in that room down the hall. If he does know, which I think he does, then the question is how did he find out. When you left Calgary, did you tell anybody about Robert?"

"Nobody. At least nobody until last night when I made arrangements to move Robert... and I can vouch for that person."

"Who was that..." Marcel quickly put up his hand. "No! don't tell me, I'll accept your endorsement. Do you think that Rico may have recognized you, and made the linkage from you to Robert?"

"I don't see how. We've never met, and I am not well known outside of the oil fraternity. To my knowledge there are no recent pictures of me in print."

"Is it possible that this young man, Rico, may be spying on you? You're smiling and probably thinking that we policemen suspect everybody. But don't forget you have been asking a lot of questions in Colombia and digging into the finances of companies controlled by the cartel. They probably want to know what you are up to, and have been watching you. I think Rico recognized you and told Bannerman."

Abruptly Craig got up and began pacing the floor, "If what you are saying is correct, then my whole family is in danger, Audrey, Donald, Robert, and me too. They will have to go into hiding... I can't, I have too many business commitments. I'll have to find a safe place for them until this is over."

Pacing past the window, Craig paused; his visual sweep along the street below had spotted two men standing beside a car parked some distance away. One, wearing white slacks and a short sleeved shirt, was the same blond orderly that had been snooping outside the telephone booth. The other man was slim, dressed in black, and wore dark glasses. The orderly was pointing to his wristwatch while he spoke to the other man.

"Commissioner! Speaking of the devil, he's down there!"

With two quick strides, Marcel was at the window gazing down to where Craig was pointing, "Is that him?"

"I'm certain that's him, and that's the orderly that has been passing information to them. He was hanging around the phone booth when I was on the phone."

The Commissioner rushed out the door and pounded down the hall, barking orders at the two policemen. Craig didn't follow. He had other priorities, the most important being his family. Instead, he stayed by the window to watch developments and ponder the threat to his family.

* * *

Although Enrique Chavez was younger and shorter than the man standing in front of him, it was the other man that was bobbing his head deferentially in response to the questions.

"Could you hear what he said?"

"No sir, not very well, and he saw me before I could get very close, but I did hear the words 'jet', and 'seven o'clock'. The rest was muffled."

"So! He's bringing in a jet to fly Robert out and it'll be here at seven tonight. Nice work, Jacques. Here take these." Rico held out a wad of hundred dollar bills. "There's more to follow if you keep us informed."

Jacques took the bills and began counting. He didn't notice the Commissioner and two policemen bounding out the front door of the hospital. Rico did.

"Carajo! That fucking Commissioner again!"

Rico opened the door to the stolen car he had been using, but realized immediately he would have to race past the three policemen. They would not hesitate to shoot him. He slammed the door and raced down the street in the opposite direction weaving rapidly. He ignored the calls to stop. Some yards in front of him a branch hanging over a high wall gave Rico an idea. He raced forward and leapt up grasping the branch in both hands. Effortlessly he swung up into the tree, crouched and skittered cat like along the branch, dropping onto a flower bed on the far side of the wall. Remaining in a crouched position, Rico was partly hidden by low bushes. Quickly he absorbed the surroundings. It was a large garden behind a gray stone building. From it's size, and the murmur of voices drifting from the open windows, it was evidently a school. A nun appeared briefly at a window but didn't see him. A girl's school most likely. The sound of grunts and curses from the other side of the wall warned Rico he had better move. He brushed past the bushes and broke into a loping run along a gravel path that curved around the building. To allay suspicions, he maintained the same easy pace out the front yard and down the street for one block. At the corner, Rico flagged a passing taxi and directed it to

Hotel de Ville on rue Notre-Dame, where he caught another taxi. Twenty minutes later the driver dropped him in front of the George Cartier statue in Parc du Mont-Royal. Rico walked to Lac des Castors, passing his station wagon on the way. There was nobody near the wagon. Sitting on a bench by the lake, Rico glanced back along the street occasionally while watching a duck searching for fleas before waddling into the water. It was still too early for the noon traffic and the few cars that passed his wagon did not hesitate. Satisfied, Rico walked back to the station wagon and peered in to make sure that none of the papers he had laid out on the dash board had been disturbed. They were as he had left them two hours before. Nobody had broken into the car. Rico opened the front door. A slight gust of air lifted the front of the papers, wafting them gently to the floor. Rico jumped in, gathered up the papers, turned the key and drove out of the park, heading for Dorval Airport. He drove past the passenger terminal and entered the airport at the commercial entrance. Rico circled completely around a trucking depot, before parking the wagon behind a small hangar. Rico rearranged the papers on the dashboard and gently closed the car door, pushing until the lock clicked. He checked to see the papers were as he had arranged them. Rico ignored the man grinning at him through a window and entered the hangar through a side door. The dispatcher, sitting at a desk in front of the window, rolled his chair back and spoke to his boss.

"Rico, I sit here all day and would see anybody fooling around with your car."

"You're not here all the time, Andre. If there's a message for the crew you have to call them, or you go to have a piss or crap. Then there's other times I've seen you stretching your legs in the hangar. I'm careful and still alive... any messages?"

"Yea, Jacques called."

"Oh did he? He must have got away."

"Yea, he said the cops raced after you so he took off. But he said he can't go back to the hospital."

"Where is he?"

"He called from a public phone. Said he was on his way home to pack up and hide somewhere for a while."

"He's no further use to us and might start talking if the police catch him... Andre, send somebody over to his room. Have him take care that Jacques doesn't talk. Do it now before he disappears."

Andre opened a desk drawer and pulled out a clip board. He ran his finger down a list of names typed on a sheet of paper. He put the clip board back in the drawer and dialed a number. Rico closed the office door behind him and walked over to where two men were servicing a helicopter; a Huey, still in its dark green army colors; war surplus from Vietman. Rico spoke to the mechanics, giving them a five o'clock deadline before returning to the office.

"Andre, Is somebody looking after Jacques?"

"Yea, Johnson is the closest to Jacques' place."

"Johnson! That bloody fool. He'd better not screw up this one or he's in trouble."

"I warned him you weren't too happy about last night." Andre began to chuckle. "Said he still finds more splinters every time he sits down."

"He won't be sitting for long if Jacques gets away. Now listen carefully, Andre. The raid tonight has to be very carefully timed. The police guarding Ronald... by the way, Ronald is not his real name, it is Robert... the police guarding Robert leave at six and we can't move in until after they leave. I don't want any dead cops now that they are... ummh friendly. I have information that a plane is arriving here at Dorval at seven tonight to pick up Robert and take him somewhere. I presume to Calgary where his parents live. This has been organized by his father, Craig Fox. He knows we're after his son and won't be wasting any time if he can help it. So he'll make sure Robert is at the airport at seven o'clock. It'll take at least a half hour for an ambulance to drive from the hospital to Dorval, which means he will leave the hospital at six thirty. We have thirty minutes, from six to six thirty, to finish off Robert, capture Craig Fox and his wife and bring them back here."

"What about Commissioner Boulanger? He'll probably be there too."

"No! He's not to be touched... at least not for a while. I'll arrange for him to be called to Ottawa for some urgent meeting."

"Wow! How will you do that?"

Rico gave Andre a menacing look. "None of your business."

Andre lowered his eyes. "Yeah, sure. I just didn't know you could do that."

"I'm going to be handling this raid myself, and I want four good men. Go through the list and pick four of the best. Also, I want a backup hit squad in case something goes wrong and they leave the hospital before I get there in the Huey. Four men should be enough to highjack the ambulance, plus one in the radio car to follow the ambulance. I'll be back in an hour to go over your list. Have the ones we select here by two o'clock. They must have silencers. I don't want the whole town to hear what we're doing." Rico glanced behind him towards the helicopter. "Make sure those two have the Huey ready by five at the latest. I've already warned them but you make sure they do."

Andre waited until Rico had finished his security routine around the car and driven off, before taking the list out of the drawer.

* * *

Craig leaned over the bed and stroked Robert's head, his fingers gently kneading the scalp. As a child, Robert had loved that, tottering over to his dad as soon as he came home, leaning his head on Craig's lap like a puppy dog to have his head massaged. A sudden gush of tears at the memory made him turn his head away from the policeman sitting on the chair beside the bed, but the man had noticed. He got up and patted Craig on the shoulder before walking out of the room. Craig lifted Robert's hand to check the pulse. The beat was more forceful. Robert's face was no longer so pale, and the breathing was stronger. A shuffling noise and creak of the springs from the other bed alerted him that Audrey was wakening. Audrey rolled on her back and rubbed her eyes. Craig leaned over her.

"Sweetheart, go back to sleep. You were up all night and we have a long night ahead of us."

"Did you call Ken Watson?"

"Yes, the helicopter will be at Dorval at five thirty and will wait until the jet lands before coming here. According to Ken the Lear jet will land about the same time. Ken's son, Doctor Roger Watson, will transfer to the helicopter and come here to help with Robert."

"What time will it be here?"

"The plan is for the helicopter to land upstairs at ten after six tonight. I don't want to leave while the two policemen are here."

"Why?"

"They will report to headquarters that we are preparing to leave and ask permission to go home. Somebody at headquarters is sure to alert the cartel... so we wait until they leave. The moment they leave at six we'll wheel the bed into the elevator and up to the roof as quickly as we can."

"Can't we ask the police to leave a little earlier?"

"Good idea! I don't see why not. You seem to have good rapport with the older one, Raymond. Why don't you speak to him. They've been on duty a long time and I'm sure they would like to leave. But don't tell them too soon, otherwise word that they are leaving early might get back to that gang. When you speak to him suggest five thirty, that's one hour from now."

"How is Robert?"

"Much better. His pulse and breathing is stronger. I think he is strong enough for the trip."

"Is Commissioner Boulanger coming back?"

"No, he left a message for me to call him, which I did. He's been summoned urgently to Ottawa for a meeting with Richard. He thinks Richard wants him out of the way when the cartel come calling tonight... I agreed with him."

"Did he catch that man?"

"No, he got away. They managed to trace his movements as far as some park. That's where he picked up the stolen car he used this morning. It belonged to some jogger."

"And the orderly?"

"They found him in his rooming house with his throat cut. They're a pretty ruthless bunch. The Commissioner is concerned we are dithering and should have moved Robert long ago. I reassured him everything is organized."

Audrey sat up in bed and swung her legs over the side. Her dress was scrunched up around her waist. She stretched her arms and legs, catlike, and ruffled her hair. Glancing up from under her hands, Audrey caught Craig admiring her legs. Pulling down her dress, she gave him a saucy look.

"You dirty old man, I better get you home before you get into trouble with the nurses."

Craig leaned over her and crushed her lips with his.

* * *

Rico closed the office door behind him and walked across the hangar floor to the men swaggering about in front of the helicopter, laughing and spewing profanities. Only the cigarettes betrayed their nervousness.

"For Christ sake! Put out those bloody cigarettes. Do you want to burn the place down. Don't you know you can't smoke around planes? That's better." Rico pointed at the pilot, "what's your name?"

"Renaud."

"Renaud, how long will it take you to fly to the hospital?"

"Ten minutes, maybe twelve."

"OK, I want you landing on the roof at five minutes after six... not four minutes, not six minutes after six... got that?"

"Bien, no problem."

"That means we lift off at ten to six... when we land, Andre you stay with the helicopter to make sure nobody interferes with our getaway... you, you, and you, will come with me. The guy we want is on the fourth floor, the top floor... I'm going to make another attempt to poison him but if there's any problem blast the hell out of him. He must not get away this time. The same with his father. I want him alive if possible. I want to know what he knows about our organization but if there is a problem let him have it... the wife too. We don't want her identifying anybody afterwards... I want the whole thing over quickly before anybody has time to react. I want us back in the air in less than ten minutes, with or without our prisoners, so keep the Huey's motor running... you all got that?" Rico glared at each man in turn. "If anybody fucks up you'll hear from me... and you all know what that means." All eyes dropped.

"Now set your watches... it is now... five thirty... move the helicopter out and start the motor. Be ready to lift off in twenty minutes."

Rico returned to the office to put through a call to the control tower. He requested clearance for immediate takeoff but was told he would have to wait until six thirty because of heavy traffic. Using his most persuasive manner Rico argued with the controller for several minutes. The man was apologetic but unswayed. Rico thanked the man and slowly put down the receiver then hurled it through the open door onto the hanger floor. Andre rushed in, glancing back at the shattered phone. Rico sat hunched forward, jaw clenched, eyebrows sliced down, lips compressed.

"Rico, what's the problem?"

"They won't give me clearance until six thirty." Rico held out his hand, "Here, give me a cigarette."

Andre, realizing his boss was in a dangerous mood, hurriedly plucked a packet out of his breast pocket and offered it to him. Rico took one. Using two hands to steady his lighter Andre spun the wheel and presented the flame. Rico lit the cigarette, inhaled, and allowed the smoke to drift out slowly through his nostrils. "Fuck em! We're taking off without their go ahead. I'll fix it up with them later." He pounded his fist on the desk. "Let's go!"

Rico quashed the cigarette under his shoe and walked through the hangar. Andre followed. The Huey was out on the tarmac. Two men were closing the hanger doors. The blades of the Huey gathered speed. Through the narrowing opening Rico noticed the pilot beckoning him from the cockpit. He increased his stride but the pilot couldn't wait. He yelled at Rico,

"You're wanted on the radio. He says it's urgent."

Rico ran forward and leaped into the helicopter through the side door without using the step. He raced forward into the cockpit and snatched the head phones out of the pilot's hand.

"This is Rico, what is it?"

"The two cops just left. They got in their car and drove off about five minutes ago."

"Shit! They weren't supposed to leave until six. Where are you?"

"Up the street from the hospital."

"Keep a sharp lookout in case they leave in an ambulance. We'll take off right now and be there in a few minutes."

"Aren't you in the air?"

"No, why?"

"Cause there's a helicopter circling the building right now and it looks as if it's getting ready to land."

"Carajo!" Rico thrust his head out the side window and bellowed at the men standing below him, "Get the fuck in here! We're leaving right now!" Turning to the pilot, he ordered, "Get this fucking machine up and out of here. Head away from the runways so the tower doesn't blow a fuse and get me to the hospital as fast as you can."

Ten minutes later the Huey was over the hospital. They were too late. The helicopter pad was deserted except for an empty hospital bed and an I.V. stand beside it. A sheet of writing paper was pinned to the pillow. It flapped in the wash from the rotating blades when they landed on the pad. Rico leapt out and strode over to the bed. He ripped the sheet of paper from the pillow. In big black letters, Craig had written.

> *"Sorry. We decided not to wait for you. Give my regards to your father - Florentino Chavez. He probably still remembers me.*
>
> *Craig Fox."*

Rico crushed the paper in his fist and shook it in the direction of the airport. "Fuck you, Mr. Fox! Don't think you can get away with this." Rico climbed back into the helicopter. No man dared to make eye contact.

- 10 -

Enrique Chavez called Richard Bannerman late one night through the secure line in Richard's apartment, "Ricardo, my friend, I have good news for you."

"Did you find Robert?"

"No! No! He's no longer important to me, but should still be important to you."

"Oh! Why?"

"I have moved everything to a new location, and I've eliminated all the people Robert knew. It's a completely new organization. He can talk all he wants to. Boulanger won't find anything."

Richard frowned, "Why is Robert important to me?"

"Because he knows you are working with us."

"Christ! Why the fuck did you tell him?"

"I didn't, but he heard me talking to you."

"Jesus! You've got to get him before he is well enough to talk. Do you still have somebody tailing Craig?"

"Yes, I'm going to put two men on his tail. I still want to get my hands on that Robert... nobody outsmarts me and gets away with it."

Richard smirked, "I thought you said he wasn't important?"

"No, he isn't, but I still want him."

"So what's the good news?"

"The good news is we have figured out a safe way to kill Craig Fox."

"Wait a minute, you can't kill him. I've told you before, you can't kill him because of all the past history between us. I'll be blamed, and nothing must interfere with my election as Prime Minister... the bugger probably has made sure that if he's killed, the finger will be pointed at me."

"Don't worry, Ricardo, no blame will fall on you. We'll kill him in Colombia."

Richard snorted, "How do you hope to get him down there?"

"Ah my friend, this is where you become part of our master plan. My uncle and I have worked out a plan, but we need you to do your part."

"And that is?"

"You told us you would be representing Canada at the Organization of American States Conference in Bogota next month?"

"Yes?"

"By the way, we are financing the Conference. Our name is not on the invitations, but we are making all the arrangements; conference rooms; hotel accommodation for the Ministers, etc."

Richard burst out laughing, "You're kidding?"

"No. We wanted to make sure we know what they decide to do. All the conference and hotel rooms are bugged. We have a nice suite picked out for you, and we promise not to bug it."

"Well I'll be damned! You guys are incredible."

"Richard, you are going to have newspaper and television coverage there, including the Canadian Broadcasting Corporation."

"Yes, I know."

"You also know Craig Fox's younger son, Donald, works at the C.B.C."

"So?"

"We want you to phone the C.B.C. and request they send one of their bright young stars to cover the meeting in Bogota. I'm sure if you ask for Donald Fox they would be happy to oblige."

"Aha! I'm beginning to get the picture. You'll kill the young man and Craig will go down to reclaim the body... and bingo! You've got him too."

"No, no, Ricardo, my friend, you are too crude. We will kidnap Donald for ransom," Rico paused chuckling softly, "and when Craig comes down to rescue him, we'll capture him and find out what he knows. Then we kill them both and make it look like they were involved with the Cartel."

"I would like to be there when you capture Craig. It will be sweet revenge for all the problems he has caused."

"Richard, where is Boulanger?"

"He's around, why?"

"Well, he's asking too many questions. You better figure out a way to shut him up."

"Oh, don't worry about him. I put one of my men into his organization and he's keeping an eye on the Commissioner."

"Ricardo, you think you are so smart. You always underestimate people like Craig Fox and Boulanger. They're smarter than you think. I have a lot of respect for Craig Fox. He has out smarted me twice. I like the man... he's macho."

"But you will kill him, won't you?"

"Yes, but it won't be me. Uncle Tino says he, and only he, will kill him."

"Glad to hear he is going to finish the job he failed to do years ago."

"I have a suspicion he has another reason for wanting to kill him. If I'm right..." Rico paused, giving meaning to the silence, "it's going to be an interesting meeting in Bogota. We'll get in touch with you when you arrive"

"Rico, good luck. I'll see you in Bogota."

"Ciao!"

* * *

Craig poured himself a second cup of coffee, adding a half teaspoon of sugar. Stirring slowly he moved over to the kitchen window. He ran his eyes along the Calgary downtown skyline then down to the driveway of the complex seven floors below. Most of the residents in Rideau Towers worked in the city. By nine in the morning the circular driveway connecting the four buildings was usually empty of cars, except for a Cadillac and a Mercedes parked in front of Cumberland House. Two widows owned them. One was nearly blind and afraid to use the underground parking; the other, the Cadillac owner, had won the car in a raffle and wanted every body to know about it. However, things had changed the day after his return to Calgary twelve days ago. Now there was a third car parked there every morning close to the exit to the underground parking in Craig's building. This morning it was the green Chevy Coupe. There were four cars altogether that rotated in a regular and predictable order. Yesterday it was a red Camaro; tomorrow it would be the black Mustang with the throaty exhaust growl. They made no attempt to hide that they followed him wherever he went. Even during the day they tagged behind when he walked to the bank; to meetings; or to the Petroleum Club for lunch. His shadower was always the designated driver of the day. Today the teenager with the wispy mustache and leather jacket would be on duty. Craig liked him. Passing the boy on the street during the day the boy usually smiled apologetically, shrugging his shoulders as if to say, "Sorry! but it's my job."

Craig finished the coffee and put the mug in the sink with the other dirty breakfast and dinner dishes. He'd been too tired to clean up last night. He eyed the dishes in the sink and for a brief moment considered washing them. "To hell with it," he muttered and headed for the front door. Craig set the alarm and locked the door behind him. He glanced up and down the hall to make sure it was empty before kneeling on the floor. Taking a roll of transparent scotch tape out of his pocket, Craig snipped off a three inch piece with his penknife, then stuck it in the corner of the door near the floor. The tape was invisible, but if broken, would alert Craig that somebody had entered the penthouse.

On his way to the elevator Craig passed the door to the penthouse across the hall. He heard voices through the door. The captain was giving Mrs. Richardson her marching orders for the day. A former naval officer, Captain Richardson, retired, was the Chairman of the Strata Council for the building. Craig was also on the Council, although at times he was tempted to resign whenever the captain became too officious. So far Audrey had managed to quell his irritation by pointing out that the building had never been so clean and shipshape. The captain patrolled the halls and grounds of the building, pen and pad poised to record the slightest infraction. Residents leaving their shopping cart in the hall in front of their unit for more than ten minutes could expect to be summoned to the door by the captain's insistent rapping. This had happened to Craig twice. When he checked the urge to slam the door in the man's face for the second time, he vowed to Audrey, who was chortling in the background, that the next time he was going to wrap the bloody cart around the captain's head.

Craig walked across the underground parkade towards the latest object of his affection, his own Jaguar XJS. It was parked next to Audrey's ten year old clunker, a Pontiac sedan, a relic of a more spartan life that she refused to part with. A soft glow bouncing off the sleek burgundy metal of the Jaguar warmed him as he approached. He took a handkerchief from his pocket to remove a streak of dirt from the front bumper and some dust on the windshield. Craig unlocked the door, carefully peering under the seat and dashboard before easing onto the tan leather seat. His bomb inspection routine was perfunctory now that he understood they were not about to bump him off until he inadvertently revealed where Robert was hidden. Craig turned the key, listening contentedly to the gentle purr of the motor while he waited for the oil to grease the bearings. He backed out then eased forward until he could reach the opener for the parkade doors. When the doors were fully raised he glided out into the driveway and turned right past the green Chevy. The young teenager was in the driver's seat but he didn't smile this time. Next to him was another man. Craig leaned forward to get a better look. The features were familiar; it was one of the other drivers; the one that drove the Camaro. Craig drove out of the complex, down the hill, over the Elbow River bridge, and followed the traffic north along Fourth Street towards the city center. The green Chevy followed. Craig was puzzled as to why a second man was now present. Perhaps things were about to change. The presence of the second man could only mean the cartel were becoming impatient at the lack of progress in the search for Robert. He would have to warn Audrey to be extra careful next time she called.

The arrangement with Audrey was that she would call once each day from a public phone across town from the hideout; never at the same time; and never speak for more than two minutes to avoid whoever might be bugging Craig's office and home phone, from tracing the call. The Avis station wagon she was driving was rented under an assumed name. Under no circumstances was she to use her credit cards. Gas, groceries, and any other supplies were to be paid for with cash. Craig was to make no effort to phone Audrey, nor visit the hideout. So far he and Audrey had made no mistakes but he could understand that the cartel might be getting a little frustrated after twelve days and was about to step up the pressure.

The pressure, when it came, was from a direction Craig had not expected.

Sandy, his secretary, handed Craig the fateful note, "It's from your son. He called a few minutes ago." Seeing the puzzled look on his face, she explained, "Your son, Donald."

"Oh! I thought for a moment you meant Robert."

Feeling guilty for neglecting Donald while trying to save Robert, Craig took the pink message slip and checked the phone number. It was a Toronto number. Under the number, Sandy had scribbled Donald's message "Just back from France. Have great news for you. Call soon. Love, Donald."

Sandy followed Craig into the office carrying a fresh mug of coffee. "How is Robert?"

"Much better, thank you. According to Audrey he is now sitting up in bed. She thinks he'll be able to get out of bed in few days and take a few steps. But he has some memory loss... we hope that will improve as he gets stronger."

"Commissioner Boulanger called late yesterday afternoon after you had gone to your meeting."

"Did he leave a number?"

"No. He said he was moving around too much to leave a number. Said he'd call you in a few days, but to let you know things were beginning to fall into place and he had made an appointment with AS for next Tuesday. Do you know what he meant by AS?"

"If he is saying what I think he's saying, he is in great danger. AS is probably the initials for Allan Sharp. Next time he calls tell him I must speak to him. I'll give Donald a call now. Sandy, could you please shut the door on your way out... thanks."

A carefully modulated female voice answered the phone at the number Craig dialed, "This is The Canadian Broadcasting Corporation, to whom may I direct your call?"

"May I speak to Donald Fox, please?"

There was a pause before the voice came on again, "I am sorry, but Mr. Fox is on a foreign assignment."

"Miss, could you please check again. He called a few minutes ago and left a message giving your number."

"Just a minute sir." There was a long pause, "My apologies, sir. He is coming to the phone now."

There was a loud clunk, followed by the noise of a phone clattering to the floor, then a muffled curse in what sounded like Donald's voice. Craig shook his head, baffled once again at how such a high energy person could be so disorganized. Craig could visualize the mess on Donald's desk.

"Blast!" Another clunk echoed in Craig's ear. "Sorry... hello, Donald Fox speaking."

"Donald, you called?"

"Dad! Yes I called. I've got some terrific news. But first tell me how's Mum? And how are you? Have you heard from Robert lately? I've been so out of touch, but it just wasn't possible to telephone from over there. Everybody was on strike and the phones weren't working. I just called your flat but nobody answered... is Mum all right?"

"Your mother is in good health but not at home just now. Robert has been badly wounded and..."

"What happened?"

"As you know, he was doing under cover work. He got shot... Donald, I don't want to go into details right now. He's going to recover but it will take time. What is your good news?"

"I've just been offered a plum assignment. Completely unexpected but I guess the powers upstairs have finally realized what terrific talent lies bundled up in this manly chest."

"I'm sure they must appreciate your modesty."

"Just kidding, Dad. They've asked me to cover the O.A.S. Conference in Bogota next month, your old stomping grounds. You'll have to fill me in on the country so I can get up to speed."

The moment the word "Bogota" was uttered Craig sat bolt upright in his chair. Carefully controlling his emotions he probed, "Do you know what the O.A.S. stands for?"

Donald replied, irritably, "Yes Dad! Of course I do!... The Organization of American States. The agenda is the Drug Cartel. I'm told the drug problem is getting worse and all the countries in the Americas would like to coordinate their responses to the cartel. It's going to be a very important conference with most of the heads of state attending. If I do a good job I can see myself, not too far down the road, taking over the National News spot."

"Donald, I have no doubt that one night in the not too distant future, I will be forced to watch you on the nightly news... and it will be a very different format after you have finished reorganizing it."

"You're right! I have some ideas that I have been working on to improve it. Dad, how are you?"

"I'm in excellent health, thank you... Donald, Sorry I can't talk longer. I'll give you a call tonight. You're still in the same flat?"

"Yes, If I'm not home Jean will be there. She'd love to talk to you. She's a fantastic person."

"What happened to Isabel?"

"Oh, we broke up a couple of month's ago. Things didn't work out."

"Sorry to hear that... I'd better go. Talk to you tonight. The assignment sounds like a terrific opportunity. We're very proud of you. Bye."

"Bye, Dad."

Craig put down the receiver and leaned back in his leather chair. Thinking of Donald a warm smile spread across his face. He reached for the morning paper in his "in" tray. Craig skimmed through the first few pages of the Calgary Herald. On page two he stopped briefly to read a short article reporting on the O.A.S. Conference coming up in three weeks in Bogota, Colombia. Heads-of-State would be attending. Canada was not a member. Instead of the Prime Minister, the Solicitor General would be representing Canada. Craig snorted in disgust, shook his head and was about to move on to the stock market quotations when an uneasy thought made him put down the paper. 'Donald and Bannerman will both be in Bogota at the same time. Donald must not go! For sure Bannerman knows I have a son, but does he know Donald is working for the C.B.C.? Probably... I must assume he does and stop Donald from going.'

Craig redialed the Toronto number.

* * *

Barbara Bannerman read the article on the O.A.S. Conference on page three of the Globe and Mail. She was enjoying her usual morning cup of tea beside the pool. It was where she planned the day's activities away from the house cleaning hubbub and the telephone. Barbara put down the paper and reached for the cup of tea cooling on the trolley beside her. Gazing absently at the waterfall at the far end of the pool, she sipped the liquid, too involved in developing a plan to have Richard to take her with him to notice the tea was cold. She had never been to Colombia, or for that matter to any country in Latin America. Holiday plans never included countries south of the American border. Twice Barbara had researched exotic locations in Central and South America and proposed them to Richard, but he was never interested, always suggesting other equally exotic places in the Caribbean, Hawaii, or Africa. Maybe now that he had to go he would take her with him. She would speak with him this evening when he came home from Ottawa. Realizing the tea was cold Barbara rang the bell for the maid.

A young Filipino girl approached carrying a jug of hot water and a slice of carrot cake. Barbara didn't hear the girl. Her head was again buried in the paper. An editorial had engrossed her. It demanded the immediate resignation of the Prime Minister and appointment of Richard Bannerman as Prime Minister without going through the farce of the expensive convention in November to select a new leader for the Party. There was absolutely no doubt that Richard Bannerman would be selected as the leader at that convention, so why go through the ritual and expense when the country needed a strong leader now. Barbara mumbled to herself, "you bet!"

"Señora?"

Startled, Barbara dropped the paper. "Oh!.. Juanita, it's you."

The girl curtsied apologetically. "Sorry, Ma'am, I frightened you."

"No,no, you didn't. Oh! Doesn't that cake look delicious. Thank you."

Pleased, Juanita curtsied again and turned to leave.

"Oh Juanita," the girl paused, "I'm expecting Mr. Sharp, Mr. Allan Sharp, in a few minutes. When he comes please bring him out here. And a fresh pot of tea and some of this delicious cake."

"Yes, Ma'am."

Barbara waited until the girl disappeared into the sun room before picking up the paper again. She never tired of watching the girl's graceful movements. Each step gliding past the other, moving her hips smoothly forward with a slight swaying motion which would have been provocative if it wasn't so natural. No wonder these girls got into so much trouble when they came to Canada.

Twenty minutes later the maid reappeared through the sun room door followed by Allan Sharp, elegantly dressed as usual; gray flannel slacks; tweed jacket, and striped tie over a blue shirt. Through Barbara's subtle influence, Allan had evolved into a cultivated executive with a keen interest in literature and the arts. His once unruly mop of hair was now iron gray and handsomely arranged by a hair dresser recommended by Barbara. His teeth had been either straightened or replaced; Barbara had not dared to ask which. Over the years the face had hollowed which, combined with the thin sharp nose and angular chin, gave him a hawkish profile. He no longer was what Barbara would have called "skinny", but was exercising more to lose the slight bulge in the middle. He had cut down on his drinking too which had improved his complexion. She noticed his eyes were not on her, but on the girl. His face flushed when he caught Barbara's amused expression. She pulled a chair out for him.

"Come and sit down you old goat."

They both watched Juanita's graceful exit. Allan sighed, "She is beautiful. The kind that makes old men wish they were young again." Turning back to Barbara, Allan continued, "Thank you for seeing me. I know how important this quiet time out here is to you, but you're the only one I can turn to for advice."

"Oh Allan, you're the one that is so good about listening to all my silly little problems. Here, let me pour you some tea and then we'll talk... it's black with one lump, isn't it?"

Barbara removed the cosey covering the tea pot, lifted the lid and checked inside the teapot before inserting a spoon to extract the soggy tea bags. She prolonged the tea ritual while she sifted through her mind the possible reasons for Allan's distress. By the time she finally offered him a cup of tea with the one lump of sugar, Barbara decided it must be that wretched boy of his that he wanted to discuss.

Allan had married his secretary and was promptly sued by a widow claiming damages for making false promises of marriage and various other charges that were later proved to be false. But his wife chose to believe the accusations and over the years poisoned the son's relationship with his father. The boy had been arrested several times for stealing and drug dealing. Allan was frequently out of the office, either searching for his son or bailing him out of Jail.

Barbara leaned back in her chair quietly stirring her tea, waiting for him to speak. She looked up after a few moments. Allan was frowning at the teacup in his hand, his lips mouthing silent words, arguing with himself over how to reveal his problem. Finally, he raised his head.

"Barbara, how do I tell Richard I am resigning from the company?"

"What! Resign! Allan, you are not seriously thinking of resigning?"

"Yes, I have made up my mind. I sat up most of the night trying to decide. I told Sarah my decision this morning. She was most unhappy." Barbara could imagine the scene. She had once witnessed one of Sarah's tantrums at a party. "I must resign immediately but I know Richard will be furious."

"Why this sudden resignation?"

"I got a call from the R.C.M.P. yesterday."

"Surely, anything that Michael has done shouldn't require you to resign. You know Richard well enough to know he wouldn't ask you to leave because of something your son has done. He has often said hiring you was the best decision he ever made. Richard is a very fair man and he needs you to run that company."

"Barbara, it has nothing to do with Michael. He's in trouble again but that's not the reason I am leaving. A Commissioner called and will be coming to see me next Tuesday. He has requested I prepare a full disclosure on the company to review with him when he comes. Shareholders, assets, etc... Barbara, that means they are onto us and we could be in big trouble."

"What are you talking about? Richard is a major share holder and I'm sure he wouldn't mind giving them the names of the other shareholders, or letting them see a list of the company's assets. Allan, you haven't done anything illegal... have you?"

Shaking his head in wonder, Allan put the half empty teacup back on the table. 'Incredible! She has been married to the man close to thirty years and still had no idea her husband is a ruthless killer working with the Colombian drug cartel... such an intelligent lady. Can she be so naive?... or is she just playing the role of the dutiful wife.' Allan searched her face for any trace of deceit. There was none. Her features still retained the frank open air freshness that he had always admired. The eyes, warm and sympathetic, yet penetrating, showed only concern. Regretfully, Allan realized too late, he shouldn't have revealed the R.C.M.P. visit... he shouldn't have come at all... now, being the kind of person she is, she will ask questions and want answers, and if he can't, or won't provide them, Barbara will ask Richard. 'You bloody fool, you should have thought of that... I shouldn't have brought her into this... Richard will kill me for this.' Realizing the implication of his thoughts, Allan murmured to himself, 'No doubt Richard probably will.'

"Barbara, of course not! I did do something foolish years ago over some stock trading. At the time I didn't know I had broken the law but I thought I had cleared that up a long time ago. That's probably why the Mounties want to talk to me. You know those people. They're like bulldogs, they never give up."

Allan gave Barbara a reassuring smile but he could see she was unconvinced. For a few moments she locked eyes with him, her gaze cooling, her lips compressing, before she sighed softly and allowed her eyes to wander off towards the pool. He had lost her trust. A trust they had both nurtured and enjoyed over the years. Allan, too, allowed his gaze to wander off across the garden. Both silent, the seconds ticked on as the gulf widened between them. Finally, after an eternity Barbara spoke.

"Would you like some more tea?"

"Barbara, I'm so sorry, I've insulted you. Please forgive me."

"Would you like more tea?"

"No thank you. I must go."

Barbara rang the bell. "Juanita will see you out."

This time, when Allan followed Juanita, his eyes were not on the girl.

Barbara's were, but they saw nothing. She was too busy trying to sort out the events of the past hour. 'Why did he tell me the R.C.M.P. were coming to look at the company, then suddenly change his story and tell me it was him they were investigating? Why did he lie? Did Allan think I knew all about the company and lied when he realized I didn't? Is the company involved in some illegal activity? If so, does Richard know about it?... No. He's always been so careful about his public image I can't imagine him allowing Allan to do anything illegal... but Richard has the controlling interest and he has always kept a tight control on the company, and on Allan... so...'

Juanita appeared with a lunch tray. She placed the tray on the table in front of Barbara, startling Barbara out of her troubled speculation. She hadn't realized she had allowed the morning to pass while she struggled to accept her husband's possible involvement in illegal activities. She put aside her troubling questions and addressed the day's decisions.

"Juanita, tell the cook Mr. Bannerman will be home for dinner and I want her to prepare his favorite dishes. I will write out the menu and you can come back in ten minutes for it. It is a special dinner for the two of us tonight to get us in the mood for Colombia so it must be perfect. I'll come to the kitchen this afternoon after tennis and talk to her about it."

Juanita curtsied and glided back to the house. Barbara didn't see her go.

* * *

Richard was in an excellent mood at dinner.

That fool Goodrich had finally conceded he was a liability to the party and announced he would resign after a new leader is chosen at a Convention in November. The Prime Minister had insisted that there should be a vote for a leader in what, Richard assumed, was a forlorn hope that somehow, somebody other than Richard would be chosen by the delegates. But there was nobody. Richard had made sure of that. The two possible rivals had been eliminated; One, the Minister of Defense was forced to resign when pictures of him in a brothel in Amsterdam were published; the other, the Justice Minister resigned abruptly without any explanation. It was rumored he had received a mysterious package the day he resigned. The campaign in the media was going well building up support for Richard to be anointed Prime Minister by acclamation without a convention.

In addition, the plan Rico had put together for the "Final Craig Fox Solution" gave him even more pleasure. It would be a fitting climax to his career to be finally rid of the bastard, just before accepting the crown he had striven to grasp for so long.

Richard scooped the last spoonful of Lobster Bisque out of the soup plate, placed the spoon in the correct position on the plate with the handle towards him, and picked up the glass of white wine. He took a small sip, swirled the liquid around before swallowing, and sniffed the glass.

"Excellent wine... Gewurtztraminer isn't?... an excellent German wine."

"Yes Dear, but not from Germany. It's from British Columbia."

"Oh!" Richard took another tentative sip, "Yes, there is a difference."

Barbara turned away to hide her smile. Richard fancied himself a wine connoisseur. He knew the names of all the fine wines, but couldn't distinguish one from another unless he could read the label. Realizing she had made an error by correcting him, Barbara decided to wait until after the main course before discussing Colombia. The maid brought in the Chateau-Briand, his favorite steak, grilled to perfection. The thick slices, charred on the outside and pink on the inside, were displayed in a semicircle on a teak platter. A small ramekin, filled with Bernaise sauce, nestled in the middle of the pink semicircle. Richard finished six slices, leaving two for Barbara. He leaned back in his chair with a satisfied sigh. Barbara refilled his glass, replacing the bottle of burgundy on the cradle in front of him with the label facing him.

"Richard, I see in the paper that you are going to attend a conference in Bogota. I would like to go with you."

About to take a sip, Richard spilled wine on his shirt. "Impossible!"

"Why not? I won't be in your way. You can go to your meetings during the day, and I can wander around on my own, or maybe with some of the other delegates' wives. I would like to go. We have never been to Colombia together and you could show me where you lived and went to school. We haven't done anything together for a long time. Please, Richard."

Trying to gain time, Richard tried flattery. "The steak was perfect, and..." glancing at the bottle in front of him, "your choice of the '68 Nuit St. George couldn't have been better. What's for dessert?"

Frustrated, Barbara picked up the small dinner bell and shook it vigorously. Richard knew he was in for a long angry debate unless he could come up with a plausible excuse. Barbara was not to be put off so easily. But he was not about to tell her the real reason she could not go. Thinking of the reception awaiting Craig Fox in Bogota he allowed himself a smile. This infuriated Barbara. She got up and stormed into the kitchen. He could hear her reprimanding the maid for being so slow. Barbara marched back into the dining room followed by the maid carrying a lemon meringue pie. Seated once again, she waited until she had calmed down before cutting off a large piece for Richard.

Barbara watched him eat in silence, studying his features. He was not looking at her but at the pie on his plate, methodically severing each forkful before lifting it carefully into his mouth. 'He's trying to figure out how he can talk me out of going... the sly devil... in about ten minutes he'll have come up with a smooth explanation as to why I can't go... and, I, like an idiot, will lap it up and agree with him.' Barbara ate her pie slowly, glancing at her husband between mouthfuls.

After so many years she could tell what he was thinking; the imperceptible movement of the lips as he developed an idea; the slight shake of the head rejecting a thought; the faint nod to approve a phrase. As much as Richard annoyed her at times, he fascinated her. He was still a very handsome man even though the thick blond hair was now fading to white and the crows feet and slight bulge under the eyes was noticeable under his tan. If anything age had accentuated the dimple in the prominent chin. Richard had converted the recreation room into an exercise Spa equipped with a rowing machine, stationary bike, and exercise gadgets that Barbara referred to as his "torture machines". No slouch in intelligence herself, Barbara acknowledged and respected his talent for absorbing information, complex technical data, reports, and financial statements; and quickly extracting the kernel from all the chaff; then putting the essentials together; and articulating the results in words easily understood by laymen. She had often wondered why it had taken him so long to become Prime Minister and had put it down to his arrogance; his impatience with other Ministers and Members of Parliament. He was ruthless with incompetents, but so was she. Yet with her he was always kind and considerate although she had realized soon after their marriage that he didn't love her. She had been chosen because of her family name which he needed for his career. Barbara was his trophy to be trotted out when required. Disappointed that Richard cared so little for her, Barbara had considered leaving him, but after reflecting on the alternatives, she accepted that Richard was the most exciting person she was ever likely to meet, and admitted to herself that she wouldn't mind being the wife of the Prime Minister, which she had no doubt Richard would become.

Richard scraped up the remains of the lemon custard on his plate. He eyed the rest of the pie dish. Deciding against another piece he put his fork down and lifted his head to face Barbara. 'Oh, oh, here it comes.' Barbara clenched her jaw determined not to give in.

"Barbara," He usually addressed her as "Barb," her full name was reserved for announcements and explanations, "I'm really sorry, no delegate wives will be allowed to attend. I tried to have them make an exception for you but they said absolutely not. The security at the conference will be extraordinary because of the drug cartel. They are very concerned that the cartel may try to disrupt or attack the conference. You may remember what they did a few years ago when they attacked the Supreme Court in Bogota and slaughtered all those judges. Also, I'm sure you have been reading about all the kidnapping that has been going on down there. I'm sorry, Barbara, that's why I said it is impossible for you to go, as much as I would like to have you with me and show you off to all the world."

Barbara studied his face for any sign of duplicity. She was almost sure he was lying but nothing betrayed him. Maybe he was telling the truth. Certainly his explanation was plausible, and if there was danger from the cartel it made sense not to allow the wives to attend. Still suspicious, Barbara decided to drop the subject for now, and maybe make some discreet inquiries to confirm what Richard had said.

Later, while drinking coffee in the living room, Barbara brought up the strange visit that morning, "Allan Sharp came to see me this morning."

"Did he come to cry on you shoulder about his son?"

"No. He's resigning from the Company."

"What!" Fortunately, Richard had just put his cup back on the coffee table, otherwise the contents would have splashed all over the chair when he propelled himself forward to the edge of his seat. "Resign? What the hell for?"

"An R.C.M.P. Commissioner is coming to see him next Tuesday to look at all his books. He said something very strange."

"Oh! What was that?"

"He said, 'that means they are onto us and we could be in big trouble'... Richard, what did he mean by that?"

"Christ! That bloody Boulanger! What else did Allan say?"

"When he realized I know nothing about Star Corporation, he lied to me by saying it was him they were investigating over something that happened years ago, but I could tell he was lying... Richard, what is going on in your company?"

Richard picked up his coffee cup. "Nothing, Barbara, don't make a big issue of this. Allan is not lying, he got into trouble many years ago over some illegal stock trades but I cleared that up for him. But I'd better talk to him and stop him resigning." Richard finished his coffee, put the cup back on the table and stood up. "I'll go and talk to Allan now."

Richard walked into his study, locking the door behind him. He dialed Rico's number. He would deal with Allan Sharp tomorrow. Right now he would have to take care of the Boulanger problem. The Commissioner would have to be eliminated before Tuesday. Richard felt a twinge of regret when the phone was answered at the other end. Marcel Boulanger was one of the few men that had earned Richard's respect.

In the living room, Barbara was again wrestling with the same questions she had asked herself that morning, 'Why is Richard giving me the same lies that Allan did?... who is Boulanger?... it must be the Commissioner that Allan said was coming on Tuesday... what's going on in that company?... I'll ask Richard when he returns... no, I can't do that, he'll only lie and that would destroy our relationship completely... and I can't ask Allan... but I must know somehow... maybe I should get in touch with Commissioner Boulanger.'

* * *

Deputy Commissioner Marcel Boulanger was very tired. He had driven in the dark all the way to Montreal from Toronto in heavy rain with only one stop to refill his gas tank. It was after midnight when he pulled up in front of his driveway. It was blocked by a trestle and a yellow painted bar. Behind the trestle there was now a foot wide ditch. Cursing the municipal workers responsible, Marcel pulled over to the kerb in front of his house. Stiffly he worked his way out of the car and reached into the back for his briefcase and bag. Inside the house Marcel poured himself a glass of red wine, threw his clothes over the chair in the bedroom and put on his night gown. He didn't finish the wine before he was asleep, too tired to worry about somebody stealing his car while it was parked outside. On Sunday he rested, did some reading on Star Corporation, the company he would be interviewing on Tuesday, washed some clothes, and repacked his bag so he could leave early on Monday for the drive back to Toronto.

On Monday morning at twelve minutes after five, the Commissioner's car blew up. The two gasoline containers behind the back seat ignited simultaneously creating a raging inferno. By the time the flames petered out there was only twisted metal left. There were few signs of human remains. Only the neighbors heard the actual bang, but the shock waves from the explosion were felt across North and South America.

In Montreal, Enrique Chavez heard the news on the radio. He shouted "Ole" before making a long distance call.

In Bogota, Rico's uncle, Florentino Chavez, congratulated Rico but asked if the perpetrators had been taken care of. When Rico finished reporting, Tino nodded and hung up.

In Ottawa, Richard Bannerman heard the news by telephone when Rico called him out of a meeting. He smashed one fist into the other palm. "Now it's your turn, Craig."

In Toronto, Allan Sharp heard the news on the radio while eating breakfast. He decided maybe he wouldn't resign after all.

In Toronto, Barbara Bannerman read the news in the Globe and Mail, but it wasn't until several days later that she made the connection between Commissioner Boulanger and Allan Sharp.

In Calgary, Craig Fox read about the explosion in the Calgary Herald when Sandy brought the paper to him. Deeply disturbed at the loss of such a fine officer and friend, Craig had to make a supreme effort not to allow despair to envelope him... but now that Boulanger was gone there was nobody to help him; nobody to stop Bannerman; nobody to stop the cartel taking over Canada. By the end of November Bannerman would be Prime Minister of Canada, and Craig had only a few weeks left with no idea what he could do to reverse the inevitable.

* * *

Walking from the elevator to the parkade on his way to work, Craig was accosted by Captain Richardson.

"Oh Craig! Could you give me a hand?"

The captain was in the laundry room straining at a massive drier, trying to tip it forward to retrieve an empty soap carton somebody had jammed behind it. Shaking his head and too polite to ignore the man, Craig moved next to the captain to help him tip the machine. It had always puzzled Craig how this potbellied baldheaded fussy little man could have risen to command Canada's only aircraft carrier. No wonder the Government eventually sold the ship. The captain grabbed the carton before it slithered to the floor and marched over to the garbage bin, leaving Craig struggling with the drier by himself. Craig eased the drier back muttering "Thank you" under his breath. The captain was too busy scribbling on his note pad to hear the remark. On his way out the door, Craig noticed a pay phone on the wall next to the door, but it wasn't until some hours later that its usefulness dawned on him.

Before noon Craig made a quick trip home to copy the telephone number. He added it to a short note to Audrey, setting up a schedule for her to call that number. The problem was how to deliver the letter. If he put it in the lobby mailbox it would be collected by whoever had bribed the mailman. Mailing it anywhere else wouldn't work either. The young men following him would report the subterfuge. The solution came in the form of Ken Watson, the man who had organized the escape from Montreal. A heavy thump on Craig's back announced his presence.

"Craig! Old friend, Where have you been? I haven't seen you around the Club for days."

Ken pulled out the chair across from Craig and plunked into it. Leaning forward on his elbows he studied Craig, head cocked to one side.

"What the hell are you looking so grim about? Roger tells me Robert is a little weak but fully recovered, so why so glum?" Ken's lips curled slightly, "Is the cartel still bothering you?" Ken Watson was still a little skeptical about the Montreal rescue. The whole episode was a bit too melodramatic; however, Craig wasn't the kind to over dramatize, so maybe there was something to it.

"Ken, you have just rescued me once again."

"What do you mean?"

"I've been trying to figure out how I can get a letter to Audrey, and you walk in the door."

"Go on."

"Is Roger still making house calls?"

"Yes, but only a couple of times a week now that Robert is so much better."

"Good! Could you give him this letter and ask him to deliver it to Audrey as soon as possible? I think I've found a phone that's not bugged and I need to talk to her and make some plans."

Ken eyed Craig cynically, "What makes you think your phone is bugged?"

"I am sure the volume on our phone is lower than it should be normally, and I'm convinced I can hear a click whenever I pick it up."

Ken whistled before nodding his head. He got up and patted Craig on the shoulder. "Craig, old friend, call if you need me."

"Thanks, Ken."

* * *

Stacking the last of the dishes into the dishwasher Craig glanced yet again at the clock on the wall. It was five to eight. "Its time to go and talk to Audrey."

He dried his hands with a soggy towel cringing under the sink, turned off the burner under the coffee pot, and switched off the kitchen light before peering out the window. Except for the two cars owned by the old ladies, the street in front of the building was empty. Puzzled, Craig walked out on the balcony and leaned out to look around the corner. Squinting into the late evening sun he checked the approaches to the Rideau Towers Complex. No Camaro. No Mustang.

"That's strange! Why have they gone?"

Craig reentered the suite. Uneasy at the change in routine, he locked the balcony door and closed the window curtains. On his way to the basement Craig double locked the door to the suite, put the tape across the door frame and hurried downstairs to the basement laundry. It was two minutes before eight when he entered the laundry room. The room was empty. Relieved, he closed the door behind him and walked over to the phone on the wall. Craig lifted the receiver to make sure the phone line hadn't been cut. Reassured by the hum in his ear, Craig put the receiver back. He pulled over a chair and sat down to wait for Audrey's call. But he was too restless. To his own surprise he found himself tidying up the place while he waited.

Promptly at eight the phone rang. Craig picked up the receiver and offered a tentative "Hello?"

It was Audrey on the other end. "Craig, it's me. Aren't you taking a big risk sending me a letter?"

"No, I trust Ken Watson, but now that we can speak on the phone I won't do it again. How is Robert?"

"Why don't you ask him yourself?"

There was some muffled voices at the other end, then, "Dad! it's me Robert."

"Robert! it's so good to hear your voice again. How are you?"

"Great!"

"Come now, I want the truth. I know you must still be weak. How's your memory?"

"Dad, really! I'm fine. Naturally still a little weak, but exercise will soon change that, and my memory is good. I'm anxious to talk to Boulanger to give him all the details on Rico. I understand from Mum that you have met Rico."

"Yes, I have. He's still looking for you. I had two men tailing me every day hoping I would lead them to you, but tonight for some reason they are gone. I think something is brewing and I don't know what. I'm pretty sure they don't know about this phone."

"Dad, please be careful. Rico is very ruthless and I'm sure he is planning some kind of revenge for rescuing me from under his nose... Dad! Thank you for saving my life, I..."

"Robert, you would have done the same for me, and don't forget, your mother is the one who really saved your life."

"I know. Dad, what is Donald up to these days? I'd like to call him."

"He left three days ago for Colombia."

"Colombia! What the hell is he doing down there?"

"The Organization of American States is holding a conference in Bogota to work on an agenda for controlling the drug traffic, and the C.B.C. has a team down there to report on the meeting. Donald was asked to go. I tried to stop him going but It's a big step for him and he insisted on going."

"Who asked him to go?"

Craig shrugged, "I suppose the C.B.C. did."

"Dad, didn't you warn him about your connection to Florentino Chavez?"

"No, I didn't think he needed to know. I told you because you were involved in undercover work and my knowledge of Chavez might have been useful."

There was silence for a few moments on the other end, then a muffled "Christ!", another pause. Then Craig heard, "Mum, I'm beginning to feel a little weak, could you please go over to that grocery store and bring me a Coke. I need that to pep me up... thanks."

"Shall I try to find a stool for you?"

"No! No! I'm O.K. Mum, just a Coke. Please."

There was another long pause. Craig could hear Audrey's footsteps fading in the background. "Dad! You must bring Donald back immediately. He will be killed by those brutes. By now they will know he is your son and they will kill him to get their revenge on you... hello!... Dad!... Dad are you there?"

"Yes, I'm here. I share your concern. As I said, I tried to talk Donald out of going, but he insisted on going. You know how stubborn he can be."

"Who is heading the Canadian delegation?"

"Richard Bannerman."

Craig sat down abruptly, the receiver clasped loosely on his thigh. Ignoring the muffled voice on his lap he stared vacantly at a box of laundry soap perched on a washer. Trying to organize his thoughts, Craig leaned forward and began reading the fine print extolling the benefits of that particular brand of soap. A loud yell "Dad!" from the receiver made him lift it just in time to have it blast through his ear.

"Dad! Are you there?"

"Jesus! Yes! I'm here!"

"Dad, please listen to me. Get in touch with Commissioner Boulanger right away and have him send somebody down there to bring Donald back, and if he won't come back, knowing Donald he probably won't, then have the man stay and protect him. Dad, please do this right away."

"Oh Robert..." Craig hesitated a moment, "Boulanger is dead!"

"Oh no! Oh God No!... no!... no! They finally did it, the bastards. When did this happen?"

"It was in the paper last week. A bomb went off in his car at about the time he goes to work. According to the paper, they think he set it off when he turned on the ignition. The car caught fire and he was... burnt beyond recognition."

"Why would they kill him now? They've known what he has been doing all along through the leaks from Ottawa. Why now?"

"I gave him what I knew about Bannerman and the Star Corporation. He was going to investigate Star Corporation, and that must have made them decide he had to be eliminated."

"Do you know where Donald is staying?"

"No. He said he would call in a couple of days, but that has not happened. He gets so involved in his work he forgets to call."

"Dad, we can't wait for him to call, I'll have to go down myself."

"Robert! that doesn't make sense! You'd be more of a liability in your condition. You're still too weak, and you don't speak the language. I speak Spanish, and I know Bogota. If anybody goes it has to be me... the more I think about it, the more I know I'm the one who has to go. Donald will listen me this time... I think?"

"Dad, please. Let's both go."

"Robert, No! I must go and make some reservations. I'll hang up before your mother comes back, otherwise she'll raise all kinds of logical reasons why I can't go. You tell her after I've hung up. Don't worry, I know my way around down there. I'll bring your brother back. Bye, my boy. Take care of your Mum while I'm away. Tell her not to worry, and that I love her."

"Dad! Listen! I..." But Craig had hung up. He opened the door and was about to step into the hall when the phone rang again. Craig ignored the desperate ringing behind him and walked to the elevator. Entering the suite the telephone buzzed. Craig ignored it. The phone buzzed four times, then the answering machine clicked on. Audrey's angry voice drowned out the recorded greeting.

"Craig! Answer the damn phone! I know you are there. Answer it! Please."

Craig rushed over and picked up the receiver. He was about to yell at Audrey to get off the phone but he noticed the volume was normal.

"Yes, Dear, I'm here."

"Craig! this is crazy! Craig! you can't go down there, they'll kill you. Call the C.B.C. and tell them it's an emergency... that I've had a serious accident and Donald has to come home immediately. Do it tonight. There must be somebody in their office all the time... why didn't you stop Donald from going down? You should have known it was another Bannerman trick."

"Audrey! You and I both know that we couldn't stop Donald going... but..." Craig paused, shaking his head in wonder, "That's a good idea of yours. I'll call the C.B.C. right away." Trust Audrey to come up with such a sensible idea. 'I wonder if I'm getting old. Why didn't I think of that?'

"Why don't you try Donald's place first? Maybe his girlfriend has his number in Bogota. Craig, I'm coming home tonight!"

"Do you think it's a good idea?"

"Whether it's a good idea or not, I'm coming home. It's very obvious you need me at home."

Craig bit off an angry retort. Instead he clenched the phone for a few moments before answering, "Audrey, be careful. They have changed the routine and I'm worried. The car outside is gone and I just noticed our phone is no longer bugged. Something is up. I think you should stay hidden for a few more days until it becomes clear what they have planned. Give me a call at seven in the morning. Don't call me here... O.K.?"

There was a long silence, followed by muffled voices before Audrey spoke into the phone, "Robert agrees with you. I'll call you at seven... Craig."

"Yes?"

"I'm sorry, I shouldn't have said that. I love you."

"I love you too, sweetheart. You're right as usual. Good night."

"Nite."

Craig unlocked the balcony door and checked the street below. It was empty except for the two luxury cars owned by the elderly ladies. He did not lean over the balcony to look around the corner. If he had, Craig might have seen an R.C.M.P. car parked a block away between two street lights. Any car entering or leaving Rideau Towers would have to pass by the car.

Craig shook the coffee pot to make sure there was some liquid left in it. He turned on the burner then promptly forgot it while he searched around for the telephone number of Donald's apartment in Toronto. He found the number pinned to the fridge with a small magnet. It was a piggy magnet; one that he had bought Audrey years ago as a joke for their wedding anniversary. Remembering the hilarious evening, Craig chuckled. Passing the stove he noticed the coffee pot. Craig turned off the burner and shook the pot. It was empty. He reached in the cupboard for the brandy bottle. He was about to hang up on the Toronto number when a sleepy voice answered,

"Hello."

"Is this Jean?"

"Who is it?"

"This is Craig Fox, Donald's father."

"Donald is not home. He's away for two weeks."

"Jean, I'm sorry to bother you at this late hour, but it is most important I talk to Donald. Do you have his number in Colombia?"

"No. He said he would call and give me his number. He hasn't called, but knowing Donald, I'm not surprised."

"Do you know the name of his supervisor?"

"No." The voice was now fully awake, "Has something happened to Donald? Who am I speaking to?"

"Craig Fox, his father. No, Miss. Nothing has happened to Donald but we want him to come home as soon as possible. His mother has been in a serious accident. When he calls please tell him it is most urgent he come home."

"Sure, I'll tell him. I'm so sorry to hear she had an accident. Will she be O.K.?"

"We don't know yet, that's why he must come home. Bye, Miss. Sorry to have wakened you."

"That's okay. Hope Mrs. Fox will be okay."

A little guilty for misleading the young lady, Craig took a large gulp of brandy and immediately regretted it as the liquid burned down his throat. With a loud "whoosh" he expelled the fumes, then rang the C.B.C. number in Toronto. A carefully modulated female voice answered the phone.

"This is The Canadian Broadcasting Corporation, to whom may I direct your call?"

"My name is Craig Fox, and I'd like to speak to whoever is in charge of your news desk tonight."

"What is the purpose of your call? Sir."

"I have to contact my son, Donald Fox. It is an emergency. I know he is in Colombia but his mother has been seriously injured in an accident and he must come home immediately."

"Just a minute, sir, and I will see if Mr. Kowalski can help you."

Craig waited. He reached over and pulled a chair towards him, sat down, and this time took a small sip of brandy. He was beginning to wonder if he had been disconnected when a man's voice boomed in his ear.

"Kowalski here! Mr. Fox, are you there?"

"Yes, I'm still here."

"I'm sorry to have kept you waiting. I understand you are trying to contact Donald?"

"That's right. His mother has had a serious accident and he must come home immediately."

"Ummh, I see... well... Mr. Fox, I don't know how to say this but Donald has disappeared. He was supposed to cover the opening ceremonies at the Conference this morning, but he didn't turn up and he's not in his room. Do you know where he might be? Does he have friends down there in Bogota that he may have gone to visit?"

"Oh Christ! I'm too late. No, Mr. Kowalski, he does not have any friends down there. If he calls please tell him to come home... Mr. Kowalski, where was he staying?"

"The C.B.C. crew are at the Tequendama Hotel, Mr. Fox..."

But Craig had hung up and was now gasping after emptying the tumbler of brandy.

- 11 -

Donald was pleased with the results so far. He had organized a helicopter ride over Bogota to capture on camera a panoramic view of a city hemmed in by peaks rising several thousand feet above the plateau, which was itself over eight thousand feet above sea level; he had arranged to have the cameras and crews put on the funicular and hauled up the mountain to Monserrat Cathedral for another city view; the crew had filmed Tequendama Falls, the underground cathedral in the salt mines of Zipaquira, and inside the "museo del Oro", the pre-Colombian gold collection. Instead of himself chattering in front of the camera about the scene behind him, experts provided the description and history of each location. Donald had enough material for two or three days, depending on how much time was available between news conferences. All of this had been accomplished in the three days before the opening of the conference, due to start the next day. Donald would not have been able to do all he planned if it hadn't been for the young lady from the travel agency. Señorita Alicia de Quesada Guzman was a marvel at cutting through all the bureaucratic objections thrown in his path by officials in the ministries. Her English was excellent. She had gone to the American School in Bogota, and to Miami as an exchange student for a year. If she understood what Donald was trying to do, Alicia would dash over to the nearest telephone and rattle off a stream of Spanish to somebody at the other end, who was able to organize helicopters, vehicles, or professors within hours of the request being made. Tonight the film crew was having a little party to celebrate their accomplishment, and Donald invited Alicia to the party.

Alicia de Quesada had met the C.B.C. crew at the airport. They were picking up their equipment and bags when Donald noticed the young lady. She was at the Avis counter talking to the agent. Her pink blouse, stretched over well formed breasts, was pressed against the counter; tight black jeans emphasized the long legs, firm buttocks, and slim waist. Donald couldn't see the face, just her black hair, held together with a silver brooch, streaming down the back of her pink blouse. The agent pointed towards where Donald was standing motionless with a bag in one hand. The young lady turned her face towards him, nodded her thanks to the agent, and walked briskly towards Donald. She was wearing hiking boots, giving her a masculine stride. But there was nothing masculine about her features; pale creamy white skin folded over an oval face, straight nose slightly flared, a dimpled chin, and a wide mouth with full lips, tinted with a trace of pink lipstick. She slowed and stopped in front of him. She surveyed each of the gawking men in turn - Donald noticed her eyes were green - returning to Donald, she smiled.

"Mister Donald Fox?"

Donald smiled back. "Yes, Miss... ah si... Señorita, I'm Donald Fox."

"I am from the Avita travel Agency. The Canadian Broadcasting crew has been assigned to my company and I am to look after you. My name is Alicia... would you please follow me, I have a bus waiting to take you to the Hotel Tequendama."

Alicia waited until the camera equipment was loaded on two trolleys, then led the way out of the terminal, not before she tilted her head slightly in Donald's direction when she passed a man wearing dark glasses, who was standing off to one side near the exit. In the bus she made sure Donald sat by himself. She sat next to him, which Donald had hoped she would. He was beginning to wonder whether his commitment to Jean, his new love waiting in Toronto, could withstand the appeal of the warm thigh pressing against his own. He decided he had better concentrate on the plan he had sketched out in the plane on the way down. Donald reached into his breast pocket for the ever handy notebook and pen to begin reviewing his notes.

Alicia's orders were clear. She was to meet the Canadian film crew, identify Donald Fox, ingratiate herself and seduce him. Anticipating that Donald Fox was probably a middle aged Prima Donna like other T.V. newsmen she had met, she had not been looking forward to the fourth part of her instructions. Sitting next to him on the bus she knew she was going to enjoy that part of her assignment. Watching Donald scribble and scratch, pen grasped firmly in the long thick fingers of the right hand and notebook locked in the powerful left hand, she imagined those hands on her. When he turned and spoke to her in his deep but gentle masculine voice Alicia began to feel her cheeks flushing and a familiar warmth creep down towards her lower belly.

Looking down at her upturned face, sparkling green eyes and slightly parted moist pink lips, Donald nearly forgot what he was about to say.

"Aah. Señorita. I would like to take some pictures of the city from the air. Can you tell me where I can rent an airplane... no. better still, a helicopter... yes, a helicopter. I would like one as soon as possible... say, tomorrow morning. Can you arrange that? Señorita?"

Afraid he had been reading her thoughts, Alicia swung away from Donald as if to check on the other passengers. She didn't answer until she recovered her composure, but still did not look at him. "Because of the drug problem, the military doesn't like helicopters flying over the city, but I will phone my office from the Hotel. Maybe they can get permission."

"Thank you, Miss. That will be very helpful. I have done some reading on your beautiful city, and with your help I would like to film some of the city's attractions to show to Canadian viewers during the conference. I have some ideas but yours may be better. After I've checked in could we meet in the lobby and go over some of my notes?"

Things were moving a little too fast for Alicia. She wasn't supposed to bed him until the night before the conference opened. She would have to phone for instructions, and the helicopter. "Mister Fox, I have to phone about your helicopter. Maybe we can meet later. I will call your room when I am free and we can meet in the lobby."

"Señorita, I look forward to working with you."

Thinking his words may have implied something more personal, Alicia gave Donald a quick look but there was no hint on his face. His expression was serious, but she could see the warmth in his brown eyes. He clearly meant what he had said. When the bus entered the city limits, Donald put the notebook and pen back in his breast pocket and turned his attention to the life and buildings passing by. Taking care not to be caught staring, Alicia studied Donald's profile. The nose was large and slightly bent in the middle as if it had been broken by a blow; a dark brown mustache, thick and bushy, and in need of trimming, hung over the full upper lip. She was pleased to see the chin was strong but not too prominent. It was covered with a day old beard. The forehead was domed and curved back to a thick mass of brown hair streaked with lighter brown patches, no doubt bleached by the sun. The hair needed combing and was surprisingly long for a T.V. reporter. Alicia decided Donald was not married.

Every few minutes Donald reached for his notebook to scribble a few words, before thrusting the book back into his breast pocket. In between those bursts of writing Donald's fingers drummed gently on his thighs. The nails needed a manicure. They were trimmed too close. Maybe he kept them short so they wouldn't interfere with his typing. Alicia had a theory about men with long powerful hands. She hoped Donald would prove her theory. Watching the long thick fingers move up and down, Alicia's pulse began to rise. Much to her relief the bus slowed and pulled up in front of the hotel. Alicia stood and rushed for the front exit, almost tripping in her haste to get out. Outside she took a deep breath and walked to and fro in front of the bus while the passengers disembarked. Donald was one of the last to emerge. Fully recovered, Alicia motioned the men to follow her into the lobby.

* * *

"Donald, where did you get this wound?"

Alicia was pointing at a scar on Donald's upper right thigh, close to his groin.

"In Angola."

"Angola! What were you doing there?"

"I was doing a documentary on the civil war there... from the Cuban side."

"Cubans in Angola?"

"Si. Castro sent Cuban troops to Angola to fight the South Africans. I thought I would report the war from their side."

"But how did you get this?"

"The platoon I was with got ambushed by the South Africans... fortunately I dress on the left..." Alicia looked puzzled, but Donald decided it was too complicated to explain, "Otherwise 'El Toro' would have been Kaput."

"El Toro?"

Donald chuckled, "That's what my Cuban soldier used to call His Highness."

Alicia's eyebrows shot up. Donald smiled and leaned over to pinch and gently shake her nose. "No, my Dear, it's not what you think. The Cuban army has many fine women in their army."

"Oh." Alicia reached up and squeezed Donald's nose. "Where did you break this?"

"In El Salvador, courtesy the rifle butt of the military. They didn't want me to take pictures of a demonstration against the government."

Alicia glanced up at the clock by the bed. It was after ten and she was supposed to have made the call over an hour ago. Rico would be getting impatient. She started to climb out of the bed to get dressed, but one look at the male animal stretched out below her made her hesitate. Pleased her theory had been confirmed, Alicia ran her fingers over his nipples and down through the hairs on Donald's chest to his belly. Quickly she straddled his hips and grabbed 'El Toro', catching it on the rise... one last time to make it four... four was her lucky number.

It had not been too difficult to get Donald to leave the party and take her up to his room, but it was becoming more and more difficult for Alicia to take the next step and turn him over to the cartel. But she had no choice. Rico had made sure she fully understood her family was at risk if she did not carry out their instructions. Also, he had pictures he threatened to publish if she balked. She regretted becoming involved with that snake, Rico, but he had been so charming and such a lover. He had led her down his perverted paths and she had loved every step of the way. Now they wanted Donald. Why, she didn't know.

Dressing by the side of the bed, Donald's mind was already on the Opening Ceremonies next morning. Alicia was making noises in the bathroom but she was not in his thoughts, at least until she came back in, stuffing a red blouse into her jeans. He looked up as she came towards him. Even though they had spent the last three hours in bed together she could still raise his pulse. Dropping his eyes Donald concentrated on putting on his socks and shoes.

"Donald..." Alicia walked nervously up and down the room in her bare feet, fluffing her hair one moment, straightening the collar of her blouse the next, "Donald..."

"Yes, Alicia, what is it?"

Suddenly, she blurted, "Would you like to interview the head of the drug cartel for your Canadian Broadcasting Company?"

With his left shoe poised over his left foot Donald stared at her for a full minute before he put his shoe on and lowered the foot. "Alicia, can you arrange that?"

"Si querido, I can."

"How?"

"My cousin works for them. I told him who you are and he asked me today if I thought you would be interested in listening to their side, and maybe give a more unbiased report. He thought he could arrange a meeting."

"Wow!" The thought the impact that such an interview would make on that stuffy Toronto office was... "Wow!" Donald leapt up and hugged Alicia. "Oh you lovely creature." He cupped her face between his hands and kissed her lips. "It would be perfect if I could interview him and broadcast it while the conference is still on. Wow! What a coup! How soon can he set it up?"

"He said that if you are interested I was to call him tonight. He said he thinks he can arrange the meeting for tonight as he knows you will be too busy over the next few days."

"Alicia, please. There's the phone."

Unaware the room was monitored, Donald was surprised at the quick response. Within minutes after she put the phone down there was a knock on the door. Alicia gave Donald a long lingering look before she walked over to the door to open it. The man that walked in was not what Donald had expected. His first impression was that the man was Chinese, but then concluded he was probably Indian with some oriental blood in his past. It was the high cheekbones, smooth skin, and straight black shiny hair that made him think he was oriental. He was dressed much like Alicia in black slacks and red shirt. If he had been asked Donald would have described the man as being of medium height, not quite up to Donald's nose, about thirty to thirty five years old, with a light springy step, a very strong grip, and spoke excellent English... "Oh, and he never took his dark glasses off."

"Donald, this is my cousin, Enrique."

The man bowed slightly but didn't move. Donald hesitated then decided he had better swallow his pride if he wanted that interview. He stepped forward, smiled, and held out his hand. "Señor, I am very pleased to meet you."

Enrique accepted the handshake, a slight sneer curling his lips as if to say 'Good! you accept I'm in control here.'

"Mister Donald Fox, I too am very pleased to meet you. I am sure we will have a very interesting time together." Acknowledging Alicia with a slight dip of his head. "From what Alicia has been telling me you are a very enterprising reporter and that is why we thought you might be the man to report on all the good things we do for the community the schools and hospitals that we have set up in many villages; the sewage and water systems that we, not the corrupt government, are installing; the housing... I can go on and on, but it is best you talk to the man that has made all this possible."

"Yes, I look forward to that. Can we do it tonight?"

"Of course. I have a car waiting outside right now."

Donald moved towards the phone. "Good, I'll get a couple of cameras and we can go."

Rico sprang forward and clamped his hand around Donald's upper arm before he could lift the phone. "No! No! No cameras!"

The pain made Donald jerk his arm down breaking the grip. He nearly followed it with a punch to the man's face. Rico stepped back quickly. In future, Rico decided he would avoid provoking Mister Donald Fox. The man was fast in spite of his size, and the biceps he had squeezed were not soft.

"Please, no cameras. The man you are meeting tonight has many enemies but few know what he looks like. He has not been photographed for many years."

"But if I don't have him on camera I have nothing for viewers in Canada."

"I repeat, no cameras. You can take that," pointing to a small cassette on the bedside chest, "and record the interview."

"Very well. Alicia, are you coming?"

Alicia was about to follow Donald out the door but Rico motioned her back. "No, I am sorry, she cannot come."

Enrique led the way to a long black limousine parked to one side of the front entrance. A wisp of exhaust fumes drifted up from the rear end. The driver jumped out the moment they appeared at the front door and opened the rear door. Taking off his peaked cap, he smiled at Donald, but the smile faded the moment he realized Donald was not the person he had expected. Rico waved Donald into the back seat. Before sliding into one of the folding seats facing Donald, Rico spoke to the driver in Spanish.

"Take us to the Casa, but, Eduardo, don't go direct. I don't want our guest to know where we are going."

"Si, Patron."

The driver slowly closed the back door until it clicked, then climbed into the driver's seat. He pushed a button on the dashboard. A louder click alerted Donald that the doors were now locked. Donald was able to follow their progress along Carrera 10A, past the Capitol buildings, the Presidential Palace, and Monserrat Peak, but within minutes the limousine turned off the main boulevards. It twisted and turned through unfamiliar suburbs before heading into a narrow road meandering along a steep valley. Enrique made no effort to cut through the hostile air between them. Nor did Donald. When he realized they were trying to confuse the route to the man's house, Donald stopped peering out the tinted windows and pulled out his pen and notebook. A small light behind each side window was barely enough to see what he was writing. Donald ignored Enrique's scrutiny, but every time he looked up the man was checking Donald's facial features against his own reflection in the side window. Finally, Donald decided a little humor might improve the atmosphere.

"Señor, I think you will agree we do not look alike."

The response was a snarl, "It is my good fortune we do not."

Donald started to respond, instead he shrugged and returned to his notebook.

Rico continued to study the man opposite him. He had to admit the man was ruggedly handsome and projected an aura of masculine power that would appeal to women. He was almost sure Donald was his brother... well, half brother... yet he bore, absolutely no resemblance to himself. If Donald wasn't his brother, why was his uncle so determined to kill Craig Fox if it wasn't to avenge the rape of his sister, Rico's mother. And wasn't he, Rico, the result of that violation? It was going to be an amusing gathering when Craig Fox arrived.

The limousine turned onto a gravel road leading into a forest. The driver picked up a microphone clamped to the dashboard and spoke a few words. Immediately powerful lights flooded the car and lit up a high wall and iron gates ahead of them. The driver spoke again. The gates slowly swung open. They drove through. Donald heard the gates clang ominously shut behind him. The limousine followed the long curved driveway and slowed as it approached the front of the mansion. Enrique spoke to the driver. The limousine continued around to the side of the building and entered an underground garage. Once again, there was the ominous clang of doors closing behind them. Enrique jumped out,

"Donald, follow me."

Donald did; up some stairs, along a hall and into a large paneled room. The curt command and familiar use of his name warned Donald to be cautious, but it was too late to turn back. He had taken a big risk for the sake of an interview with one of the most notorious drug lords and he intended to go through with it. It didn't make sense for them to bring him here if it wasn't to grant him an interview. He was of no value to them. Unless... unless they planned to ransom him to the C.B.C. The thought of the ruckus that a ransom demand would create in that budget conscious company amused him. Rico heard the chuckle behind him and gave Donald a puzzled backward glance. 'He won't think it is so funny in a few minutes when he finds out the truth.' Enrique motioned towards an overstuffed leather armchair.

"Sit here."

Enrique took up a position in front of Donald, far enough away that Donald could not spring up to reach him. "Donald, you are now our prisoner. See those men," pointing at two young men that had appeared in the doorway they had just passed through,"They are here to guard you so do not attempt to escape. They will escort you to a room. It is comfortable with a bed, bathroom, and T.V. No harm will come to you if you behave."

Stunned, Donald's head jerked up, "But this is nuts! What possible harm can I do you. I didn't come to spy on you. I came for an interview, and it was your idea I come."

"You are terribly naive to think we would give anybody an interview. No. You are here because you are to be ransomed."

"You are crazy if you think my company will pay a ransom. And, anyway, your cartel makes that kind of money in an hour, so why bother with a few hundred thousand dollars."

"I agree, the ransom is pennies to us, but it's not the money. It's your father we want."

"Dad! What's he got to do with all this. Just because he rescued my brother is no reason to destroy him. He probably hardly knows you exist except for what Robert has told him."

"Your father knows we exist. In fact, he probably knows more about us than any other man in North America. He and my uncle, Florentino Chavez, the man you came to interview, go back many years. That's why my uncle wants to kill him for something your father did when he was a young man."

"What was that?"

"I will leave it to my uncle to explain the deed to you. In the presence of your father."

"How much is the ransom?"

"A million dollars."

"Christ! You'll ruin him."

"Precisely! That's enough for now. The men will take you to your room. I'll have our office in Canada deliver the ransom note to your father and we'll see what happens. I expect we'll see your father within the week. Ciao for now."

"What about your cousin, are you going to harm her?"

"Cousin? Oh, Alicia. She's not my cousin. No, she works for us. She is good, Isn't she?"

Donald stood up and glared at Rico for a few moments, trying to decide whether to hurl himself at the man, but a slight movement by the door when the two men moved forward convinced him not to. He shrugged and headed for the door.

* * *

Early the next morning Rico escorted Alicia to the train station and bought her a first class ticket to Girardot. She was to go home; not return to Bogota; nor contact anybody in the city, particularly the C.B.C. crew, until he gave permission. He waited until the train pulled out of the station before walking back to where Eduardo was waiting beside the limousine. On his return to his uncle's compound Rico was intercepted at the front door by his mother.

"Who is that man you have locked up in the basement room?"

"Why don't you ask your brother?"

"He won't tell me, he just laughs and says he has a surprise for me. What is it?"

"I'm sorry, Mama. If he won't tell you, you know I cannot. Sorry."

"The maid said he is an American."

"No, Mama, he is Canadian."

Rico put his arms around his mother and gave her a gentle hug. He kissed her lightly on the forehead before releasing her. "Mama, please, I am expecting a phone call. I must go."

Teresa patted his shoulder. "You are a good son." She watched him sprint up the stairs, two steps at a time. Teresa allowed a sigh to escape. Shaking her head she turned towards the kitchen at the back of the house. 'He was such a beautiful boy before Tino corrupted him. Now Tino makes him do such terrible things.'

* * *

At noon the following day the phone rang in Rico's study. He picked it up on the second ring, "Si?"

"Rico?" It was Richard Bannerman. He had arrived in Bogota the previous evening.

"Si, Ricardo. It's me."

"Rico, your plan is working. Craig left Calgary this morning and is on his way down here to Bogota."

"Huh! He can't be! We have yet to deliver the ransom note. It's to be delivered this afternoon."

"Well, he's on his way."

"Who told you that?"

"Inspector Calder called me from Montreal."

"Who is he?"

"Inspector Calder is the man I put into the drug counterintelligence unit to watch over Boulanger. When you blew up Boulanger I put Calder in charge of the team... clever don't you think?"

"But he's in Montreal and Craig is in Calgary?"

"When you pulled your men out of Calgary, I had him send a Mountie to find Craig and keep an eye on him. I wanted to be sure he would come."

"I wonder how he found out we have his son? Is he alone?"

"Yes. His son Robert wasn't with him. According to the Calgary check-in agent at Air Canada, Craig is arriving on an Avianca flight out of Miami at 9:50 PM tonight."

"I had better organize his reception immediately."

"Don't forget, I want to be there when you bring him in."

"Oh, you are going to be there my friend. It's going to be a very interesting gathering with many surprises... many surprises... I'll let you know when he arrives. Ciao."

"I will be at a reception and dinner at the Tequendama Hotel until ten. Leave a message in my room."

"Okay."

* * *

On the flight from Calgary to Toronto, Craig tried to convince himself that Donald was still alive, and if so, he would have to try to figure out a way to rescue him. Flying from Toronto to Miami, Craig ordered aspirin and a couple of stiff drinks. They didn't take effect until he boarded the Avianca plane, a ten year old Boeing 707. He slept all the way to Bogota. The shudder and thud of the wheels descending and locking into place woke him up. The plane slowed and bucked slightly when the flaps extended. Creaking and heaving up and down in the rough air, the plane descended between a peak on the right and a bank of clouds on the left. The lights of the city came into view, extending for miles to the airport in the distance. Craig leaned forward to get a glimpse of the city below. A city he left more than thirty five years ago.

Looking out the window at the buildings drifting by below him Craig tried to locate his old school. He recognized the street but not the school. Thinking of the school triggered boyhood memories, long buried and covered by other memories. His capture by Joaquin, the bandit, and rescue by his father... Teresa... 'my first love... where is she now? Her brother, Tino, will know. I must ask him when we meet, as I'm sure we will meet. Eduardo... I wonder what happened to him after Mother and Dad were killed by Tino. Mum was teaching Eduardo to read before sending him to school in Gachala... he was a good friend... so brave. Nearly killed trying to rescue me... after I rescue Donald, I must see if I can find Eduardo.'

Craig had no idea how he was going to rescue Donald, much less look for Eduardo. The problem at the moment was... where was he going to start looking for Donald? According to Kowalski, the C.B.C. crew didn't have a clue where Donald might have gone. The only lead was that Donald had left a party with his arms around the girl from the Avita travel agency; but according to the Canadian Embassy in Bogota, there was no Avita Travel Agency; and the girl had disappeared. The only helpful suggestion the Embassy could offer was to contact Richard Bannerman, the Solicitor General, who was in Bogota attending a Conference. He might be able to influence the authorities to look for Craig's son.

Even though he arrived without a visa, Craig was hustled through the airport formalities. Craig attributed the efficiency to the Conference and the government's desire to impress the delegates. The passport official, sitting in a little glass enclosure took one look at Craig's passport and immediately motioned to a young man standing behind him. The young man, part indian, with a roundish face and large curved nose, leaned over the official's shoulder to examine the document. He glanced up at Craig and back to the passport. He said something in a low voice before moving into the hall at the side of the passport booth. The official returned the passport and pointed at the young man in the hall.

"Señor, siga con ese hombre."

Pretending he didn't understand the language, Craig asked in English, "Do you want me to follow him?"

"Si, Señor."

The young man waited for Craig, smiled, and reached down to take Craig's bag. "Welcome to Bogota, Mr. Fox. Are you here for the Conference?" He spoke heavily accented English.

"Yes."

"We like to help delegates get through passport control and customs as quickly as possible. Do you have reservation at a hotel?"

Craig didn't, but hoped Donald's room was still available. "The Tequendama Hotel."

"A good choice. You have no other baggage?"

"No."

"Then we can go right through and get a taxi for you."

The taxi was parked away from the taxi stand with the overhead sign on, indicating it was busy. The driver was leaning against the hood smoking a cigarette until they appeared through the exit doors. He threw his cigarette away and hurried forward to relieve the young man of Craig's bag. The young man opened the rear door. Craig got in wondering whether a tip was expected, but the young man was already striding towards the entrance doors. Inside the terminal he waited until the taxi moved off before entering a phone booth to report Craig's arrival.

The taxi driver did accept a tip and carried Craig's bag to the hotel porter. The receptionist, a severe woman, dressed in black with slashing black eyebrows, black hair pulled back in a bun and heavy makeup, gave Craig her professional smile. She spoke English,

"Sir, welcome to the Tequendama Hotel. You have a reservation?"

"My son is registered here. I will share his room."

"And his name is?"

"Donald Fox."

She ran her finger down a cardex file on the desk beside her. When her finger stopped Craig heard a low exclamation. "Ah!" She looked up. She gave him another professional smile.

"Your son is in room 401." She reached behind her and lifted a key from a letter box marked #401. Craig noticed several messages in the box and asked to see them. The receptionist handed Craig the key and the pink slips.

"Do you need assistance with your bags?"

"No thank you, I have this small bag."

But a bellhop was at his elbow, bag in hand before Craig could reach for it. The middle aged man escorted Craig to room #401, then returned to the lobby. Passing the reception desk he nodded to the dark haired lady. She picked up a telephone and dialed a number.

Craig dumped his bag on the bed and took off his tie and jacket, dropping them next to the bag. Sitting on the bed Craig let his eyes do the "walking" while he organized his thoughts. The room had been cleaned but Donald's things were still scattered about. A crumpled gray shirt and khaki trousers lay on one of the chairs. An exotic snake skin belt had slid partly out of the loops. A small pile of dirty clothes lay in a heap on the floor next to an open suitcase containing, what Craig assumed, were clean clothes. Papers were scattered over the desk and on the chair next to the desk. Craig noticed the small fridge and liquor cabinet under a side board. A small tray with glasses was on the sideboard. Craig walked over to the liquor cabinet. It was locked. Using the small key attached to the room key he unlocked the cabinet. It was empty except for a small two ounce bottle of Creme-de-menthe. Muttering, "I guess Donald doesn't like Creme-de-menthe. Neither do I." Craig next tried the fridge. This time he was lucky. There were two beers left in a six pack. Craig opened one and put it on the desk while he read the messages on the pink slips. They were all frantic appeals from the film crew, except one, it was from himself. It was a call he had made the previous evening in a forlorn hope that Donald might have returned. Next, Craig shuffled through Donald's papers. They appeared to be a mess. Scraps of paper with the names of places of interest around the city, sketches showing setups for cameras and lights with stick figures for people. It all seemed so disorganized, but then Craig noticed the various topics were in different piles. Personal stuff in one pile, Conference material, tourist attractions etc., in others. But none that might provide information about Donald's whereabouts. The closet was empty except for Donald's leather windbreaker and a scarf badly in need of cleaning. Two books of traveler's cheques and Donald's passport were in the inside pocket of the windbreaker. Craig didn't count the cheques but estimated several thousand dollars in hundred dollar denominations. He added these to the money belt around his waist. Craig checked his watch. It was after midnight. He would try to sleep and talk to the C.B.C. crew in the morning.

Donald's toilet and shaving kit were still in the bathroom. Wherever Donald had gone he had expected to return the same day. A brown metal lipstick tube lay next to the cold water tap. Craig pulled the top off and checked the color. It was pink, probably belonging to that girl from the Agency. The phone rang.

Holding the lipstick tube in his hand Craig went back to the bedroom to answer the phone. He hovered over it wondering who, other than the Embassy, would know he was in town. The ringing became more insistent. Craig picked up the phone.

"Hello?"

"Mister Craig Fox?" the accent was Canadian but Craig detected a trace of the Latin background.

"Speaking. Who is this?"

"My name is Enrique Chavez. You probably know me as 'Rico'... you may remember we have met."

"Yes, I remember, you tried to kick my head in."

"Mister Fox, I will not waste time, we have your son Donald. He is alive and well..."

"Donald knows nothing about your goddamn cartel. Let him go!"

"He was the bait. It is you we want. He will remain alive and well as long as you do exactly what we request, otherwise we will not hesitate to kill him... at nine o'clock tomorrow morning you will go downstairs and out the front entrance. You will see a long black limousine parked to your left. You will enter that limousine and will be driven to see your son... I must warn you your room is monitored. Do not... I repeat, do not make any phone calls nor leave your room until nine tomorrow."

"But..." The line was dead. Craig spewed a stream of curses into the mouthpiece before he put the phone down. He hadn't sworn like that in years and was gratified he remembered so many. It made him feel better but that wasn't going to help rescue Donald. Craig opened the second beer and retreated to the bed.

What to do now? Once again he had been outmaneuvered by the opposition. Craig knew he would eventually have to confront the cartel, but had hoped to arrive in the city unobserved and be able develop a plan before they were aware he was in Bogota. Now he was trapped in the room and could do nothing. The room was bugged and they could monitor his movements and phone calls. Not that there was anybody he could call for assistance. Craig had arranged to call Sandy, his secretary, at seven the next morning and have her pass on to Audrey any news he might have gathered. Now they would worry. He didn't dare do anything... unless... unless he could find the bug. His eyes roaming around the room Craig tried to think of all the spy movies he had seen over the years, then began a methodical check of all the likely places. Half an hour later, feeling somewhat foolish, Craig gave up and returned to the bed. He lay on the bed, awake, fully dressed, until morning, with no solution to the trap he was in.

At seven Craig phoned for room service. He didn't think whoever was listening would object. Not knowing when he might get another meal, Craig ordered bacon and eggs, toast and marmalade, and fresh papaya. He showered, shaved, and was dressed in casual clothes in time to answer the door to admit the waiter. While the waiter was arranging the breakfast trolley Craig debated bribing him to deliver a note to the Canadian Embassy, but decided against it when he noticed the young man casting his eyes around the room while he arranged the cutlery.

Promptly at nine Craig marched downstairs and out the front door feeling much like a condemned man on his way to the gallows. He had no delusions what his fate might be once in the hands of his old nemesis, Florentino Chavez.

* * *

Robert heard the crunch of tires on the gravel driveway. Quickly he switched off the TV, pushed himself off the easy chair with the help of the walking stick and limped over to the window. Through a gap in the curtains he saw Audrey getting out of the station wagon and reaching in the back for bags of groceries. Robert opened the side door and hopped down the steps to the driveway. With her hands loaded down with grocery bags his mother was trying to close the car door.

"Mom! Wait! I'll help."

"Robert, you're not supposed to be lifting things. You'll start to bleed again."

"Mother, please. I'm okay."

Robert was about to to wrap his hands around three of the bags when the police car drove by. It slowed briefly then accelerated. If it hadn't slowed down Robert probably wouldn't have paid attention. Even though there was nothing to identify the car as a police car; no lights; no logo; Robert knew it was a police car. He had been in the Service long enough to recognize an R.C.M.P. car when he saw one. And the young man with the short blond hair peering at them through the open window was a Mountie he knew. A Mountie who should be in Montreal chasing drug peddlers, not spying on him. The moment he realized that Robert had seen him the Mountie mouthed a silent curse. Robert limped out to the sidewalk. He watched the police car until it turned into a side street and disappeared.

Robert hopped back to the car and in a low urgent voice called his mother who was about to climb the steps to the side door of the bungalow.

"Mother! Drop everything! We've been discovered. We must leave immediately!"

"But?"

"Mother! Please, let's go! Now!"

Audrey refused to drop the groceries. She carried them back in each hand and dumped them in the back of the wagon. She jumped into the front seat. Robert backed out into the street. Taking care to avoid squealing the tires he accelerated in the opposite direction to that taken by the police car. Keeping an eye behind him to make sure he wasn't being followed Robert drove along the street until he came to a small shopping mall. Glancing behind him once again he pulled into the parking area and eased into a spot between two cars well back from the street. Five minutes later the police car came racing down the street and drove past the shopping mall without slowing down.

"Mom, we'll stay here for about half an hour while we make some plans. What have you got in those bags that we can eat while we wait?"

Not used to being ordered around, particularly by her son, who was supposed to be an invalid under her care, Audrey had been tempted to reassert her authority until she saw his grim countenance. The face was pale, but that was due to his wounds and the lack of sun; the eyes, although alert had yet to recover their former blue luster, and the cheeks were hollow; but there was no weakness in the chin. It was thrust forward with lips compressed and jaw muscles flexing. Whatever had triggered his demand they flee there was no doubt he was now very much in charge. She decided she was rather proud of her son. Audrey leaned over and extracted a bag of potato chips from a grocery bag. She ripped it open, placing it on the seat between them.

"Robert, will you please tell me what is going on? Why this sudden panic to flee?"

"Didn't you see that police car drive by?"

"No. Why should a police car be a danger to us?"

"The police car was following you... now, why would a police car be following you? Were you speeding? Did you go through any stop signs? Hit any pedestrians?"

"No! Of course not!"

"Where have you been this morning?"

"Robert! I told you last night I had arranged to meet Sandy for breakfast at six this morning. We ate at McDonalds on the Macleod Trail. Then I came straight home after picking up some groceries."

"The Mountie must have been following Sandy figuring she might lead him to us."

"But, Robert, why would the R.C.M.P. be a menace to us? Aren't they supposed to be on our side?"

"They are supposed to be but these days that is not necessarily true. Commissioner Boulanger was very concerned that the Service had been corrupted. The Mountie in that police car should be in Montreal... so why is he out here if not to try and find me?"

"But aren't you supposed to be part of the team?"

"I was, but I'm sure Rico told Bannerman that I know he is connected to the cartel, so Bannerman has to find and eliminate me."

"Robert, your father did not call Sandy this morning."

Trying to keep his voice calm, Robert asked, "When was he supposed to call?"

"He was to call Sandy at home at seven o'clock this morning. That was seven Bogota time which is five o'clock our time. There was no call. Sandy waited until nearly six o'clock before she came to meet me."

"Dad gets things screwed up sometimes. Maybe he thought he was supposed to call at seven Calgary time."

Audrey swung around, snapping, "Your father does not get things screwed up!"

"Sorry, I was just trying to reassure you."

"I know. Robert, what are we going to do? Your father is in trouble and we have nobody we can turn to for help."

"Mom, at the moment we can't help Dad. We have to solve our problem first. Whatever we do we have to do it quickly before they organize surveillance on the highways, airport, train, and bus - that's it! We must get to the Greyhound bus depot right away. That's the only place they don't ask for your name when you buy a ticket."

"But where shall we go?"

"We'll figure that out on our way to the bus depot. We have to forget the car. He will have radioed the license number and description to the dispatcher... see those phones over there, Mom, you phone Sandy and find out if Dad called. Also have her meet us at the bus depot with all the money she can get, and any mail addressed to us. I'll use the other phone and call a taxi. Please hurry, Mom, we don't have much time."

* * *

"Damn!Damn!Damn!" Pounding his fist on the steering wheel Constable Johnson cursed his stupidity. He shouldn't have slowed down. "Stupid! Stupid!" In spite of all his training he did the one thing that's a sure giveaway. The Academy had said over and over, "Don't slow down if your quarry stops." And he had done just that. Everything had been going so well up to that point. He had followed Craig Fox to the Airport; obtained Craig's flight schedule from the check-in agent and passed that on to Inspector Calder; and he had figured out that the best way of finding where that bugger, Robert Fox, was hidden would be through Craig Fox's secretary. According to the file he had been given when he left Montreal, her name was Sandra Reagan. She had been Craig Fox's secretary for over twenty years and must be a trusted employee to have been with him for so long. She would know where Robert was and would be contacting him or Craig Fox's wife, while Craig was in South America consorting with the cartel. It turned out to be easier then expected. Just one day tailing her while she took care of company business, and one night parked down the street from her apartment. Early that morning he had followed her to McDonalds and parked across the street opposite the entrance. At this early hour it was mostly men going in but none looked like Robert. A white station wagon slowed down, drove past the entrance, then proceeded down the street. a few minutes later it was back and eased slowly into a parking spot near the exit. A lady got out. Constable Johnson checked the pictures in his file.

"Ah! That's her. Mrs. Audrey Fox."

It had all gone so well and now he had screwed it up! He would just have to hope that bastard, Robert, hadn't recognized him. He would wait a few minutes and drive back up the street past the house.

This time he didn't slow down when he passed the house, but quickly backed up the moment he realized the station wagon was gone. In spite of warnings that Robert Fox might be armed and could be dangerous, Constable Johnson, desperate to rectify his mistakes, parked the police car in the middle of the street, snapped a gun out of a shoulder holster and raced up the driveway on the balls of his feet. He bounded up the steps to the side door. It was ajar. Diving through the open door, Johnson spun around in mid air landing on his back, gun grasped in both hands. The kitchen was empty. So was the rest of the house. Angrily, he slammed the side door shut behind him and raced for his car.

Four hours later Constable Johnson made his report to Inspector Calder, including details of his skill in tracking the women that led him to Robert Fox's hideout; in locating the abandoned white station wagon, and organizing surveillance at the airport and other exits from the city. It was Constable Johnson's opinion that Robert and his mother were still in the city and it would not be very long before Mr. Fox's secretary would try to get in touch with them. No mention was made of the fact that the station wagon was found in the parking lot of a shopping mall less then four blocks from Robert's hideout.

* * *

The black limousine was not parked where he had been told it would be. To the left of the hotel entrance the parking spaces were occupied by cars and two white limousines. No black limousine. Uncertain as to whether he should attempt to flee Craig paused on the steps leading down to the driveway. A porter approached to inquire if he wanted a taxi, but before he reached Craig a voice beside him made Craig swivel around.

"Señor Fox?"

A man was standing to the left of Craig several steps below him, a chauffeur's hat clutched in both hands. He appeared to be tense, looking up anxiously scanning Craig's face, a tentative smile playing across his face as if waiting to be recognized.

"Craig?"

It was not the use of his first name that surprised Craig. Rico had probably given his full name to the driver. The inflection, the way the driver pronounced the word was what startled Craig. It was an unusual pronunciation of his name. It sounded like "Kra-go". Only one other person had ever placed the emphasis on the last syllable and that was long ago. Craig leaned forward and mouthed the question, hesitantly,

"Eduardo?"

Quickly the man put a finger to his lips. Nodding his head vigorously he whispered, "Si! Si!" Then turning and beckoning, he spoke in a louder voice,

"Señor, venga, por favor."

His emotions in turmoil Craig followed the driver. The man in front of him was average height for an Indian, fairly stocky, with a fleshy face and an incipient belly. The Indian boy he remembered was slender and shorter, but that was thirty five years ago. 'If he is Eduardo, what is he doing working for the cartel?'

"Eduardo...?"

The response was a quick negative wave of the hand and a low hiss,"Sssh." Not a moment too soon. A few feet in front of the driver a man stepped out from a doorway. Craig recognized him immediately. It was Enrique Chavez. He waited, smiling at Craig.

"Mr. Fox, I see you haven't tried to escape."

"The thought occurred to me but I'm sure you made suitable arrangements to prevent that."

"Yes. The porter... and there are others. Please come with me."

The driver led the way, Rico walking beside Craig. Around the corner the limousine was parked by the curb. Two men were standing beside it, one at the front, the other next to the taillight. The driver opened the rear door. Craig glanced at him as he entered but Eduardo stared coldly through him. Rico pulled down a jump seat and sat down facing Craig. The two men got in beside the driver. Rico pulled out a kerchief and motioned Craig to lean forward.

"I am sorry, but this is necessary. You went to school here and know the city well. It is better if you don't know where we are going."

Craig shrugged, "Does it matter... unless the fare includes a return ticket."

"That is up to Florentino Chavez."

"Then this must be a one way ticket."

Rico placed the kerchief over Craig's eyes and tied it. The limousine pulled away from the kerb, ignored a horn blaring behind it, and accelerated into the morning traffic. Craig leaned back in his seat and stared into the orange gloom in front of him wondering why this cunning young man was being courteous? Why Eduardo was working for the cartel? What would he say when he met Teresa? Was Donald still alive?

"Will I see my son?"

"Yes, your son is alive and well. But very angry that he was responsible for your being here. We have to be careful we don't get too close."

Craig smiled, "That sounds like Donald."

"We have many questions we wish to ask you, but that can wait until we meet with my uncle and your old friend..."

"Let me guess. Richard Bannerman!"

"Ricardo is very anxious to see you."

"I have no doubt Richard will be gloating."

Enrique studied the features of the man before him. He was taller than himself, broad shouldered, and as he had been able to flip Rico when they first met, obviously very fit. Under the blindfold the face was tanned, clean shaven, and from the few creases just visible under the blind his age must be around fifty. Could this man be his father? There was no physical resemblance, in build, nor in skin and hair color, except the eyes. It was the eyes that convinced him. The same brilliant blue as his own. The eyes were now covered but he had noticed them the moment he saw Craig. His uncle, Florentino Chavez, claimed Rico's mother had been raped by a Canadian. Florentino had revealed few details about Craig except that Craig had gone to school in Bogota. Craig could have met Teresa in Bogota, and if what his uncle said was true, raped her. But this man did not look like a rapist, so it must be true what his mother had confided to him years ago that she had not been raped. They had been lovers. Whether it was love or rape had been of no consequence to him at the time, but now he hoped it had not been rape. Rico was quite surprised at his own emotions. He had to admit he liked the man. Even though humiliated by having to wear the blind he retained his dignity and humor, projecting an aura of calm confidence in himself. 'He must have been just a boy when he slept with my mother... muy Macho!' In many ways he was much like Richard Bannerman, and it was puzzling why Ricardo hated Craig so much. 'Could it be because he is jealous of Craig?... no, not Ricardo. He's too arrogant. He's constantly dismissing Craig as a minor nuisance, yet Craig has been able to frustrate so many of Ricardo's plans. Not to mention some of my own. There was a lot of ancient history between Ricardo and Craig... and between them and my uncle. It should be an interesting meeting'.

Craig heard the squeak of gates opening and closing. He guessed they must have entered a compound. Rico pulled the kerchief off without loosening the knot. They were in a large underground garage. The two men jumped out and positioned themselves at the front and rear of the limousine. Eduardo opened the rear door nearest him and stood beside the door, eyes on the ground, cap pulled down. Rico folded the jump seat and stepped out. Craig followed. Aware that Rico was watching him Craig ignored Eduardo. Rico led the way along a hall and the two men fell in behind Craig. Part way down the hall a flight of stairs led up to the main floor. Passing the stairs Craig glanced up briefly, to be confronted by an Indian lady descending the stairs. She had stopped with one foot frozen in mid air, hands clutching the railing, and a startled expression on her face. Abruptly she sat, murmuring, "O Dios Mio!"

It was Teresa. Of that he was certain. Her black hair, pulled back into a bun, was now streaked with gray but the face was much the same as he remembered; the light brown skin smoothed over high cheekbones; large nose with slightly flared nostrils; and the thin unhappy lips. Craig quickly averted his eyes, but in front of him Rico looked back. Craig's flushed cheeks was his proof!

At the end of the hall Rico unlocked a heavy metal door and waved Craig in, slamming the door shut behind him. Rico ordered the two men to guard the door before he walked back to the stairs knowing his mother would be blocking the way upstairs to demand answers.

* * *

Donald was stretched out on a sofa, watching a Spanish program on the TV. He cocked his head around at the intrusion. Seeing his father he leapt over the sofa and wrapped his arms around Craig.

"Dad!... Dad, I'm so sorry... I..."

"Donald! Thank God you're alive and well. Rico said you were alive but I don't trust him."

"Dad, I'm so sorry I got you into this."

"Ssh. Things had to come to a head very soon. I know too much about the cartel, so they have to eliminate me. Your presence in Bogota provided them with an opportunity that's all. They would have had to try something else soon. They've murdered Commissioner Boulanger so I'm the last obstacle... Donald don't blame yourself."

"But I was stupid to think they would give me an interview."

"Is that how they got you out here? I thought you had been seduced by Mata Hari."

"Who?"

"Never mind. We have to make plans and..."

Quickly Donald raised a finger to his lips then pointed at the ceiling. He walked over to the television, raised the volume, and beckoned his father. He whispered in Craig's ear,

"I know they can hear what we say but I haven't been able to find the bloody thing."

Craig whispered, "I was going to say, there is a glimmer of hope but I won't explain what that is just now. Let's wait and see what develops." Craig turned down the volume and resumed speaking in a normal voice, "Your mother sends her love and hopes you are not forgetting to take your malaria pills." Craig smiled in response to Donald's and went on, "Robert is much better but still a little weak. I talked to your girl in Toronto. She's fine but a little upset you haven't called... and the C.B.C. is sending John McCabe to replace you."

"What! Him? He'll screw everything up besides getting all the credit for my work."

Craig leaned over and whispered, "All the more reason for you to get out of here."

"Blast them. I'm going to have a drink." Donald opened the door of a buffet and pulled out a bottle half full of a colorless liquid. "Here, have some of this, Dad. It'll put hair on your chest."

"If that's what I think it is, no thanks."

Donald read the label, "Aguardiente, it says."

"No thanks. In English that means 'burning water' It's almost pure alcohol. Donald come sit down and relax. It will be a while before we are summoned. They have to wait for Richard Bannerman to arrive."

"Richard Bannerman! You mean..."

"Yes, Bannerman is in cahoots with the cartel."

"Jesus!"

"I know. The cartel has been financing all the propaganda to get Bannerman elected Prime Minister of Canada. That's another reason I had to be eliminated now before he becomes Prime Minister. Come and sit down and we'll see what develops."

"Dad! How can you be so calm? We're trapped in here in the middle of a hornet's nest with two guards outside the door. Nobody knows we're here... and I'm sure that little bastard, Rico, is dying to cut my throat."

"For once in your life, Donald, you're going to have to sit quietly and await developments. There is nothing we can do so sit down and sip your joy juice."

* * *

Teresa confronted Rico as he was about to mount the stairs, "Enrique! What is going on? That man is Craig Fox. I recognized him right away. Why is he here?"

"Mama! If your brother has not told you why my father is here, then I cannot."

"How did you know he is your father?"

"I have suspected for some time and when I saw both your reactions when you met, I knew for sure."

"Enrique, Florentino will kill him. You must help him escape."

"Mama, you know very well Tino will kill me if I do that. Besides, I have no desire to see him escape."

"But he is your father."

"I am sorry, Mama. He is too dangerous. He knows too much about our organization in Canada. He has to die, and his son too."

"Is that his son in there?"

"Yes."

"He is your brother. You must help them escape."

"Mama! I can do nothing for them. Now, please let me pass, I have to tell Tino his old friend is here."

"Enrique! I shall never forgive you if you don't help."

Rico shrugged. He stepped around Teresa and continued up the stairs. Teresa didn't move for a long time, sitting where she had collapsed, caressing an image she had nurtured and held close to her heart for so many years. ‘He is still handsome ... the same blue eyes that mesmerized me long ago.’ Finally, she reached a decision. She put her hand on the railing and pulled herself upright. Teresa leaned over to check on the two guards. Quietly she tiptoed down the last few steps and went out to the underground garage to look for Eduardo.

- 12 -

Allan Sharp was sure somebody was tailing him. In fact he was certain he had been under surveillance for some time, at least for the last four days. He had seen the same Chevy sedan everywhere he went; at the bank; the super market; outside the Granite Club, and across the street from his office. Although there are probably over ten thousand gray Chevy sedans cruising the streets of Toronto, Allan was sure it was the same car. He had been unable to identify the driver but Allan was convinced Richard Bannerman was responsible for the stakeout.

Even though Richard had talked him out of resigning from the Company, Allan was left in no doubt that he was under suspicion; the tone of voice; the frequent phone calls demanding detailed information on Company business; details that he had previously left to Allan's control; and the recent clumsy attempts by his secretary to open his safe. Allan had been aware for several years that Roberta Masse reported to Richard Bannerman and had provided her with carefully selected material for her to pass on while keeping personal correspondence in his safe. From habit the pointer was always on zero. No longer. Every time Allan checked the safe the pointer was at some other number. It had to be Roberta. A professional would have been more careful.

Pulling out from the detached garage Allan checked up and down the street. The gray Chevy was parked across the street halfway along the block. It followed Allan.

"Enough is enough!"

Angrily, Allan pulled into a service station and parked his car. The Chevy sedan followed him in, easing into the slot next to Allan's car. Allan jumped out, slammed his car door behind him, and strode over to the driver's side of the Chevy. The driver opened his door and stood up. Allan was not sure what he was expecting to confront, but it was certainly not this well dressed gentleman in tweed sports jacket and expensive gray slacks standing before him, very straight, very military. The surprise only slowed him momentarily. Allan halted three feet in front of the other man. Shaking his fist he growled,

"I'm sick and tired of you following me. What the fuck do you want with me?"

"Mr. Sharp? Mr. Allan Sharp?"

"Yes! Yes! it's me. You bloody well know it's me. What the hell do you want?"

"Mr. Sharp, I'm arresting you for attempted murder."

"Murder! Me!... You're crazy! Who the hell are you any way?"

"I am Deputy Commissioner Boulanger."

"But you're..."

"Dead. No Mr. Sharp, I'm not dead... you failed. I was not in the car you blew up."

"It wasn't me,I swear it. It was..."

The steel blue eyes flashed, "Who? Mr. Sharp. Who was it? Please explain to me why an attempt would be made on my life on the day before I was to meet you, if it wasn't to prevent me from conducting an investigation of your company. You must have arranged to have my car blown up. I'm charging you with attempted murder."

"Officer... Commissioner, it was not me!"

"Who, then?"

"I don't know... and anyway how do I know you're Commissioner Boulanger. The police identified the body in the car and I watched his funeral on T.V."

"If you watched my funeral you must have seen my picture. It was in all the papers and on T.V. I am Commissioner Boulanger."

Allan nodded reluctantly. There was no denying the face was the same as in the pictures.

"Mr. Sharp, you're under arrest. Lock your car and get into my car... don't try to run away."

Allan had started to walk back to his car but the Commissioner's words spun him around. He retorted angrily,

"I never run away, Commissioner!"

Marcel Boulanger waited until Allan sat in the front passenger seat before getting in the car. He turned to face Allan, who in turn was studying the Commissioner. Marcel was fairly certain that Allan Sharp was telling the truth. He didn't think Allan had planted the bomb himself, but he must know who did. He had followed Allan Sharp for days hoping Allan might make contact with whoever had planted the bomb, but Allan had made no contact with any suspicious persons. Still, he must know who organized the job. Marcel suspected it was Richard Bannerman and was determined to keep the pressure on Allan until he revealed the perpetrator, and more importantly, disclosed the secrets of his company, the Star Corporation. But from the man's outburst Marcel knew that getting him to talk would not be easy, particularly a war hero like Allan Sharp with 12 planes to his credit. The Commissioner backed out into the street. He turned right at the next corner and followed the signs pointing to Highway #401.

"Where are you taking me?"

"To a safe house where we can talk."

"I must phone my office. They are expecting me... also my wife."

"No! Later tonight you and I will pay a visit to your office. As far as your wife is concerned I doubt if she cares whether you return."

"You seem to know a great deal about me, Commissioner."

"Through the help of a mutual acquaintance I have learned about you, your company, and your connection to the Colombian Drug Cartel. Those connections should be enough to put you behind bars for the rest of your life, without the additional charge of attempted murder."

"Commissioner, you are barking up the wrong tree. I have no connection to the Cartel. I have never met them. I have never spoken to them."

"My information says you do have connections with them."

"Well, you're wrong." Allan turned to face the Commissioner. "Who is our mutual acquaintance?"

"Craig Fox."

"Craig! I'll be damned. So Craig Fox has risen again." Allan chuckled, "Richard won't be pleased to hear that."

"If you mean Richard Bannerman, he knows... and you're right, he is not too pleased."

Angry with himself for blurting out Richard's name, Allan slumped back in the seat and tried to ignore the commissioner. He should have resigned and not allowed Richard to talk him out of it. In fact he should have resigned years ago and gone back to England. Now he would have to rely on Richard to to get him out of this mess and at the moment he wasn't Richard's favorite.

* * *

It had been an exhausting eighteen hours: the frantic flight from the house; the three taxis they took to the Greyhound bus depot; the bus to Red deer; the second bus to Edmonton; and two taxis to the Edmonton airport; with his mother insisting on lugging those wretched bags of groceries from taxi to taxi and bus to bus. Waiting for his father's secretary to appear had been the most nerve-racking. Acutely aware that it was through her being tailed that they had been discovered, Robert wouldn't have asked Sandy to meet them at the Calgary bus depot if they weren't desperate for money. Without money they didn't have the means to escape.

At the bus station Robert had positioned his mother at the far end of the waiting room near the door leading to the buses, where she would be clearly visible from the front entrance. He stationed himself to one side of the main entrance hidden behind a pillar, where he would be able to observe Sandy when she came in, and whoever might be following her.

They waited... and waited

From time to time his mother glanced at him, shrugging her shoulders silently indicating, "I don't know what's happened to her." Twice, Robert was forced to go up to the counter to change their tickets for the next bus to Red Deer. Finally Sandy came running in carrying a large brown envelope in her right hand and a packet of letters in her left. She raced over to Audrey and shook her awake. Startled, Audrey jerked upright, gasping.

"I'm so sorry Audrey, I didn't mean to frighten you."

"It's okay, It's okay. I fell asleep."

"I'm sorry I'm so late but the bank put up a fuss about my taking out so much company money without authorization from Craig. I finally talked them into letting me have twenty thousand in hundred dollar denominations." Sandy looked around the waiting room. "Where is Robert?"

"He's over there," pointing behind her, "waiting to see if you were followed."

Sandy looked around frantically, "Oh God No! I hope not, not again. Audrey, I'm so sorry about this morning. How could I have been so careless?"

"Sandy, please don't worry about it... it was time we moved anyway... have you heard from Craig?"

"Not a word. I'm sorry."

"Here comes Robert. Thank you Sandy. We'll be in touch."

"Where are you going?"

"It's better if you don't know. We'll call you when it is safe."

Robert walked up and hugged Sandy. He kissed her on the cheek. "Sandy, you are a gem. How much money were you able to get?"

"Twenty thousand."

"Perfect. We're catching the next bus to Vancouver. We'll stay there until we hear from Dad. Sandy would you mind leaving us now. Thanks again."

"Sure. Here's the money and the mail I grabbed when I left the office."

"Thanks Sandy. Bye."

"Good luck."

Sandy was barely out of earshot when Audrey asked, "Why did you tell her we are going to Vancouver? You shouldn't have misled her."

"Just a precaution, Mother. Just a precaution."

"Sandy would never betray us."

"I know that Mother, but I'm just being cautious."

He had been cautious: on each bus; in Red Deer; in Edmonton, and getting on the plane to Toronto. Even when calling Aunt Valerie from the Edmonton airport he was cautious. He made the call loaded down with enough quarters to feed the machine for an hour. Fortunately she was home and not out at her cottage on Georgian Bay. She assured him they could stay at the cottage as long as they wanted.

"Brian is about to close it down for the winter but I'll call him to leave the water on... yes, the phone at the cottage is working but remember it is a party line and neighbors can listen in." She was upset to hear Craig was missing. "Richard Bannerman must have done it." Robert agreed.

But Audrey was puzzled, "Why do you want to go there? It's so isolated."

"Yes. it's isolated but you'll be safe there."

"But your father will never be able to find us."

"I'll think up something to leave on your answering machine in Calgary."

Audrey gave him one of her skeptical looks. "A secret code I suppose?"

"Oh Mother! Have a little faith in your son."

"Robert, I'm so sorry!" Contritely, she took his hand in both hers and pressed it to her chest, "I'm so sorry. You're doing so well in spite of your wounds and I'm not helping. It's just that I'm so tired... so tired of hiding and running... when will it ever end?"

"I don't know, Mom, but I have a feeling that one way or another it will be soon."

Audrey tipped her seat back, murmuring, "I hope so. God I hope so." Two minutes later she was asleep. Robert leaned over her and pulled down the blind to shut out the early morning sun, before standing to look for a pillow to put behind his mother's head.

Robert searched the overhead rack. He found two pillows. Spying a blanket he took that and the two pillows. He tucked one pillow behind his mother's head and wrapped the blanket around her legs. Audrey murmured something in her sleep which he interpreted to mean "Thanks". A strand of hair had fallen across her face. Gently he picked it up with his thumb and index finger and threaded it back in her hair. Looking at her Robert realized for the first time that his mother was no longer young; the hair was tinged with gray; her cheeks, though still round, were losing their rosy bloom; and the lines radiating from her eyes were sharper. She had dark circles under her eyes but that was probably from exhaustion. He was dead tired too but didn't dare relax until they were safely in the cottage on Georgian Bay.

He put a second pillow behind him to ease the pressure on the scars on his back. Robert was sure one of the wounds had broken open again. He felt no pain but putting his hand behind him he could feel moisture on his shirt. He took out his handkerchief and wedged it between his shirt and the pillow to make sure no blood got on the pillow. He leaned back and closed his eyes.

A sudden thought popped his head up, eyes wide open, 'What if Dad is dead? What if they've killed him?' Before it had never occurred to Robert that his father might not survive. Growing up he had thought his father indestructible. Able to confront and overcome obstacles with ease. A pillar to lean on. The realization that his mother was getting old disturbed Robert. 'And Dad is older than Mum. He must be in his fifties... he'll be an old man soon... that's if he's still alive.' Robert shook his head and tried to think of something else.

Remembering the letters Sandy had given them when she delivered the money, Robert reached under the seat in front of him and pulled out the one remaining grocery bag. Inside, under a bag of nuts, he found the packet of letters bound together with a thick rubber band. He pulled off the rubber band and sorted through the envelopes. Halfway through the small pile he was surprised to find one addressed to himself. His name and his fathers company address was printed in large black letters, but there was no return address. It had been mailed in Toronto three days before. Robert sorted through the remaining letters before putting the rubber band back on and replacing them in the grocery bag under the seat. Intrigued and puzzled Robert held the letter addressed to him in his hand for several minutes, wondering who it was from and how that person had found out he was in Calgary. The only persons that knew were his mother, father, Sandy, and the drug cartel. One other person had known but he was dead, blown up in his car. Robert stuck his finger under the flap and ripped open the envelope. Inside was a folded sheet of white paper. He opened it and let out a loud gasp,

"It's him!"

Audrey stirred. "Who?"

"Sssh, Mom, I'm sorry, I didn't realize I was so loud."

"Who is him?"

Robert handed her the sheet of paper, "See, it's him. He's alive!"

"For Heaven's sake, Robert! Who is alive?"

Robert leaned over. Speaking in a low voice he said, "Boulanger... Boulanger is alive."

"But...?"

"Mom, look at this," pointing to the paper in his hand. "It says 'Robert I need you in Toronto. TSH.3'."

"What does 'TSH.3' mean?"

"That means that Boulanger is alive, in Toronto, and staying at a safe house that only he and I know about."

"But Robert, you and I watched his funeral on T.V. Somebody else could be using that house."

"Impossible! He set up safe houses in Montreal and Toronto, maybe in other places I don't know about, but only he knew where they all were. Each undercover officer in his squad was given the location of one safe house in Montreal and one in Toronto. Each officer was assigned a safe house and only Boulanger and that officer knew the location of that house... TSH.3 is my safe house in Toronto. It's not really a house, just a run down one bedroom apartment on the eastern outskirts of Toronto that I used when I needed to get in touch with Boulanger."

"If he wasn't killed why would he hide and allow them to go ahead with a funeral? Wouldn't he tell somebody?"

"When they blew up his car Boulanger must have seen it as an opportunity to do his investigation while the cartel assumed he was no longer a threat."

"Then who was in the car? The police said it was him."

"Good question... Mom, this changes everything! I must go to him. We must organize something to rescue Dad. When we get to Toronto I'll phone the safe house and have Boulanger pick me up."

"Can you remember the number?"

Robert tapped his head. "It's imprinted here. I'll arrange for Aunt Valerie to drive you to Georgian Bay."

"What! And have me sit there in total isolation not knowing what is happening to your father or to you."

"Mother, please. Boulanger and I will be trying to find Dad and Donald and I have to know that you are safe. You've been to the cottage. It's lovely and Uncle Brian has it full of books."

"Very well. If I'm stuck out there I might as well do some painting. I'll pick up some stuff, but you keep me informed... promise."

"I promise, Mom. Thank you."

Robert knew his mother too well to think she would accept her banishment to the cottage without a struggle. At the moment, she was too tired to argue while they were still in the air. Hopefully in two hours he might be able to enlist Aunt Valerie's help.

* * *

Beginning to lose patience with his son, Craig walked over to prevent Donald from pouring himself another half tumbler of alcohol. He placed one hand over the bottle the other on Donald's shoulder. Leaning into Donald's ear Craig pleaded in a low voice,

"Donald, please! I need you. I need you sober not drunk. You have to help me organize our escape. We have been locked up for many hours so I suspect we will be taken upstairs soon. There's nothing we can do until we know what they plan to do with us. Then with an awful lot of luck we make our escape."

"Escape! How?"

"Sssh! Not so loud! We have a..."

Both heads turned at the sound of a bolt sliding back. The door opened. Rico entered followed by the two guards. Rico glanced quickly around the room taking in the open bottle of "Aguardiente" and the tumbler in Donald's hand. His lips curled in a sneer.

"So! Daddy doesn't want you to drink anymore so you can escape. Tell us Mr. Fox, how do you plan to escape?"

Donald lurched toward Rico, hands clenched. Quickly Craig stepped between the two.

"Donald! Calm down! Don't let him provoke you." Craig was about to add, "He's not worth it." But didn't. Besides the situation was tense enough without adding to the hostility between the two men.

Bowing slightly towards Rico, Craig said, "I presume your guest has arrived and you would like to invite us upstairs for drinks?"

Rico laughed, "I like that." Bowing in turn he waved his hand in the direction of the door, "You are invited. Please follow the guards."

Craig nudged Donald past Rico, who had stepped well away to one side out of Donald's reach. Craig followed Donald out the door. The guards positioned themselves at the foot of the stairs blocking the hall leading to the underground garage. Standing some distance behind them near the entrance to the garage was Teresa, head clasped between her hands. Craig paused one hand on the railing. He gave Teresa a reassuring smile. Her hands opened palms toward him in a gesture, 'I had nothing to do with this'. Craig understood. He nodded and smiled again. Behind her in the dim light of the garage he could see Eduardo, a dark shape in a peaked cap. Donald reaching the top of the stairs turned around to look for his father. He wondered what his father was smiling about.

Rico bounded up the stairs behind Craig and led the way into a very long large room. At the far end seated on each side of a huge rock studded fireplace sat two men, Florentino Chavez, head of the Cali Cartel, and Richard Bannerman, soon to be Prime Minister of Canada.

Donald was stunned.

Craig's first thought was, 'God! If I could splash that picture all over the newspapers in Canada, Richard would be finished forever'.

They were both watching Craig approach, Florentino with a scowl, Richard with a smug look on his face. On the right a huge picture window held back the pitch black night. In the distance a low ridge blocked the city lights visible only as a glow against the low lying clouds. Rico waved Craig to a leather armchair, Donald to a bench against the wall.

Craig was amazed at how little his two opponents had changed in the thirty odd years since their last confrontation. Florentino was still slim, perhaps slimmer, with the same flashing eyes, straight black shiny hair, and high cheekbones that gave him the oriental caste. The only visible sign of aging was the skin now dry like parchment and beginning to wrinkle. Richard on the other hand was beginning to put on weight. His cheeks were thicker, less sculptured, making his chin less prominent; the hair, still blond but fading to white; and as usual his bearing carefully arranged to display his best features; face tilted slightly to one side to profile the straight nose and dimpled chin and one long elegant leg crossed over the other. Craig had seen Richard on T.V. many times and that was the way Richard liked to be viewed by the public. The only difference now was the tumbler in his right hand, a half empty bottle of Scotch, and a silver tray full of ice on a table beside him.

Richard spoke first, "Craig, it is a pleasure to see you again particularly in these surroundings."

Craig ignored Richard. He addressed Florentino, speaking in Spanish slowly to make sure he chose the right words, "Tino, your business is with me. My son knows nothing about your drug cartel. I beg of you, as a father, let my son go."

Florentino chopped his hand down in a dismissive gesture. "Ridiculous!" Pointing at Richard, "And have your son tell the world this man is sitting next to me. Impossible! And I'm not a father."

"But Rico is your son."

Florentino shook his head waving the suggestion away, "Rico is not my son. I have no sons... at least that I know about."

Rico walked over to stand beside Florentino, facing Craig, "Uncle, tell him who my father is. Tell him."

Florentino rose slowly. Pointing a finger at Craig he growled, "You raped my sister!" In a higher pitch, he yelled, "You raped Teresa, my sister!... and he..." pushing Rico towards Craig, "is your son!"

Donald leapt to his feet. "What! It can't be!" Turning to his father, "Dad?"

Craig said nothing for a few moments. Shaking his head he muttered, "Impossible." but, his mind flashing back to a night many years ago, he knew it was possible. "No! It's impossible! Look at him. He's totally different."

Rico whipped off his dark glasses. "Except for the eyes. They are blue like yours." Rico thrust his head forward. "Look! Yes Father, look."

Richard slapped his hand on his knee, bellowing out a guffaw. He chortled, "This is rich! Fantastic! Craig Fox the man who can do no wrong... the man who single handed thinks he can destroy me... the man in shining armor out to save Canada. He rapes a girl. Knocks her up and produces a son. A son who is the Chief Honcho of the cartel in Canada! Oh, I love it! Tino, I want pictures of Craig standing next to his son Rico. I'll make sure Rico's face is blurred then I'll plaster the pictures in every newspaper across Canada... and when they find your body, Craig, there will be one in your pocket... Tino, I insist, I want pictures."

Florentino gave Rico a quizzing look. He had not understood the outburst. Rico explained. Florentino shrugged dismissing the request. Instead he spoke to his nephew,

"Rico, go and fetch Teresa. I want her to confront the man who raped her."

"Uncle, she won't come. I asked her. She said she wants no part of the games you play. She said Craig did not rape her."

"She's right, I never did."

Florentino shook his fist at Craig, "You raped her! And for that I'm going to kill you."

Donald thrust his chin forward, "Over my dead body you will!"

This time Florentino understood the threat, "That I'll be happy to arrange... later... Rico take them back, I have business to discuss with the next Prime Minister of Canada."

In heavily accented Spanish Richard insisted, "No wait! I want that picture. Rico, get a camera."

Florentino nodded at Rico and pointed to a cupboard beside Donald. Rico circled around Donald, took a large camera out of a drawer and carried it over to where Richard was now standing in front of Craig's leather chair. Craig continued to sit quietly. Donald did not. Moving forward he pleaded,

"Dad? Don't let him take a picture of you with him." pointing at Rico.

Craig waved him back, "Donald it's not important. Let Bannerman play his little games."

The remark infuriated Richard. He slashed his hand across Craig's face leaving a red streak where Richard's ring bruised Craig's cheek. Donald was about to hurl himself at Richard, but stopped when Richard thrust his hand in his jacket and whipped out a small black revolver. Craig leapt up and placed himself in front of Richard at the same time shoving Donald angrily behind him.

"Goddamn it! Donald! Go and sit down before you get us both killed."

Richard motioned with the revolver for Craig to move aside, "Craig, move over and I'll finish him off for you before he gives you any more headaches."

Florentino slammed his hand on the table beside him. "Enough! Ricardo stop that! Take your picture then Rico can take them away."

Richard took two pictures; one of Rico seated in front of Craig; the second of Rico standing beside him. Richard handed the camera to Rico. "I want those developed right away so can give them to the C.B.C. tomorrow."

Richard strutted back to his chair, put three ice cubes in his glass, poured in some whiskey and sat down, legs crossed, the revolver visible on his lap. He spoke slowly, trying to recall his Spanish, "Tino, I want to hear what Craig knows about me and the cartel. Question him now."

"No Ricardo. There are some things it is better for you not to know about our business. Rico, take them back to the room."

Craig studied the faces of the two men seated in front of him. His lips curled slightly as his eyes passed over Richard, but remembering who was responsible for his parents murder, his lips tightened and eyes narrowed as they focused on Florentino Chavez. Turning, he nodded to Rico, giving him a slight smile.

The smile ripped a tiny tear in Rico armor. How could this man stand there so self confident, so serene even though he knew he would probably be tortured and killed. He was the only one that had remained cool in spite of all the squabbling around him. Rico placed his hand on Craig's shoulder and guided him towards the door. In a low voice he said, "You heard what he said, Father."

Donald muttered in a low voice, "Father my foot!" as he led the way back down the stairs.

Florentino Chavez sat quietly, his eyes following Rico, a pensive look on his face.

Richard lifted his glass to Florentino. He stumbled though the little Spanish he could remember, "Tino, that was brilliant the way you got Craig to walk right into your trap. I congratulate you." Richard took a large drink before he put the glass back on the table. He poured more whiskey into the glass. Florentino noted the bottle was emptying fast and Richard was showing the effect. That suited his purpose. A few minutes later Enrique reentered the room.

"Rico, did you lock them up?"

Irritated, Enrique snapped, "Yes Uncle! Of course I did."

"Well, he is your father."

"The door is locked and bolted and there are two guards in front of it."

"Bueno." Florentino motioned Rico to pull up a chair. "I want you to translate for me to make sure Ricardo understands me, and that I understand what he plans to do when he becomes Prime Minister."

Turning to Richard who had just taken another drink, "Ricardo, why is it necessary for you to have this... what do you call it... Convention? Why don't you just give everybody some money and tell them to vote for you?"

Richard didn't wait for the translation. He chuckled,"In Canada it's not so easy." Rico noticed Richard's English was beginning to sound fuzzy. "That's what I wanted to do. We spent a great deal of money on editorials, talk shows, and interviews to build up support to get me appointed Prime Minister by acclamation, but that stupid bastard Trevor Goodrich insisted on holding a Convention to pick the next leader of the Party. He was hoping somebody else would creep out of the woodwork and beat me... silly ass!"

"When is the Convention?"

"In eight days. Starting on November the eighteenth."

"Is there any possibility you may lose?"

"None! I've eliminated the two serious contenders." Richard started to laugh, "That ass Goodrich has nominated a French Canadian lawyer from Montreal that nobody heard of before... I can't even remember his name."

"Bueno! And after the Convention?"

"I intend to move fast. I have to. Under the current rules we have to hold an election in the next twelve months so I don't have much time. I've got enough votes, bribes some might call it, in Parliament to push through some Emergency Laws, much like Trudeau did in nineteen seventy. He brought in The War Measures Act when he had that trouble with terrorists. I am going to use... you'll like this... the drug cartel menace as a reason."

"Is that a good idea?"

Rico chipped in,"Yes, Uncle. That was my idea. It will deflect any suspicion from Richard."

"And what will you do with these Emergency Laws?"

Richard was beginning to slur his words. "It will give me the power to suspend the Constitution and provide the R.C.M.P. with the authority to do anything I ask them to do... I will abolish the Senate. That will be popular. Nobody likes the Senate anyway... kick out that lady in London and declare Canada a Republic... hold an election for President for which I will "arrange" the results. Every five years I will hold an election until I think the climate is right for a President... a President For Life."

It was obvious to Florentino the man was very drunk. "I think you underestimate the Canadian people, but that is your problem... of interest to me is what can you do for us?"

"I still need Rico's help and your money to continue to undermine the R.C.M.P. There are many stubborn officers imbued with a sense of honor and pride in the Force and will not accept bribes. I am gradually weeding them out but that takes time. We must not arouse suspicion. We are making good progress with Customs. Most of them look the other way when Rico brings a drug shipment into Canada... Star Corporation is gaining control over more T.V. stations and we now own close to seventy percent of the newspapers in the country... I could even make drugs legal in Canada."

"You do that and we'll kill you! That would drive the price down."

"Just joking."

"Well don't!"

"Rico and I are working on some ideas for changing some of the drug laws as part of my Emergency Laws."

"Bueno." Florentino turned to Enrique, "Rico, go and bring him in."

Rico left the room. Richard emptied his glass and sloshed in the remaining ice cubes. He added a large slug of whiskey. Florentino noted the bottle was less than quarter full.

Enrique entered the room followed by a young man in his late teens. The youth was dressed in black from head to foot; a wide brimmed hat held in place by a black cord under his chin; tight fitting jacket and pants and high heeled boots. Only the blouse was white. The pale face was striking; thin black eyebrows; high cheek bones and a thin sharp nose. The lips however were thick, sensuous.

"Ricardo. I have a present for you. I want you to meet Miguel. He's a Flamenco dancer from Andalusia... a 'Gitano'... a gypsy... and by reputation has much to offer. I'm sure you will enjoy him."

Richard was suspicious, but... the young man was attractive. His movements graceful... those flashing black eyes... Richard felt a stirring in his groin... but Florentino never gave gifts for nothing. "Tino, what do you want from me?"

"Nothing." Florentino opened his hands motioning towards the young man. "It is a gift for old times sake. We have a room arranged for you. You will stay the night. Rico will show you to the room."

Richard stared at the boy for a full minute, eyes roving from head to toe. He took another drink, emptying the glass. Slamming it down on the table he stood up, steadying himself on the back of the chair. He followed Rico and the dancer out the door.

Florentino slammed a fist into the other palm. "Caramba! We've finally got him! Now at last he will have to do what we tell him. I hope it's all on the tape."

A few minutes later Rico came back in. Gently he closed and locked the door behind him. He was grinning. "I thought for a minute he wasn't going to take the gypsy but I guess he was drunk enough. He takes too many risks when he is drunk. In Canada I make sure the boys are taken care of as soon as he's finished with them." Waving a black cassette in his left hand, "I've got the tape. Now we have him. "

"Bueno. Did you turn on the tape in the bedroom?"

"Si."

"Bring the tape into the studio and we'll check it out."

It was all there, in color, from the moment of Richard's arrival to his exit with the Flamenco dancer... and the sound was good too.

"Rico, I want you to go back to Canada. You have much to do. Make a copy of this tape and take it with you. Show it to Ricardo whenever he refuses to do what we want. I'll keep the original here."

"What are you going to do with Craig?"

"First I'm going to cut off his cock for raping Teresa, then I'm going to throw him over the Tequendama Falls like I did with that girl that started the whole problem with him."

"When?"

"Tomorrow night, after you and I have some answers from him."

Rico deliberately shrugged for his uncle's benefit. "I'm going back to the city. I have to meet somebody. Eduardo will drive me to the hotel. I'll be back in the morning."

Florentino ignored him. He was busy dialing a long distance number.

* * *

The problem was the two guards. How to get them away from the door. Teresa and Eduardo could open the locks and bolts easily and let Craig and his son escape from that room and into the garage in seconds, with the door re-bolted before anybody noticed... but how were they going to get the guards to move? Their plan was for Eduardo to hide Craig and Donald in the trunk of the limousine then wait until Mr. Bannerman was ready to go back to his hotel. Eduardo would release them after dropping Mr. Bannerman. The trunk lid was unlocked with the lid down, ready for a quick entry.

Teresa was becoming agitated. Time was slipping by and they had been unable to figure out how to get the guards away from the locked door. She pulled Eduardo further back into the dark garage, away from the light streaming out of the open hall door to whisper in his ear,

"Eduardo, what are we going to do?"

Eduardo put his hands on her shoulder to calm her, "Sssh, they will hear us... I have to think... there's a gun in the glove compartment. Maybe you can ask them to come out here and I will put the gun on them... but there's two of them. No! That won't work... I don't know."

They both looked back at the two men at the far end of the hall, quietly sitting on chairs on each side of the door reading comic books. Precious time was slipping away. Bannerman might leave at any moment and they could only stare helplessly at the two guards.

Suddenly Rico appeared in the hall at the foot of the stairs.

"Eduardo!"

Hurriedly Eduardo pushed Teresa to one side and walked forward into the light from the door. "Si, Patron?"

"Señor Bannerman will not be returning to his hotel tonight..." In the dark, Teresa threw her arms up in despair... "But I will be leaving in thirty minutes." Teresa clasped her hands together in prayer.

"Si Patron, I am ready."

Rico walked towards the garage. Quickly Eduardo moved forward through the hall door. Rico was holding a cassette in his right hand. He gave it to Eduardo.

"Take this to the file room and make me a copy."

"Si, Patron." Eduardo held the cassette up to the light. "It will take me more than thirty minutes to copy this."

"Bueno. One hour no more. The copy is for me. The original is for Florentino. Give it to him when you have made a copy."

"Si, Patron."

Teresa moved further back in the garage but positioned herself where she could look down the corridor. Rico walked back down the hall to speak to the guards. She overheard him ordering them to the kitchen for a quick meal while he spoke to the prisoners. One of the guards handed him a pistol before following the other guard up the stairs. Rico entered closing the door behind him.

A movement to his right alerted him. Rico leapt forward and sideways to his left at the same time swinging the gun to the right. Donald crashed into the door behind him.

"Christ!" Craig bounded out of his chair. He had been reading a magazine. "Jesus! Donald! Rico don't shoot... please."

Rico moved backwards warily, the gun aimed at the figure picking itself off the floor. "You tell your son to sit in that chair over there or I will kill him."

"Donald, you heard him. Do it, please."

Massaging his bruised shoulder Donald glared at the gun, scowled at Rico, and sat down in a chair across the room.

"Mr. Fox. I want you to know, and this is hard for me to say, I respect you. You are a brave and honorable man."

Donald spoke up sarcastically, "I do hope you don't start crying crocodile tears."

Rico ignored him and stretched out his hand to Craig. "I've come to say goodbye and am sorry it has to end this way. There is nothing I can do. Knowing my uncle I am sure you understand."

For a brief second, Craig considered grabbing the hand and wrestling the gun from Rico but it was cocked firmly in Rico's left hand and aimed at Craig's chest. Rico's finger tightened on the trigger. He had read Craig's thoughts, and surprised at himself, hoped Craig would attack him. He could kill Craig and save him from his uncle's torture. He could explain that it was in self defense that he had to kill Craig. However the hand that clasped his own was firm but relaxed. The moment had passed.

"Enrique, I am sorry I didn't know I had a son... things would have been different had I known."

Rico shrugged. He shook Craig's hand, turned and walked out the door giving Donald a scowl before he closed the door behind him. Rico locked the door, closing the bolts. The guards had not returned. Rico looked at his watch then along the hall. He walked to the foot of the stairs to look up. No sign of the guards. Muttering angrily to himself Rico bounded up the stairs and disappeared.

Teresa was in a panic. Here was the opportunity she had been praying for but Eduardo was in the file room at the other end of the house.

"Oh Dios Mio! What shall I do? What can I do?"

Gingerly she stepped into the hall, hands trembling, and so nervous she was afraid her legs would give way under her. Her heart was thumping so loud she put her hands over her chest hoping to muffle the sound. Teresa paused at the foot of the stairs. The stairway was empty. Gathering courage she raced down the hall, eased back the bolts, unlocked the door, opened it a crack and whispered,

"Craig! It is me, Teresa, come quickly!"

There was rapid movement inside and the door was flung open. It was Craig standing at the door. Teresa grabbed his hand and pulled him out.

"Quickly, Caro, Rico will be back any minute. Run-run-run and get in the trunk of the limousine."

Craig and Donald ran down the hall glancing up the stairs as they went by. Teresa followed, but realizing the door was wide open she ran back, closed and locked it, sliding the bolts back gently. She raced into the garage. Donald was already in the trunk legs tucked against his chest and head scrunched against his chin. Craig was standing by the taillight one hand on the trunk lid waiting for her.

"Teresa, I don't know how to thank you." He opened his arms and folded them around her. She started to cry. At last she was in his arms again. "Teresa. Please don't... Teresa, why didn't you tell me you were going to have our son? I would have married you."

"Florentino wouldn't let me. Said he was going to kill you... anyway your father would not have allowed you to marry so young."

"I could have helped to give him a better life."

"Rico is very happy doing what he is doing. Florentino has totally corrupted him. Don't feel sorry for him. Quickly, Craig, get in. Rico and the guards must be coming back by now."

Teresa squeezed him one last time then pushed Craig towards the trunk. He stepped in folding himself next to Donald. She closed the lid slowly until it clicked. Hearing a noise in the hall she moved back behind the limousine away from the light. Peering over the top of the car she saw the guards return to take up their previous positions in front of the locked door. Feeling weak and realizing she might collapse she searched around for a chair. Teresa sat in the dark on a stool to wait for Eduardo.

* * *

Either Allan Sharp was a consummate liar or he really did not know much about the drug cartel. A day of intensive probing at the safe house by Commissioner Boulanger was unable to coerce Allan into admitting any connection with them. By the end of the day Allan was so frustrated with the persistent questioning that he sat back in his chair and refused to answer any more questions. Neither threats of imprisonment nor offers of immunity made any difference. He ignored the Commissioner and concentrated on manicuring his finger nails.

Finally, Allan had had enough. "Jesus fucking Christ! Commissioner, can't you get it through your fucking head I have never! - I repeat, never! - had any dealings with the cartel. You're talking to the wrong person."

"Mr. Sharp, perhaps you can tell me who I should be talking to?"

A night of sifting through the files of Star Corporation had produced no evidence that the cartel controlled the Company. What was very evident was that Richard Bannerman owned the company and the money invested in the company came through him or his family trust. Boulanger had established that the Bannerman family was very wealthy, but not even they had the kind of money that had been poured into the Corporation over the years. If the money had come from legitimate sources there should be records of their investment. There were none, therefore the money must have come from an illegal source. But there was no documentation to prove it. If Allan Sharp had had no dealings with the cartel and the money was funneled into the Company through Richard Bannerman, then it had to be Bannerman that was laundering drug money, but Allan Sharp must have been aware drug money was coming into the Company through Bannerman.

"Mr. Sharp, I think you and I can agree that Richard Bannerman is a very wealthy man but even he does not have the financial resources to fund the huge acquisitions that your Company has made."

Allan nodded without looking up. He continued cleaning his finger nails.

"Mr. Sharp, I think you and I can agree, that if the money came from legitimate investors you would have the names of these individuals and a record of the amounts of money invested."

Allan nodded again.

"Mr. Sharp, then the money must have come from illegal sources and only the drug cartel has that kind of money... is Richard Bannerman laundering their money?"

Allan's eyes flicked up briefly. He stopped fiddling with the nail file, staring at the floor for almost a minute before taking a deep breath. Allan sat up.

"Commissioner, you are finally asking the right questions. For many years I have suspected Richard was laundering drug money."

"Why didn't you do something about it?"

"Commissioner, you, yourself, have gone through the company files. Did you find anything in them to indicate that the money is from the cartel?"

"No, but Richard must have said something over the years. He must have shown you papers, documents... something."

"Nothing. When I asked him where the money was coming from he said it was none of my business. My job was to run the company."

"Why didn't you go to the R.C.M.P. with your suspicions?"

Allan snorted, "Because Richard has many admirers in the R.C.M.P."

"Yes, I know. I used to be one of them until I met Craig Fox."

"I call them 'admirers', but they are more than that, they follow his orders... and if I went to them, Richard would be told and within hours I would be dead. You may not know this, Commissioner, but Richard is a killer. Ask your friend Craig Fox. Richard has been trying to kill him for years."

"Yes, I know. Craig gave me all the details."

"Where is Craig?"

"In Calgary looking after his son... Mr. Sharp, I need your help. Very soon Richard Bannerman will become Prime Minister of Canada. If he is appointed, and there is nothing to stop him becoming Prime Minister, he will in effect be turning the country over to the drug cartel. Somehow I must find evidence to connect him to the cartel. If you can help me I will make sure that you are protected from Richard and are not prosecuted."

"Commissioner, I will help you but I don't think you can protect me from Richard. He will kill me eventually."

"Not if I can break him. The moment he loses power, the cartel will dump him. Maybe even kill him to protect their business."

"You are an optimist. You have nothing on him. He has been too careful."

"Is there nothing you can give me that will help me build a case against him?"

Allan made one final inspection of his nails, and almost in slow motion, took out a leather case from his breast pocket and inserted the nail file in its proper slot, before putting the case back in his pocket. He looked up at Commissioner Boulanger who was standing in front of him with one hand in his trouser pocket the other on the mantel of the fireplace.

"Commissioner, In my safe in the office there are four black notebooks. They are my diaries. In them I have recorded everything I know about Richard Bannerman. They go back many years. I think I started them soon after he joined my Squadron."

"Why did you?"

"Originally I thought he might end up being court-martialed for the things he was doing and I wanted to make sure I had an accurate record. I realized he was utterly ruthless. Later when Richard became famous I continued with the diaries for my own protection. He strafed enemy pilots in their parachutes. This was reported to me by the army but I ignored it as he was my best pilot and at the time we were being decimated by the Germans. He shot down one of our own pilots just because the young man was getting too much publicity. He corrupted some of the young airmen, one committed suicide. He made several attempts to get Craig Fox killed by leading him into a gaggle of Jerry fighters and then leaving him to battle them on his own. I'm sure Craig has told you all about that."

"No, not that one."

"Incidentally, Craig didn't tell me that. I heard it from one of the pilots in Richard's flight. And then Richard came back one day without Craig. He said Craig was hit by flak and killed when his plane crashed and blew up, yet a few weeks later Craig turns up unhurt. He said nothing at the time but after the war Craig claimed Richard attacked him after he crash landed behind enemy lines."

"Yes, I have read the transcript of the trial... did you know that there were two witnesses to the attack?"

Allan looked up surprised. "I didn't know that, Craig never mentioned them. Why weren't they at the trial?"

"Richard found out about them and had one of them killed. The other one... Well, he was killed by an irate husband."

"So Craig was telling the truth."

"Yes, He was. I checked with the Italian Police. They corroborated the murder of the witness and convinced me Craig's accusations against Bannerman were true."

"When Pilot Officer Fox arrived on the Squadron he didn't want to be in Richard's Flight, but I put it down to some school boy fight and ignored his request. When Richard came back from his patrol without Craig I suspected Richard might have been up to his tricks again, but Craig said nothing when he came back."

"What else is in those diaries?"

"Richard insisted it was none of my business who was investing in the Company. I became suspicious when I found out he was receiving phone calls from Colombia. That's when I started keeping track of the date and amount invested in the Company."

"Excellent! May I have those diaries?"

"Off course." Allan allowed a small grin to spread across his face, "Provided some of the personal stuff in them remains confidential."

"I can guarantee that, Mr. Sharp. We'll pick them up tonight."

"Commissioner, while we've been talking I've been toying with an idea that might help you beat Richard."

"I'm listening."

"Don't Members of Parliament, particularly Cabinet Ministers, have to document all their assets and put them in trust?"

"Absolutely!"

"I will lay a bet with you that Star Corporation is not mentioned in Richard Bannerman's list of assets."

"Mon Dieu!" The Commissioner's fist slammed into the mantel. "If you're right, and I think you are, we have got him. Thank you, Mr. Sharp, I will check into that. Tonight we'll retrieve your diaries from your safe."

But when they opened the safe, the diaries were gone. The safe was empty.

* * *

Robert dialed the number and hung up on the fifth ring. Eyes glued to his watch he waited while the minutes ticked by. Audrey watched the performance. Robert lifted his eyes for a second, seeing his mother's amused expression he gave her a sheepish smile and went back to checking the time.

Audrey couldn't resist, "Double-O-Seven Code?" She was immediately sorry she had said that.

The quip annoyed him but he didn't lift his eyes from his watch. At the end of the fifth minute he dialed again. Immediately the receiver at the other end was picked up but nobody spoke. Robert counted to five before speaking.

"This is Robert."

A familiar voice answered, "Robert! So you got my message. I have been hoping to hear from you. Where are you?"

"Commissioner, you've no idea how wonderful it is to hear your voice. When I heard you had been killed I was..."

"Yes, I know, but it was necessary for me to disappear. Where are you?"

"Here in Toronto at the airport."

"Are you alone?"

"No. My Mother and I had to flee Calgary. Our hideout was discovered."

"How did Rico find you?"

"It wasn't him, it was Johnson from our detachment... you remember him?... Constable Eric Johnson. He joined us about a month before I was attacked."

"Johnson... Johnson... ah yes, I remember. A bright young man. A little cocky, but I liked him. I wonder why he... never mind, we'll go into that some other time. Robert, I need your help. We haven't much time. I'll pick you up in one hour. Please give my fondest regards to your mother. She is a wonderful lady."

"Yes! She is... Commissioner, my father has disappeared."

"Isn't he in Calgary?"

"No. He went to Bogota to try to find my brother, Donald, who has been abducted, we think, by the cartel... Commissioner, I have to go down there to find them."

"That is bad news. We need him. Robert, I'll pick you up in an hour and we'll talk about it. Be at the main entrance and I'll honk twice."

"Yes sir, but I have to do something."

"I understand. Don't come out until I'm there."

"Yes sir."

Robert replaced the receiver. He gave his mother a hug. "It's him. He's alive and well. Sends you his fondest regards. Sounds like you've made another conquest."

"He is a very attractive man, but what did he say about your father?"

"He was disturbed to hear Dad has disappeared. He was hoping Dad could help. The Commissioner is picking me up in an hour. Where's Aunt Valerie?"

"She's waiting for us in the coffee shop."

Ever vigilant, Robert checked up and down the hall. Satisfied he placed a hand on his mother's elbow and nudged her forward towards the coffee shop at the far end of the hall. A hand beckoning at the end booth signaled Valerie's location. Valerie was smoking her second cigarette of the day, inhaling the smoke slowly, holding it in her lungs for a few moments with her eyes closed before exhaling the smoke through her pursed lips. Her back was straight, pressed firmly against the padded back. She was wearing a navy blue jacket, that together with the long straight nose and prominent chin, gave her an imposing almost masculine air. Her hair was white and elegantly styled. A solitary pearl decorated each ear and a simple string of pearls nestling over a pale blue blouse was her only acknowledgment of her femininity. 'A handsome take charge lady' was Robert's appraisal when he approached the booth. Audrey sat next to Valerie. Robert eased himself into the opposite bench. Audrey noticed he was favoring his back again.

"Is it bleeding again?"

"No, I don't think so. It's itchy that's all." Robert changed the subject before his mother could start mothering him again, "Aunt Valerie, I'm so sorry we've dragged you and Brian into this but there was nowhere else we could go."

Valerie put her cigarette down on the ashtray, reaching over she folded her hands around his right hand, "Robert, please. I'm so pleased that you did. Ever since you told us Donald and your father have disappeared we have been determined to help, even though we know how ruthless those people can be."

"If they find out you are sheltering us they may..."

"I know. They may kill us."

"Hopefully It will take them a few hours to track us to Toronto so I'm going to leave you now. You should leave for Honey Harbour as soon as possible. I haven't been to your cottage for some time. If I remember correctly it's on Home Island in Monument Channel."

"Yes, it's easy to find."

"I'll come out as soon as I can. I'll find it."

Robert put his hands on the table and stood up slowly. He leaned over to kiss Valerie on her forehead. "Thank you."

Audrey got up and pulled her son down towards her, "Robert dear,take care and don't worry about me. Valerie convinced me I should stay at the cottage so as not to create problems for you. I'll get some paints and wait to hear from you. Please keep in touch."

"I will, Mother. Bye."

Audrey didn't reply. She sat down abruptly turning her face toward Valerie to hide the tears bubbling up. Valerie reached for her hand. When Audrey looked up again Robert was half way down the aisle. She watched until he disappeared down the hall. Valerie's hand was fidgeting anxious to get back to the cigarette. Audrey released it and made an effort to be social.

"Now that he's gone, let's talk about you, Valerie... what is Dick doing? The last we heard about him he was with a company that provided the electronics and lighting for rock concerts and conventions?"

Valerie loved to talk about her son. She took another small puff and put her cigarette back on the ashtray. She only allowed herself two cigarettes a day and she was already half way through the second one. She eyed it regretfully before taking a sip of coffee. Valerie allowed her thoughts to drift back in time.

"Ever since he was a little boy Dick has been fascinated with stage settings... you may remember our garage. He built a small stage in there with lights and curtains. He used to borrow Brian's movie camera and make movies with puppets... well, he's still at it and just loves all the arranging... he's become well known and in great demand." Valerie leaned forward confidentially, "I'm not supposed to tell anybody but Dick got the contract to organize all the lights and sound for the big Convention. You know, the one that will crown Bannerman. He said he'll be using some new gimmicks. Things have I have never heard of."

"I remember the stage settings he made. A real talent."

"They're going to show a movie of Bannerman. War hero, and all the things he has accomplished. It should be sickening. Brian is going but I refuse to go. Such a hateful man... and the things he has done to Craig."

"How is Brian? Is he fully recovered from his heart attack?"

"Yes, he's fine but has to watch his diet and no more golf. He loves being out at the cottage with all his books. His room is so chaotic but I've decided not to fuss over it. I just shut his door and try not to think about the mess in there."

Valerie drained her cup, examined the cigarette butt and took a quick puff before crushing it in the ashtray. "Come along Audrey, we have to be on our way to Honey Harbour. I have to be back by six... did I tell you I've had another story published in The New Yorker?"

"No. I didn't know."

"It came out in the August issue. There's a copy at the cottage. Be sure to read it... I have to read extracts from it tonight at our Writer's Club."

"I'll be sure to read it... Valerie, please, can we hurry?"

"Yes! Yes! I'll follow you out."

- 13 -

The wait was becoming unbearable, not only for Teresa but for Craig as well. Teresa paced back and forth between the trunk of the limousine, which held her beloved Craig as well as his son Donald, and the front of the limousine, where she had a clear view of the hall and the two guards sitting at the far end guarding the now empty room.

'Dios Mio. What if the guards decide to unlock the door to check inside? What if Rico comes back and decides to put something in the trunk? Where is Eduardo? What's taking him so long?'

Craig was having similar worries on top of his concern that he was getting a cramp. He and Donald would have to move. A whisper; a nod; and both changed positions.

The limousine rocked up and down. Frantically Teresa rapped on the trunk lid.

"Craig! Don't move! Somebody is coming."

It was Eduardo. Glancing back along the corridor towards the guards he entered the garage looking around for Teresa.

"Eduardo, over here."

Eduardo joined her behind the limousine. Nodding towards the guards he whispered, "They're still there. I don't know what we can do to get them away from the door."

Barely able to contain herself, Teresa pulled his head down to hiss in his ear, "They're in the trunk!"

A quick glance confirmed the trunk lid was closed. Eduardo clapped his hands together before wrapping them around Teresa in a crushing hug. Teresa sprang back gasping, both shocked and surprised. Eduardo shrugged sheepishly. Teresa smiled to reassure him then gave him a gentle pat on the cheek.

Rico appeared in the corridor at the bottom of the stairs. Eduardo pointed Teresa towards the storeroom at the back of the garage before hurrying into the corridor to meet Rico.

"Where are the tapes?"

Eduardo handed Rico an envelope. "Aqui Patron."

Rico was about to open it, but seeing it was sealed he shook it instead. The cassette rattled inside the case. Satisfied Rico put the envelope in his breast pocket.

"Where is the other one?"

"I gave it to your uncle."

Rico headed for the limousine. Eduardo pulled out his handkerchief with trembling hands to wipe his cold sweaty brow. It had been close. He didn't know what he would have done if Rico had ripped open the envelope and opened the cassette case. Eduardo hurried to catch up with Rico but Rico was already opening the rear door.

Anxious to warn Craig, Eduardo spoke in a loud voice, "Patron, where would you like to go?"

"I can hear. You don't have to shout. Take me to the Hotel Bogota... and hurry. I'm late."

"Si, Patron."

Eduardo slid into the driver's seat but had trouble getting the ignition key into the lock. He used his left hand to steady the other one. Waiting for the garage doors to open, Eduardo watched Rico in the rear view mirror, fearful he might open the envelope, but Rico was staring at nothing out the side window. Driving out of the garage Eduardo caught a glimpse of Teresa in his side mirror. She was leaning out of the storeroom door with a clenched fist thrust above her head in triumph.

Nervously Eduardo approached the front gate. If the alarm had been raised this is where he would be stopped. He picked up the microphone from the dashboard and in a hoarse voice informed the gate keeper he was taking Rico to the city. When the gate closed behind him Eduardo pressed his foot down on the accelerator, but eased off when he realized he was going to fast.

"I said hurry. I'm going to be late."

"Si Patron."

He increased speed, gaining confidence with each spin of the car wheels. Their daring gamble might yet succeed and his friend, Craig, freed... as long as Rico did not open the cassette case.

The increased motion and the ping of gravel against the bottom of the car could only mean they were outside the compound. The road and gravel noise muffled the voices from the passenger compartment preventing Craig from hearing Rico's instructions for more speed. Craig became increasingly concerned Eduardo was driving too fast but there was nothing he could do about it. He put his hand under his head to soften the impact of the metal bouncing against his head. Donald did the same.

The car slowed, turned, and accelerated again. The gravel noise stopped. The ride was smoother. They were approaching the city. Ten minutes later Craig was surprised by a loud snort from Donald. Quickly he covered Donald's mouth while shaking him. A muffled sound escaped through his fingers before Donald awoke. The effects of all the alcohol Donald had consumed was wearing off plus the combination of exhaust and gas fumes had given him a throbbing headache. Craig heard a muttered "Shit!"

A sudden thought alarmed Craig. Was there a suitcase, briefcase, or other bags in the trunk that Rico would need and open the trunk to retrieve? Carefully he felt around with his hands and with his feet in the far corners. There was nothing. Relieved he turned his thoughts to what they would do once they were out of the trunk.

Going back to the hotel was out. Rico had boasted that most of the staff were on their payroll. In any case there was no need to go there. The money belt wrapped around his waist held their passports, American Travelers cheques, and a bundle of Colombian currency... how much? Craig wasn't certain but it should be enough to get them out of the country. The clothes and other personal effects in their room were not essential. They could be replaced.

The airport was also out. At this late hour there would not be flights out of the country. They would have to hang around the airport lobby until morning and it would be the first place searched the moment their escape was discovered.

If they could get to another large city they might be able to catch an overseas flight in the morning. The closest large city was Girardot on the Magdalena River. Trying to remember his schoolboy geography, Craig estimated Girardot was about two hundred kilometers by road... a four or five hour drive depending on the condition of the road. Eduardo could take them there in the limousine... very quickly Craig realized that was not going to work either. The limousine was too conspicuous. The police would be alerted and they would be intercepted before they reached Girardot... a rental car?... No. They would have to provide passport identification... what about a bus?... No. Buses carried Indians and peasants not "Gringos". His options were being eliminated one by one... the only option that was reasonably safe was an overnight train. They could seclude themselves in a private compartment and Craig was fairly sure the ticket agent didn't require identification. Eduardo could purchase the tickets and give a false name if the agent asked for one.

At that moment a sudden screech of the rear tires flung Craig and Donald against the forward wall of the trunk compartment. Off to the right more squealing and a crash, followed by a stream of curses from Rico. Craig's impact was cushioned by Donald whose head hit the front wall first. It didn't improve Donald's headache. They didn't dare move while the car was stationary. The moment the car began moving again they worked themselves back from the wall praying that Eduardo would control his speed. To have the whole gamble fail because of a car accident was more than Craig could bear to think about.

The limousine slowed to a stop. The rear door opened. Craig heard Rico get out and slam the door. Craig tensed ready to leap out and attack Rico if Rico unlatched the trunk lid.

"I don't need you tonight, Eduardo, you can go home to your family. Pick me up at eight tomorrow morning... at eight, no later."

"Si Patron. Muchas gracias."

With muscles coiled Craig waited. He felt Donald's buttocks tighten against his lap. Donald, too, was ready to spring. The sound of footsteps came closer, paused, passed the car then faded away.

Eduardo collapsed in the driver's seat, mopping his brow with his wet handkerchief. He didn't dare start the motor for a few minutes. When his hands stopped shaking he turned the ignition key. Slowly he pulled out into the evening traffic taking care to allow the late night revelers in their hotrods plenty of space.

Eduardo followed the traffic for several blocks while trying to decide on a safe place to park. He chose a street in an affluent residential suburb where a limousine would not attract attention. Donald was first out of the trunk, gasping for air. Eduardo reached into the trunk to help Craig climb out.

The two men faced each other; the tall white man and the stocky Indian; one well dressed in now rumpled slacks and shirt; the other in a threadbare gray uniform; one tanned and fit; the other a brown puffy face and expanding middle. They both stepped forward and embraced. Silently they hugged each other: Eduardo with joy and relief at saving his friend; Craig with a heavy mantle of guilt wrapping around him... guilt for abandoning his boyhood friend when he left to go to school in Canada... guilt for not trying to contact Eduardo after Craig's parents were killed... guilt for devoting his life to making money while his friend was forced to work for the cartel in order to survive. Somehow he would try to make amends. Reluctantly Craig released Eduardo.

"Eduardo, my dear dear friend. Once again I owe my life to you."

"No! No! Craig. It was Teresa that saved you. She's the one that worked out the plan. She's the one that got you out of the room. But we must hurry. Please get in the car and I will take you to the hotel." Suddenly Eduardo held up his hands in horror. "No! No! You must not go there. It is full of spies... Craig, do you have any money?"

"Yes, I have money and passports... Eduardo, could you please take us to the train station... That is our only chance of getting away. The airport here will be watched but if we can get to Girardot maybe we can catch a plane before they alert the police to look for us."

Eduardo opened the front passenger door motioning Craig to sit. Donald sat on the jump seat behind his father. He was anxious to apologize for his drunken behavior, but his father's attention was on his friend. He would have to wait for a more suitable occasion.

Once again Eduardo turned the ignition key. Slowly he pulled away from the kerb but this time there was nobody in the trunk and his hands were not shaking.

In the little time available to him before they parted once again, Craig hoped he could fill the huge gap between the boy he had known and the man beside him.

"Eduardo, I overheard Rico say you could go home to your family tonight. Do have any children?"

"Si. I have two daughters... sixteen and eighteen... they are good girls. They look after my wife. She is not well and I am allowed so little time to visit them."

"How long have you worked for... for them... for the cartel?"

Eduardo spoke up in a louder voice, "I don't work for them. I work for Teresa. She pays me... not them!"

"But...?"

"Yes, I drive them around in this or other cars but they know I only do what Teresa wants me to do."

"When did you start working for her?"

"Teresa knew your parents were paying for my school and board in Gachala... she was broken hearted when you left to go to Canada, and knowing you and I were good friends she kept in touch with me... after your parents were killed in the accident she came to Gachala and took me to Bogota. She supported me until I finished school... she didn't want me to work for them but I insisted. I had to look after her. She had nobody else except her brother and he ignores her. I have been there ever since."

"Eduardo, you cannot go back. They will kill you!"

"I know, but not because you escaped... I don't think they could suspect me for that because Rico would have to confirm that he was the only one in the limousine when I brought him into the city... they will kill me after Rico discovers I switched tapes and gave him a broken cassette instead of this one." Eduardo lifted a black box out of his breast pocket and held it in front of Craig.

Craig plucked the black box from Eduardo's hand. Switching on the overhead light he examined the box. Turning to Donald, "Is this what I think it is?"

Donald reached over his father's shoulder to explain, "Yep, this a Beta Max cassette."

"Eduardo, why would they kill you for this cassette?"

"Because on this tape they have recorded your visit upstairs including what Mr. Bannerman said about you, and everything that went on after you were taken back to your room... on the tape Mr. Bannerman said what he was going to do when he becomes Presidente of Canada. How he is going to change the laws and destroy your government... Rico asked me to make a copy. I was to give the original to his uncle and the copy to him. I saw everything on the tape while I was making the copy but I didn't have time to make a copy for you. I decided you should have the tape I was supposed to give Rico... Craig, I'm giving the tape to you. Maybe it will help you destroy these evil people."

"What did you give Rico?"

"I couldn't find another blank tape so I had to put some broken pieces in another cassette case and put it in a sealed envelope, hoping he wouldn't open the envelope."

"But if you give the tape to me it is your death sentence."

"Si. It is."

"You must not go back. Do they know you have a family?"

"Si, they know, and that is the first place they will look for me. After I take you to the station I must go home and take them away."

"Where will you go?"

"My wife is from Gachala. That's where I met her when I was going to school. Juanita has many relatives there. They will hide us for awhile." Eduardo glanced at the clock in the dashboard. "A bus leaves every morning at six for Gachala. We will be halfway to Gachala before I am supposed to pick up Rico at eight."

Craig unbuttoned his shirt, zipped open a pouch on his money belt and extracted a bundle of Colombian pesos. "Let me give you some money."

"No! No! I have enough money for the bus."

Craig separated the money into two halves. He put one half on the seat between them. "Eduardo, please take it for the sake of your family please take it."

Eduardo shook his head, but realizing how little money he had in his pocket and no means of getting more, he relented. "For the sake of my wife and daughters, I accept. Thank you, thank you."

"When all this is over I would like you and your family to come to Canada. I will pay your way up there, find you a good job and pay for your daughters education."

"My dear friend. You are very kind but it is too late for that... Juanita and I would not be happy there. We are too old now. Our life is here. Thank you... did you know your parents wanted to adopt me?"

"Yes, I did, and I was very happy when they asked me to approve."

"They were on their way back to Gachala from Bogota with the papers when they had the accident."

"It was no accident. Florentino killed them."

"Oh Dios Mio! How?"

"He tampered with the steering mechanism and it broke going around the curves in the mountains."

"How terrible! If I had known he did that I would have killed him... my oldest daughter has your mother's name, Margarita."

"She would have been pleased you did that... Eduardo, if you will not come to Canada would you consider allowing your daughters to come? I will pay their way to Canada and for their education. They can live with us as part of our family... if they wish to return for visits or to live I will pay their fares... Eduardo, you have done so much for me, please allow me to do this for you?"

"Craig, you are too kind." Eduardo turned towards Craig, "I can look after my family." He continued speaking with pride, "I can provide them with food clothes and a place to live but..." Giving a gentle shake of his head, "I cannot give my daughters the education they would like. Margarita wants to be a teacher, Teresa, a nurse... we named her after your Teresa... Craig, I will have to discuss this with Juanita. It will be her decision."

"I understand." Craig looked through the glove compartment until he found a pencil and an old envelope. He wrote his name and address on the back of the envelope. "Eduardo, this is my address. Write to me in two or three months when you think it is safe for you to do that, and I will make arrangements for your daughters to come to Canada... that is if your wife agrees."

"Thank you. You are a good friend. Thank you."

Eduardo drove past the front of the train station and continued around the block. There were no police cars; just two parked taxis and a third unloading passengers at the front entrance. Eduardo passed the front entrance once again then pulled around the corner to a side entrance. Craig handed Eduardo ten large bills explaining what he wanted. They waited with tinted windows rolled up. Eduardo was back in twenty minutes with two train tickets and a handful of loose change.

"Your train to Girardot is on platform one. It leave in twenty five minutes. You're in compartment "C" in carriage fifteen. The agent said it is the third carriage from the front."

"Did you have to give a name?"

"Yes, but he just wanted to put a name on his register. I told him it was for my Patron... I gave him Spanish names."

Craig lowered his window to check along the sidewalk. Other than a few travelers entering the station all was clear. Eduardo opened the front door for Craig. They both embraced once again. This time both their cheeks were wet. When they parted there was nothing more that could be said. Silently Craig turned away, walking briskly towards the station entrance. Donald clasped Eduardo's right hand in his.

"Muchas Gracias, Eduardo. Thank you, thank you."

"Vaya con Dios. Look after your father, he is a fine man."

Donald understood. "Yes, I know."

At the entrance they both turned for one last glimpse of their friend, a solitary Indian in a shabby driver's uniform standing alone under the glow of a dirty yellow light. Craig waved before turning away quickly. He knew his friend had little chance of surviving the wrath of the cartel, but "Come-hell-or- high-water" he was going to make sure the daughters got their education.

* * *

The insistent ring of the telephone woke the girl. Before she could roll over to pick up the phone Rico rushed out of the bathroom.

"Don't pick it up! I'll answer it."

Quickly she reached behind her to put on her glasses, the better to observe his approaching nakedness. She never tired of looking at him as he glided forward on the balls of his feet as if ready to spring, with his penis swinging from side to side with each step. Immediately the old familiar ache flared in her belly. An ache he had so thoroughly healed the night before. She ran her fingers up his inner thigh and was about to lean forward but he had picked up the phone.

"What! They escaped!" Rico pushed her face away. "Tino, of course I didn't let them out! No! I didn't bring them into the city. You can ask Eduardo when we return. He'll tell you I was alone when he brought me here. What do the guards say? You shot them! Didn't they say anything? Yes, I went in there to see if if I could get Craig to tell me what he knew but he wouldn't talk. I locked the door when I left and the guards were back at their post when I got into the limousine. Have you told Bannerman? He's still asleep! Don't wake him until I get there. I can handle him better than you can. Maybe we will have found them by the time he wakes up... have you searched all the compound?" Rico pulled the phone away from his ear when a stream of curses blasted it. "I will get Eduardo to pick me up right away. Did he give you the cassette tape? Yes, I have the other one."

Rico hung up. He dialed Eduardo's number. Waiting for the call to be answered he ran his free hand over and under the girl's breasts. Taking each nipple in turn he rolled them between thumb and index finger gradually increasing the pressure. Moaning softly she leaned forward slipping her hands around him to clutch his buttocks. Nobody answered the phone. Rico glanced at the clock on the dresser. It was seven o'clock. Eduardo must have left home early. Rico had an hour before Eduardo was due to pick him up. He replaced the receiver and leapt over the girl into bed. Quickly she straddled him.

Promptly at eight Rico was at the front entrance of the hotel. By ten minutes after eight he was pacing up and down. At twenty minutes after eight he was back in the lobby renting a car from Avis. He had nearly finished filling out the contract when a disturbing thought occurred to him. Rico dropped the pen and raced back to his room. The girl was asleep on her back, naked, arms akimbo, mouth open, snoring softly. Leering at her, Rico had difficulty remembering where he had put the envelope Eduardo had given him, he'd been in such a hurry to get into bed last night. It was in the breast pocket of his jacket. The jacket was on the floor under the girl's clothes. Rico ripped open the sealed envelope and opened the video cassette case. Two broken pieces of plastic fell on the floor. Rico stared down at the broken pieces, the implication of the missing tape and Eduardo's disappearance sinking in. Reluctantly he dialed his uncle's private number.

"Tino, did you check the tape Eduardo gave you?... Good, because he stole my copy... I know! I know! I should have checked but I was in a hurry... no, he's not here. He was supposed to pick me up at eight but he didn't turn up and he's not at home... Yes, yes, I'm coming right now."

Rico put the phone down. The girl was still asleep. He leaned over her and pinched one of her nipples. She awoke with a yelp.

"Monica, it's after eight thirty. You'll miss your flight."

"Will I see you on the plane?"

"No, I've been delayed. I have some business to attend to."

"Will you call me when you get back to Montreal?"

"Sure, I'll call you next week."

She watched him close the door behind him. She knew he wouldn't call.

* * *

Other than the dubious look the conductor gave them when he saw the Spanish names on their tickets the trip from Bogota was uneventful.

Craig was pleased he was able to have a long and frank conversation with his son. It had been years since they had had the opportunity to talk, what with Donald flitting around the world and himself immersed in the oil business. Donald apologized for his behavior, attributing it to his embarrassment at thinking he could interview the head of the drug cartel, and for being responsible for luring his father into a trap. Sensitive to the feelings of his proud son Craig glossed over the apology quickly moving on to more important subjects, their return to Canada, and what to do with the tape Eduardo had risked his life to give them.

The first priority was to get out of Colombia. It was agreed they would take the first available international flight regardless of its destination. Once out of the country and out of the clutches of the Colombian police they would make their way to Canada.

If what Eduardo said was in the tape turned out to be correct, then what Craig was carrying in his money belt was dynamite. Properly used it would mean that Bannerman's political career was over, and hopefully put him in prison. But they had to move fast. In one week the Convention in Toronto would elect Richard Bannerman Party Leader and Prime Minister of Canada. Once in power Bannerman could smother any scandal, and with his control of the R.C.M.P. suppress any opposition. Donald proposed giving the tape to his employer, The Canadian Broadcasting Corporation, and have them broadcast excerpts on all T.V. stations across Canada. Aware that the head of the C.B.C. was a personal friend and admirer of Bannerman, Craig was certain the tape would not be broadcast and most likely end up in Bannerman's pocket. But Donald did not give up the idea without a struggle. He could see himself before the cameras announcing the "Coup of the Century". Other possibilities were reviewed and discarded. Most of the independent T.V. stations were controlled by Star Corporation, Bannerman's company. The few that were not could not provide coverage across Canada. The national newspapers were wholly or partly owned by Star Corporation. They agreed to think about it, and for now concentrate on getting back to Canada.

Donald was able to get a couple of hours sleep. Craig didn't. Every time he was about to drift off something woke him; the clatter of wheels going over a crossing; the occasional snort from Donald; the creak of the carriage adjusting to a curve; or what he thought was somebody trying the door to their compartment. He was relieved when the train pulled into Girardot station.

Girardot was hot and humid. Even at seven in the morning it was humid. Stepping onto the platform from the air conditioned carriage the moist clammy air enveloped Craig's face like a wet towel. In less than a minute his shirt was soaked.

Donald muttered, "Christ! Its stifling."

Craig put his finger to his lips hoping Donald would quit attracting attention to themselves by speaking English. Craig steered Donald away from the station cafeteria and from a nearby cafe. He chose instead a small cafe on the other side of the park across from the station. The cafe was nearly empty, nevertheless Craig moved to a cubicle at the back. Donald's irritation was beginning to show. He was used to taking charge. He didn't like being led around like a little boy. Craig realized he had better explain before there was a confrontation. Keeping his voice low he tried to justify his actions.

"Donald, I know you think I am paranoid but please understand. I have been fighting Bannerman since I was sixteen years old... I have never burdened you and Robert with all the details... but when I was sixteen Bannerman paid Florentino Chavez five thousand pesos to murder me."

"Whatever for?"

"I overheard Florentino telling Bannerman that he had murdered an Indian girl that was pregnant by Bannerman... that he failed to kill me was due to the courage of my father... Bannerman has been trying to kill me ever since, and all my life I've had to walk with one eye cocked over my shoulder, always apprehensive of what that man might do to my family. I know what he is capable of doing... if our escape has been discovered, and we must assume it has been, then we must make ourselves as inconspicuous as possible. He has the power of the cartel behind him. They cannot afford to let us escape, particularly if they conclude that Eduardo gave us the tape. The whole gang will be looking for us, and I have no doubt, the police have been alerted as well... so please go along with my paranoia... okay?"

"Okay. Its just that I am not used to sneaking around."

"I know, but we have to get used to the idea we are fugitives... not only here, but in Canada too."

Startled Donald lifted his head, "In Canada too?"

"Shush! Not so loud. Yes, in Canada. You can be sure the Canadian Cartel will be alerted... and Bannerman will alert the R.C.M.P. the moment he hears we have escaped. He will have them scouring the country for us."

"On what possible charge?"

"Oh, I'm sure Bannerman will think of something."

"Good Lord, Dad! You do paint a grim picture."

"I just wanted you to fully understand our situation. I just try to keep focused on our immediate problem and move forward one step at a time. Donald, I do believe we can win... as you know I am not a religious person, but I have faith in humanity. I believe most people want to do good things and at some point they will stand up and destroy the evil ones. If we can show them this tape they will turn on Bannerman. Once he is gone we have to find all the tentacles the cartel has stretched across Canada and cut them off."

"What about your... your son?"

"Rico? I don't know. Maybe I can convince him to tell us about the cartel."

"Oh Dad, You don't really believe that... do you?"

"You never know. He seemed to be softening towards me... Donald, I think we had better eat before I go to check on flights out of here." Craig raised his hand signaling to a girl watching them from behind the front counter. "Here comes the girl, let me order for you. My Spanish is better than yours."

Craig was hungry. He hadn't eaten in twenty four hours. He ordered a Spanish omelette, corn bread, papaya, and coffee for two. The girl delivered the omelettes with a big smile for Donald.

"El guapo tiene mucha hambre."

Donald turned towards his father, "What did she say?"

"She said, the ugly one is very hungry."

"I thought 'guapo' meant handsome?"

Craig chuckled, "So you do know some Spanish."

"Mostly swear words I picked up from the Cubans."

Donald finished his omelette before Craig was half way through his, and from his glances, had designs on Craig's.

"Donald, I will order you another omelette and leave you to practice your Spanish on the young girl. I'll ask her to direct me to the Avianca Agency and I'll come back for you."

Twenty minutes later Craig was back, looking grim. "Donald, finish your coffee and let's get out of here."

Donald paid the bill and left a large tip and a smile for the girl. Eyes glowing she watched them enter the park. With a gentle sigh she picked up the dishes and carried them into the kitchen.

Craig led the way to the center of the park. He picked a bench close to a fountain, hoping the splashing water would muffle their voices enough to garble their English.

"There are no direct International flights out of Girardot. The agent said she could book us through Bogota where we could pick up an overseas flight to Miami or New York. We would have to go through customs and passport control in Bogota... you can imagine the reception we would get if we tried that... the alternative is a flight to Barranquilla that leaves at three this afternoon and connects with a flight to Panama this evening. I made reservations on both those flights. Donald, I don't like sitting around until three... the longer we delay getting out of the country the more likely we will be detected, but I don't see any alternative... any suggestions?"

"I know a girl that lives here. Maybe she has returned from Bogota and can help us."

"Is she the one that set you up?"

Donald nodded. "Yes, that's her, but she did it because she had to."

"And she will probably be forced to do the same again. Sorry, Donald. We can't take that risk."

"You're right. Just a thought... Dad! How much money do you have?"

"Together with your traveler's cheques we have over ten thousand dollars, and a wad of Colombian pesos. Why do you ask?"

"See that plane over there," Donald pointed up at a float plane in the distance. It was descending, flaps extended. It disappeared behind a building.

"Dad, why don't you charter a plane to take us to Panama?"

Craig smacked his son's knee. "Perfect! We could be airborne and gone within the hour. Donald, you are brilliant. Let's go and get us a plane. The Magdalena River must be that way." Pointing in the direction the plane had disappeared. "Come let's go!"

* * *

Florentino Chavez was glowering. "Rico, I am sure Teresa had something to do with their escape."

"My mother is much too timid to have organized something like that. You've bullied her so much she wouldn't dare cross you."

"She has been avoiding me. Every time she sees me she moves away quickly... Rico, I don't care if she is your mother I am going to get a confession out of her."

Rico did something he had never done before; threaten his uncle. He leapt out of his chair, and with two quick steps grabbed the arms of Florentino's chair. Leaning over he thrust his flushed face inches from Tino's,

"You touch my mother, I'll kill you! There is no way she could have helped them escape. She's just happy her old lover got away. Don't you dare touch her!"

Florentino clamped his hands over Rico's. "Don't you ever threaten me again! If I didn't need you in Canada you'd be dead by now. You get back to Canada but first you help me find Craig... now, get back in your seat... I won't touch your mother, but don't you ever threaten me again."

Rico returned to his seat massaging his bruised hands, not too surprised they were shaking. It had been close. He had seen his uncle in action before, flashing the slim dagger he kept strapped to his leg with deadly effect. Rico waited until tempers cooled before speaking.

"Have you alerted your men to look for Craig?"

"Yes. Also the police. He is not in his hotel and he has not turned up at the airport. In case he shows up at the Canadian Embassy I have some men there. They will shoot him if he tries to get in."

Rico insisted, "Craig and his son were not in the limousine when I went to the hotel. Eduardo must have come back for them."

"No. The guards at the gate said nobody came in or out after you left, and there is no way they can get over the walls even if they were able to avoid the dogs."

The only possibility dawned on them simultaneously.

"Rico, did you open the trunk of the limousine?"

"No, there was no reason for me to open it. I had no baggage with me... Eduardo must have put them in while we were upstairs. He must have bribed the guards. Did they confess before you shot them?"

"No, they said you must have let them out."

"Eduardo must have bribed them with Craig's money... Tino, have you alerted the men to look for Eduardo?"

Florentino shook his head irritably, "Of course! The men found the limousine in a shopping mall. He's taken his family with him and gone into hiding. He's stupid. He won't get very far."

"He can't be stupid if he was able to organize Craig's escape in spite of all our guards dogs and electric fences."

"He won't get far... did you know he and Craig were boyhood friends?"

"What! Why did you hire him if he was Craig's friend?"

Florentino sneered. "Because it gave me pleasure to think that Craig's friend was working for me... Eduardo thought he was working for Teresa, but Teresa doesn't have any money."

"Tino, if Eduardo is Craig's friend I have no doubt Eduardo has given the tape to Craig. If Craig gets to Canada with that tape he will destroy Bannerman and wreck all our plans."

"It's all your fault. You should have made the copy of the tape yourself and not given it to Eduardo. Because he saw everything on it I would have been forced to kill him even if he had not stolen the tape. Make another copy and this time do it yourself. Don't forget to add the tape of Bannerman and the gypsy boy."

"Have you told Bannerman about the tape?"

"Rico don't be stupid! Of course not!. I told him Craig had escaped. He went storming out of here calling us a bunch of idiots for letting him get away."

"Where is the gypsy?"

"I think he is in the kitchen. Teresa was patching him up a little while ago. Richard must have tried some of his rough stuff on the boy."

Rico shook his head, "Bannerman can be pretty mean when he is drunk. Can you get rid of the boy?"

"Yes. He has no relatives here. I will send him back to Spain."

* * *

The river front was a jumble of tin warehouses, old broken paddle steamers, abandoned railway cars on tracks that seemed to go nowhere, and punctured leaky oil drums. Many of the warehouses had huge irregular gaps where rust had eaten through. Rust was everywhere, giving the whole dock area a mottled brown color splattered over remaining patches of gray, green, or on, what at one time may have been, white.

Craig and Donald wandered along the dismal scene looking for any building that might house an airplane office. Unsure whether they should go north or south along the waterfront. They chose to go north. An hour later they realized they should have gone south. They could see ahead for at least a mile along the waterfront and there were no planes out there. Just a paddle steamer taking on bananas to be delivered downstream. For a few minutes they watched a long continuous line of bare chested indians carrying huge bundles of green bananas from a dock to the steamer, sweat glistening in the glaring sunlight, horny brown feet moving confidently along narrow wooden planks. They too, were soaked. Craig was beginning to worry about the money belt. Was it waterproof? In that neighborhood he did not want to check.

By the time they found the airplanes the sun was directly overhead. Both were feeling irritable with the heat, their soaked clothes, and the time they had wasted. They wisely avoided any communication between them that might spark a flash of temper.

There were three float planes in the water. Two were tied to a low wooden raft which was connected to the concrete breakwater by a rusty metal stairway. The third plane was tied with a short chain to a buoy some fifty yards beyond the raft. Eddies in the fast current were making it bob up and down. Craig could feel the heat on his face from the bright sunlight bouncing off the windshield. A little used railway track ran along the breakwater. Behind the tracks a long two story building, with offices on the ground floor and sleeping quarters above, looked like it might be the airplane office although there were no signs outside to indicate what was inside.

Craig chose an office with an open door. Inside a young man was seated at a desk with his back to the entrance. He was listening intently to a news bulletin from a small T.V. sitting on the counter in front of him. Craig moved forward towards the desk but was stopped by a fierce grip on his upper arm. He turned to snap at Donald, instead he followed the direction of Donald's pointing finger to be confronted by a T.V. picture of himself and Donald standing next to Rico. The T.V. was less than twelve inches across but the picture on it was sharp. They were easily recognizable. Only Rico's image had been blurred. The picture faded, replaced by a clip of their train conductor explaining how he had recognized and reported the fugitives. Quietly Craig and Donald walked out the door and ambled along the dockyard in the direction they had come. Cautiously they moved into an abandoned warehouse selecting an office well removed from local traffic. Through a broken window they could see the three float planes less than two hundred yards downstream; so tantalizingly close yet totally out of reach. Although Craig expected their escape would be broadcast on T.V. and newspapers, he had hoped they would be out of the country before that occurred. Now they were trapped.

* * *

Richard Bannerman was not feeling well. Any sudden move escalated the throbbing pain in his head. Flashes of red lightning flicked across his eyes every time he moved his head. He was supposed to chair a meeting at eleven o'clock. Instead he delegated the assignment to his deputy even though the man was unfamiliar with the topic of the meeting he was to chair. Richard retired to his room. But he had to know what progress, if any, those idiots were making in finding Craig. He called Rico, who did not appear to be in a happy mood.

The police had been alerted that the two canadian fugitives were involved with the drug cartel. They had been able to establish that Craig and his son took the overnight train to Girardot. They were definitely identified by the train conductor. Also, Craig had made inquiries with the Avianca agent in Girardot about international flights and made reservations to catch the three o'clock flight to Barranquilla with connections to Panama.

"The police have the airport surrounded and will get them when they show up. So don't worry, Ricardo, my friend. In another four hours they will be dead. The police have been told they are armed and very dangerous. They have instructions to shoot them on sight for resisting arrest. The pictures you took last night have been most helpful."

"I'm looking at their picture on the T.V. right now. Rico, I want the negative of that picture. I'm going to give it to the C.B.C. crew here and have them transmit the picture to Canada. I want the picture of them standing next to the head of the Canadian Cartel shown across Canada."

* * *

It was now late afternoon. A violent thunderstorm had clashed overhead, flushing the dock clean of garbage. The temperature and humidity dropped so much both Craig and Donald began to shiver in their damp clothes. The storm moved east. The humidity and perspiration began to rise again. Donald had found an old sack and was sitting on it, watching his father with increasing puzzlement. Craig was standing at the window staring out at the river. He hadn't moved in close to an hour.

"Dad, what are you looking at?"

"I'm keeping a lookout for any logs that might come floating downstream... logs or other large objects. I've seen a dead cow go by."

"Huh? I hope you don't plan to float six hundred miles down the river to the coast holding onto a log."

Smiling Craig turned around, "Why? Don't you think that's a good idea?"

"Come on. You're cooking up some wild scheme. What is it?"

Craig beckoned, "come over here and I will show you... do you see that plane out there. The one tied to the buoy?"

"Yes?"

"See how fast the current is flowing past the plane."

"So?"

"Well, tonight we are going to steal that plane and fly to Panama."

Donald smacked his first into his father's arm. "Fantastic!"

"Jesus Christ, Donald!" Craig sputtered massaging his sore arm, "You nearly broke my arm!"

"Sorry... Dad, do you think you can fly that thing?"

"I haven't flown since the war but I've been told flying is a skill one doesn't lose. Much like riding a bicycle... I hope they are right."

"But this is a float plane. Your plane had wheels under it."

"I don't think that will be a problem... what is a problem is how are we going to steal it without being discovered."

"Is that why you are watching for logs? To see where the current will take the plane when we untie it from the buoy?"

"Exactly. It has to float clear of any obstructions until we are far enough downstream to start the motor."

"What if the gas tank is empty?"

"That is a chance we will have to take. There is no other way we can get away. Let's hope it has been fully serviced ready to go. Most planes are usually serviced as soon they return from a flight."

"What if we run out of gas before we get to Panama?"

"Donald, for heavens sake! We'll cross that bridge when we come to it. If we come to it. In the meantime take my place and watch for any driftwood passing close to the buoy. I'll sit for awhile. I didn't get much sleep last night."

Half an hour later Donald summoned his father to the window. "See that log? It hit the buoy and spun around end to end, and is now snagged under the floats. Any second it will break loose... look! There it goes."

It was a long log almost totally submerged. For some reason the current was rotating the log. Every few minutes the stump of a branch reared up out of the water then disappeared when the log rolled over. In the fading light the branch was the only guide to the log's progress.

"Donald, can you still see it?"

"Yes, it has passed the dock, and there is nothing more to stop it."

"Good. We'll wait until everybody in that building has gone to sleep before we make a move. Any suggestions as to how we get out to the float plane without being swept downstream in that fast current?"

"If we start swimming from a good distance upstream we should be able to get out far enough by the time the current carries us down to the plane."

"And what if we miss? The current is too strong for us to swim upstream. If we miss, for sure we'll be floating to the coast on a log."

"Are there any piranhas or alligators in the river?"

"I doubt it, but if you feel anything nipping at your heels please let me know before you are dragged under."

Donald chuckled. "Depends where it bites me... we'll have to find a rowboat somewhere. Dad, after it is dark I'll scout along the waterfront while you try to get some rest."

"Good. Any old thing will do as long as it has paddles."

* * *

Rico knew it was Bannerman calling before he answered the phone. He had avoided speaking to Bannerman but his messages, passed on by Teresa, were becoming angrier by the hour. Reluctantly Rico picked up the phone.

"Hello?"

"Rico, it's me. Did you get him?"

"No. He didn't turn up at the airport to catch the three o'clock flight to Barranquilla."

"Christ! You mean your whole organization and your police force can't catch two men that have 'Gringo' written all over them... what about charter flights?"

"They have all been warned he may try to use them to fly out of the country."

"He must have seen his picture on T.V. or in the papers so he knows you're after him. That's why he wasn't at the airport and won't try to hire a plane... he's going to steal one."

"But he doesn't know how to fly."

Richard yelled into the phone, "Bullshit! He knows how to fly. He was on my squadron during the War."

"Shit! I'd better warn the police to guard the planes at the airport."

"Jesus! You fucking idiots! There's one probably missing by now. If not at the airport then a float plane on the Magdalena River. Don't you morons know that Girardot is on the river or do I have to do all your thinking for you?"

"Yes. Caramba! Float planes! They'd better check those too."

"You've got to be pretty stupid to let a guy like Craig Fox outsmart you. He's probably on his way back to Canada."

"Don't worry, Ricardo, we'll get him."

"Just in case I'm heading back to Ottawa tomorrow to prepare a reception committee."

Rico heard several choice curses before Richard hung up.

Rico leaned back in his chair and reached into his shirt pocket for a crumbling packet of cigarettes. He flicked one part way out and wrapped his lips around it. For several minutes he stared out the window. A guard with a dog on a leash was patrolling the perimeter fence. He reached for a lighter on the desk and lit the cigarette while watching the guard. When the man disappeared, Rico shifted his gaze to the phone in front of him. He would have to phone the police and warn them of the latest developments, yet he hesitated. If he did phone, Craig would die. If he didn't phone, Florentino Chavez, would not hesitate to kill his nephew. Rico picked up the phone and dialed.

* * *

Craig was snoring when Donald returned. It was so black in the room Donald couldn't see anything. He followed the snores and knelt beside the dark outline of his father lying on the floor with his head on the sack.

The moment he did so the snoring stopped. Realizing that he had better identify himself before he was assaulted Donald whispered,

"Dad! it's me, Donald."

"Thank goodness! I was just about to grab your throat. It didn't take you long to get back."

"Dad, I've been gone for several hours."

"Oh! What time is it?"

"I don't know. It's too dark to see the time and my watch doesn't have a fluorescent dial."

"Neither does mine."

"It's probably around ten or eleven o'clock."

"Time to go." Craig rose slowly, giving time for his cramped limbs to recover. "Did you find anything?"

"I came across several rowboats but they were too heavy to push into the water. I have a native dugout tied to a dock close by. It's very unstable but it has two good paddles."

"Have the people living above the airplane office gone to bed?"

"Yes, it's all dark over there."

The dugout was very narrow. Twice they nearly flipped over. Craig sat in the back Donald in the front. After the second near mishap, Craig hung onto the dock with his right hand, steadying the dugout until they could organize themselves better. He whispered to Donald,

"You paddle on the left, I'll paddle on the right, and I'll time my strokes with yours."

"Okay. Are you ready?"

Donald held the paddle poised above the water for a few seconds then leaned forward and plunged it into the river. The dugout shot forward. Craig did the same when they cleared the dock. Immediately they felt the tug of the current pulling the bow downstream. Gently Craig adjusted their direction, sending them on a diagonal course across the river. It was a clear night, no clouds, no moon, just a canopy of stars brilliant in the ebony sky above them. The eddies and wavelets in the river sparkled with myriad dots of reflected star light making it easier for Craig to steer in the direction of the float plane. It was clearly visible before them less than half a mile downstream and approaching rapidly.

"Dad! You've gone too far out, we'll miss the plane."

"No, we're okay."

"Back up! Back up! or we'll miss it."

"Oh! Oh! You're right. Paddle backwards as hard as you can... there, that's better... get ready... here it comes!"

The dugout slammed into the buoy with a loud metallic clang, it was loud enough to wake everybody in the neighborhood, or so they thought. Immediately the dugout rolled over and they were thrown into the river. Donald lunged for the cable holding the float plane and managed to grasp it in his right hand, at the same time he reached behind him with his left hand, to grab his father by his shirt as the current swept him by. Desperately he fought to drag Craig close enough to the chain until Craig was able to clutch the heavy chain in both hands.

"Thanks... whew! That was close."

They hung on to the cable fighting the pull of the river threatening to drag them under the floats of the plane. Both were beginning to tire. Donald heaved himself up on one of the floats straddling it. Leaning forward he helped Craig move along the chain, lifting him until he too was able to straddle the float. Grinning in triumph they clasped hands. They were safe, soaked, and shoeless; their shoes sucked off by the current.

Using Donald's shoulder and the wing struts for support Craig pulled himself upright. He reached for the handle of the cockpit door.

"Blast!"

"What's the matter?"

"The door is locked... I hadn't considered that."

"Is that the only way in?"

"There's a passenger door back here, and if that's locked there's another door on the other side."

Taking care not to slip in his wet socks Craig moved back along the float, steadying himself by pressing his hands against the fuselage. He turned the handle on the passenger door. It too was locked but there was enough play in the lock to allow him to wrap his fingers around the edge of the door. He pulled. The door rattled but didn't give.

"Donald, come and give me a hand. I think we can force this door open."

They did. The bolt scrapped across the door frame complaining all the way until it suddenly released almost dumping them back into the river. Craig climbed in and moved forward into the pilot's seat. Donald followed him and sat in the passenger seat opposite Craig. Barely able to see in the dark, and unfamiliar with the layout of the controls, Craig ran his fingers over the throttle and pitch controls and along the instrument panel trying to identify the location and type of instruments. With increasing skepticism, Donald watched his father fumbling around.

"What kind of plane is this?"

"It's a DeHavilland Beaver. They were made in Canada in the fifties. I have flown in them when I was doing geological field work in northern

Alberta, but only as a passenger." Craig couldn't see the dubious look his son was giving him but from the tone of Donald's voice he detected doubts about his father's flying ability. "Before you have a nervous breakdown watching me locate where everything is why don't you take a look at the cable? When I give you the word you can cast off."

The only instruments critical for their flight was the compass, to give them a bearing for Panama, and the altimeter to keep them from plowing into the ground. Having located the two instruments Craig adjusted the controls; the pitch on fine; the throttle one quarter open; the flaps down; and the elevator and rudder trim in the middle. Those were the settings he remembered for the Spitfire and hoped they applied to the Beaver. Remembering that the bush pilots had to prime the motor of the Beaver before they turned on the ignition Craig looked around for the primer. He located it below the instrument panel on the right hand side. He pulled the plunger back ready to squirt gas into the cylinders of the radial engine. Craig tried to recall how the bush pilots started the engine. At the time he was intrigued by how involved the procedure was compared to starting a Spitfire. Master, starter switches, and mags had to be on; blades rotated several times; then several strokes with the primer to shoot gas into the cylinders, before hitting the starter switch... and pray it would start. Craig opened the window beside him and leaned out. Donald was bent over struggling to unhook the chain. Craig spoke in a low voice, aware sound carried easily over water,

"I'm as ready as I'll ever will be. Cast off whenever you can then hop back in."

"The current is keeping the chain very taut. I should have it untied in about five minutes."

A few minutes later Craig heard the rattle of the chain slipping through the ring on the float. Immediately the plane surged down river, rotating slowly in a clockwise direction. Donald scrambled into the plane, closed the passenger door behind him, and moved up into the passenger seat. He strapped himself in, very tightly. Craig noticed Donald's lack of faith, decided it was a wise move and strapped himself in as well.

"Dad, we're well clear of the wooden dock. When are you going to start the motor?"

Craig peered out the side window. The current had carried them out into the middle of the river well away from the docks and warehouses. Ahead was all clear for over a mile before the river curved off to the left.

"I'm almost afraid to turn on the ignition switch in case nothing happens."

"I know what you mean."

"Here we go. Keep your fingers crossed."

"I have. All of them."

Craig pushed in the primer plunger six times just to be sure, turned on the switches and pressed the starter. The propeller jerked around a half turn. The motor coughed black smoke out of the exhaust. Craig pushed the primer twice squirting more gas into the cylinders and tried again. The propeller spun around, the motor caught and roared into life, then died. Quickly Craig worked the primer in and out before the propeller could stop. This time the motor blew out a sheet of flames from the exhaust as it started. Ready to prime it again Craig kept his hand on the plunger, but it was no longer needed. Black smoke spewed out of the exhaust for a few seconds then disappeared. The motor settled into a steady roar. Craig throttled back, careful not to throttle back too far and stall the motor. The plane was facing upstream when the motor started and was now moving slowly against the current. Craig switched on the instrument panel lights and checked the gas gauges, first one wing tank then the other.

"Donald, are you religious?"

"No, not particularly."

"Well, maybe you and I should go to church and give thanks to whoever is looking after us. Both tanks are full!"

"Fantastic! Will that take us to Panama?"

"I don't know, but I'll let you know if we run out of gas."

"Are you going to take off upstream?"

"No. Now that the motor has warmed up I'm going to turn around and take off downstream. The current will help us get airborne quicker."

Craig rechecked the control settings then applied right rudder. The plane turned to head downstream. Craig glanced out the window checking to make sure the river was choppy. A smooth surface would not allow the floats to break clear from the surface. Craig moved the throttle forward, slowly increasing power until the throttle was fully forward. He shouted at Donald over the rising crescendo of noise from the motor and propeller thrashing through the air,

"Keep a sharp lookout for logs. I don't want us to go arse over tit before I get this thing up."

Within seconds the plane began to bounce. Craig pulled the stick back a fraction to lift the floats up onto the step. In less than a minute the plane was airborne and climbing. At a safe height Craig raised the flaps, and to conserve fuel, throttled back to three quarters power, and changed the pitch on the propeller to a coarser setting. Immediately the propeller noise died away. Climbing steadily to two thousand feet Craig flew down river in a northerly direction, making sure the Magdalena River was within gliding distance in the event of engine failure.

"Donald, I'm going to follow the river for awhile until I'm satisfied the engine won't quit, but I don't think we have enough fuel to go all the way north to the coast and then west to Panama. That distance must be close to a thousand miles... We'll have to take the direct route to Panama and that is over jungle... I'm sure I don't have to paint you a picture of what that means if we are forced to land."

"Dad, you're flying this thing as if you had been doing it for years. I'm sure you'll get us to Panama safely. You're doing great."

"There should be some maps around somewhere. See if you can find one."

Donald found several tattered maps in a pocket behind the pilot's seat. "There's four here. Is there a cabin light so I can figure out what they are?"

Craig tried several switches. He found one on a rheostat that turned on the light. With the help of the cabin light he located the cabin heater and turned it on. The air at two thousand feet was cool and he was beginning to shiver in his wet clothes.

"Three of the maps are local maps but this one should help us. It covers all the country and includes a little bit of Panama. Hey! I thought Panama City was on the east coast?"

"No, it's on the Pacific side."

"How are we... never mind, we'll cross that bridge when we come to it. Here's the map."

Craig spread the map across his lap, smoothing out the wrinkles and fitting together the torn pieces. The map was covered in smudges and in the dim light he could barely see the features he needed to decipher, but one thing was very clear.

"Damn!"

"What's the problem?"

"Lean over and I'll show you... the Andes is a single chain of high mountains along the west coast of South America until it reaches the southern boundary of Colombia where it splits into three, the Eastern, Central, and Western Cordillera. The Central Cordillera is to the west of the Magdalena River and blocks our direct route to Panama. We won't be able to turn west until we're two thirds of the way to the coast."

"Why don't you just climb over them?"

"The map is so dirty I can't read the elevations, but from the number of contour lines those mountains are very high. I don't know if this plane can go so high, and in any case we would probably use up more fuel trying to climb over than going around... I'm sorry, Donald, I think we should follow the river until we are north of the Central Cordillera before we turn west."

"You're a better judge of that than I am."

"Why don't you try to get some sleep? If you find a jacket or a spare blanket I could use one, I'm cold."

Donald released the straps and moved to the rear of the plane. In the overhead storage bins he found several blankets and a pillow. He sniffed one of the blankets and gasped. He wrapped a blanket around Craig's shoulders.

"Dad, don't take any deep breaths, you'll pass out."

"I don't have to, I can smell sweat, unwashed feet, and God knows what else."

"At least it'll keep you warm."

Donald squeezed his father's shoulder. "You're doing great, Dad," and went off to find a place to sleep.

- 14 -

Craig was frustrated. He didn't know where he was. He could see the Magdalena River faintly visible below him, a broad band of gray flowing north. On each side there was nothing he could identify. Nothing but a black void beyond each bank of the river. The slight tone changes in the black void hinted at hills and valleys along each bank. Hills he was careful to avoid by flying directly over the river and following its gentle meanders. He had flown over a number of villages, tiny clusters of dull yellow lights huddled on the bank of the river, but he had been unable to identify any of the villages on the map on his lap. The dim glow from the overhead light, the smudges on the map and the small print, reduced the names to a blur. If only he had a magnifying glass... or... maybe he needed reading glasses. That admission didn't help his mood. Donald's snoring in the background was equally annoying.

Craig was about to admit defeat and summon Donald, when coming around a curve in the river a large town burst into view from behind a hill. Dim lights streamed along the east bank of the river for at least a mile and for half a mile inland. He waited until he was past the town before trying to pinpoint it. On the map the only large town on the river with letters large enough to read was "Barrancabermeja". It too was on the east side of the river. It had to be Barrancabermeja.

Using his thumb and index finger to measure off the distance between Girardot and Barrancabermeja, then checking that distance with the scale on the bottom of the map, Craig determined they had traveled a little over three hundred kilometers, or about two hundred miles. Next he checked the fuel level on each tank. The gauges indicated one tank full, the other, the one he was using, more than half full. Again using his thumb and index finger, Craig measured the distance north along the river to the point where he could turn west, and the distance from that point to Panama. Based on the rate they were consuming fuel, they had more than enough gas to reach Panama and could even climb over the Isthmus to the Pacific side to land in Panama City.

"How are we doing?"

Donald had wakened himself up with a loud snort and was moving into the seat across from Craig.

"Good. I've pinpointed our position; calculated how much gas we've used so far, and worked out the estimated amount of gas we'll need to get to Panama."

"How did you do that?"

"It's a system we used in the R.A.F. It's a little too technical to explain."

"Come on, Dad. You're pulling my leg."

Craig held up his hand with thumb and index finger extended, "Like this."

"That's too technical for me."

"Here I'll show you where we are... see this town, it's called Barrancabermeja. We passed it fifteen minutes ago... in another half hour we'll reach this point where the river makes a ninety degree turn and heads west for awhile. That's where we turn west and head straight for Panama. We've got enough gas to allow us to climb over the mountains on the Isthmus of Panama and land in Panama City."

"Wouldn't it be easier to follow the Panama Canal instead of flying over the mountains?"

Craig shook his head, "I thought of that but I suspect it is forbidden to fly over the canal for security reasons. We're liable to get shot down."

"You're probably right. You think of everything. I'm more and more impressed."

"If I remember correctly, you stopped being impressed by me soon after your thirteenth birthday... I am honored to be worthy of your respect."

Donald leaned over and squeezed his father's shoulder. "Dad, that wasn't fair. I've always admired and looked up to you... why don't you let me take over for a few minutes while you get up and stretch your legs... I'll let you know if anything happens."

"Good idea. My clothes are still damp where I've been sitting."

Craig fine tuned the aileron and elevator trim and was half way out of his seat when the motor coughed, faltered, coughed again, and quit.

Craig dropped back into his seat. Quickly he worked the throttle back and forth. Nothing happened. The propeller was wind milling but the motor wouldn't start. Craig moved the pitch control to fine to make sure the propeller didn't stall, and frantically worked the primer pump. The primer was sucking air! That could only mean the tank was empty... but the fuel gauge showed the tank was half full! Craig switched to the other wing tank and continued working the primer. It was still sucking air.

"Donald! Quick! Come over here. We might have an air lock in the fuel lines blocking off the gas to the engine. Keep working this primer pump until you feel it sucking gas. We are coming down fast and I've got to get ready to land on the river if we can't get that bloody motor going."

Donald leaned over Craig's shoulder to work the primer. Craig lowered the flaps part way to give the plane more lift and hopefully keep them in the air a little longer. He eased back on the elevator control to reduce their rate of descent. The altimeter showed they were down to less than a thousand feet but Craig was not sure what their true elevation above the river might be. Craig continued down the middle of the river descending steadily. At what he judged to be about five hundred feet above the river he turned and headed upstream. High cloud had drifted in from the west blotting out the stars. Below him the river was barely visible, murky gray, opaque, without waves or ripples, making it almost impossible for Craig to judge his height above the water.

"Donald, you better go back to your seat and strap yourself in. I can't tell how high I am above the water and could easily slam into the river before I can pull up... Donald! Did you hear what I said? Donald!"

"Wait! Wait! I feel something. it's sucking gas! Dad, It's coming, do something!"

A sheet of flame spewed out of the exhaust. The motor coughed, sputtered, and caught, propelling the plane forwards and upwards with a loud roar. Glancing out the side window Craig saw a log floating by not more than thirty feet below. He eased back on the pitch and throttle, then climbed slowly back up to two thousand feet, heading once more down river.

Craig rechecked the fuel gauges. The wing tank they were now using was full. The tank he had been using was half full according to the gauge. Craig rapped the gauge with his knuckle. The pointer began to descend. Both he and Donald watched it move down, slowly, steadily, until it registered empty. Craig checked the other tank again. He rapped the gauge. The pointer didn't move nor did it move after he banged even harder. They had enough gas to get to the coast but not to Panama.

* * *

Rico reached over and slammed his hand down on the electric clock alarm, choking off the irritating noise. It had been set for six. He sat on the side of the bed trying to decide whether to phone Richard Bannerman or wait until Bannerman called. He decided the bathroom was more urgent. He finished relieving himself when the phone rang. Before Rico picked up the phone he leaned over to pull the covers off the girl in the bed. She shot him a dirty look and pulled the sheet back as far as her neck.

"Si?"

"Rico, did you find him?"

"No, but we know Craig stole a float plane last night..."

"What! You let him get away again."

"The owner heard a plane take off at midnight. This morning he found one of his planes missing."

"Jesus! I told you to keep an eye on the float planes."

"We did. A policeman was guarding the planes, but he was guarding the planes tied to the dock. Craig stole a plane tied to a buoy out in the river... I don't know how the hell he got out there. Apparently the current is very fast."

"So, he got away on you."

"No. Not yet. I have been informed that Craig is not likely to risk going west over the high mountains at night so his only choice is to fly north to the coast. According to the plane's owner Craig has only enough gas to reach the coast. He will have to head for Barranquilla and try to pick up an international flight there... Florentino knows a commander in the air force and has arranged for him to shoot Craig down before he reaches the coast... He'll go down in the jungle or the river and that will be the end of him."

"You'd better get him this time... I'm leaving for the airport in an hour. I've arranged for my plane to take off at ten. I'll call before I leave. Where will you be?"

"I'm going back to the compound. Call me there."

Rico heard Bannerman bang the phone down. He put his phone down gently, a rare smile on his lips. He enjoyed Richard's obvious frustration with Craig's skill in avoiding capture. The young woman was now sitting up in bed, a sheet folded over her breasts, a smirk lighting her face.

"Rico. I'm beginning to believe that Donald is smarter than you. He's rescued his Dad; organized the train to Girardot and managed to steal a plane. He'll get away."

"Alicia. I didn't bring you back from Girardot to get smart with me. Donald might be the greatest in bed, as you made a point of telling me last night, but it is his father, Craig Fox, who has managed to be one step ahead of us; ahead of the police, and maybe ahead of the air force... I'm going to have a shower then I'll explain your next assignment. I regret it won't be as enjoyable as your last one, but you'll be well paid."

* * *

Teniente Colonel Miguel De Toro Y Galtier understood his mission. The man who spoke to him had made it clear that failure to carry out his instructions would force the speaker to reveal the Colonel's involvement in the drug business and would imperil his family. The Colonel had never met the man but he had no doubt who he was, and that he meant what he said. The Colonel commanded the Air Force Base on the outskirts of Barranquilla. An ideal location, only a short hop by jet to Panama or Miami, where he could interact with his peers in the American Air Force and deliver drugs on the side. These illegal activities had financed the purchase of a large estate in "Altos Del Prado" suburb, an expensive car, plus membership at the prestigious Country Club two blocks from his home. The Colonel had no intention of sacrificing his career or life style. An additional incentive to make sure the plane was destroyed, was the knowledge that the two occupants of the plane were American agents carrying a complete list of all the drug couriers. Included in that list was the Colonel's name, or so he was told.

Colonel De Toro entered the main gate of the Air Base promptly at six. He parked the Mercedes in front of the crews' Ready Room, turned off the headlights and activated the alarm in the car before entering the building. A quick glance out the back window satisfied him the ground crew had rolled his Hawker Hunter out of the hanger and were making final preparations to start up the Rolls Royce Avon jet engine. The Hawker Hunter was his personal plane, the only one still flying. It was obsolete, but fast, sleek, graceful, and very maneuverable. It flew like an airplane should. Not like the modern jets his pilots preferred. Jets that barreled through the sky, propelled by monstrous engines, and barely held up by stubby protrusions on each side of the engines.

The Colonel waited until it was light enough to see the cockpit instruments before waving the ground crew away and taxiing to the end of the runway. He didn't want to risk taking off in the dark when he couldn't see the runway. He did not call the control tower to request permission to take off. At this hour of the morning the tower was not manned. He was breaking one of his own rules by taking off without permission but would justify the unauthorized takeoff as a "National Emergency".

The sun, yet unseen in the east, was beginning to paint the clouds a soft pink. The Colonel faced down the runway to began his takeoff. In less than thirty seconds the Hawker Hunter was off the ground, tucking its undercarriage into its wings before hurling itself up into the sky. Streaking up to ten thousand feet the Colonel looked to the east, waiting for the sun to pop up like a yellow balloon, before turning his attention back to flying. He never tired of seeing the sun come up so fast each time he zoomed up into the sky. At ten thousand feet the Colonel flew east over the city, then south to follow the Magdalena river towards his quarry, a DeHavilland Beaver aircraft. The information he had been given described his target as a silver colored high wing monoplane with a radial engine and equipped with floats. It would be flying north towards the coast at less than five thousand feet and would probably follow the river fairly closely in case of engine failure. The Colonel was to shoot it down and make sure it burned when it crashed.

Five minutes later the Colonel spotted the plane, a bright silver against the dark green of the jungle. It was flying at about two thousand feet above the jungle a half mile west of the river, but it was going in the wrong direction. It was going south instead of north towards the coast. Wondering what had made the pilot of the Beaver decide to reverse course, Colonel De Toro prepared to attack. He moved off to the east to put the rising sun behind him, turned on the gun sight and cannon switch, then made a gentle diving turn towards the Beaver. It was moving steadily south, oblivious to its fate. The Colonel closed to three hundred meters before pressing the button. An instant later he had to haul back on the controls to avoid hitting the wing the exploding cannon shells had sheared off. Pulling around in a tight turn he prepared to make another attack but there was no need. The Beaver was on fire, tumbling and spinning towards the jungle. Two bodies had been flung out by the violent spinning and were fluttering down behind the stricken plane, arms and legs akimbo. The Beaver plunged into the jungle, breaking off branches as it broke through the forest canopy, and exploded on impact with the ground, sending up a sheet of flame towards the bodies plunging into the inferno. The Colonel regained altitude, circling slowly while he climbed to ten thousand feet. The attack had been flawless. Perfectly executed according to the manual; attacking from the rear with the sun behind him; not firing until he was so close he couldn't miss; and firing a one second burst only. But something was gnawing at him. It wasn't until he was making his landing approach to the base that the Colonel realized what it was that was bothering him... one of the bodies tumbling down was a woman! The man had said there were "two American agents". He had neglected to mention one was a woman. The Colonel was a gentleman of the old school and the thought that he had killed a lady bothered his notion of chivalry. He decided not to reveal this shameful lapse from tradition.

* * *

"Rico, It's me, Richard. Are you going to tell me your air force couldn't find him?"

"No, Amigo. The pilot phoned an hour ago. He located their plane about a hundred kilometers south of Barranquilla and gave it a good burst with his cannons. A wing came off and the plane went down in flames. He said two bodies fell out of the fuselage on the way down and crashed into the burning plane."

"Rico, you don't sound very pleased. You wouldn't be going soft on your father, would you?"

"Course not! I'm tired that's all... late night.... Craig Fox and his son are dead."

"Are you sure?"

"They were shot down in flames."

"Maybe the second time I'll be lucky."

"What's that mean?"

"That's the second time Craig Fox has been shot down in flames."

"Oh? Where was the first time?"

"Long ago in Italy. He survived, but that's... oh, never mind... this better not be a repeat performance."

"Impossible, if the pilot is telling the truth."

"Would he lie?"

"No. He knew the consequences of failure. But in case he couldn't find the plane we had alerted our people in Panama."

"Good! That removes the last obstacle to our plans. My plane leaves in ten minutes... when are you returning to Canada?"

"Not for a few days. I have to track down our driver. He stole some money from us and Tino wants me to find him before I go back. Ricardo, I'll give you a call when I return. We have to have a talk. Ciao!"

"Bye!"

* * *

The realization that they did not have enough fuel to fly to Panama plunged both Craig and Donald into a somber mood. Only minutes before they had been euphoric at the prospect of being able to reach Panama. Now they would have to land somewhere within Colombia with the strong possibility of capture. Donald moved back to the passenger seat without saying a word. With an effort Craig forced himself to concentrate on finding a solution to the fuel problem.

They had enough fuel to reach the coast, but where on the coast should they land? To go north and land at or near Barranquilla, or Cartagena, would mean certain capture. The authorities in those cities would have been alerted as soon as the theft of the plane was discovered. The only hope was to go west to the coast, and land at some small coastal fishing village where the villagers had not been alerted to the fugitives. There, they could refill the gas tanks, or if no gas was available, hire a boat to take them to Panama.

In a few minutes they would reach the point where the Magdalena River makes a sharp angle turn to the west. At that bend they would be far enough north, beyond the northern edge of the Central Cordillera, and able to go west towards the coast and Panama without having to struggle over the mountains.

It was still cloudy overhead but the river was becoming more visible, less opaque, more clearly defined. The hills and valleys more distinguishable, no longer a black void. Dawn was approaching from the east. Some miles ahead Craig could now see the bend in the river.

"Donald, see that bend ahead? That's where we turn and go west... if we go north to Barranquilla we're flying into their arms. Our best chance is to go west and hit the coast south of Cartagena." Craig pointed to where the map showed the coastline extending in a southwesterly direction from the City of Cartagena towards the "Golfo De Uraba" and Panama. "Somewhere along that coast we should be able to find a fishing village and maybe some gas. Your eyes are better than mine. Take a look at the map and pick the largest village you can find... not a town, a village."

Donald spread the map against the instrument panel and ran his eyes up and down the coastline. Southwest of the City of Cartagena there were no large towns, just a few small villages. Craig had reached the bend in the river and was making the turn to the west before Donald noticed a peculiar symbol next to the little town of Covenas in the Gulf of Morrosquillo. It was red and looked like a flying horse.

"Dad. There's a town here with a symbol of a flying horse next to it. Does that mean anything to you?"

"Yes! That's a Mobil Oil Logo. It must mean they have a fuel depot there. We'll go there. Where is it?"

"Go due west and you're sure to hit it... here, I'll show you."

Two hours later, in brilliant sunshine, they crossed the coast and circled the town of Covenas. It was a small fishing village, but clearly visible behind a small wooden dock was the Mobil Oil fuel depot, two round gray tanks with rust streaming down the sides, and the Flying Horse Logo faintly visible on the crumbling gray paint. A small rusty tin shack lay between the tanks and the wooden dock. Two fishing boats were tied up at the dock, one on each side. At the end of the dock several large drums were lined up. They looked like gasoline drums. Craig pointed them out to Donald.

"See those drums? There's a hose coiled up right next to them. That's what they use to transfer the gas from the drums to the boats. Let's hope some of the drums are full."

The sea was calm. Craig was able to land the plane with no more than two bounces. He taxied slowly to the dock. Donald stood on one of the floats until it scrapped the end of the dock before jumping out to tie the plane to a wooden post. Craig, not sure whether he could restart the motor if he shut it down, kept the motor idling in case of trouble. Following Craig's instructions Donald rapped each of the drums with a wrench. Two were full, the rest empty. Enough to get them to Panama City, if only they could transfer the gas to their wing tanks, eight feet above the drums. The hose was there next to the drums, but no pump.

"Donald, Go over and check that shack. There might be a pump inside."

At that moment a door at the side of the shack opened slowly, rusty hinges screeching. A man emerged scratching his armpit with one hand and peering at them in the bright sunlight from under the other hand. He was short, fairly slim, and wearing dirty overalls pulled tight over a large belly. Approaching the dock his face was wary but not hostile. Craig greeted him in Spanish.

"Buenos Dias, Señor."

The man's face relaxed into a smile. "Buenos Dias Señores. How may I help you?"

"We would like to buy gasoline for our airplane."

"I can sell you gas but first you have to pay at the office in the town, then bring a note saying you have paid. I am not allowed to give you gas without the note... but the office does not open until nine o'clock... Señor, you have to turn off your motor."

Reluctantly Craig turned off the ignition. He stepped down onto the float in his stocking feet and jumped on the dock holding a large wad of Colombian pesos in his hand. Craig began stripping one bill after another from the wad, laying each bill on top of the other on a gasoline drum. The man didn't take his eyes away from the growing pile in front of him. Craig straightened the last bill, put it on top of the others, and placed the wrench on top of the pile.

"Señor, I know that gasoline must be difficult to get here and is very expensive. I hope there is enough money there to cover the cost. If you could fill our tanks now we would be very grateful. When you have finished you can take this money to the office and give it to them... do you agree there is enough money here to cover the cost of the gas?"

"Si! Si! Señor, there is enough. I will get the pump right away."

While the man was in the shack looking for the pump Donald gave his father a sly grin. "That was the slickest bribe I've ever seen."

"You and I know it is a bribe. He doesn't consider it a bribe... he will deliver the right amount to the office and keep the rest for services rendered. This way I haven't hurt his pride."

"Sometimes you amaze me."

"Thank you."

Forty minutes later the two wing tanks were full. Craig thanked the man, but he barely nodded in response mentally adding up the amount as he recounted the money. The motor started on the first attempt. Donald waited until the motor was running smoothly before untying the plane and leaping back on the float. The wind had picked up, blowing onshore towards the rising temperature on land. The sea was becoming choppy. Craig pointed the plane out to sea and gunned the motor. Picking up speed the plane began to bounce from wave to wave, throwing up spray over the windshield. Afraid the spray might douse the motor, Craig pulled down the flap lever to full flaps and hauled back on the controls, sucking the floats out of the water. The plane bounced once more before staggering into the air with minimal flying speed. Craig climbed slowly to two thousand feet before heading west across the Caribbean to Panama.

"Donald, I think we are going to make it this time. Don't you?"

"I'll reserve judgment until we land in Panama."

"Fair enough."

* * *

For the first time Robert was upset with the Commissioner, and that upset him even more. Commissioner Boulanger was Robert's idol, but the Commissioner was refusing to allow Robert to go to Colombia. Boulanger had tried to convince Robert that a rescue attempt could not possibly succeed: Robert was not fully recovered from his bullet wounds; couldn't speak the language; was unfamiliar with the country; couldn't expect help from the authorities; and had no idea where to start his search. Moreover if Craig Fox couldn't rescue himself with his knowledge of Spanish and his familiarity with the country, then nobody could. Robert was unconvinced. Finally Commissioner Boulanger was forced to assert his authority, by reminding Robert he was still in the R.C.M.P. and under the Commissioner's command. Moreover as much as he respected Robert's father, his first priority was to gather enough evidence against Richard Bannerman in order to prevent Bannerman's election to the office of Prime Minister. Robert would be allowed to search for his father when Boulanger was satisfied he had enough evidence to arrest Bannerman.

Knowing that Boulanger was an admirer of his mother, Robert phoned her at the cottage hoping to enlist her help in persuading the Commissioner to change his mind. Much to his surprise she agreed with the Commissioner. Audrey was beginning to doubt whether she would ever see Craig or Donald again. The CBC had heard nothing from Donald ever since the evening he disappeared. Aunt Valerie had phoned the Hotel Tequendama in Bogota and was informed Craig's and Donald's personal effects were still in the room registered in their names. The staff were going to remove their things that day, and would she please send money to settle the bill. If Craig and Donald were dead, Audrey was determined not to lose Robert also. She insisted on speaking to the Commissioner to thank him for forbidding Robert to go to Colombia.

The next day she was glad she had. A short item on the six o'clock evening news made her sit up and listen. Unsure she had heard correctly Audrey waited for the seven o'clock news. A few minutes before seven she summoned Brian from his study at the back of the cottage,

"Brian, come and listen to the radio. I'm sure they said something about Craig on the six o'clock news... I think he has escaped."

Brian shuffled into the living room, slippers clacking softly on the wooden floor, and eased himself into his favorite rocking chair. He peered at Audrey over his thick glasses before pushing them back higher on his nose with the index finger of his right hand, using his left hand to smooth back the thin strands of gray hair drifting down over his forehead.

"What did they say?"

"Craig wasn't mentioned by name but the announcer said a prominent Western Canadian oil man has been identified as working for the drug cartel and has escaped from the Colombian police."

"That sounds like Craig. Did they mention Donald?"

"No. Sssh! Listen."

Audrey waited impatiently through the first part of the news. Again the announcer did not identify the "prominent oil man", but at the end of the broadcast there were two special announcements. The first one was from the Solicitor General's office to the effect that the Solicitor General, the Right honorable Richard Bannerman, had been aware for some time that a prominent Western Canada oil man, Mr. Craig Fox, was being funded by the drug cartel, and while attending the Drug Conference in Bogota, Colombia, the Solicitor General had organized the capture of Craig Fox and his son, who is also involved in the drug business. Unfortunately the two men were able to escape and are now being pursued by the Colombian Police. The second announcement was from the Canadian Broadcasting Corporation confirming that one of their T.V. announcers, Donald Fox, was missing in Colombia and was suspected of being a courier for the drug cartel.

Brian switched off the radio. Neither one spoke for almost a minute. Brian spoke first, and immediately wished he hadn't asked such a stupid question.

"Do you think Craig can elude their police?"

Audrey shrugged, "I don't know... he speaks Spanish but doesn't look Colombian. He'll be easy to spot... I must phone Robert."

Audrey went into the kitchen and picked up the receiver from the wall phone. She was about to crank the handle to ring the operator but there was somebody on the line. Two minutes later she tried again, and again a few minutes later. Audrey debated asking the chatty lady to hang up for an emergency call but Brian talked her out of it.

"That's probably Mrs. McPherson. She'll listen in if you make the call. She does it all the time... I always hear the click when she picks up her phone. Better wait for half an hour until she goes off somewhere."

Audrey made the call after ten hoping Mrs. McPherson was in bed asleep. Robert was thrilled.

"Fantastic! Mom, Dad will make it I'm sure... if he was able to rescue Donald and escape the cartel, the Colombian Police won't get him... in a day or two you can expect to hear from him."

"But he won't know where I am?"

"Yes he will. I left a message on your answering machine in Calgary. He should be able to figure it out."

"Oh Robert, I hope you didn't make it too difficult. You know how hopeless your father is with crossword puzzles."

"Don't worry, Mom. If he can't, I'm sure Donald can... you go to bed and have a good sleep. I'll go out and see if there's anything in the paper."

There was, on page one. Plus a picture of his father and brother standing next to the slightly blurred image of a young man who the paper claimed was the head of the Canadian drug organization.

* * *

Barbara was exhausted. She leaned over the side of the bed to search for her nightgown. It was in a heap on the floor where Richard had flung it. She picked it up and slid it down over her head. The silk crackling over her nipples sent tingling sensations coursing through her body once again. Barbara propped herself up against the headboard with two pillows and reached for a comb and small mirror on the bedside cabinet. Richard had gone downstairs to make some late night phone calls but left a brandy snifter on the cabinet by the bed. He had barely touched the brandy. Barbara reached over and helped herself to a sip. She was about to put the glass back but changed her mind and took another sip. Leaning back against the pillows, glass in hand, Barbara contemplated her husband's unusual behavior.

Something must have happened while he was in Colombia to put him in such a sexy mood. Richard arrived home late that evening bubbling over with energy. Barbara was getting ready for bed when she heard his limousine pull up. She came downstairs in her dressing gown to meet

Richard. No sooner was he in the door he picked her up, wrapped his arms around her and gave her a passionate kiss on the lips. By his actions he left no doubt what he had in mind. He tore off her dressing gown and would have done the same to her silk nightgown if she hadn't eluded him and run back upstairs. Richard followed a few minutes later with a snifter half full of brandy in his hand.

What followed was the best love making Barbara had experienced in years. Richard was inexhaustible, and so was she. He had toyed with her emotions, caressing her body with his gentle touch, lifting her, step by step to a shuddering climax, and repeating it time and again until she pleaded with him to stop.

Barbara had been planning to ask Richard what he knew about Commissioner Boulanger's murder, and to tell him that Allan Sharp had disappeared. She decided to wait until morning. Barbara took another sip of brandy, put the glass back on the cabinet and switched off the light. In what seemed to her like seconds later she was being shaken awake by a very angry husband. She was startled and a little frightened at the fierceness of his features. He leaned over and spat the words at her,

"Why the hell didn't you tell me Allan Sharp has disappeared?"

"You didn't give me a chance, lover boy."

"Well, you should have."

"Richard, if you think I was going to interrupt what you were doing to tell you about Allan, your priorities are very different to mine."

"I just called his house and that bitch wife of his gave me an earful."

"I know. She has been calling me twice a day. Even accused me of having an affair with him."

For some reason that struck Richard as funny. He snorted and stomped out of the room. Barbara took another sip of brandy and switched off the light once again.

Downstairs in his study Richard poured himself another brandy before looking up Allan Sharp's secretary's number on his cardex. Miss Roberta Masse answered the phone on the first ring. She had been expecting Richard's call. She had heard the news that he was back from Colombia.

"Roberta, I just talked to Mrs. Sharp. What do you know about Mr. Sharp's disappearance?"

"Nothing. He left his house last Friday morning at his usual time and promptly disappeared. His wife knows nothing and has been bugging me every day."

"I know. She's been calling Barbara as well."

"I contacted the Police the next day. They found his car parked at a service station just up the street from his house. It was locked. It had been there since early Friday morning. He must have gone straight there from the house, parked the car and gone somewhere... Mr. Bannerman, somebody went through our files one night."

"Are you sure?"

"Absolutely! I'm very meticulous and I know exactly where everything is. The files have been put back carefully but not carefully enough... I know somebody was in them after Mr. Sharp disappeared."

"You say it happened after Mr. Sharp disappeared?"

"Yes. I think he must have been kidnapped and the kidnappers are going through our files."

"You could be right. I'll call Inspector Calder tonight and have the R.C.M.P. find Mr. Sharp... Roberta, were you able to get into Mr. Sharp's safe?"

Roberta hesitated too long.

"Well! Did you?"

"Yes sir... my cousin did it for me. He's an expert with safes."

"Well! What did you find?"

Again Roberta hesitated.

"For Christ sake! Roberta, I haven't got all night."

"I'm sorry Sir... there was mostly stock in various companies... some gold coins... and... several diaries."

"Roberta, get on with it. What diaries?"

"Mr. Bannerman, In the diaries we recovered from Mr. Sharp's safe he has recorded everything you have done since he first met you during the war... the shooting down of enemy pilots... the murder of one of your pilots, Rene Gauthier... the murder attempts against Craig Fox and many other exploits that we are sure the media would love to hear about, including details of your involvement with the Colombian drug cartel... these diaries must be worth a great deal to you... something in the order of a million dollars... we will be in touch again."

"You fucking bitch! I'll get you for this!"

But the line was dead. She had hung up. Richard redialed her number. No answer. He dialed several more times. Still no answer. Richard slammed down the receiver. He sat at his desk for several minutes trying to decide his next move. He had to get those diaries back, and he had to eliminate Roberta and her cousin. Even if he recovered the diaries he couldn't have those two running around dropping hints to the press. This was not something for Inspector Calder.

"Blast Rico! Why aren't you back here where I need you? You should be here instead off chasing after some measly little driver."

Richard dialed long distance. This was the first time he had dialed Colombia from his house but he had to get Rico back as soon as possible.

* * *

They were flying over the San Blas Islands. Ahead and some miles to the right Craig identified the Gulf of San Blas. Pleased with his navigation skills Craig pushed the throttle forward a notch, increasing power for the climb over the mountains directly ahead. There were a few wispy clouds hovering over the top of the peaks of the Cordillera of San Blas but he anticipated going over them without any problems. In one hour they would be over the Pacific and landing in Panama City. The increased noise from the engine roused Donald from his private thoughts.

"Dad."

"Yes?"

"I've been thinking. Does the cartel have connections in Panama?"

"I have no doubt they do... in fact, I've read reports the President of Panama might be involved."

"By now they know we stole the plane, and probably expected us to fly to Barranquilla. if we didn't land there wouldn't the cartel realize where we were headed and warn Panama?"

"You're thinking there will be a reception committee waiting for us in Panama City?"

"Yes."

"Good thinking. What do you suggest we do?"

"How much gas do we have?"

Craig checked the fuel gauges, tapping the gauges to make sure they were reading correctly. "One tank is full, the one I'm using is nearly empty."

Donald pointed at the map on his lap, "According to this map it's about three hundred miles to Costa Rica. Do we have enough gas to get us there?"

"Costa Rica? Yes, we can get there if I throttle back as much as possible."

"On this map the only big town is San Jose and it is not on the coast."

"I doubt if we could pick up an international flight from any coastal town. We would have to land on the coast and somehow make our way to San Jose... that's going to delay us another day."

"But safer than Panama City."

"Let's see that map for a moment." Craig pointed to the port of Limon located half way up the east Coast of Costa Rica. "How about this town? It's the biggest one on the coast."

"Let's go, Dad. We can hire a car to take us to San Jose and we can be home by tomorrow."

Craig made a slow turn to the right, reduced power and revs, and followed the coast line to Costa Rica, unaware the cartel had called off Panama.

* * *

Marcel Boulanger heard the slam of a car door outside. He closed a small notebook and put down his pen. Allan Sharp walked in carrying a briefcase in one hand and a folded newspaper in the other. He opened the paper displaying the picture of Craig Fox. Under a large headline the paper reported Craig had been killed by the Colombian Police while resisting arrest.

"Commissioner, have you seen this?"

"I heard it on the news but they didn't give any details."

"The paper doesn't mention his son."

"Neither did the newscast."

"Where is Robert?"

"He was so sure Craig would turn up soon he went to the cottage to be with his mother."

"I guess Bannerman will be drinking a toast when he hears the news."

Boulanger shook his head, "He probably knew."

"Oh, you think so?"

"I don't think Craig was ever a fugitive. I think the cartel killed him and concocted the story of escape and resisting arrest to justify the murder."

"You're probably right. Are you going to phone Robert?"

"I will call him later. It is something I must do... such a fine family... Mrs. Fox is a wonderful lady. Did you know she is a well known artist?"

"No."

"Yes, I have several of her paintings... Mr. Sharp, tell me about your trip to Ottawa."

"There is no mention of Star Corporation in the list of assets submitted by Richard Bannerman when he was appointed to the Cabinet."

"Excellent! Did you make copies?"

"Yes, I have them here in my briefcase."

"Good. Now all we have to do is impound Star Corporation's files and prove Bannerman controls that company... did you have any problems getting access to his files?"

"Yes, they kept me hanging around while they got clearance from somebody. It took several hours."

"Oh! Oh! That doesn't sound good. Were you followed?"

"No, I don't think so."

But Allan Sharp was wrong.

* * *

Craig listened to the recording on the answering machine at his home in Calgary. Muttering to himself he held the telephone receiver out in front of him. He glared at it, as if this would decipher the strange message his son had left on the answering machine. Cursing Robert's penchant for secret codes, Craig shoved the receiver back on its cradle and looked around for Donald. Maybe he could figure out what his brother was trying to convey. Donald was limping towards him from the Pan American counter. Watching Donald's approach Craig's frustration quickly dissipated. He greeted his son with a chuckle,

"I think those clothes suit you."

"I was going to say the same about your outfit."

Donald's denim pants were so tight around the hips and buttocks. He had been forced to leave the two top buttons unhooked, depending on a leather belt to keep the pants up. The legs ended three inches above his reddish brown shoes which were two sizes too small and decorated with leather tassels. Unable to find a shirt large enough to accommodate the wide shoulders and brawny chest, Donald was wearing a brilliantly colored Guatemalan serape. Craig's more modest frame was able to fit into a white shirt, but it too had round pearl buttons and frilly things up and down the front. His pants were properly buttoned and only two inches above his shoes. Their clothing was hardly suitable for First Class on Pan American but it was the best they had been able to find after padding around San Jose for several hours in their stocking feet and muddy clothes, much to the amusement of the Costa Rican sales clerks.

"Dad, did you get through to Calgary?"

"Yes, it took a while but nobody's home. Robert left one of his cryptic messages on the answering machine... I couldn't figure it out what he meant... I think he was trying to tell us where he and your mother are hiding."

"What did he say?"

"Something about going to visit my cousin at Granite Island in Saskatchewan. I don't have any cousins in Saskatchewan. In fact, I don't have any cousins... and, Donald, where the hell is Granite Island?"

"Good question."

"Sometimes Robert gets carried away with his Mountie training."

"Wait a minute Dad. Maybe he meant my cousin. If that's what he meant it makes sense. I have a cousin, your sister's son, Dick... and Aunt Valerie and Brian have a cottage on Georgian Bay. I'm pretty sure it is located on a granite island. That must be where they've gone."

"But Robert said they were going to Saskatchewan."

"But Dad, he couldn't tell us they were going to Ontario. That would have given the cartel too many clues."

"I guess what you're saying makes sense... at least it's a start. I'll go and change our booking from Calgary to Toronto... I'll call Aunt Valerie when we get to Toronto."

* * *

Richard was tired, very tired. He had spent the whole day dealing with routine paper work and answering calls from reporters asking for details on how he organized the capture of Craig Fox. By the end of the day he had regretted trying to paint himself as a diligent Solicitor General. The phone rang. Richard turned on the bedside light in the apartment to check the time. It was nearly three in the morning. Gearing up to yell at whoever was calling at such a stupid hour, Richard picked up the phone.

"Yeah, who is it?"

"It's me."

"Jesus Christ Rico, couldn't this wait until the morning?"

"Ricardo, I have some bad news for you."

"Let me guess... Craig is not dead."

"Well, maybe... the pilot shot down the wrong plane and the shit's hit the fan... turns out the head of Ecopetrol and his wife were flying in the same kind of plane on their way to inspect one of their oil fields along the Magdalena River. Now Ecopetrol wants to know why the Air Force shot it down."

"What's Ecopetrol?"

"Our National Oil Company."

"So? Where's Craig?"

"He's disappeared... he didn't land in Barranquilla or Cartagena and wasn't supposed to have enough gas to get to Panama. Just in case I checked with Panama but he never showed up there. He's either crashed in the jungle or somehow made it back to Canada."

"I bet he's in Canada by now. He's too smart for your people."

"Sounds like Craig has gone up in your estimation."

"Bullshit! Your people made him look good that's all... I'll have to alert the R.C.M.P. They'll get him."

"Ricardo, I don't think you should do that."

"Why?"

"He has on him a film that if it is ever released will destroy you."

"Oh! What film?"

"I don't want to discuss it on the phone. I'll be back in Montreal tomorrow. I'll explain everything to you when I get back. In the meantime have the Mounties find out where he is but do not arrest him... I repeat, do not arrest him. Once they have located him I'll take over."

"How soon can you take care of those two blackmailers?"

"I've got a couple of men working on it. They've searched her apartment. She'd written the address of their hideout on a grocery list... bunch of amateurs... we'll get them tonight."

"I want those diaries."

"Have you found Allan Sharp?"

"Yes. He's holed up in some apartment in Toronto. I can't figure out why unless he's hiding from his wife. He came to Ottawa and looked into some of my records, made copies, and went back to Toronto. I've got the Mounties keeping an eye on him until I figure out what he's up to."

"Be careful how you handle him. If the President of Star Corporation turns up dead there will be too many questions."

Richard leaned forward in bed. "Rico, I've just about had it with our Mr. Sharp. I want you to take care of him soon."

"You're getting to be very bloodthirsty."

"I have too much at stake to pussyfoot around."

"Well. Take it easy until I get there. Ciao!"

* * *

Commissioner Boulanger was beginning to suspect that Allan Sharp had indeed been followed from Ottawa. He should have known better than allow the man to go blundering around Ottawa. If it wasn't so important for him to remain incognito, Boulanger would have preferred to go himself. He was almost sure they were under surveillance. The green car across the street had been there all day in the same spot.

"Mr. Sharp, could you come over to the window please... don't get too close... see that green car parked across the street?"

"Yes?"

"I am almost certain you were followed and this apartment is being watched."

"Oh, you think so?"

"To make sure I want you to go down to the store around the corner and buy something. A paper or groceries... and come back. If you are followed it will confirm my suspicions."

Allan Sharp was followed. The man in the car waited until Allan had disappeared around the corner before stepping out of the car and hurrying after him. He reached the corner just as Allan reappeared, blundering straight into him and knocking the paper out of Allan's hand. The man apologized, but had no choice. He was forced to continue around the corner. Ten minutes later he returned, gave the front right tire a couple of vicious kicks and aimed a couple of curses towards their window. He slammed the car door behind him and drove off down the street. The Commissioner watched the performance before turning to Allan who was standing beside him.

"I know that young man. Constable Johnson is one of my recruits. A bright kid... very ambitious. Maybe too ambitious."

"You mean that's the R.C.M.P. watching us?"

"It is. They must have been alerted when you requested Bannerman's records. You were identified and followed. Bannerman must have asked them to look for you."

"So, why didn't they arrest me?"

"On what charge? You did nothing illegal by looking at Bannerman's records."

"Then why are we being watched?"

"It is you who is being watched. They still think I'm dead. Bannerman is probably wondering why you're checking his records and hiding here. Whatever the reason we have to leave immediately before they bring in another man to watch you. Quick! Down the back stairs."

"What about your car parked in the front?"

"They've got the license number of that car by now. We wouldn't get very far in it... I've got another car parked in a garage a couple of blocks from here. Come! Hurry!"

"Commissioner, where are we going?"

"We're going to the only safe place left, to Georgian Bay to meet up with Robert and to organize our attack on Mr. Bannerman."

* * *

Valerie dreaded making the call to the cottage. Ever since she had heard the terrible news, she knew she had to call, but kept postponing the ordeal, hoping a later broadcast might make a correction. There had been no correction. Craig was dead. Her brother was dead. He had survived attacks from bandits, German fighters, and anti aircraft guns. He had survived Bannerman's attempts to kill him, and had eluded the drug cartel, only to have some stupid policeman gun him down as if he was some vicious criminal. Audrey would be devastated. They were so close those two. Valerie paced up and down the living room, alternatively approaching the telephone on the side table by the sofa, each step slower than the last, and turning away, unable to commit to the final act of lifting the receiver to deliver the horrible news that Craig was dead.

The phone rang. Startled and relieved that the dreaded call could be postponed, Valerie picked up the receiver.

"Hello?"

"Valerie, it's me, Craig."

Valerie dropped the phone and collapsed on the sofa. The receiver banged against the leg of the side table, swinging back and forth on the end of the cord. whoever was calling continued speaking but the voice was too faint to decipher. It had to be some cruel hoax... but... but the voice did sound like Craig. Gingerly she picked up the receiver.

"Hello?"

"Valerie, it's me, Craig. Are you all right?"

"Oh God! Oh God! Thanks be to God you're alive!"

"Yes, we're alive... I don't know how much God had to do with it but Donald and I are very much alive in spite of Bannerman and the cartel."

"Where are you?"

"Here in Toronto at the airport. We're trying to keep out of sight as much as possible... can you come and pick us up?"

"Of course. It will take me an hour to get there but first I must phone Audrey and tell her you are alive."

"Yes, please call her. Is she at the cottage?"

"Yes. How did you know?"

"Donald was able to figure out Robert's message... we have no baggage so you can pick us up at the Departure entrance. They won't be looking for us there."

"I'll be there in an hour... Craig?"

"Yes?"

"Thanks for coming back. I love you."

"I love you too."

Valerie dialed the long distance operator to put a call to the cottage. Robert answered the phone. Immediately Valerie heard another click.

She growled into the phone, "Mrs. McPherson! Get off the bloody phone!"

A second click confirmed Mrs. McPherson had retreated. Robert put the receiver to his ear again, although his ear was still ringing.

"Is that you, Aunt Valerie?"

"Sorry, but I had to get that nosy woman off the phone... Robert, I can't say too much over the phone but tell your mother that the two dogs managed to escape from the pound and were not killed as was reported by radio and T.V... I am bringing them out tonight."

"Huh? Oh! Is this true?"

"Yes! Fantastic news. Your mother will be so pleased."

"Are both... dogs... in good shape?"

"Yes."

"Thank you! Thank you! I must tell mother. Goodbye."

Usually a meticulous dresser, Valerie slapped on some makeup and lipstick, rushing out of the house without bothering to change her dress or shoes. Forty five minutes later she drove up to the Departure entrance of Pearson International Airport. Craig and Donald came out before she had pulled up to the kerb. They strolled towards the car at a leisurely walk. Valerie waited impatiently until they were both in the car. She drove off as soon as they were seated.

"Slow down, Valerie. We don't want to attract attention."

"Oh! Is that why you were ambling along like a couple of tourists?"

"According to the papers we're supposed to be dead, but I'm sure Bannerman knows we're not. He's either got the cartel or the Mounties looking for us. I'm hoping we can slip by before they start checking the airports."

Valerie glanced over at her brother sitting in the front seat beside her, then at Donald in the back seat. "You two are looking very well dressed for two fugitives."

Both men chortled. "You should have seen the outfits we had on when we landed in Miami. We had trouble getting through Passport Control. We bought these clothes at a shop in Miami... Valerie, did you call Audrey?"

"Yes, I talked to Robert. It's a party line so I had to be careful but he understood what I said... I'll take you out there tonight."

"How is Robert?"

"Almost fully recovered... we had a hard time trying to keep him from rushing off to Colombia to look for you. Fortunately Commissioner Boulanger wouldn't let him go."

Craig's head jerked around, "Commissioner Boulanger! But he's dead!"

"No! He is very much alive, much to our surprise... he got in touch with Robert and they have been trying to gather evidence against Bannerman."

"But we saw the funeral on T.V."

"He wasn't in the car when they blew it up."

"Who was?"

"The Commissioner thinks it was somebody from a car stealing gang... If it had been a teenager, he would have been reported missing."

"I have no doubt it was Bannerman that arranged for the car bomb."

"Craig, I don't know if you will be very pleased when I tell you what my son, Dick, is doing."

Donald leaned forward resting his arms on the back of the front seat. "What is Dick up to now?"

"He has been hired to set up the lights sound and pictures for the convention."

"Which convention?"

"The convention here in Toronto in three days time, at which your great leader, Richard Bannerman, is to be anointed Prime Minister of Canada."

Donald pounded his fist on the back of the seat, "That's it! That's the way to do it."

"Valerie, you'll have to excuse my son he hasn't been normal lately. Donald, what are you talking about?"

"Dad, I'll explain later... Aunt Valerie, can I call Dick?"

"Of course, I'll give you his number as soon as we get home."

Donald called Dick and arranged to meet him at Dick's apartment within the hour. While Valerie was preparing lunch in the kitchen, Donald spoke to his father and talked him into parting with the money belt that had been wrapped around Craig's waist for several days. Ostensibly, Donald wanted to convert all his traveler's cheques into Canadian money. Donald didn't return until late afternoon, just in time to get in the car as Valerie and Craig were about to leave for the cottage. In the car Donald returned the money belt to his father. Craig checked the contents before once again wrapping the belt around his waist. The cassette was in it but Donald's travelers cheques were gone. On the road to Honey Harbor, they were unaware Commissioner Boulanger and Allan Sharp were also on their way to the cottage.

* * *

Inspector Calder was not sure if he should give the Solicitor General the bad news or the worse news first. He still hadn't decided until the moment Richard Bannerman returned his call. The tone of his superior's voice convinced him to give the bad news first. What he didn't realize was that it was actually the worse news that he was giving first.

"Sir, you were absolutely right, Craig Fox is alive. He arrived in Toronto at ten thirty this morning."

"Good work, Calder. Where is he now?"

"I... I don't know. He gave us the slip at the airport. Must have worn some disguise... He didn't rent a car or take a taxi so he must have been picked up."

"Jesus Christ Man! You're as bad as the Colombian police. His son is a big man. The two men exiting together should have been easy to pick out."

"He didn't come out the Arrival exit."

"You're telling me you didn't have all the exits covered?"

"Sir! There must be over fifteen major airports across Canada. We don't have the staff to cover them all and didn't know which one he would use to get into Canada, so we concentrated on Calgary, Toronto, and Regina... I'm sorry, sir."

"Why Regina?"

"There was a message on his answering machine that alerted us he might go there."

"He has a sister living somewhere in Eastern Canada, probably right here in Toronto. She must have picked him up. Calder, find out where she lives."

"Yes Sir." Inspector Calder knew he had screwed up badly in the Solicitor General's eyes. Revealing the other bad news couldn't make things any worse so he took the plunge. "Sir, Mr. Sharp has also disappeared."

"What! How did that happen?"

"Constable Johnson got suspicious after there was no movement in the apartment for several hours, so he decided to check it out. It appears Mr. Sharp left in a big hurry. The car he had been using was still parked in front of the building... sir?"

"Yes?"

"The car Mr. Sharp was using is an R.C.M.P. car."

"How the hell did he get hold of one of your cars?"

"We're checking that out right now... the car was one of several we use for our under cover work. How he got hold of it I have no idea."

"Well, you can deal with him later. I want you people to get your finger out and find Craig Fox for me. Find him but do not arrest him... I repeat, do not arrest him... check out his sister. He may be with her."

"Yes sir."

An hour later, a policeman was parked down the street from Valerie's house. Craig, Donald, and Valerie had left only minutes before.

- 15 -

Robert Richard Shirley-Dale was named after the grandfather that had been murdered in Colombia, but to avoid confusion with his older cousin, Robert Fox, he answered to the name of "Dick". In any case it was a name he preferred. "Dick" had a more intriguing ring to it, but still very masculine. Not that anybody ever had any doubts about Dick's masculinity. Certainly his many intimate girlfriends didn't. It was the brooding gypsy look he cultivated that first attracted their attentions. The smoldering brown almost black eyes, the prominent cheek bones, angular chin with only a wisp of a beard clinging to the end, and the shoulder length dark hair tied in the back with a black ribbon, enhanced the look. To reinforce the image Dick usually wore black, and a black fedora, the kind favored by the Chicago gangsters, whenever he was outside. Initially the gold earring on each earlobe were intended to defy and irritate his mother, but became a permanent feature when he realized they added to the image he wanted.

Besides women Dick had two loves in his life, hockey and the theater. Thanks to his parents he was good at both. His father, Brian, encouraged and supported Dick's ambition to be a professional hockey player. His mother, Valerie, recognized Dick's artistic talents and was equally determined to develop them by helping him with his growing interest in stage craft. She won and there was no more talk of professional hockey after Dick graduated from high school. Nevertheless, nothing was allowed to interfere with his Saturday "Hockey Night in Canada" ritual on the radio or TV.

Dick had no interest in politics and when offered the visual and audio contract for the Party Convention, he ignored his mother's objections, and on being assured by the organizers he would have a free hand, signed the contract. It was an opportunity, if he was able to pull it off, that would move him to the top of his profession.

Initially Dick was given to understand the Convention was going to be held at the Royal York Hotel in Toronto, which would have been a breeze to organize. But very soon after signing the contract he was informed by a bureaucrat from the Prime Minister's Office that the Convention would be held at Maple Leaf Gardens. At first the management of Maple Leaf Gardens refused to make the Arena available, but changed their minds after considerable pressure from Ottawa. They agreed provided the Convention's use of the Arena was restricted to three days. Dick's crew would have two days to set up the equipment, but must be out of the Arena with everything removed by Saturday morning in time for Saturday night hockey. This changed his whole approach to the problem. Instead of a hall holding two thousand he had a whole Arena capable of seating over fifteen thousand with very different acoustic and lighting problems. He informed the bureaucrat he would need a much larger crew than originally envisioned which would add considerably to the price of his contract. Dick named a price double what he thought he would need. The man didn't even quibble at the sum Dick quoted. He even hinted there was more available if Dick performed well.

Given the time constraints, Dick determined he would need a crew of at least fifteen professionals to be able to set the show up in two days. The crew would include carpenters, sound technicians, light technicians, a couple of spot operators, and three or four cameramen, plus a stage manager to make sure technicians, cameramen, and sundry stage hands were at the right spot at the right time. Lighting and audio equipment would have to be purchased assembled and tested at another location, then disassembled and reinstalled in the Arena at predetermined locations for proper lighting and sound. Chairs and desks for each delegate, plus a stage and podium, would have to be constructed and brought in at the last moment.

The ink was hardly dry on the contract before Dick was tempted to to tear it up and go on to other work. Within hours of signing he realized there were two opposing factions in Ottawa battling for control of the Convention. He could be caught in the middle and crushed between them. The Prime Minister's Office were determined to have a regular Convention, while the Solicitor General's bureaucrats didn't want a Convention at all. For days, days Dick could ill afford to waste, the polite but vicious infighting continued. Finally it was agreed the Convention would be held on Friday, November the Eighteenth, and restricted to a few hours late in the afternoon and early evening.

Dick assumed he would receive his instructions from the bureaucrat in the Prime Minister's Office. Instead it was the Solicitor General's office that began giving Dick their interpretation on how he should organize the Convention. The "free hand" he was promised very quickly became less so. Dick thought of quitting several times, but by controlling his irritation, decided his artistic freedom was not too compromised, and was able to make enough changes in their demands to satisfy himself. They instructed him to close off the back half of the Arena by hanging huge canvas sheets across the middle. Instead Dick hung large Canadian flags and colored bunting. This not only added color to the drab Arena, but, also improved the acoustics. They demanded he install a huge television screen in front of the flags right behind the podium. The screen to be at least sixteen by twenty feet. He was to prepare a film covering Richard Bannerman's life from boyhood in Colombia to the present. Two weeks before the Convention boxes of film and photographs were dumped in Dick's office. The old film and photos were black and white, the recent ones in color. He hired two photographers to sort out the mess. Initially he didn't think it was technically feasible, considering the present level of technology, to project a television film of Richard Bannerman's exploit on such a large screen, but with the help of experts, he developed a method using a Beta Cam player.

Although extremely busy preparing for the Convention Dick still took time to phone his mother every few days to find out what was happening with Uncle Craig and his cousin Donald. He knew they had been captured in Colombia and had escaped. Nevertheless he was surprised when Donald called one afternoon and invited himself over. When he arrived at the apartment Donald's first question was,

"Where's your Beta Max? We've got to see this film right away. According to Eduardo it's dynamite."

"Donald! Aren't you even going to say Hello?... and who the hell is Eduardo?"

Donald was halfway down the hall on his way to the living room before he remembered his manners. He turned back to Dick who was closing the front door a frown creasing his brow. Donald gave Dick a hug and ruffled his hair. That annoyed the younger man even more. Donald knew it would. He was very fond of his cousin but didn't have much patience with Dick's sartorial aspirations. Donald walked into the living room. Dick checked his hair in the hall mirror before he followed. The film was in the Beta Max and Donald was switching on the TV by the time Dick joined him.

"You haven't answered my question."

"Oh? What was that?"

"Who is Eduardo?"

Donald was on the point of answering, instead he waved for silence. The picture of Richard Bannerman and Florentino Chavez popped up on the T.V. screen. Donald exclaimed,

"Christ! Look at that!"

Dick leaned forward to get a better look. "Isn't that the guy I'm preparing this convention for. Richard Bannerman, our next Prime Minister?"

"Yep, that's him... and you'll never guess who is sitting next to him."

"Who?"

"Florentino Chavez, the head of the Colombian drug cartel."

"Why would he be talking to him?"

"Because Bannerman is in cahoots with the cartel."

Dick, knowing Donald's penchant for embellishment, was suspicious and a little irritated to be fed such nonsense. His skepticism evaporated by the end of the film. Dick shook his head in astonishment.

"Is he really going to get rid of the Queen, make himself President for Life, and do all that stuff with the cartel?"

"Unfortunately Bannerman has convinced most of the public that he is the only one who can provide strong leadership, improve the economy, and make the streets safe again. Once he's in, there's nothing to stop him."

"What about the R.C.M.P., won't they stop him?"

"According to Dad, he's already corrupted them."

"How can he be stopped?"

"You can."

"Me!"

"Yes, you... only you can stop him."

"Donald, for Christ sake! For once quit the bullshit!"

"No, I'm serious. Aunt Valerie said you are organizing the lights and sound for the Convention." Dick nodded. "She also mentioned something about you preparing a film on Bannerman."

"Yes, the film is all ready except for some minor editing that I'm doing right now."

"Good. I want you to splice this film on the end of your film."

Dick exploded. "No way! Absolutely not! If you think I'm going to throw away my whole career for some crazy idea of yours you're nuts."

"Dick, please listen... please hear me out... according to Dad, Bannerman committed murder during the war; has arranged the murder of many people, and has been helping the drug cartel acquire control over most of the newspapers and T.V. stations in this country... if we can show who Bannerman really is by projecting this film just as he starts his acceptance speech, everybody will turn against him and he'll be arrested... Dick, just close your eyes and imagine the scene... it'll be the most dramatic comeuppance you will ever see... the delegates are on their feet, madly cheering the man they have voted unanimously to be the next Prime Minister... he saunters to the podium to give his acceptance speech... up on the screen behind the podium a film of their hero's exploits unfolds... suddenly as he faces the cheering the film changes and they are confronted by this film... can you imagine the pandemonium."

Dick snorted in amusement. "Donald, you're incorrigible... I suppose at this climactic moment, while the delegates gape in stunned silence, you and your father step forward, handcuffs jangling in your hands, to make a citizen arrest."

"No. Not by us. There's a Mountie that hasn't been corrupted, Commissioner Boulanger. He'll make the arrest."

"Are you serious about all this? Do you mean to tell me that the Prime Minister of Canada is about to be arrested?"

"Yes! That will be the news story of the century... but it depends on you."

"Wow!" Dick began pacing around the living room. "Is there no other way to expose him?"

"Dad has been trying for years but Bannerman is too clever. If we don't stop him now it will be too late. You heard him say what he is going to do. You've got to do it, Dick. You're our only hope. If you do this you'll be the hero that saved Canada."

"Now you are bullshitting me."

Donald wisely said nothing while he watched Dick pace back and forth.

Dick paused in front of a small wall mirror. He pushed a stray hair back into place then resumed his pacing. After what seemed for ever to Donald, Dick faced him. "Okay! I'll do it!"

Donald jumped up and hugged him, taking care not to mess Dick's hair. "Terrific! Dick, thank you."

"But I won't be able to splice it right away, those nosy bureaucrats from Ottawa check everything I do. I will have to do it at the last minute... maybe the night before... no, late afternoon before the Convention is better, after they've run through the film for the last time. Yep! That's when I'll do it."

"Good!... Dick, two more things."

"What's that?"

"Once you have the film running properly I want you to leave as fast as you can."

"Why?"

"In case things go wrong I want you out of there."

"You think it could be dangerous?"

"If things fall apart it could be very dangerous for you."

"Okay, I'll leave as soon as I'm sure there are no problems with the film... what's the other thing?"

"In case this film is destroyed, I want you to make a copy."

"No problem. Go and get yourself a beer while I run off a copy."

Sometime after Donald left Dick realized he had forgotten to ask about the mysterious Eduardo.

* * *

Richard refused to meet with Rico in Ottawa. It was far too risky. Rico had demanded a meeting the moment he passed through Montreal's Dorval Airport Customs. Over the phone he had warned Richard that he had a film with him, which if it ever became public, would destroy Richard. Rico offered to come to Richard's apartment very late at night but Richard vetoed that. Too many security guards wandering around that might start to wonder who was visiting the Solicitor General so late at night. Regardless of whatever Rico wanted to show him their meeting would have to be somewhere else. They agreed to meet at a cheap motel in Hull after midnight.

Richard parked his BMW five blocks from the motel in an alley he had used before. Coming out of the alley Richard checked up and down the street. Satisfied he had not been observed, he put on dark glasses, turned up his collar, and pulled down the peak of an old golfing cap, before walking briskly through the gloomy streets towards the motel. He hadn't wandered around this part of town for years, not since becoming a Cabinet Minister. He had almost forgotten the adrenaline rush this late night prowling gave him, the stronger pulse, springier stride, alert eyes and ears, chest thrust forward, and hands clenched ready to confront any danger; daring the hidden enemy to attack just like the old days during the war. He even remembered the motel and had hesitated going there in case the desk clerk recognized him, but Rico assured Richard he now owned the motel and the clerk had been replaced long ago. The street was empty except for an older 'lady' that initially approached, but quickly backed off when Richard emerged from the shadows. The younger prostitutes were not patrolling their turf. By now, no doubt earning their fees. A workman, returning home from a late shift, crossed the street rather than confront the sinister figure coming towards him.

Richard avoided the front entrance by walking around to the side of the building looking for room twenty one. Rico's station wagon was parked in front of it. Before he could knock on the door, it opened. Rico motioned Richard inside and locked the door behind him.

"How did you know I was standing there?"

"I had you shadowed to make sure nobody followed you. The desk clerk just phoned to say you had arrived."

Richard grunted, somewhat chastened he hadn't been as alert as he thought.

"So! What is this film I must see?"

Rico peered at Richard's outfit and chuckled. "You look like a gangster."

"Rico, it is one o'clock in the morning. Let's get on with it."

Rico moved a chair in front of the television. "Sit here, please."

Richard dumped his hat and glasses on the bed and moved the chair closer, leaning forward to watch the TV. Rico took a black cassette tape out of his briefcase and held it in front of Richard. "This is a film that contains enough images of you to put you in prison for the rest of your life... unfortunately it is a copy of an identical film that is in the hands of Craig Fox... if he is alive and is able to reach Canada your career is over."

"He is alive and in Canada."

"Where?"

"He arrived at the Toronto Airport this morning and promptly disappeared."

"You mean your famous Mounties lost him?"

"Rico! Do I get to watch the goddamn film or do I go home?"

Rico inserted the cassette into the Beta Max machine he had set up on the dresser next to the television. He turned on the TV and pressed 'play'. Suddenly Richard jerked forward, gasping,

"Jesus Christ!"

Unfolding before his eyes was a picture of himself sitting next to Florentino Chavez, the head of the Cali Cartel. This was followed by the appearance of Craig Fox and his son, Donald. Richard began to squirm in his seat at the picture of himself slurping down Scotch after Scotch, more and more inebriated as the film progressed. At one point Richard muttered, "You idiot! You've had enough!" But it was Richard's speech following Craig's departure from the room that made Richard explode. He leapt to his feet and lunged at Rico bellowing,

"You fucking bastard! I'll kill you for this!"

Rico jumped lightly onto the bed behind him, facing Richard knees bent legs apart, and a knife in his right hand. Richard glared at Rico and at the knife. Slowly he regained control. Turning back to the TV he was just in time to watch his exit with the gypsy boy. Richard slumped in the chair. Slowly Rico got off the bed. He turned off the Beta Max and TV.

"God Almighty! What the fuck do you guys think you were doing filming all this and giving a copy to Craig Fox?"

"We didn't give a copy to Craig. He stole it." Rico paused briefly. "Actually it was our driver who stole it and gave it to Craig."

"How did your driver get hold of it?... and why would he give it to Craig instead of selling it?"

"Tino told me later that the driver and Craig were boyhood friends. The driver stole my copy of the tape from my briefcase. It was in the front seat of my limousine when I went into Bogota. He stole it when I wasn't looking."

"I find it hard to believe you would be so careless with this tape. It's dynamite if it ever gets out."

"I know, Richard, that's why you had to see it. Now you know how urgent it is that you find Craig and recover the film before he goes public."

"Craig is somewhere in the Toronto area. His picture is on TV and will be in the papers in the morning. Inspector Calder has his men out scouring the town for him and watching all the exits. We think it was his sister that picked him up at the airport. She returned to her house late tonight so we don't think she could have taken him very far."

"You'd better find him quickly or all our plans are wrecked."

"God damn you! I know that! It's all your stupid fault anyway... Rico, what the hell got into you and your uncle to make such a tape?"

"We have invested a lot of time and money in you, and when you become Prime Minister we don't want you to get ideas that you don't need us anymore."

This time Richard was quicker than Rico. While still in his chair his hands jerked forward and wrapped around Rico's wrists in a crushing grip before Rico could reach for his knife. Moving forward and up Richard forced Rico's hands behind his back as he stood. Bending over the smaller man he shoved his nose inches from Rico's.

"Nobody will be telling me what to do when I take over... nobody!... Not you. Not your uncle. Nobody! Is that understood? You and your gang will help me make the changes I am planning, and are there when I need you to take care of people that might not like what I am doing. In exchange I will make it easier for you to move your stuff into the States. Is that understood?"

"Ricardo, if you break my wrists I will kill you. Calm down. We have to work together or we are both lost... let go. I won't go for my knife."

Richard moved his left hand back until it was close to the hilt of the knife strapped to Rico's belt. He released Rico's wrist and jerked the knife out of the leather scabbard. He stepped back ready to repel any attack. Rico didn't move other than rubbing his wrists.

"Ricardo, I told you I wouldn't attack you, but don't ever do that again!"

Richard put the knife on the TV behind him and hit the 'eject' button on the Beta Max. Rico made no move to stop him. Richard put the tape in his breast pocket.

"I'll keep this thank, you very much."

Rico shrugged, "Florentino has the original. He can send me another copy by courier... there's more on that tape. You might enjoy watching it."

"Christ! What else?"

"Pictures of you and the boy in your bedroom."

"Does Craig have that too?"

"No, Craig doesn't have that part. Your bedroom scene is only on this film. A little more encouragement to follow orders."

"Fuck you! What did you do with the boy?"

"Florentino sent him back to Spain. You beat him up badly."

"Serves him right. He shouldn't have pulled a knife on me."

"You were hurting him. You really like that rough stuff, don't you?"

Richard changed the subject. "Did you recover the diaries from Roberta Masse?"

"Yes, I have them here in my car. I had no idea you were such a ruthless killer in your younger days."

"You read them?"

"Of course. I'll give them to you in the car."

"What did you do with her?"

"She and her cousin have disappeared. You don't need to know the details."

Richard was about to insist but quickly changed his mind. Other than being curious he really didn't care. "Rico, let's go. I have to warn our stations and papers against accepting anything from Craig... and I have to work out some damage control in case that bastard does manage to get that film shown."

* * *

Richard parked the BMW in his underground parking stall, threw the coat and cap into the back seat and took the elevator up to his apartment. The answering machine was flashing. He checked the number of messages. Fifteen. Richard had no doubt who were calling. Frantic Members hoping to be included in the Cabinet or in a cushy job on some committee. Over the last few days he had been bombarded by phone calls from anxious Members promising to vote for him at the Leadership Convention while dropping none too subtle hints on where they would like to sit. Some had even taken to waiting in his outer office in the hope they would be noticed. There were still some holdouts that supported the Prime Minister's candidate. If he couldn't bribe or blackmail them he would take care of them later.

Richard placed the tape on top of his Beta Max machine and walked over to the small teak bar at the other end of the living room. His mind on the danger that the cartel's blackmail threat presented, Richard reached into the cupboard, grabbed a bottle and poured a jigger of liquor into a goblet. He took a large gulp and was about to swallow it when he realized it was rum. Angrily he spate it out and flung the goblet across the room. The glass shattered against the far wall, above Barbara's favorite Audrey Fox painting. The rum splashed across the painting leaving a streak of dark brown liquid dripping over the water color. Richard had often wondered whether the artist was related to Craig Fox.

He leaned down, lifted the correct bottle, and poured a double jigger into another goblet. Holding the brandy in his left hand, Richard headed for the TV. He turned it on and inserted the tape in the Beta Max. He dropped into an easy chair and kicked off his shoes. He watched the screen while he sipped the brandy. Every once in a while he shook his head muttering to himself. When the tape was finished Richard wound it back, and ran it again... and again... and again. Finally, he switched off the two machines. Slowly sipping his brandy he stared at the blank screen. By the time the goblet was empty Richard had made up his mind... Rico and the cartel would have to be eliminated... not now while they were taking care of some of his dirty work, but later when the opposition had been destroyed. In the meantime he would make sure that Craig was neutralized.

Satisfied with his decision, Richard headed for the bedroom. He paused briefly in front of the answering machine, but decided the messages could wait until morning. The next morning he went to his office without checking them. If he had he would have known his wife, Barbara, had decided to come to Ottawa.

* * *

Rico was back in Montreal and fretting that he should have remained in the Ottawa area to keep an eye on Richard Bannerman.

"Lover boy! What's the matter?"

Rico pushed her away and slid out of bed, his rejection of her charms very much on display. Monica reached up for him hoping to generate a spark of interest but he brushed her hand away.

"Rico, what's the problem? Is it me?"

Rico shook his head, "No, I'm just not in the mood."

But it was more than that... Enrique Chavez was worried. Besides his confused feelings about his father, things were not as they should be between Bannerman and himself. Maybe they had pushed Bannerman too far by trying to control him with that film. It had shaken Richard up. Made him realize how much power they had over him. Rico couldn't quite put his finger on it but he was astute enough to know that something had changed. Maybe it was the slight change in tone of voice, or maybe the lack of communication, or the fact the cartel was having difficulty accessing funds from Star Corporation.

He was familiar enough with the Canadian Parliamentary system to know that Prime Ministers wielded enormous power. Canadians liked to think of themselves as a democracy even though the Prime Minister had the power to appoint or dismiss Ministers or whomsoever he wished. He appointed judges to the Supreme Court and Members of Parliament to the Senate; he controlled the military and the R.C.M.P., decided who represented the Party in each riding; and decided when to call an election. The only curb on his power was the law and his caucus, and he easily controlled the caucus by awarding plum positions to his supporters.

Richard Bannerman would be Prime Minister in forty eight hours. When Richard Bannerman became Prime Minister he could turn on the cartel. He could use the R.C.M.P. and the military to destroy their organization in Canada. He would know where to look for them. He could use the resources of Star Corporation to bribe, or offer huge rewards for information on the cartel. The more Enrique Chavez thought about it the more his concern increased, and the more certain he was that his whole organization, an organization that he had created and built, might be at risk. But what to do about it? Bannerman was crucial to the success of the whole operation. They had planned to put him in that spot to make sure the cartel was protected.

Enrique Chavez decided to discuss his problem with his uncle in Bogota. He checked his watch. It was still too early to call. He got back into bed.

Monica gurgled happily, "Oh! That's better, lover boy."

* * *

Richard Bannerman, too, was worried. At the moment it was not the cartel that concerned him. It was Barbara he was worried about. She had disappeared and he had a pretty good idea what had caused her disappearance. It was that fucking tape. He had forgotten to remove it and she must have played it and run away, shocked at what she had seen. When he had returned to the apartment after a late meeting, it was empty, all the lights on, and Barbara's overnight bag on the bedroom floor, open with her nightgown laid out neatly on the bed besides his pajamas. Remembering the tape he rushed into the living room. The TV was switched off but the Beta Max was still on, and the tape was wound almost to the end. He was certain he had not left the machine on and had rewound the tape when he finished looking at it the night before.

He sat up most of the night waiting for her to return. But by eight o'clock in the morning Richard conceded he had a serious problem. He had to find Barbara before she did something crazy and wrecked everything. She hadn't taken the tape with her but he couldn't have her turning up at the Convention making all sorts of accusations. 'Where could she have gone? if I was Barbara and had found out my husband had done something dreadful, what would I do, where would I go?'

Richard canceled the nine o'clock limousine, rescheduling it for eleven o'clock. For the next hour he sat at his desk with an open phone book. He dialed all their mutual friends in Ottawa but nobody had seen Barbara and were surprised to hear she was in Ottawa, as she usually let them know in advance when she was coming. He tried several friends in Toronto with negative results. He called the house in Toronto. The maid answered.

"Juanita, Is my wife, Barbara, there?"

"No Sir. She left for Ottawa yesterday morning."

Reluctantly he dialed Barbara's mother in Toronto. Mrs. Bourne-Smith and Richard Bannerman had not spoken to each other in years. She had opposed her daughter's marriage to Richard when she realized that he was only interested in her daughter because of the family name, and only attended the wedding to avoid giving the gossips something to crow about. Richard had tried all his wiles on her but she was not to be beguiled. She had also seen through his veneer of charm and was suspicious of what lay underneath. Mrs. Bourne-Smith resented having her daughter used as a trophy for Richard's political benefit. She had wanted grandchildren and when Richard refused to oblige, she never spoke to him again.

The maid answered the phone, then went off to call her mistress. A few minutes later she returned,

"Sir, Madam does not wish to speak to you."

"Blast her! Go and ask Mrs. Bourne-Smith if she has spoken to Barbara recently. Tell her Barbara has disappeared."

A few minutes later Richard was startled when Mrs. Bourne-Smith bellowed in his ear. "So! She has finally done it! Good for her. She should have left you years ago. Let me tell you, Mr. Richard Bannerman, that if Barbara does call me the last thing in this world that I would do is to call you!"

The phone at the other end slammed down before Richard had a chance to respond. He debated calling her back just to curse her but changed his mind.

"Fuck you! You old bitch!"

Richard debated phoning the hotels in Ottawa but quickly vetoed the thought. Too risky. Some nosy reporter would be sure to find out he was looking for his wife and would want to know why the soon to be anointed Prime Minister's wife had run away.

It was important to find Barbara... but how? He couldn't phone Inspector Calder. The Inspector would be shocked to learn Barbara had run away. He had no other choice, he would have to do it - call Rico and put up with his derisive laughter - but first he would have to decide what they would do with her when they found her.

* * *

Usually the neighbors didn't leave their cars parked on the street at night, nor did any own a black van. Valerie had noticed the van the previous evening when she returned from Honey Harbor and assumed it was making a delivery to the house down the street. But it was still there in the morning when she stepped out to pick up her copy of the Star. Immediately suspicious, she dug out Brian's binoculars from the back of the hall closet and walked upstairs to her studio. Through the studio window Valerie had a good view of the van. Several other cars were now parked on the street, some in front, and some behind the van. Focusing the binoculars she was able to look into the front passenger compartment and determine it was empty, but the side windows were blacked out or heavily tinted. Valerie returned to the kitchen and lit a cigarette. Sipping her luke warm coffee and taking slow puffs on the cigarette, Valerie tried to decide whether she was being watched, and whether she should warn the cottage... but the van appeared to be empty... maybe it had been abandoned... Maybe she should wait and keep an eye on it while she worked in her studio. Valerie took a final puff from the butt that was about to burn her fingers and dropped it into the empty coffee cup. It sizzled for a second before dissolving into a black smelly goo. Valerie opened the paper and promptly slammed it down on the table. Craig's picture took up nearly one quarter of the front page under the headline

FUGITIVE DRUG DEALER ELUDES POLICE
BELIEVED HIDING IN TORONTO
REWARD OFFERED FOR CAPTURE

She must phone Craig and warn him to stay out of sight. Valerie left the paper on the table and walked into the living room. Halfway to the phone she stopped, realizing that if the van outside was keeping watch over her, then most likely her phone was bugged. Annoyed her privacy was being invaded, Valerie wrapped her dressing gown more tightly around her waist and marched out the front door to confront whoever might be spying on her. There was nobody in the passenger compartment and all the doors were locked, including the rear access door. She tried peering in through the painted rear windows but could see nothing. Deciding the van was abandoned, Valerie was about to walk away when she thought she heard a noise from inside. Putting her ear to the metal side Valerie heard a faint hum, as if some electrical equipment was turned on. Angrily she pounded on the side of the van.

"I know there is somebody in there! Open Up! Open up!"

She banged on the side once more. "Open up, or I'll call the police!"

There was no response from inside, but the humming noise was still there. Valerie marched back into the house and ran upstairs. Standing well back from the studio window, she waited. A few minutes later, a man emerged from the rear of the van and hurried into the driver's seat. The van eased away from the curb and disappeared down the street. Valerie looked into the large mirror hanging on the wall and gave herself the thumbs up sign.

"Gotcha, you bastards."

By the time she had showered and dressed, Valerie realized she had made a mistake. Now they would bring in some other vehicle. She had exchanged the known for the unknown. At least she now knew she couldn't call Craig from the house. She would have to go to a pay phone.

* * *

Craig put the receiver back on the hook and turned to face the expectant faces arranged around the kitchen table.

"That was my sister, Valerie. The house is being watched. My picture is in the papers and a reward is being offered for me." Grinning, Craig moved back to his seat next to Commissioner Boulanger. "I wonder how much they think I'm worth?"

"Did she phone from the house?"

"No, Commissioner, she called from a pay phone."

"Good, but still risky. That call can be traced."

They had cleared away the breakfast dishes, and were just settling down at the kitchen table to organize their campaign against Richard Bannerman when the phone rang. The night before the Commissioner had refused to discuss plans while everybody was tired. Instead they were to meet after breakfast. Boulanger sat at the head of the table and arranged Craig and Audrey on his right, Robert and Donald on his left, Brian Shirley-Dale next to Donald, and Allan Sharp at the far end. By placing him at the bottom end of the table, Allan had no doubt he was being tactfully reminded he was still on probation.

The Commissioner waited until Craig was seated before beginning. "Gentlemen, I beg your pardon, Madame." The Commissioner bowed towards Audrey, "Madame... Gentlemen... I know some of you were surprised to see me arrive with Mr. Sharp. I will explain his presence later, but Mr. Sharp has been instrumental in helping me build a case against Mr. Richard Bannerman."

The Commissioner paused and took a sip from his coffee cup. He curled his lips in distaste and put the cup down. Audrey noticed and reached for the cup. She dumped the cold coffee in the sink and gave him a fresh cup.

"In two days Richard Bannerman will be elected Prime Minister of Canada... everybody here knows what that means, but it is important that we all appreciate how serious his election will be for our institutions and for the rule of law... Mr. Bannerman is very intelligent, charismatic, and very popular. Many people, and I was one of them, believe he is the one person that can provide good strong government, reverse our economic decline, and do something about the crime in this country... when he becomes Prime Minister... let us have no doubt, when he becomes Prime Minister, he will use his popularity to pass draconian laws in Parliament. Laws that no Member of Parliament will risk opposing. These laws will give him the authority to control all our institutions. The Armed Services, the Supreme Court, the Bank of Canada, the News Media, and the remaining departments of the R.C.M.P. that he does not already control. He will be a dictator! And everything that Canada stands for will be destroyed. It is bad enough for him to assume dictatorial powers, but we now know that he has been financed by the Colombian drug Cartel, and I have no doubt is controlled by them. The thought that the drug cartel could end up running Canada has kept me awake for many nights... we have to prevent this happening!"

The commissioner paused to take a drink of coffee. Craig glanced across the table at his sons. Robert was leaning forward, absorbing every word. Donald, on the other hand, was visibly restless, impatiently waiting for the opportunity to present his report on the contents of the Beta Max tape. The Commissioner put his cup down, nodding appreciatively to Audrey.

"Merci, Madame. My good friend, Craig," the Commissioner bowed slightly towards Craig, "convinced me that Bannerman was being funded by the drug cartel... I shouldn't say 'convinced', as a policeman I am skeptical by training. I checked Craig's allegations through other sources and they supported what he had told me... unfortunately we have been unable to confirm a direct link between the cartel and Bannerman, nor is there any paper trail in the company files showing Bannerman's control of the company, nor did Mr. Bannerman list Star Corporation as one of his assets when he became a Minister."

Marcel emptied his coffee cup, and shook his head at Audrey at her offer to refill it. Donald was squirming in his chair and was about to speak, but his father gave him a frown and a brief negative head shake.

"However Mr. Sharp is prepared to testify that Mr. Bannerman controls Star Corporation, and that he takes orders from Mr. Bannerman and nobody else, and as it is a criminal offense not to give full disclosure of all one's assets on becoming a Minister, we have something we can use against Mr. Bannerman." The Commissioner splayed his hands out apologetically, "I'm sorry, gentlemen, it is all we have been able to come up with, but..."

"Commissioner..." Donald ignored his father's scowl and placed the Beta Max tape on the table in front of him, "Commissioner, I have here a tape that will destroy Bannerman."

Surprised at the interruption, the Commissioner recovered quickly. He gave Donald a stern look, "Young man, from the expression on your father's face I suspect you have displeased him. However, please proceed."

"This tape was made by the drug cartel and records a meeting between Richard Bannerman and the head of the Cali drug cartel, Florentino Chavez."

"Mon Dieu! How did you get it?"

Hoping to mollify his father Donald motioned to Craig, "Dad, why don't you tell them? You know more about it than I do... because... because... Dad won't tell you, but I will... because I was drunk at the time."

"Donald, you weren't drunk. You were upset that they used you to lure me into their trap. We wouldn't have made it back without your help."

"Gentlemen, please. Tell us how you got the tape."

"Sorry, Commissioner. While Richard Bannerman was in Bogota attending the Drug Conference he had a meeting with Chavez at the man's compound outside of Bogota. The meeting was recorded on this Beta Max tape. The man that helped us escape gave a me a copy that he had made."

"Unbelievable! Have you viewed the tape?"

"No, but Donald has. Go ahead, Donald."

"It is absolutely fantastic! I wish you had a Beta Max here, it would blow you away!" Donald jumped up, tipping his chair over with a crash. He grabbed the chair and carried it over to the far side of the room, thrusting it to the floor beside the kitchen stove. "Robert give me your chair." Robert barely had time to get up before his chair was swished away from under him and carried over to the other side of the stove. "Okay, imagine this stove to be a fireplace. Sitting here on the right is Florentino Chavez, the head of the Cali drug cartel. Here on the left sits Richard Bannerman, the next Prime Minister of Canada... when I saw them together I was stunned. At the time I had no idea Bannerman was involved with the cartel... it's all on this tape. Bannerman gives a long speech outlining what he proposes to do as soon as he becomes Prime Minister, and you are absolutely right, Commissioner, he intends to ram The War Measures Act through Parliament .. the same Act Trudeau used in the 1970's... give himself dictatorial power, suspend the Constitution, declare Canada a Republic, abolish the Senate, and make himself President for life... but there's more, Bannerman talks about increasing drug shipments to the States through Canada!"

"Mon Dieu! This is incredible... incredible that a man as intelligent as Bannerman would allow himself to be trapped like that... but why would the cartel make such a dangerous film?"

Craig held up the tape for all to see. "Commissioner, this tape is a copy, they have the original. I'm sure they intended to threaten Bannerman with it should he refuse to follow orders. I have no doubt he has seen it by now and has been warned to obey them... also, he will have been told I have a copy, and must make sure to eliminate me before I can publish the tape."

The Commissioner thrust his clenched hands forward. "We've got him! We've got him! He is finished! We must show that tape to all the TV stations, the newspapers. We must make copies and send them to everybody."

"I am sorry, Marcel, Bannerman will stop most of the media from accepting the tape. He will claim it is a fake... Donald has come up with, what I think, is a brilliant plan. It can't fail... Donald, please explain it to us."

"For many years, my cousin has been organizing the lighting and sound system for rock concerts, conventions, and whatever else you can think of. He's one of the best in Canada... he got the contract for the Leadership Convention, and in addition has been asked to put together a film extolling the achievements of the next Prime Minister of Canada... pictures of his childhood, youth helping the poor in Colombia, newsreels of his exploits in the R.A.F. His whole history including his years in government. This film will be projected on a huge screen in front of the delegates just as Bannerman goes to the podium to give his speech... my cousin, Dick, has made a copy of our Beta Max tape and will splice it to the end of Bannerman's film... it will come on in the middle of Bannerman's speech... I can't wait to see the pandemonium when it comes on the screen."

The Commissioner leaned back in his chair and buried his chin on his chest, eyes closed. Unsure whether he was praying or planning, all eyes watched him. Donald was beginning to show signs of restlessness by the time the Commissioner lifted his chin and opened his eyes. He nodded his head to Donald.

"I agree with your father. It is brilliant! Well done, young man... I will be there, waiting in the wings, ready to move in and arrest him. I will have a long list of charges to read to him, including murder, attempted murder, and drug trafficking."

Craig spoke up, "Commissioner, we will all be standing beside you."

"Bien! I don't think there is anything more we can do between now and the day of the Convention." The Commissioner eyed each person around the table. "Good. In the meantime I suggest we stay here until Friday morning, the day of the Convention. It is the safest place, remote and isolated... the safest place as long as they don't trace the phone call your sister made."

"She said she made sure she wasn't followed."

"Maybe, but we have to assume she was followed and plan accordingly... Robert, any suggestions?"

Robert had said nothing throughout the meeting, sitting quietly in the background while his younger brother took center stage. Craig had been wondering how he could encourage his more modest son to contribute to the decisions they were making, and was pleased the Commissioner had noted Robert's tendency to fade into the background in Donald's presence and had asked the right question.

Robert sat up and leaned forward, the sparkle back in his blue eyes. "Brian, do you have a map of Georgian Bay showing the location of your island?"

Brian went into the living room and came back with a topographic map. He spread it out on the kitchen table in front of Robert. Donald stood up and leaned over the table. Craig gave him a fierce scowl. Donald sat down again.

Robert located the island on the map, pointing it out to the group. "The island is small, about a half mile across and three quarters of a mile long. You will note it is fairly heavily wooded... correct me if I'm wrong, Brian, but when we visited you when we were kids, there used to be a trail around the island close to the shore?"

"It's still there but a little overgrown."

"Good." Robert looked up at the Commissioner. "Sir, we have three boats. The big inboard-outboard that Brian uses for water skiing, the quarter horsepower outboard he uses for fishing, and the eighty horsepower outboard Dad rented in Honey Harbor. I would like to suggest we keep the small boat in front of the cottage, loosely tied to the dock, and hide one of the big boats in this little cove on the north side of the island, and the other big boat in this cove on the back side of the island... whoever is planning on attacking us will not be very familiar with the area, and most likely will approach the island along the channel in front of the cottage. This will allow us to escape in the two big boats... however, if they come from behind the island, one or two persons might get away in the small boat, and we have to hope they don't find both big boats."

"Très bien, Robert."

"Commissioner, it is essential that you and my father escape... you will want to be present at the Convention to arrest Bannerman, and my father will be killed if he is captured... I recommend you plan to take one of the large boats, and Dad you take the other one."

"No! No! I want you, and Donald, to take your mother in the big outboard. I'll take the small boat."

Craig's sons objected, simultaneously. "No! Dad!"

Pointing his finger at his father, Robert insisted, "Dad! You and Mom are going in the big outboard!"

The Commissioner interjected, "They are right, Craig. You have to take the big boat. I need you with me when I arrest Bannerman... you and Madame will go in the big boat... I, and Mr. Sharp will take the other one. Mr. Shirley-Dale you will come with me."

"Why do I have to go, Commissioner? I'm not involved. I'm not a threat to Bannerman."

"No, but you are a witness and they don't want any witnesses. You will come with me."

"Marcel. I'm sorry, I cannot agree to this arrangement. I will not leave my two sons behind."

"I don't intend to leave them behind, Craig. We will make a slight change to Robert's excellent plan. The small outboard is light enough for two men to lift... Robert and Donald will hide the boat in the trees down here at the south end... Mr. Shirley-Dale, do you have a camera?"

"Yes, but it is an old eight millimeter movie camera that I've owned for years."

"Does it have any film in it?"

"I'll check. If there is, it's very old. I haven't used the camera for several years."

"The risk of our being discovered is small, nevertheless we have to assume there will be an attack. I want Donald to film the attack from a good hiding place. I want the attackers identified and brought to justice when all this is over. Robert and Donald will remain hidden until it is safe for them to leave. They will not be exposed to any more risk than the rest of us. Craig, is this acceptable to you?"

Craig looked at Audrey. She hesitated for a few seconds, then nodded. "Yes, I guess it is necessary."

"Merci, Madame... gentlemen, make sure the gas tank in each boat is full. I will move the big boat to the north end. Craig, you take the rented boat to the backside. Robert, you and Donald hide the little boat... Mr. Sharp, Mr. Shirley-Dale, and I, will take turns patrolling along the trail to make sure we are not surprised from the rear... and the Fox family will keep an eye on the front channel... gentlemen, be prepared to move at a moment's notice if we are attacked."

* * *

Inspector Keith Calder was becoming impatient. He had been sitting in the Solicitor General's waiting room since eleven o'clock, watching the powerful parade through the anointed one's door to plead or demand a seat in the Cabinet. He looked at his watch for the umpteenth time. Less than ten minutes had expired since he last checked the time. It was now two minutes after one o'clock.

Usually, when the Right Honorable Minister summoned him and kept him waiting, Inspector Calder was not impatient. Just to be sitting in a room near the man he admired most in the whole world was enough. Richard had given him opportunities for advancement he knew he didn't deserve. He owed everything to the man in the other room. He should be glad to be there, he told himself, and not be so impatient.

Looking around the waiting room, Keith remembered the first time he had been summoned to the Ottawa office of the Solicitor General. It was exactly one week after Mr. Bannerman was appointed. Over the objections of the R.C.M.P. Commissioner, the Solicitor General promoted Staff Sergeant Calder to the senior rank of Inspector and instructed him to form a secret "Elite Force" reporting, through Inspector Calder, to the Solicitor General.

"I want you to recruit young men who are ambitious and who think because they are Mounties they can push people around; the ones disliked by the locals and by the other officers. They're the ones that thrive on the power of their uniform and will have no qualms about doing whatever we require."

The Solicitor General had explained the urgent need for such a Force... too many drug peddlers, criminals, and murderers, were getting off with light sentences, or being released by corrupt judges, who in many cases were being paid off by the drug cartel. There was too much crime and too few criminals going to jail. The Force would stand guard against crime.

Each Officer in this "Elite Force" would be nominally assigned to other detachments in towns and cities across the country, but when required, could be assembled by Inspector Calder. In addition each Officer was to gather information on important people in his community; their family status, including names of children, and mistresses; their business relationships, and financial data; plus any other information that would enable the Solicitor General's staff to develop a profile on that person. The Solicitor General would use this profile, when he became Prime Minister, to select outstanding Canadians to serve in his Government.

Inspector Calder assumed his "Elite Force" was the only one in existence, and was surprised when the Solicitor General informed him that Deputy Commissioner Boulanger was in charge of another undercover "Force" that had successfully penetrated the higher Canadian echelons of the Colombian drug cartel. When the Solicitor General became suspicious that Commissioner Boulanger had been corrupted by the cartel, he moved the Inspector into Boulanger's unit with instructions to watch the older man. Inspector Calder took over the squad when Boulanger was killed by the drug cartel, and quickly replaced most of the men with his own officers.

The Mounties assembling in Honey harbor belonged to the "Elite Force" Inspector Calder had selected and trained for the last two years; young ambitious men from poor families; preferably from broken homes. Men who were prepared to bend the rules to accomplish any mission assigned to them by the Right Honorable Richard Bannerman.

But today was not the day to be wasting his time reading old magazines, while his men were preparing to go out to Georgian Bay to capture Craig Fox. That guy had slipped through too many traps and there could be no more mistakes. Inspector Calder was determined to lead the attack team that was at this moment gathering in Honey Harbor. He, and he alone, would drag Craig Fox before Mr. Bannerman, then put the bastard into a secure prison, and throw the key away.

* * *

Richard was confident he had enough votes at the Convention to win the leadership of the Party, but just to be sure, he was soliciting Members that had not committed themselves. The Member of Parliament from Calgary Southwest was pleasantly surprised that the Solicitor General knew the name of his oldest daughter, and was inquiring if she did well at the Calgary horse jumping competition the previous weekend. The M.P. from Thornhill received a sympathetic pat on the back, when the Right Honorable Bannerman offered his condolences on the death of his son in a car accident. The M.P. from St. John's East Riding was shocked to learn that his secret affair was not so secret after all.

By one o'clock in the afternoon, Richard was satisfied. He had overwhelming support. The remaining delegates that refused to endorse him in spite of his effort to seduce, or bully them, were too few to matter. They could never muster enough votes to prevent his election. Ushering out the last M.P. Richard allowed a satisfied smile to spread over his face. Signaling over the man's shoulder, he motioned Inspector Calder to come into the room. Keith replaced an old magazine on the side table and entered the Solicitor General's office.

Richard pointed the Inspector in the direction of the sofa at the far end of the room and sat across from him in an easy chair. Richard leaned back to study the younger man for several minutes. The Inspector became increasingly restless. He straightened his tie, checked the shine on his shoes, and flicked imaginary dust from his jacket. He knew this was a ritual Richard inflicted on him to establish Richard's dominance over him but he could never get used to it. Keith made another effort to maintain eye contact, but those eyes burned right into his head, forcing him to drop his eyes. Finally Richard spoke. His voice was pleasant, friendly.

"Keith, it's good to see you again. We talk often on the phone, but how long is it since we last met?"

"Eight months, sir. On the third of March."

"Ah yes, I remember... you are looking well as usual."

Inspector Calder smiled, pleased at the compliment. But he knew it was not true. The strain of trying to fulfill the many demands placed on him by the Solicitor General was affecting his health. He didn't know how much longer he could carry on. He could only sleep at night with the help of sleeping pills. During the day he frequently took a Valium pill to calm his nerves. The promotion to Inspector had catapulted Keith Calder above his abilities and he knew it. Inspector Calder was close to a nervous breakdown. The brilliant red hair had faded to a dull brown, now streaked with gray on the temples; the eyes, once sparkling green, were dull, pouchy,with black circles underneath and crow's foot creases on each side. His posture was still erect but it was becoming an effort. All this would have been obvious to most men, but not to Richard. Richard had little interest in anybody other than himself.

"Have you been able to find out where Craig Fox has gone?"

"Yes sir."

"Please, call me Richard."

"Yes sir... Richard. We traced the call his sister made. It was to a cottage near Honey Harbor in Georgian Bay. The cottage is owned by Craig Fox's brother-in-law, Brian Shirley-Dale."

"That name is familiar."

"He used to be the Editor of the Star. He retired because of ill health some years ago."

"Ah yes, I remember him now. Go on."

"Unfortunately it is a party line and there are eight cottages on that one line, so we had some difficulty determining which cottage belonged to this Shirley-Dale."

"Why didn't you check with the land titles office?"

"We are doing that now, but because the cottage is in an isolated area, and because of concern Craig might move again, I decided to move in without waiting. My men should be in Honey Harbor by now and are waiting for me to join them... there's a helicopter waiting to take me there, and I can be there in less than one hour. I have two more helicopters and three fast boats organized."

"But you still don't know which cottage Craig is in?"

"Yes we do. One of my electronic experts is in Honey Harbor and has been listening in on that party line... somebody in one of the cottages keeps picking up his phone every time a call is made on that line. We are certain that person is monitoring all the calls on that line to make sure nobody is attacking them. Using our electronic equipment we have been able to determine which cottage is checking the calls."

"Good work, Keith. Now, listen carefully... the drug cartel is winning. They have to be stopped and we cannot allow them to defeat us. We have to be ruthless. I have found out through some of my secret sources that Craig Fox's illegitimate son is the head of the Colombian Cartel in Canada. His father, Craig, is part of that gang... he must not escape this time. He must be eliminated... burn the cottage and everybody in it. Position your men around the building and do not let anybody escape. Make sure the building and everything in it burns completely to remove any trace of them... you understand?"

"Yes sir."

"I mean it... burn everything!"

"Yes sir."

The Solicitor General stood up. The Inspector did likewise. Richard patted him on the back. "Good man, I won't keep you any longer... on your way. Good luck!"

The Inspector checked the impulse to salute. "Thank you, sir... Richard."

Richard Bannerman waited until the door closed behind the Inspector before returning to his desk to continue writing his acceptance speech.

* * *

- 16 -

The attack began at precisely three o'clock in the afternoon.

Craig was relaxing on the front verandah of the cottage... well, maybe not entirely relaxing. Taking the occasional sip from the bottle of beer in his left hand, he listened to Brian reminisce about his youth in Nova Scotia, while keeping an eye on the boats passing through the channel between Brian's island and the McPherson's island half a mile away. He caught the faint sound of the "Sluff... sluff... sluff" of helicopter rotors slapping through the air. He held up his hand to silence Brian. The slapping sound increased rapidly from the direction of Honey Harbour. Craig jumped up and ran towards the front door.

"Quick! Brian, inside!"

The moment Brian struggled through the door, Craig slammed it shut. Just in time. Three motor launches appeared from behind one of the islands and roared up the channel at high speed. Each boat held five men in steel helmets and bulky jackets. Three helicopters appeared above the island on the other side of the channel. The Commissioner heard the noise and came running out of the kitchen.

"Commissioner, I think we have company."

"Is everybody here?"

"Yes, except for Allan Sharp. He's patrolling the trail."

"Good! He will have heard the helicopters and know they are coming from the front. Everybody move to the kitchen and get ready to make a run for it out the back door. Try to keep the house between you and the helicopters."

Donald grabbed the movie camera from the top of the bookcase and joined the rush to the kitchen. Craig was about to open the back door when the distant rattle of automatic fire made them stop and look at each other, the same question etched on all their faces. They raced back to the living room to peer out the front window. The three boats were halfway up the sandy beach on the island across the channel. Men were leaping out of the boats and spreading out on each side of the McPherson's white two story house. One helicopter was hovering over the roof while the other two helicopters were circling and firing into the building. Donald propped the movie camera against the window sill and began filming. An elderly lady came rushing out of the front door. She was promptly mowed down by a burst from the helicopter above her.

Horrified, Brian blurted. "Oh my God! That's Mrs. McPherson!"

An elderly man came running out to bend over the body on the verandah. A second burst jerked him upright. He tottered a few steps before pitching headfirst down the front steps.

"Oh God! That's Jimmy! They've killed him too!"

The Commissioner barked, "They've hit the wrong house! We've no time to lose. Quick! Out the back door before they realize their mistake. Move!"

The Commissioner held the back door open and ushered them out, one by one. Silently they glided into the trees behind the cottage.

* * *

"Inspector, you're wanted on the radio."

Inspector Calder was leaning out over the open doorway of the helicopter, the AK-47 pointing down at the figure on the grass at the foot of the steps. Doubt was beginning to gnaw in his gut. Though it had been many years since he had seen Craig, he knew the body down there was not Craig Fox, and the woman he had just killed was too old to be Craig Fox's wife.

"Inspector! The dispatcher on the radio says it's urgent."

Dreading what he now knew he would hear, Inspector Calder reached forward and took the headphones from the pilot, "Calder here."

"Sir, do not attack that house! It's the wrong house! According to the Title Office your target is across the channel from you."

"Jesus fucking Christ! We've already hit the bloody house. Why the fuck didn't you call me sooner?"

"Sorry Sir, but they had trouble finding the title file as the name 'Shirley-Dale' is not hyphenated in the title records."

Inspector Calder flung the head phone at the pilot and ordered him to land on the lawn in front of the house. Before it landed he jumped out, and over the noise of the swishing rotors, screamed at the men gathering around the helicopter,

"It's the wrong house!" Pointing across the channel, he yelled, "It's that one! Corporal Lowe, take your squad over and hit that cottage."

"They will be long gone by now, sir."

"God damn you! I know that! Check inside... and search the area. They couldn't have gone far."

The Inspector reached in and motioned for the pilot to hand him the radio microphone. The pilot noticed the Inspector's hands were shaking, and the voice, ordering the two helicopters circling overhead to search the other island, was pitched higher than normal. The inspector handed back the microphone. He walked over to where the old man lay face up staring blankly up at the sky. Keith stared back, his eyes equally blank. His eyes were blank but his mind was not. Keith Calder had no doubt that this latest fiasco marked the end of his career. Mr. Bannerman would never forgive this blunder. He would be dismissed. His life would no longer have any purpose.

The Inspector was tempted to give the head a vicious kick with his boot. A sharp voice behind him stopped him.

"Sir! What are your orders?"

Keith shook his head and turned to face the man behind him. It was his sergeant, a disgusted scowl on his beet red face.

"Aah, Sergeant Ritchie... take these bodies inside the house and burn the place down... make it look as if they died in the fire."

"Yes sir, we'll take care of them... why don't you go over and help look for the fugitives?"

The Inspector nodded and climbed back into the helicopter, vaguely aware he was obeying orders instead of giving them.

* * *

Donald switched off the camera and was about to move further back into the trees, but a hissed warning from Robert froze him in his tracks.

"Don't move! There's a helicopter coming."

In case the glint of metal attracted undesirable attention Donald slowly covered the camera with his parka. As an extra precaution he tucked his chin on his chest. The helicopter moved slowly along the shore, pausing briefly overhead before moving on. Robert waited for a few minutes before signaling Donald to follow him. He glided swiftly through the trees quickly leaving Donald blundering behind. Robert's brown parka and woolen cap blended with the fall colors of the trees and in less than a minute Donald lost sight of his brother. He stopped unsure of the direction Robert had taken. He listened hoping to hear his brother. Voices in the distance were communicating by radio, but he heard nothing to tell him where Robert had gone. Silently cursing his brother, Donald moved forward again, more cautiously this time. He hadn't gone far when Robert stepped out from behind a tree holding a finger to his lips. He leaned forward to whisper in Donald's ear,

"They have found our boat."

Donald flung up his arms, exclaiming, "Shit! My rucksack was in the boat and the tape is in it."

"Not so loud. What the hell did you do that for?"

Donald shrugged, "It seemed like a good idea at the time. I thought I could dash for the boat and not be held up by a heavy rucksack. What do we do now?"

"We find a clump of trees and hide until it's dark, then swim to another island and hope we find a boat or canoe to steal."

"Did the others get away?"

"I didn't hear any shooting, so they must have."

"Thank Christ for that."

"Donald, get on your knees and crawl under that bush. I'll take this one... and keep quiet."

"Yes sir!"

* * *

Inspector Calder walked through the smashed door into the living room of the cottage. Inside he came to an abrupt stop, aghast. Constable Johnson was methodically ripping the room to pieces; pulling books off the bookcase that stretched all along one wall; flinging the books halfway across the room; pulling drawers out of an old oak desk and dumping papers, that only a moment before had been neatly filed, onto a growing pile on the floor. He bellowed at the young Mountie,

"Stop that, you bloody fool! Those papers might tell us where they went."

Startled, Johnson turned to face his superior an empty drawer in both hands, "Sorry sir, I thought you wanted the place burnt down."

"It's too late for that. Now we have to find them again. Start looking through all those papers."

"Yes sir."

The Inspector walked into the kitchen. The evidence was all there. The half empty bottle of beer on the sideboard; a beef sandwich on a plate in front of a partly pulled out chair, and a steaming pot of coffee on the stove. Proof of a recent departure. Inspector Calder picked up the sandwich. The bread was fresh. He checked the coffee pot. It was still hot, but somebody had taken the time to turn off the element. They didn't flee in panic. They must have moved out as soon as the firing began in accordance to some prearranged plan. It was an orderly withdrawal. That bastard, Craig Fox, must have been expecting us. 'Now I don't have a bloody clue where he's gone. What am I going to tell Mr. Bannerman?'

Corporal Lowe entered through the back door, startling the Inspector. For a moment they confronted each other, both AK-47's aimed and ready to fire.

"Christ! Corporal, I nearly shot you. Did you find anything?"

"There's no sign of them. I don't think there was anybody here, sir."

"Oh, they were here all right. That coffee pot is hot. They couldn't have gone very far. Get some more men from Sergeant Ritchie and make a thorough search."

"Yes sir."

After the corporal left, Keith Calder pulled out a kitchen chair. He slumped into it exhausted. He leaned forward cupping his chin in both hands, fingers over his ears, elbows on the table, his mind unable to break out of the dark gray mist beginning to swirl around inside his head. Constable Johnson was shuffling through the papers on the floor in the living room when he heard the sound. Unsure what it was he paused and listened. There was silence for a few seconds then he heard it again. It was coming from the kitchen. Quietly he tiptoed to the kitchen door and listened again. It was the Inspector moaning! His superior was hunched over the kitchen table swaying slowly back and forth. Every so often the Inspector gave a low moan. Concerned the Inspector might be having stomach cramps, Constable Johnson moved up behind the Inspector's chair. He hesitated touching his superior's shoulder in case it would be considered impertinent, but obviously the man was in pain. Johnson shook Inspector Calder's shoulder,

"Sir! Sir! Are you all right?"

There was no response. Johnson shook more vigorously. The Inspector's hands parted and the head jerked up, eyes staring wildly.

"What! What!... oh! It's you Johnson. Did you find something?"

"No Sir, I thought you were ill."

"Of course not! I was just resting."

"But you were moaning."

"Don't be ridiculous... maybe snoring. I've been up for over twenty four hours. But moaning? Never!... here, have this sandwich and a cup of coffee. The coffee is still warm."

"Thank you, sir."

Johnson used the chair the Inspector vacated. Eating the sandwich he kept his head down except for surreptitious glances at his superior. The Inspector walked unsteadily through the back door. Outside, he placed one hand on a pillar as if to support himself and rubbed the back of his neck with the other hand. He straightened his shoulders and was about to walk off, out of sight, when Corporal Lowe appeared holding a rucksack in his hand. He shook his head in response to the Inspector's question.

"No sir, there's no sign of them, but I found this in one of their boats. We'll keep looking until it gets dark."

The corporal wandered off, leaving the Inspector holding the rucksack in one hand while he rubbed the back of his neck with the other. Constable

Johnson finished the sandwich and refilled his coffee cup. Before going back into the living room he glanced once more in the Inspector's direction. The Inspector was leaning against the pillar, head bowed, the rucksack dangling from his right hand.

* * *

Donald was losing patience with his older brother. Sure, there had been one scare, but that had been over two hours before when some lumbering boozo came thrashing by. Even in the fading light the man should have seen Donald's foot. He nearly stepped on it but was too busy venting his anger at some stupid corporal, who was keeping him out in the freezing cold looking for fugitives that were long gone. Donald too was cold, and getting colder. In fact if Robert didn't move out soon Donald's feet would begin to freeze. He had lost all feeling in them. The helicopters had left over an hour ago. Thrashing over them before heading in the direction of Honey Harbour. The speed boats followed soon after but Robert still refused to move. All they could hear was the soft rustle of leaves in the gentle breeze and the occasional crackle of burning logs from the McPherson's house. Donald rolled over and got up on his hands and knees. He reached up to a branch for support and slowly pulled himself upright.

"Jesus, I'm cold! Robert you can stay here and freeze your family jewels off but I'm moving on before I freeze mine."

"Okay! Okay! let's go. It should be safe now. I wanted to make sure they didn't leave anybody behind, but there's been no sound since they took off. Just in case, try not to thrash around too much."

But it was not possible to be quiet. The temperature had dropped well below freezing and each step produced a crunching snapping sound of crushed leaves and breaking twigs. Progress was slow, and was even slower as Robert approached the cottage. At the edge of the forest he paused for several minutes. Satisfied he motioned Donald to follow him. The inside of the cottage was a shambles. There was just enough light from the night sky to reveal the extent of destruction; books and papers strewn all over the living room; mattresses and pillows ripped open, and the kitchen a mess with broken dishes littering the floor. Robert growled.

"I used to be proud to be a Mountie. Not any more. They didn't have to wreck the place. Those bastards are going to pay for all this."

"Robert, let's get some heat going before we freeze to death."

"No! It's too risky to put a fire on. We'll close the doors as best we can to keep out the draft and roll up in some blankets. In the morning I'll see if they left Brian's little boat behind."

Donald went out the back door to take a leak and stumbled over his rucksack. The Beta Max tape was not inside. He showed the empty rucksack to Robert.

"The tape is gone."

"That was a stupid thing to do leaving it in the boat."

"Actually it might be the break we need. If the R.C.M.P. look at the tape they should realize that they have been chasing the wrong man and that Bannerman is the man to arrest."

"Let's hope you're right."

* * *

Anton Kowalski was not a happy man. His authority was being eroded more and more by top management. Somebody in the Executive Suite upstairs was determining what could and could not be broadcast on the news. The TV news was often slanted to present a particular point of view, and it didn't take a genius to figure out what they were trying to do. Somebody up there was rooting for Richard Bannerman. The last commandment to come down from upstairs was the one that convinced him he should quit. 'He was to ignore any attempt by that fugitive, Craig Fox, to slander Richard Bannerman with fake films. He was to destroy immediately any material sent by Fox.' But, If he quit where could he go? Anton had received offers from a competing networks, but on checking into the offers decided it wasn't much better there either. Maybe he was just getting old... going through the male menopause. The long hours trying to put together interesting and provocative programs had wrecked his marriage and his health. The once tall muscular frame was collapsing; the shoulders rounded; an incipient pot belly from hunching over miles of film; gray sallow cheeks, and bifocal glasses, tinted yellow to hide bloodshot, strained, pouchy, eyes. He didn't like what he had to face in the mirror each morning. Why not quit and go back to Edmonton? Maybe he could get his old job back... back where he started this long frustrating journey.

Anton had never accepted C.B.C. Management's decision to brand Donald Fox "a drug cartel courier". He knew Donald better than that. He had argued vehemently against their decision to announce on the Six o'clock News hour that he was a "courier" and had shown them Donald's assignments for the last five years, pointing out that except for the one to Colombia, none involved traveling to South America. A courier would be expected to make frequent trips to pick up the drugs. Donald had never been down there except for the last trip. They nodded their heads as he ticked off each point, yet they went ahead anyway. Somebody at the top must have given the order. Anton was furious. Donald was his brightest foreign correspondent, difficult at times, unpredictable, but the young man let nothing stand in the way of getting a story. Where others hesitated Donald would plunge ahead and usually returned with something unusual. Anton also had his doubts about Donald's father's involvement with the cartel. Although his telephone conversation with Craig Fox had been very brief, Anton had been left with the favorable impression of an anxious father trying to contact his son to inform him his mother was ill. He certainly was not trying to contact Donald to deliver orders for drugs. Every time it was reported that Donald and his father had, yet again, eluded the police, Anton would thrust a clenched fist into the air and whoop "Go for it, Donald! You can beat'em!" Much to the annoyance of his superiors.

Anton had hoped that Donald would get in touch with him after Donald's escape from Colombia, but had heard nothing. When the contact was made it was not by telephone. Instead a small package was delivered to his office by a teenage boy who disappeared before Anton could question him. The package was addressed to him, marked "Personal" without any indication who the sender might be. Inside was a roll of eight millimeter film and a note from Donald,

"Anton,

I am enclosing a roll of film I shot yesterday. I developed it this morning.

Your morning news reported the death of an elderly couple in a fire at a cottage near Honey Harbour. This film shows exactly who set the fire. It was the R.C.M.P.! They murdered the elderly couple then set fire to the cottage to hide the evidence. They were after us but they hit the wrong cottage [we were across the channel and saw the whole thing]. I hope you get a chance to use this footage before the yo-yos upstairs shut you down. It should help to raise questions about our rogue police and the man to whom they report, Mr. Bannerman.

Whatever you do, my friend, do not miss the Convention.

And bring your cameras!

Ciao! D."

Anton put Donald's note and the film in his pocket and slipped down the back stairs to the cutting room on the floor below. He muttered a curse when he saw who was in the room. John McCabe, the reporter Anton Kowalski had been forced to send to Colombia when Donald disappeared, was busy cutting and splicing film for the One PM News. McCabe had been around for years and had built a respectable reputation interviewing guests, mostly women, on his morning talk show. His chubby pleasant features and gentle manners endeared him to the ladies, and to management, but he did not have the aggressive Gung-ho personality that makes a good reporter. Anton had resisted pressure to move McCabe to the Newsroom but agreed to send him to Colombia to replace Donald at the Drug Conference. He had made a hash of that assignment, and even Management had agreed McCabe should be moved if his performance didn't improve.

There was no eight millimeter projector on any of the work tables, nor on the shelves under the tables.

"John, do you know where I might find an eight millimeter projector?"

McCabe pointed to the storeroom at the far end of the room, "I saw one in there a couple of weeks ago."

It was there, covered in dust, but in good working order. Anton projected the film onto the white wall opposite the work table. A few minutes later, John McCabe was startled to hear whistles, exclamations, and a loud, "Christ! Look at that!" Unable to restrain his curiosity, he got off his stool and peered over Anton's shoulder, just in time to see a police officer leaning over two bodies.

"Who's that?"

The film zoomed in and focused on the Mountie's face just as he turned towards the camera. Anton shook his head in disbelief.

"I know that man! I've seen him before. He's the one that was promoted to Inspector by the Solicitor General over the objections of the then Commissioner... I've heard rumors he runs a secret squad reporting to Richard Bannerman... what the hell's his name? Caulfield... Caldwell... Calder, that's it, Keith Calder!"

In silence they watched the Mounties dump the bodies into the burning house. Muttering "How terrible! How terrible!" John returned to his stool. Anton rewound the film, an idea germinating in his head. When he finished rewinding he left the film in the machine ready for editing. He moved over behind John to check the splices of news John was putting together. It would later be transcribed into a video by the technical staff before news time. It was pretty routine stuff, heavily weighed towards human interest stories.

"John, that's pretty dull material you have there."

"Oh! You think so?"

"I do, John. Why don't you edit the film we just saw and put in some of the more exciting bits to give your presentation some pizzazz. It'll show the brass you have what it takes to be a good reporter."

"But it won't fit in with the rest of the news I am putting together."

"John, I've been meaning to talk to you about your work. Management is not too happy with you. They want to move you out of the newsroom because our ratings are falling off, but I've asked them to give you more time. If you add some of this stuff you will get the attention of the public right away."

"You think so?"

"John, I sure do. I sure do."

Feeling a little guilty, Arnold walked out of the room. At the door he motioned towards the door lock.

"John, Why don't you lock the door after I leave so nobody comes in here and steals your thunder?"

John's pleased expression made him feel even more guilty. On his way back to his office Anton debated quitting immediately... chuckling to himself, he made a decision.

"No way! I gotta stay to watch the fireworks."

* * *

It had been nagging him for several days, but it wasn't until the morning after their escape from Honey Harbour that Allan Sharp made up his mind he would have to phone home. So much had happened since his abduction by Commissioner Boulanger he hadn't realized it was exactly one week ago he had left home. It was not his wife he was concerned about; she was probably relieved to have him out of the house; it was his son. Michael was his only child; the only person he had ever loved; the only person that had ever loved him; at least until a few years ago, before Michael was lured into drugs. Now he was seldom home, and when he was, he avoided his father. Michael had stormed out of the house ten days before, after a confrontation with Allan, and had not returned. Allan was anxious to find out if Michael had come home. Brian Shirley-Dale, too, was concerned about Valerie. But the Commissioner opposed them calling home. He insisted they were so close to victory; so close after so many setbacks; just one day before Richard Bannerman's ambitions would be crushed forever, that it would be foolish to expose their group to any unnecessary risk.

In accordance with their prearranged plan, they had moved into the Penthouse Suite of The Camberley Club Hotel late the night before. The hotel was less than a block from the Executive Offices of Star Corporation, and was maintained by the Company for the benefit of any out of town Senior Executives visiting from subsidiary companies. Allan was the only person in Star Corporation authorized to book the Suite. He assured the Commissioner it was empty and the best place for them to hide. It contained two bedrooms, a large living room, and a well stocked kitchen with a large selection of canned food and other staples, enough to last for a couple of days, plus plenty of liquor and wine behind the bar in the living room. Audrey and Craig moved into the Master Suite. Brian and Allan agreed to use the other bedroom, but only after the Commissioner insisted he would sleep on the pullout sofa.

Marcel Boulanger waited until all had gone to bed before going to the bar and checking the wine selection. Nodding his approval, he chose a half bottle of red and decanted it into a glass jug. Placing the jug and a wine glass on the desk by the window, the Commissioner closed the drapes and sat down to prepare the charges against Bannerman. Later that night he opened another half bottle.

Craig and Audrey lay awake most of the night worrying about Robert and Donald. Twice during the night Craig went into the living room in a borrowed dressing gown, only to have the Commissioner shake his head. On his third visit, the Commissioner was asleep with his head on the desk, an empty jug and wine glass beside him, but no sign of the two boys. Craig did not disturb the Commissioner, covering him as much as he could with a blanket. In the morning, Brian, knowing the Commissioner often deferred to Craig, appealed to Craig for support on behalf of himself and Allan Sharp. It didn't take much to convince Craig. Hoping the boys might have gone to Valerie's house, Craig supported Brian's desire to phone home. Craig and the two men worked out a plan. The phone in the Suite was too risky to use, instead the calls would be made from pay phones some distance from the hotel. Allan and Brian would walk in opposite directions for ten minutes, locate a pay phone, and make their calls. Boulanger approved the plan with a small rider. They were to make their phone call at exactly the same time and talk for no longer than three minutes. The simultaneous calls would make it difficult to pinpoint the area where they were hiding.

"Gentlemen, there is still some risk you may be recognized, but in this huge city I think the risk is minimal... good luck!"

At ten o'clock they made their calls. Valerie was relieved to hear they were safe, but had no news of Robert or Donald. She made no attempt to ask where they were. Allan's wife, Sarah, did. She threw a screaming tantrum when he refused to tell her, accusing him of hiding a mistress. Allan held the phone away from his ear until she paused for breath. Afraid she might hang up on him he quickly interjected,

"Sarah, is Michael there?"

"Huh? Of course he is, stupid."

"Can I speak to him, please?"

A piercing shout in his ear reverberated through his head, "Michael! Pick up the phone, it's your Dad!"

Michael came on the line, "Dad?" Allan could hear Sarah breathing.

"Yes, Michael, it's me."

"Dad, please come home. I'm sorry about the other day. I didn't mean any of it. You've always been a wonderful Dad." Sarah snorted. "Mom! Please let me talk to Dad... Dad, I promise to get off the stuff. Please come home."

"Michael, I'll be home in a couple of days. Hang in there, son. It's not what your mother thinks, but I can't talk about it right now. You'll understand when I get home..."

Sarah interrupted, "A couple of days! You come home right now. There's somebody here that says she must speak to you."

"Who's that?"

"Barbara Bannerman."

"Barbara!"

"Yes. She arrived this morning in a terrible state. Wouldn't tell me what the problem is. Said she had to talk to you. Said you were the only person she could trust. I gave her a sleeping pill and put her to bed in your room. She's still asleep. So! you'd better come home, Mr. Sharp, and talk to your lady friend."

Something must have happened between Barbara and Richard. The only possible conclusion was that she had found out who her husband really was and was devastated. Allan knew if he went home it would jeopardize everything, but his son needed him, and his best friend was calling for his help. He would have to think this through. He checked his watch. He was well over the allotted three minutes.

"Sarah, I have to hang up now. I'll call again later today." The screaming continued until the receiver was back on the cradle.

On the way back to the hotel Allan struggled with the two competing obligations. Tugged first one way then another, he couldn't make up his mind which was more important, his loyalty to Barbara and his son, or his duty to help the Commissioner and Craig Fox. For one of the few times in his life, Allan was in a quandary. He deferred a decision until he could discuss his problem with the group.

Entering the Suite, Allan was pleased to see Donald and Robert had returned. Donald was helping himself to a beer from the bar, and Robert was at the other end of the room talking to his mother and father. Brian was back, browsing through the books in the bookcase next to the desk. Donald took his beer to the easy chair in front of the TV and switched it on. He turned down the volume to a murmur, and checked the different channels until he found the C.B.C. He knew the main news wouldn't come on until one o'clock but sometimes they interrupted programing to broadcast important developments.

The Commissioner was writing at the desk. He looked up when Allan entered and motioned him over. Allan dragged a dining room chair across the room and sat on the opposite side of the desk.

"Did you speak to your wife?"

Nodding, Allan made a face. "Yes. My son is home."

"Bien, so all is well?"

Allan shook his head. "No. My son is begging for me to come home. But there is one more thing. Barbara Bannerman is at my house and wants to talk to me."

"Is she a good friend of your wife?"

Allan laughed. "No. Sarah resents her and is jealous we are good friends... Barbara is very upset about something. I suspect she discovered something about Richard and doesn't know what to do about it. She must have found out he works with the cartel."

"You mean she didn't know?"

"No, she doesn't, or at least didn't know a couple of weeks ago when I last talked to her."

"You mean all the years they have been married he was able to keep her in the dark?"

"Yes. Incredible, isn't it?"

"Mr. Sharp, what would you like to do?"

"I want to see my son, and I want to talk to Barbara. We have been good friends for many years and now she has turned to me in her distress. I cannot let her down. But I realize my going home is very risky."

"Very! Mr. Sharp, if you have made up your mind to go I will not stop you. I doubt if we could physically stop you, but please consider the consequences for your companions here. Why don't we ask them, maybe we can all come up with a solution that minimizes the risk."

"Please. That's why I came back rather than going straight home."

Except for Audrey, there was no support for Allan going home. They shook their heads when the Commissioner explained the purpose of the meeting. Audrey was more sympathetic.

"Mr. Sharp..." She had never forgiven him for not supporting Craig during his libel trial years ago, and continued to address him formally, "Are you afraid your son will drift back into drugs if you don't go?"

"Yes, it is a possibility, although for the first time he has said he is prepared to try to give it up. I need to be there to support him."

"Couldn't your wife provide that support?"

Allan shook his head vigorously. "No! She's part of the problem."

"Would he leave the house if you asked him to come with you?"

By now all eyes were on Audrey. Craig was not sure where she was leading them with her questions, but knowing Audrey, he was beginning to worry.

"In his present mood I'm sure he would... why?"

"I think it is very important for him to have your support at this delicate time in his life. But if you go home you are sure to be captured and taken away from the house as soon as Bannerman hears you are back, which cancels the whole point of your going home. Your son has to come here, and bring Mrs. Bannerman with him."

The commissioner tried to frame his negative comments in language that respected her femininity. "Madam, what you have made is an excellent suggestion but the difficulty is giving him our address without revealing our location. We cannot give it to him over the telephone, nor can we send him a letter."

In spite of his respect for the Commissioner, Robert was irritated his superior Officer dismissed his mother's suggestion without more consideration. He spoke up for the first time, "Mother, you have obviously thought this through. Please tell us what you propose."

"Mr. Sharp's wife reported his disappearance to the police so it is reasonable to assume they expect her to call them if he returns... therefore I doubt the house is being watched, nor do I think they are monitoring incoming phone calls. But it may be too risky to make that assumption."

This time, the Commissioner was listening attentively, "Madam, please proceed."

"Mr. Sharp, why don't you, Robert and Donald, just drive up to the house without any warning and bring them back?"

Except for the background murmur of the TV, the room was silent, all eyes on Audrey. Donald clapped his hands together, startling everybody. "Bingo! That's great, Mom. Let's go!"

Craig's eyes glowed with pride. He got up and walked around behind Audrey's chair and folded his arms around her. He whispered in her ear, "You had me worried for a minute, now you've scared me. What other bold scheme are you going to come up with next?"

"Craig, it was so obvious that's what we had to do."

"You were the only one thinking clearly."

* * *

Allan drove past his house without slowing down. There were no suspicious cars parked in front of the house. The cars that were, he recognized as belonging to the neighbors. He continued to the end of the block and turned into the lane behind the houses. Allan stopped the car behind his house. Robert and Donald followed Allan as he entered the back yard and rushed towards the back door. Sarah threw tantrum when the three men came rushing in through the door. Barbara was sitting in the living room drinking tea with Sarah when they entered. Sarah started yelling. Allan ignored her, which infuriated her even more. He waved at Barbara and headed upstairs to Michael's room. A few minutes later he reappeared with a slim young man, more boy than man. Other than being the same height as his father, there was no resemblance between father and son. The pale almost translucent skin, soft blue eyes, and thin blond hair, were features that once might have belonged to Sarah. She was still yelling. Allan raised his voice.

"Sarah! For Christ sake, shut up! We are leaving, and taking Michael and Barbara with us."

"What! You're leaving? Where are you going?"

"Sorry, Sarah, I can't tell you. We'll be back in a few days."

"Well! Don't bother, just send Michael home. You can go to Hell!"

"Thank you."

From the kitchen window, Sarah watched them drive away along the back lane. She had a good idea where they were going. Allan often escaped to the Suite in the hotel after one of her screaming sessions. Even before the car disappeared down the lane, she picked up the phone to dial Richard Bannerman's number in Ottawa. She knew he would be interested in knowing where Allan had gone. She left a message on his answering machine.

* * *

Richard was not in a good mood, and he knew by the end of the day, after Question Period in the House of Commons, he would be in a far worse frame of mind.

Richard should have been serenely confident, but he was not. By tomorrow night he would be Prime Minister with his hands on all the levers of power. After all his hard work, all the hand shaking, back patting, and promises of patronage, he had the votes. It was a shoe-in. Tomorrow night Maple Leaf Gardens would witness his coronation. But at the moment there were a couple of unresolved issues that continued to sour his disposition. That bastard Craig Fox was still at large with an incriminating Beta Max tape, and Barbara's disappearance.

The longer Craig Fox is free the more worrisome he becomes. 'When, where, and how, is that bugger going to use that tape? There's sure to be some maverick editor, or TV station that won't be able to resist publishing parts of the tape in spite of my warnings... Craig's going to have to do something soon or after tomorrow night it'll be too late... but what will he do? Damn him! Damn Rico too!'

When Richard had called Rico about Barbara's disappearance, he hadn't been greeted with the expected derisive laughter. Instead Rico dumped a bucketful of profanities in his ear, including many Colombian ones Richard had not heard since he was a teenager. This was followed by derogatory remarks questioning Richard's qualifications for Canada's highest office. Richard lost his temper. The shouting match ended when both slammed down their receivers.

But now Richard didn't have anybody he could call to look for Barbara, other than Inspector Calder, and Inspector Calder was nowhere to be found. He was not at the office, nor at home.

* * *

The Inspector was home in his apartment, but not answering the phone, nor the occasional ringing of the security phone downstairs. He was trying to drink himself into a stupor to stave off the cold morbid thoughts closing in. The terrible dressing down he had endured from the Solicitor General had been unbearable. He could accept criticism from most superiors but not from the man he had dedicated his life to serving. The cruel slur on his character and on his competence had, on top of the failure of the Honey Harbour attack, and the sneers from his fellow Officers, destroyed whatever confidence he had left.

With Richard Bannerman's curses still ringing in his ears, Keith Calder had put the phone down and buried his head on his arms. Hours later somebody opened his office door, snickered, and closed it again. Pulling himself upright Keith left the office, keeping his composure under control until he was home. Inside the apartment he locked and bolted the door. He stumbled into the kitchen and reached for a bottle of vodka in the cupboard above the sink. He tried filling a tumbler by holding it in his left hand and pouring with his right but the vodka sloshed over his hand. Keith put the tumbler on the counter, held the bottle with both hands, and filled the glass to the brim. He swallowed half of the liquid in one long gulp. It seared his throat. He expelled a swoosh of air and leaned on the counter until he recovered his breath. He refilled the tumbler and took it and the bottle into the living room, dribbling vodka on the carpet. He swallowed another gulp before plunking the glass and bottle on the coffee table in front of the chesterfield. Keith unbuckled his belt and dropped belt, holster, and service revolver on the coffee table between a half empty tin of baked beans and a plate of dried potato salad he had purchased two days before from the deli around the corner. He stripped off his tie and dropped it on the floor before unbuttoning his tunic. He dropped it on the table. It landed with a dull "thunk". Keith took out a Beta Max tape from the side pocket. He examined it briefly, and unable to remember where he had acquired it, dropped it next to the tin of beans.

Keith slumped into the chesterfield. He leaned back and closed his eyes, but quickly opened them again. The images inside were more frightening than those outside. Another gulp of vodka didn't help. The dark tunnel spiraling down into the abyss still beckoned.

A fly settled on the dried potato salad, then flitted to the open can of beans. It landed on the edge and slowly working its way inside. Several minutes later it buzzed back to the potatoes. Keith followed its movements but made no effort to wave it away. The fly moved to the holster to begin cleaning its wings. Keith waved it away and picked up the holster. He slid the revolver half out of the holster, then quickly slid it back in. He hurled the the gun across the room. A low groan welled up.

"Oh God, no!"

About to take another drink of vodka, Keith's eyes moved beyond the glass in his hand. They focused on a framed certificate hanging on the wall above the television. Inside the frame, above the certificate, an R.C.M.P. sergeant stared solemnly down on him. The certificate had been awarded to him for outstanding valor for saving a baby and two year old child from a burning house. Sergeant Calder had plunged into the burning building and brought out the two year old only to be told by the screaming mother that her baby was still inside. With only a brief hesitation, Sergeant Calder had raced back into the flames, emerging, unscathed, with the baby in his arms. The certificate was presented to him by Richard Bannerman at a ceremony in Ottawa.

Keith put down the glass.

Clenching his teeth, Keith straightened his shoulders and stood up. He put the liquor back in the cupboard, dumped the tin of beans and potatoes in the garbage, picked up his tunic and tie, and brushed the tunic carefully before placing it in the bedroom closet. The tie he hung on the tie rack with his other service ties. His civilian ties were on a separate rack. Keith was a fastidious housekeeper, a bachelor, with no women in his life to distract him from his commitment to Richard Bannerman. Socks were separated by color and in different drawers. Same for undershirts and shorts. Shoes and boots were lined up precisely on a rack, again separated by color. Each morning he went through the ritual of making his bed according to regulations. The finished product was a masterpiece, and a source of great pride. Without a wrinkle, so smooth the bed cover appeared to have been ironed.

But not today. The bed was unmade and had not been straightened for several days even though Keith had slept in it most nights. Agitated at the sight of the rumpled bed, Keith fought the temptation to take another drink. He forced himself to go through the ritual of making the bed. This calmed his nerves. Finishing with his flat palm over the one remaining wrinkle, Keith moved to the kitchen and prepared a mug of instant coffee. The clock in the kitchen was one minute fast. It was not quite one o'clock. Keith carried the mug into the living room and switched on the television. He turned the knob to the C.B.C. channel and eased into the chesterfield. The One O'clock News came on with John McCabe anchoring.

* * *

Normally Richard Bannerman looked forward to Question Period. It had become the highlight of his parliamentary life. The place where he could skewer those that dared challenge him, reducing them to sputtering buffoons with his rapier retorts, sarcasm, and innuendo. Richard Bannerman on the floor of the House was a show that quickly filled the benches by MPs that had wandered off to escape a dull afternoon. The word would spread quickly that Richard had arrived. Members promptly abandoned coffee breaks to rush back into the House. Whenever he entered there was always an appreciative murmur. Richard's favorite target was the Leader of the Opposition, The Right Honorable Winston Connought, the Member from Calgary North. Winston Connought was a short tubby man, bald with a round cherubic face and pink cheeks that flared a bright red when angry or flustered, particularly by Richard's barbs. He dreaded Richard's appearances and often left the House if he knew Richard was coming.

Today Richard was not looking forward to the afternoon session. He had other things on his mind. He was too preoccupied to notice the sudden hush when he entered. He nodded briefly towards the Speaker of the House and took his seat on the Front Bench beside the Prime Minister. Trevor Goodrich was looking very uncomfortable and wishing he hadn't rushed back from Toronto to attend Parliament on his last day as Prime Minister. The Leader of the Opposition was asking too many embarrassing questions and he didn't know the answers.

For many months Trevor Goodrich had been asking himself why he had been foolish enough to think he should be Prime Minister. He had worked and schemed to get it, then discovered he was supposed to have vision to lead the country. But all he had wanted was to *be* Prime Minister, live at twenty four Sussex Drive, and go to International Conferences where he could hobnob with other world leaders. He had selected his Ministers for their loyalty rather than their competence. He received bad advice from them; dithered making decisions for as long as he could; and usually made the wrong ones. The stress had aged him prematurely. His hair was still brown, but too brown. The bags under his eyes had reappeared in spite of the facelift two years ago, and he avoided using his bifocals in public even though he could barely see without them. His four years in office had been disastrous for the country. The value of the Canadian Dollar had plummeted; inflation and interest rates were sky high, and polls put the Party's popularity below twenty percent. Two years ago, Trevor, facing a revolt in the Party, was forced to give Richard Bannerman a Cabinet position and appoint him Deputy Prime Minister. It had not been a cordial arrangement.

Trevor Goodrich may have been incompetent but he was no fool. He had realized very soon after Richard Bannerman became Solicitor General that Richard had powerful friends in the newspaper and television industry who were orchestrating a campaign to make him leader of the Party, and he could foresee a disaster for the country if Richard Bannerman became Prime Minister. For that reason he had delayed as long as possible his resignation hoping that somebody else would step forward. But the only potential candidates had unexpectedly resigned from Parliament leaving only Bannerman. When it became obvious Bannerman was intimidating potential candidates, Trevor approached the one man he was certain Bannerman could not touch, Andre Courcel, an old friend and a distinguished lawyer from Montreal. Courcel accepted, more to please his friend than out of any real interest in becoming Prime Minister. The big problem was that Courcel was unknown except within the legal profession. This problem was highlighted at the next Party caucus. Trevor was greeted with a chorus of "Who?" when he submitted Courcel's name as a candidate for the leadership of the Party.

To overcome this problem Trevor embarked on a secret campaign. He insisted on booking the Maple Leaf Gardens in Toronto over Richard's objections. Bannerman didn't see the need for such a large arena for the Party Convention that would be attended by a small number of delegates, and in any case it would be over in a couple of hours. But Trevor had plans that he hoped would derail Richard's nomination. He sneaked out of Ottawa and attended a series of meetings in Toronto, Windsor, and Winnipeg, with the Mayors of those cities and some of the smaller municipalities. He convinced them of the merits of supporting Andre Courcel; the danger to Canada if Bannerman became Prime Minister; and the urgent need to recruit new members to the Party. If they could send enough delegates to the Convention they might be able to defeat Bannerman. Trevor had returned to Ottawa satisfied he had the Mayors' support, but wished he hadn't bothered to come back to Ottawa to answer questions he couldn't answer.

Richard looked across to the Opposition Benches and was puzzled by Connought's behavior. The man was practically having apoplexy. He was bobbing up and down trying to attract the Speaker's attention, who at that moment happened to be talking to one of the young pages.

Richard leaned over and spoke to the Prime Minister, "What's Winston so worked up about?"

Trevor Goodrich's head swung around, "Christ man! Don't you know?"

"No, what's happened?"

"Haven't you been watching TV or reading the papers?"

"No, I've been too busy."

"Didn't your staff warn you?"

"No, I sent them to Toronto to prepare for the Convention tomorrow."

"Well, hold your breath, here it comes."

Just then the Leader of the Opposition managed to catch the eye of the Speaker, who nodded. Winston Connought bounced up waving a newspaper in his right hand. His cheeks were red.

"Mr. Speaker, will the Solicitor General explain to the House why he has authorized the R.C.M.P. to go on a rampage attacking old men and women, setting fire to houses, and dumping the bodies of this old couple into the flames?"

Richard growled into the Prime Minister's ear, "Why the hell didn't you warn me?"

"I assumed they were following your orders."

Richard ignored the sarcasm and glared across the aisle at Connought. The man was still standing, rocking backwards and forwards expectantly.

"Well? Is the Solicitor General going to respond?"

Richard rose. "Mr. Speaker, I wonder whether you would be so kind as to have one of your pages come over and escort the Right Honorable Leader of the Opposition to the men's room. He is bobbing up and down and appears to be in some distress."

A ripple of laughter washed around the room. Connought's cheeks flared brighter. He shook his fist at Richard. "God damn you! I don't need a piss! Answer the question."

The Speaker stood. "Order! Order! Sir, that is not acceptable language."

"But he hasn't answered the question."

"Mr. Speaker..." Richard smiled across the aisle, "I think this is the first time we have been privileged to see the Right Honorable Member with printed material in his hand. I wasn't aware he could read," laughter... "I congratulate him... If he did a little more reading he would be aware that we have been pursuing a notorious and slippery criminal by the name of Craig Fox, who heads up the drug cartel here in Canada. With the help of the cartel he has concocted a series of films that purport to show our Mounties in an unfavorable light. The news media had been warned about these films and I can only assume the film you saw was shown by some scandal-hungry station."

Connought smirked, chubby chin thrust forward, "It was on the one o'clock C.B.C. news. And the man in charge of this rampage was one of your men... Inspector Calder!"

"Mr. Speaker, I repeat this is one of Craig Fox's schemes. The man in the Inspector's uniform was not Inspector Calder. The Inspector was in my office yesterday morning. He couldn't be in two places at once, although that is a feat the Honorable Leader of the Opposition often accomplishes... physically here... mentally somewhere else."

Richard sat down amid laughter, a smile on his lips but not in his eyes. 'Okay you little bastard, I'll get you for this.'

Winston Connought saw the look and decided not to provoke the Solicitor General further. The Minister had a reputation for ruthlessness and Winston was not a man that went looking for trouble.

The Prime Minister warned Richard. "You may have won this round but don't think this is the end of it."

"After tomorrow, who cares?"

"You may not, but the country does."

Richard shrugged. He stood up and leaned over to whisper in the Prime Minister's ear, a tight smile on his lips,

"Hope your trip to Winnipeg was successful?"

The Prime Minister looked shocked. Richard nodded to the Speaker and left the House. He returned to his apartment for the last time to pick up the speech he would deliver at the Convention. Richard did not check his answering machine. If he had, it might have solved his two remaining problems; the whereabouts of Craig Fox and Barbara.

* * *

Florentino Chavez was not pleased with the way things were developing in Canada and he was beginning to believe that his nephew was the problem. Tino was becoming suspicious that his nephew was getting soft on Craig Fox, his father. The young man was devoting too much of his time to women and avoiding doing anything about Craig Fox.

The last phone call from Rico convinced Florentino. Right in the middle of Rico's explanation of his problems with Bannerman, Florentino heard a woman's voice pleading with Rico to come back to bed. Florentino exploded over the phone.

"Get that fucking woman out of your room, pronto!"

"Tino, she's leaving in a few minutes."

"I said get her out now!"

Florentino heard muffled voices and assumed Rico's hand was covering the phone. A few seconds later the hand was removed.

"She's gone... Tino, as I was saying, I think we went too far with that film. Bannerman is furious with us and I'm afraid he might try to eliminate us when he becomes Prime Minister."

"Well, you tell him that if he tries that we'll kill him and put somebody else in that position."

"Tino, this is Canada not Colombia. You couldn't do that here."

"Rico, it's about time you learned you can do anything if you have enough money. I'm sure if we offered big money to one of their politicians he would gladly do what ever we want. You tell Bannerman that he is not irreplaceable."

"Bueno, I'll speak to him at the Convention."

"Rico, what are you doing about Craig Fox?"

"Me! Nothing. The Mounties are supposed to be looking for him."

"Caramba hombre! You mean he is still out there with that film and you are not looking for him?"

"Bannerman said his Mounties would take care of him."

"Rico, stop screwing around with women and start looking for Craig. You are going soft on him because he is your father."

"No! No! He means nothing to me."

"Well, find him! Rico, tell me why Craig hasn't used that film?"

"Bannerman has warned the papers and TV stations about fake films."

"That film can't be faked. It shows Bannerman talking about what he is going to do. There has to be some reason why Craig Fox hasn't released the film. Why hasn't he shown it? What is he going to do with it? He has to use it before Bannerman is elected... when is the Convention?"

"Tomorrow."

"Tomorrow!"

"Si, tomorrow evening."

"So, Craig has to use that film before tomorrow night. Rico, you put your randy cock back in your pants and don't take it out again until you find Craig Fox and recover that film... and find out what is going on at that Convention. Bannerman thinks he is so smart and he has probably screwed up."

"Okay! Okay! Tino, I'll get going."

Rico lowered the phone gently. Monica was peering through the half open bathroom door. He motioned her back in and wiggled his hips from side to side, slapping his penis against his thighs. Monica squealed and made a beeline for him.

* * *

Florentino was certain, knowing Rico, that the girl was still in the room. He had caught the faint sound of a giggle before Rico lowered the phone. He kept listening but was reminded the connection was broken by a sharp buzzing in his ear. Tino slammed the phone down just as Teresa walked in carrying his lunch tray.

"I am going to kill that son of yours if he doesn't stop screwing every girl that smiles at him."

"It's all your fault. You're the one that arranged for him to go to your brothels when he was a boy. That's where he learned all those vices."

"He's just like his father, Craig."

"Tino, how many more times do I have to tell you, I seduced Craig when he was still a boy. Why don't you forget about him? He has never done you any harm."

"He raped you, that is why. I have to satisfy the family honor."

"What honor! Tino you have no honor... you cheat, you steal, you murder. You corrupt everything with your drugs. Don't talk to me about your honor."

"Don't bother me. I have to figure what to do in Canada. Your son spends too much time in bed with women and is not taking care of our business. He is supposed to find Craig and take back the film that your Eduardo stole."

At the mention of Eduardo's name, Teresa made no further comments. She busied herself pouring coffee for her brother. She was aware that Tino was still looking for Eduardo, and had tracked Eduardo's movements as far as Gachala. He had not been captured, of that she was sure. Otherwise Tino would have made certain she knew.

"Teresa, I am thinking of going to Canada."

"That's crazy! They won't give you a visa to enter and you don't speak English."

Tino dismissed her objection with a wave of his hand. "I don't need visas to go anywhere... I don't go through airports."

"When are you leaving?"

"This evening. I have to find out what is going to happen at this Convention."

"What's a convention?"

"Tomorrow night Bannerman will be elected President of Canada, and I want to make sure he understands he must obey me... maybe your lover, Craig, will be there too, and I will kill him like I promised. Now leave me alone, I have to think."

Teresa left the room, wondering how she could warn Enrique his uncle was on his way to Canada.

* * *

Miss Vera Butler, startled by a muffled thud against her living room wall, lost a stitch. The bump was so heavy the large landscape painting on the wall slithered off balance and was now tilted to the right. A few flecks of paint, scratched off the wall by the heavy lacquered frame, floated down to settle on the oak cabinet below. She put aside her knitting, eased her feet off her old leather footstool, and with a heavy grunt, got up to straighten the painting. She was no sooner comfortably back in her rocker, there was another thud against the wall, louder this time, with the same result. Miss Butler clucked in exasperation and heaved herself upright once more. Turning off the sound on the TV, Miss Butler removed her bifocals, wondering why that nice Mountie next door was home so early in the afternoon, and on a Thursday too. She pressed her left ear to the wall. Just then another thud bruised her ear. There was something going on in Inspector Calder's living room. Rubbing her sore ear, Miss Butler reached down and took out an old milk carton from the back of the bottom drawer in the cabinet. Both ends of the carton had been cut off. She put one end against the wall, and her bruised ear in the other end. That was her good ear. There was definitely something going on next door. More thuds, not so loud this time, but enough to echo in the carton and make her ear ring. Plus the sound of glass shattering and strange muffled noises she couldn't figure out.

It was unusual for Inspector Calder to be home so early. He was so punctual. She could set her watch by his departure in the mornings, and return at night, always alone. Miss Butler knew. She could see the length of the corridor through her peephole, and made it her business to know who and what was going on on her floor. Vera Butler also kept another carton hidden in the bedroom to listen to the young couple who shared bedroom walls with her. Inspector Calder never brought women nor friends home. He was frustratingly quiet in the evenings. Occasionally she could hear the television but it was never loud. Sometimes, with the help of the milk carton she could hear him speaking on the phone. The only words she could decipher was “Yes sir” or “No sir”. The rest was a low monotone.

But this afternoon there was certainly something wrong. Miss Butler decided to investigate. She kicked off her slippers, she would have been embarrassed to have Mr. Calder see them, put on a pair of sensible low heeled shoes and wrapped a shawl around her broad shoulders. She made sure the corridor was empty before venturing out. Leaving her door open in case she had to flee, Miss Butler tiptoed along the hall, and looking around once more, put her good ear against the Inspector’s door. She could hear bumps, thuds, and more glass shattering. She tried peeking through his peephole, but it was just a blur on the other side. Tentatively, Vera Butler lifted the knocker on the door. She hesitated. She had never knocked on a man’s door before. A thump against the door made her yelp and jerk her hand down, banging the knocker against the brass base. There was silence on the other side of the door for a few moments, then a bolt scraped back and the door opened abruptly. The Inspector stood before her, tears streaming down his cheeks, an agonized expression on his face. He thrust his left arm towards her,

“I couldn’t do It! Oh God, I couldn’t do it!”

A large green towel, soaked in blood, was wrapped around his wrist. A corner of the towel hung down, dripping blood on the floor. His shirt and pants were streaked with blood. Shocked, Miss Butler lurched backwards, hands clutched around her chin.

“It was on the TV! Miss Butler, did you see it? It was on TV! Oh God! I’ll never be able to face him now.”

The Inspector leaned towards her. Paralyzed with fear, Miss Butler clutched her shawl to her chest and pressed herself back against the wall of the corridor.

“Did you see me on TV?”

She shook her head vigorously. Placing her hands behind her against the wall she eased herself along the corridor. Gaining confidence with each step, Miss Butler walked backwards until she was sure he wasn’t following. She turned and hurried back to the safety of her door as fast as her ample girth would allow. She heard the Inspector’s door slam shut just before she reached her own. Miss Butler ran inside and bolted the door. Suddenly a terrible pain streaked through her chest. Desperately she lurched towards the nitroglycerin pump spray on the little table beside her rocker. The pain stabbed up into her neck and along one arm. Another sharp searing bolt hit her chest. Miss Vera Butler crumpled to the floor her right arm reaching for the pump spray, but it was too late.

* * *

Barbara Bannerman hesitated offering her hand to him. This was the man that had falsely accused her husband, Richard, of trying to kill him. The man that, according to Richard, was a notorious drug peddler. Two days ago she would have refused to shake his hand. Today she could, but nevertheless with some reluctance. Everything Richard had told her about Craig Fox couldn't be all lies. She knew Richard well, although apparently not well enough according to that horrible tape, to know he would not stoop to murder a fellow airman. The tall middle aged man with the brilliant blue eyes waited, head cocked slightly to one side, a tentative smile hovering on his face. She gritted her teeth and thrust out her hand. Craig grasped it in both his.

"Mrs. Bannerman, I know that recent events have been a terrible shock to you and I fully appreciate how difficult it must be for you to accept that I am not the monster portrayed by your husband. Please believe me, I am not part of the drug cartel."

Barbara removed her hand as soon as courtesy permitted. The abrupt motion was not lost on Audrey. She moved up beside Craig and introduced herself.

"Mrs. Bannerman, my name is Audrey Fox..."

Barbara's head started back in surprise, "Are you Audrey Fox the artist?"

"Yes, I am Audrey Fox."

Barbara recovered quickly, "I'm sorry, I just didn't connect you to Mr. Fox... I have admired your work and have a couple of your paintings at home."

"Thank you... Mrs. Bannerman, my husband is no monster, although like most men, can be difficult at times... Mr. Sharp, as you know, is one of your admirers and has told us a great deal about you. You are most welcome here. Don't let all these men intimidate you. They are quite harmless. Please let me introduce you... Michael you know... these two young men, Robert and Donald, are my sons. You met them on your way here. This gentleman is Brian Shirley-Dale. You two may have met before. Brian used to be the Editor of the Star before he retired." Barbara shook her head and offered her hand.

Marcel Boulanger had never met Barbara Bannerman before but had often seen her picture in the newspapers and on television where she seemed aloof with a trace of snobbishness. Marcel watched her movements with growing interest a strange uneasiness in his chest. A feeling he had not experienced since his wife had died. Mrs. Bannerman moved with the grace of an athlete, extending her hand with a firm handshake and giving a gentle movement of her head at each introduction, but there was a shyness there that probably explained her apparent aloofness in public. Her hair, brown with a few streaks of gray over her right ear, was pulled back in a loose bun; a strong chin, straight nose, and a sprinkling of freckles on her cheeks, visible under her tan, projected a strong character and glowing good health. She wore no jewelry. Her clothes were elegant but simple.

Marcel Boulanger stood well back quietly trying to signal Audrey not to introduce him, but she didn't notice the faint shake of his head as she maneuvered Mrs. Bannerman towards him, "And I'd like you to meet Deputy Commissioner Boulanger."

The Mountie standing before her was not in uniform but his bearing was military, square shoulders, salt and pepper hair cut short, a chiseled face, and steel blue eyes, which although gentle and warm now, she imagined could bore a hole through one if their owner was provoked. The name sounded familiar but she couldn't recall where she had heard it before. Barbara smiled and offered her hand. Her warmth sparkled in her eyes even though she was clearly puzzling over the name.

Marcel bowed, "Madam, I am honored." He wrapped his hand gently around hers. "It is a pleasure I have looked forward to for many years." Reluctantly he released her hand. He motioned to Allan Sharp. "Mrs. Bannerman, I understand you wish to speak privately with Mr. Sharp. Why don't you use the bedroom?"

Allan followed Barbara into the bedroom, closing the door behind him. Barbara confronted him. "What am I doing here with these people? Why did you bring me here?"

Startled at her uncharacteristic forcefulness, Allan spluttered, "But, but, Barbara I thought you were fleeing from Richard. All of us here are hiding from Richard. If he finds out we are here he will kill us all."

"Nonsense! He wouldn't do that... Allan, I'm not fleeing from Richard. I just wanted to talk to you and get your advice about something."

"Is it about Richard's involvement with the Colombian drug cartel?"

"How did you know?"

"Barbara, Richard has been helping the cartel for many years. Most of the financing for Star Corporation's acquisitions comes from the cartel. With his help the cartel is about to take over the country unless the people in the next room can stop him."

Barbara began pacing up and down in the narrow space between the twin beds. "You mean all that stuff he said on that horrible tape is true?"

"So you've seen the tape. Is that what upset you?"

Barbara sat down abruptly on the edge of one of the beds. She rubbed her hands together as if washing away dirt. "Oh God yes! I was hoping you would tell me it is a fake."

"No, Barbara, please believe me, it is not a fake. If Richard becomes Prime Minister tomorrow, he will do everything he said he would. We intend to prevent his election tomorrow."

"How?"

"I am sorry, Barbara, I... I don't know. Why don't you ask Commissioner Boulanger?"

"Boulanger? Boulanger? Now I remember, Richard mentioned his name recently."

"Richard arranged to have him killed by the cartel. He had his car blown up but Boulanger wasn't in the car."

Barbara looked skeptical. "Why in the world would Richard want to do that?"

"Because Boulanger wanted to investigate Star Corporation, and Richard was afraid he would connect the Company with the cartel."

Barbara shook her head. "Oh, Allan, I just don't know what to think anymore."

Allan sat down next to Barbara and put his arm around her shoulder. "It has been a terrible shock for you. I wish there had been some way for you to learn the truth without being jolted by that tape."

"Allan, I want to be alone. Could you please leave and tell them not to disturb me for awhile?"

"Sure, I'll have Audrey bring you some tea in about an hour."

"Thank you."

An hour later Audrey knocked on the bedroom door. There was no response. She knocked again and waited for a few moments before opening the door. The room was empty. So was the bathroom. Audrey hurried back into the living room.

"Did anybody see Mrs. Bannerman go out?"

They were all watching the news on TV except Brian Shirley Dale. He looked up from his book.

"Yes, she went out about twenty minutes ago."

"Brian! Nobody is supposed to leave. Did she say where she was going?"

"No, I heard a noise and saw her going out the door."

Commissioner Boulanger leapt out of his chair and hurried over to the front door. Allan followed him. Boulanger peered out into the hall. It was empty. He closed the door and turned back to face Allan.

"Mr. Sharp, please tell us what you and Mrs. Bannerman discussed?"

"She has seen the tape and is devastated by it. She has difficulty believing her husband is involved with the cartel."

"Did you reveal our plans?"

"Absolutely not! She wanted to know what we were planning. I told her I didn't know, and to ask you."

"But you did say we were planning something?"

The implication of his casual remark to Barbara dawning on him, Allan nodded grimly, "Yes! I said we were going to prevent his election tomorrow."

"Mr. Sharp, you know her well, do you think she will contact Richard Bannerman and warn him?"

"Commissioner, I really don't know. She is very upset and confused."

"If she does contact him it means they will have much tighter security." Commissioner Boulanger walked over to the TV and turned it off. He faced the group. "Ladies and gentlemen, we have a more important question right now... do you think Mrs. Bannerman will tell them where we are hiding?"

There was a long silence with all eyes on the Commissioner. Allan spoke first, "Commissioner, Mrs. Bannerman may warn Richard we are trying to stop his election. He is after all her husband. But I am absolutely certain she will not reveal our location. She knows I am hiding from Richard. We have been friends for many years. She won't betray me."

The Commissioner looked at each one in turn. One by one they nodded. "Bien, we stay here, but just to make sure we will take turns sitting in the lobby downstairs. If anybody suspicious enters the lobby phone here and we leave by the back stairs."

- 17 -

Inspector Keith Calder headed west on highway 401. His mood was bleak, determined. He left Montreal at midnight and drove all through the night. He set the car's cruise control five kilometers below the limit. He didn't want some young 'Gung Ho' Mountie pulling him over and alerting the Force to where he was headed. Inspector Calder was going to Toronto, grimly resolved to appear at the Leadership Convention to confront Richard Bannerman; the man he had admired; the man to whom he had dedicated his life; the man that had manipulated and deceived him; the man that had destroyed him; the man Inspector Calder was determined expose and crush... his own life was over, ruined by the man he would gladly have given his life for not twenty four hours before... Keith Calder's last act would be his redemption.

After his botched attempt to commit suicide, Keith had collapsed on the chesterfield oblivious to the shards of glass crunching against his buttocks. Exhausted and despondent, a long sigh escaped unnoticed from deep within his chest. Not only had he screwed up his efforts to capture Craig Fox, he had even failed to kill himself. To top it off, that nosy lady down the hall was sure to alert the police about his strange behavior and they would come pounding on his door any minute... but nothing happened. Nobody pounded on the door... exhausted, he slept.

When he woke it was dark outside. The green towel wrapped around his left hand was caked with dried blood and stuck to the front of his shirt. Keith gazed around the room slightly puzzled at the chaos around him. The remains of the framed certificate, the one he had treasured for so many years, hung at an angle held up by a nail, the glass shattered, the picture of the handsome Mountie ripped in two, with the bottom half on the floor on slivers of glass and bits of the frame. The deep dents all over the wall mystified him for a few moments until he remembered the cause. The empty liquor bottles scattered around the floor were the culprits.

The sleep refreshed him. Keith sat up and was immediately reminded he was sitting on broken glass. He stood, carefully removing the shards stuck to his buttocks. Slowly he began to unwind the towel from his wrist, pulling gently until the three slashes across his wrist were exposed. None were deep, too shallow to cut any tendons but deep enough to cause extensive bleeding. The bleeding had stopped, sealed by a crust of dried blood. Keith tiptoed across the room in his stocking feet avoiding the glass underfoot. He dumped his clothes in the bathtub, taped his wrist, showered and put on some old clothes. Back in the living room he began to clean up the mess he had created. On the coffee table under a dirty napkin he came across a Beta Max cassette. Keith held the cassette up to the light but there was no writing to indicate what it contained. He placed the cassette on top of his Beta Max and was about to resume cleaning the room. Instead, his curiosity sparked, Keith inserted the cassette in his Beta Max machine. He turned on the TV and adjusted the volume before activating the video.

Richard Bannerman appeared on the TV screen. Keith checked to see there was no glass on the chesterfield before he sat, preparing, once more, to enjoy watching his hero. Keith did not recognize the man sitting beside Bannerman and was dumbfounded when it became obvious who he was. He recognized Craig Fox when he was marched into the room but it was the last half hour of the tape that stunned him. Finally the tape stopped. The TV went blank. No sound. Just a blue color on the screen. Keith stared at it, his mind numb, frozen, in shock. In shock to learn his hero was a villain, a rogue, a traitor selling his country to the drug cartel. In shock that he, Inspector Calder, had been doing his best to help that man betray Canada. Upset to learn that the information gathered for Bannerman by Keith's secret squad was being used for blackmail, not as he had been led to believe, for the selection of qualified and morally upright citizens. Misled too, for being sent on a wild goose chase to capture Craig Fox that ended in the terrible fiasco that ruined his career. Craig Fox, who is now revealed to be innocent, the one man trying to stop Bannerman.

Later, he didn't know how much later, Inspector Calder came to a decision. There was no alternative. It was something he would have to do. It was the only way he could redeem himself.

"Yes! That's what I must do!"

Two hours later Inspector Calder left his apartment. He was wearing his best uniform, with his service holster and revolver strapped to his belt. The apartment was clean, no broken glass, no dirty dishes, nor rumpled bed. The dents in the wall were covered by a Canadian flag and by pictures from the bedroom. The incriminating Beta Max tape was on the TV under a letter addressed to the Commissioner of the R.C.M.P.... Inspector Calder did not plan to return to his apartment.

* * *

Fleeing from the suite at the Camberley Club Hotel, Barbara wandered around Toronto more confused than ever, unable to resolve in her mind what to believe; whether to believe the monstrous tape she had watched and Allan Sharp's confirmation of what it revealed about her husband; or believe the years of association with a man who, although he had never truly loved her, treated her with respect. A man she had always assumed to be honorable. Taking care to avoid locations where she might be recognized, Barbara sat in a park for part of the afternoon then checked into a motel in the evening, giving a false name and paying cash. She ordered a meal in the motel cafeteria but left after fiddling with the food. Unable to sleep Barbara watched TV and the news at midnight. The scene showing the Mounties killing an old couple horrified her and added to her mental turmoil. She was aware the R.C.M.P. reported to the Solicitor General, her husband. 'Did he authorize the murder of that old couple? If so, why?... surely not... the Mounties must have done it on their own... but if what's on that tape is correct then maybe Richard did authorize the attack'... Mentally and physically she thrashed back and forth... back and forth... on and on.

Barbara woke late. A bible lay open on her lap, the light was on and the sun was streaming in through a rip in the curtain. By the time she was fully awake Barbara knew what she had to do. She would go to the Convention but remain in the background, hopefully unrecognized. In need of suitable clothes, a hat and dark glasses, she dare not risk going home. Richard would be there and she didn't want to be influenced by his smooth explanation of the Beta Max tape. She had enough time and money to buy the clothes before the Convention. She would slip into the arena with the crowd, sit somewhere unobtrusive and wait until the voting was over. If Richard was elected Prime Minister it would prove that he is innocent and the tape was a concoction of his enemies. She would stand by his side. If he lost or was arrested, as Allan Sharp claimed he would be, Barbara would leave the Convention unrecognized.

* * *

The phone rang three times before the sound penetrated through Rico's slumbering brain. He reached over Monica's exposed breasts, turned on the light and checked the time. It was five o'clock. The phone rang once more. He lifted the receiver. Forgetting where he was, Rico spoke in Spanish.

"Rico aqui!"

"Rico, it's me, Teresa, your mother."

"Mama! What is it? Are you all right?"

"Si! Si! I'm fine. Your uncle, Florentino, left last night for Canada."

"Carajo! Why?"

"Enrique! This is your mother, don't use such language with me."

"Sorry, Mama. But why is he coming here?"

"He said you spend too much time sleeping with women and are letting things fall apart in Canada. He said something about going to a convention."

"Caramba! He'll ruin everything if he goes there. How is he going to get into the country?"

Monica's eyes popped open. "Rico, who's that?"

Angrily Rico clamped his hand over her mouth, but Teresa had heard.

"Rico, you have a girl there and that is exactly what your uncle is complaining about. Tino is very angry with you. Get rid of the girl before he comes."

"Si! Si! Mama, I will. Did he say how he will come here?"

"No, he wouldn't tell me. Said he doesn't go through airports."

"That means he's flying into one of our airstrips."

"Take care, Rico, he's very angry with you."

"I will, Mama. How did you get my phone number?"

"I went through Tino's desk after he left."

"Mama, gracias para todo."

"Adios, Hijo mio."

Twenty minutes later the phone rang again. Anticipating who the caller might be, Rico made sure Monica was in the bathroom before he answered. He warned her not to come out while he was on the phone.

"Hello?"

"Rico, it's me, Florentino."

"Tino, is there something wrong? Is Mama ill?"

"No! Rico, don't play games with me. Knowing my sister, I'm sure she has warned you I was on my way to Canada... So! I want to know why you are still in Montreal when you should be in Toronto?"

Rico decided it might be prudent not to mention his argument with Richard Bannerman nor Barbara Bannerman's disappearance. "I am catching the eight o'clock plane to Toronto."

"That's better. Where is the Convention, and what time will Bannerman be elected tonight?"

"The Convention is at Maple Leaf Gardens. The voting is supposed to be finished by seven o'clock."

"I will meet you there one hour before the voting. That is six o'clock."

"Si! Si! I'll be there. Where are you?"

"I am in Canada, that's all you need to know."

"How will you get there? You don't speak English?"

"I have somebody with me who does. An old girlfriend of yours."

"Who?"

Rico heard a mirthless chuckle at the other end just before he was disconnected. He replaced the receiver. Absentmindedly scratching an itch under his armpit, Rico rifled through his list of current and former girlfriends. The only one he knew, other than air hostesses, that spoke fluent English was Alicia de Quesada, the girl he had used to trap Donald Fox. 'But why is she with my uncle? How long has she been working for him? Has Tino been using her to spy on me while I thought she was working for me?'

"The bitch! I'll fix her!"

* * *

Alicia De Quesada was delighted to accept, not that she had any choice. When Florentino Chavez summons you obey. But on being told she was flying to Canada that night, and to meet him at the Bogota International airport no later than nine o'clock, Alicia made sure she was there with half an hour to spare. Tino noticed her early arrival and assumed she was keen to see his nephew, Enrique. But Rico was not the partner she had in mind for a romp. The evening with Donald Fox was etched into her mind and body and still caused her blood to rise the moment she allowed her thoughts to drift back. Alicia paid off the taxi driver. Entering the main terminal a voice stopped her in mid stride,

"Señorita Quesada?"

"Si!"

Alicia swung around. A young man in a leather flying jacket was standing behind her, eyeing her up and down. His look was cold, appraising. She took an instant dislike to him, not that he wasn't handsome, it was the calculating way he checked out her feminine features that irritated her. He beckoned her to follow and led the way to a limousine parked across the street. He held the back door open and with a firm grip on her arm, which she tried to shake off, pushed her inside. She nearly tripped over Florentino and another man. Florentino motioned to the jump seat in front of him. The limousine glided to the other end of the airport, slowing to a halt in front of a small twin engine jet plane. The pilot was waiting at the bottom of the steps. The driver opened the back door. Florentino pointed up the steps. Inside she chose a single seat near the front of the cabin, well away from the looks of the two young men who persisted in mentally stripping her.

Florentino sat across from her for a few minutes, long enough to make sure she understood what she was required to do, before moving to the back of the plane. Her instructions were brief. On their arrival in Canada she was to be his interpreter. She was to translate his orders into

English, accurately, emphasizing he understood enough English to be able to determine the accuracy of her translation. He didn't have to describe the punishment for failure, she already knew her family would suffer if he wasn't satisfied.

On the eight hour flight to Canada, Florentino made no reference to Donald nor to his father, but Alicia had read reports of their progress in the paper and was sure they had eluded the cartel and escaped to Canada. She prayed that somehow Donald would help her escape from the cartel's clutches.

Alicia had hoped that Florentino would be detained when they arrived at a Canadian airport, but instead of landing at an international airport, the plane bounced into a remote airstrip illuminated by a long row of flashlights. A large motorhome was parked besides the airstrip. The driver was a heavy set man, round faced, with two pigtails extending down his back to his waist. The motorhome carried Quebec license plates. Florentino disappeared into the bedroom at the back and the two men commandeered the seats in the living room. Alicia squeezed herself into a small cubicle and locked the sliding door. She didn't sleep long before sharp rapping on the sliding door dragged her awake.

"Florentino wants you. Get up!"

Alicia checked the little window by her head. It was still dark outside but she could see they were parked by a small convenience store. She unlocked the door and stood up, straightening her clothes. Florentino was sitting in the living room.

"Come with me." He held up a small sheet of paper. "I want you to call this number, and when you get through give me the phone. It is your boyfriend's number but you are not to talk to Rico."

Inside the store, a young man was sleeping with his head resting on his crossed arms. He raised his head at the sound of the door opening. Three men and a woman entered. The men were grim faced, menacing. The young man's left hand slid off the counter and moved slowly under the counter top until the hand contacted the emergency button that would summon the police. The men moved towards the coffee stand located against one wall. A pay phone hung next to the coffee machine. The woman came up to the counter smiling reassuringly. The young man didn't press the button.

"How do I make a long distance call?"

Her soft Spanish accent reassured him. "Where do you want to call?"

"This number." Alicia showed him the sheet of paper.

"Oh! That's a local Montreal number, Miss. Just put in a quarter in the machine and dial the number."

So this is Montreal. Alicia knew Donald didn't live in Montreal. He lived in Toronto. There was no point in trying to escape in Montreal. She would have to wait.

* * *

All was ready, desks, chairs, flags, lights, sound system... and balloons. The last item was the final touch that gave Dick the most pleasure. Thousands of multi colored balloons hovering high above the delegates, packed into four huge fishnets, all to be released after Richard Bannerman gave his acceptance speech. In preparation for the Convention, Dick had checked through some old films covering American conventions. He noticed the release of balloons at the climax of the convention always brought the delegates to a high pitch of excitement and a finality to the activities. Dick had insisted on the expense in spite of the objections from the man from Ottawa.

Dick was pleased with what they had accomplished in the limited time available, and so was his crew. The only one still fluttering around was the "Nervous Nelly" from the Solicitor General's office. The wretched man insisted on viewing the Bannerman tape again and again. Each time he sat at a different location, staring up at Richard Bannerman's huge image, making sure the great man could be seen from every seat. The crew stood to one side, arms folded, and depending on personalities, a range of expressions from contempt to amusement on their faces.

All except Dick. He was beginning to worry he wouldn't have time to add the drug cartel tape to the Bannerman tape before the place filled up with delegates, making it impossible to have the privacy he needed. The delegates were due to begin arriving in one half hour. One of the hockey players' locker rooms had been set up as the "Command Center" for operating the lighting and audio systems, for monitoring the TV coverage, and for the Beta Max equipment. There was enough privacy there for him to do the splicing, but it would have to be done before the delegates arrived and Dick's crew took up their monitoring positions.

The other piece of unfinished business was the whereabouts of the C.B.C. television crew. They were supposed to have all their equipment set up by now and they were not there, nor had they phoned to give their time of arrival. Fuming at their autocratic ways, Dick was about to call the C.B.C. when they marched in. With barely controlled anger Dick voiced his disapproval of their late arrival to the supervisor in charge. The man, obviously under some stress, gave him a sharp retort.

"What! Do you think the C.B.C. has nothing else to do but attend your bloody Convention. Young man, don't you watch television? All hell has broken out in the C.B.C. so we're lucky to be here at all. Anyway I've been told to expect some unusual developments tonight so we had to be here."

"Oh! Where did you hear that?"

"I have my sources... could you show me where we can set up our monitoring system?"

Dick led the way into the second locker room and pointed to where the C.B.C. crew could set up their equipment. He didn't want them interfering with his operation in the other locker room. The man's comment was unnerving. Dick had to find out what the man meant by "unusual developments". Leaning against a locker, hands worriedly jiggling coins in his pant's pocket, Dick watched the C.B.C. crew lay out their equipment... 'what "unusual developments" is he talking about? Did he mean the pandemonium that will envelope the place when I put on the drug cartel tape? if so, how had this leaked out... who else knows? Who told him?'... Dick would have to try to get some answers from the supervisor, but other than an occasional glance in Dick's direction the supervisor ignored him. Dick moved forward to help the man uncoil some cables.

"I hope I didn't sound unwelcome, It's just that nobody told me you would be delayed... my name is Dick, Dick Shirley-Dale."

"No problem." The man's hand shot forward. Dick responded. They shook hands. "Pleased to meet you. The name's Anton Kowalski."

"Oh! That explains it!"

"Explains what?"

"Yesterday morning I sent you a film my cousin, Donald Fox, asked me to deliver to you. He must have told you to expect something tonight."

"So you're his cousin... interesting... what's supposed to happen tonight other than the coronation of Richard Bannerman?"

The man was being cagey. Dick could be too. "I have no idea. Donald told me nothing. He just asked me to develop the film and forward it to you with his note... you know they are still looking for him and his Dad."

"I know. It's stupid. The Mounties should be looking elsewhere."

Although Dick was fairly certain to whom Anton was referring, and would have liked to get a different perspective on Bannerman, he didn't have time. He had to get that tape spliced. On his way to the "Control Room" in the other locker room Dick walked through the arena for a final check. He had arranged the desks in two sections with a wide fifteen foot aisle running between them the length of the arena. A few of the Bannerman delegates, Dick had no doubt who they were, with "Bannerman" splashed on the large placards waving over their heads, were filtering into the right hand section. Raised voices at the Carlton Street entrance alerted Dick to trouble brewing. He rushed down the wide aisle to the front lobby. He didn't have time to take his usual pause to admire his hockey heroes glaring down at the chaos developing under their stern black and white eyes, King Clancy,Turk Broda, Punch Imlach, Dave Keon, Dave Sittler, and Doug Gilmour, but he did give them a brief apologetic nod before going to the street entrance to find out what the shouting was about.

The security staff had been given a list of delegates authorized to attend the Convention. The lists were in alphabetical order but the delegates were not arriving in that order, and by the time Dick appeared the guards were being overwhelmed, frantically flipping pages while more and more irritated delegates piled up in front. Quietly, Dick touched each guard on the shoulder.

"Forget it, let them in."

One of them, the one doing his best to start a confrontation with an aggressive delegate, muttered, "Thank Christ somebody is taking charge here!"

The doors were opened wide and the mob pushed through. The Captain of the security guards came over shaking his head.

"Mr. Dale, you've allowed everybody in, now I can't guarantee the security here... I take no responsibility for what may happen."

"Jim, I understand your concern and nobody will blame you if anything goes wrong. It is Ottawa's fault. Instead of giving us a list Ottawa should have provided name tags for the delegates before they arrived. All I can expect you to do is break up any fight that might develop. Some of these people have a lot at stake and may get carried away."

"I'm still not happy. There's some sleazy looking characters coming in. They don't even look Canadian."

"All you can do is keep an eye on them."

The man turned away shaking his head, muttering to himself.

Wondering what a typical Canadian was supposed to look like Dick joined the crush pushing into the arena. Many of the new arrivals were not from the Bannerman faction. Hugging cardboard placards to their chests to protect them from being crushed they moved into the left hand section. Dick managed to read the name on one of the boards, "Andre Courcel". It was a name he'd never heard before... and from the whispered questions around him, many of the delegates had not heard of the man either. The surge of opposition delegates filling the left hand desks galvanized the Bannerman delegation. The organizers orchestrated a chant of "Richa-a-rd... Richa-a-rd." A few braver delegates in the other faction responded with tentative shouts of "Andre Courcel... Andre... Andre." But the effort to generate enthusiasm soon dissipated. It was very obvious somebody needed to take charge of that group, but Dick had no intention of getting involved.

"Nervous Nellie" was living up to his moniker. Dick caught a glimpse of him rushing back and forth in front of the opposition delegates. He was frantically waving them back, eyes practically popping out, mouth wide open, evidently shouting something that could not be heard over the din. Spotting Dick emerging from the crowd he rushed over. The hum inside the arena was becoming a roar and he had to shout to be heard.

"Who the hell are all these people?"

"You're the one who should know. I am responsible to makes sure everything works. Who is or is not a delegate is your responsibility."

"But, but, I was told there would be only a few delegates supporting Mr. Courcel... look at them! They're filling up the whole place. Mr. Bannerman will kill me when he comes in and sees this mob... Jesus! What am I going to do?"

Dick pointed to a familiar figure entering the arena. "There's the Prime Minister, the Right honorable Trevor Goodrich. Why don't you ask him?"

The man glanced towards the approaching Minister and took a few quick steps in the opposite direction as if preparing to run. He stopped, straightened his shoulders, wheeled around and marched resolutely past Dick towards the Prime Minister. But the Prime Minister was too busy shaking hands and introducing his protégé, Andre Courcel, to the delegates to pay attention to the man fidgeting beside him.

* * *

Late Friday afternoon the motorhome entered the outskirts of Toronto. The driver, not familiar with the city, stopped at a service station to fill up with gas and buy a city map. He dropped Florentino and Alicia a block away from the Maple Leaf Gardens. Florentino, a large black case in his right hand, kept a grip on Alicia's upper arm while he maneuvered her around the pedestrian traffic. The two men remained with the driver until he parked then rejoined Florentino and Alicia at the entrance to Maple Leaf Gardens.

The front lobby was full of frustrated delegates bunching up in front of security guards checking identification. Alicia's hopes began to rise. Florentino was not a registered delegate and might be prevented from entering, maybe arrested. Should she point him out to the guards then make a dash for freedom, but a quick glance at the two men beside

Florentino convinced her not to even think about it. They were standing behind Florentino, their cold eyes on her. A young man came into the lobby from the arena and whispered something to the security guards. The guards folded their sheets and waved everybody in.

Alicia followed Florentino into the arena. The two men positioned themselves close behind her. Florentino moved to one side away from the bunched up delegates slowly filtering into their seats and paused for a few minutes to assess the situation. He motioned with his head and eyes to an area high up in the near corner of the arena, a dark section close to the rafters unlit by the overhead lights. Moving slowly to avoid attracting attention they walked up an aisle between two banks of seats. On reaching the top row of seats Florentino turned to survey the arena below him. Unable to see the podium at the far end of the arena he moved slowly along behind the row of seats until the view of the podium was unobstructed.

* * *

Dick headed towards the ramp leading down to the locker room, the Control Room, where the Beta Max and other equipment had been set up, but looking around Dick realized he had run out of time. Somebody was tapping the microphones on the podium, the sound technicians, light technicians, spot operators, and cameramen, were already in position around the arena. By now the Stage Manager would be in the Control Room checking to make sure everything was in proper working order. The tapes would not be spliced together. Dick would have to think of an alternative.

On his way down to the Control Room, Dick passed a slim young man on his way up. The man smiled briefly.

"Hello, I was looking for the bathroom... I guess it isn't down here."

The man looked oriental but didn't speak like one. Dick pointed at the sign indicating the area was off limits to unauthorized persons before proceeding into the Control Room. The Stage Manager looked up from the control panel. Cocking his head towards the door he spoke.

"Who was that guy?"

"Who?"

"The young fellow that just left. He was asking a lot of questions about how all this stuff works and what each operator does."

"You mean that Asian guy I just passed in the hall? The one looking for the bathroom?"

"He wasn't looking for the loo while he was here. Didn't sound Chinese to me. I'd say he had a trace of a Spanish accent."

"Jack, you better keep your door closed and I'll put a 'Do not enter' sign on it."

Dick checked the clock above the control panel. It was time to unlock the back entrance. The R.C.M.P. Commissioner, Donald, and the others were due to arrive in a few minutes. According to the plan he and Donald had thrashed out, and which had been approved by the Commissioner, they would enter the building through the rear door and proceed to the rear of the arena, the large area blocked off behind the podium separated from the rest of the arena by the large Canadian flags. There they would wait until Bannerman was speaking at the podium, and the drug cartel film was unfolding on the big screen, before moving forward to arrest him.

A quick look at the equipment satisfied Dick all was well. He headed for the back door. But Dick still hadn't figured out how he was going to slip the drug cartel tape into the Beta Max machine without being observed.

* * *

Barbara Bannerman instructed the driver to drop her off on Church Street around the corner from the main Carlton Street entrance to Maple Leaf Gardens. She gave him a generous tip even though the man didn't bother to get out to open the door for her. He barely looked at her when she handed him the money. For a brief second she was tempted to pull his beard, but controlled her irritation and turned into Carlton Street, thinking 'I wish they would make an effort to assimilate'. She didn't consider herself a racist but on occasion worried about the effect all this immigration would have on "Canadian Culture". Not that she was entirely certain what that was.

Before approaching the front entrance to the arena Barbara adjusted the heavy wraparound sunglasses and brown wide brimmed hat. Brown was not her favorite color, blue was, but she had chosen a brown hat hoping it would add to her disguise. She rarely wore hats. Trying to decide whether she looked best with the hat at the back of her head, like "Mrs. Miniver", or better with the forward sophisticated look. She chose the sophisticated look and pulled the hat forward to hide her face as much as possible.

The front lobby was nearly empty except for several grumpy looking security guards and clumps of men, some arguing, some speaking in low voices. A guard unfolded his arms, hoisted himself up from a stool and ambled over to where Barbara was trying to decide what to do next.

"Madam, are you a delegate?"

"Ah-h, yes I am."

The guard spoke, his face puckering, relishing the bad news he was about to impart. "Sorry, Madam, the voting is over. The scrutineers are counting the votes right now... come I'll show you."

With a gentle hold on her arm, he led Barbara to the entrance of the arena and pointed to a table at the far end of the long wide aisle. The scrutineers, five men and a lady, were studiously ignoring the cheers and boos from the delegates while they checked and rechecked every slip of paper the lady extracted from a black box.

"They've been at it for over half an hour. I expect they'll be announcing the results pretty soon. Not that there's any doubt who's the winner." The guard gave a disdainful nod of his head towards the delegates on the left side of the aisle. "If you were going to vote for that French guy it wouldn't have made any difference. He didn't have a hope."

Barbara ignored him. Concerned that if she sat among the delegates supporting her husband she might be recognized, she deliberately choose to sit on the left hand side of the arena. She selected an empty desk in the middle of the last row. Carefully checking around Barbara was relieved to see that Richard had not arrived. The only familiar figure was the man clutching the microphone on the podium. She recognized him as one of Richard's bureaucrats from Ottawa. Every few seconds he would lean over to hiss something to the scrutineers below him then peer nervously at his wristwatch. This prompted her to look at hers. The time was ten minutes to seven. She guessed that something was supposed to happen on the hour.

Repeating her visual sweep of the arena Barbara noticed an R.C.M.P. Officer sitting next to the aisle, two rows in front of her. With her attention focused on the man on the podium Barbara initially ignored the Officer, but it gradually registered that she had seen him somewhere before. Glancing at him from time to time she was struck by his stiff posture, ramrod straight back and shoulders, arms stiffly by his side, elbows bent and hands clasped together. His head did not move nor did his eyes react to the noise around him They were locked forward. The only movement was the occasional twitch of his fingers, followed immediately by a tighter clasp of the hands.

The scrutineers handed their tally sheets to the lady who appeared to be in charge, at least Barbara assumed she was by her demeanor. The lady murmured something to them. Each man nodded agreement. The moment she stood and reached above her to hand over the results of the vote to the man at the microphone, the shouting and noise died out as if by command. Barbara heard the bureaucrat sputter "About time!", and saw him snatch the sheet out of her hand. The man rechecked his watch, so did Barbara. It was seven o'clock.

* * *

Florentino opened the black case he had been carrying. Alicia gasped. Inside, bedded in green felt, she could see the barrel of a rifle, a wooden butt, and what she took to be a telescope.

"Tino! What are you going to do with that?"

Florentino ignored her. He lifted the barrel and screwed it into the wooden butt. Next he used a small screwdriver to attach the telescope. This was followed by a black fluted piece he screwed into the front of the barrel. He pointed the rifle at a tiny figure of man standing at the podium and squinted through the telescope. Satisfied he addressed Alicia's question.

"I am going to kill your friend Donald Fox and his father Craig Fox. I am certain they will be here tonight. I will finish the job your boyfriend, Rico, didn't do... now, I want you to go down there and find Rico and bring him to me. He is supposed to be here. If he isn't I will kill him too."

Florentino reached over and squeezed her arm above the elbow. He was hurting her but she didn't dare to jerk her arm away.

"Alicia, remember your family, so do not do anything to hurt them. You understand?"

"Si! Si! Florentino, I understand."

Florentino released her. Alicia walked down to the floor of the arena rubbing her sore arm. Ten minutes later she was back. Rico was walking beside her.

"So! You are here."

"I've been here for over an hour checking everything."

"And what have you found?"

"They are counting the votes now."

"Did you give them any money?"

Rico shook his head in annoyance, "No! I didn't!" He was about to add, "You don't do that in Canada." Instead, knowing his uncle would argue about it, he said, "It wasn't necessary, Bannerman has won easily."

"Good. Now, as to the reason I am here. Where is Craig Fox, and what is he going to do with our tape?"

"I was just coming to that. Craig is not here and I don't think he will come."

"Por que no?"

"Why not? Because he's too smart. He knows the moment he appears he would be arrested or killed."

"Rico, so you think he's smart... I don't. I've said all along he is going to be here and that's why I am here."

Rico pointed towards the podium, "See that huge TV screen behind the podium. They have made a movie of Bannerman's life. As soon as he enters the arena it will be projected on that screen."

"So?"

"I have checked the room where the video equipment is located. That is where Bannerman's video is supposed to be played but I suspect that Craig has managed to substitute it for his."

"Is Craig in that room?"

"No! I told you he's not here. I checked the room and I've looked all around the arena. He is not here."

"But you think that Craig will, somehow, put our tape on instead of Bannerman's?"

"Yes, as soon as Bannerman enters the arena, I will be in that room to make sure the correct tape is run and hopeful recover the one that Craig had."

An announcement came bouncing off the rafters, "Ladies and Gentlemen! May I have your attention please... I would like to announce the results of the voting... five hundred and sixty three delegates voted for Mr. Andre Courcel..." Loud boos. "Sixteen hundred and eight votes for the Right Honorable Richard Bannerman... thirty five percent for Courcel, sixty five percent for Bannerman." Wild cheering and chants of "Richa-a-rd" echoed around the arena but were cut off on cue by a gesture from the podium.

"Ladies and Gentlemen... ladies and Gentlemen. Please welcome the next Prime Minister of Canada, the Right Honorable Richard Bannerman!"

"The screen behind the podium lit up, and faint sound of bagpipes began to wail over the arena. At that precise moment Richard entered.

"Rico! If you don't get moving, you are going to be too late."

"Si, I'm going. I need Alicia to keep watch so I'm not interrupted." Turning to retrace his steps Rico spotted the butt of a rifle on the floor under the seats. "What the hell! What is that doing here?"

"That is for killing your father."

Startled, Alicia exclaimed, "Your father?"

Enrique ignored her. He hissed at his uncle,"You're crazy! You'll wreck everything!"

"No I won't. I have a silencer on the rifle. Nobody will hear the shot and we will quietly slip away in the confusion... remember Craig is supposed to be a fugitive. When he appears they will think some policeman shot him. Rico, get moving before it is too late."

Rico hesitated. The look on his uncle's face convinced him. He ran down the aisle hoping he was right about his father's smarts. Alicia followed him.

* * *

Dick ran down the ramp leading to the locker room, unlocked the door and entered. The Stage Manager pointed to the Beta Max machine.

"Now?"

"Yes please, Jack. He is just about to enter the arena."

The Stage Manager pressed the "on" button. The black and white picture of a young boy appeared on the small monitor screen. Slowly he turned up the volume until the faint sound of bagpipes could be heard.

According to Donald's instructions, the moment the tape was on, Dick was to leave the building as quickly as possible. But that assumed he had been able to splice the cartel tape to the end of the Bannerman tape. He had not had time to do that. The cartel tape was sitting in locker number nine and the key was in his pocket. Now he would have to wait until Bannerman's tape finished before he could insert the cartel tape. But he needed privacy to do that.

"Jack."

"Yea?"

"Why don't you take a break? Go get yourself a cup of coffee. I'll look after things here until you come back. I know how all this stuff works."

"Thanks, Dick. I could do with a break... is twenty minutes okay with you?"

"Sure, I'll keep an eye on these monitors to make sure there's no foul up."

Dick waited until the door closed behind the Stage Manager before unlocking locker number nine. He put the drug cartel tape beside the Beta Max machine and sat down facing the Beta Max monitor. On the screen, Squadron Leader Bannerman was leaning against the wing of his Spitfire. The swastikas painted on the fuselage and the decorations on Bannerman's chest were prominently displayed. Dick estimated there was about three minutes left on the tape. According to the time table the Ottawa bureaucrat had given him, Bannerman should be standing on the podium by now, acknowledging the cheers from the floor. Dick checked the other monitors. Bannerman was on the podium. Dick was about to reach for the drug cartel tape when he heard the slight squeak of the door opening. Dick swiveled around.

* * *

Florentino Chavez was not about to concede that his eyesight was no longer sharp enough to recognize the man walking up towards the podium. He knew it was Bannerman but only because his entrance had been announced. Florentino picked up the rifle and leaned it across the back of the seat in front of him, closed his left eye and squinted through the telescope. With his left hand he adjusted the focus until Bannerman's head was sharply etched in the middle of the cross hairs. He would have to rely on the telescope to identify Craig Fox. When his honor had been satisfied he would leave. Florentino ordered one of the young men to get the motorhome and have the driver bring it to the front entrance.

* * *

Richard Bannerman paused for a full minute at the entrance to the arena, waiting for the cheering to taper off. When it didn't, he raised both hands gently motioning for silence. The cheering subsided immediately. The bagpipes were louder now. The huge screen behind the podium came alive, black and white images of a boy faded to color pictures of a young man. Slowly Richard proceeded down the center of the aisle smiling at delegates he recognized.

Barbara had to admit he was magnificent, charismatic, elegantly dressed in a blue gray single breasted suit that enhanced his tall athletic figure; the silvery gray hair glinted softly under the bright lights, and his tan was darker than she remembered. Barbara saw he was wearing the "Countess Maria" tie she had given him for his birthday. This precipitated a flood of tears and an urge to rush over to stand by his side.

Barbara glanced at the R.C.M.P. Officer. She noticed only because he had moved, even though it was just a movement of his head. But it was the expression on his face that held her attention. His eyes were on Richard as he approached, his face imploring, pleading for recognition. Richard's eyes swept over the Officer when he passed with only a slight flick of the eyebrows to indicate he had seen him. Richard continued along the aisle. The Officer resumed his rigid pose, eyes and face locked forward, but now Barbara could see moisture on his cheeks. The man was crying!

* * *

Trevor Goodrich and Andre Courcel sat in the front row waiting for the results of the vote. When it was announced Trevor Goodrich slumped in his seat. Leaning his elbows on the desk in front of him, he clasped his head between his hands. He had failed to stop Richard and knew he was partly responsible. If only he had organized the opposition weeks ago instead of leaving it so late. Trevor estimated that less than twenty five percent of the delegates were on the left side of the arena, yet Andre

Courcel was able to get thirty five percent of the vote. This indicated weak support for Richard Bannerman. Maybe he could have defeated Richard If he hadn't let things slide until it was too late.

Andre Courcel was not depressed. He was relieved. He had agreed to allow his friend Trevor to put his name on the ballot only because he was confident the popular Richard Bannerman would win easily. Andre was living in comfortable retirement in Montreal; enjoying life with his extended family, old friends, and a twice a week bridge game. Andre Courcel had no desire to be Prime Minister. But while the voting was in progress it gradually dawned on him that Bannerman was not as popular as he had thought and that the impossible might happen. When the results of the voting was announced Andre allowed the pent up air in his lungs to be exhaled with a loud sigh of relief.

Out of the corner of his eye Trevor saw Richard approaching up the aisle. He straightened his shoulders a fixed a smile on his face. A heavy hand squeezed his shoulder. Above the skirl of the bagpipes, a voice hissed in his ear.

"Good try, Trevor. I won't forget this."

Surprisingly, Richard's veiled threat lifted Trevor's spirits. Instead of being acclaimed Prime Minister without a convention he had forced Richard to hold a convention, and demonstrated that Richard did not have a hundred percent support. But Trevor had no doubt Richard would find a way to get his revenge.

Richard squeezed Trevor's shoulder once more, harder this time, before moving towards the podium.

* * *

Through a small gap between the Canadian flags, Robert and Donald watched Richard's victory promenade up the aisle. Off to the left something caught Donald's eye. He swiveled his eyes left to where a woman was standing in front of the entrance to the locker room where the Beta Max equipment was located. Even though her back was turned to him she looked vaguely familiar. When she turned he exclaimed.

"Christ! It can't be her!"

"Who's her?"

"Jesus! It is her. It's Alicia! What the hell is she doing here?"

"Donald, please. Who are you talking about?"

"I am talking about a young woman I met in Bogota, Alicia De Quesada, who happens to be working for the Colombian drug cartel."

"You mean the one that talked you into..."

Donald gave Robert a dirty look. "Yes, that one."

"Where is she?"

"There in front of the entrance to Dick's locker room."

"I see her. What's she so agitated about?"

Alicia was pacing back and forth, one second peering down the ramp towards the locker room, the next stretching up on her toes desperately looking for somebody over the heads of the delegates. Robert stepped back, closed the gap between the flags, and gestured for Donald to do the same.

"If she is here that means the drug cartel are here in the building. Come, the Commissioner should be told right away."

But an idea was growing in Donald's head. He grabbed Robert's sleeve. "Wait! Wait! Take another look. All the delegates have their eyes glued to that screen over our head and Bannerman is bending over to talk to the Prime minister Goodrich. Let's you and I go and talk to her. Nobody will notice us and maybe we can find out what they're up to."

"I think we should talk to the Commissioner first."

"Robert! For Christ sake! We've got to do it now! In a few moments it will be too late."

"Okay! Okay! You do it. I'll go and tell the Commissioner."

Robert headed back up to the tenth row bleachers where the others were waiting for his report.

Donald turned left and moved quickly along behind the flags. He stepped out from behind the curtain of flags. He walked, purposely towards Alicia, fighting the urge to turn his head to look for Bannerman. Her head was turned away from him, eyes focused beyond the heads of the delegates. Donald prayed she would turn her head enough to see him before he was too close, otherwise she might scream if he startled her. Fortunately she saw him while he was still some distance away. Her face flooded with relief. Frantically she motioned him towards her, one finger on her lips. Donald moved around in front of Alicia, making sure his back was to the arena. She grabbed his hand and pulled him closer.

"Oh Donald! Gracias a Dios! They said you and your father would be here for sure. I've been standing here for the last ten minutes hoping they were right and that you would see me."

"Alicia, what are you doing here?"

"I came with Florentino. He's up there," Pointing up to to dark corner near the roof of the arena, "He's waiting for your father to appear. He's going to kill you and your father."

"How?"

"He brought a gun and it's got a telescope."

"Christ!" Donald leaned over to whisper in her ear but loud cheering from the delegates forced him to shout, "Alicia, come, we've got to warn the others. Follow me."

Alicia pulled him back. Pointing down the ramp towards the locker room, she warned him, "Donald, Rico is down there." Alicia pointed up at the huge screen behind the podium. Donald looked up. Bannerman was now standing at the podium. Behind him on the screen, Squadron Leader Bannerman was leaning against his Spitfire, demonstrating with his hands how he shot down an ME109. "Rico wants to stop them showing that movie."

"Damn! Dick is still down there. Rico will kill him."

For a few precious moments Donald dithered. Knowing that the Commissioner and his Father could be just about ready to move forward to arrest Bannerman, they needed to be warned. But Dick was in danger too.

"Alicia! Listen carefully... behind those flags, my father, my mother, my brother, and a police officer is waiting to arrest that man standing on the podium. Walk over there." Pointing to the corner from which he had recently emerged, "Walk, don't run. Walk over there and warn them that Florentino is here with a rifle to kill my father. Will you do that please? They will protect you from the cartel."

Alicia nodded. She gave him one last lingering look before walking briskly towards the curtain of flags. Donald waited until she disappeared behind the flags. He ran down the ramp to the locker room.

* * *

With three quick steps, Richard was on the podium. Immediately the sound of bagpipes faded away. Richard glanced behind him up at the huge image of himself leaning against the wing of a Spitfire before moving forward to the lectern. Richard tapped the microphone in front of him. The two taps echoed around the arena breaking the hushed silence of the delegates. He reached into his breast pocket as if to extract his notes, but pushed whatever it was back into the breast pocket. Richard lifted his chin, surveyed his audience and gave them what Trevor called the "Famous Bannerman smile".

A scowl replaced the Bannerman smile. The delegates did not have their eyes on him, instead something above and behind him had diverted their attention. Richard swung around, to be confronted with the image of himself running backwards around the wing of the plane and leaping backwards into the cockpit. A titter behind him quickly swelled into roars of laughter. Furious, Richard bellowed into the microphone.

"Somebody turn that bloody thing off!"

Richard looked around, but his man from Ottawa was nowhere in sight, instead three men were emerging from behind the curtain of Canadian flags. Craig Fox and Allan Sharp were following another man he did not recognized immediately. The fact that the third man was not in uniform and was supposed to be dead took a little longer to register.

* * *

Unsure what the reaction from the delegates would be, the Commissioner had insisted Audrey and Robert remain behind, while he, Craig, and Allan Sharp moved out from behind the curtains to arrest Bannerman. The Commissioner was in civilian clothes and unarmed. The only weapon between the three of them was a small Swiss army knife that Craig habitually carried. It was hardly a weapon to be used to intimidate a group of delegates that had just elected their favorite Prime Minister. Nevertheless the Commissioner was supremely confident that the delegates would support the arrest once they had seen the film of Bannerman consorting with the drug cartel.

The Commissioner led the way through a gap between two flags, followed by Craig and Allan Sharp. The Commissioner took a quick look up at the screen behind him to reassure himself the drug film was on. He gasped. Craig jerked his head around and cursed under his breath. The drug film was not playing on the screen, instead Bannerman was jumping backwards into the cockpit of his plane. The arena was convulsed in laughter. There was no alternative but to proceed. The Commissioner moved forward.

* * *

Alicia moved behind the curtain of Canadian flags. For a few moments she paused allowing her eyes to adjust to the gloom behind the curtains. Half way up the bank of seats she spotted a man and a woman. They were looking at her. Quickly, and quietly, she moved along a row of upturned seats, and up to where they were sitting. Both stood as she approached. Robert recognized her as the woman Donald had pointed out.

"Mom, this is the lady Donald knows. The one that works for the cartel."

"Please, Señor, Sir. Donald sent me to warn you," Pointing to far corner high up in the arena, "There is a man up there with a gun waiting to kill Señor Fox and his son Donald."

Audrey gasped, "Oh my God! Oh my God! Craig just stepped out there. Robert, go and get him back. No! No! I'll go. He'll kill you too!"

Robert grabbed his mother around the waist and pushed her back into a seat. He kept both hands on her shoulders until she calmed down.

"Mom, Please... please stay here. I'm going! Miss, where's Donald?"

"He's gone after Rico... Enrique."

"Christ..." Robert nearly blurted. "He'll kill Donald!", but swallowed the words before he upset his mother further. Robert hesitated while he resolved a brief mental struggle. Donald would have to look after himself, Robert's first priority was to save his father. He motioned Alicia to sit beside his mother. With one more look to make sure Audrey remained seated, Robert ran down the steps of the aisle and jumped out onto the podium through the same gap in the flags his father had used. At that moment two quick shots echoed around the arena followed by a third. Multi colored balloons descended over him. Robert didn't hesitate, he ran towards the sound of the shots.

* * *

The door to the locker room was closed but Donald didn't hesitate. He threw his shoulder against the door. It slammed open nearly dumping him on the floor. Donald recovered his balance and was about to rush forward, but the sight of Rico's dagger at Dick's throat stopped him.

"Don't move, Donald, or this goes in."

Dick was in an office chair, Rico beside him, the knife in his right hand and his left hand behind him fiddling with the controls of the Beta Max. He had evidently done something to the machine and it was making a whirring sound. A quick glance at the monitor confirmed the machine was in reverse. Dick dripped blood from a small puncture on his throat. Rico nodded towards the wound.

"That happened when you smashed in the door."

"I thought you were supposed to have nerves of steel."

"Don't provoke me, Donald, or I will finish him off."

"What is it you people want?"

"We want our friend Bannerman to become Prime Minister."

"Then why did you stop that tape? It's all about what a great guy he is."

"Because I think you plan to show our cartel tape with it and that would have been, to put it mildly... unfortunate for our plans."

The cassette was in plain view, only inches from from the hand fiddling with the Beta Max controls. Unfortunately Donald's glance alerted Rico. Rico grabbed the cassette and stuck it in his pocket. Still holding the knife to Dick's throat, he wrapped the other hand around Dick's pigtail.

"OK Donald, I'm leaving now. Nobody gets hurt if you control that temper of yours. I'll release him once I'm through that door."

Rico pushed Dick towards the open door. Donald moved to one side close to where the Beta Max machine was still rewinding. Rico's eyes strayed from Donald to a second TV monitor. He stopped abruptly. Craig Fox was walking towards the podium!

"Caramba! He'll be killed!"

Rico hurled Dick to one side and ran out the door. He raced up the stairs three steps at a time, whispering an unaccustomed prayer, "Dios, for favor, no mi padre."

Donald took one look at the TV and he too uttered an unaccustomed prayer, "Oh Dear God! Please not Dad... please."

Realizing he couldn't possibly reach his father in time, Donald grabbed Dick, who was busy rearranging his hair, and pushed him towards the desk. "Dick, do something! What about all those balloons, can you release them?"

"But they are not supposed to be released until after he gives his acceptance speech."

"Jesus fucking Christ! Forget the fucking speech. My Dad is about to be killed!

Reluctantly Dick nodded towards the button at one end of the desk. Donald punched it and dashed for the door. Two shots in quick succession boomed out through a microphone on the desk. Another shot, muffled, followed some ten seconds later. Donald ran up the ramp towards the arena. Pandemonium confronted him. Men and women elbowing each other aside, frantically wading through thousands of multi colored balloons, trying to head for the exits.

* * *

Things were not going according to the script Richard had so meticulously crafted with his staff. At this precise moment he should have been delivering his acceptance speech to a hushed audience while a larger than life portrait of himself filled the screen behind him. Instead the audience was roaring with laughter at the ridiculous scene of Richard jumping backwards into his cockpit. The laughter faded when three men stepped onto the podium from between two Canadian flags. It was obvious from Richard Bannerman's behavior that the three men had not been expected. Instead he was gaping at the three intruders as if he had seen ghosts.

Richard recovered quickly and tried to turn the situation to his advantage. He moved away from the microphone to make sure he was not overheard by the audience.

"Commissioner Boulanger, I am pleased to see you are alive and well."

"No thanks to you, sir."

"Commissioner, I will ignore that impertinence." Pointing at Craig, he spoke in a louder voice, "Commissioner, arrest that man. He works for the drug cartel."

The Commissioner replied in a low voice. "Sorry sir. You know as well as I do that he is not the guilty one. You are the guilty one, and I have come to arrest you, sir."

"Don't be ridiculous!" The audience heard his retort and strained to hear more.

Inspector Calder recognized Commissioner Boulanger the moment he appeared on the podium. Concerned the Commissioner might thwart his plans, Keith Calder rose from his seat and walked rapidly up the center aisle towards the podium. When he approached, Richard noticed him for the first time and beckoned.

"Inspector Calder, come here quickly." Pointing again at Craig Fox, and speaking in a loud voice, he ordered, "Inspector Calder, this is the man you have been searching for. He is a criminal. He works for the drug cartel. I order you to arrest him, and if he resists arrest I authorize you to shoot him."

Inspector Calder stepped up onto the podium. Holding the holster strapped to his belt with his left hand he undid the cover with his right hand and extracted a pistol. He moved forward until he was standing beside Craig. He raised his right arm, but the gun was not pointed at Craig. It was pointing at Richard's chest. Angrily, Richard moved forward.

"You idiot! Don't point that bloody thing at me. Point it at him!"

Realizing Calder's finger was tightening on the trigger, Craig hurled himself against the inspector. Craig's shoulder smashed into the him while his right hand reached for the pistol. The impact triggered two shots from the inspector's gun and a series of pops as the bullets exploded dozens of balloons drifting down. Both men crashed to the floor of the podium. Frantically Craig tried to wrestle the pistol out of the inspector's hand, but the man seemed to have super human strength, gradually forcing the pistol into his own chest. Craig tried to thrust his thumb behind the trigger to prevent it being pulled. Suddenly a heavy person collapsed on Craig's back jarring his hand. The gun went off. The inspector murmured something unintelligible and relaxed his grip.

* * *

Florentino trained the telescope on the men on the podium. He identified Craig Fox. Quickly Florentino removed the safety catch, adjusted the butt of the rifle against his shoulder and squinted through the telescope. He was too late. Craig Fox was flinging himself against a man in uniform.

His nephew Rico came panting up the aisle. Holding up a cassette tape he yelled at Florentino. "I have the tape. You don't have to shoot. We can leave now."

"I came here to kill Craig Fox, then I will leave."

Florentino readjusted the rifle. Two shots from the podium echoed up to Florentino, followed by a third. Startled Florentino momentarily lost his concentration. He readjusted the butt of the rifle against his shoulder and squinted through the telescope once again aiming for the two figures on the floor, but a cloud of multi colored balloons obliterated his view. Florentino was about to take aim at where he estimated Craig to be and fire three three quick shots. Rico suddenly leaned against him just as he pulled the trigger. The bullet hit the back of a man's head spinning the head around. Florentino gasped. It was not Craig!

"Carajo! Hombre, look what you made me do. I will kill you for this."

Florentino swiveled the rifle around towards Rico, but Rico wrestled it out of his hands and threw the rifle behind a row of seats. "Caramba Florentino! Go before it is too late."

Florentino pointed a menacing finger at Rico before racing down the aisle to the floor of the arena. Rico and the guard ran down after him. More balloons floated down, hiding whatever was taking place on the podium. Florentino joined the frantic delegates fleeing the arena out of the Maple Leaf Gardens. The motorhome slowly filtered its way through the mob streaming out into the street. The door opened while it was still moving. Florentino climbed aboard. Rico ignored Florentino's beckoning hand and followed the crowd down the street.

* * *

Warm blood trickled down Craig's neck and splattered on the inspector's uniform beneath him. But it wasn't the inspector's blood. It was coming from whoever was lying on top of him. Craig tried to wriggle out from the heavy weight on him. Somebody removed the heavy weight. Craig heard an exclamation.

"Mon Dieu! Mon Dieu!"

Craig lifted himself off the still form of Inspector Calder. He sat up pushing away the balloons covering the face of the man lying next to him.

"Oh my God! How did that happen?"

Blood was flowing out of a bullet hole in Richard Bannerman's left temple.

Robert ran up, terrified at what he might find. He batted the balloons away revealing his father sitting on the floor, his neck and shoulder covered in blood.

"Dad! You've been..."

"No! No! It's his." Pointing to the lifeless body beside him.

Craig reached over and picked up the pistol lying on Inspector Calder's chest.

"Commissioner, that couldn't have come from this pistol. I am certain I was able to deflect the inspector's aim."

"Dad, Quickly get up and move behind the curtain. That bullet was meant for you. He'll try again."

"Who?"

"Florentino Chavez. He's up there with a high powered rifle."

"Christ!"

Craig stood just as Audrey, panicked by the shooting, rushed up. She gave a quick intake of breath before echoing Robert's words.

"Craig! You've... !"

"No, I'm fine."

The arena was now empty except for a small crush of delegates scrambling out the exit through the lobby. Three figures approaching the group on the podium, Barbara Bannerman, Trevor Goodrich, and Andre Courcel. The sound of police sirens could be heard wailing in the distance.

Robert tried to push his father towards a gap in the curtains, but Craig brushed him aside when he saw Barbara Bannerman approaching. She was walking hesitantly towards them knowing that something terrible must have happened. Richard was not standing among the group on the podium, and there were two bodies lying on the floor. She recognized the tie on one of the bodies. A loud anguished cry of "Richard!" followed. Barbara kneeled down and cradled Richard head in her arms. She wiped the blood from his face gently closing his eyelids. Looking up at Craig she cried,

"You brute! Why did you have to kill him?... why couldn't you just arrest him?"

Craig started to move forward to explain but the Commissioner held him back. He pointed to the body next to Bannerman.

"Mrs. Bannerman, Mr. Fox did not kill your husband. That man killed your husband. Mr. Fox tried to save your husband's life but he was too late."

Barbara straightened Richard's tie. She noticed a spot of blood on it and tried to rub it off. Tears streaming down her face she shook her head. "You didn't have to kill him."

Commissioner Boulanger put his arms around Barbara's shoulders. Gently he helped her to her feet.

"I am so sorry, Mrs. Bannerman. We had no intention of killing your husband. We were about to arrest him, not kill him."

The Commissioner motioned to Audrey. She led Barbara off the podium to a desk in the front row.

Donald and Dick came racing up the aisle, kicking balloons out of the way. They slowed down when they saw Craig standing next to Robert.

"Did anybody see Rico?"

Robert shook his head. "No."

"He got away with the tape."

"It doesn't matter any more." Robert tipped his head towards Richard's body, "He's dead."

"But that was the only proof we had he was involved."

Commissioner Boulanger held up his hand warning them to be silent. Trevor Goodrich and Andre Courcel were approaching.

"Commissioner Boulanger, I had been told by Richard Bannerman that you were dead and now it is him that is dead."

"Sir, at the time it was convenient for me to go underground."

"How was Mr. Bannerman killed?"

"We have to assume Inspector Calder had a nervous breakdown and decided to kill the man he had worked for all his life."

"Why in the world would he want to kill the man he idolized?"

"Sir, May I speak to you privately, please?"

The Commissioner disappeared behind the Canadian flags with the former Prime Minister and Andre Courcel. Robert watched their departure with a puzzled look on his face. He queried his father, making sure to keep his voice low enough not to be overheard by Barbara Bannerman,

"Why is the Commissioner insisting the Inspector killed him when he knows that's not true?"

"I don't know. I'm sure he must have a reason. Until we know the reason, I think we should stick to his version."

And that's the story they told Anton Kowalski when he asked. Anton was skeptical, but said nothing. He would review his tapes when he got back to the C.B.C. office. Unfortunately, the tapes showed nothing but multi colored balloons floating down, obscuring whatever took place on the podium.

* * *

Late that evening they assembled at the Star Corporation suite in the Camberley Club Hotel. The only persons missing were the Commissioner and Dick Shirley-Dale. Dick stayed behind to clean up the mess at the arena. The Commissioner had escorted Barbara to her home, and was then closeted with Trevor Goodrich for several hours. He sent word with Andre Courcel, who was on his way back to Montreal, that they were to wait for him in the Penthouse Suite. Craig removed his bloody clothes, showered, dressed in borrowed pajamas and dressing gown, and while waiting for the Commissioner, relaxed in an easy chair, a brandy in his right hand.

It was after midnight when the Commissioner entered. He looked very tired. Audrey poured him a glass of red wine. He bowed slightly before easing himself into the couch opposite Craig. The Commissioner sipped his wine quietly while he organized his thoughts.

"Trevor Goodrich has withdrawn his resignation and will be arranging a new Leadership Convention early next year."

"What about Andre Courcel?"

"He does not want to be Prime Minister."

Marcel Boulanger sipped some more wine.

"Thanks to Miss Alicia de Quesada's description we were able to set up a road block and stop the drug cartel motorhome."

Alicia leaned forward, but kept her hand on Donald's knee. "Señor Boulanger, Did you capture Florentino?"

Boulanger shook his head. "No, they opened fire so we had to respond... he is dead. The Indian survived and is cooperating."

"Gracias a Dios!"

Reluctantly Marcel continued with what he had to say. "The Prime Minister insists Richard Bannerman's connection to the drug cartel is not to be revealed under any circumstances."

Craig exploded, spilling the brandy on his dressing gown. "What! That is unacceptable! I demand that he be exposed!"

Both Robert and Donald jumped up. "No way! We want him brought to justice!"

The Commissioner held up his hand pleading for the chance to be heard. "Gentlemen, please allow me to explain. Initially I reacted as you have, but the Prime Minister convinced me that if it became public knowledge that one of the highest Ministers in Canada's Government, who had just been elected Prime Minister of Canada, was part of the drug cartel, it would destroy whatever is left of the public trust in our government."

"Marcel, I have enormous respect for you, but I cannot agree. For years I have fought this man, and now you are asking me to forgive and forget everything... I cannot accept that... and, Commissioner, I'm surprised you did."

Audrey moved behind Craig's chair, worried he might say something to insult the Commissioner. "Craig, I think the Commissioner is right. Over the past few years people have become increasingly upset with high taxes, high inflation, and increasing crime, and blame the government. The government needs the public's help. A scandal like this could demoralize the public."

Craig said nothing, but shook his head repeatedly. The Commissioner decided to wait a few more minutes before delivering the next blow. He finished his glass of wine, refilled it at the bar, and returned to his seat. He took a sip and put the glass on the table beside him.

"The Prime Minister wanted to give Bannerman a State Funeral." Before Craig could leap to his feet, the Commissioner held up both hands. "Wait! Wait! I said no, I could not accept that."

"Thank you, Marcel. I will never agree to that."

"That's what I told him. I said I would go public if he insisted on a State Funeral."

"Good!"

Marcel Boulanger took a deep breath. "I eventually agreed he could have a Military Funeral."

Craig, Robert, and Donald shook their heads, vigorously, "No! Never!"

Audrey interjected again. "Craig, why don't you go along with that. He was, after all, a decorated hero during the war and is entitled to a Military Funeral."

Craig whipped around, to face Audrey.

She persisted. "I am sorry, Craig. I know how much you have suffered, but surely we can give him that, if only for the sake of his wife."

Craig strode over to the bar to pour a large dollop of brandy in his snifter. Unwilling to concede, he tried once more. "Don't forget he has ruined my reputation. In case you've forgotten, the whole country has been told I am a dangerous criminal to be arrested or shot on sight... I am a fugitive, and Bannerman is to get a hero's funeral... Marcel, that is not justice."

"I agree, it is not. I pointed that out to the Prime Minister and he agrees. We had a long discussion. We have a proposal that will not only clear your name, but will also reward you for helping to expose the Canadian Cartel. At a special investiture next week you are to be awarded the 'Order of

Canada' by the Governor General in recognition of your undercover work posing as a member of the drug cartel. There will be announcements of the award on TV and in the papers with details of the work you have done over the years in helping to expose the drug cartel."

"But Marcel, you are the one who should be awarded that medal."

"I will be awarded the 'Order of Canada' at the same time. I told Trevor Goodrich I would not accept it unless you also received the award."

"What am I to do in return for receiving the medal?"

"You are to agree to the military funeral for Bannerman and never to reveal his connection to the cartel."

Craig looked at Audrey, she nodded. He looked at Robert, he nodded. He looked at Donald, Donald hesitated, then nodded.

"Commissioner, reluctantly I accept Bannerman can have his Military Funeral but don't expect me to attend."

"Thank you, Craig. I will pass that on to the Prime Minister."

"However, don't expect me to lie if I am asked."

"I accept that. Knowing you, I do not expect you to lie."

The Commissioner continued. "The Prime Minister has authorized a search warrant for the offices of Star Corporation. As it is owned by the cartel, the government will seize all the company's assets and sell them to the public. Mr. Allan Sharp, I hope you will assist us to identify and dispose of everything."

"I will be delighted to help," Allan added, hopefully, "With Florentino's death, will that put an end to the cartel?"

The Commissioner shook his head, smiling sadly. "I'm afraid not. Somebody else will take over, probably the man Florentino trained, Enrique Chavez."

Craig hesitated, but decided he should ask anyway. After all the man was his son. "Did the police find Enrique Chavez?"

"No! No trace of him."

Craig lifted the snifter and swished the liquid around in the glass. He didn't want anybody to notice the relief on his face. Audrey noticed.

"Craig, can I count on your help to break up the drug cartel in Canada."

Audrey spoke up, very forcefully, "Commissioner, Craig will not be helping you! He and I are going home to Calgary. Our son, Robert, is in the R.C.M.P. He will help you. Craig has done enough."

"Bien, Madam. I shall miss him."

The Commissioner finished his wine and put the glass back on the bar. "Now, Gentlemen, if you will excuse me I must report your decision to the Prime Minister."

Audrey couldn't resist asking, "How is Mrs. Bannerman?"

That was the first time anybody had seen the Commissioner blush. "A-ah, the maid gave her a sleeping pill. She is doing as well as can be expected."

Donald waited until the Commissioner closed the door behind him.

"Dad, there's only one problem."

"What is it?"

"The tape Rico took with him is a copy of the one Eduardo gave you. The original was in my rucksack at the lake and was taken by Inspector Calder. It is out there somewhere. Somebody is bound to find it and Bannerman's involvement will come out."

Craig digested the implication of what Donald had said, then smiled. "Come Audrey, let's go to bed... tomorrow I have to figure out how to contact Eduardo."

About the Author

Peter W. Rainier grew up on a remote emerald mine, high in the Andes of Colombia, two days ride from the nearest motor way, in an area infested with bandits. His playmates were young Chibcha Indians.

Peter Rainier served in the Royal Air Force during the Second World War as a fighter pilot on a Spitfire squadron in Italy.

As a geologist and later an oil executive he pursued a long career in petroleum geology in Western Canada, Australia, Europe, Africa, South America, and the United States.

Many of the locations and scenes in this novel owe their roots to actual experiences during the writer's formative years in Colombia, wartime service in the Royal Air Force, and as a geologist in the petroleum industry. Naturally, liberties have been taken with actual experiences.

E-mail:- pwr76@shaw.ca